NEGIMA!

3

Ken Akamatsu

TRANSLATED BY
Douglas Varenas

ADAPTED BY
Peter David and Kathleen O'Shea David

LETTERED BY
Steve Palmer

DEL
REY

BALLANTINE BOOKS · NEW YORK

A Word from the Author

Here it is, Volume 3 of *Negima!* Volume 3 is the first *Negima!* that uses a whole volume for a single story. It's called the "Evangeline Edition."

How in the world will Negi-kun, who as an honor student who graduated top of the class from a magic school, and has yet to run into any particularly serious barriers, continue to grow up when he encounters new formidable enemies and friends he comes to depend on? What is the secret of the Thousand Master who pursues Negi!? And what is the partner binding system!?

Usually there are only nine chapters in a volume but, this time, we've packed in ten, so there's plenty to enjoy. Well then, take your time and enjoy (ha ha)!

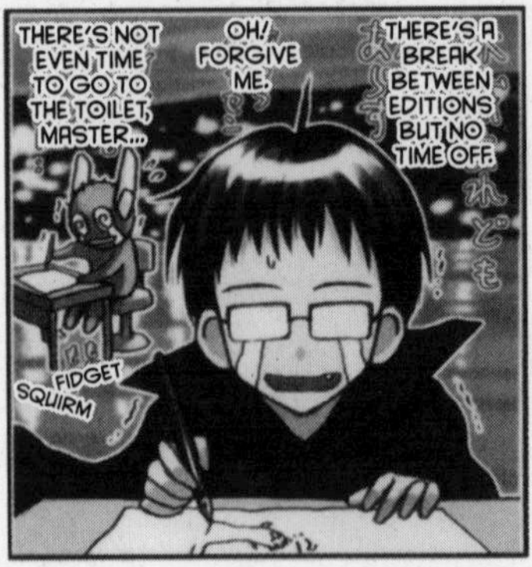
THERE'S A BREAK BETWEEN EDITIONS BUT NO TIME OFF.
OH! FORGIVE ME.
THERE'S NOT EVEN TIME TO GO TO THE TOILET, MASTER...
FIDGET SQUIRM

By the way, looks like there's gonna be a stream of some pretty big news through autumn 2004. For more information, please check out the official site below. You can also access it from your mobile phone. I update my blog every day.

Ken Akamatsu
http://www.ailove.net

Translator—Douglas Varenas
Adaptors—Peter David and Kathleen O'Shea David
Lettering—Steve Palmer
Cover Design—David Stevenson

A Del Rey® Book
Published by The Random House Publishing Group

Published in the United States by Del Rey Books,
an imprint of The Random House Publishing Group, a division
of Random House, Inc., New York, and simultaneously in
Canada by Random House of Canada Limited, Toronto.
First published in serial form by Shonen Magazine Comics and subsequently
published in book form by Kodansha, Ltd., Tokyo in 2003.

www.delreymanga.com

Cataloging-in-Publication Data is available from the Library of Congress.

ISBN 0-345-47180-6

Manufactured in the United States of America

First Edition: November 2004

Honorifics

Throughout the Del Rey Manga books, you will find Japanese honorifics left intact in the translations. For those not familiar with how the Japanese use honorifics, and more important, how they differ from American honorifics, we present this brief overview.

Politeness has always been a critical facet of Japanese culture. Ever since the feudal era, when Japan was a highly stratified society, use of honorifics — which can be defined as polite speech that indicates relationship or status — has played an essential role in the Japanese language. When addressing someone in Japanese, an honorific usually takes the form of a suffix attached to one's name (example: "Asuna-san"), or as a title at the end of one's name or in place of the name itself (example: "Negi-sensei," or simply "Sensei!").

Honorifics can be expressions of respect or endearment. In the context of manga and anime, honorifics give insight into the nature of the relationship between characters. Many translations into English leave out these important honorifics, and therefore distort the "feel" of the original Japanese. Because Japanese honorifics have nuances that English honorifics lack, it is our policy at Del Rey not to translate them. Here, instead, is a guide to some of the honorifics you may encounter in Del Rey Manga.

-*san:*   This is the most common honorific, and is equivalent to Mr., Miss, Ms., Mrs., etc. It is the all-purpose honorific and can be used in any situation where politeness is required.

-*sama:*   This is one level higher than -*san*. It is used to confer great respect.

-*dono:*   This comes from the word *tono*, which means *lord*. It is an even higher level than *sama*, and confers utmost respect.

-*kun:* This suffix is used at the end of boys' names to express familiarity or endearment. It is also sometimes used by men among friends, or when addressing someone younger or of a lower station.

-*chan:* This is used to express endearment, mostly toward girls. It is also used for little boys, pets, and even among lovers. It gives a sense of childish cuteness.

Bozu: This is an informal way to refer to a boy, similar to the English term "kid" or "squirt."

Sempai: This title suggests that the addressee is one's "senior" in a group or organization. It is most often used in a school setting, where underclassmen refer to their upperclassmen as *sempai.* It can also be used in the workplace, such as when a newer employee addresses an employee who has seniority in the company.

Kohai: This is the opposite of *sempai,* and is used toward underclassmen in school or newcomers in the workplace. It connotes that the addressee is of lower station.

Sensei: Literally meaning "one who has come before," this title is used for teachers, doctors, or masters of any profession or art.

-[blank]: Usually forgotten in these lists, but perhaps the most significant difference between Japanese and English. The lack of honorific means that the speaker has permission to address the person in a very intimate way. Usually, only family, spouses, or very close friends have this kind of permission. Known as *yobisute,* it can be gratifying when someone who has earned the intimacy starts to call one by one's name without an honorific. But when that intimacy hasn't been earned, it can also be very insulting.

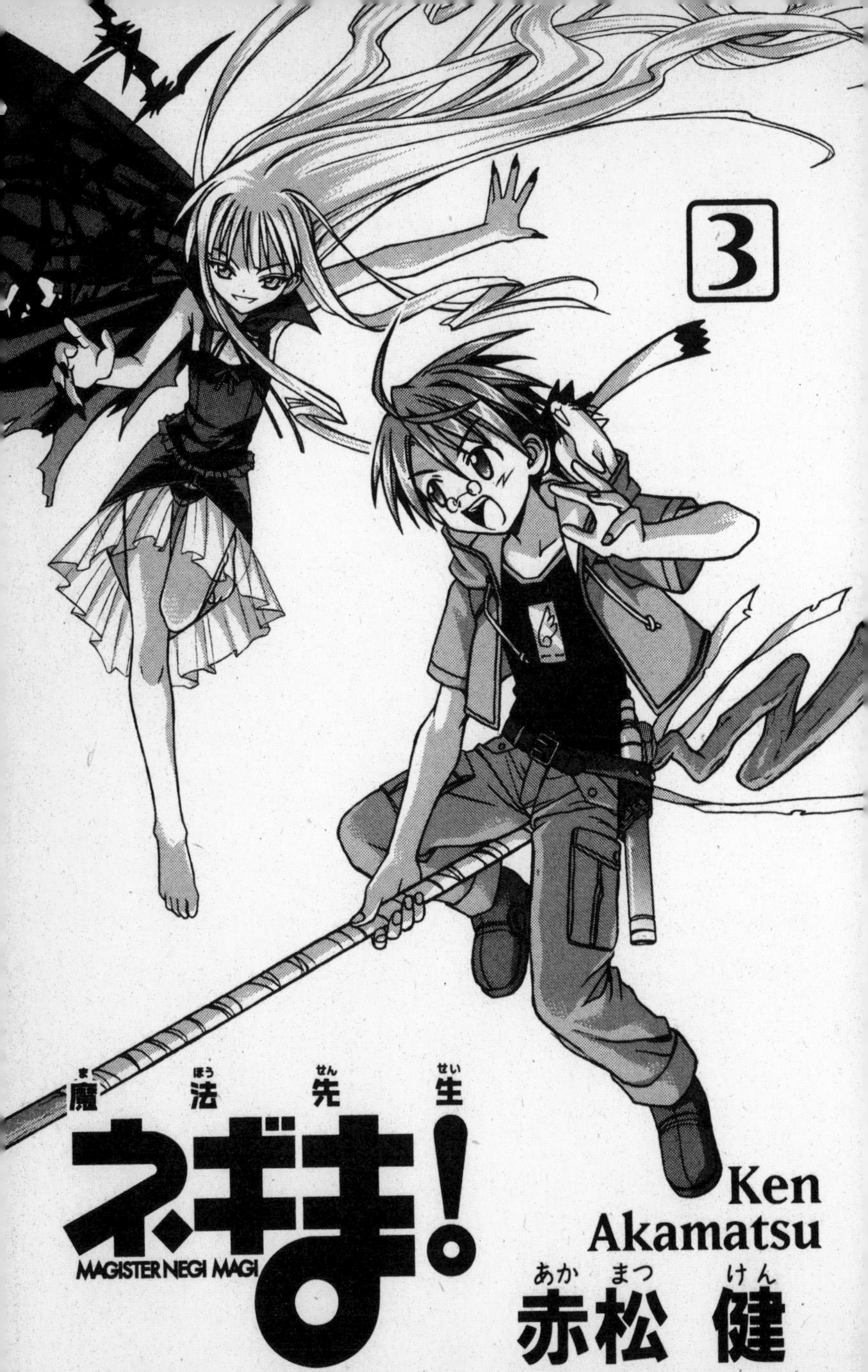

3

魔法先生ネギま!

MAGISTER NEGI MAGI

Ken Akamatsu

赤松 健

WRITTEN APPOINTMENT. NEGI SPRINGFIELD.
APRIL 2, 2003. APPOINTMENT OF TEACHER,
JUNIOR HIGH DEPARTMENT MAHORA ACADEMY.

HEADMASTER, MAHORA ACADEMY.
麻帆良学園学園長　近衛近右衛門

CONTENTS

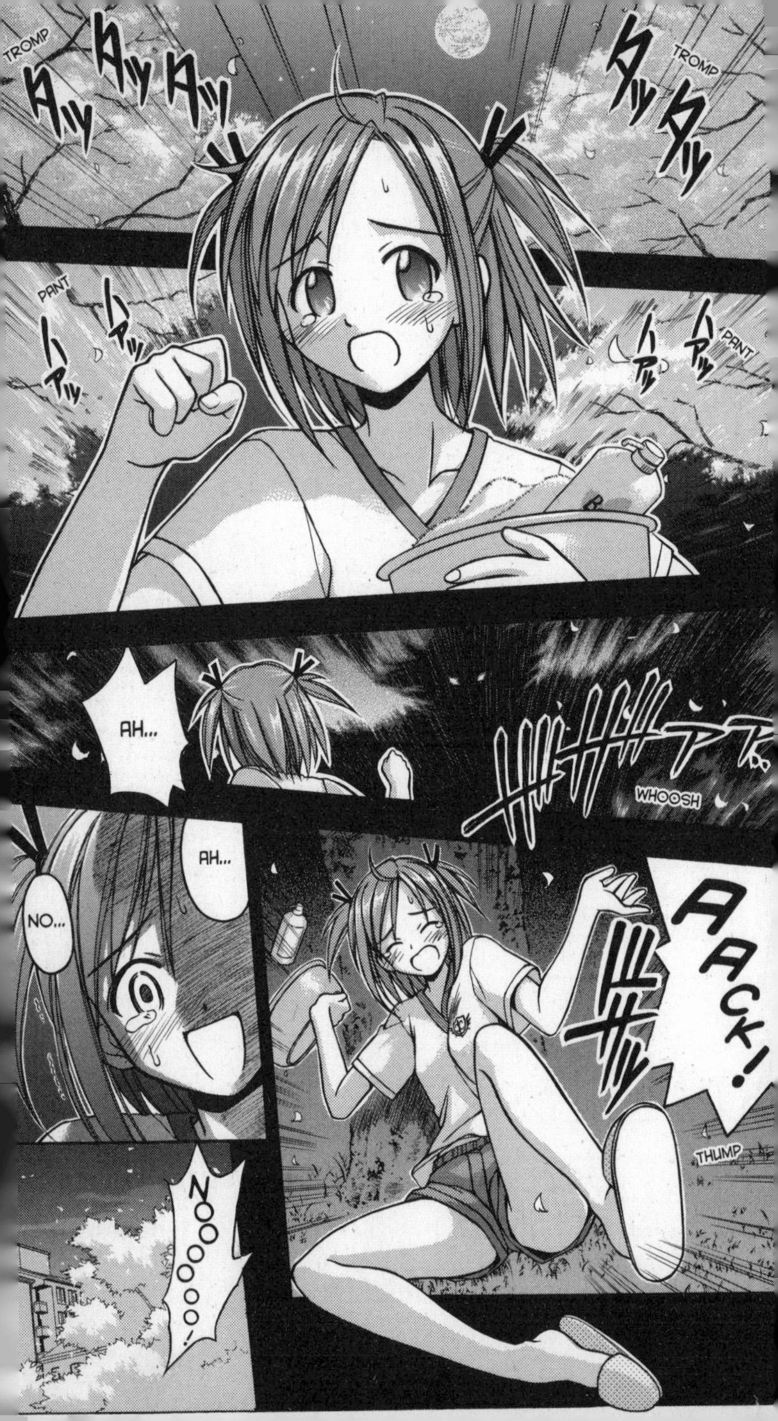
TROMP
TROMP
PANT
PANT
WHOOSH
AH...
AACK!
THUMP
AH...
NO...
NOOOOOO!

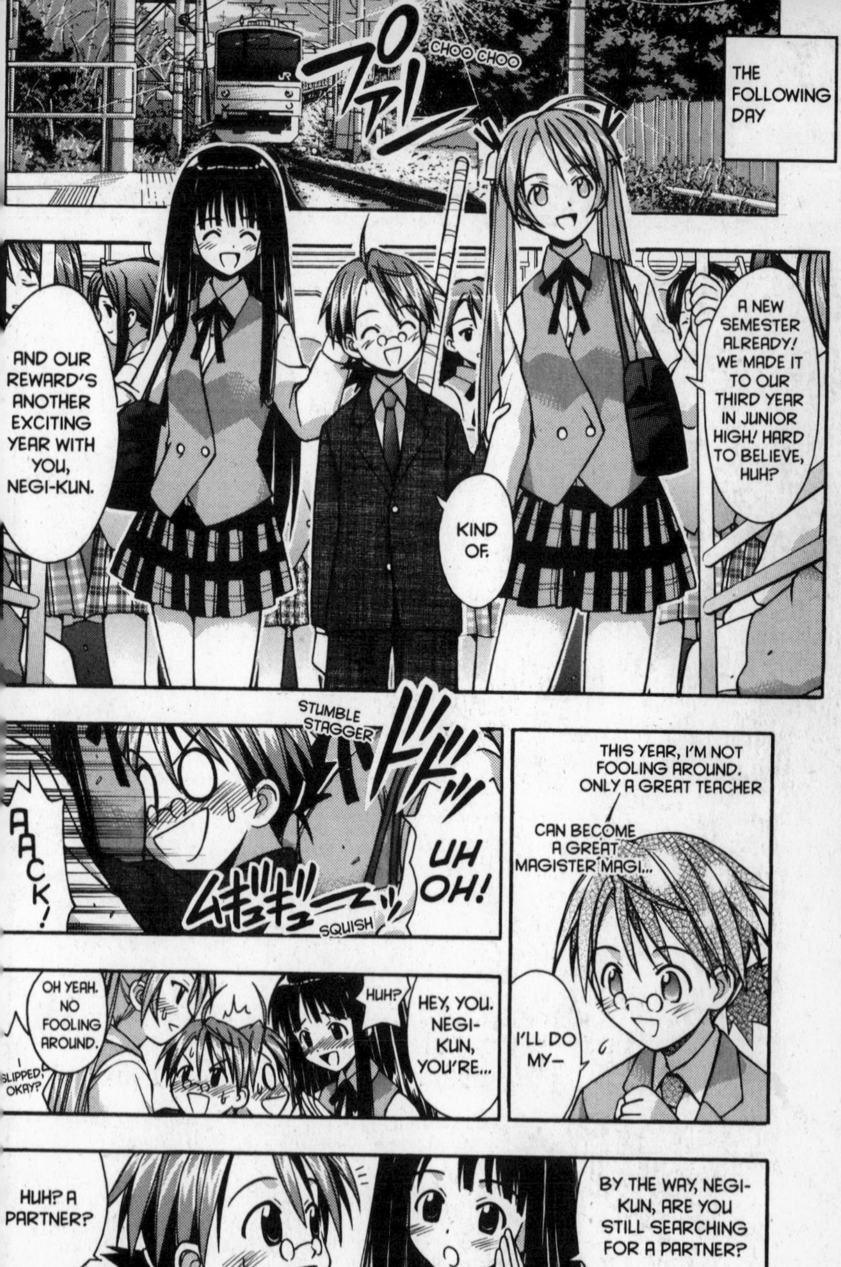
THE FOLLOWING DAY
CHOO CHOO
A NEW SEMESTER ALREADY! WE MADE IT TO OUR THIRD YEAR IN JUNIOR HIGH! HARD TO BELIEVE, HUH?
KIND OF.
AND OUR REWARD'S ANOTHER EXCITING YEAR WITH YOU, NEGI-KUN.
THIS YEAR, I'M NOT FOOLING AROUND. ONLY A GREAT TEACHER
CAN BECOME A GREAT MAGISTER MAGI...
I'LL DO MY—
STUMBLE STAGGER
UH OH!
SQUISH
AACK!
HEY, YOU. NEGI-KUN, YOU'RE...
HUH?
OH YEAH. NO FOOLING AROUND.
I SLIPPED, OKAY?
BY THE WAY, NEGI-KUN, ARE YOU STILL SEARCHING FOR A PARTNER?
HUH? A PARTNER?

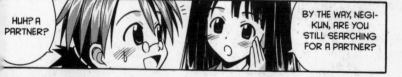

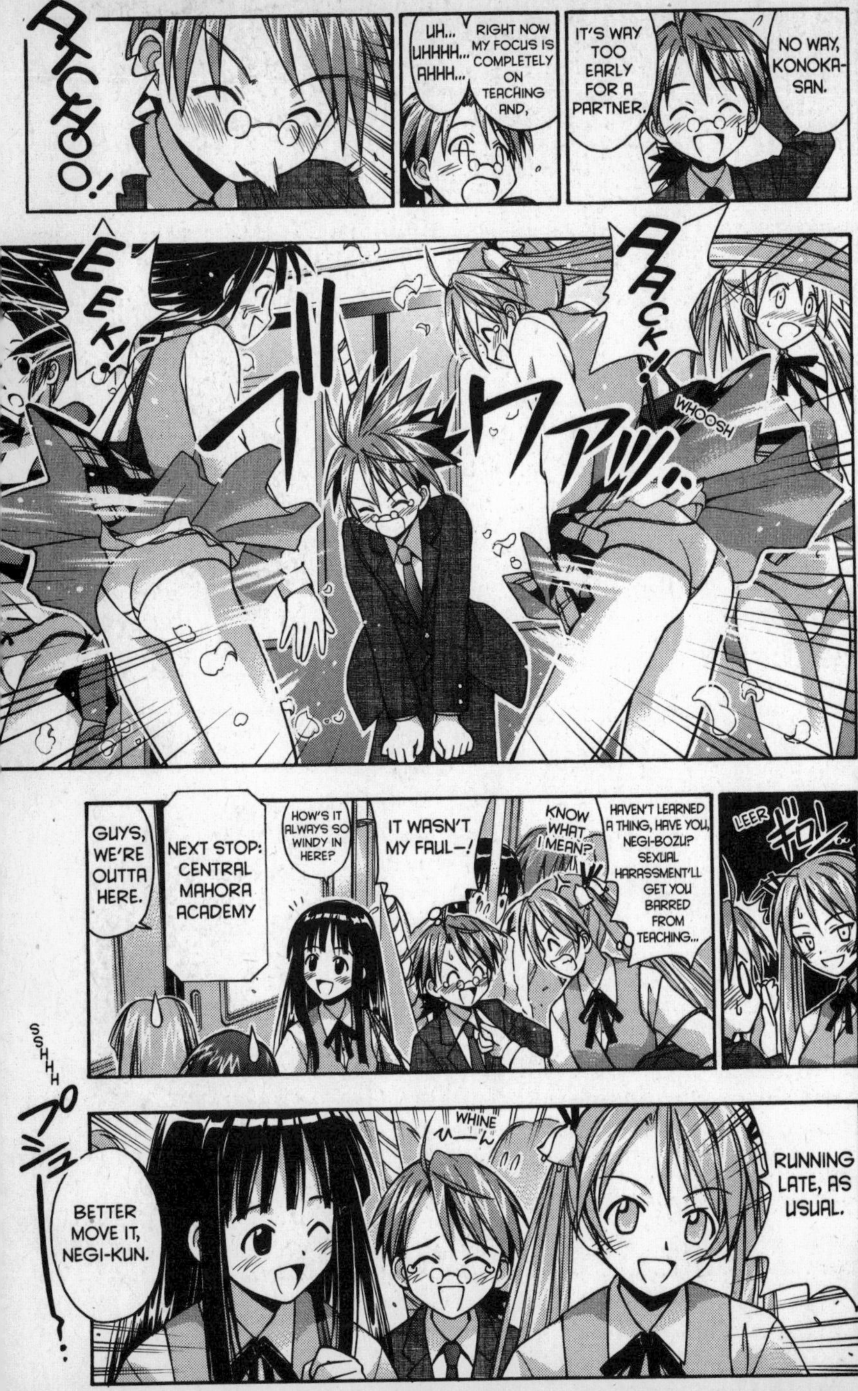
NO WAY, KONOKA-SAN.
IT'S WAY TOO EARLY FOR A PARTNER.
RIGHT NOW MY FOCUS IS COMPLETELY ON TEACHING AND,
UH... UHHHH... AHHH...
ATCHOO!
AACK!!
WHOOSH
ÊEEK!!
LEER
HAVEN'T LEARNED A THING, HAVE YOU, NEGI-BOZU? SEXUAL HARASSMENT'LL GET YOU BARRED FROM TEACHING...
KNOW WHAT I MEAN?
IT WASN'T MY FAUL—!
HOW'S IT ALWAYS SO WINDY IN HERE?
NEXT STOP: CENTRAL MAHORA ACADEMY
GUYS, WE'RE OUTTA HERE.
RUNNING LATE, AS USUAL.
WHINE
BETTER MOVE IT, NEGI-KUN.
SSHHH

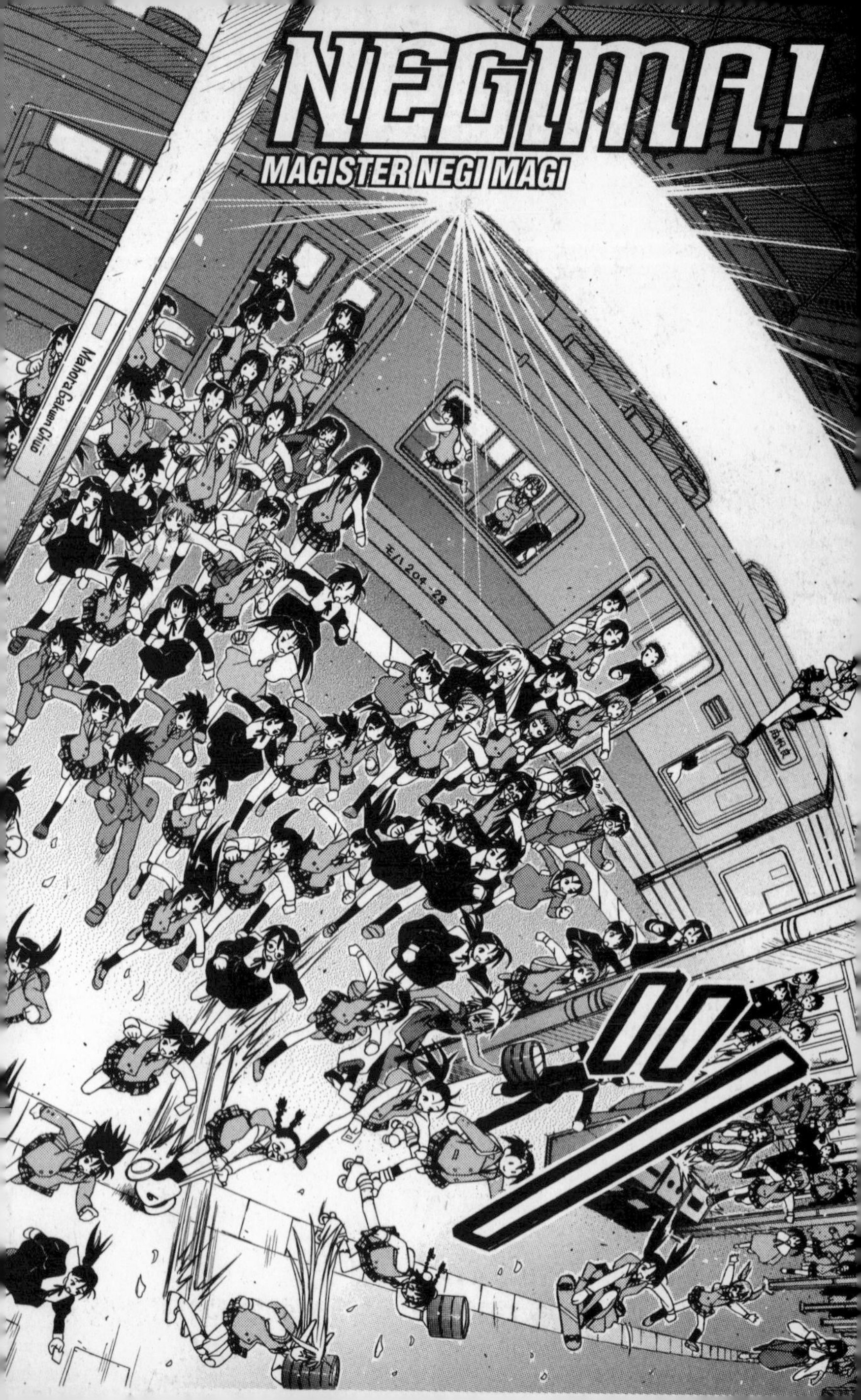
NEGIMA!
MAGISTER NEGI MAGI
Mahora Gakuen Chūō

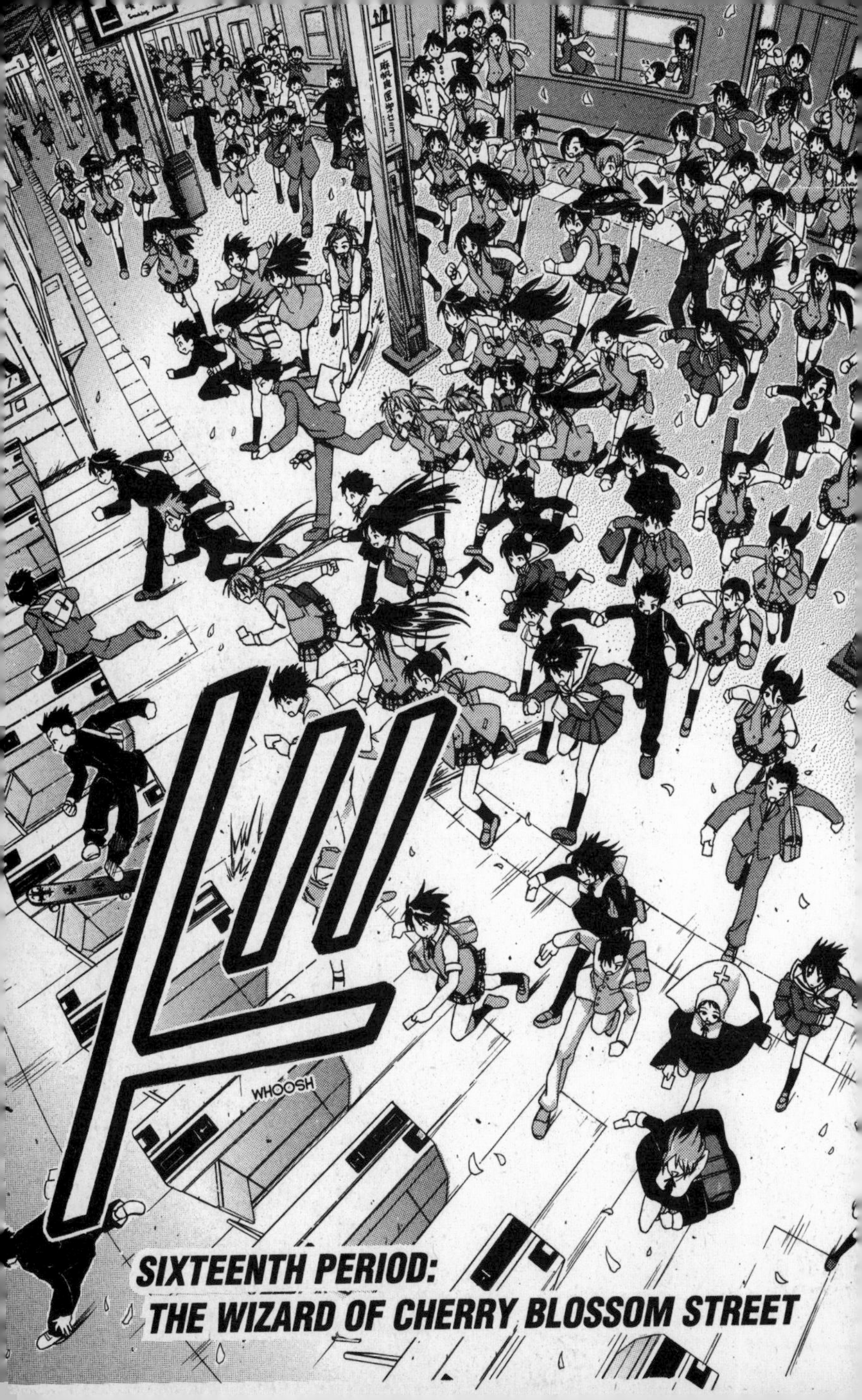
WHOOSH
SIXTEENTH PERIOD:
THE WIZARD OF CHERRY BLOSSOM STREET

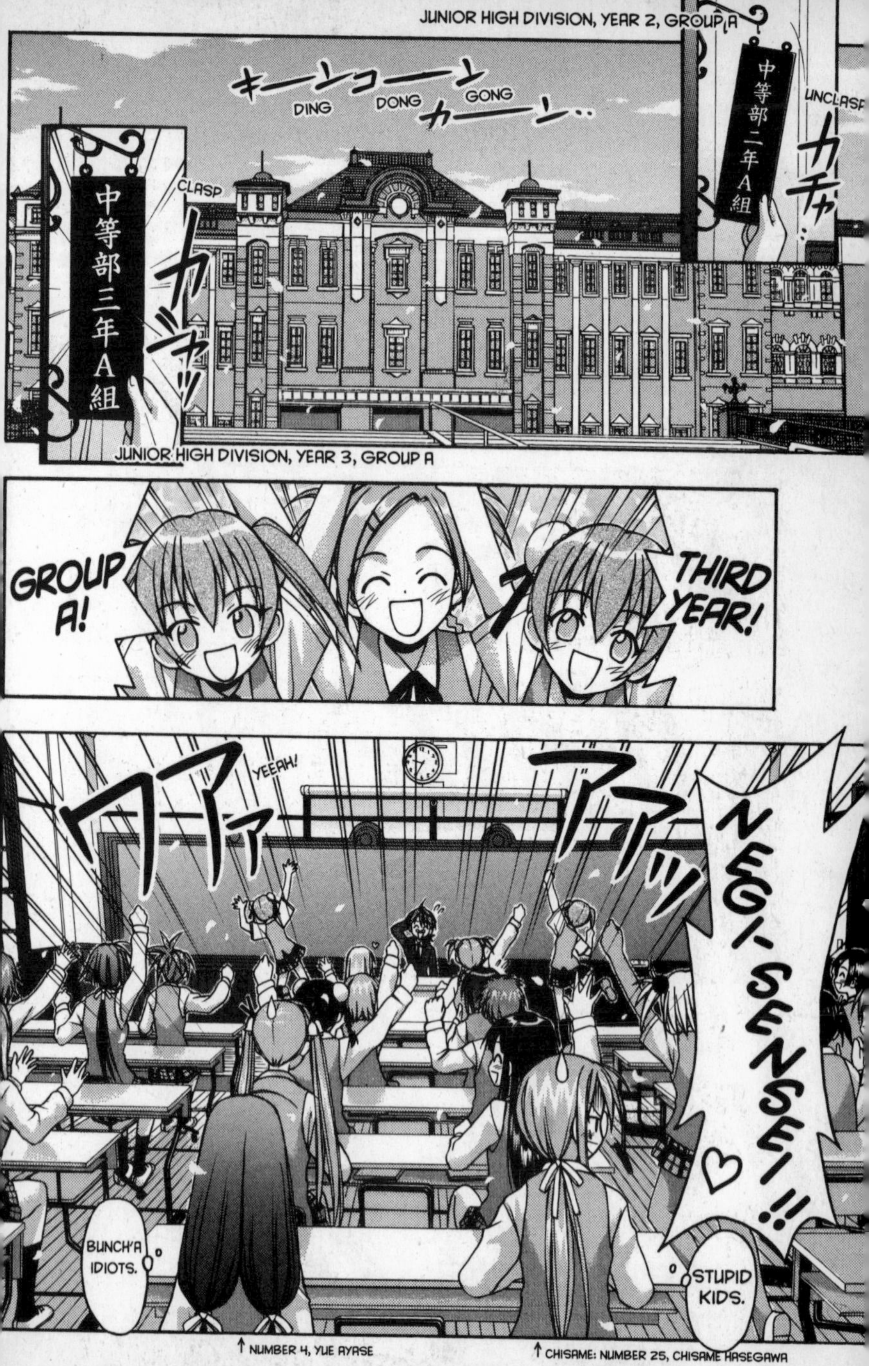
JUNIOR HIGH DIVISION, YEAR 2, GROUP A
中等部二年A組
UNCLASP
カチャ
キーンコーン
DING DONG GONG
カーン..
CLASP
カシャッ
中等部三年A組
JUNIOR HIGH DIVISION, YEAR 3, GROUP A
THIRD YEAR!
GROUP A!
NEGI SENSEI ♡ !!
アアッ
ワーァァ
YEEAH!
STUPID KIDS.
BUNCH'A IDIOTS.

↑ NUMBER 4, YUE AYASE

↑ CHISAME: NUMBER 25, CHISAME HASEGAWA

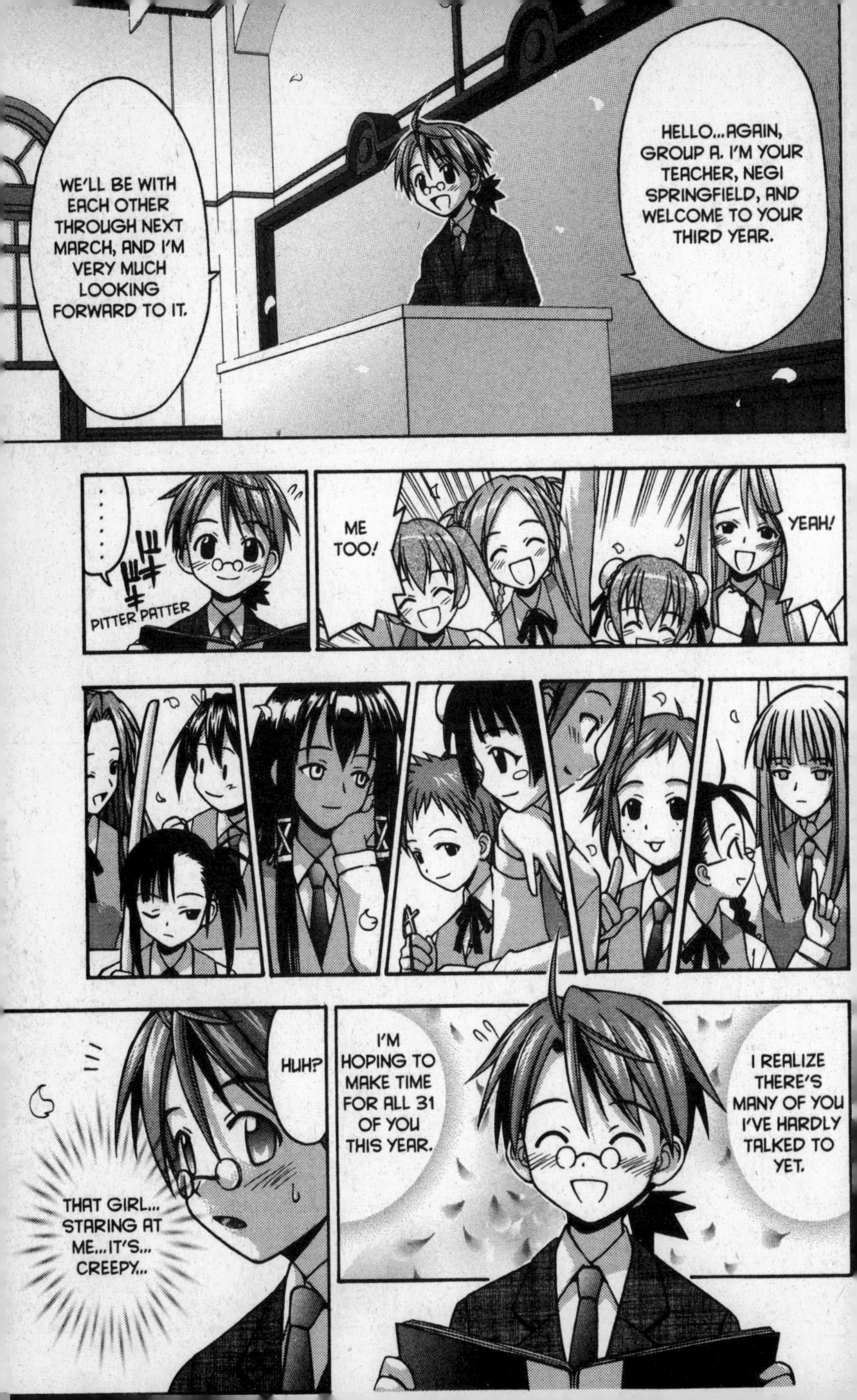
HELLO...AGAIN, GROUP A. I'M YOUR TEACHER, NEGI SPRINGFIELD, AND WELCOME TO YOUR THIRD YEAR.
WE'LL BE WITH EACH OTHER THROUGH NEXT MARCH, AND I'M VERY MUCH LOOKING FORWARD TO IT.
YEAH!
ME TOO!
......
PITTER PATTER
I REALIZE THERE'S MANY OF YOU I'VE HARDLY TALKED TO YET.
I'M HOPING TO MAKE TIME FOR ALL 31 OF YOU THIS YEAR.
HUH?
THAT GIRL... STARING AT ME...IT'S... CREEPY...

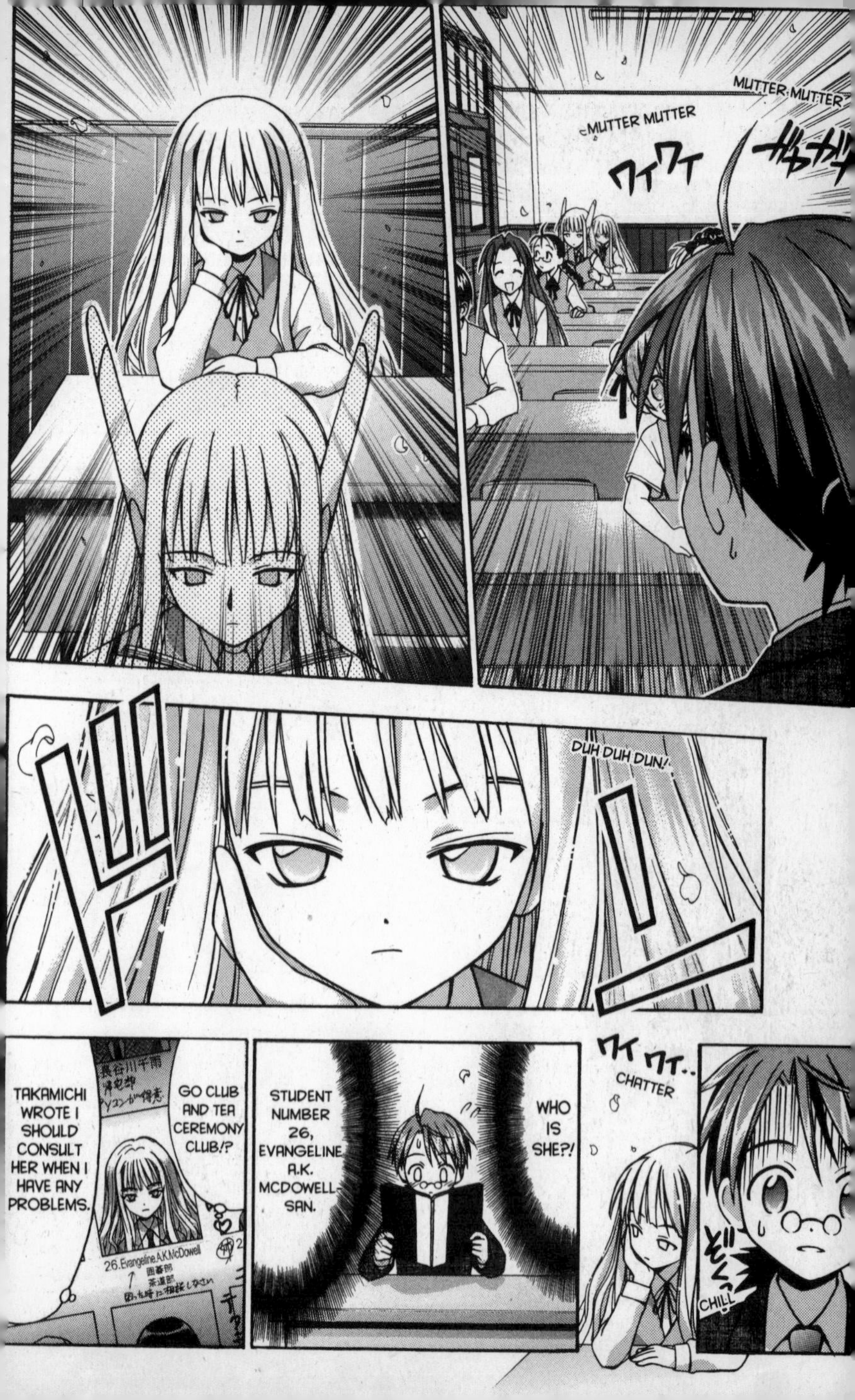
MUTTER MUTTER
MUTTER MUTTER
DUH DUH DUN!
CHATTER
CHILL!
WHO IS SHE?!
STUDENT NUMBER 26, EVANGELINE A.K. MCDOWELL-SAN.
GO CLUB AND TEA CEREMONY CLUB!?
TAKAMICHI WROTE I SHOULD CONSULT HER WHEN I HAVE ANY PROBLEMS.
26.Evangeline.A.K.McDowell

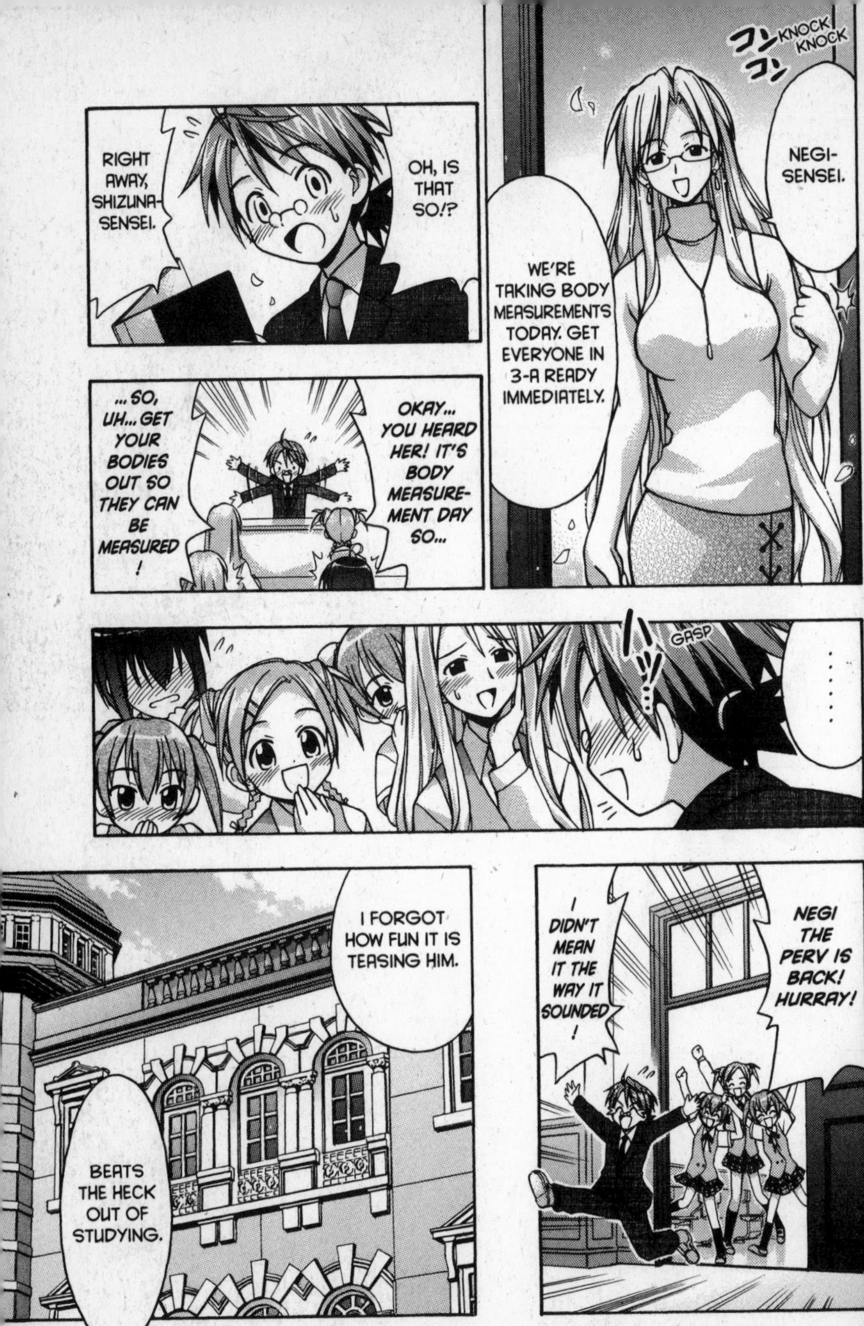
KNOCK KNOCK
NEGI-SENSEI.
WE'RE TAKING BODY MEASUREMENTS TODAY. GET EVERYONE IN 3-A READY IMMEDIATELY.
OH, IS THAT SO!?
RIGHT AWAY, SHIZUNA-SENSEI.
OKAY... YOU HEARD HER! IT'S BODY MEASUREMENT DAY SO...
...SO, UH... GET YOUR BODIES OUT SO THEY CAN BE MEASURED!
GASP
......
NEGI THE PERV IS BACK! HURRAY!
I DIDN'T MEAN IT THE WAY IT SOUNDED!
I FORGOT HOW FUN IT IS TEASING HIM.
BEATS THE HECK OUT OF STUDYING.

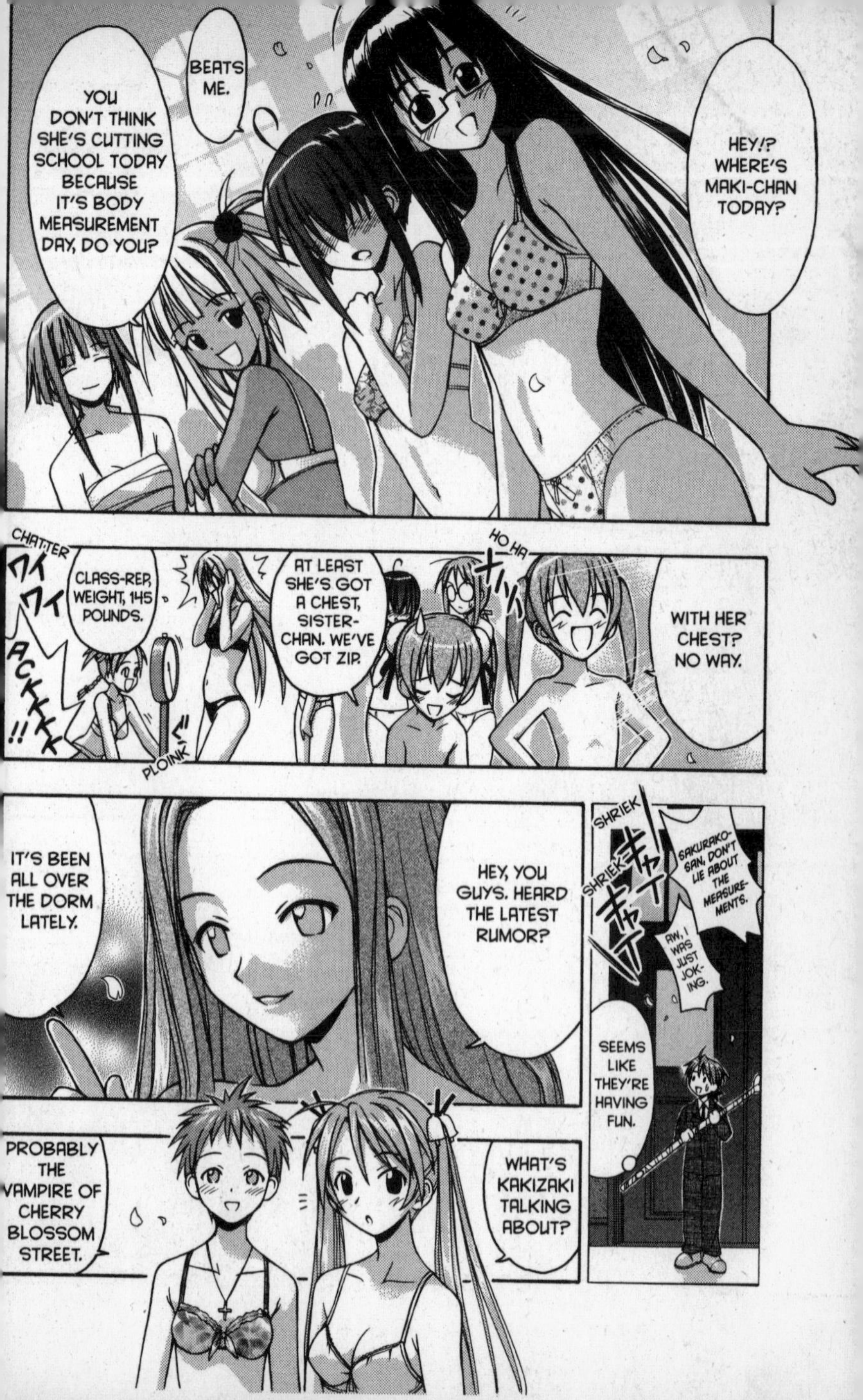
HEY!? WHERE'S MAKI-CHAN TODAY?
BEATS ME.
YOU DON'T THINK SHE'S CUTTING SCHOOL TODAY BECAUSE IT'S BODY MEASUREMENT DAY, DO YOU?
WITH HER CHEST? NO WAY.
HO HA
AT LEAST SHE'S GOT A CHEST, SISTER-CHAN. WE'VE GOT ZIP.
PLOINK
CLASS-REP, WEIGHT, 145 POUNDS.
ACKKKKK!!
CHATTER
ワイワイ
SHRIEK
SHRIEK
キャ キャ
SAKURAKO-SAN, DON'T LIE ABOUT THE MEASUREMENTS.
AW, I WAS JUST JOKING.
SEEMS LIKE THEY'RE HAVING FUN.
HEY, YOU GUYS. HEARD THE LATEST RUMOR?
IT'S BEEN ALL OVER THE DORM LATELY.
WHAT'S KAKIZAKI TALKING ABOUT?
PROBABLY THE VAMPIRE OF CHERRY BLOSSOM STREET.

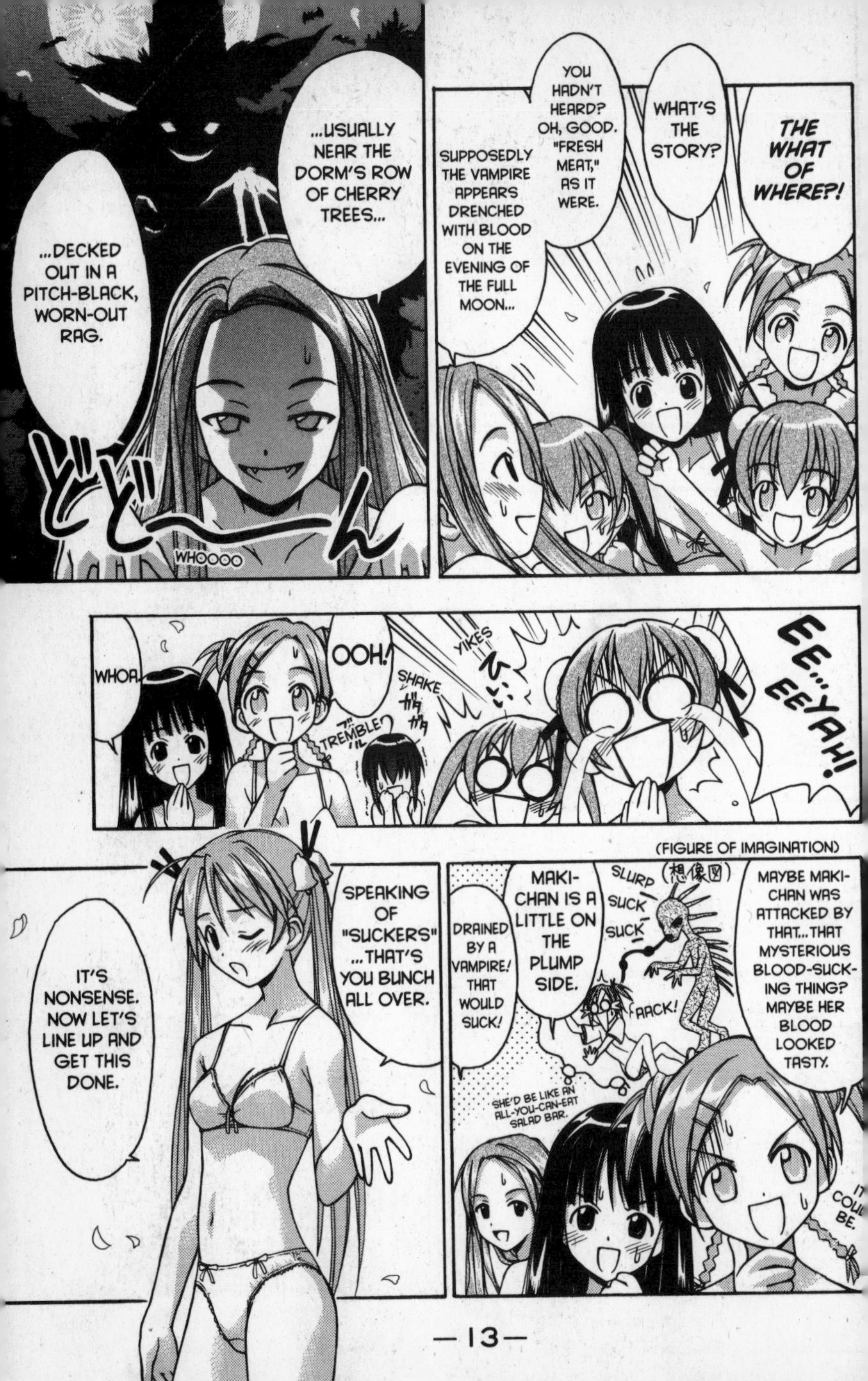
THE WHAT OF WHERE?!
WHAT'S THE STORY?
YOU HADN'T HEARD? OH, GOOD. "FRESH MEAT," AS IT WERE.
SUPPOSEDLY THE VAMPIRE APPEARS DRENCHED WITH BLOOD ON THE EVENING OF THE FULL MOON...
...USUALLY NEAR THE DORM'S ROW OF CHERRY TREES...
...DECKED OUT IN A PITCH-BLACK, WORN-OUT RAG.
どど〜ん
WHOOOO
EE... EEYAH!
YIKES
ひぃぃ
SHAKE
ガタガタ
TREMBLE
ブル
OOH!
WHOA.
(FIGURE OF IMAGINATION)
想像図
MAYBE MAKI-CHAN WAS ATTACKED BY THAT... THAT MYSTERIOUS BLOOD-SUCKING THING? MAYBE HER BLOOD LOOKED TASTY.
MAKI-CHAN IS A LITTLE ON THE PLUMP SIDE.
SLURP
SUCK
SUCK
AACK!
DRAINED BY A VAMPIRE! THAT WOULD SUCK!
SHE'D BE LIKE AN ALL-YOU-CAN-EAT SALAD BAR.
IT COULD BE.
SPEAKING OF "SUCKERS"... THAT'S YOU BUNCH ALL OVER.
IT'S NONSENSE. NOW LET'S LINE UP AND GET THIS DONE.

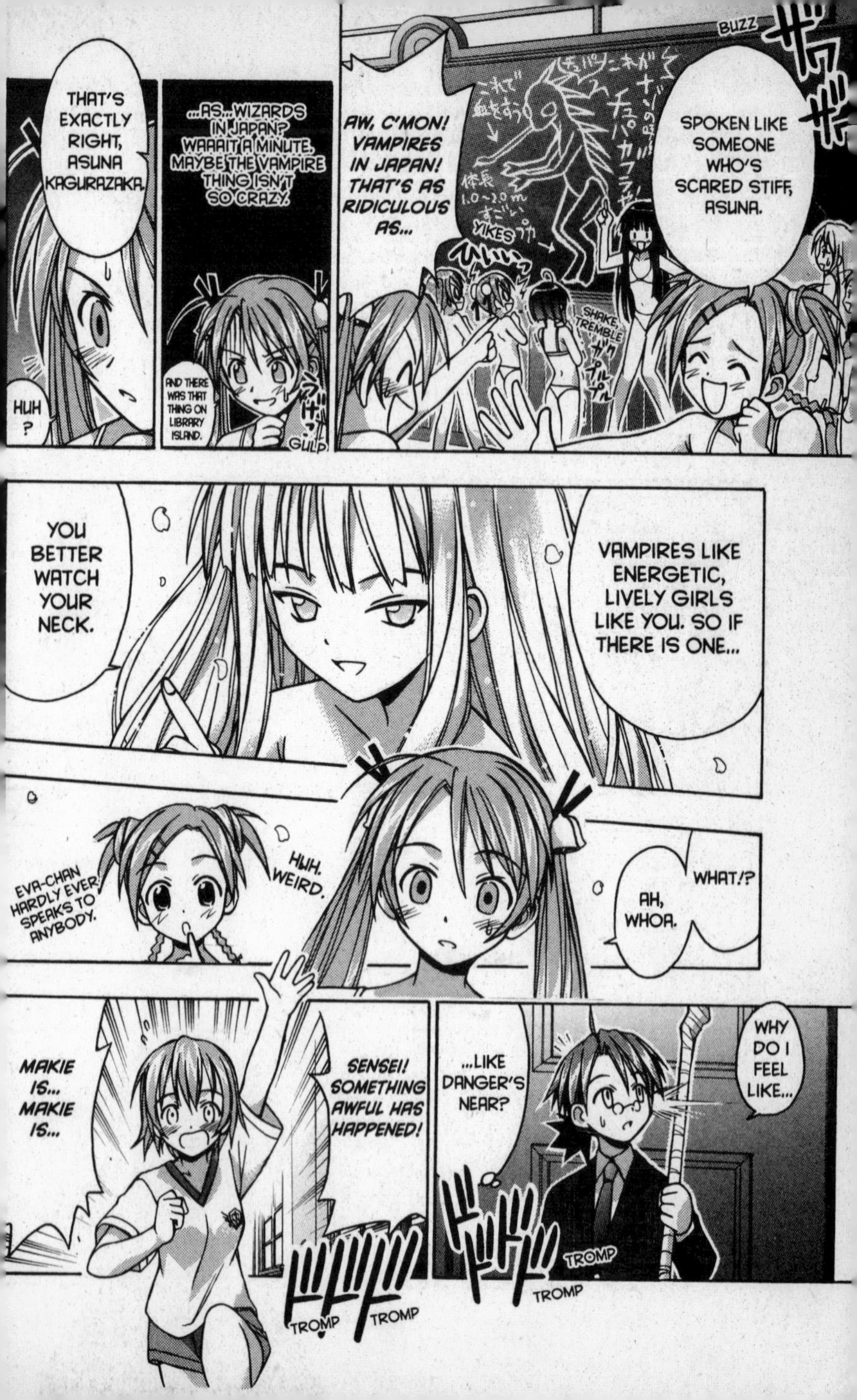
BUZZ
SPOKEN LIKE SOMEONE WHO'S SCARED STIFF, ASUNA.
YIKES
SHAKE, TREMBLE
AW, C'MON! VAMPIRES IN JAPAN! THAT'S AS RIDICULOUS AS...
...AS... WIZARDS IN JAPAN? WAAAIT A MINUTE. MAYBE THE VAMPIRE THING ISN'T SO CRAZY.
AND THERE WAS THAT THING ON LIBRARY ISLAND.
GULP
THAT'S EXACTLY RIGHT, ASUNA KAGURAZAKA.
HUH?
VAMPIRES LIKE ENERGETIC, LIVELY GIRLS LIKE YOU. SO IF THERE IS ONE...
YOU BETTER WATCH YOUR NECK.
WHAT!?
AH, WHOA.
HUH. WEIRD.
EVA-CHAN HARDLY EVER SPEAKS TO ANYBODY.
WHY DO I FEEL LIKE...
...LIKE DANGER'S NEAR?
TROMP
TROMP
SENSEI! SOMETHING AWFUL HAS HAPPENED!
MAKIE IS... MAKIE IS...
TROMP
TROMP

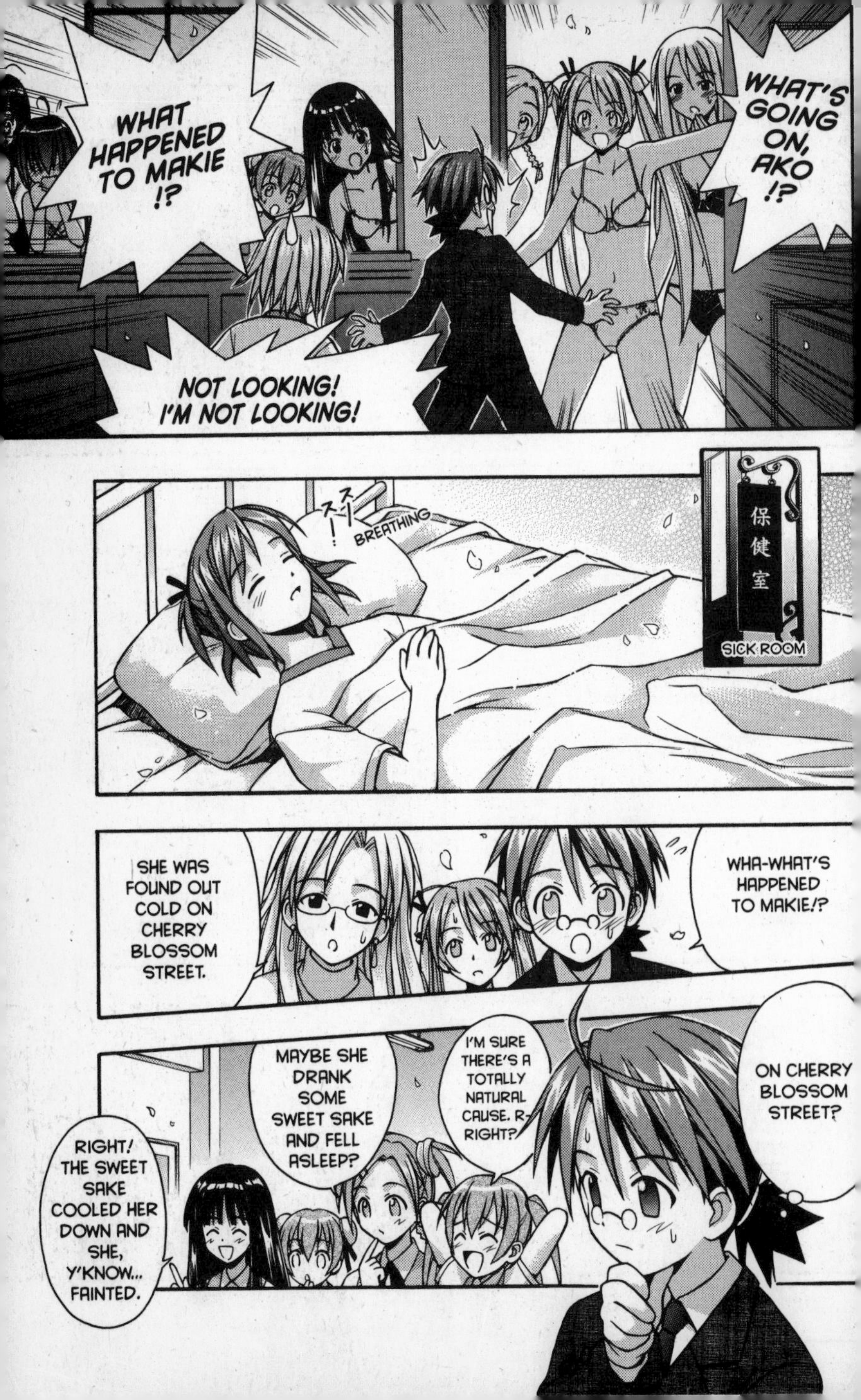
WHAT'S GOING ON, AKO!?
WHAT HAPPENED TO MAKIE!?
NOT LOOKING! I'M NOT LOOKING!
保健室
SICK ROOM
スー
BREATHING
WHA-WHAT'S HAPPENED TO MAKIE!?
SHE WAS FOUND OUT COLD ON CHERRY BLOSSOM STREET.
ON CHERRY BLOSSOM STREET?
I'M SURE THERE'S A TOTALLY NATURAL CAUSE. R-RIGHT?
MAYBE SHE DRANK SOME SWEET SAKE AND FELL ASLEEP?
RIGHT! THE SWEET SAKE COOLED HER DOWN AND SHE, Y'KNOW... FAINTED.

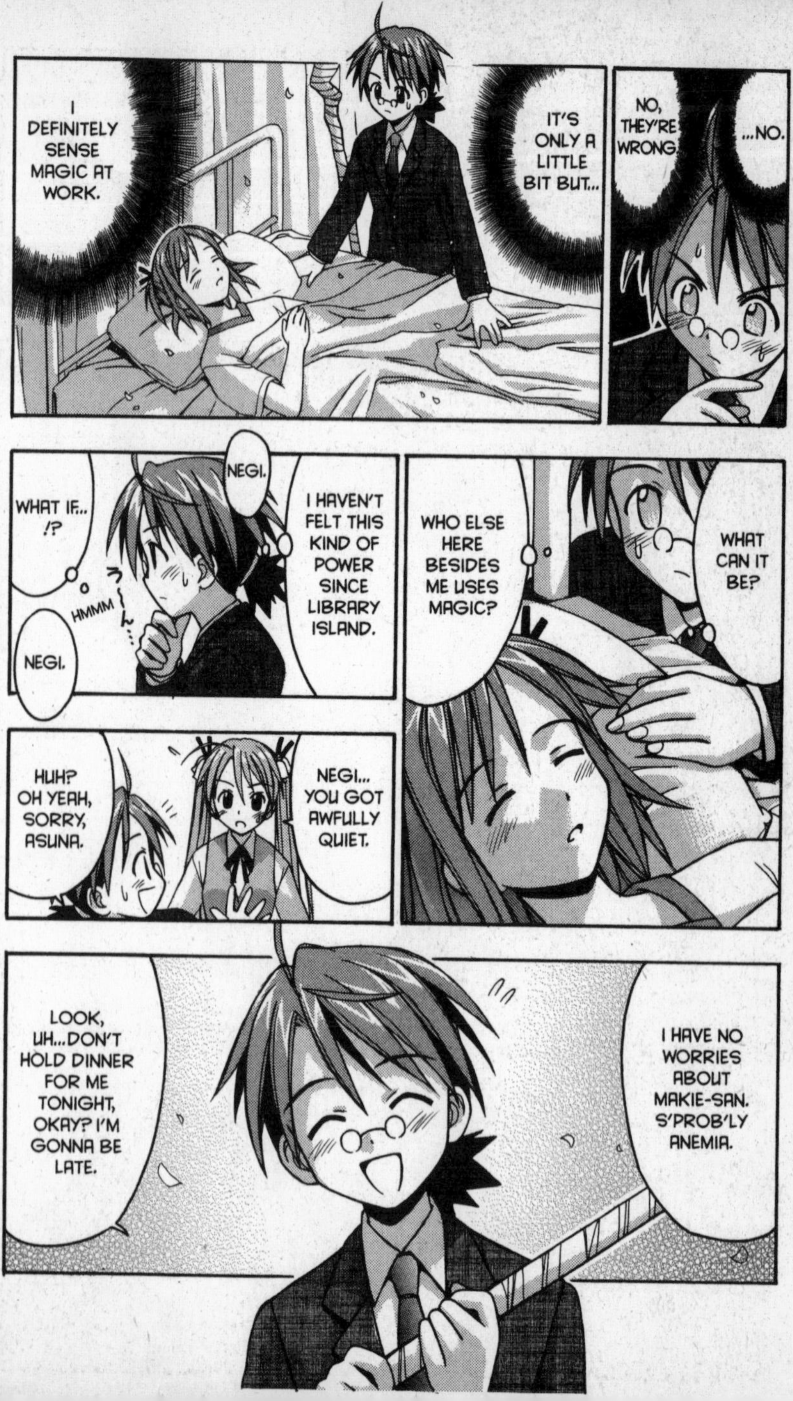
...NO.
NO, THEY'RE WRONG.
IT'S ONLY A LITTLE BIT BUT...
I DEFINITELY SENSE MAGIC AT WORK.
WHAT CAN IT BE?
WHO ELSE HERE BESIDES ME USES MAGIC?
I HAVEN'T FELT THIS KIND OF POWER SINCE LIBRARY ISLAND.
NEGI.
WHAT IF... !?
HMMM
NEGI.
NEGI... YOU GOT AWFULLY QUIET.
HUH? OH YEAH, SORRY, ASUNA.
I HAVE NO WORRIES ABOUT MAKIE-SAN. S'PROB'LY ANEMIA.
LOOK, UH...DON'T HOLD DINNER FOR ME TONIGHT, OKAY? I'M GONNA BE LATE.

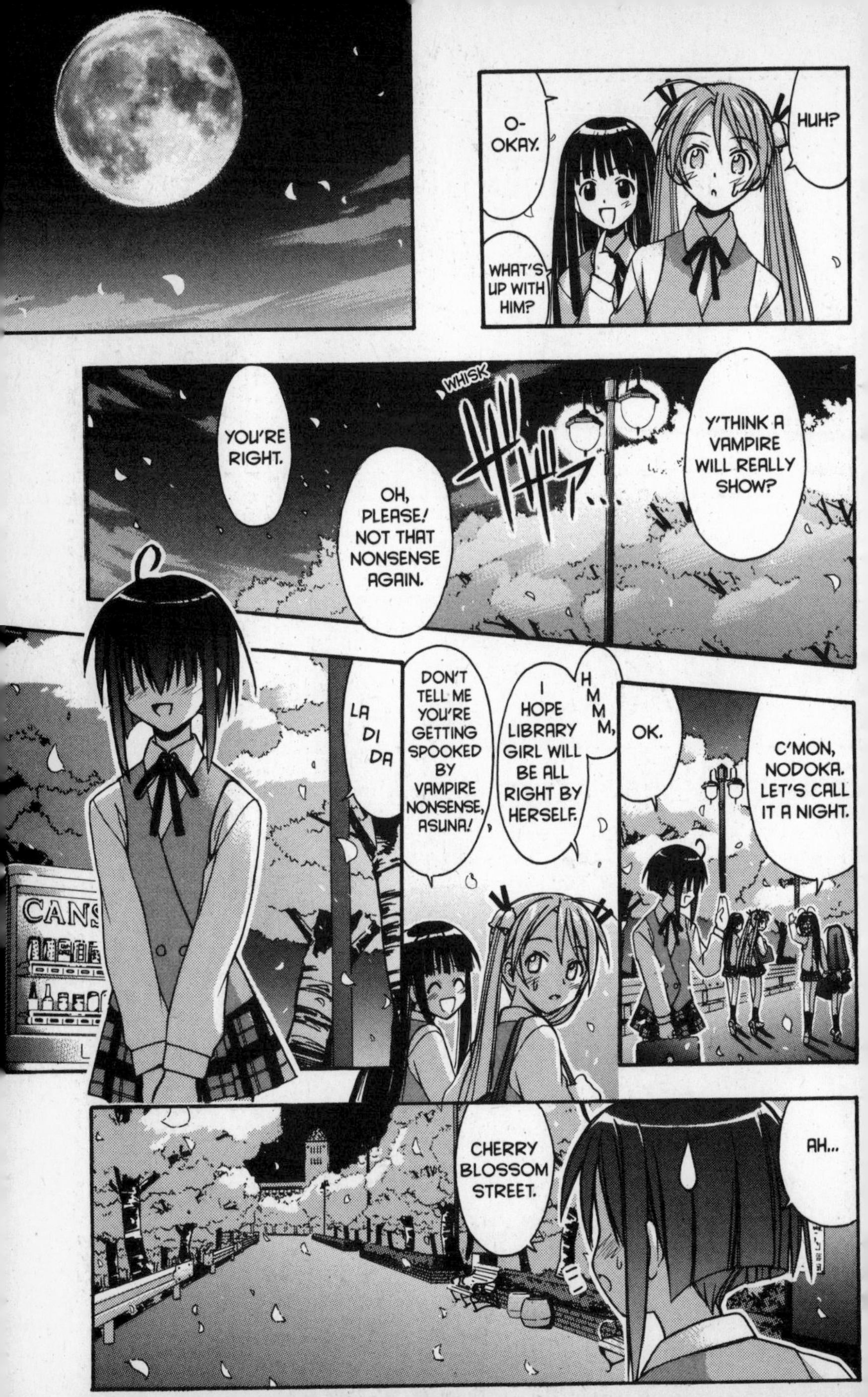
HUH?
O-OKAY.
WHAT'S UP WITH HIM?
Y'THINK A VAMPIRE WILL REALLY SHOW?
WHISK
OH, PLEASE! NOT THAT NONSENSE AGAIN.
YOU'RE RIGHT.
C'MON, NODOKA. LET'S CALL IT A NIGHT.
OK.
HMMM,
I HOPE LIBRARY GIRL WILL BE ALL RIGHT BY HERSELF.
DON'T TELL ME YOU'RE GETTING SPOOKED BY VAMPIRE NONSENSE, ASUNA!
LA DI DA
CANS
AH...
CHERRY BLOSSOM STREET.

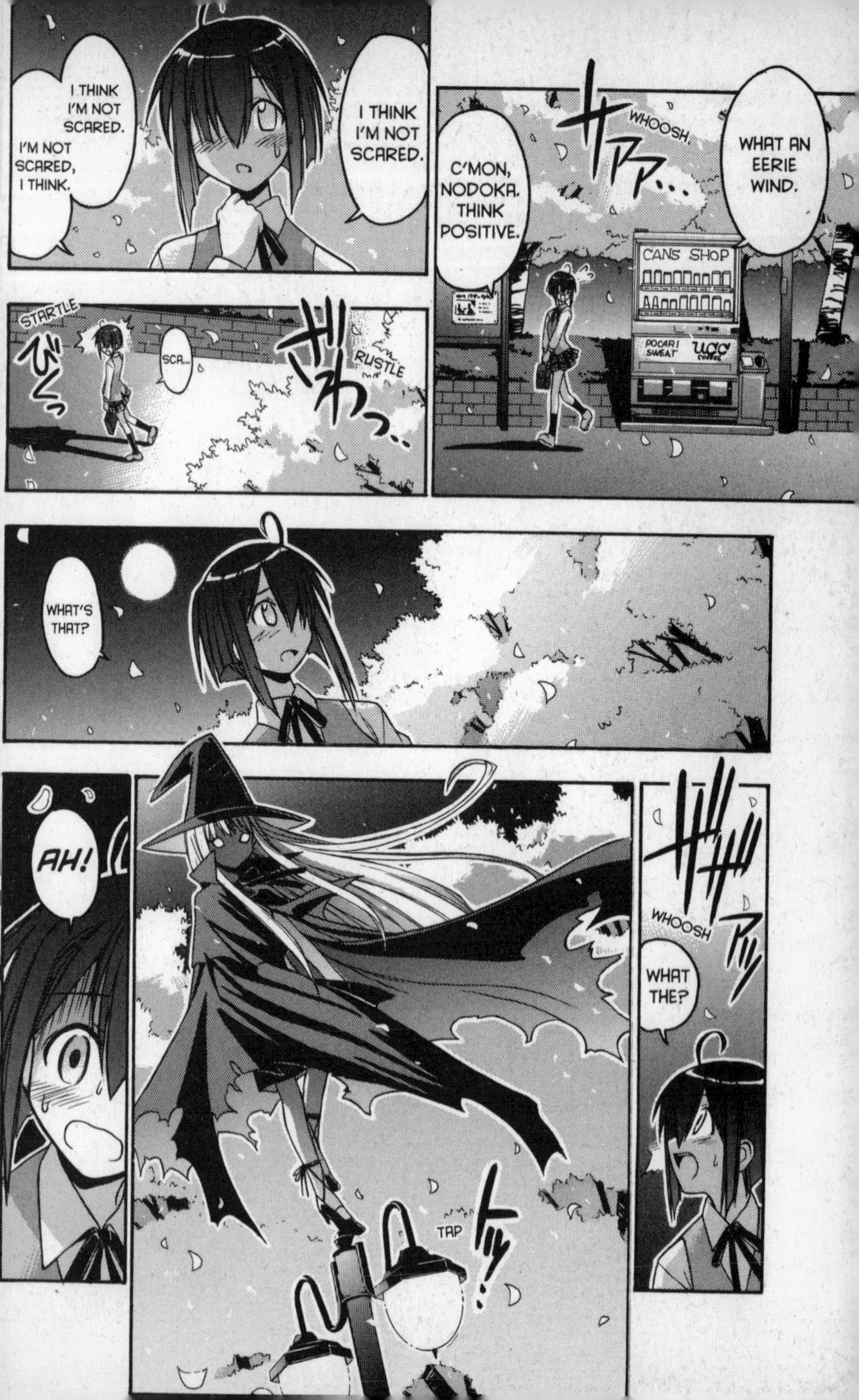
I THINK I'M NOT SCARED.
I THINK I'M NOT SCARED.
I'M NOT SCARED, I THINK.
WHAT AN EERIE WIND.
WHOOSH.
C'MON, NODOKA. THINK POSITIVE.
CANS SHOP
POCARI SWEAT
UCC COFFEE
RUSTLE
SCA...
STARTLE
WHAT'S THAT?
WHOOSH
WHAT THE?
TAP
AH!

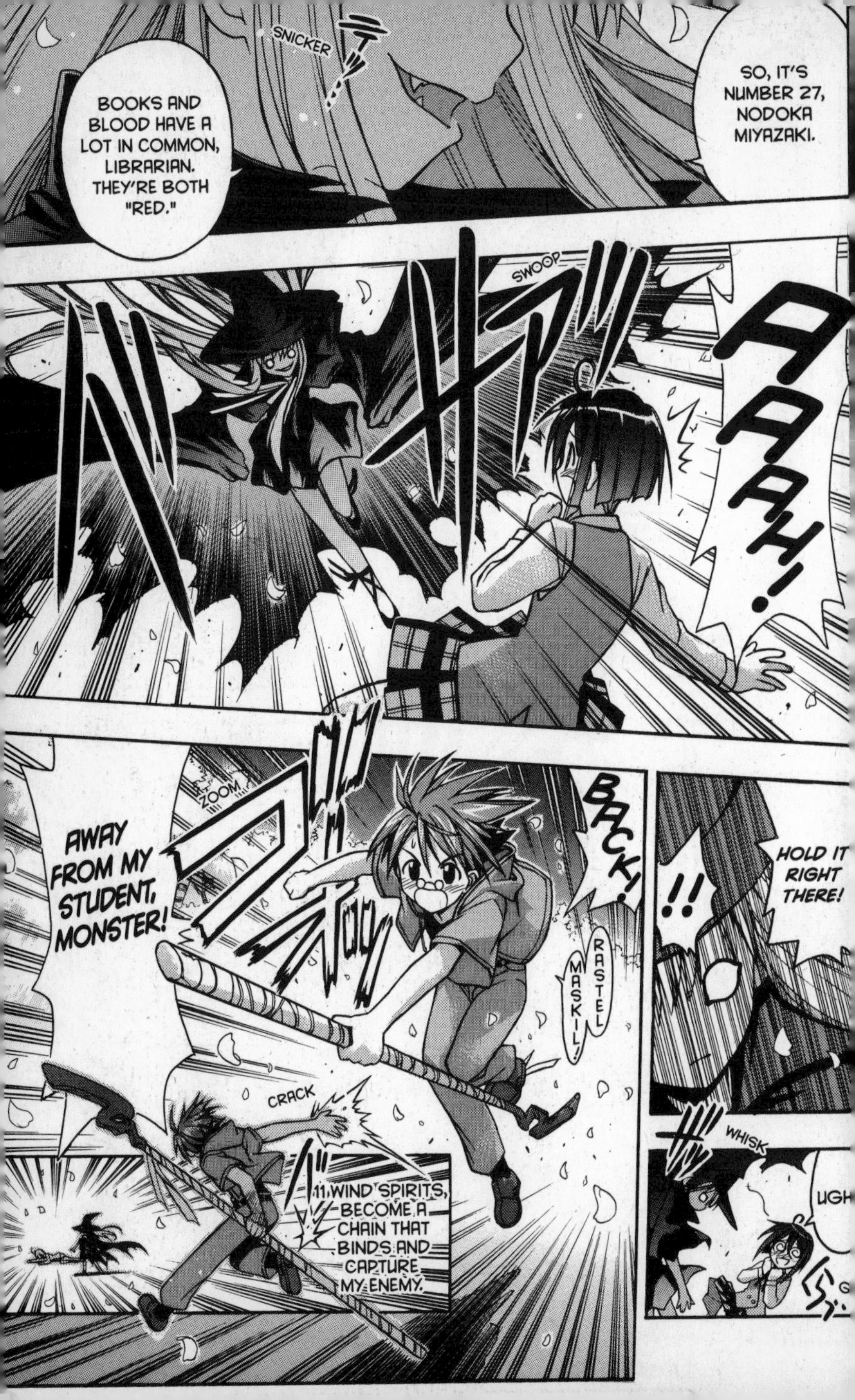
SO, IT'S NUMBER 27, NODOKA MIYAZAKI.
SNICKER
BOOKS AND BLOOD HAVE A LOT IN COMMON, LIBRARIAN. THEY'RE BOTH "RED."
AAAH!
SWOOP
HOLD IT RIGHT THERE!
!!
WHISK
UGH
BACK!
ZOOM
RASTEL MASKIL
AWAY FROM MY STUDENT, MONSTER!
CRACK
11 WIND SPIRITS, BECOME A CHAIN THAT BINDS AND CAPTURE MY ENEMY.

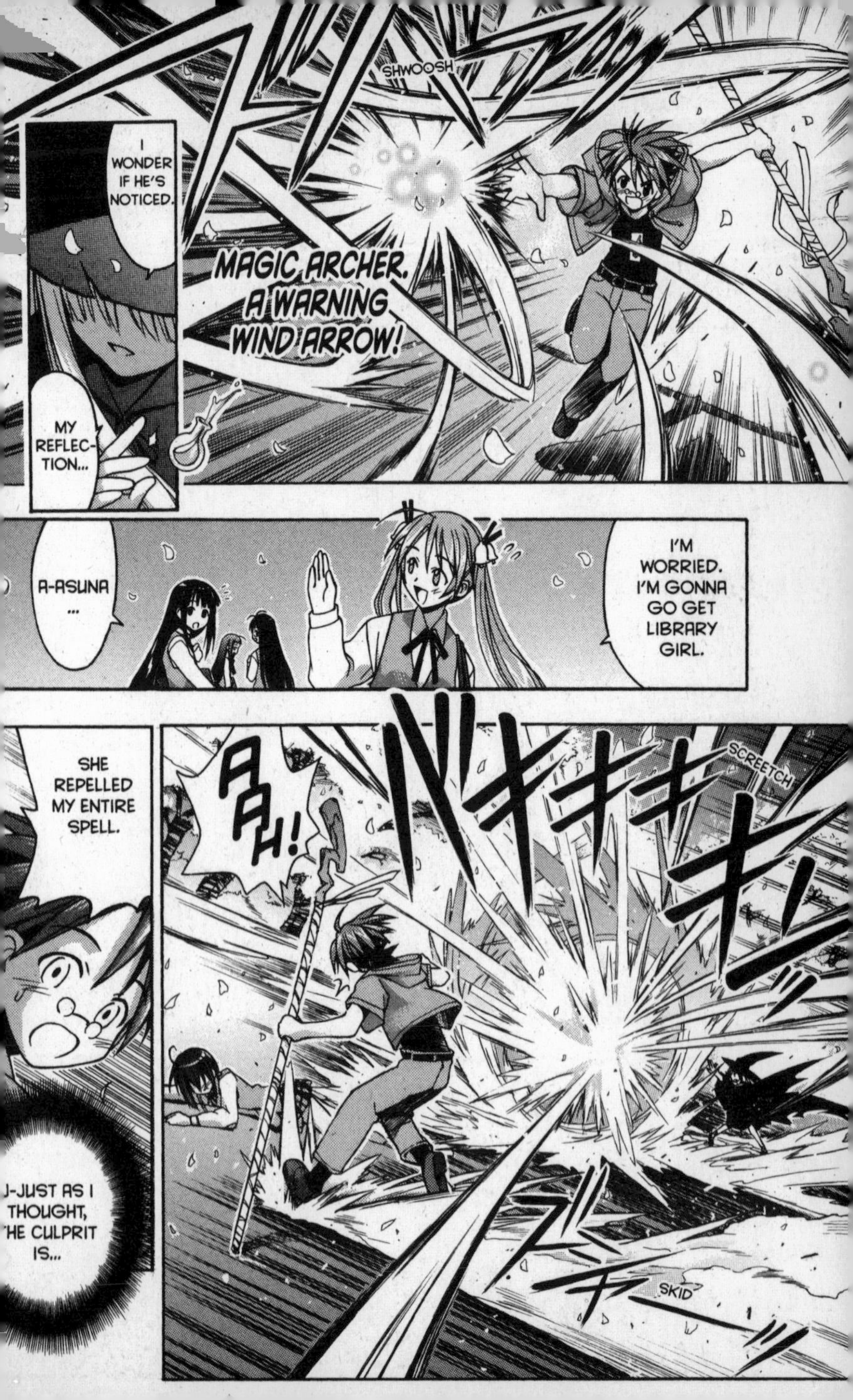
SHWOOSH
MAGIC ARCHER. A WARNING WIND ARROW!
I WONDER IF HE'S NOTICED.
MY REFLECTION...
I'M WORRIED. I'M GONNA GO GET LIBRARY GIRL.
A-ASUNA ...
SCREETCH
AAH!
SKID
SHE REPELLED MY ENTIRE SPELL.
J-JUST AS I THOUGHT, HE CULPRIT IS...

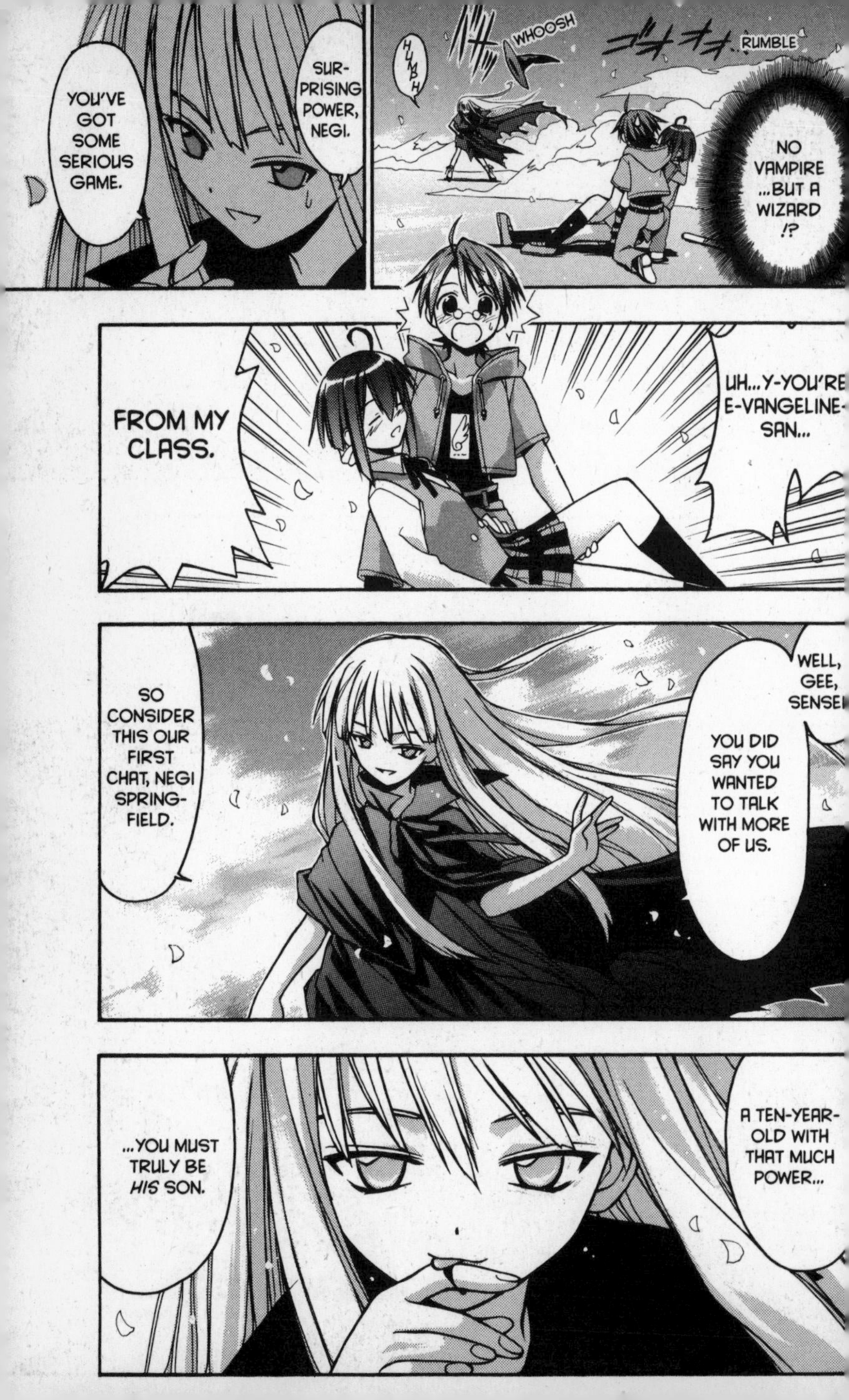
RUMBLE
NO VAMPIRE ...BUT A WIZARD !?
WHOOSH
HUMPH
SUR-PRISING POWER, NEGI.
YOU'VE GOT SOME SERIOUS GAME.
UH...Y-YOU'RE E-VANGELINE-SAN...
FROM MY CLASS.
WELL, GEE, SENSE
YOU DID SAY YOU WANTED TO TALK WITH MORE OF US.
SO CONSIDER THIS OUR FIRST CHAT, NEGI SPRING-FIELD.
A TEN-YEAR-OLD WITH THAT MUCH POWER...
...YOU MUST TRULY BE *HIS* SON.

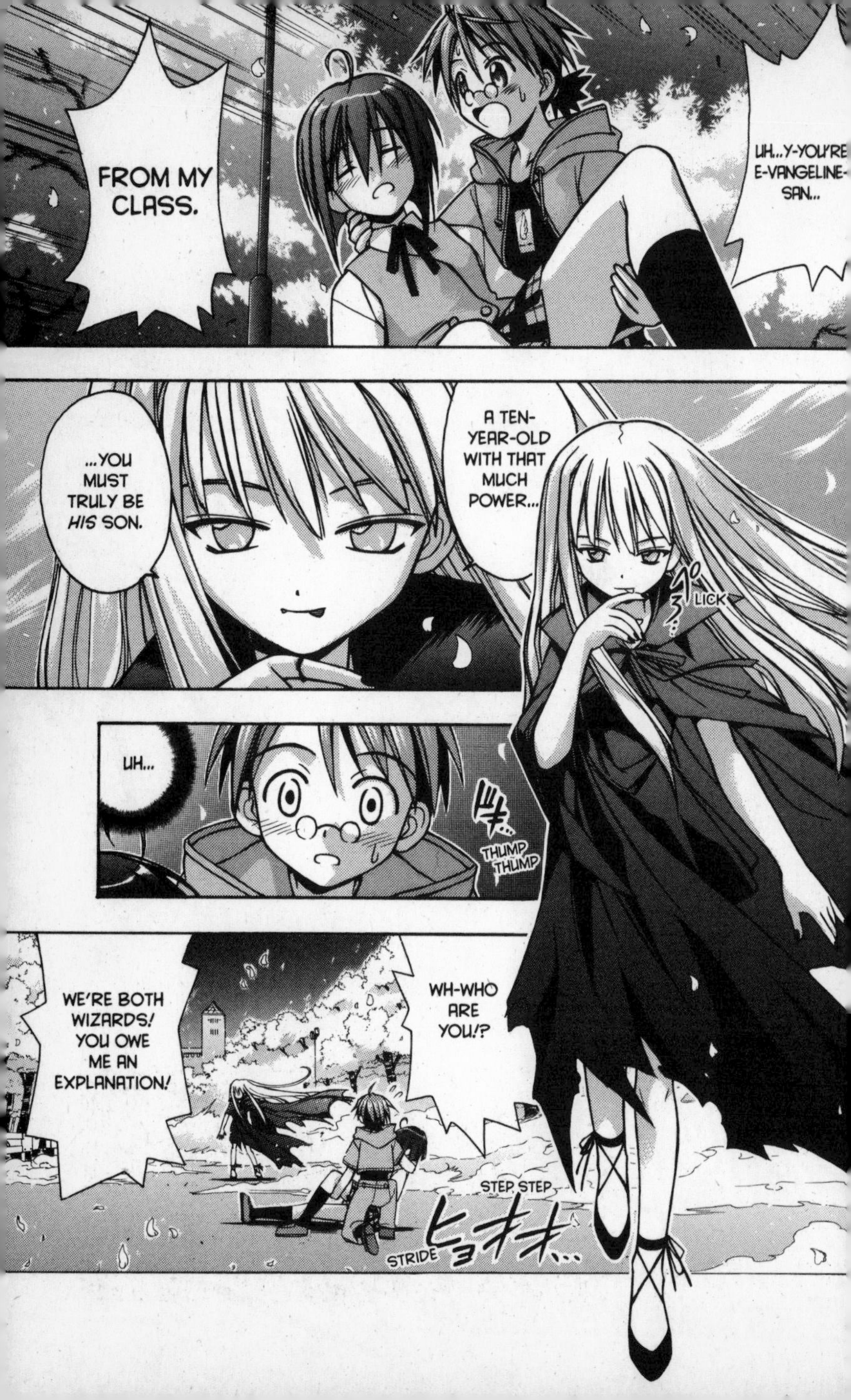
UH...Y-YOU'RE E-VANGELINE-SAN...
FROM MY CLASS.
A TEN-YEAR-OLD WITH THAT MUCH POWER...
...YOU MUST TRULY BE *HIS* SON.
LICK
UH...
THUMP THUMP
WH-WHO ARE YOU!?
WE'RE BOTH WIZARDS! YOU OWE ME AN EXPLANATION!
STEP STEP
STRIDE

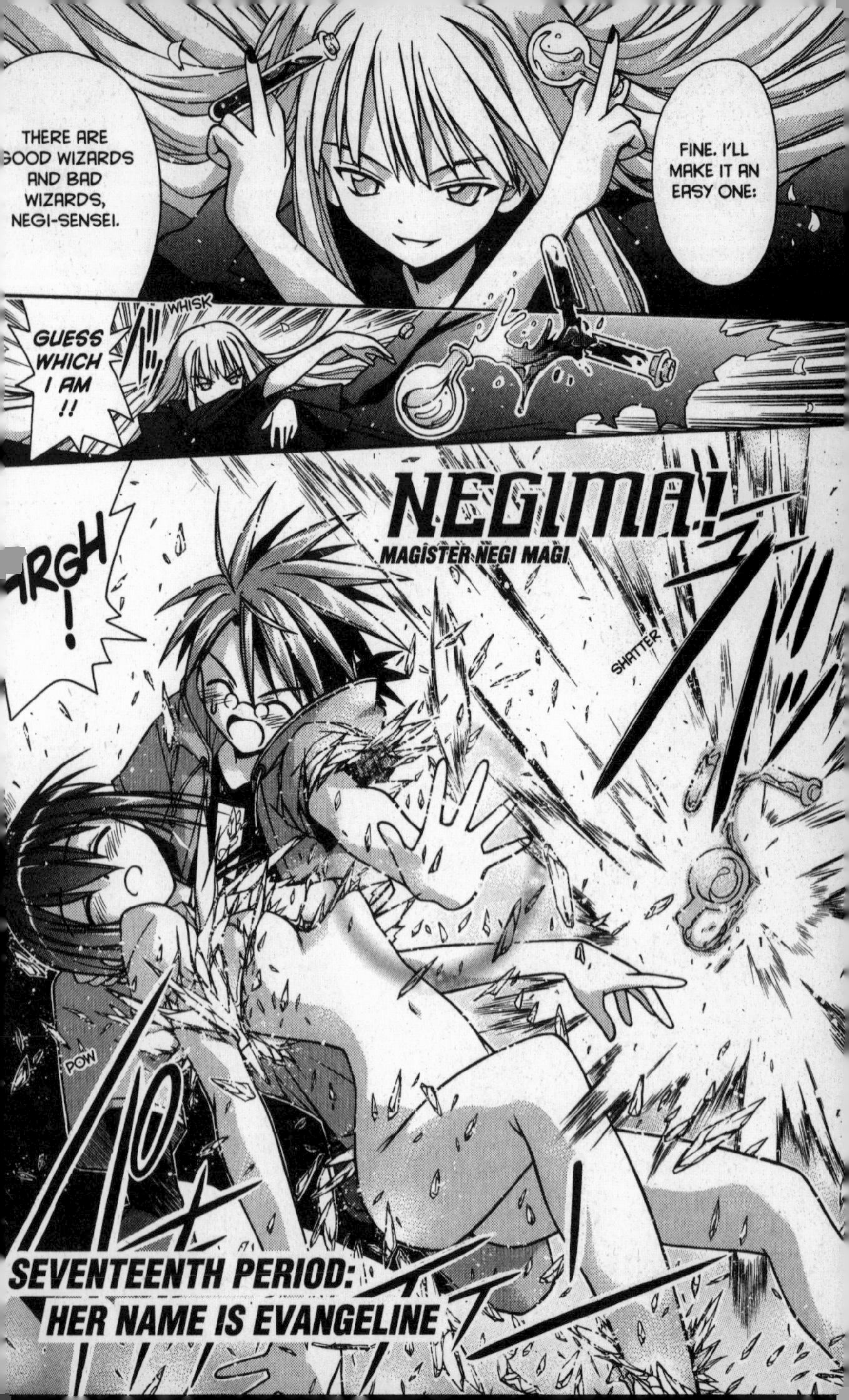
FINE. I'LL MAKE IT AN EASY ONE:
THERE ARE GOOD WIZARDS AND BAD WIZARDS, NEGI-SENSEI.
WHISK
GUESS WHICH I AM !!
NEGIMA!
MAGISTER NEGI MAGI
SHATTER
RGH !
POW
SEVENTEENTH PERIOD:
HER NAME IS EVANGELINE

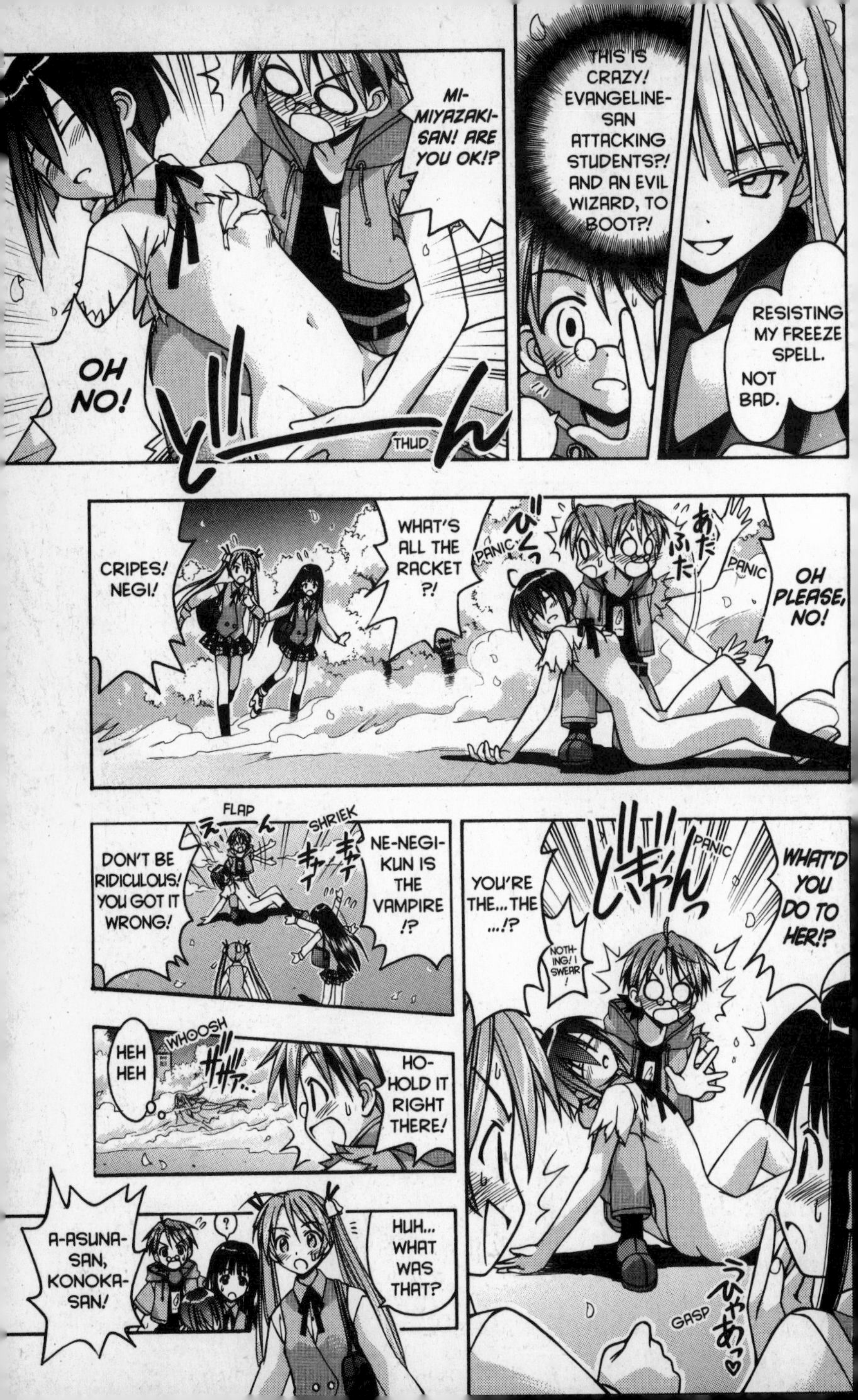
THIS IS CRAZY! EVANGELINE-SAN ATTACKING STUDENTS?! AND AN EVIL WIZARD, TO BOOT?!
RESISTING MY FREEZE SPELL.
NOT BAD.
MI-MIYAZAKI-SAN! ARE YOU OK!?
OH NO!
THUD
PANIC
OH PLEASE, NO!
PANIC
WHAT'S ALL THE RACKET?!
CRIPES! NEGI!
WHAT'D YOU DO TO HER!?
PANIC
YOU'RE THE... THE ...!?
NOTHING! I SWEAR!
GASP
NE-NEGI-KUN IS THE VAMPIRE!?
SHRIEK
FLAP
DON'T BE RIDICULOUS! YOU GOT IT WRONG!
HO-HOLD IT RIGHT THERE!
WHOOSH
HEH HEH
HUH... WHAT WAS THAT?
A-ASUNA-SAN, KONOKA-SAN!

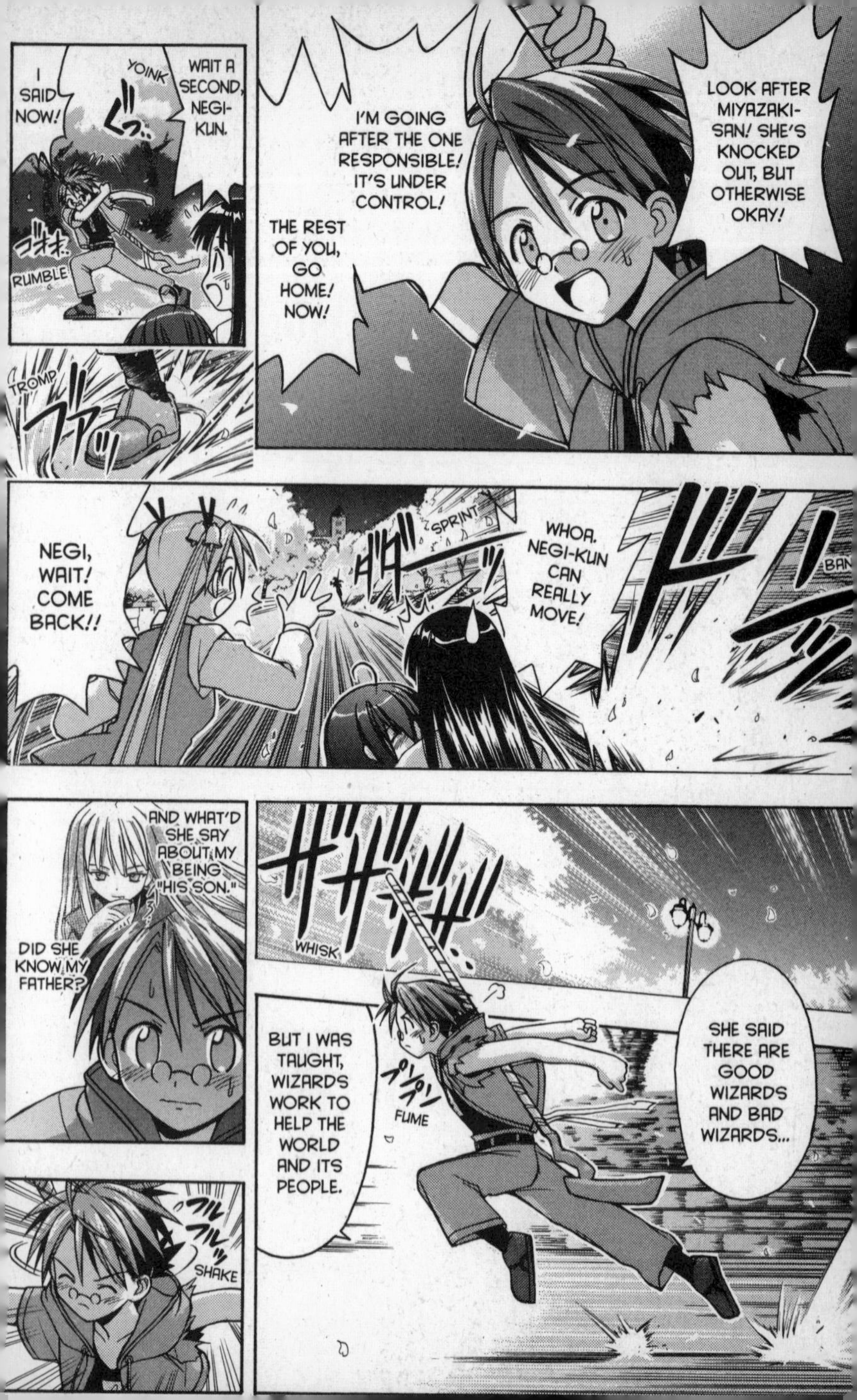
LOOK AFTER MIYAZAKI-SAN! SHE'S KNOCKED OUT, BUT OTHERWISE OKAY!
I'M GOING AFTER THE ONE RESPONSIBLE! IT'S UNDER CONTROL!
THE REST OF YOU, GO HOME! NOW!
WAIT A SECOND, NEGI-KUN.
YOINK
I SAID NOW!
RUMBLE
TROMP
BAN
WHOA. NEGI-KUN CAN REALLY MOVE!
SPRINT
NEGI, WAIT! COME BACK!!
SHE SAID THERE ARE GOOD WIZARDS AND BAD WIZARDS...
BUT I WAS TAUGHT, WIZARDS WORK TO HELP THE WORLD AND ITS PEOPLE.
FUME
WHISK
AND WHAT'D SHE SAY ABOUT MY BEING "HIS SON."
DID SHE KNOW MY FATHER?
SHAKE

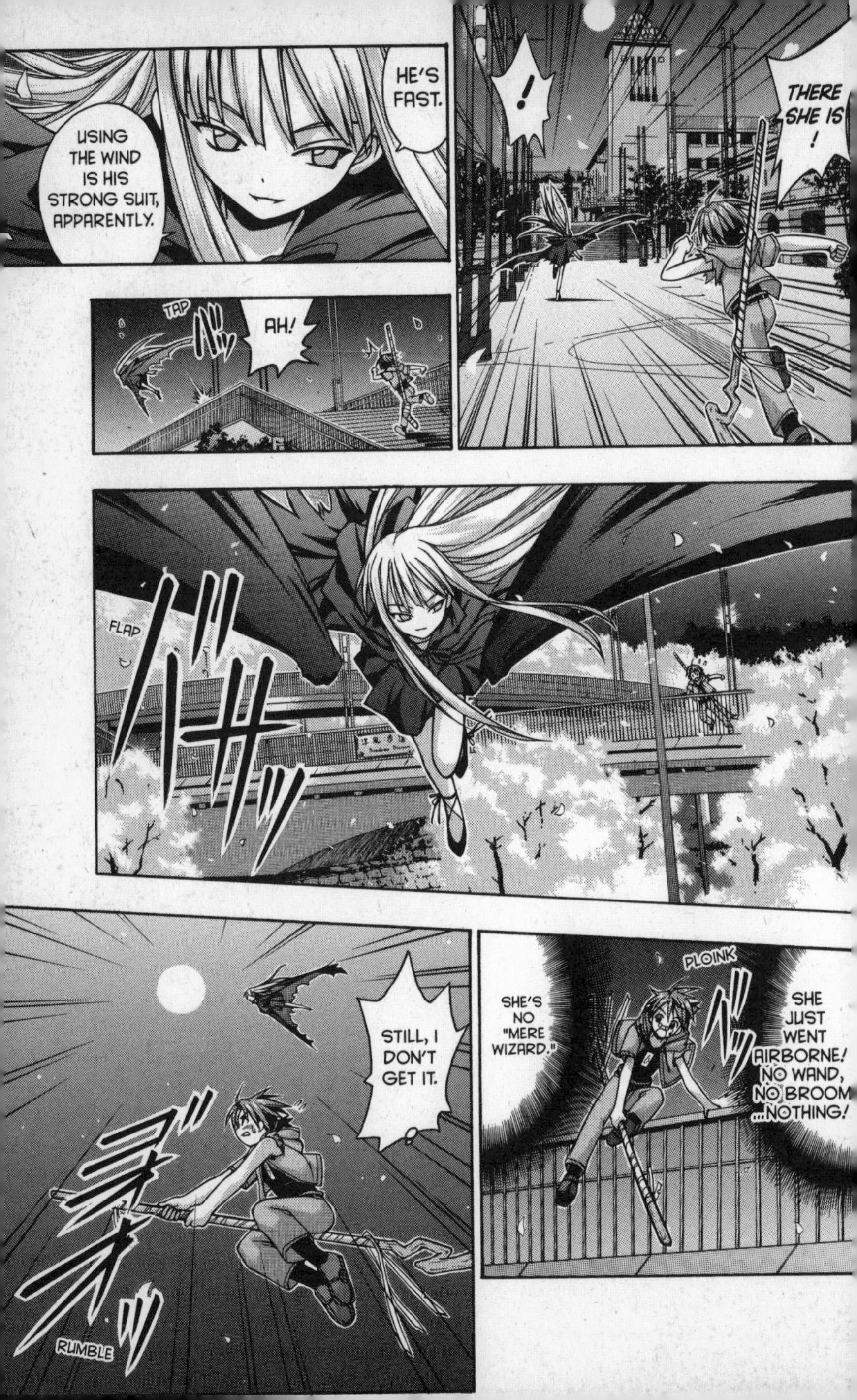
!
THERE SHE IS!
HE'S FAST.
USING THE WIND IS HIS STRONG SUIT, APPARENTLY.
TAP
AH!
FLAP
PLOINK
SHE JUST WENT AIRBORNE! NO WAND, NO BROOM ...NOTHING!
SHE'S NO "MERE WIZARD."
STILL, I DON'T GET IT.
RUMBLE

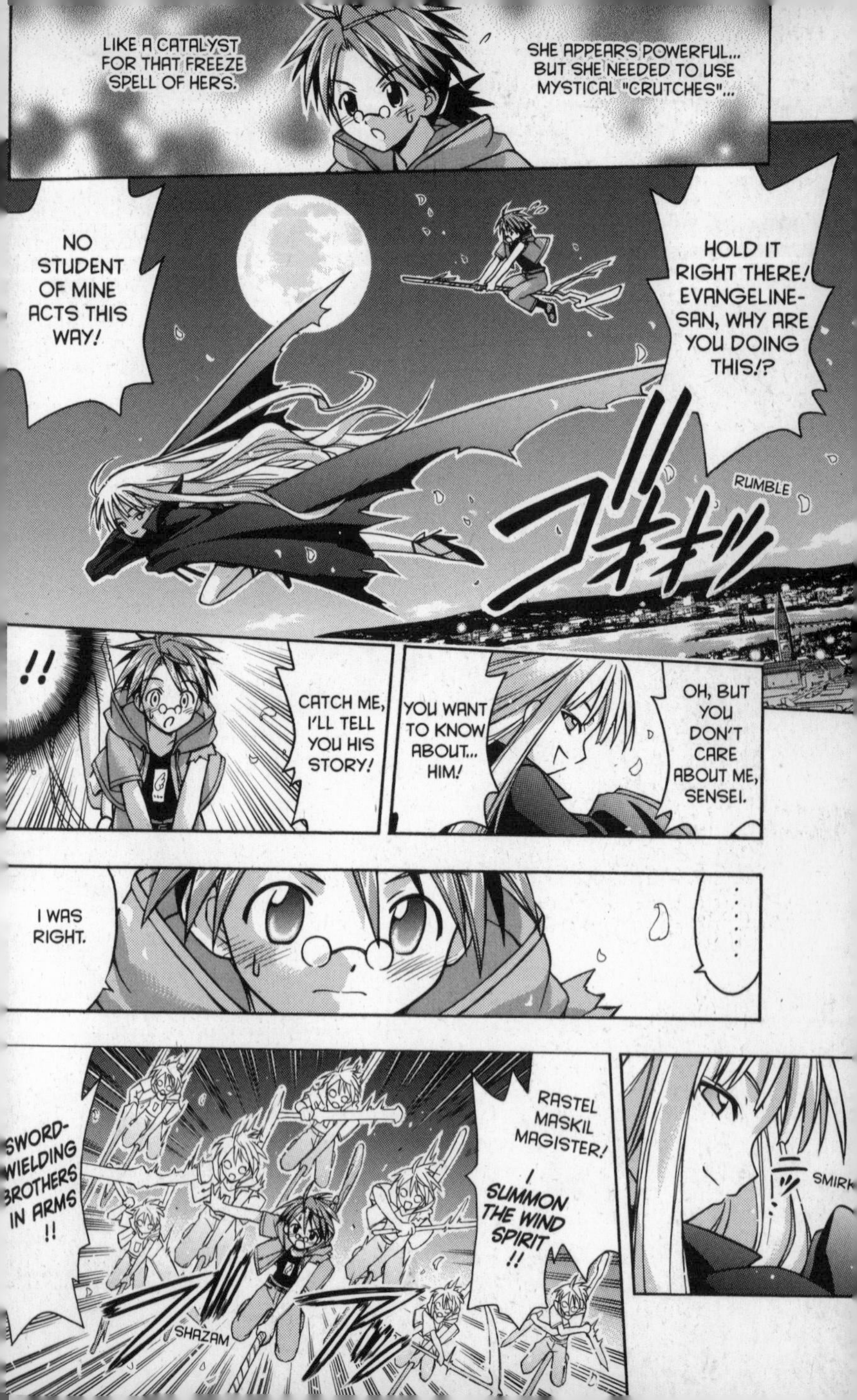

SHE APPEARS POWERFUL... BUT SHE NEEDED TO USE MYSTICAL "CRUTCHES"...
LIKE A CATALYST FOR THAT FREEZE SPELL OF HERS.
HOLD IT RIGHT THERE! EVANGELINE-SAN, WHY ARE YOU DOING THIS!?
NO STUDENT OF MINE ACTS THIS WAY!
RUMBLE
OH, BUT YOU DON'T CARE ABOUT ME, SENSEI.
YOU WANT TO KNOW ABOUT... HIM!
CATCH ME, I'LL TELL YOU HIS STORY!
!!
......
I WAS RIGHT.
SMIRK
RASTEL MASKIL MAGISTER!
I SUMMON THE WIND SPIRIT!!
SWORD-WIELDING BROTHERS IN ARMS!!
SHAZAM

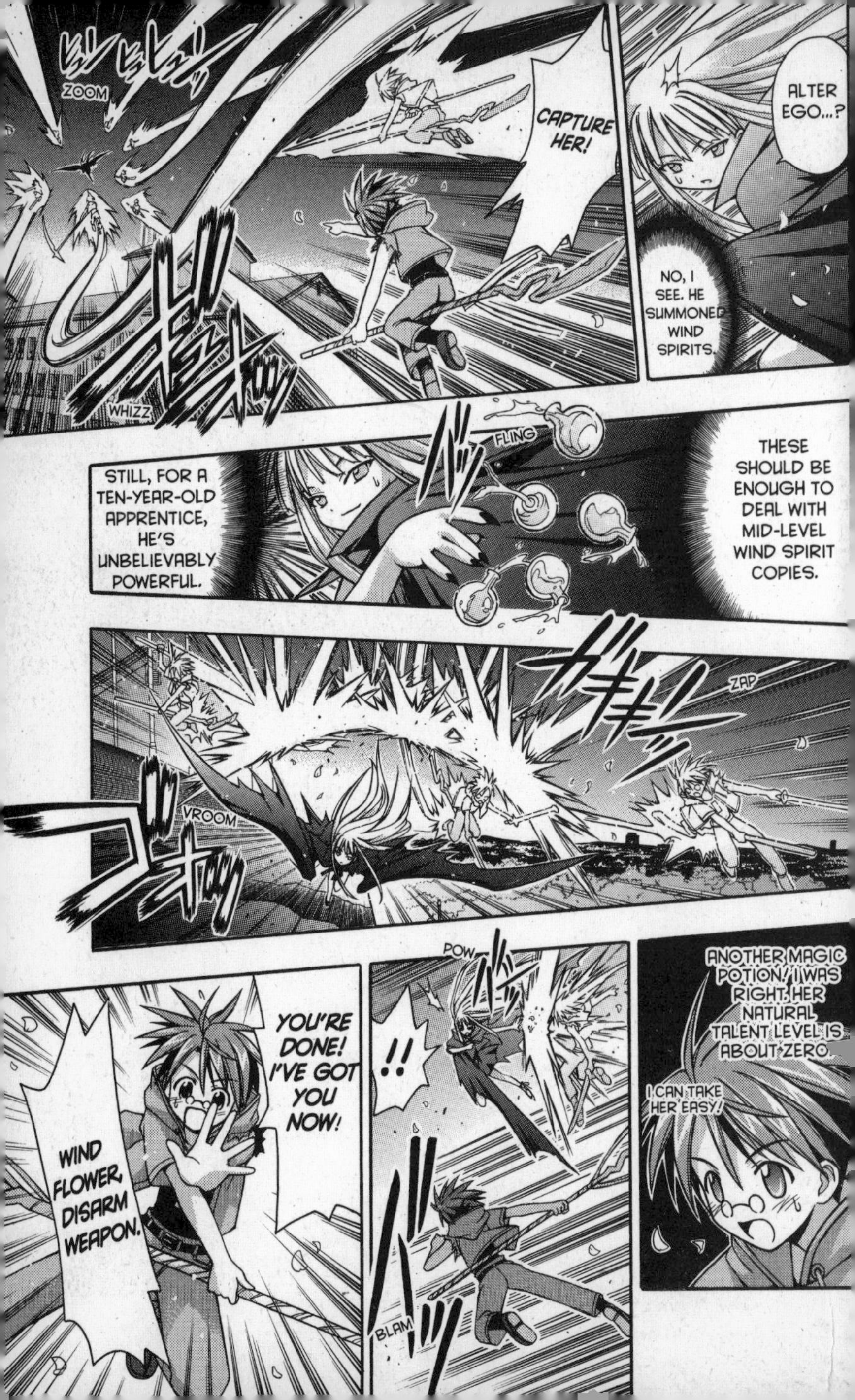
ALTER EGO...?
NO, I SEE. HE SUMMONED WIND SPIRITS.
CAPTURE HER!
ZOOM
WHIZZ
THESE SHOULD BE ENOUGH TO DEAL WITH MID-LEVEL WIND SPIRIT COPIES.
FLING
STILL, FOR A TEN-YEAR-OLD APPRENTICE, HE'S UNBELIEVABLY POWERFUL.
ZAP
VROOM
ANOTHER MAGIC POTION! I WAS RIGHT. HER NATURAL TALENT LEVEL IS ABOUT ZERO.
I CAN TAKE HER EASY!
POW
!!
BLAM
YOU'RE DONE! I'VE GOT YOU NOW!
WIND FLOWER, DISARM WEAPON.

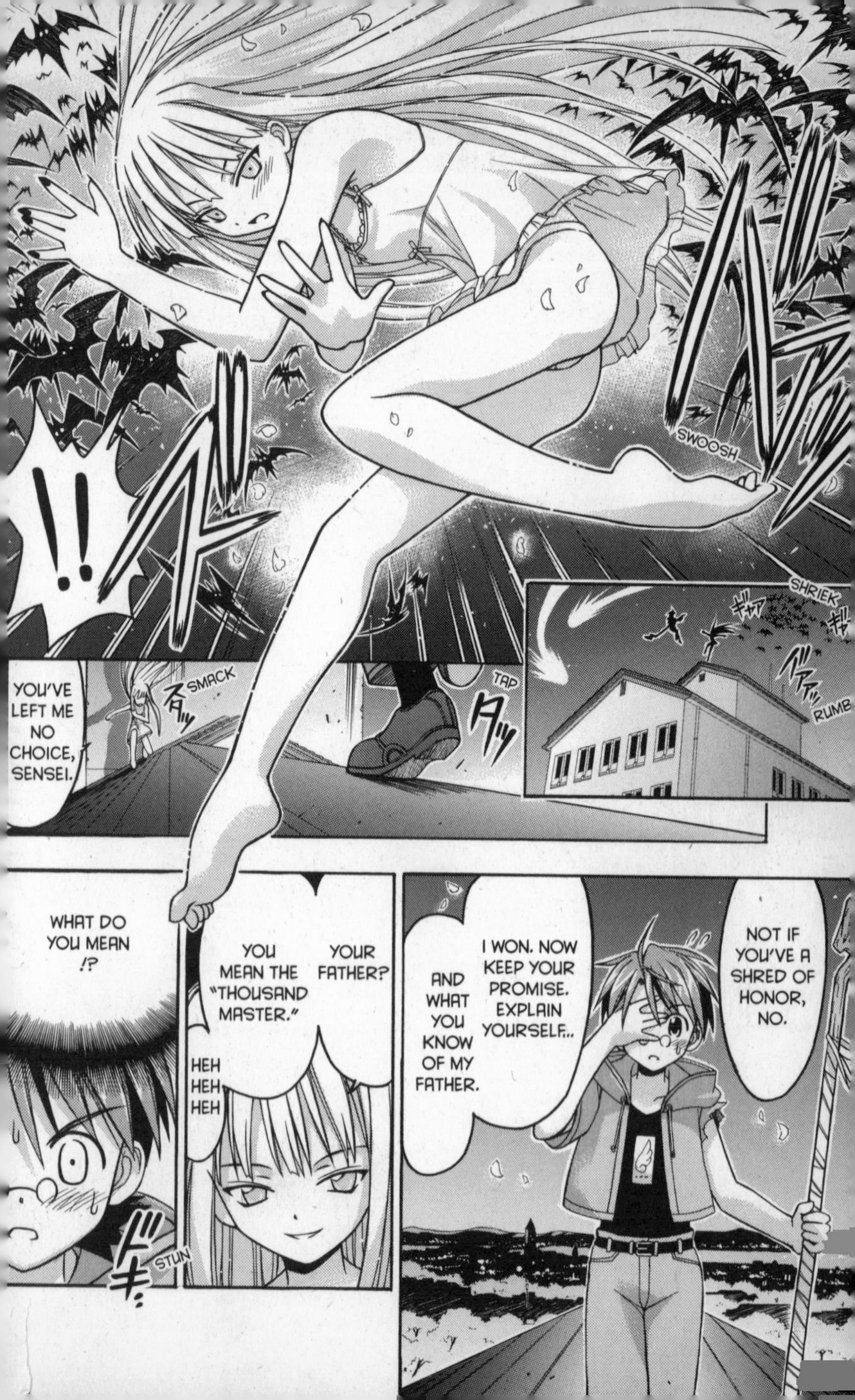

SWOOSH
!!
SHRIEK
RUMB
TAP
SMACK
YOU'VE LEFT ME NO CHOICE, SENSEI.
NOT IF YOU'VE A SHRED OF HONOR, NO.
I WON. NOW KEEP YOUR PROMISE. EXPLAIN YOURSELF...
AND WHAT YOU KNOW OF MY FATHER.
YOUR FATHER?
YOU MEAN THE "THOUSAND MASTER."
HEH HEH HEH
WHAT DO YOU MEAN !?
STUN

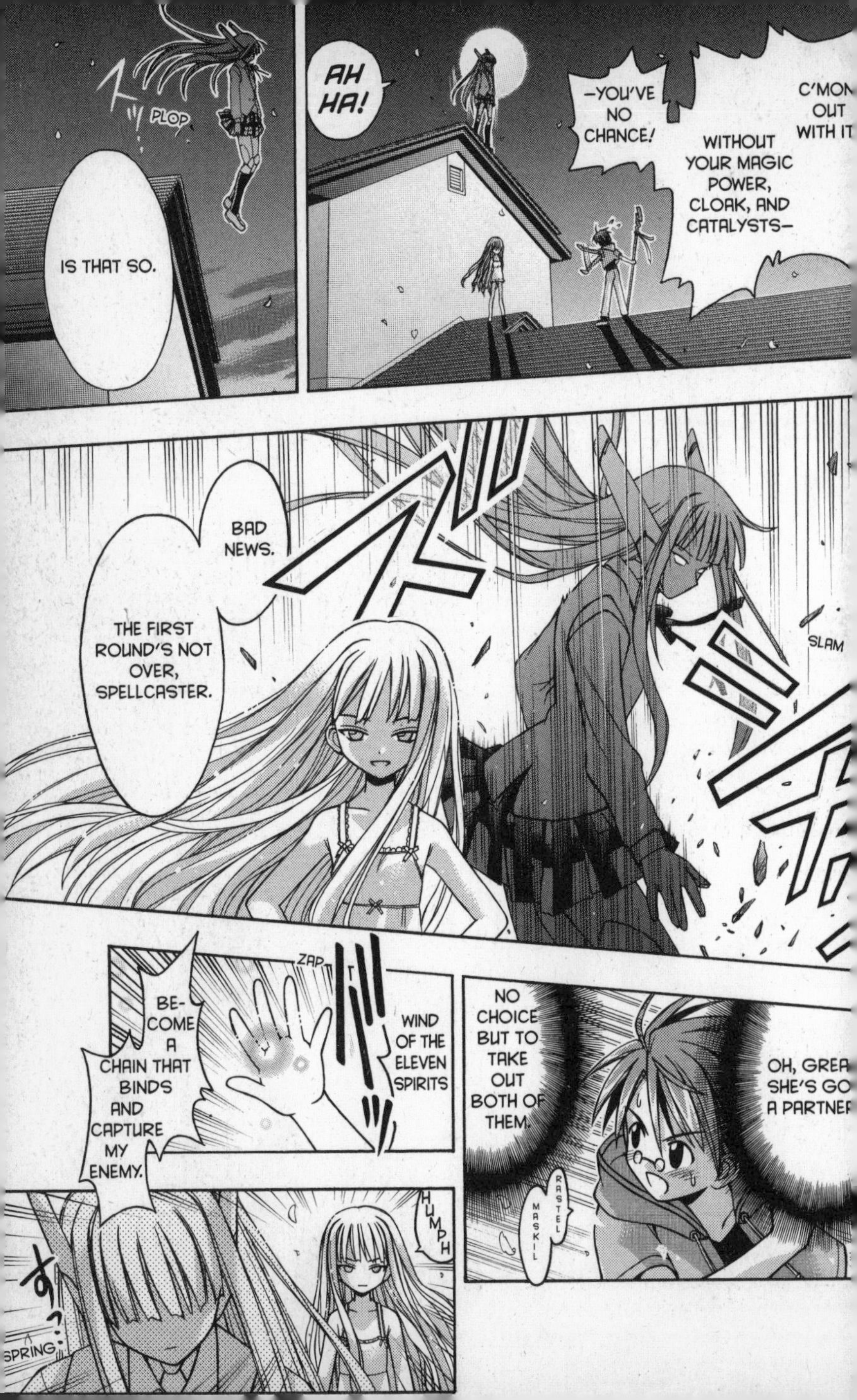
C'MON OUT WITH IT
WITHOUT YOUR MAGIC POWER, CLOAK, AND CATALYSTS—
—YOU'VE NO CHANCE!
AH HA!
PLOP
IS THAT SO.
SLAM
BAD NEWS.
THE FIRST ROUND'S NOT OVER, SPELLCASTER.
OH, GREA
SHE'S GO
A PARTNER
NO CHOICE BUT TO TAKE OUT BOTH OF THEM.
RASTEL MASKIL
WIND OF THE ELEVEN SPIRITS
ZAP
BE-COME A CHAIN THAT BINDS AND CAPTURE MY ENEMY.
HUMPH
SPRING

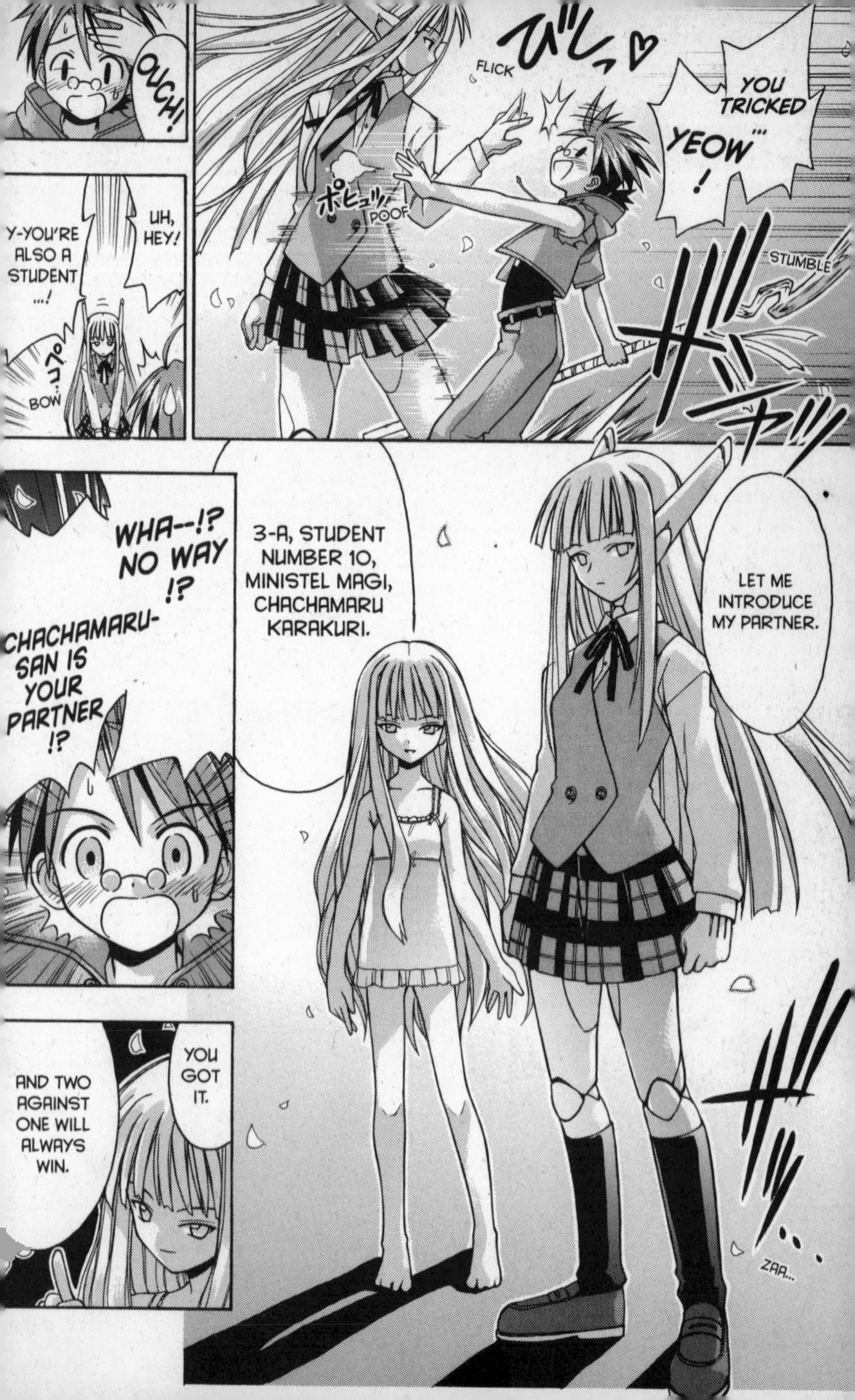

びしっ♥
FLICK
YOU TRICKED...
YEOW!
ポヒュッ
POOF
STUMBLE
OUCH!
UH, HEY!
Y-YOU'RE ALSO A STUDENT ...!
ペコ
BOW
LET ME INTRODUCE MY PARTNER.
3-A, STUDENT NUMBER 10, MINISTEL MAGI, CHACHAMARU KARAKURI.
ZAA...
WHA--!? NO WAY!?
CHACHAMARU-SAN IS YOUR PARTNER!?
YOU GOT IT.
AND TWO AGAINST ONE WILL ALWAYS WIN.

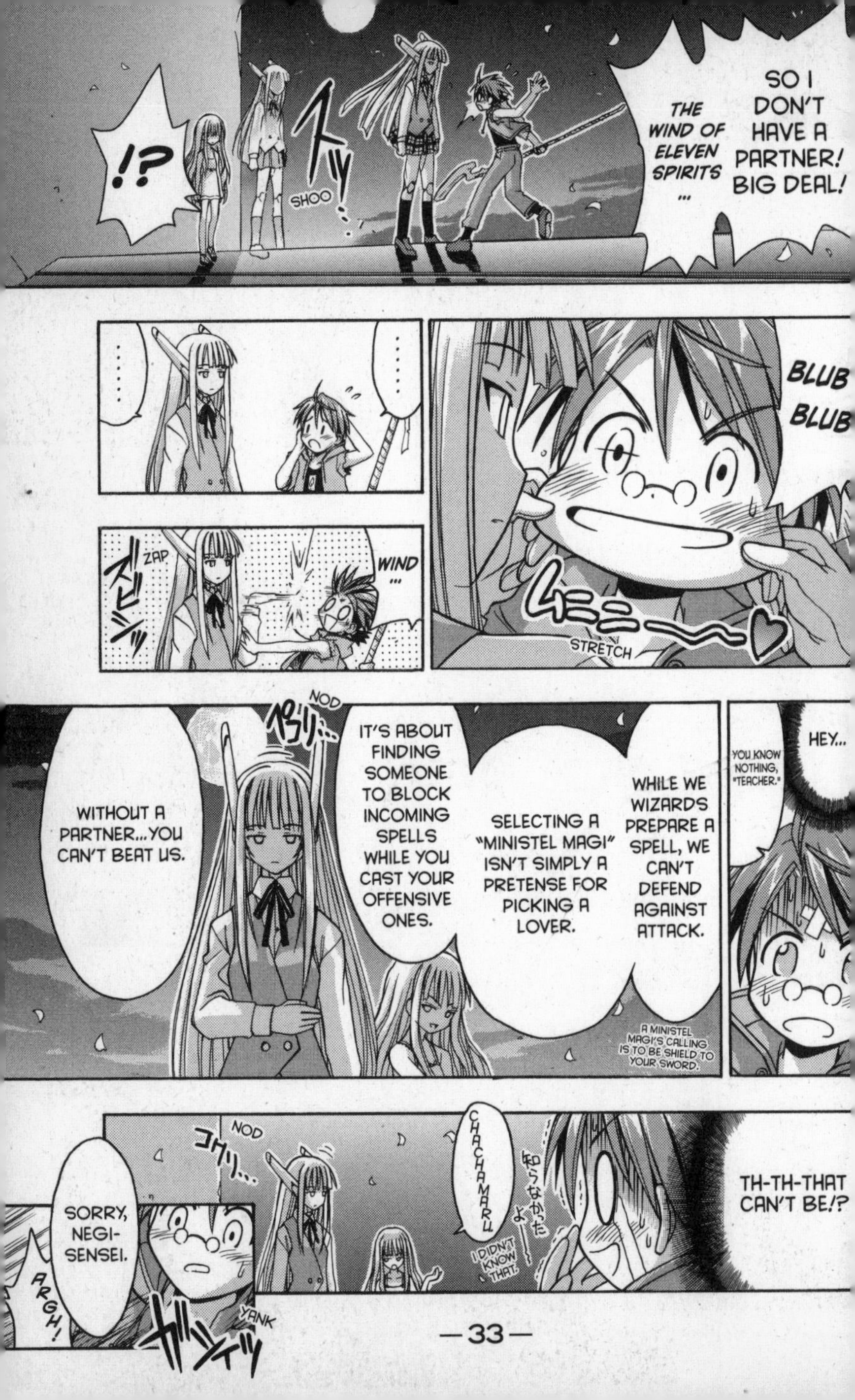
SO I DON'T HAVE A PARTNER! BIG DEAL!
THE WIND OF ELEVEN SPIRITS ...
SHOO
!?
BLUB BLUB
STRETCH
......
......
WIND ...
ZAP
HEY...
YOU KNOW NOTHING, "TEACHER."
WHILE WE WIZARDS PREPARE A SPELL, WE CAN'T DEFEND AGAINST ATTACK.
SELECTING A "MINISTEL MAGI" ISN'T SIMPLY A PRETENSE FOR PICKING A LOVER.
A MINISTEL MAGI'S CALLING IS TO BE SHIELD TO YOUR SWORD.
NOD
IT'S ABOUT FINDING SOMEONE TO BLOCK INCOMING SPELLS WHILE YOU CAST YOUR OFFENSIVE ONES.
WITHOUT A PARTNER...YOU CAN'T BEAT US.
TH-TH-THAT CAN'T BE!?
I DIDN'T KNOW THAT.
CHACHAMARU
NOD
SORRY, NEGI-SENSEI.
YANK
ARGH!

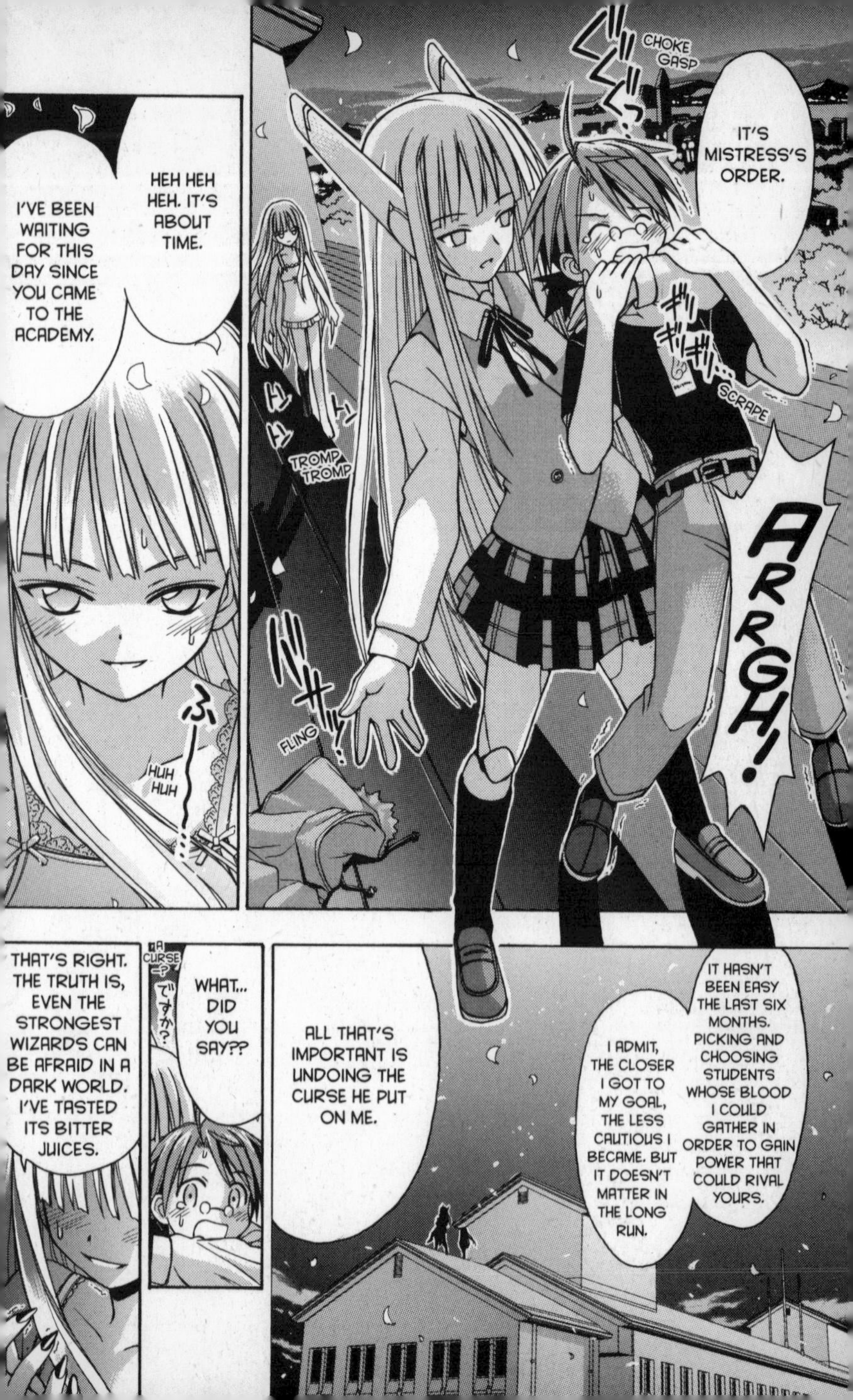
CHOKE GASP
IT'S MISTRESS'S ORDER.
SCRAPE
ARRGH!
TROMP TROMP
FLING
HEH HEH HEH. IT'S ABOUT TIME.
I'VE BEEN WAITING FOR THIS DAY SINCE YOU CAME TO THE ACADEMY.
HUH HUH
IT HASN'T BEEN EASY THE LAST SIX MONTHS. PICKING AND CHOOSING STUDENTS WHOSE BLOOD I COULD GATHER IN ORDER TO GAIN POWER THAT COULD RIVAL YOURS.
I ADMIT, THE CLOSER I GOT TO MY GOAL, THE LESS CAUTIOUS I BECAME. BUT IT DOESN'T MATTER IN THE LONG RUN.
ALL THAT'S IMPORTANT IS UNDOING THE CURSE HE PUT ON ME.
WHAT... DID YOU SAY??
A CURSE--?
ですか?
THAT'S RIGHT. THE TRUTH IS, EVEN THE STRONGEST WIZARDS CAN BE AFRAID IN A DARK WORLD. I'VE TASTED ITS BITTER JUICES.

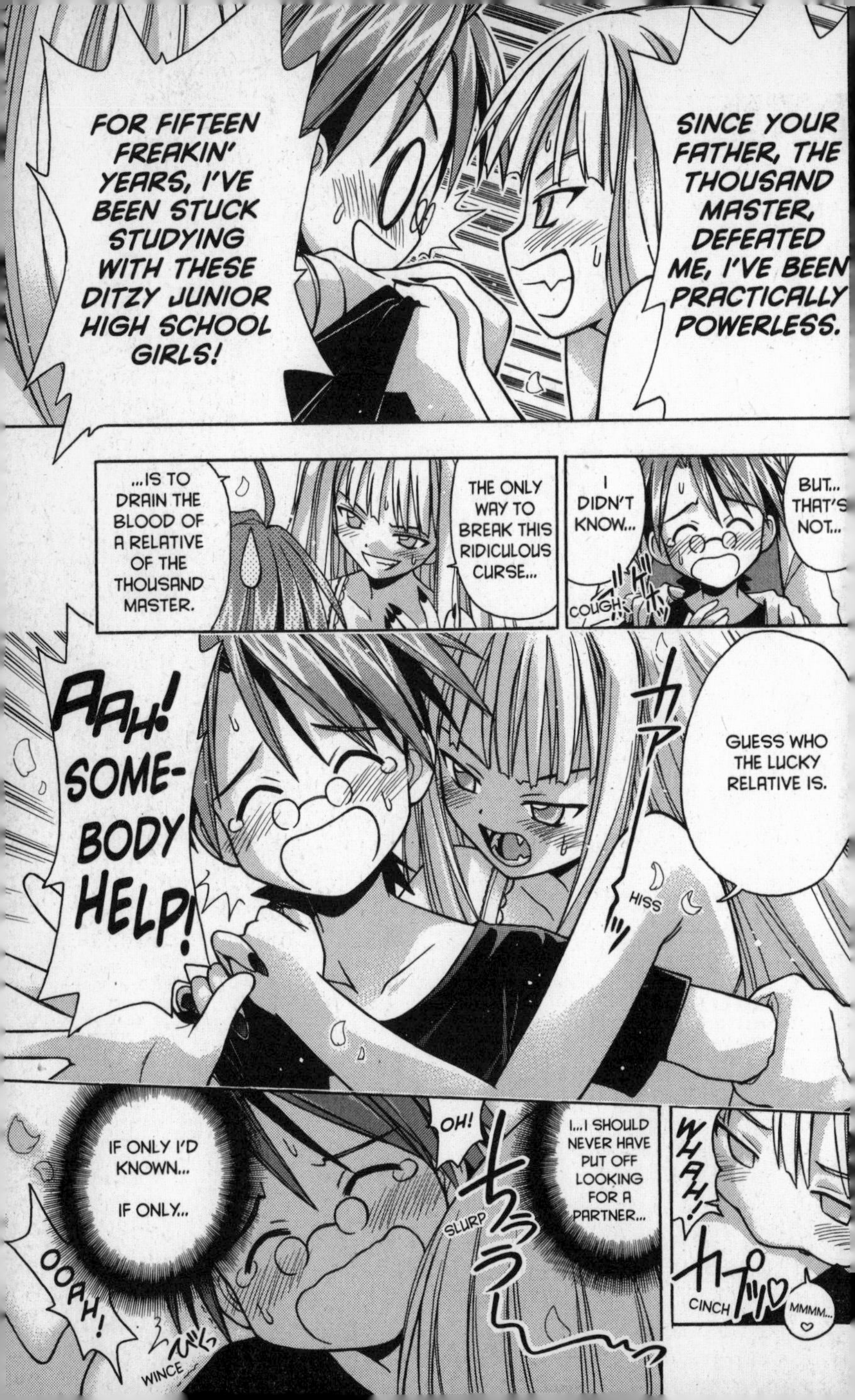
SINCE YOUR FATHER, THE THOUSAND MASTER, DEFEATED ME, I'VE BEEN PRACTICALLY POWERLESS.
FOR FIFTEEN FREAKIN' YEARS, I'VE BEEN STUCK STUDYING WITH THESE DITZY JUNIOR HIGH SCHOOL GIRLS!
BUT... THAT'S NOT...
I DIDN'T KNOW...
COUGH
THE ONLY WAY TO BREAK THIS RIDICULOUS CURSE...
...IS TO DRAIN THE BLOOD OF A RELATIVE OF THE THOUSAND MASTER.
GUESS WHO THE LUCKY RELATIVE IS.
HISS
AAH! SOME-BODY HELP!
WHAH!
CINCH
MMMM... ♡
I...I SHOULD NEVER HAVE PUT OFF LOOKING FOR A PARTNER...
OH!
SLURP
IF ONLY I'D KNOWN...
IF ONLY...
OOAAH!
WINCE

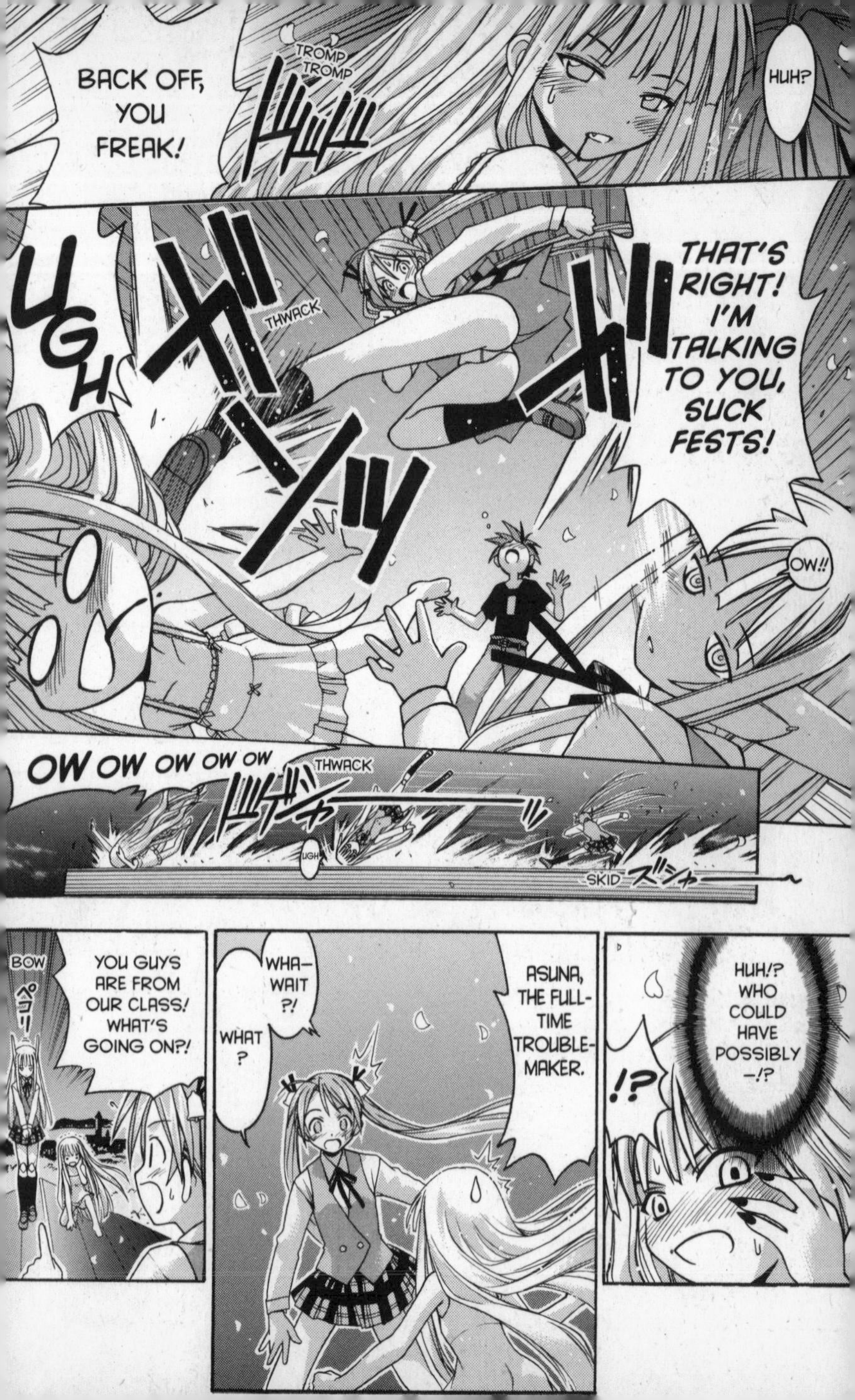
HUH?
TROMP TROMP
BACK OFF, YOU FREAK!
THAT'S RIGHT! I'M TALKING TO YOU, SUCK FESTS!
THWACK
UGH
OW!!
OW OW OW OW OW
THWACK
UGH
SKID
!?
HUH!? WHO COULD HAVE POSSIBLY—!?
ASUNA, THE FULL-TIME TROUBLE-MAKER.
WHA—WAIT?!
WHAT?
YOU GUYS ARE FROM OUR CLASS! WHAT'S GOING ON?!
BOW

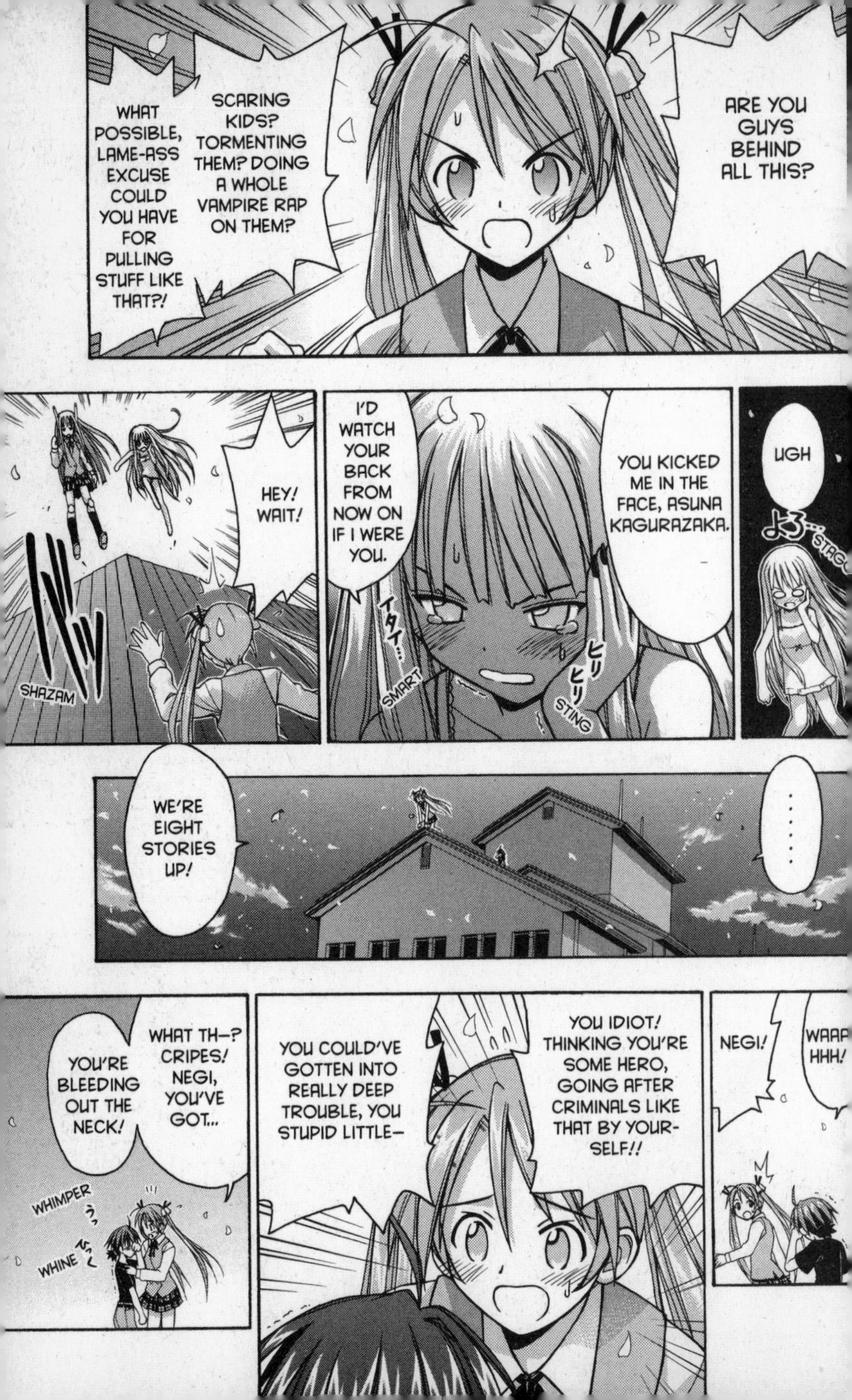
ARE YOU GUYS BEHIND ALL THIS?
SCARING KIDS? TORMENTING THEM? DOING A WHOLE VAMPIRE RAP ON THEM?
WHAT POSSIBLE, LAME-ASS EXCUSE COULD YOU HAVE FOR PULLING STUFF LIKE THAT?!
UGH
よろ… STAGG
YOU KICKED ME IN THE FACE, ASUNA KAGURAZAKA.
I'D WATCH YOUR BACK FROM NOW ON IF I WERE YOU.
ヒリヒリ STING
イタイ… SMART
HEY! WAIT!
SHAZAM
......
WE'RE EIGHT STORIES UP!
WAAAHHH!
NEGI!
YOU IDIOT! THINKING YOU'RE SOME HERO, GOING AFTER CRIMINALS LIKE THAT BY YOUR-SELF!!
YOU COULD'VE GOTTEN INTO REALLY DEEP TROUBLE, YOU STUPID LITTLE—
WHAT TH—? CRIPES! NEGI, YOU'VE GOT...
YOU'RE BLEEDING OUT THE NECK!
うっ WHIMPER
ひっく WHINE

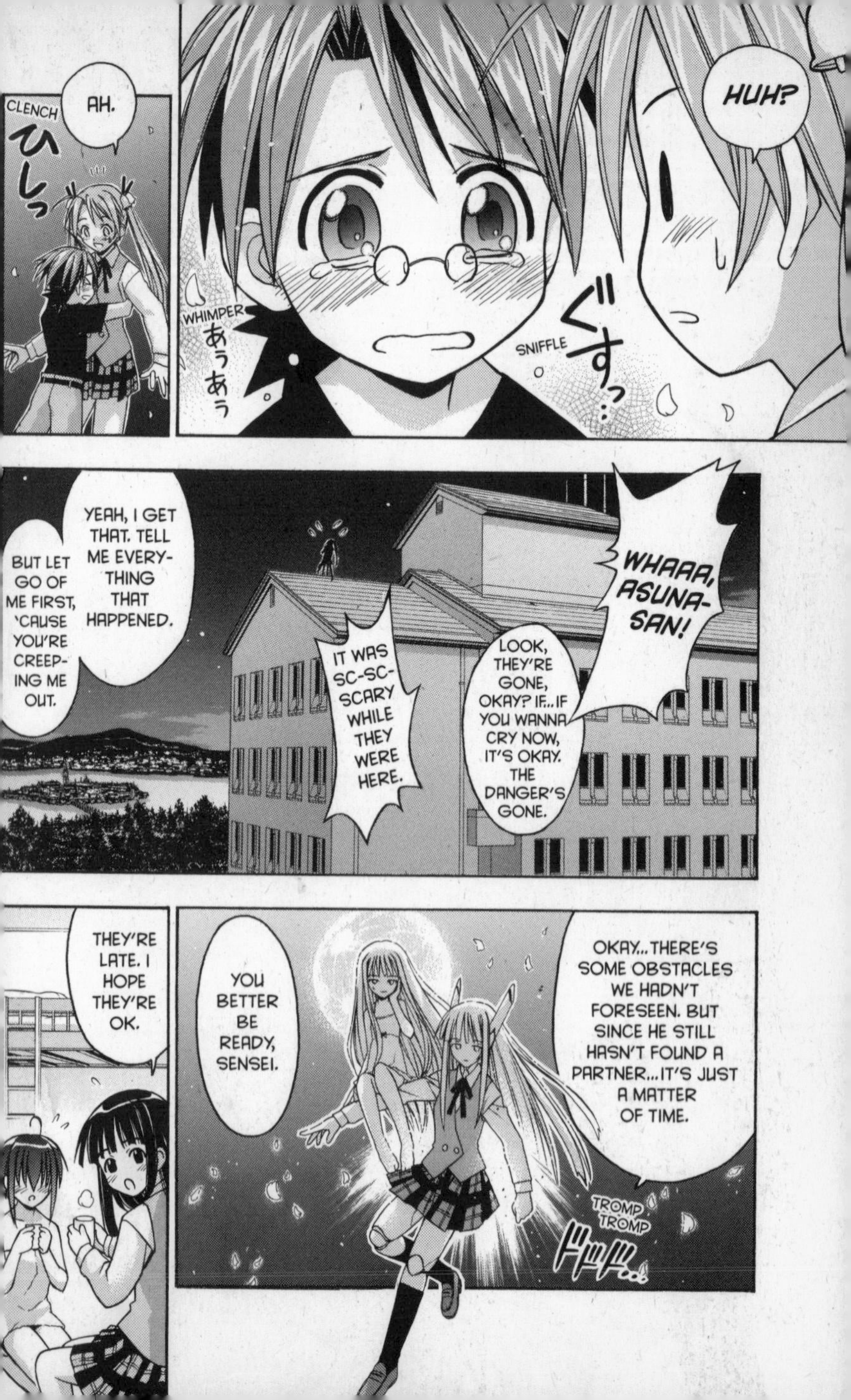
HUH?
SNIFFLE
ぐすっ
WHIMPER
あぅあぅ
CLENCH
ひしっ
AH.
WHAAA, ASUNA-SAN!
LOOK, THEY'RE GONE, OKAY? IF... IF YOU WANNA CRY NOW, IT'S OKAY. THE DANGER'S GONE.
IT WAS SC-SC-SCARY WHILE THEY WERE HERE.
YEAH, I GET THAT. TELL ME EVERYTHING THAT HAPPENED.
BUT LET GO OF ME FIRST, 'CAUSE YOU'RE CREEPING ME OUT.
OKAY... THERE'S SOME OBSTACLES WE HADN'T FORESEEN. BUT SINCE HE STILL HASN'T FOUND A PARTNER... IT'S JUST A MATTER OF TIME.
YOU BETTER BE READY, SENSEI.
TROMP TROMP
ドドド...
THEY'RE LATE. I HOPE THEY'RE OK.

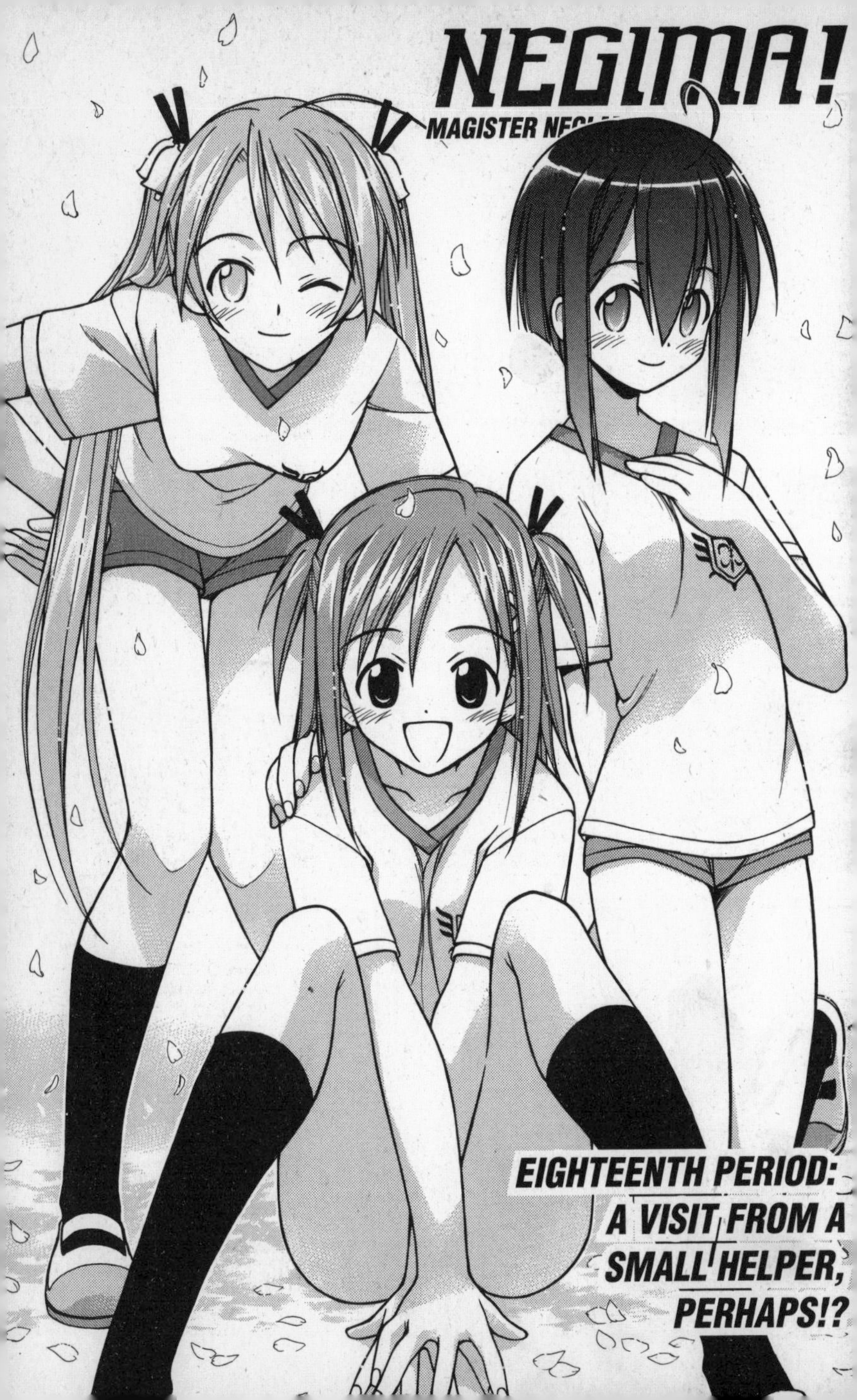
NEGIMA!
MAGISTER NEGI
EIGHTEENTH PERIOD:
A VISIT FROM A
SMALL HELPER,
PERHAPS!?

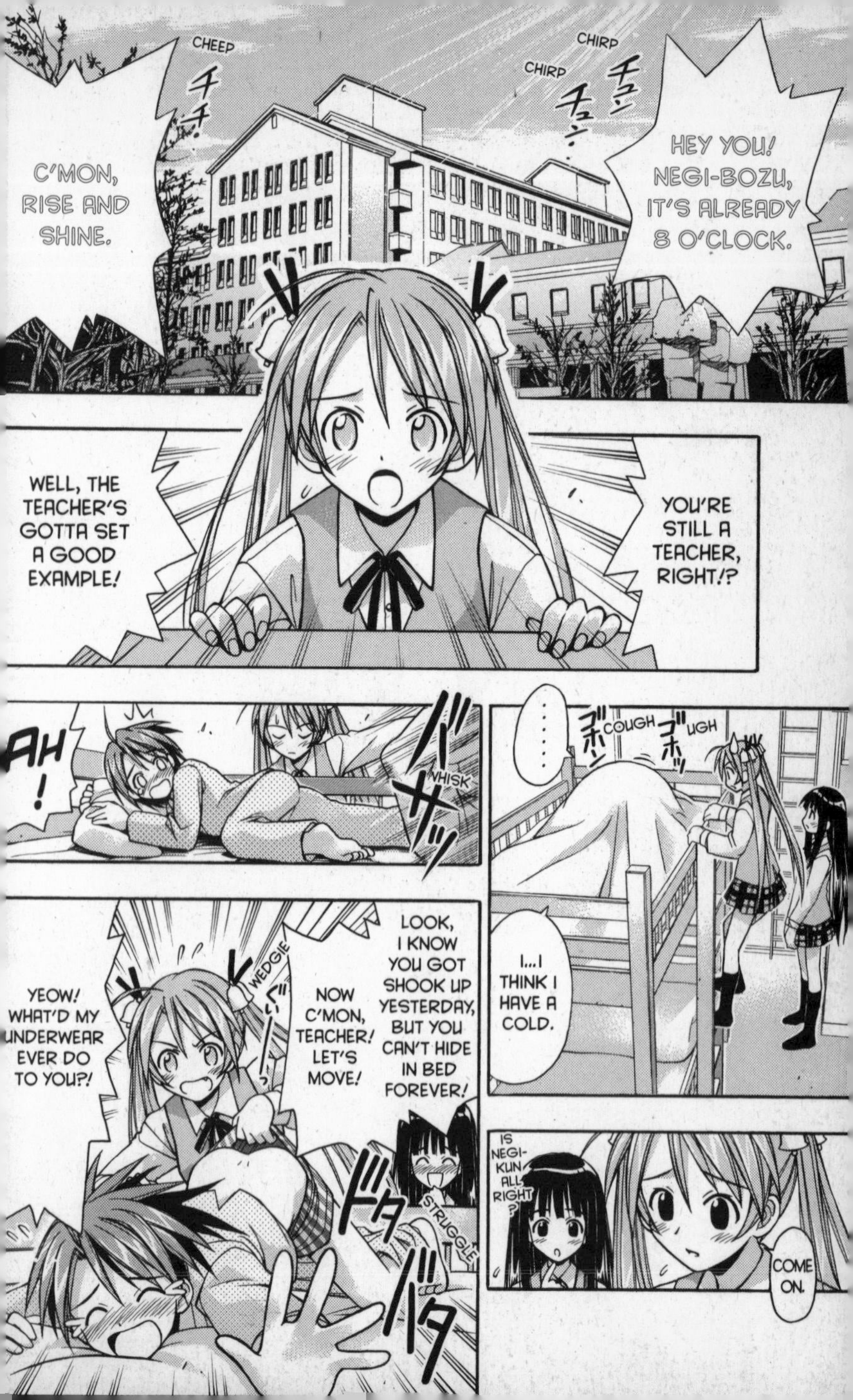
HEY YOU! NEGI-BOZU, IT'S ALREADY 8 O'CLOCK.
CHIRP
CHIRP
CHEEP
C'MON, RISE AND SHINE.
YOU'RE STILL A TEACHER, RIGHT!?
WELL, THE TEACHER'S GOTTA SET A GOOD EXAMPLE!
......
COUGH
UGH
I...I THINK I HAVE A COLD.
WHISK
AH!
LOOK, I KNOW YOU GOT SHOOK UP YESTERDAY, BUT YOU CAN'T HIDE IN BED FOREVER!
NOW C'MON, TEACHER! LET'S MOVE!
WEDGIE
YEOW! WHAT'D MY UNDERWEAR EVER DO TO YOU?!
STRUGGLE
IS NEGI-KUN ALL RIGHT?
COME ON.

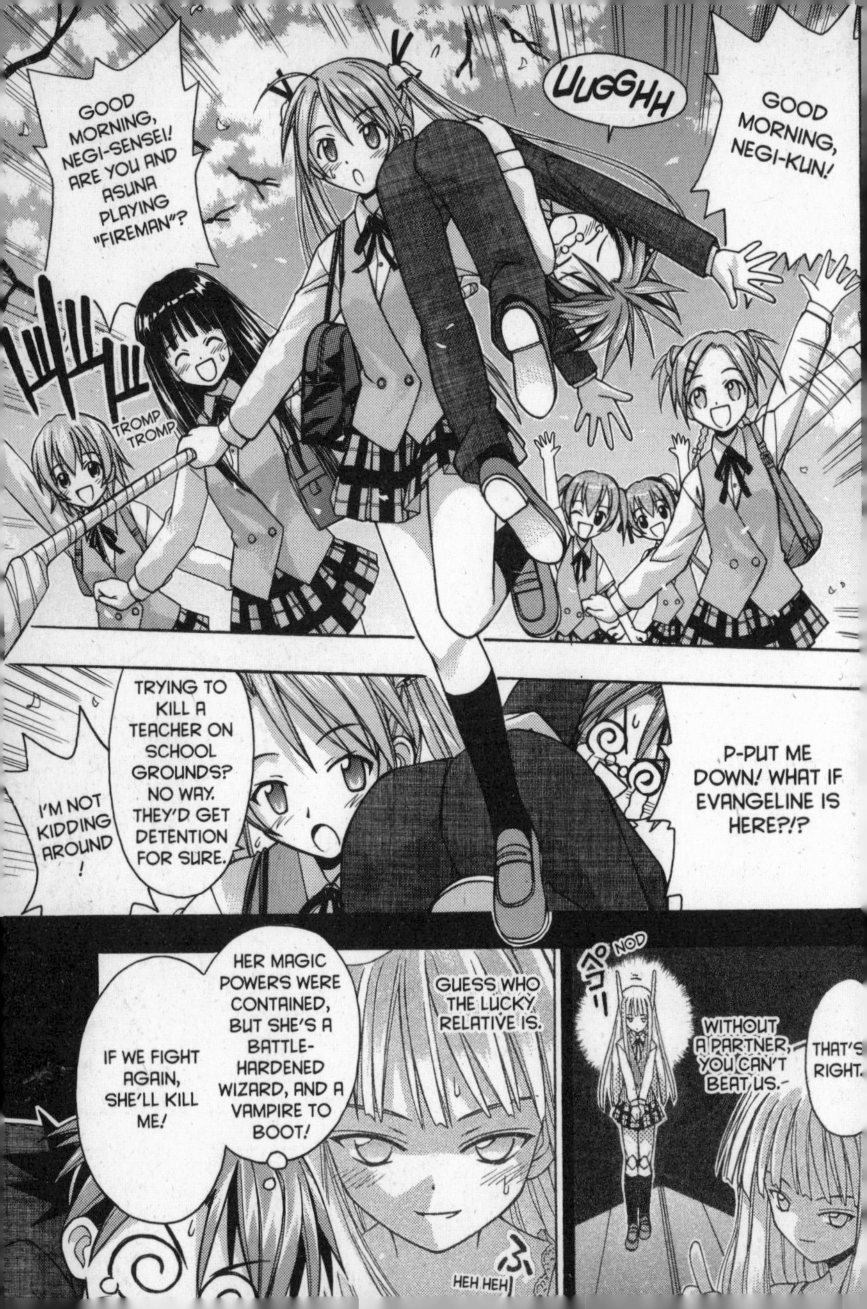

GOOD MORNING, NEGI-KUN!
UUGGHH
GOOD MORNING, NEGI-SENSEI! ARE YOU AND ASUNA PLAYING "FIREMAN"?
TROMP TROMP
P-PUT ME DOWN! WHAT IF EVANGELINE IS HERE?!?
TRYING TO KILL A TEACHER ON SCHOOL GROUNDS? NO WAY. THEY'D GET DETENTION FOR SURE.
I'M NOT KIDDING AROUND!
THAT'S RIGHT.
WITHOUT A PARTNER, YOU CAN'T BEAT US.
NOD
GUESS WHO THE LUCKY RELATIVE IS.
HER MAGIC POWERS WERE CONTAINED, BUT SHE'S A BATTLE-HARDENED WIZARD, AND A VAMPIRE TO BOOT!
IF WE FIGHT AGAIN, SHE'LL KILL ME!
HEH HEH

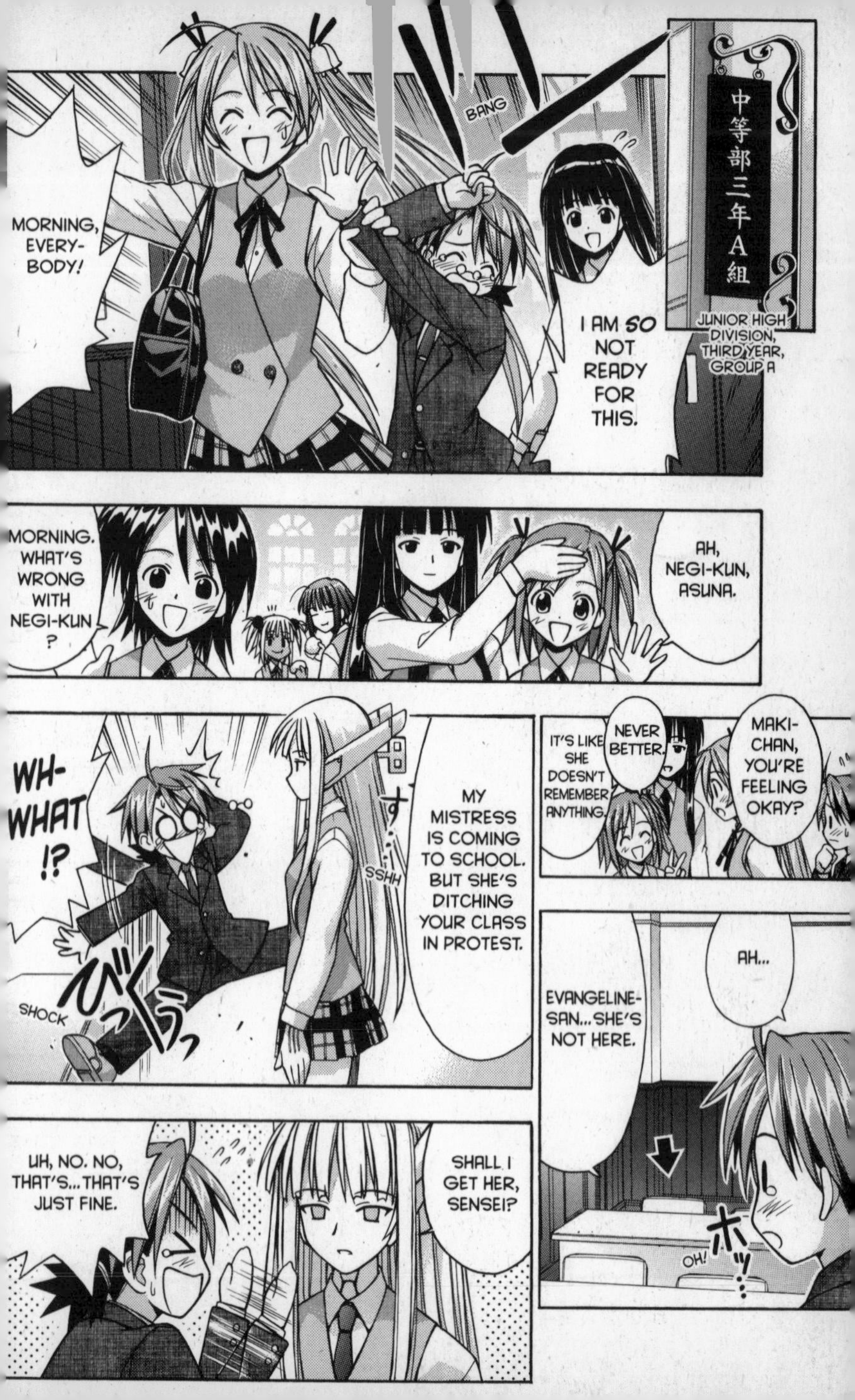
中等部三年A組
JUNIOR HIGH DIVISION, THIRD YEAR, GROUP A
BANG
MORNING, EVERY-BODY!
I AM SO NOT READY FOR THIS.
AH, NEGI-KUN, ASUNA.
MORNING. WHAT'S WRONG WITH NEGI-KUN?
MAKI-CHAN, YOU'RE FEELING OKAY?
NEVER BETTER.
IT'S LIKE SHE DOESN'T REMEMBER ANYTHING.
AH...
EVANGELINE-SAN...SHE'S NOT HERE.
OH!
MY MISTRESS IS COMING TO SCHOOL. BUT SHE'S DITCHING YOUR CLASS IN PROTEST.
SSHH
WH-WHAT!?
SHOCK
SHALL I GET HER, SENSEI?
UH, NO. NO, THAT'S...THAT'S JUST FINE.

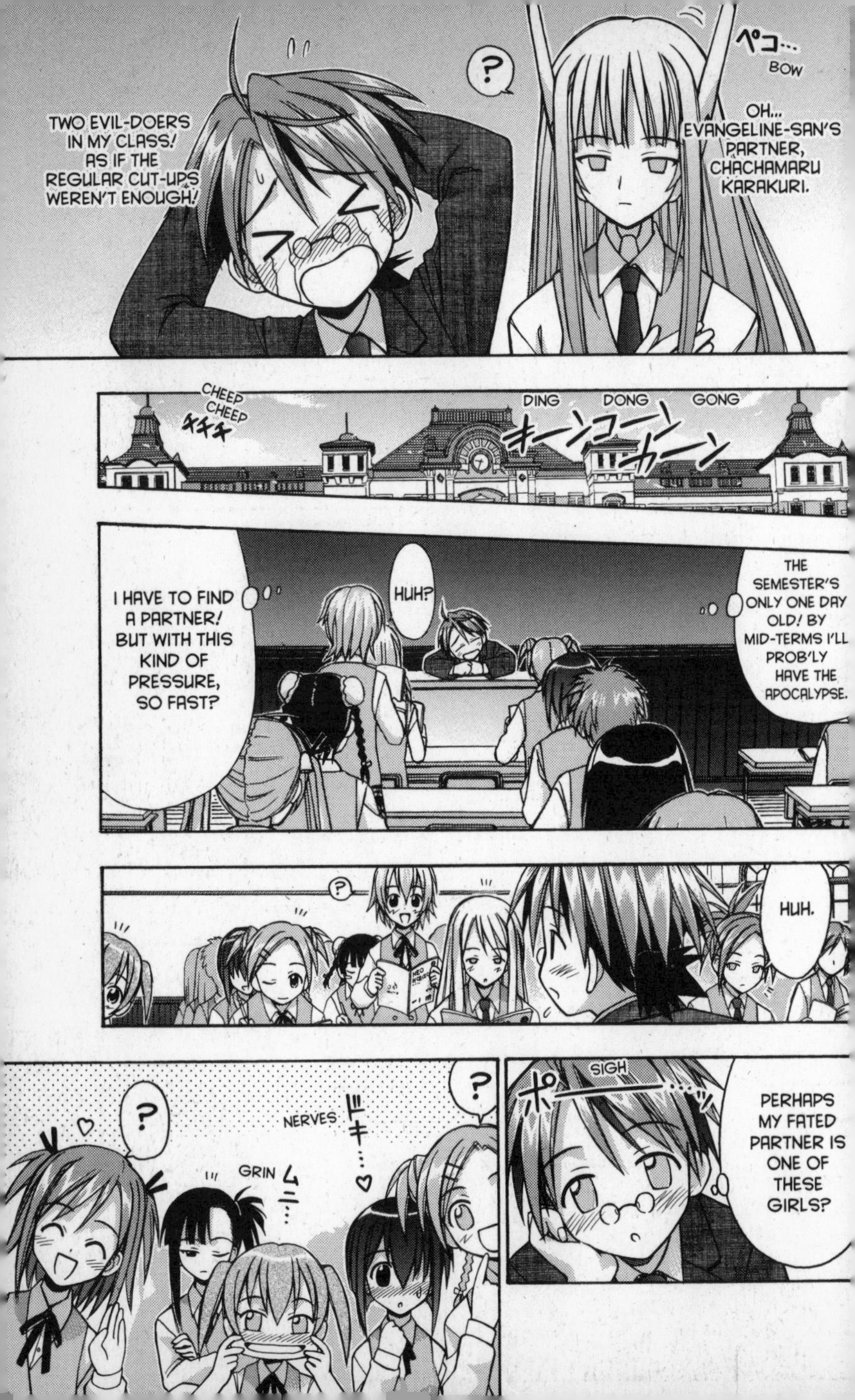
ペコ…
BOW
OH... EVANGELINE-SAN'S PARTNER, CHACHAMARU KARAKURI.
?
TWO EVIL-DOERS IN MY CLASS! AS IF THE REGULAR CUT-UPS WEREN'T ENOUGH!
DING DONG GONG
キーンコーンカーン
CHEEP CHEEP
チチチ
THE SEMESTER'S ONLY ONE DAY OLD! BY MID-TERMS I'LL PROB'LY HAVE THE APOCALYPSE.
HUH?
I HAVE TO FIND A PARTNER! BUT WITH THIS KIND OF PRESSURE, SO FAST?
HUH.
?
SIGH
ポー…ッ
PERHAPS MY FATED PARTNER IS ONE OF THESE GIRLS?
?
NERVES
ドキ…♡
GRIN
ムニ…
?

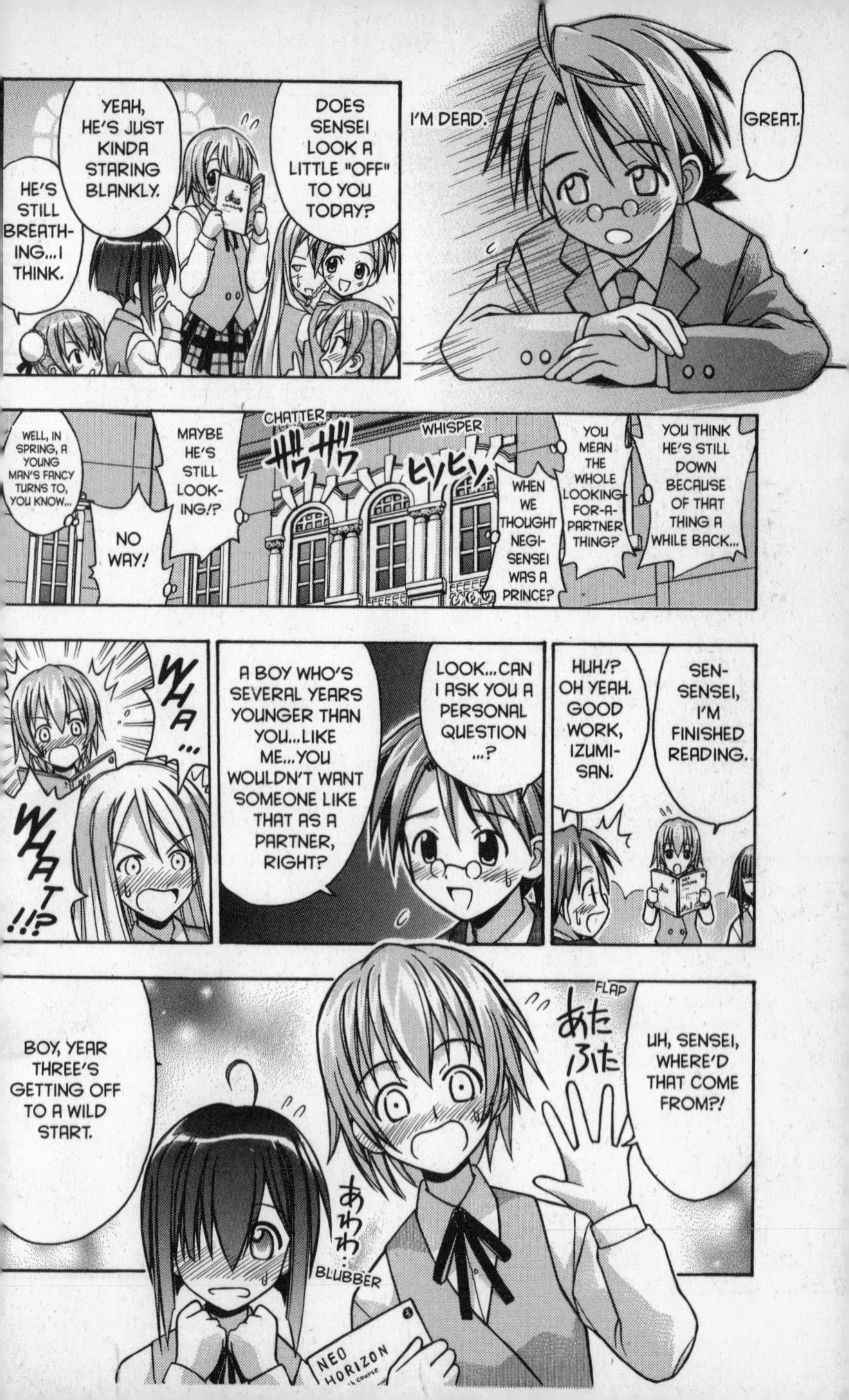
GREAT.
I'M DEAD.
DOES SENSEI LOOK A LITTLE "OFF" TO YOU TODAY?
YEAH, HE'S JUST KINDA STARING BLANKLY.
HE'S STILL BREATHING...I THINK.
YOU THINK HE'S STILL DOWN BECAUSE OF THAT THING A WHILE BACK...
YOU MEAN THE WHOLE LOOKING-FOR-A-PARTNER THING?
WHEN WE THOUGHT NEGI-SENSEI WAS A PRINCE?
ヒソヒソ
WHISPER
ザワザワ
CHATTER
MAYBE HE'S STILL LOOKING!?
NO WAY!
WELL, IN SPRING, A YOUNG MAN'S FANCY TURNS TO, YOU KNOW...
SEN-SENSEI, I'M FINISHED READING.
HUH!? OH YEAH. GOOD WORK, IZUMI-SAN.
LOOK...CAN I ASK YOU A PERSONAL QUESTION...?
A BOY WHO'S SEVERAL YEARS YOUNGER THAN YOU...LIKE ME...YOU WOULDN'T WANT SOMEONE LIKE THAT AS A PARTNER, RIGHT?
WHA...
WHAT!!?
UH, SENSEI, WHERE'D THAT COME FROM?!
FLAP
あたふた
あわわ
BLUBBER
BOY, YEAR THREE'S GETTING OFF TO A WILD START.
NEO HORIZON

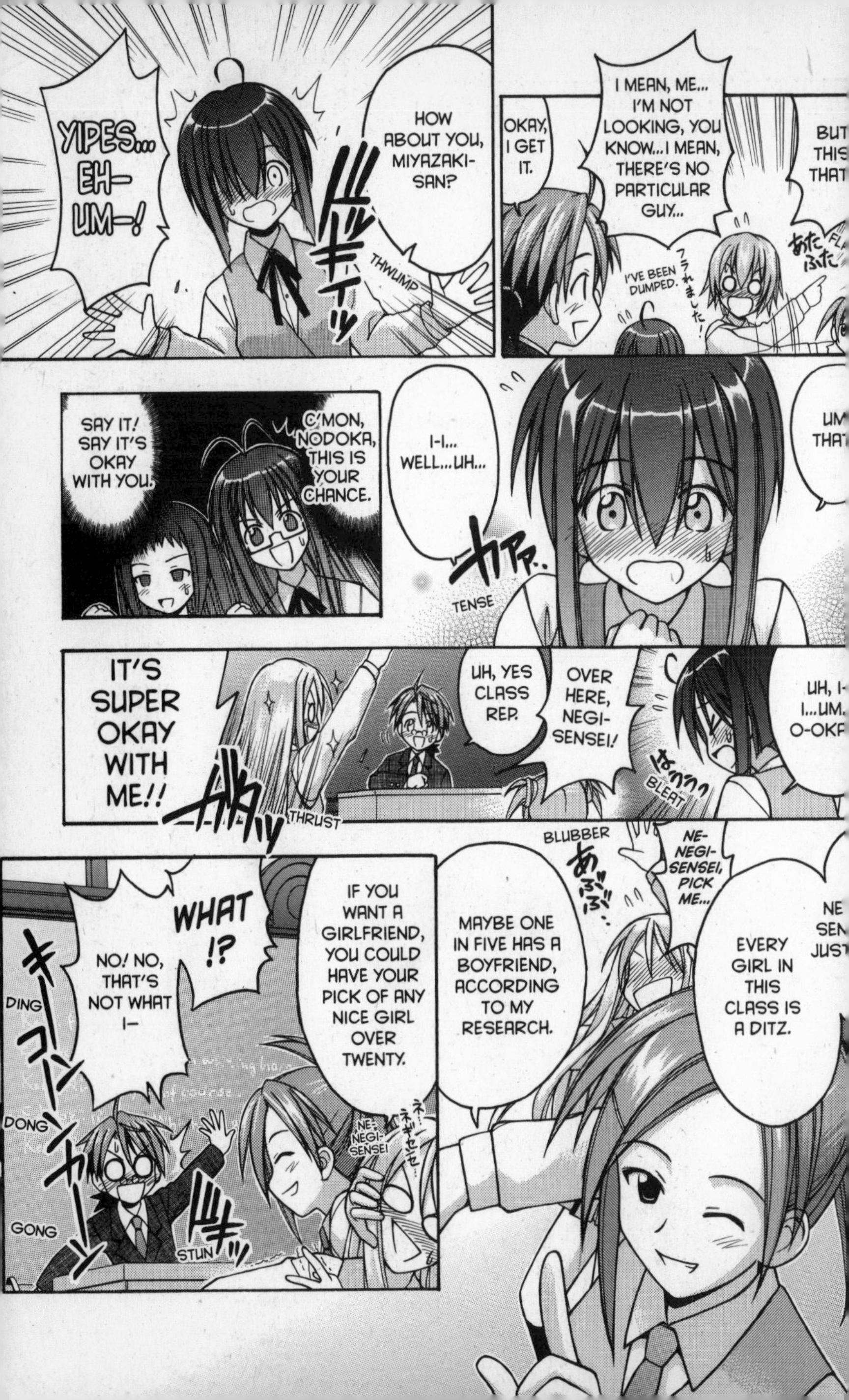
BUT THIS THAT
I MEAN, ME... I'M NOT LOOKING, YOU KNOW...I MEAN, THERE'S NO PARTICULAR GUY...
OKAY, I GET IT.
FLA
あたふた
フラれました!
I'VE BEEN DUMPED.
HOW ABOUT YOU, MIYAZAKI-SAN?
THWUMP
YIPES... EH— UM—!
UM THAT
TENSE
I-I... WELL...UH...
C'MON, NODOKA, THIS IS YOUR CHANCE.
SAY IT! SAY IT'S OKAY WITH YOU.
UH, I- I...UM. O-OKA
BLEAT
OVER HERE, NEGI-SENSEI!
UH, YES CLASS REP.
IT'S SUPER OKAY WITH ME!!
THRUST
NE SEN JUST
EVERY GIRL IN THIS CLASS IS A DITZ.
NE-NEGI-SENSEI, PICK ME...
BLUBBER
MAYBE ONE IN FIVE HAS A BOYFRIEND, ACCORDING TO MY RESEARCH.
IF YOU WANT A GIRLFRIEND, YOU COULD HAVE YOUR PICK OF ANY NICE GIRL OVER TWENTY.
ネ…ネギセンセー…
NE-NEGI-SENSEI
STUN
WHAT!?
NO! NO, THAT'S NOT WHAT I—
DING
DONG
GONG

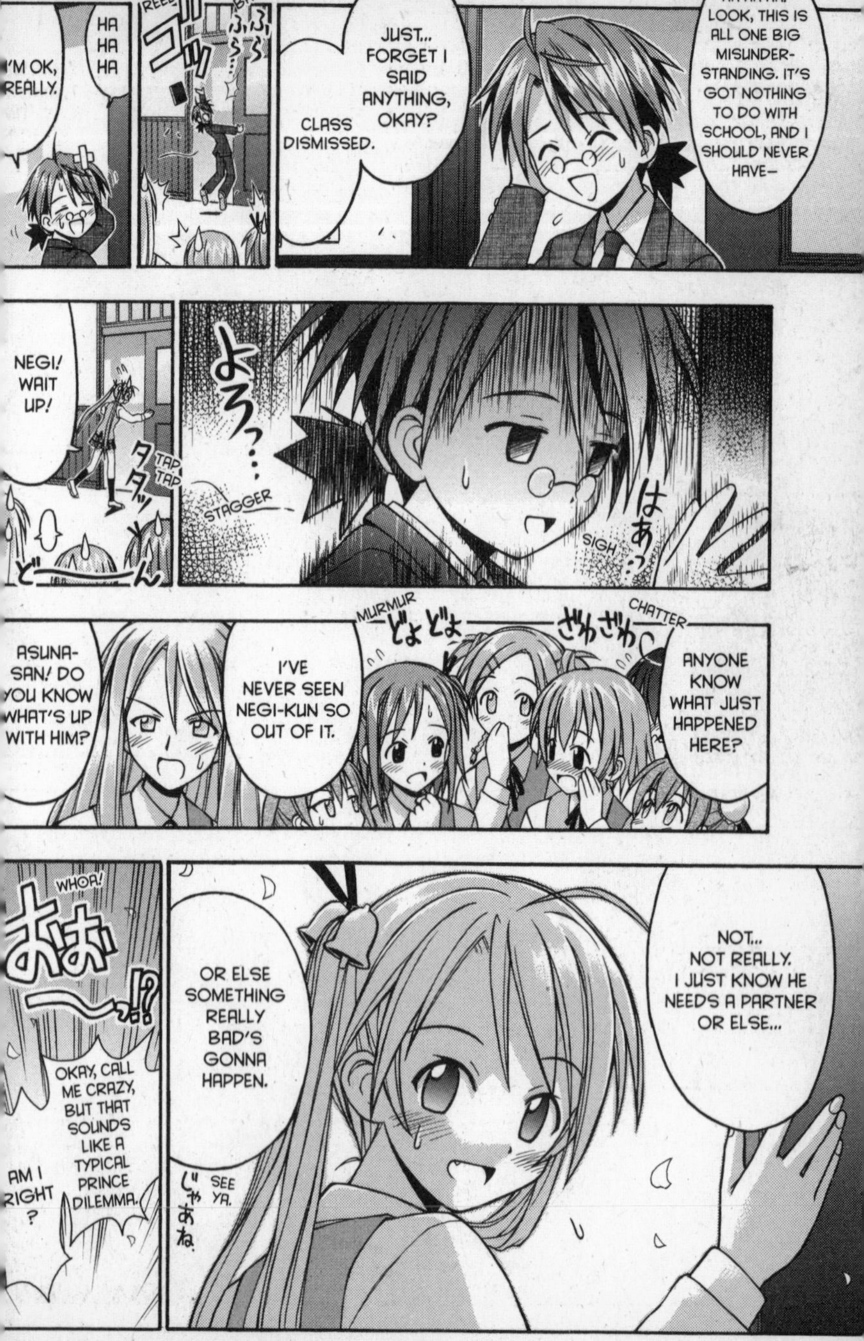
HA HA HA! LOOK, THIS IS ALL ONE BIG MISUNDERSTANDING. IT'S GOT NOTHING TO DO WITH SCHOOL, AND I SHOULD NEVER HAVE—
JUST... FORGET I SAID ANYTHING, OKAY?
CLASS DISMISSED.
ゴッ
REEL
ふらふら...
BANG
HA HA HA
I'M OK, REALLY.
よろっ...
STAGGER
はあっ...
SIGH
NEGI! WAIT UP!
タタッ
TAP TAP
どーーーん
ANYONE KNOW WHAT JUST HAPPENED HERE?
ざわざわ
CHATTER
どよどよ
MURMUR
I'VE NEVER SEEN NEGI-KUN SO OUT OF IT.
ASUNA-SAN! DO YOU KNOW WHAT'S UP WITH HIM?
NOT... NOT REALLY. I JUST KNOW HE NEEDS A PARTNER OR ELSE...
OR ELSE SOMETHING REALLY BAD'S GONNA HAPPEN.
じゃあね.
SEE YA.
おおーっ!?
WHOA!
OKAY, CALL ME CRAZY, BUT THAT SOUNDS LIKE A TYPICAL PRINCE DILEMMA.
AM I RIGHT?

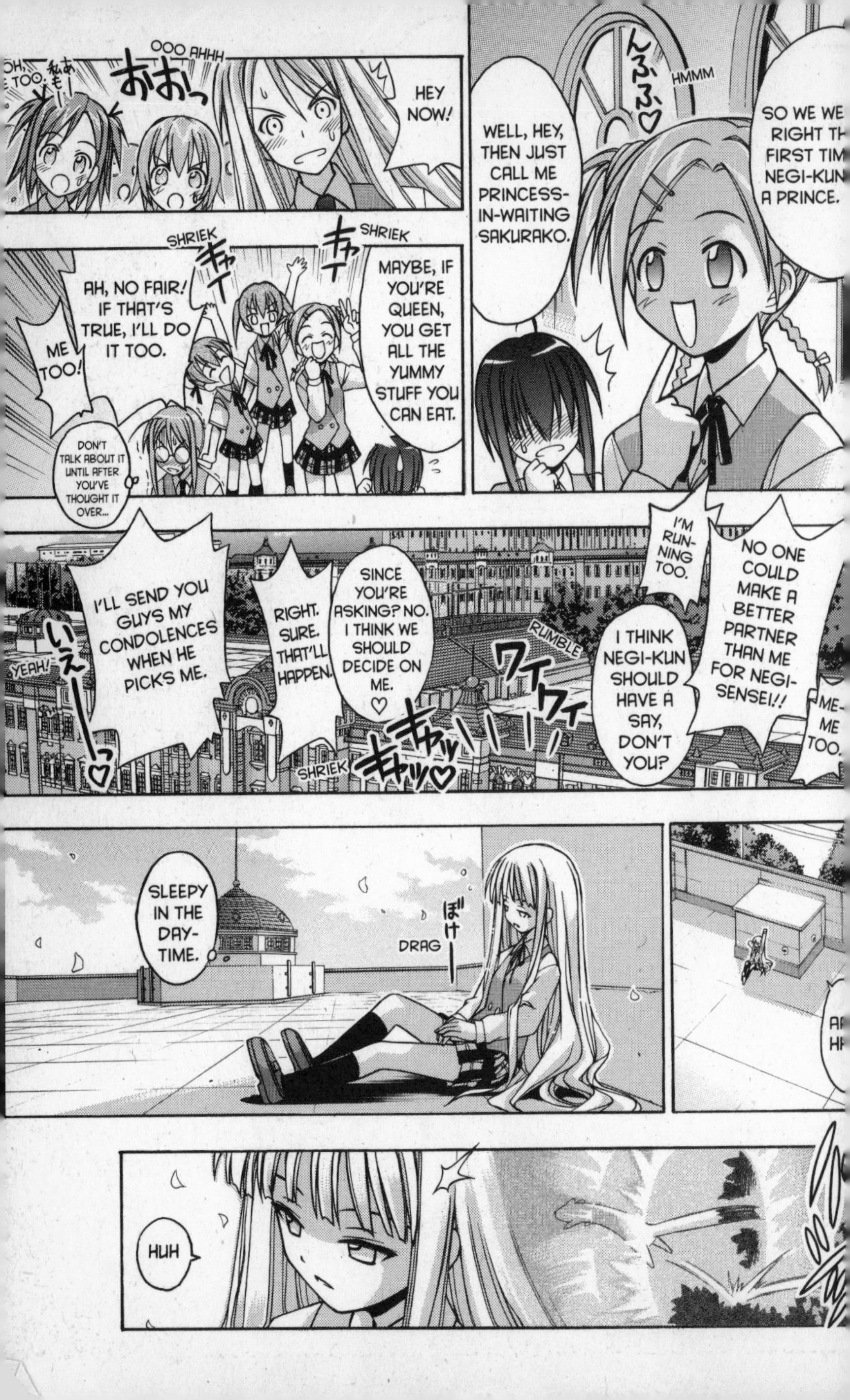

SO WE WE
RIGHT TH
FIRST TIM
NEGI-KUN
A PRINCE.
んふふ♡
HMMM
WELL, HEY, THEN JUST CALL ME PRINCESS-IN-WAITING SAKURAKO.
HEY NOW!
おおっ
OOO AHHH
私あも！
OH, ME TOO.
MAYBE, IF YOU'RE QUEEN, YOU GET ALL THE YUMMY STUFF YOU CAN EAT.
キャ
SHRIEK
キャ
SHRIEK
AH, NO FAIR! IF THAT'S TRUE, I'LL DO IT TOO.
ME TOO!
DON'T TALK ABOUT IT UNTIL AFTER YOU'VE THOUGHT IT OVER...
ME- ME TOO.
NO ONE COULD MAKE A BETTER PARTNER THAN ME FOR NEGI-SENSEI!!
I'M RUNNING TOO.
I THINK NEGI-KUN SHOULD HAVE A SAY, DON'T YOU?
ワイワイ
RUMBLE
キャッキャッ♡
SHRIEK
SINCE YOU'RE ASKING? NO. I THINK WE SHOULD DECIDE ON ME. ♡
RIGHT. SURE. THAT'LL HAPPEN.
I'LL SEND YOU GUYS MY CONDOLENCES WHEN HE PICKS ME.
いえーっ♡
YEAH!
ぼけー
DRAG
SLEEPY IN THE DAY-TIME.
HUH

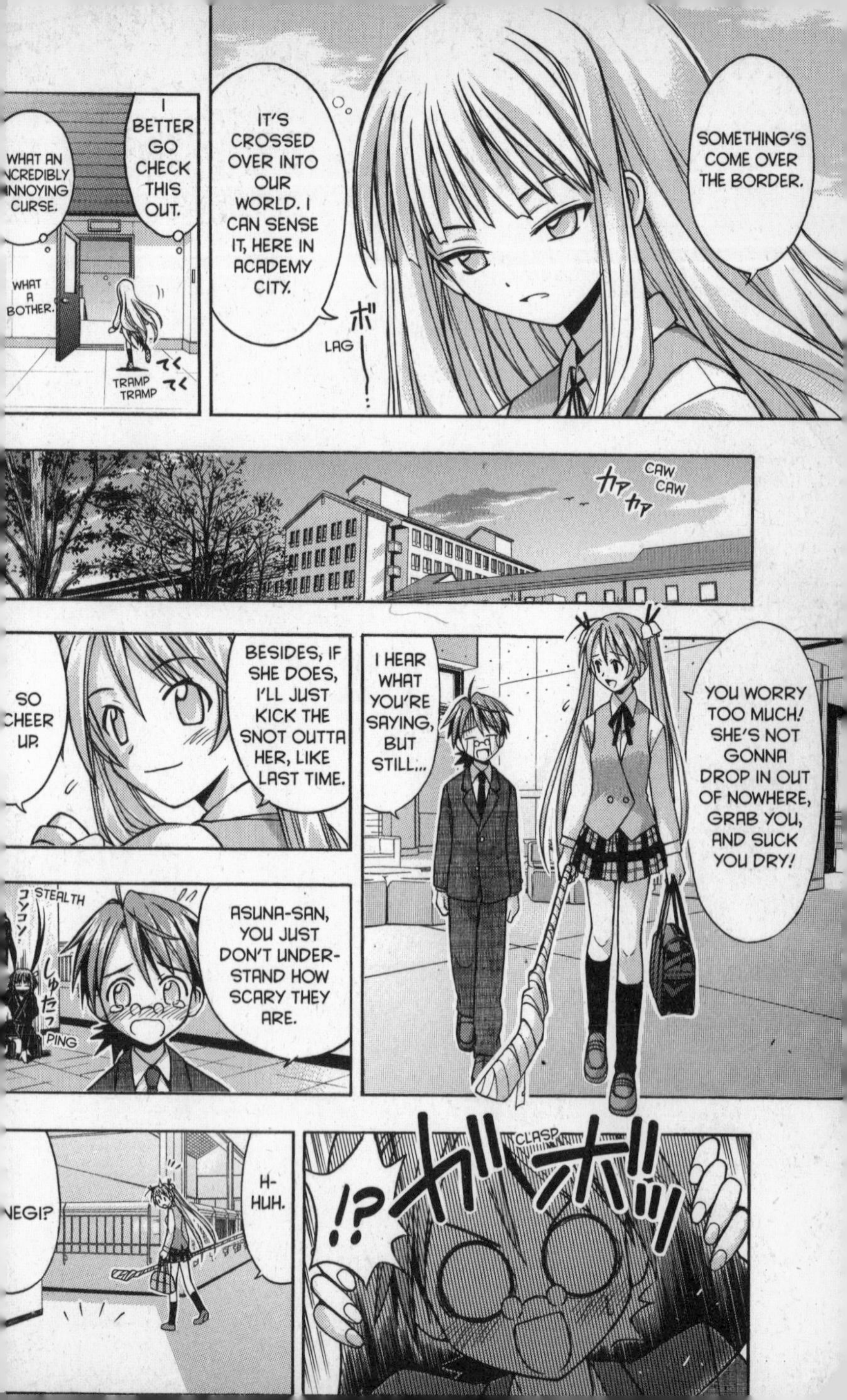
SOMETHING'S COME OVER THE BORDER.
IT'S CROSSED OVER INTO OUR WORLD. I CAN SENSE IT, HERE IN ACADEMY CITY.
LAG
I BETTER GO CHECK THIS OUT.
WHAT AN NCREDIBLY NNOYING CURSE.
WHAT A BOTHER.
TRAMP TRAMP
CAW CAW
YOU WORRY TOO MUCH! SHE'S NOT GONNA DROP IN OUT OF NOWHERE, GRAB YOU, AND SUCK YOU DRY!
I HEAR WHAT YOU'RE SAYING, BUT STILL...
BESIDES, IF SHE DOES, I'LL JUST KICK THE SNOT OUTTA HER, LIKE LAST TIME.
SO CHEER UP.
ASUNA-SAN, YOU JUST DON'T UNDER-STAND HOW SCARY THEY ARE.
STEALTH
PING
CLASP
!?
H-HUH.
NEGI?

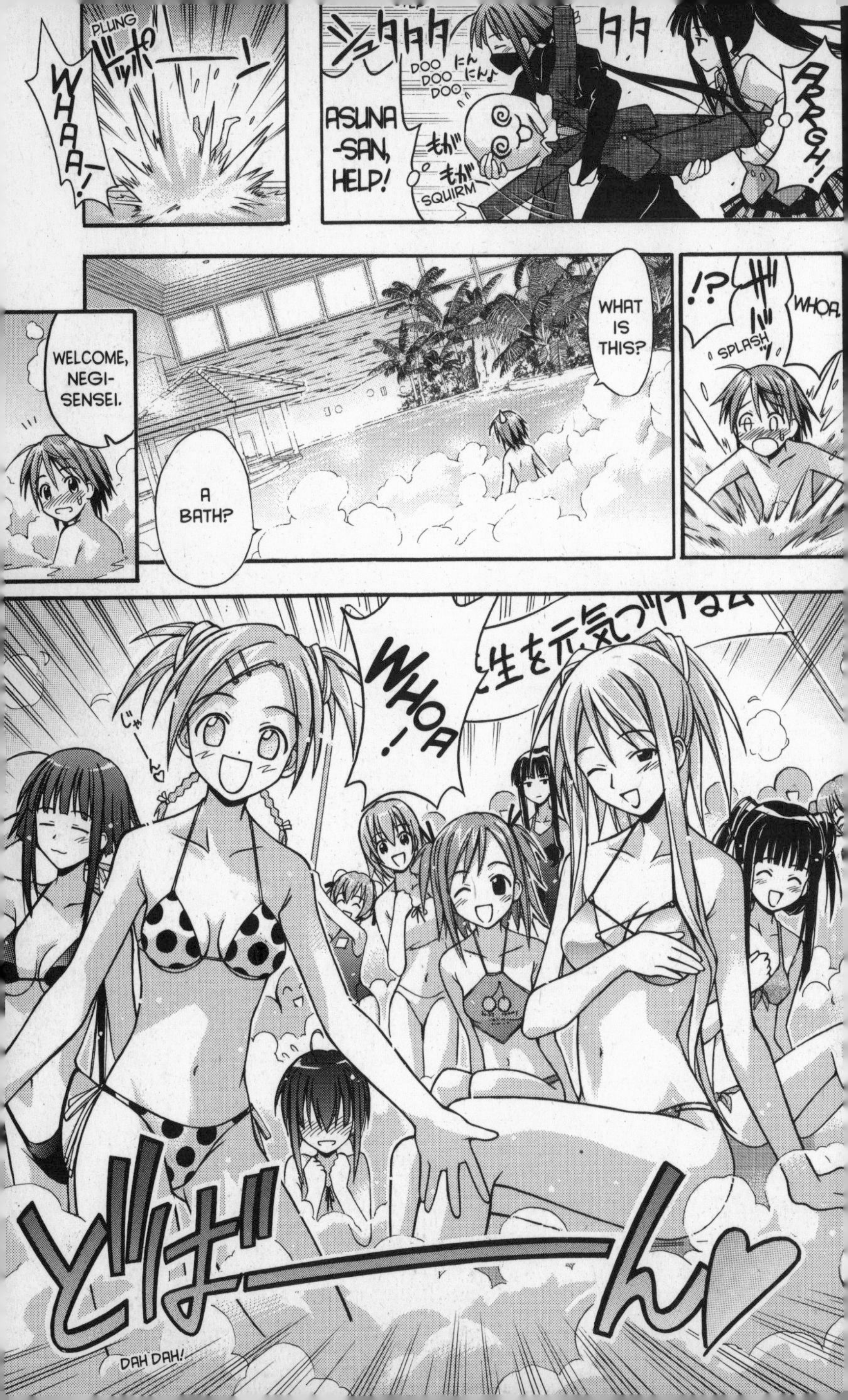

ARRRGH!
タタ
シュタタタ
DOO DOO DOO
にんにん♪
ASUNA-SAN, HELP!
もが もが
SQUIRM
PLUNG
ドッポーーン
WHAAA!
!?
ザバ
SPLASH
WHOA.
WHAT IS THIS?
A BATH?
WELCOME, NEGI-SENSEI.
生を元気づける
WHOA!
じゃーん♡
どばーーん♥
DAH DAH!

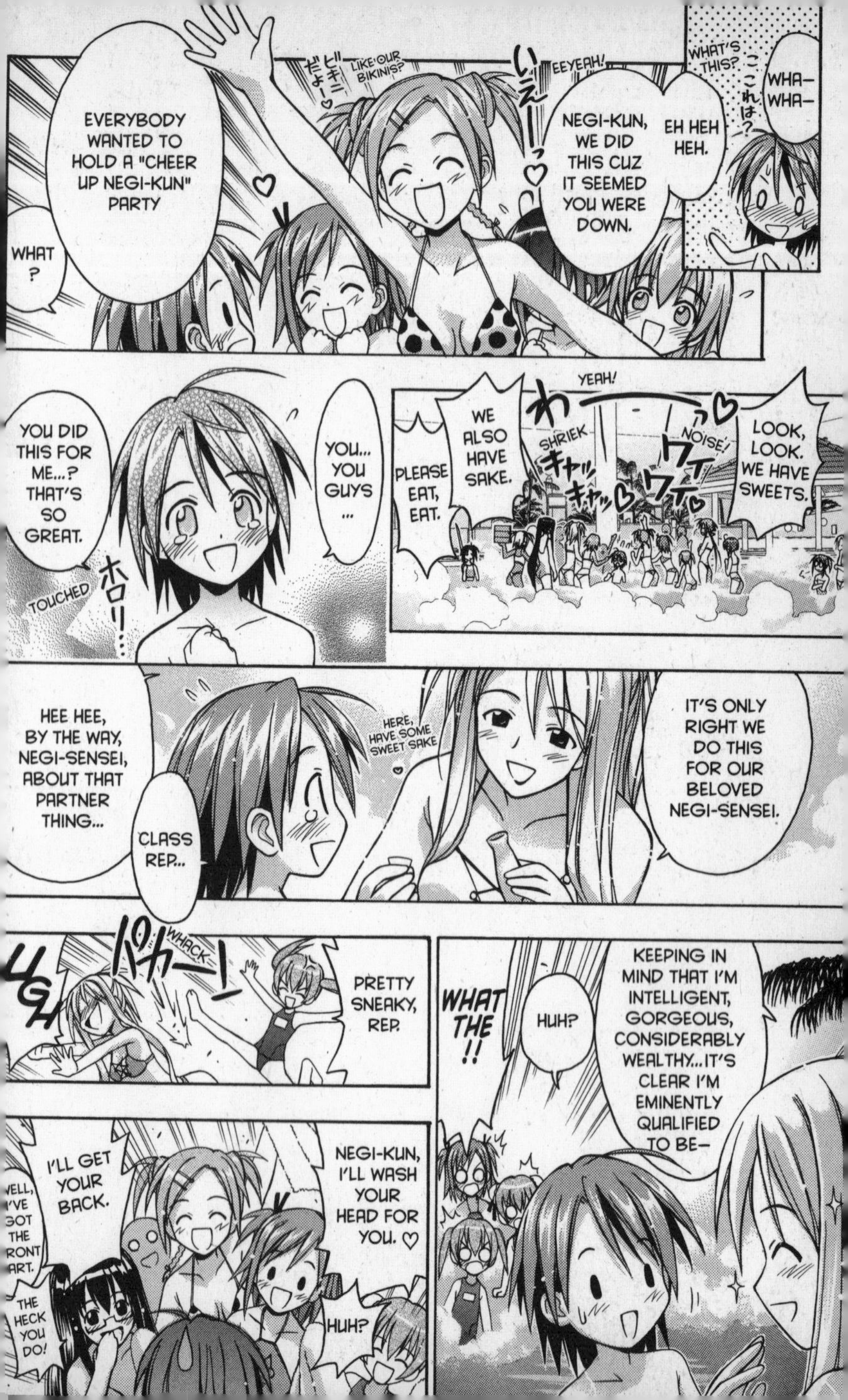

WHA- WHA-
これは？
WHAT'S THIS?
EH HEH HEH.
NEGI-KUN, WE DID THIS CUZ IT SEEMED YOU WERE DOWN.
いえーっ♡
EEYEAH!
ビキニだよー♡
LIKE OUR BIKINIS?
EVERYBODY WANTED TO HOLD A "CHEER UP NEGI-KUN" PARTY
WHAT ?
LOOK, LOOK. WE HAVE SWEETS.
わーっ♡
YEAH!
ワイワイ
NOISE!
キャッキャッ♡
SHRIEK
WE ALSO HAVE SAKE.
PLEASE EAT, EAT.
YOU... YOU GUYS ...
YOU DID THIS FOR ME...? THAT'S SO GREAT.
ホロリ…
TOUCHED
IT'S ONLY RIGHT WE DO THIS FOR OUR BELOVED NEGI-SENSEI.
HERE, HAVE SOME SWEET SAKE ♡
CLASS REP...
HEE HEE, BY THE WAY, NEGI-SENSEI, ABOUT THAT PARTNER THING...
KEEPING IN MIND THAT I'M INTELLIGENT, GORGEOUS, CONSIDERABLY WEALTHY...IT'S CLEAR I'M EMINENTLY QUALIFIED TO BE-
HUH?
WHAT THE !!
PRETTY SNEAKY, REP.
パカーン
WHACK
UGH
NEGI-KUN, I'LL WASH YOUR HEAD FOR YOU. ♡
I'LL GET YOUR BACK.
HUH?
ELL, 'VE GOT THE RONT ART.
THE HECK YOU DO!

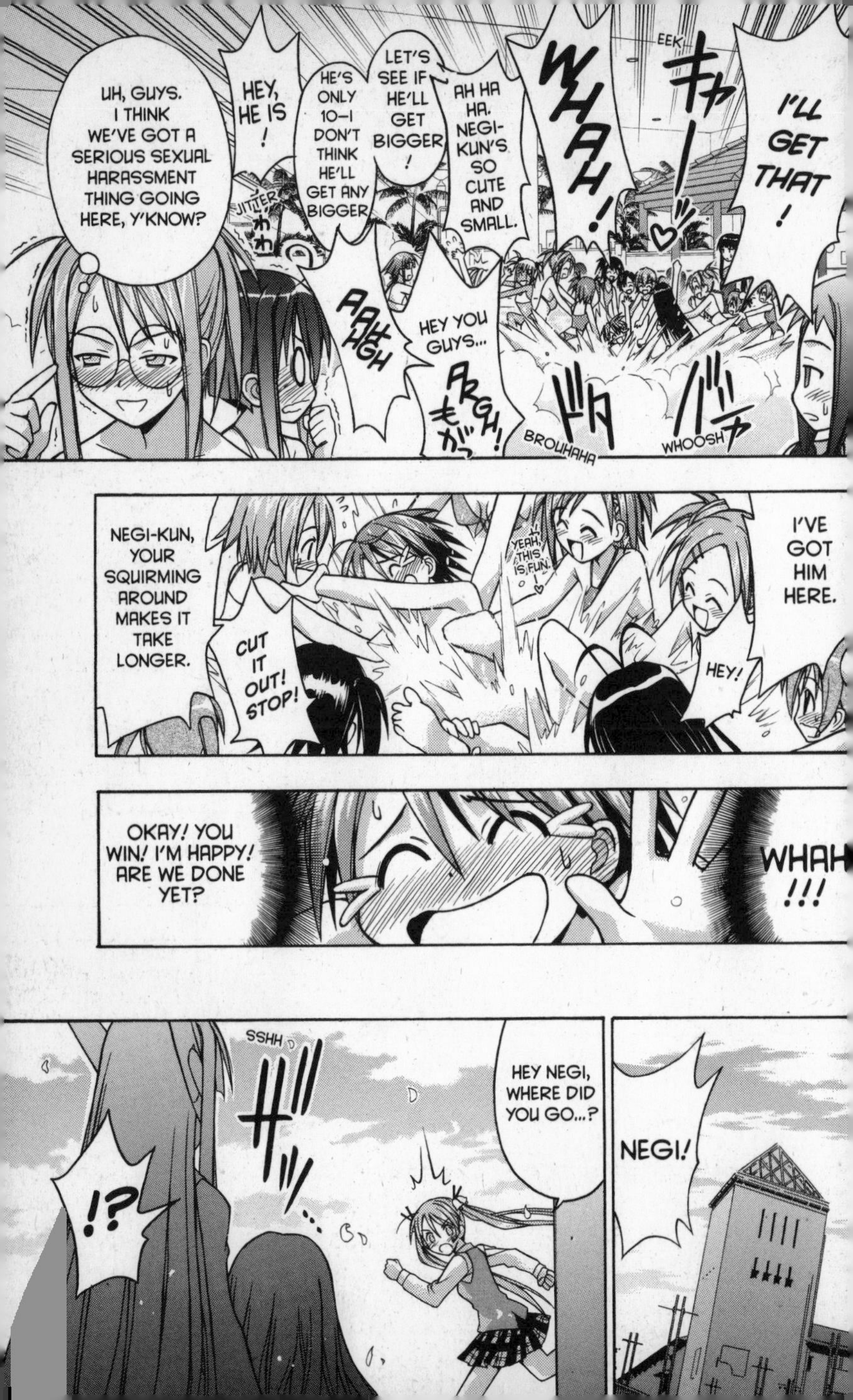

I'LL GET THAT!
EEK
キャー♡
WHAH!
AH HA HA. NEGI-KUN'S SO CUTE AND SMALL.
LET'S SEE IF HE'LL GET BIGGER!
HE'S ONLY 10—I DON'T THINK HE'LL GET ANY BIGGER
HEY, HE IS!
UH, GUYS. I THINK WE'VE GOT A SERIOUS SEXUAL HARASSMENT THING GOING HERE, Y'KNOW?
JITTER
WHOOSH
BROUHAHA
HEY YOU GUYS...
ARGH!
もがっ
AAHHGH
I'VE GOT HIM HERE.
HEY!
YEAH, THIS IS FUN.♡
CUT IT OUT! STOP!
NEGI-KUN, YOUR SQUIRMING AROUND MAKES IT TAKE LONGER.
WHAH!!!
OKAY! YOU WIN! I'M HAPPY! ARE WE DONE YET?
NEGI!
HEY NEGI, WHERE DID YOU GO...?
SSHH
!?

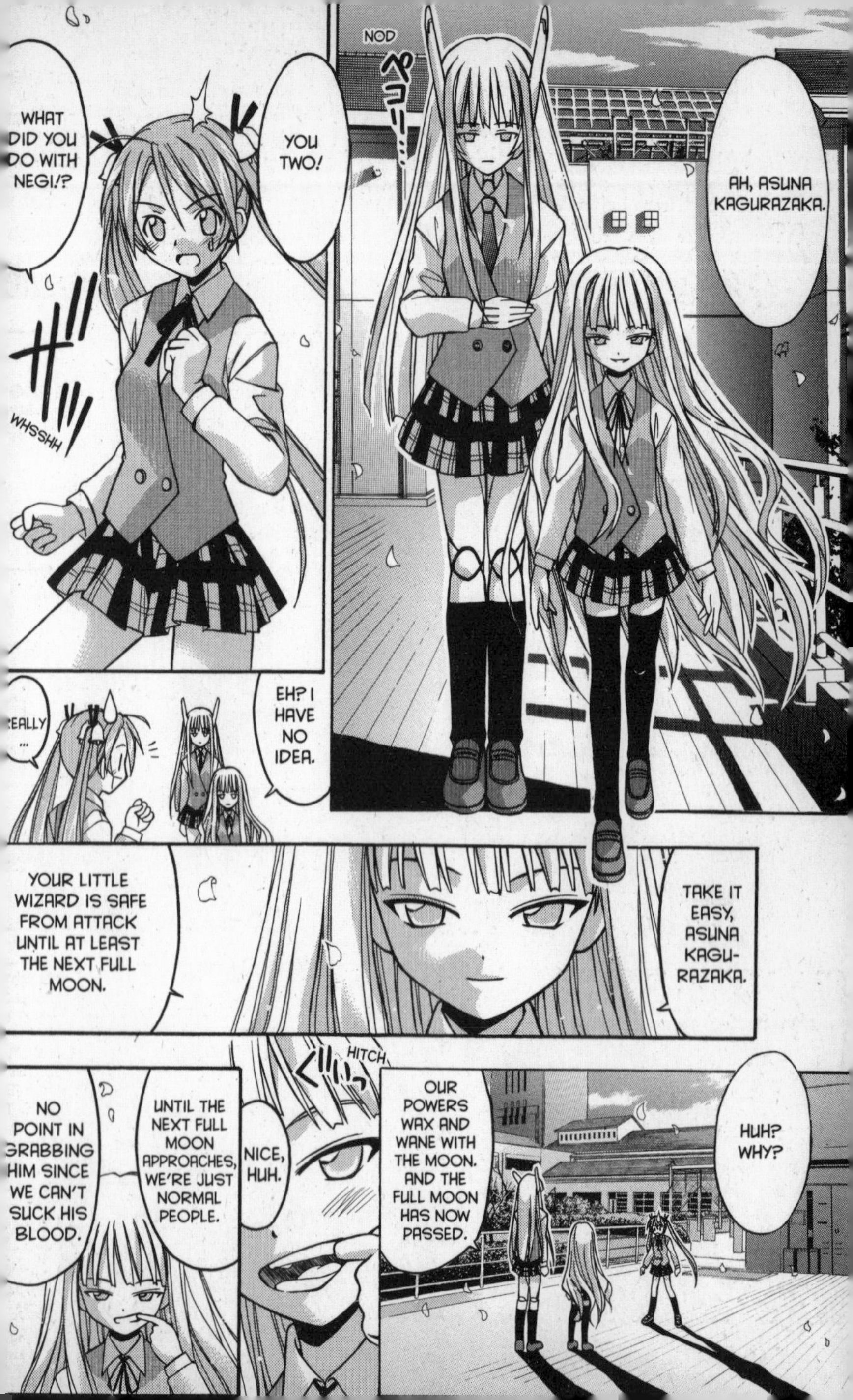
NOD
AH, ASUNA KAGURAZAKA.
YOU TWO!
WHAT DID YOU DO WITH NEGI!?
WHSSHH
EH? I HAVE NO IDEA.
REALLY ...
TAKE IT EASY, ASUNA KAGU-RAZAKA.
YOUR LITTLE WIZARD IS SAFE FROM ATTACK UNTIL AT LEAST THE NEXT FULL MOON.
HUH? WHY?
OUR POWERS WAX AND WANE WITH THE MOON. AND THE FULL MOON HAS NOW PASSED.
HITCH
NICE, HUH.
UNTIL THE NEXT FULL MOON APPROACHES, WE'RE JUST NORMAL PEOPLE.
NO POINT IN GRABBING HIM SINCE WE CAN'T SUCK HIS BLOOD.

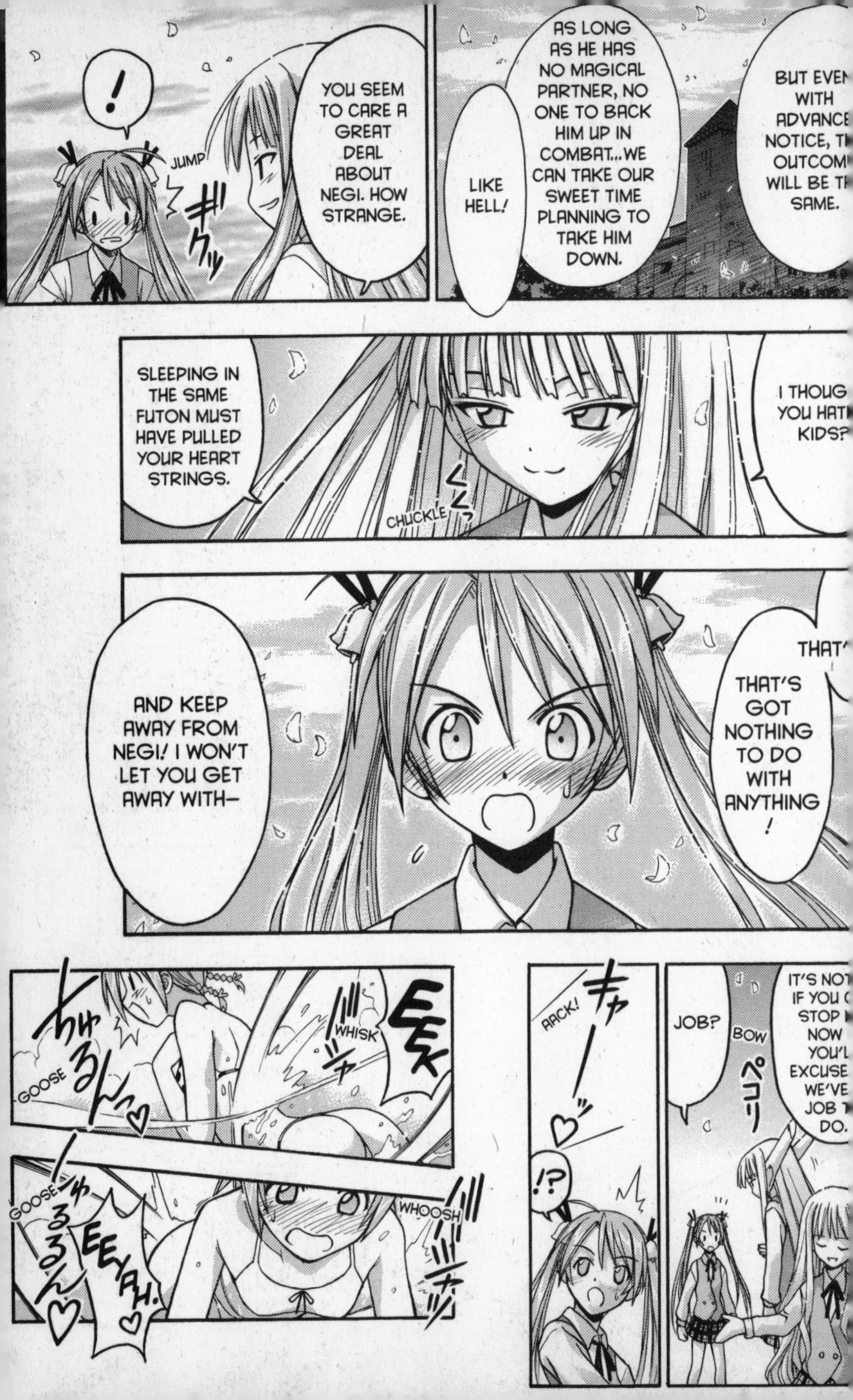
BUT EVEN WITH ADVANCE NOTICE, T OUTCOM WILL BE T SAME.
AS LONG AS HE HAS NO MAGICAL PARTNER, NO ONE TO BACK HIM UP IN COMBAT...WE CAN TAKE OUR SWEET TIME PLANNING TO TAKE HIM DOWN.
LIKE HELL!
YOU SEEM TO CARE A GREAT DEAL ABOUT NEGI. HOW STRANGE.
!
JUMP
I THOUG YOU HAT KIDS?
SLEEPING IN THE SAME FUTON MUST HAVE PULLED YOUR HEART STRINGS.
CHUCKLE
THAT'
THAT'S GOT NOTHING TO DO WITH ANYTHING!
AND KEEP AWAY FROM NEGI! I WON'T LET YOU GET AWAY WITH—
IT'S NOT IF YOU STOP NOW YOU'L EXCUSE WE'VE JOB TO DO.
BOW
JOB?
!?
RACK!
EEK
WHISK
GOOSE
WHOOSH
GOOSE
EEYAH!

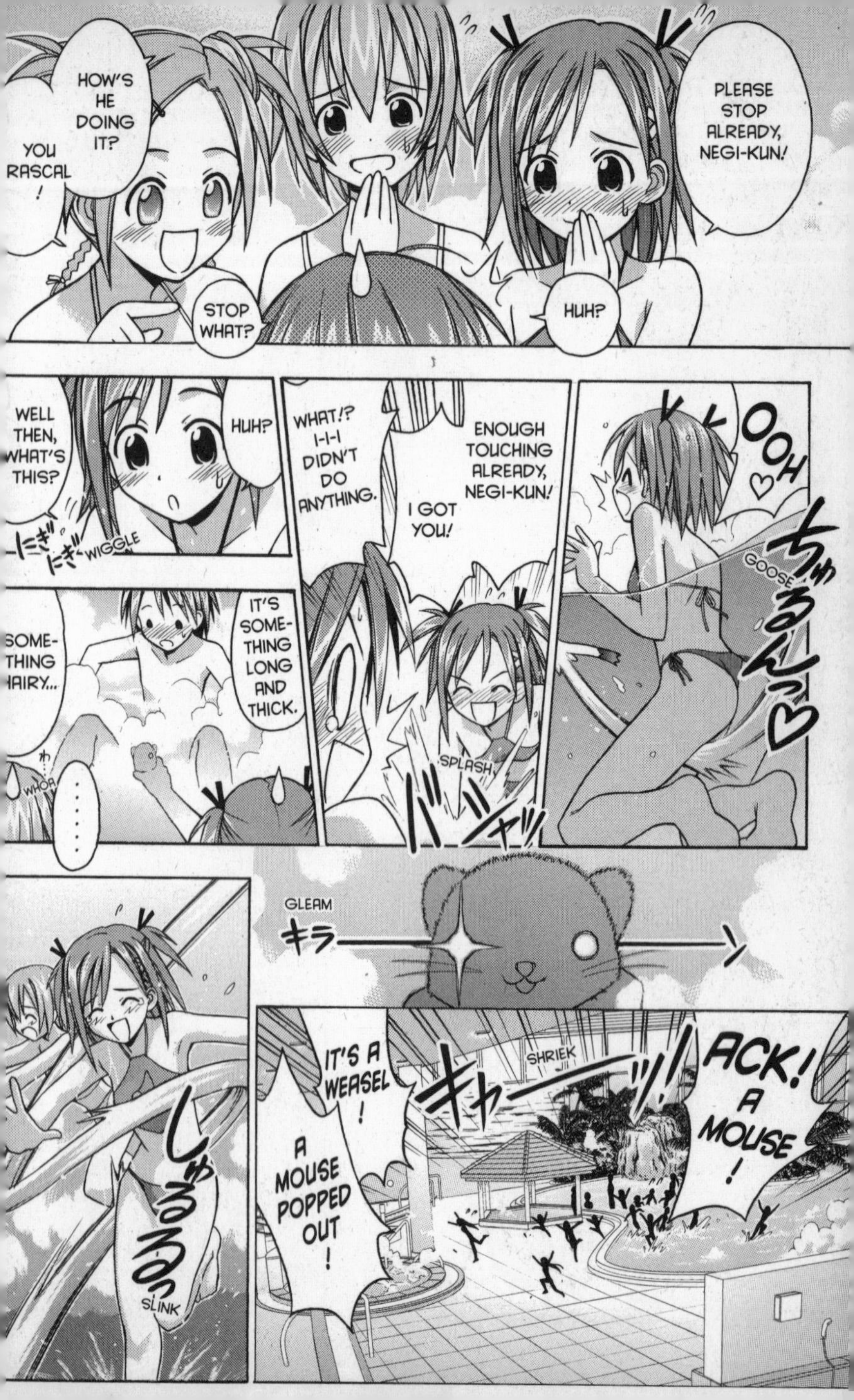

PLEASE STOP ALREADY, NEGI-KUN!
HOW'S HE DOING IT?
YOU RASCAL!
HUH?
STOP WHAT?
OOH ♡
GOOSE
ENOUGH TOUCHING ALREADY, NEGI-KUN!
I GOT YOU!
WHAT!? I-I-I DIDN'T DO ANYTHING.
SPLASH
HUH?
WELL THEN, WHAT'S THIS?
WIGGLE
IT'S SOMETHING LONG AND THICK.
SOMETHING HAIRY...
......
WHOA
GLEAM
ACK! A MOUSE!
SHRIEK
IT'S A WEASEL!
A MOUSE POPPED OUT!
SLINK

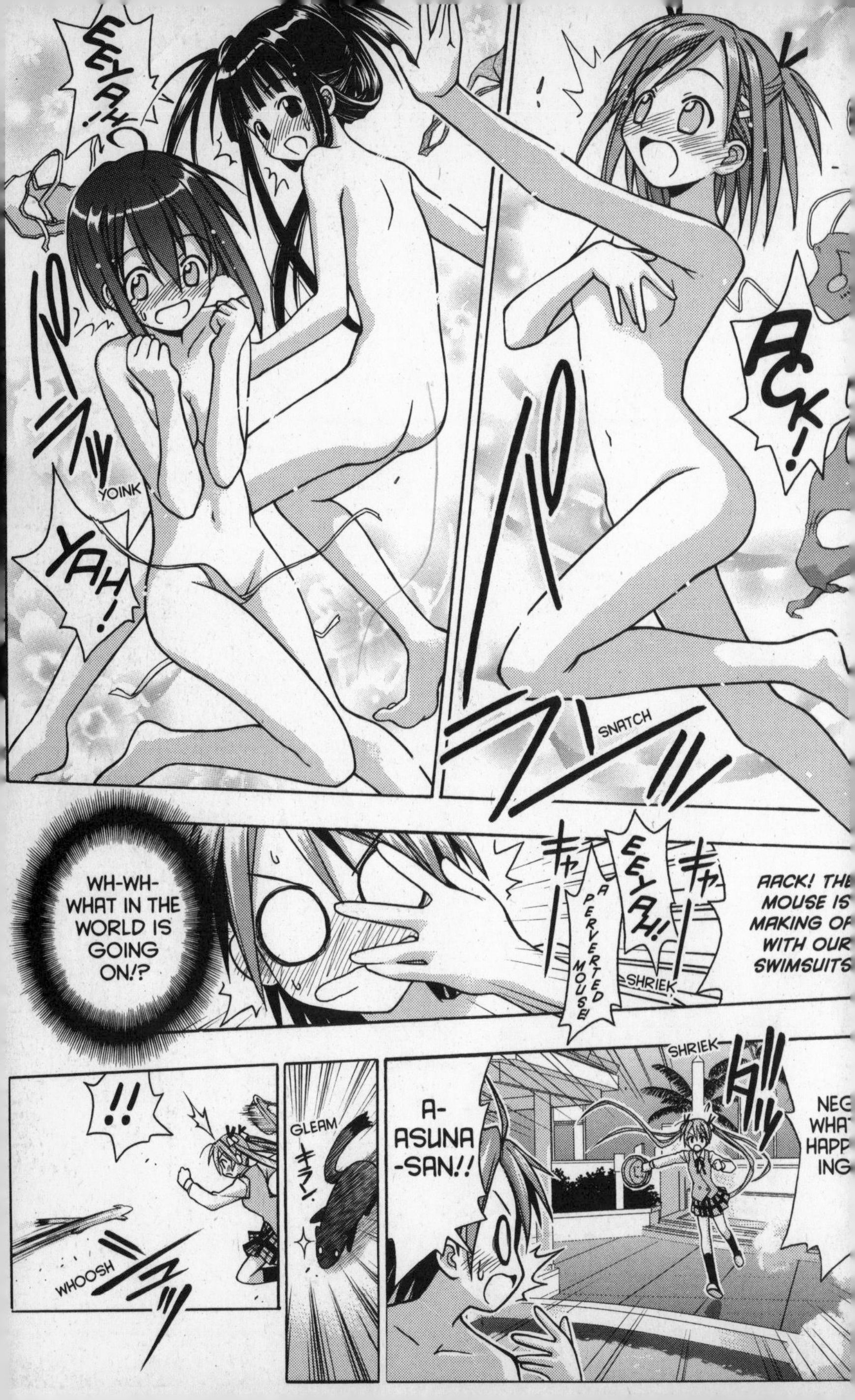
AACK!
SNATCH
EEYAH!!
YOINK
YAH!
AACK! THE MOUSE IS MAKING OF WITH OUR SWIMSUITS
EEYAH!!
A PERVERTED MOUSE
SHRIEK
WH-WH-WHAT IN THE WORLD IS GOING ON!?
NEG WHAT HAPP ING
SHRIEK
A-ASUNA-SAN!!
GLEAM
!!
WHOOSH

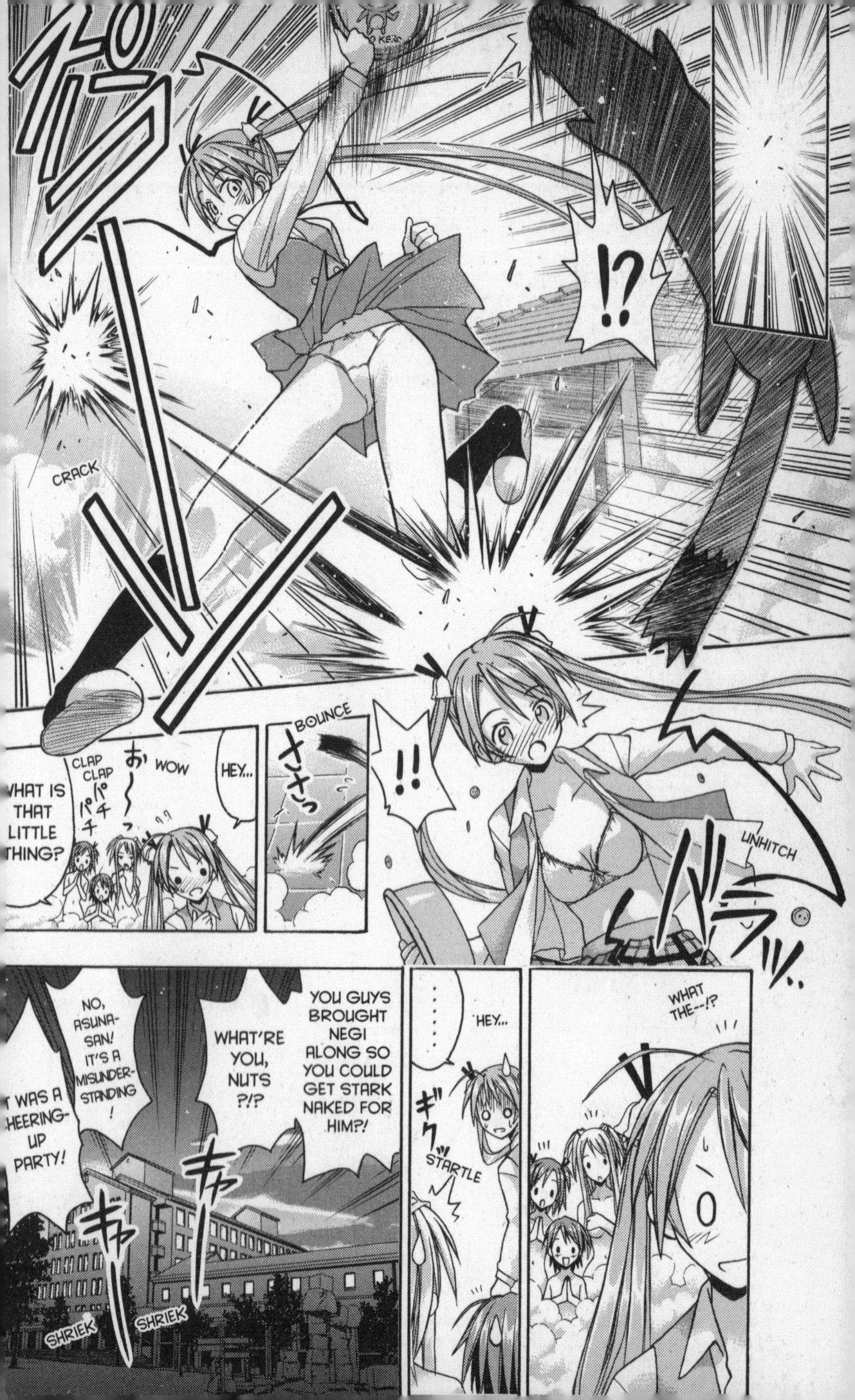

スパン
!?
CRACK
!!
UNHITCH
パラッ
BOUNCE
ささっ
HEY...
WOW
おーっ
CLAP CLAP
パチパチ
WHAT IS THAT LITTLE THING?
WHAT THE--!?
HEY...
......
ギクッ
STARTLE
YOU GUYS BROUGHT NEGI ALONG SO YOU COULD GET STARK NAKED FOR HIM?!
WHAT'RE YOU, NUTS?!?
NO, ASUNA-SAN! IT'S A MISUNDERSTANDING!
T WAS A HEERING-UP PARTY!
キャー
ギャー
SHRIEK
SHRIEK

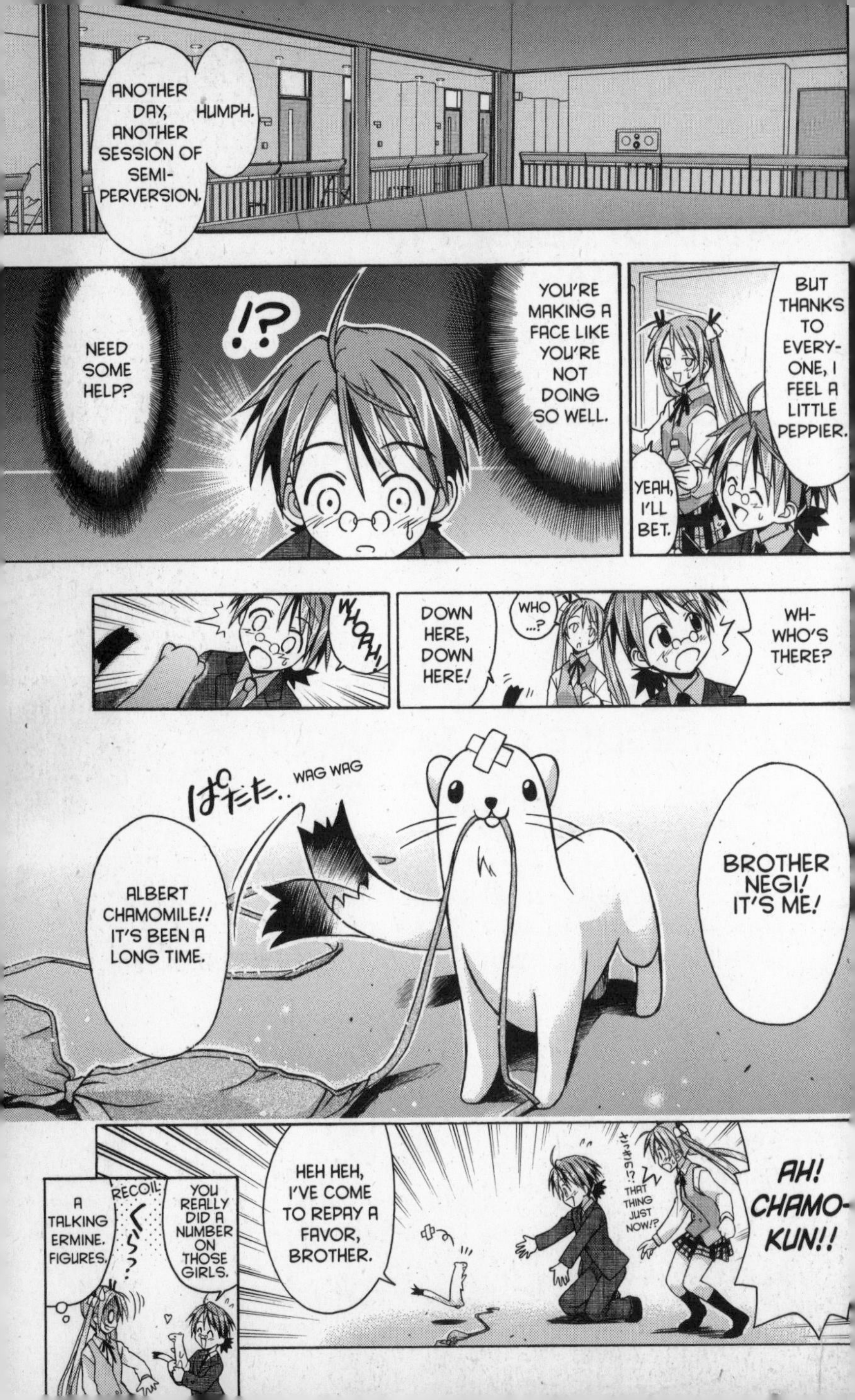
HUMPH.
ANOTHER DAY, ANOTHER SESSION OF SEMI-PERVERSION.
BUT THANKS TO EVERYONE, I FEEL A LITTLE PEPPIER.
YEAH, I'LL BET.
YOU'RE MAKING A FACE LIKE YOU'RE NOT DOING SO WELL.
!?
NEED SOME HELP?
WH-WHO'S THERE?
WHO ...?
DOWN HERE, DOWN HERE!
WHOAH!
BROTHER NEGI! IT'S ME!
WAG WAG
ぱたた..
ALBERT CHAMOMILE!! IT'S BEEN A LONG TIME.
AH! CHAMO-KUN!!
THAT THING JUST NOW!?
HEH HEH, I'VE COME TO REPAY A FAVOR, BROTHER.
YOU REALLY DID A NUMBER ON THOSE GIRLS.
RECOIL
A TALKING ERMINE. FIGURES.

STUDENT NUMBER 10
CHACHAMARU KARAKURI

ACTIVATED: APRIL 1, 2001
POWERS: SPRING-BASED (JUST AFTER
        COMPLETION AN OUTSIDE POWER SOURCE
        WAS USED)
LIKES: SERVING TEA, HAVING HER SPRINGS WOUND
DISLIKES: NOTHING IN PARTICULAR.
AFFILIATIONS: GO CLUB, TEA CEREMONY CLUB

STUDENT NUMBER 26
EVANGELINE A.K. MCDOWELL

DATE OF BIRTH: UNKNOWN
BLOOD TYPE: UNKNOWN
LIKES: TEA PREPARED BY CHACHAMARU,
       SCENERY OF JAPAN, GO
DISLIKES: GARLIC AND LEEKS, CLASS
AFFILIATIONS: GO CLUB, TEA CEREMONY CLUB

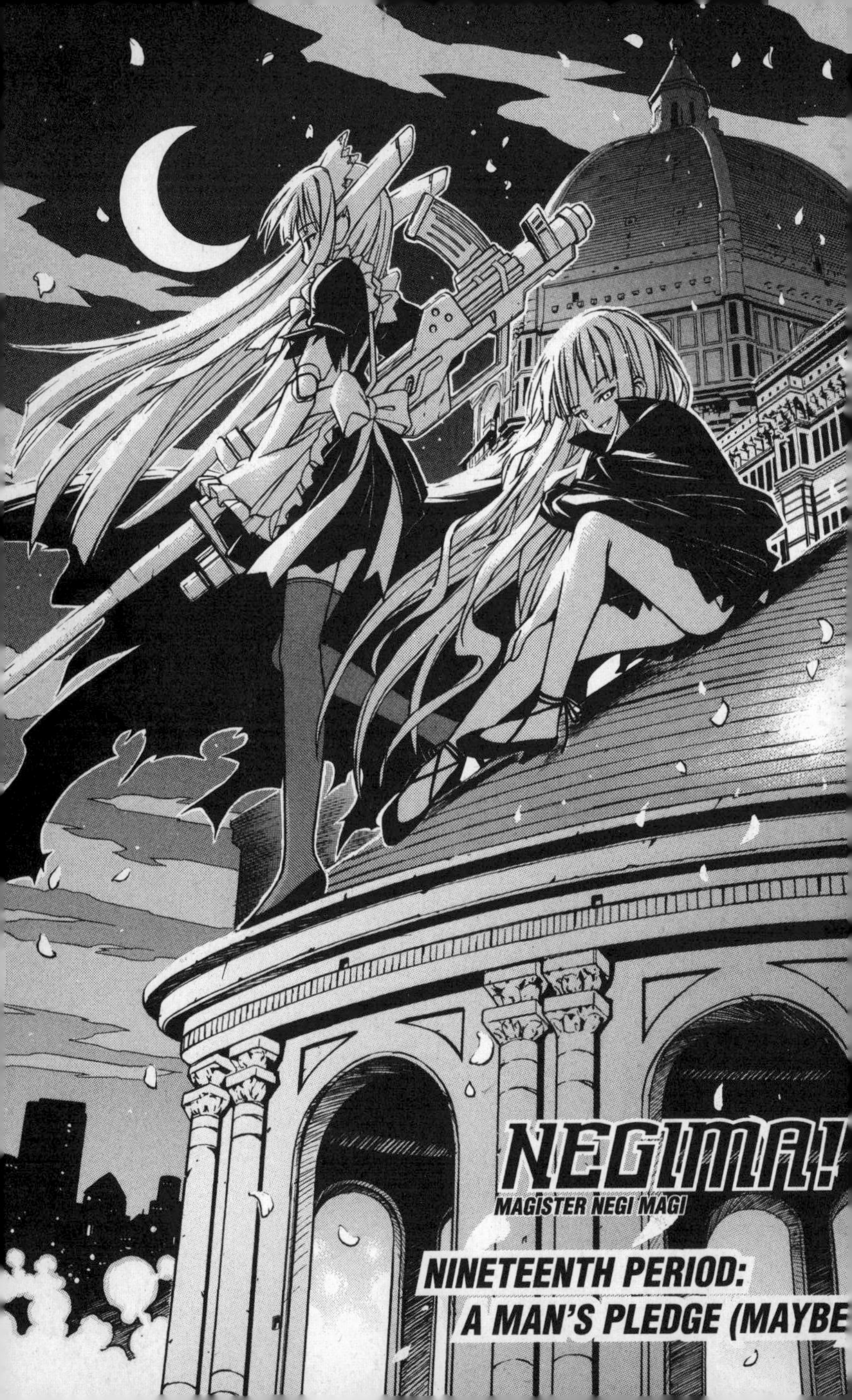
NEGIMA!
MAGISTER NEGI MAGI
NINETEENTH PERIOD:
A MAN'S PLEDGE (MAYBE

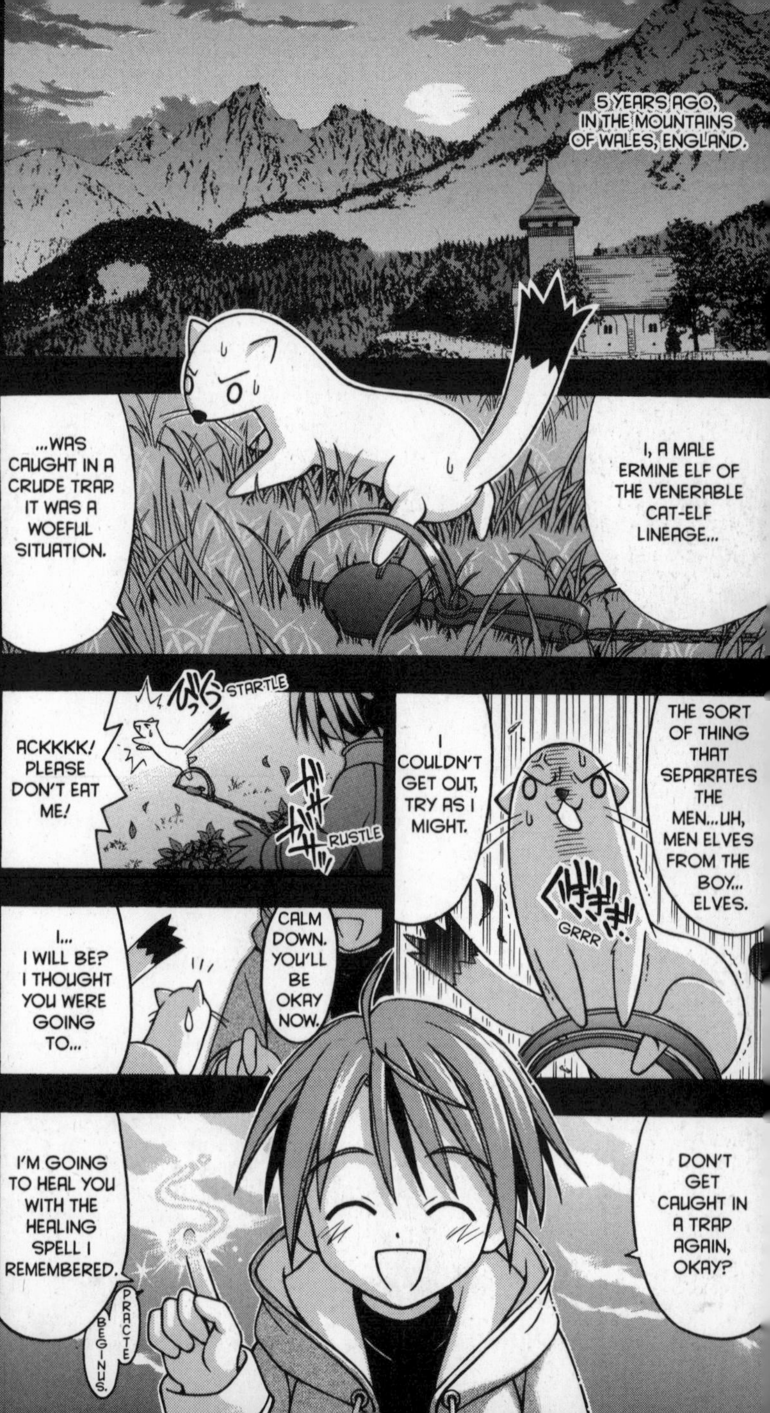
5 YEARS AGO, IN THE MOUNTAINS OF WALES, ENGLAND.
I, A MALE ERMINE ELF OF THE VENERABLE CAT-ELF LINEAGE...
...WAS CAUGHT IN A CRUDE TRAP. IT WAS A WOEFUL SITUATION.
THE SORT OF THING THAT SEPARATES THE MEN...UH, MEN ELVES FROM THE BOY... ELVES.
I COULDN'T GET OUT, TRY AS I MIGHT.
GRRR
STARTLE
ACKKKK! PLEASE DON'T EAT ME!
RUSTLE
CALM DOWN. YOU'LL BE OKAY NOW.
I... I WILL BE? I THOUGHT YOU WERE GOING TO...
DON'T GET CAUGHT IN A TRAP AGAIN, OKAY?
I'M GOING TO HEAL YOU WITH THE HEALING SPELL I REMEMBERED.
PRACTE BEGINUS.

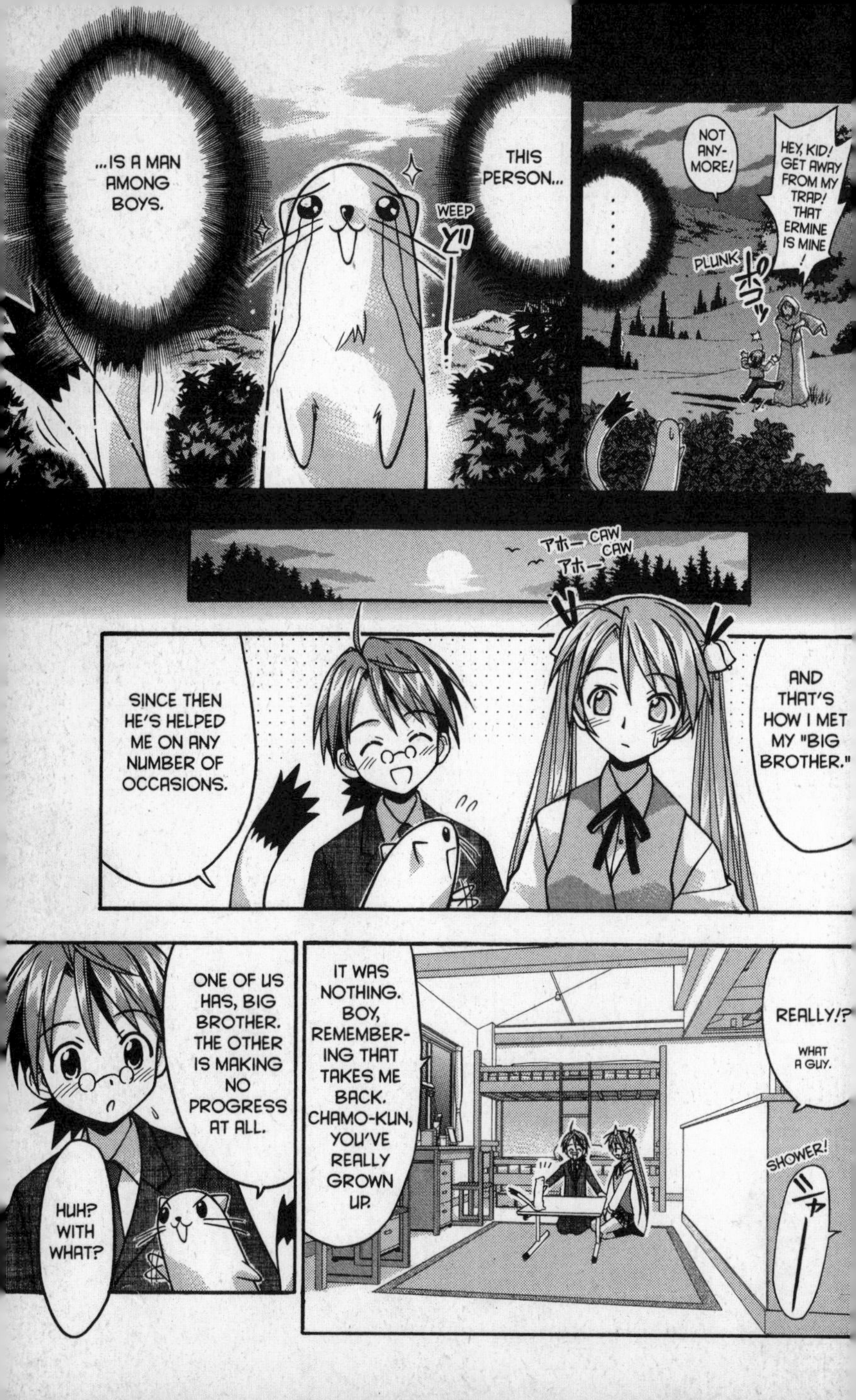
HEY, KID! GET AWAY FROM MY TRAP! THAT ERMINE IS MINE!
NOT ANY-MORE!
...
PLUNK
THIS PERSON...
WEEP
...IS A MAN AMONG BOYS.
CAW CAW
AND THAT'S HOW I MET MY "BIG BROTHER."
SINCE THEN HE'S HELPED ME ON ANY NUMBER OF OCCASIONS.
REALLY!?
WHAT A GUY.
SHOWER!
IT WAS NOTHING. BOY, REMEMBER-ING THAT TAKES ME BACK. CHAMO-KUN, YOU'VE REALLY GROWN UP.
ONE OF US HAS, BIG BROTHER. THE OTHER IS MAKING NO PROGRESS AT ALL.
HUH? WITH WHAT?

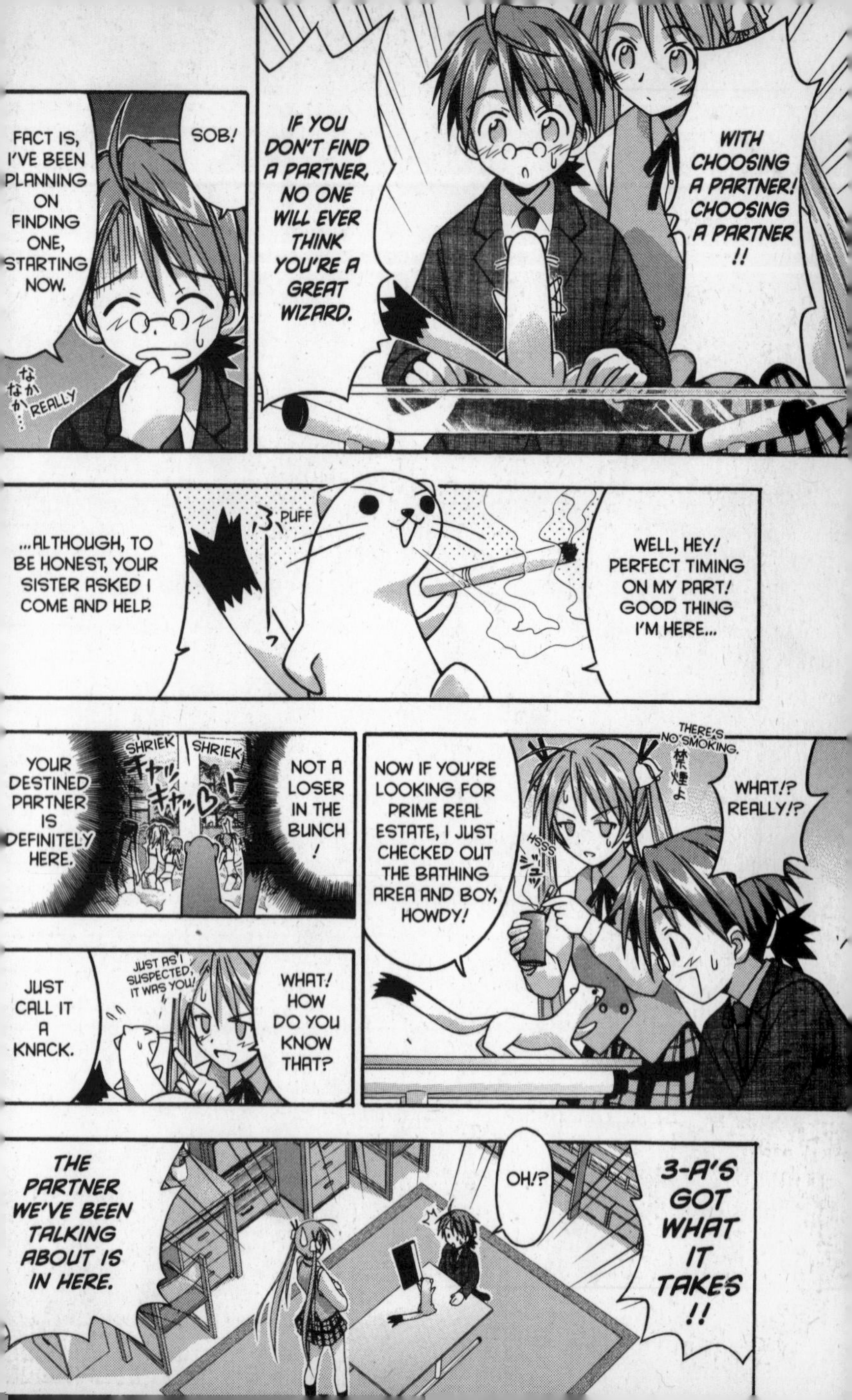
WITH CHOOSING A PARTNER! CHOOSING A PARTNER!!
IF YOU DON'T FIND A PARTNER, NO ONE WILL EVER THINK YOU'RE A GREAT WIZARD.
SOB!
FACT IS, I'VE BEEN PLANNING ON FINDING ONE, STARTING NOW.
なかなか… REALLY
WELL, HEY! PERFECT TIMING ON MY PART! GOOD THING I'M HERE...
ふ PUFF
...ALTHOUGH, TO BE HONEST, YOUR SISTER ASKED I COME AND HELP.
WHAT!? REALLY!?
THERE'S NO SMOKING. 禁煙よ
HSSS
NOW IF YOU'RE LOOKING FOR PRIME REAL ESTATE, I JUST CHECKED OUT THE BATHING AREA AND BOY, HOWDY!
NOT A LOSER IN THE BUNCH!
SHRIEK
SHRIEK
YOUR DESTINED PARTNER IS DEFINITELY HERE.
WHAT! HOW DO YOU KNOW THAT?
JUST AS I SUSPECTED, IT WAS YOU!
JUST CALL IT A KNACK.
3-A'S GOT WHAT IT TAKES!!
OH!?
THE PARTNER WE'VE BEEN TALKING ABOUT IS IN HERE.

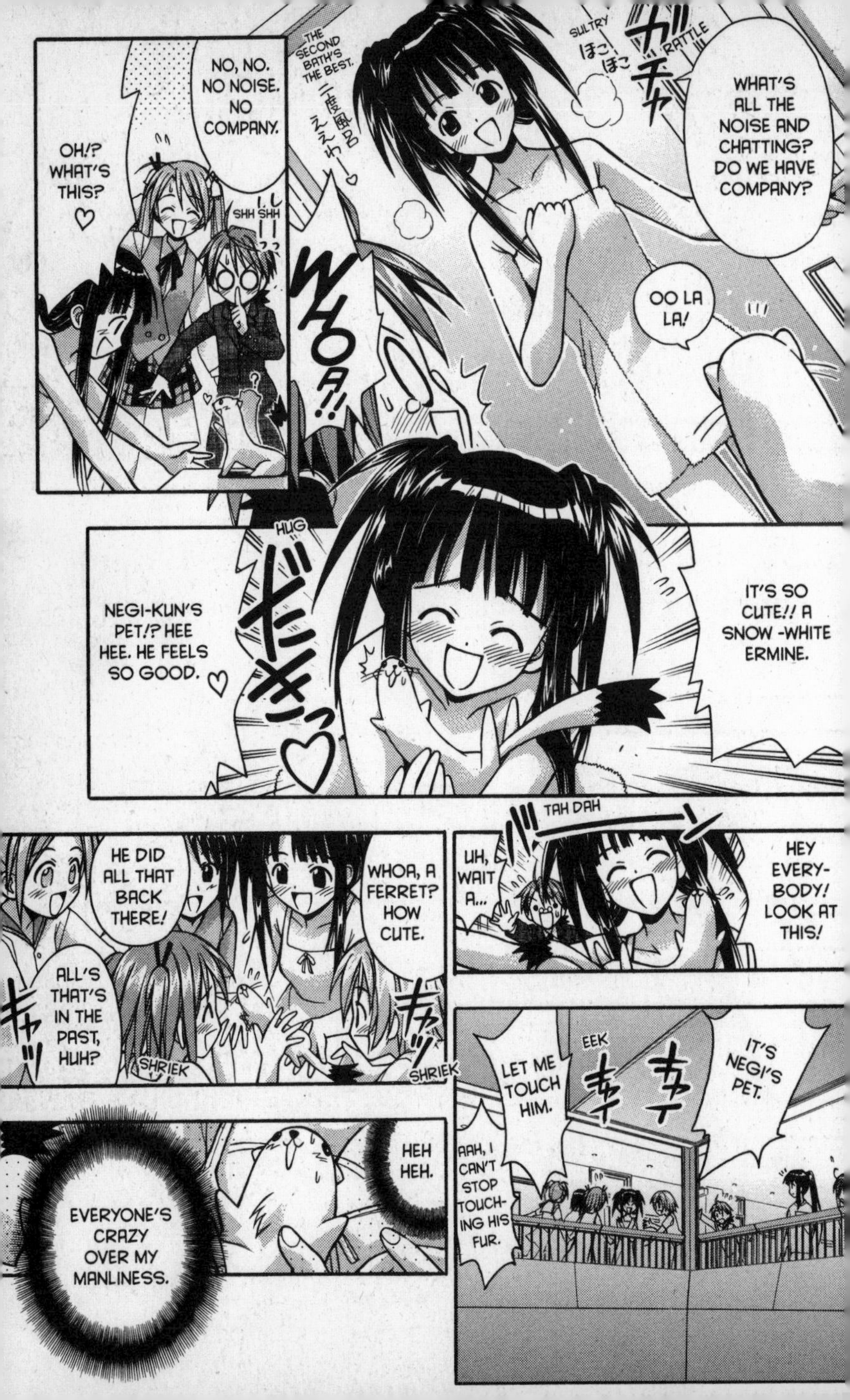
RATTLE
SULTRY
ほこほこ
WHAT'S ALL THE NOISE AND CHATTING? DO WE HAVE COMPANY?
THE SECOND BATH'S THE BEST.
二度風呂ええわ~♡
OO LA LA!
WHOA!!
NO, NO. NO NOISE. NO COMPANY.
SHH SHH
OH!? WHAT'S THIS? ♡
HUG
IT'S SO CUTE!! A SNOW -WHITE ERMINE.
NEGI-KUN'S PET!? HEE HEE. HE FEELS SO GOOD. ♡
TAH DAH
HEY EVERY-BODY! LOOK AT THIS!
UH, WAIT A...
WHOA, A FERRET? HOW CUTE.
HE DID ALL THAT BACK THERE!
ALL'S THAT'S IN THE PAST, HUH?
SHRIEK
SHRIEK
IT'S NEGI'S PET.
EEK
LET ME TOUCH HIM.
AAH, I CAN'T STOP TOUCHING HIS FUR.
HEH HEH.
EVERYONE'S CRAZY OVER MY MANLINESS.

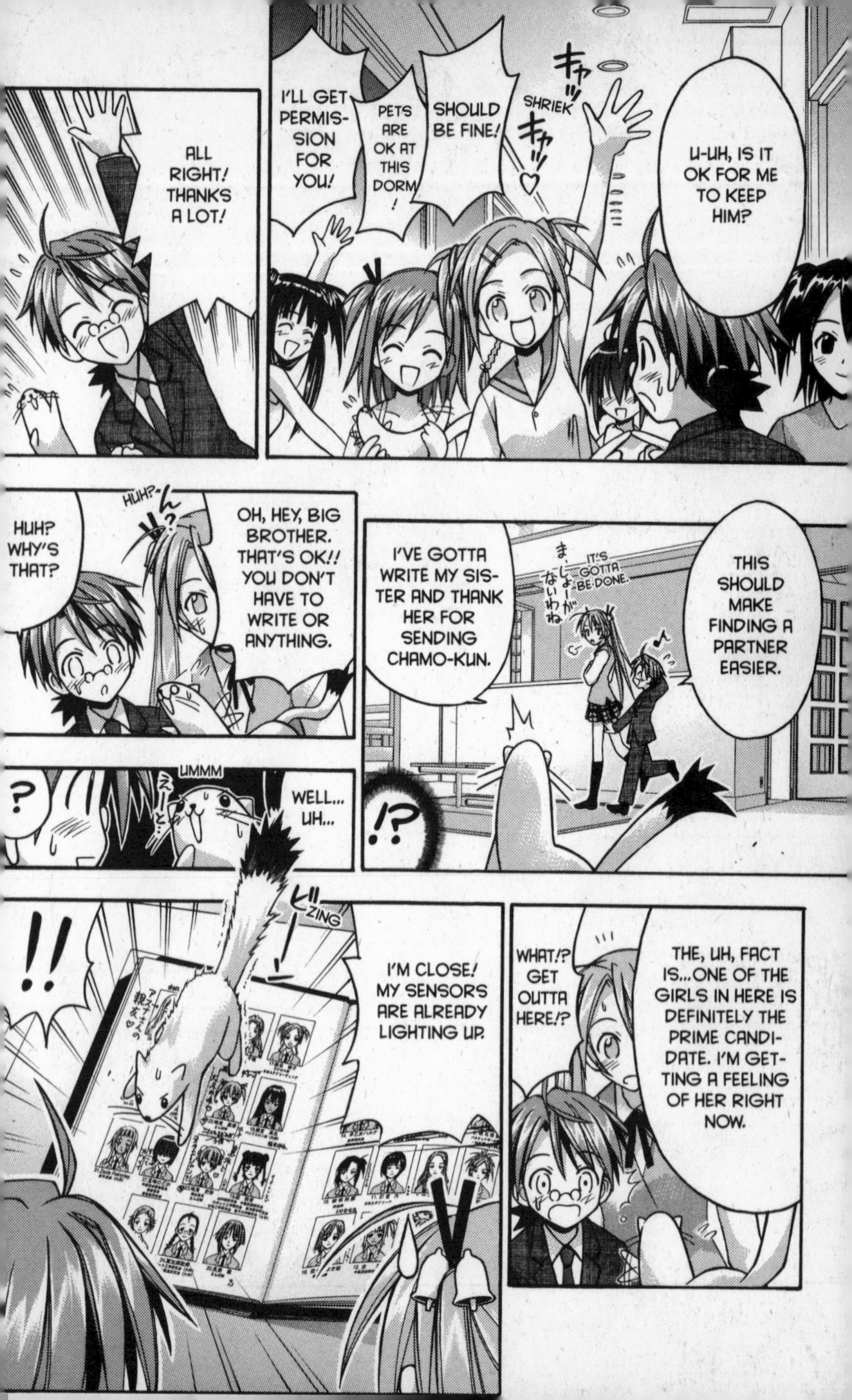
U-UH, IS IT OK FOR ME TO KEEP HIM?
SHRIEK
SHOULD BE FINE!
PETS ARE OK AT THIS DORM!
I'LL GET PERMISSION FOR YOU!
ALL RIGHT! THANKS A LOT!
THIS SHOULD MAKE FINDING A PARTNER EASIER.
I'VE GOTTA WRITE MY SISTER AND THANK HER FOR SENDING CHAMO-KUN.
ま、しょーがないわね
IT'S GOTTA BE DONE.
!?
OH, HEY, BIG BROTHER. THAT'S OK!! YOU DON'T HAVE TO WRITE OR ANYTHING.
HUH?
HUH? WHY'S THAT?
WELL... UH...
UMMM
?
THE, UH, FACT IS...ONE OF THE GIRLS IN HERE IS DEFINITELY THE PRIME CANDIDATE. I'M GETTING A FEELING OF HER RIGHT NOW.
WHAT!? GET OUTTA HERE!?
I'M CLOSE! MY SENSORS ARE ALREADY LIGHTING UP.
ZING
!!

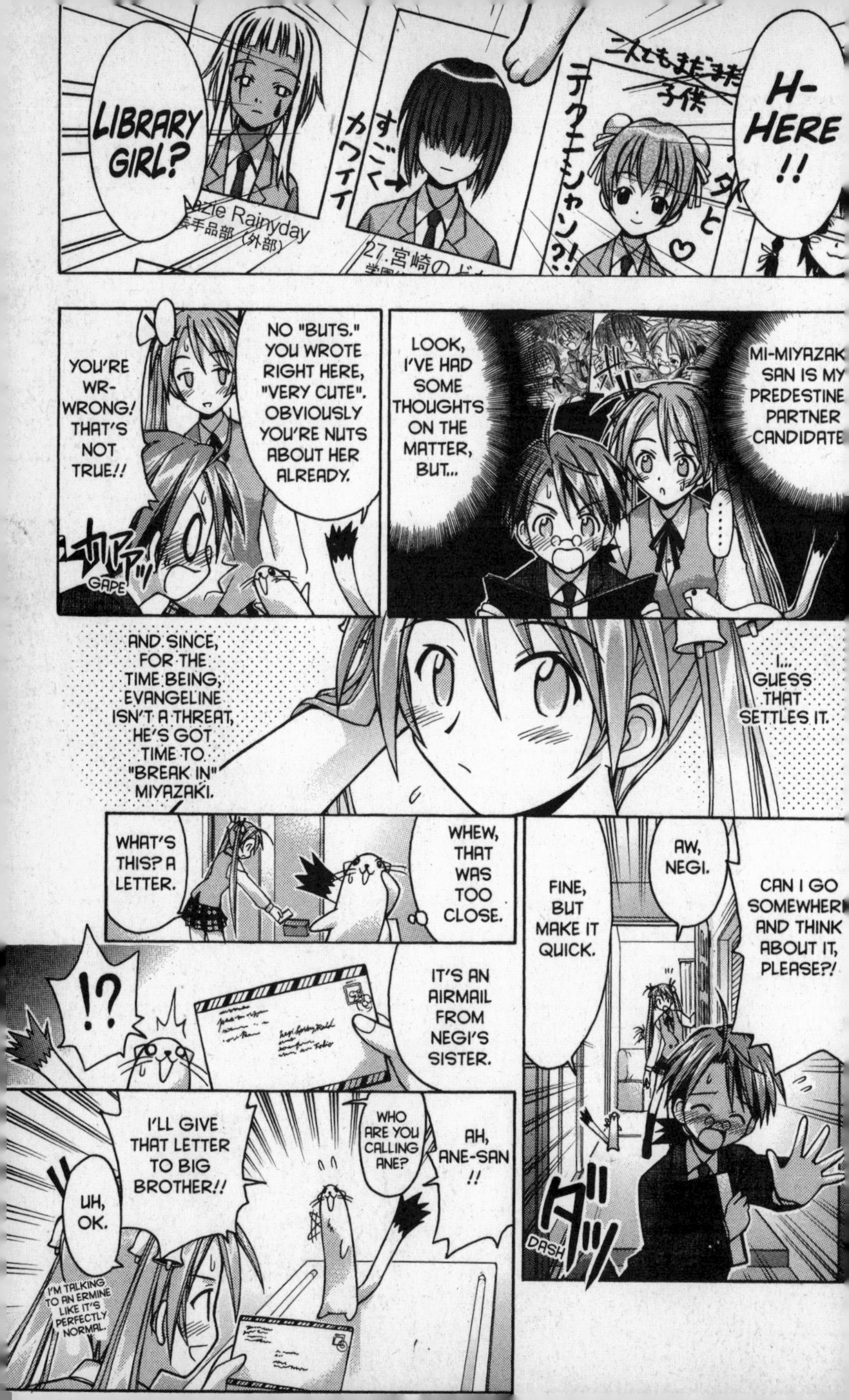
H-HERE!!
テクニシャン?!
すごくカワイイ
LIBRARY GIRL?
Zazie Rainyday
MI-MIYAZAK SAN IS MY PREDESTINE PARTNER CANDIDATE
......
LOOK, I'VE HAD SOME THOUGHTS ON THE MATTER, BUT...
NO "BUTS." YOU WROTE RIGHT HERE, "VERY CUTE". OBVIOUSLY YOU'RE NUTS ABOUT HER ALREADY.
YOU'RE WR-WRONG! THAT'S NOT TRUE!!
GAPE
I... GUESS THAT SETTLES IT.
AND SINCE, FOR THE TIME BEING, EVANGELINE ISN'T A THREAT, HE'S GOT TIME TO "BREAK IN" MIYAZAKI.
CAN I GO SOMEWHER AND THINK ABOUT IT, PLEASE?!
AW, NEGI.
FINE, BUT MAKE IT QUICK.
DASH
WHEW, THAT WAS TOO CLOSE.
WHAT'S THIS? A LETTER.
IT'S AN AIRMAIL FROM NEGI'S SISTER.
!?
AH, ANE-SAN!!
WHO ARE YOU CALLING ANE?
I'LL GIVE THAT LETTER TO BIG BROTHER!!
UH, OK.
I'M TALKING TO AN ERMINE LIKE IT'S PERFECTLY NORMAL.

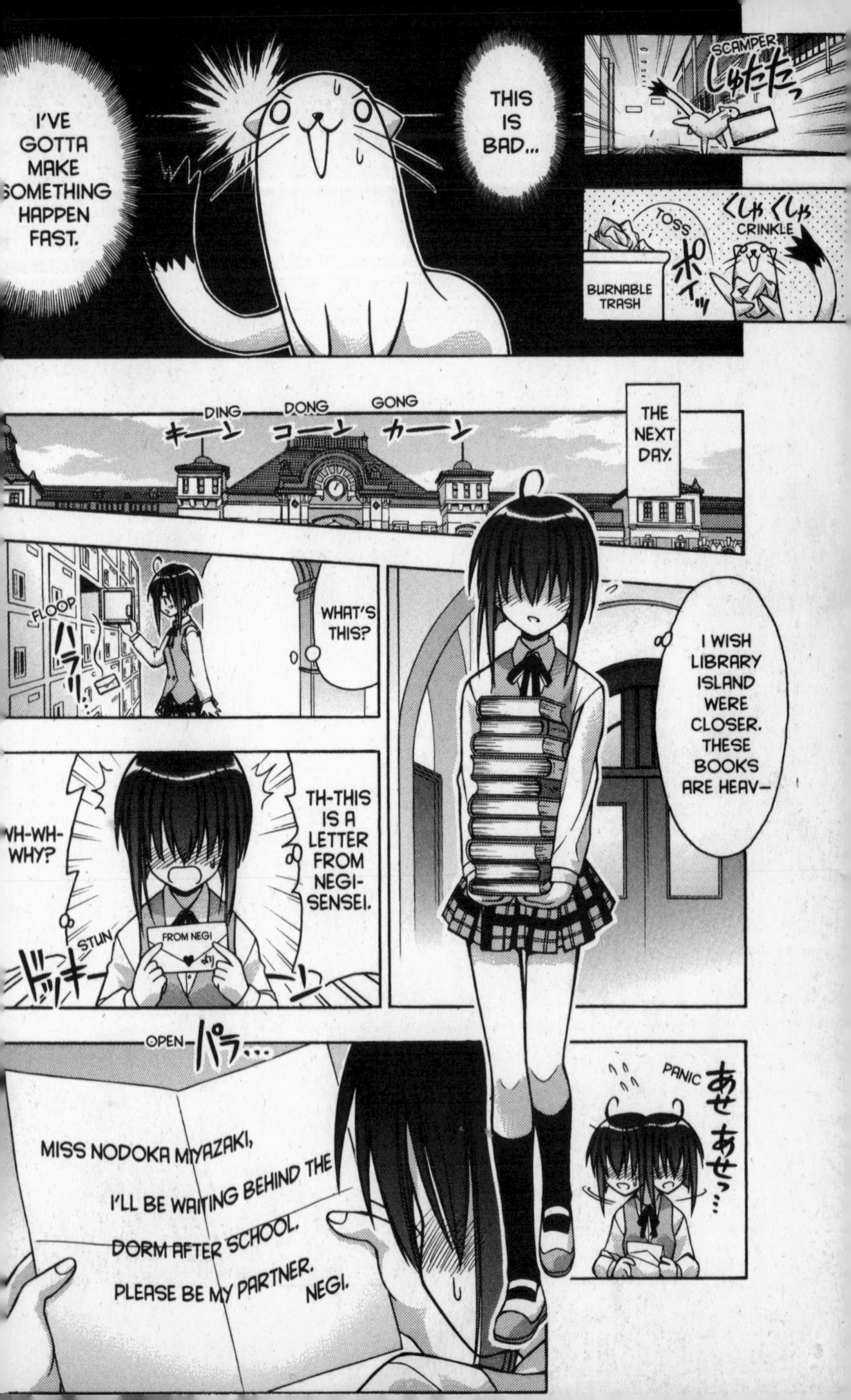
SCAMPER
しゅたたっ
TOSS
ポイッ
くしゃくしゃ
CRINKLE
BURNABLE TRASH
THIS IS BAD...
I'VE GOTTA MAKE SOMETHING HAPPEN FAST.
THE NEXT DAY.
GONG
カーン
DONG
コーン
DING
キーン
I WISH LIBRARY ISLAND WERE CLOSER. THESE BOOKS ARE HEAV—
WHAT'S THIS?
FLOOP
パラリ…
TH-THIS IS A LETTER FROM NEGI-SENSEI.
WH-WH-WHY?
FROM NEGI
STUN
ドッキーン
PANIC
あせあせっ…
OPEN
パラ…
MISS NODOKA MIYAZAKI,
I'LL BE WAITING BEHIND THE DORM AFTER SCHOOL.
PLEASE BE MY PARTNER.
NEGI.

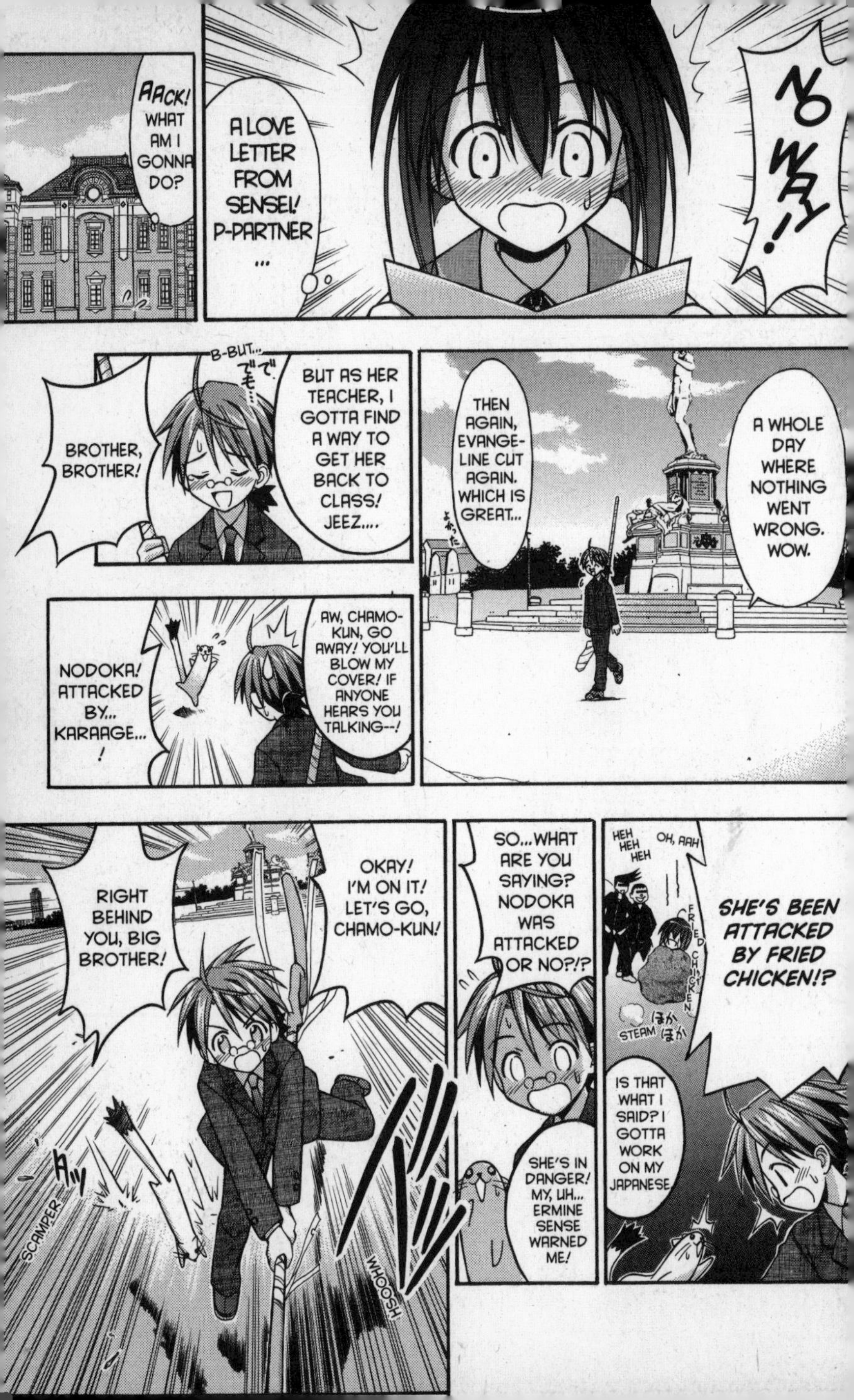
NO WAY!
A LOVE LETTER FROM SENSEI! P-PARTNER...
AACK! WHAT AM I GONNA DO?
A WHOLE DAY WHERE NOTHING WENT WRONG. WOW.
THEN AGAIN, EVANGELINE CUT AGAIN. WHICH IS GREAT...
よかった
BUT AS HER TEACHER, I GOTTA FIND A WAY TO GET HER BACK TO CLASS! JEEZ....
B-BUT...
でも…で
BROTHER, BROTHER!
AW, CHAMO-KUN, GO AWAY! YOU'LL BLOW MY COVER! IF ANYONE HEARS YOU TALKING--!
NODOKA! ATTACKED BY... KARAAGE...!
SHE'S BEEN ATTACKED BY FRIED CHICKEN!?
OH, AAH
HEH HEH HEH
FRIED CHICKEN
STEAM
ほかほか
IS THAT WHAT I SAID? I GOTTA WORK ON MY JAPANESE
SO...WHAT ARE YOU SAYING? NODOKA WAS ATTACKED OR NO?!?
SHE'S IN DANGER! MY, UH... ERMINE SENSE WARNED ME!
OKAY! I'M ON IT! LET'S GO, CHAMO-KUN!
RIGHT BEHIND YOU, BIG BROTHER!
WHOOSH
SCAMPER

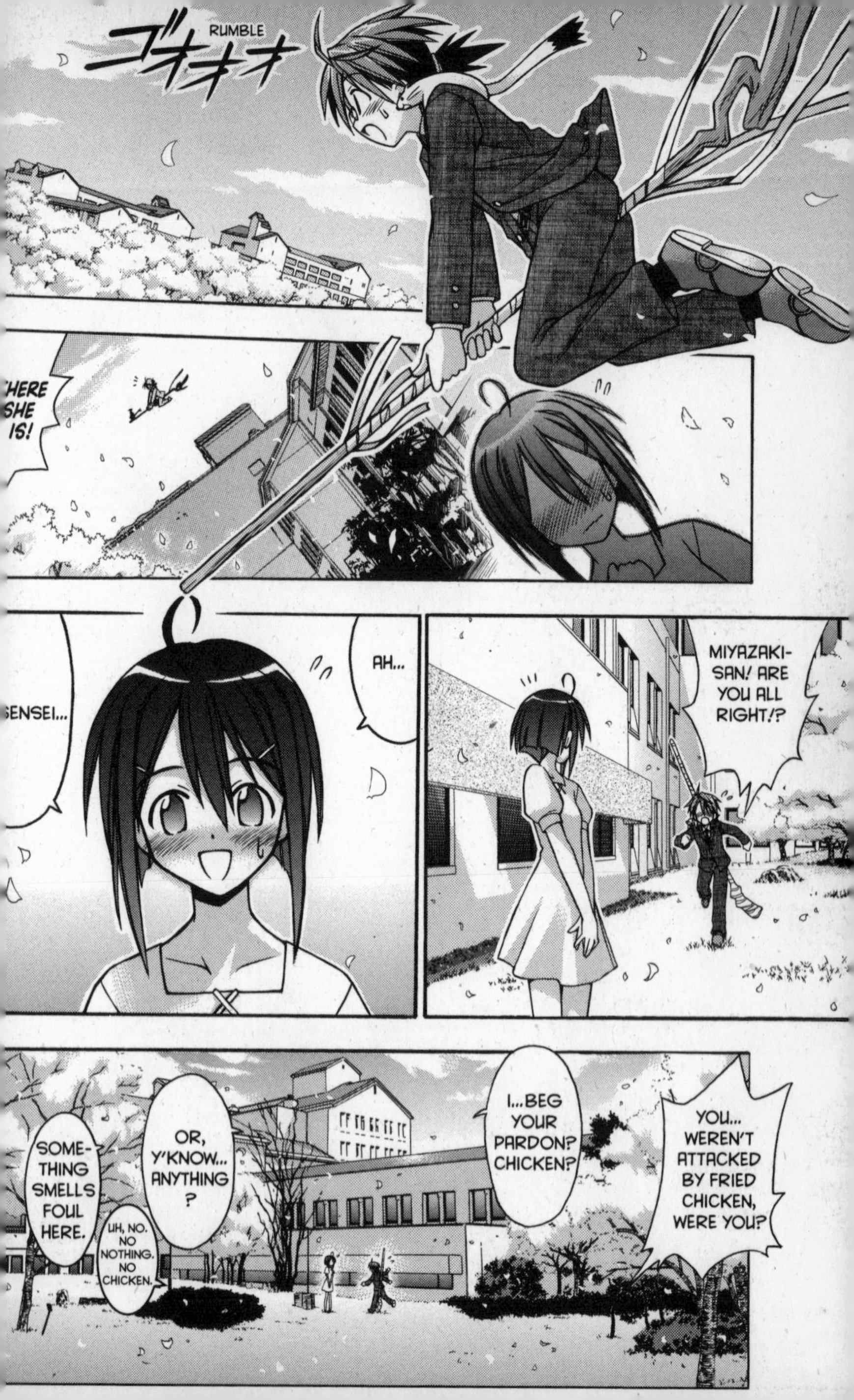
RUMBLE
THERE SHE IS!
MIYAZAKI-SAN! ARE YOU ALL RIGHT!?
AH...
SENSEI...
YOU... WEREN'T ATTACKED BY FRIED CHICKEN, WERE YOU?
I...BEG YOUR PARDON? CHICKEN?
OR, Y'KNOW... ANYTHING?
UH, NO. NO NOTHING. NO CHICKEN.
SOME-THING SMELLS FOUL HERE.

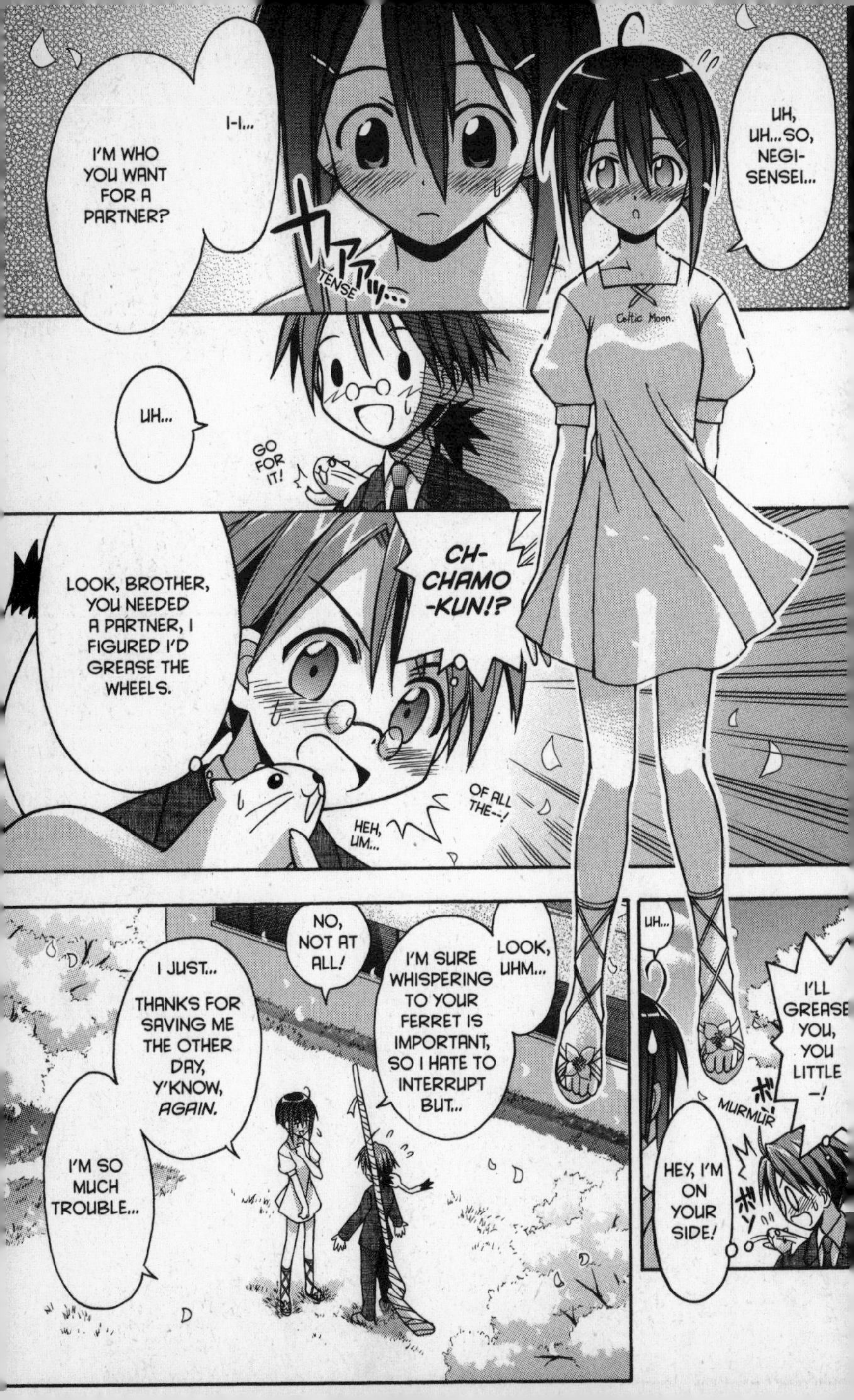
UH, UH...SO, NEGI-SENSEI...
I-I...
I'M WHO YOU WANT FOR A PARTNER?
TENSE
Celtic Moon.
UH...
GO FOR IT!
CH-CHAMO-KUN!?
LOOK, BROTHER, YOU NEEDED A PARTNER, I FIGURED I'D GREASE THE WHEELS.
OF ALL THE--!
HEH, UM...
UH...
I'LL GREASE YOU, YOU LITTLE--!
MURMUR
HEY, I'M ON YOUR SIDE!
LOOK, UHM...
I'M SURE WHISPERING TO YOUR FERRET IS IMPORTANT, SO I HATE TO INTERRUPT BUT...
NO, NOT AT ALL!
I JUST...
THANKS FOR SAVING ME THE OTHER DAY, Y'KNOW, *AGAIN.*
I'M SO MUCH TROUBLE...

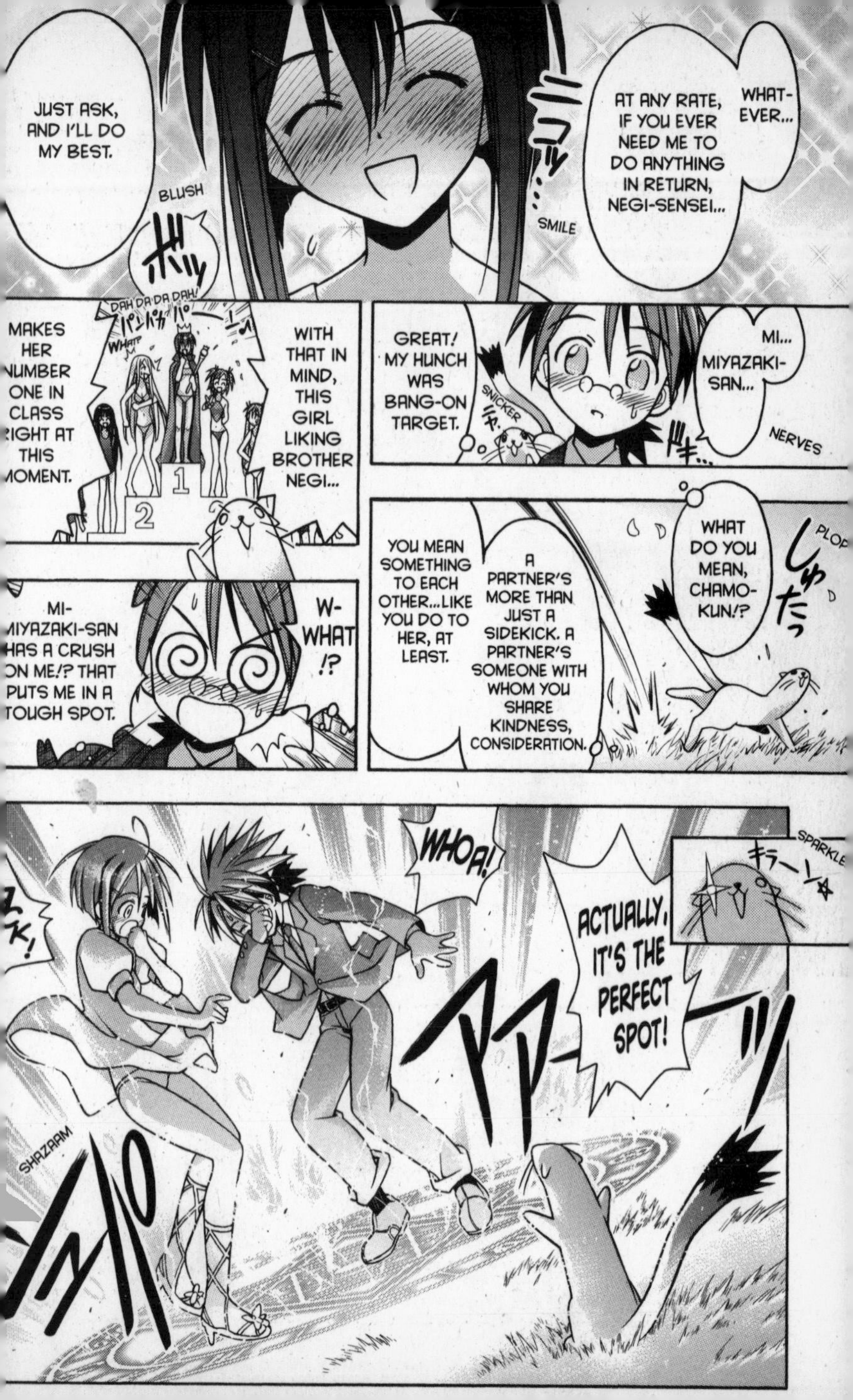
WHAT-EVER...
AT ANY RATE, IF YOU EVER NEED ME TO DO ANYTHING IN RETURN, NEGI-SENSEI...
SMILE
BLUSH
JUST ASK, AND I'LL DO MY BEST.
MI... MIYAZAKI-SAN...
NERVES
SNICKER
GREAT! MY HUNCH WAS BANG-ON TARGET.
WITH THAT IN MIND, THIS GIRL LIKING BROTHER NEGI...
DAH DA DA DAH!
WHAT
MAKES HER NUMBER ONE IN CLASS IGHT AT THIS OMENT.
PLOP
WHAT DO YOU MEAN, CHAMO-KUN!?
A PARTNER'S MORE THAN JUST A SIDEKICK. A PARTNER'S SOMEONE WITH WHOM YOU SHARE KINDNESS, CONSIDERATION.
YOU MEAN SOMETHING TO EACH OTHER...LIKE YOU DO TO HER, AT LEAST.
W-WHAT!?
MI-MIYAZAKI-SAN HAS A CRUSH ON ME!? THAT PUTS ME IN A TOUGH SPOT.
SPARKLE
ACTUALLY, IT'S THE PERFECT SPOT!
WHOA!
SHAZAAM

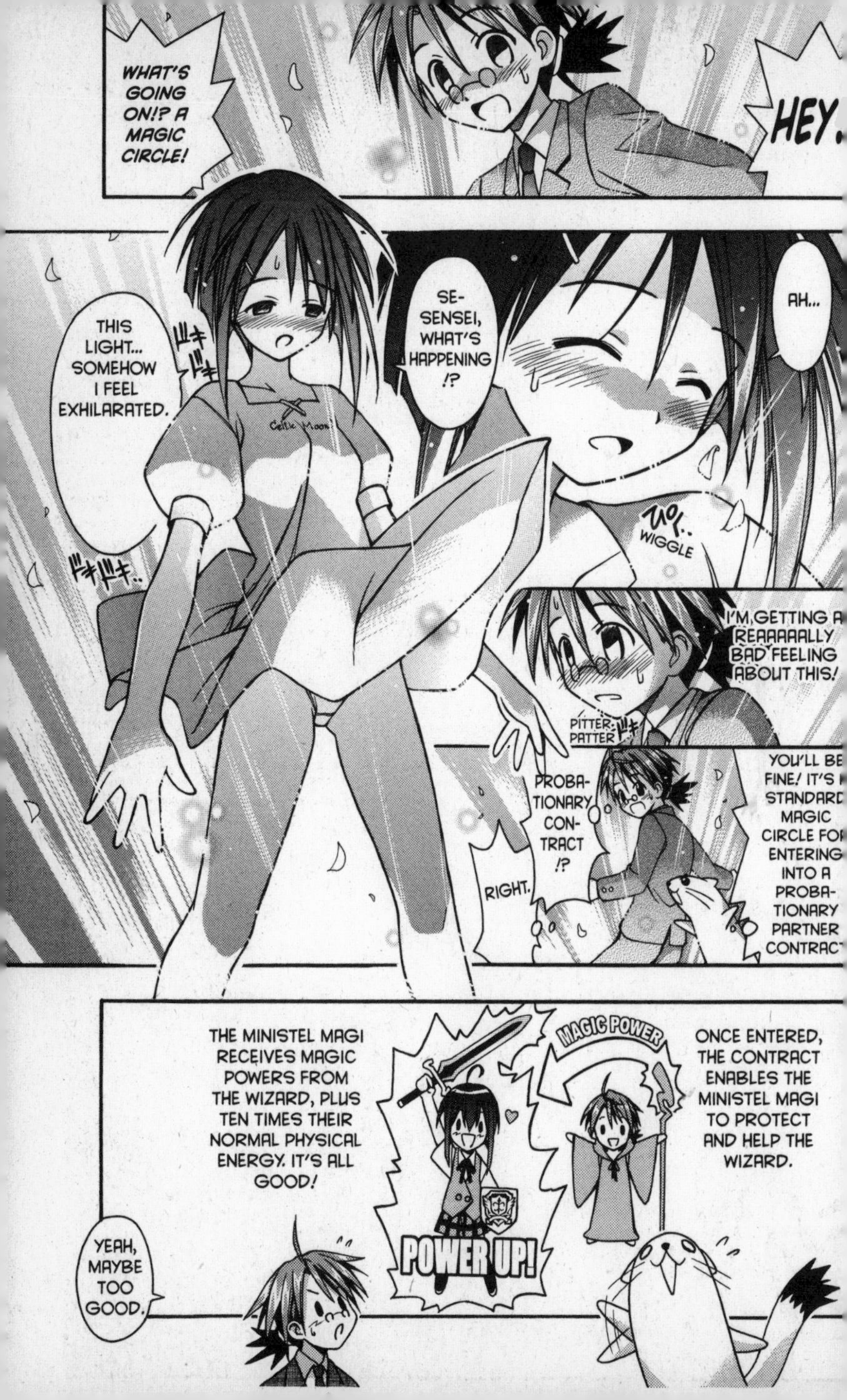
HEY.
WHAT'S GOING ON!? A MAGIC CIRCLE!
AH...
SE-SENSEI, WHAT'S HAPPENING!?
WIGGLE
I'M GETTING A REAAAAALLY BAD FEELING ABOUT THIS!
PITTER-PATTER
YOU'LL BE FINE! IT'S A STANDARD MAGIC CIRCLE FOR ENTERING INTO A PROBATIONARY PARTNER CONTRACT
PROBATIONARY CONTRACT!?
RIGHT.
THIS LIGHT... SOMEHOW I FEEL EXHILARATED.
ONCE ENTERED, THE CONTRACT ENABLES THE MINISTEL MAGI TO PROTECT AND HELP THE WIZARD.
MAGIC POWER
THE MINISTEL MAGI RECEIVES MAGIC POWERS FROM THE WIZARD, PLUS TEN TIMES THEIR NORMAL PHYSICAL ENERGY. IT'S ALL GOOD!
POWER UP!
YEAH, MAYBE TOO GOOD.

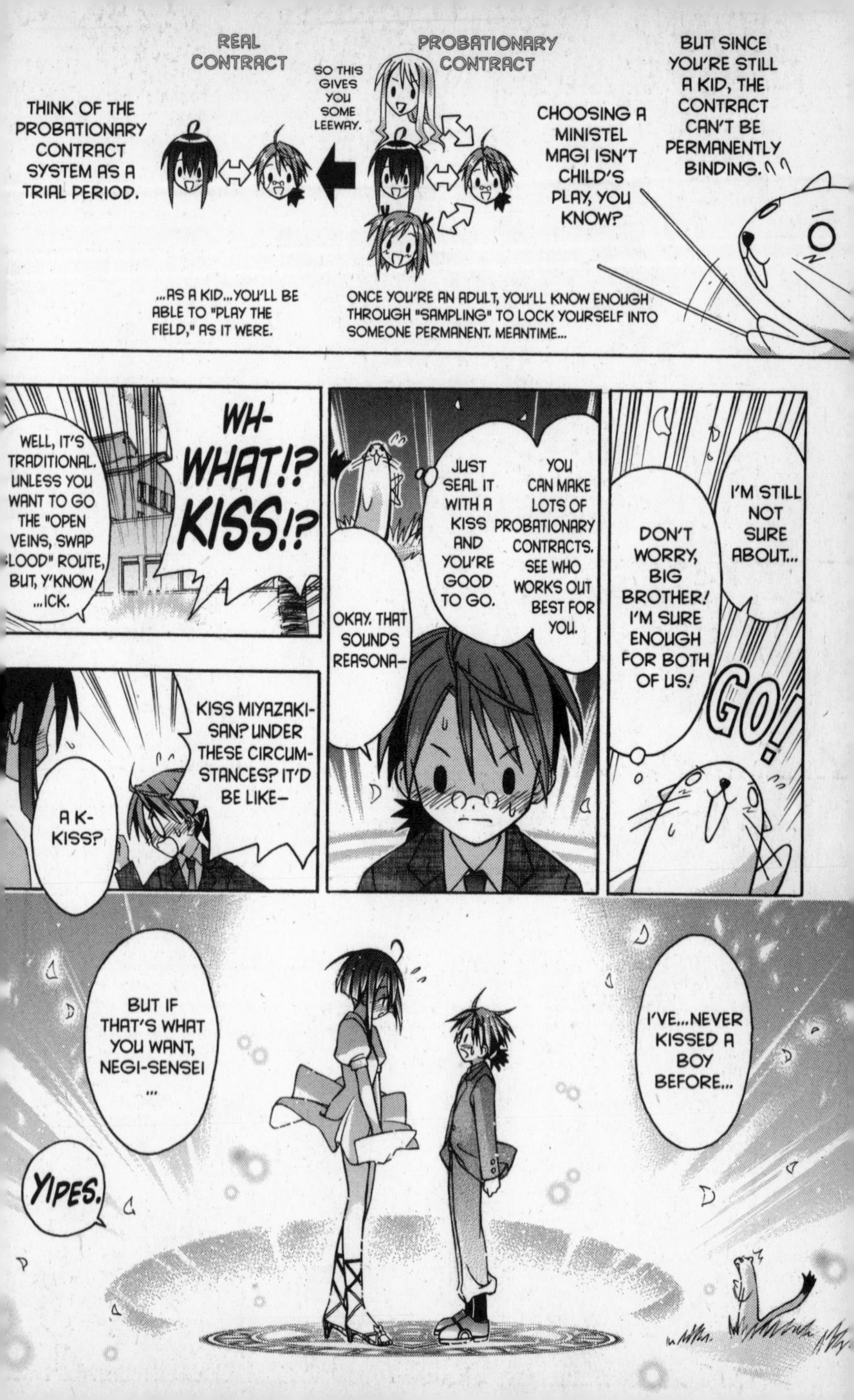

BUT SINCE YOU'RE STILL A KID, THE CONTRACT CAN'T BE PERMANENTLY BINDING.
CHOOSING A MINISTEL MAGI ISN'T CHILD'S PLAY, YOU KNOW?
PROBATIONARY CONTRACT
SO THIS GIVES YOU SOME LEEWAY.
REAL CONTRACT
THINK OF THE PROBATIONARY CONTRACT SYSTEM AS A TRIAL PERIOD.
ONCE YOU'RE AN ADULT, YOU'LL KNOW ENOUGH THROUGH "SAMPLING" TO LOCK YOURSELF INTO SOMEONE PERMANENT. MEANTIME...
...AS A KID...YOU'LL BE ABLE TO "PLAY THE FIELD," AS IT WERE.
I'M STILL NOT SURE ABOUT...
DON'T WORRY, BIG BROTHER! I'M SURE ENOUGH FOR BOTH OF US!
GO!
YOU CAN MAKE LOTS OF PROBATIONARY CONTRACTS. SEE WHO WORKS OUT BEST FOR YOU.
JUST SEAL IT WITH A KISS AND YOU'RE GOOD TO GO.
OKAY. THAT SOUNDS REASONA–
WH-WHAT!? KISS!?
WELL, IT'S TRADITIONAL. UNLESS YOU WANT TO GO THE "OPEN VEINS, SWAP LOOD" ROUTE, BUT, Y'KNOW ...ICK.
KISS MIYAZAKI-SAN? UNDER THESE CIRCUMSTANCES? IT'D BE LIKE–
A K-KISS?
I'VE...NEVER KISSED A BOY BEFORE...
BUT IF THAT'S WHAT YOU WANT, NEGI-SENSEI ...
YIPES.

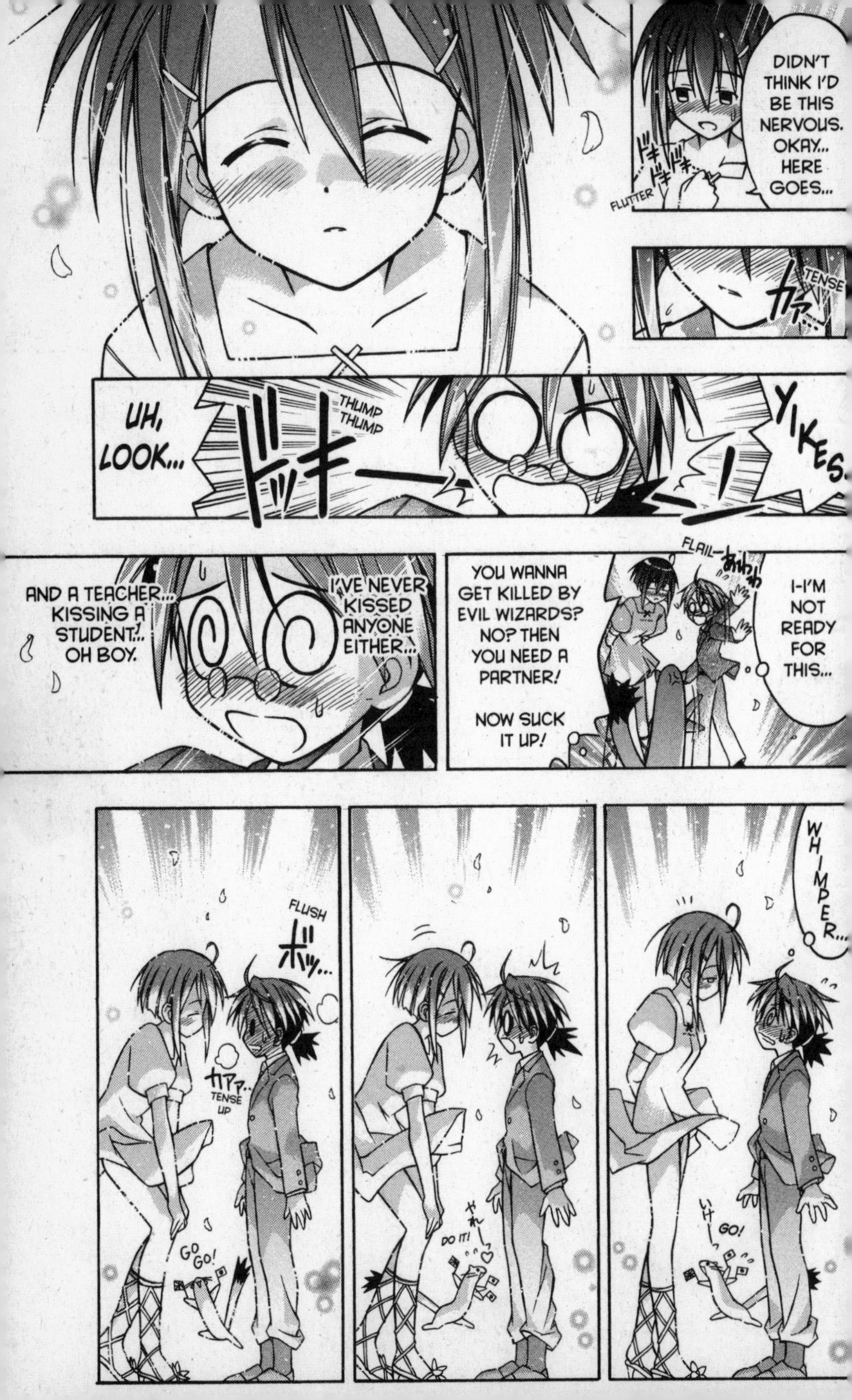
DIDN'T THINK I'D BE THIS NERVOUS. OKAY... HERE GOES...
FLUTTER
TENSE
YIKES.
THUMP THUMP
UH, LOOK...
I-I'M NOT READY FOR THIS...
FLAIL
YOU WANNA GET KILLED BY EVIL WIZARDS? NO? THEN YOU NEED A PARTNER!
NOW SUCK IT UP!
I'VE NEVER KISSED ANYONE EITHER...
AND A TEACHER... KISSING A STUDENT... OH BOY.
WHIMPER...
GO!
DO IT!
FLUSH
TENSE UP
GO GO!

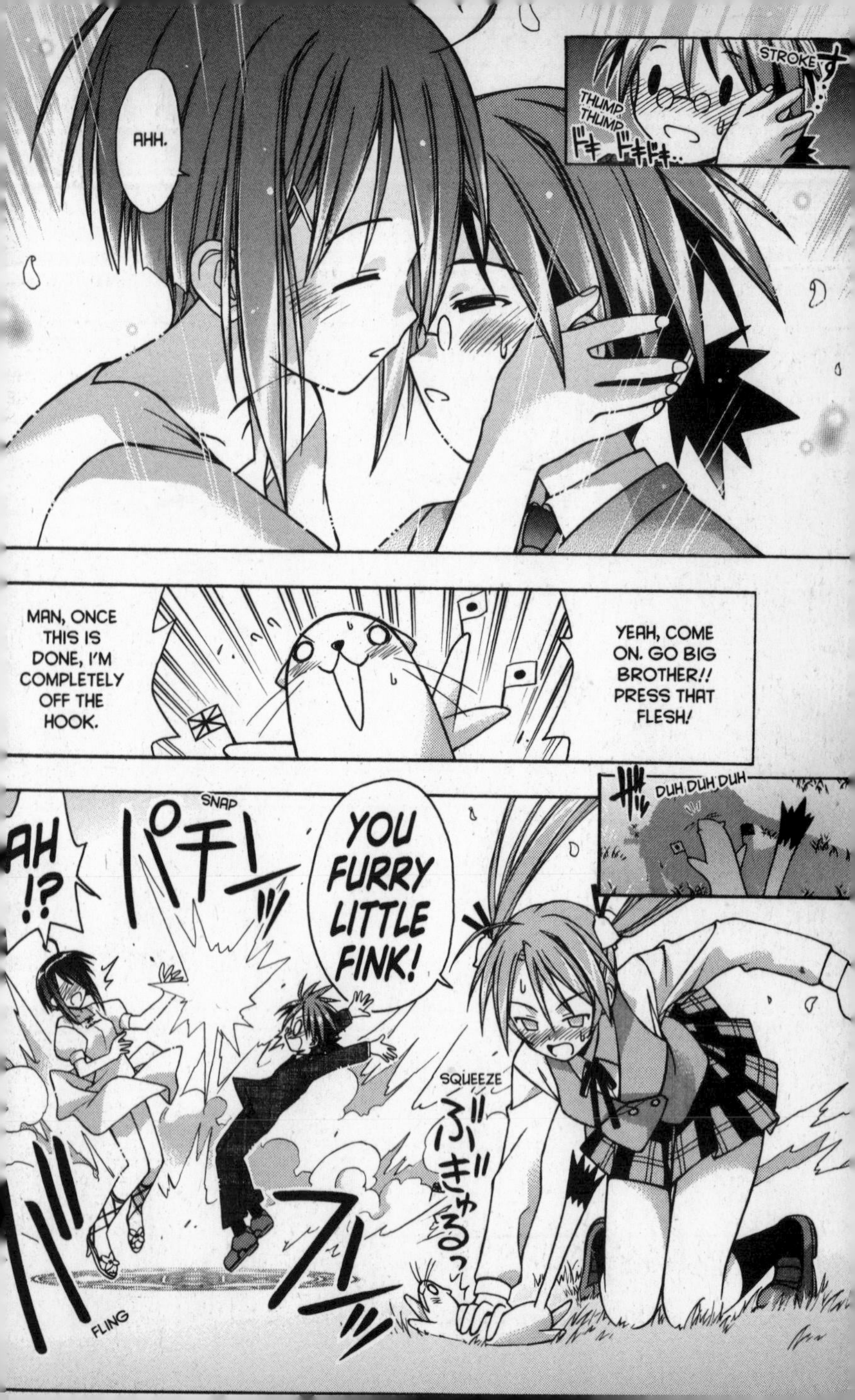
STROKE す
THUMP THUMP
ドキ ドキドキ…
AHH.
YEAH, COME ON. GO BIG BROTHER!! PRESS THAT FLESH!
MAN, ONCE THIS IS DONE, I'M COMPLETELY OFF THE HOOK.
DUH DUH DUH
YOU FURRY LITTLE FINK!
SQUEEZE
ぶぎゅるっ
SNAP
パチーッ
AH!?
FLING

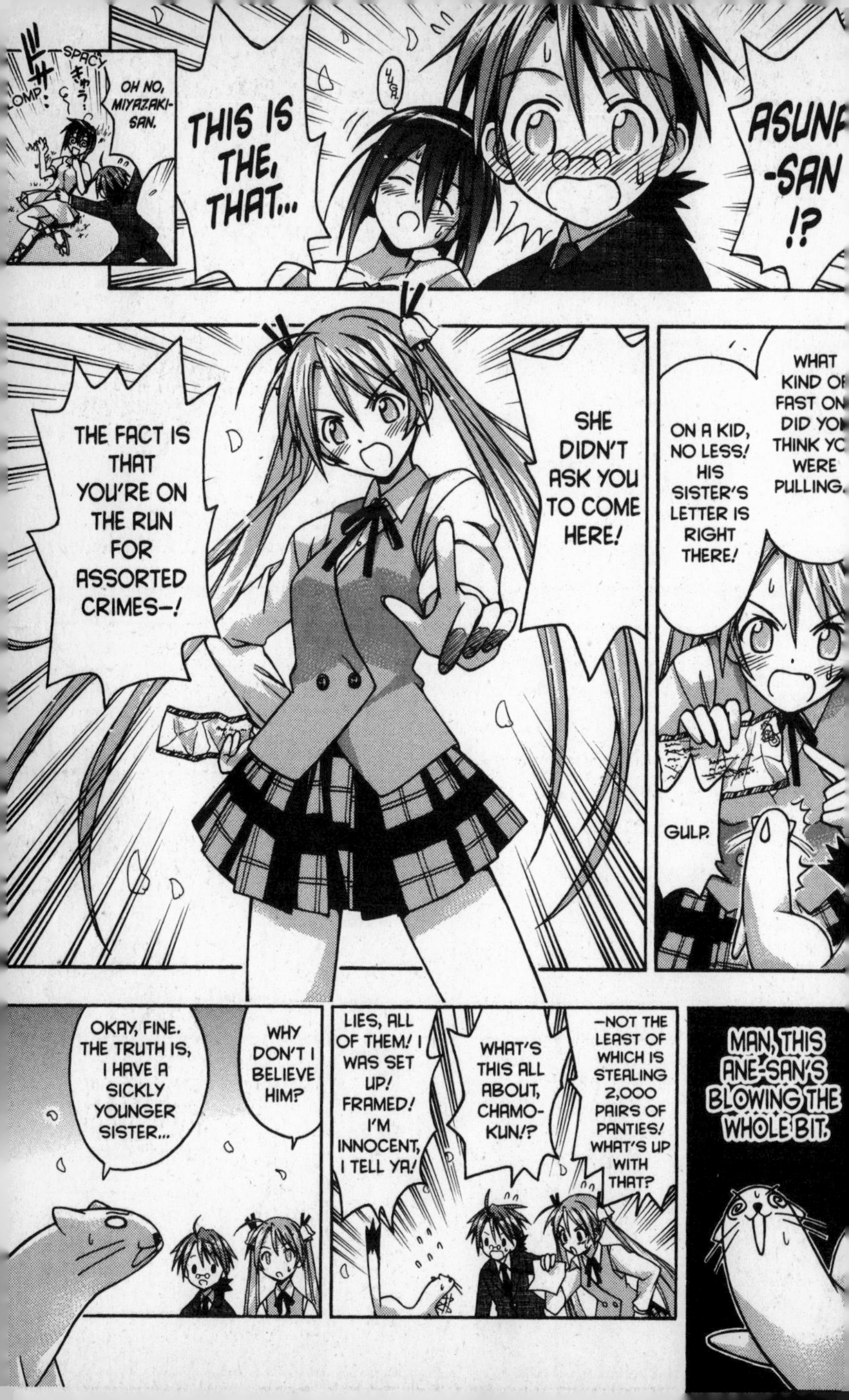
ASUNA-SAN!?
THIS IS THE, THAT...
OH NO, MIYAZAKI-SAN.
SPACY
CLOMP!
WHAT KIND OF FAST ON DID YO THINK YO WERE PULLING.
ON A KID, NO LESS! HIS SISTER'S LETTER IS RIGHT THERE!
GULP.
SHE DIDN'T ASK YOU TO COME HERE!
THE FACT IS THAT YOU'RE ON THE RUN FOR ASSORTED CRIMES–!
MAN, THIS ANE-SAN'S BLOWING THE WHOLE BIT.
–NOT THE LEAST OF WHICH IS STEALING 2,000 PAIRS OF PANTIES! WHAT'S UP WITH THAT?
WHAT'S THIS ALL ABOUT, CHAMO-KUN!?
LIES, ALL OF THEM! I WAS SET UP! FRAMED! I'M INNOCENT, I TELL YA!
WHY DON'T I BELIEVE HIM?
OKAY, FINE. THE TRUTH IS, I HAVE A SICKLY YOUNGER SISTER...

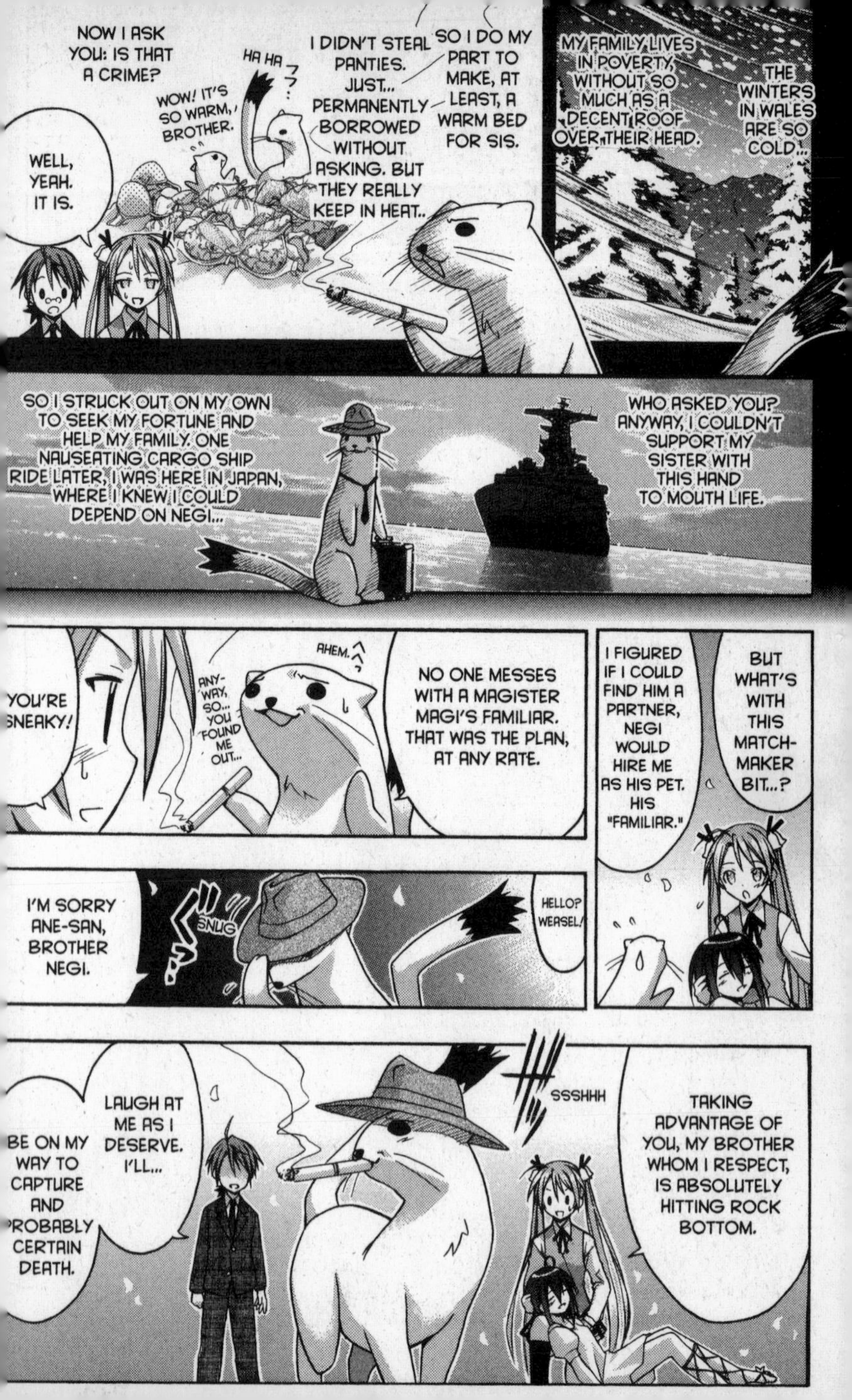
THE WINTERS IN WALES ARE SO COLD...
MY FAMILY LIVES IN POVERTY, WITHOUT SO MUCH AS A DECENT ROOF OVER THEIR HEAD.
SO I DO MY PART TO MAKE, AT LEAST, A WARM BED FOR SIS.
I DIDN'T STEAL PANTIES. JUST... PERMANENTLY BORROWED WITHOUT ASKING. BUT THEY REALLY KEEP IN HEAT..
HA HA
WOW! IT'S SO WARM, BROTHER.
NOW I ASK YOU: IS THAT A CRIME?
WELL, YEAH. IT IS.
WHO ASKED YOU? ANYWAY, I COULDN'T SUPPORT MY SISTER WITH THIS HAND TO MOUTH LIFE.
SO I STRUCK OUT ON MY OWN TO SEEK MY FORTUNE AND HELP MY FAMILY. ONE NAUSEATING CARGO SHIP RIDE LATER, I WAS HERE IN JAPAN, WHERE I KNEW I COULD DEPEND ON NEGI...
BUT WHAT'S WITH THIS MATCH-MAKER BIT...?
I FIGURED IF I COULD FIND HIM A PARTNER, NEGI WOULD HIRE ME AS HIS PET. HIS "FAMILIAR."
NO ONE MESSES WITH A MAGISTER MAGI'S FAMILIAR. THAT WAS THE PLAN, AT ANY RATE.
AHEM.
ANY-WAY, SO... YOU FOUND ME OUT...
YOU'RE SNEAKY!
HELLO? WEASEL!
SNUG
I'M SORRY ANE-SAN, BROTHER NEGI.
TAKING ADVANTAGE OF YOU, MY BROTHER WHOM I RESPECT, IS ABSOLUTELY HITTING ROCK BOTTOM.
SSSHHH
LAUGH AT ME AS I DESERVE. I'LL...
BE ON MY WAY TO CAPTURE AND ROBABLY CERTAIN DEATH.

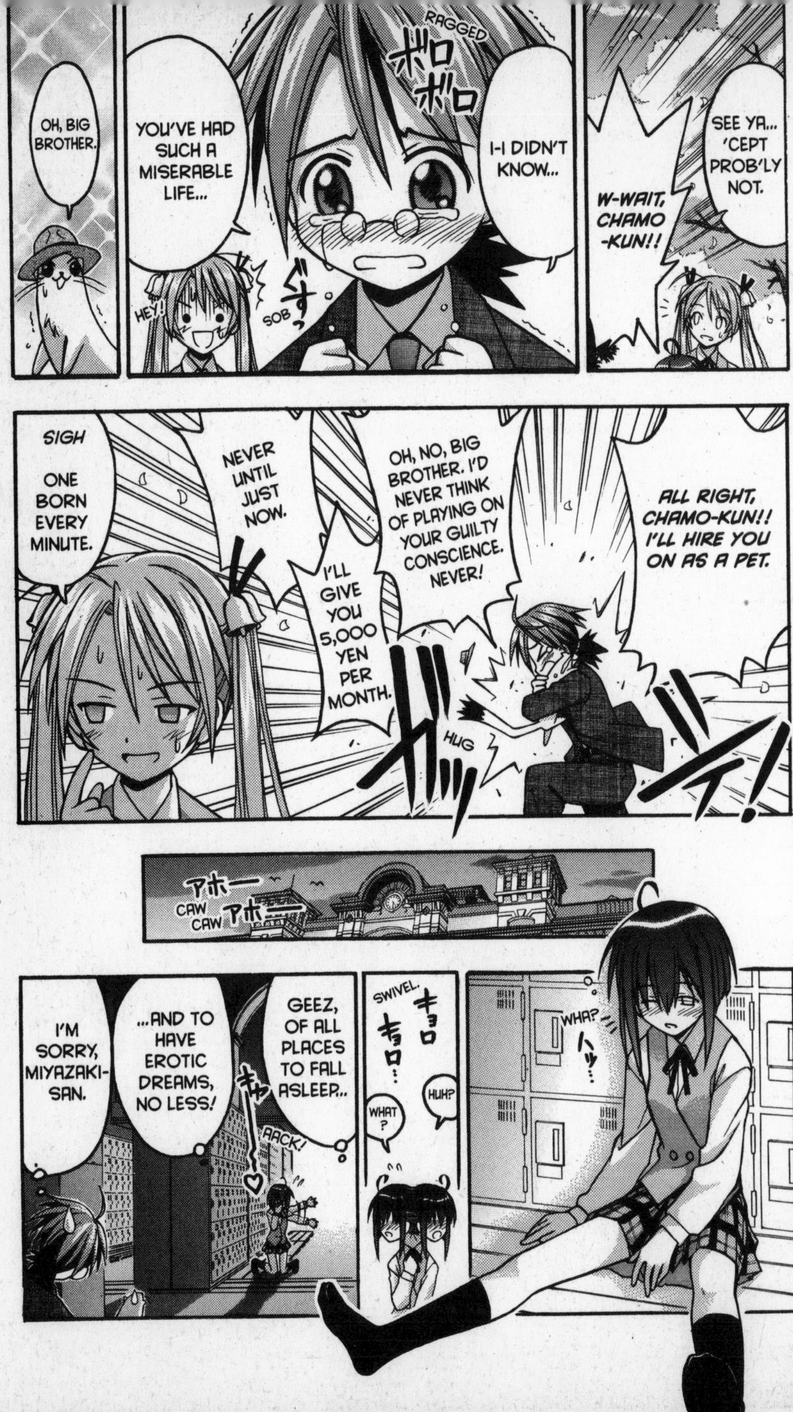
SEE YA... 'CEPT PROB'LY NOT.
W-WAIT, CHAMO-KUN!!
ボロボロ
RAGGED
I-I DIDN'T KNOW...
YOU'VE HAD SUCH A MISERABLE LIFE...
ぐすっ
SOB
HEY!
OH, BIG BROTHER.
ALL RIGHT, CHAMO-KUN!! I'LL HIRE YOU ON AS A PET.
HUG
OH, NO, BIG BROTHER. I'D NEVER THINK OF PLAYING ON YOUR GUILTY CONSCIENCE. NEVER!
I'LL GIVE YOU 5,000 YEN PER MONTH.
NEVER UNTIL JUST NOW.
SIGH
ONE BORN EVERY MINUTE.
アホー
CAW
アホー
CAW
WHA?
ハッ…
HUH?
WHAT?
SWIVEL
キョロキョロ…
GEEZ, OF ALL PLACES TO FALL ASLEEP...
...AND TO HAVE EROTIC DREAMS, NO LESS!
キャ
AACK!
I'M SORRY, MIYAZAKI-SAN.

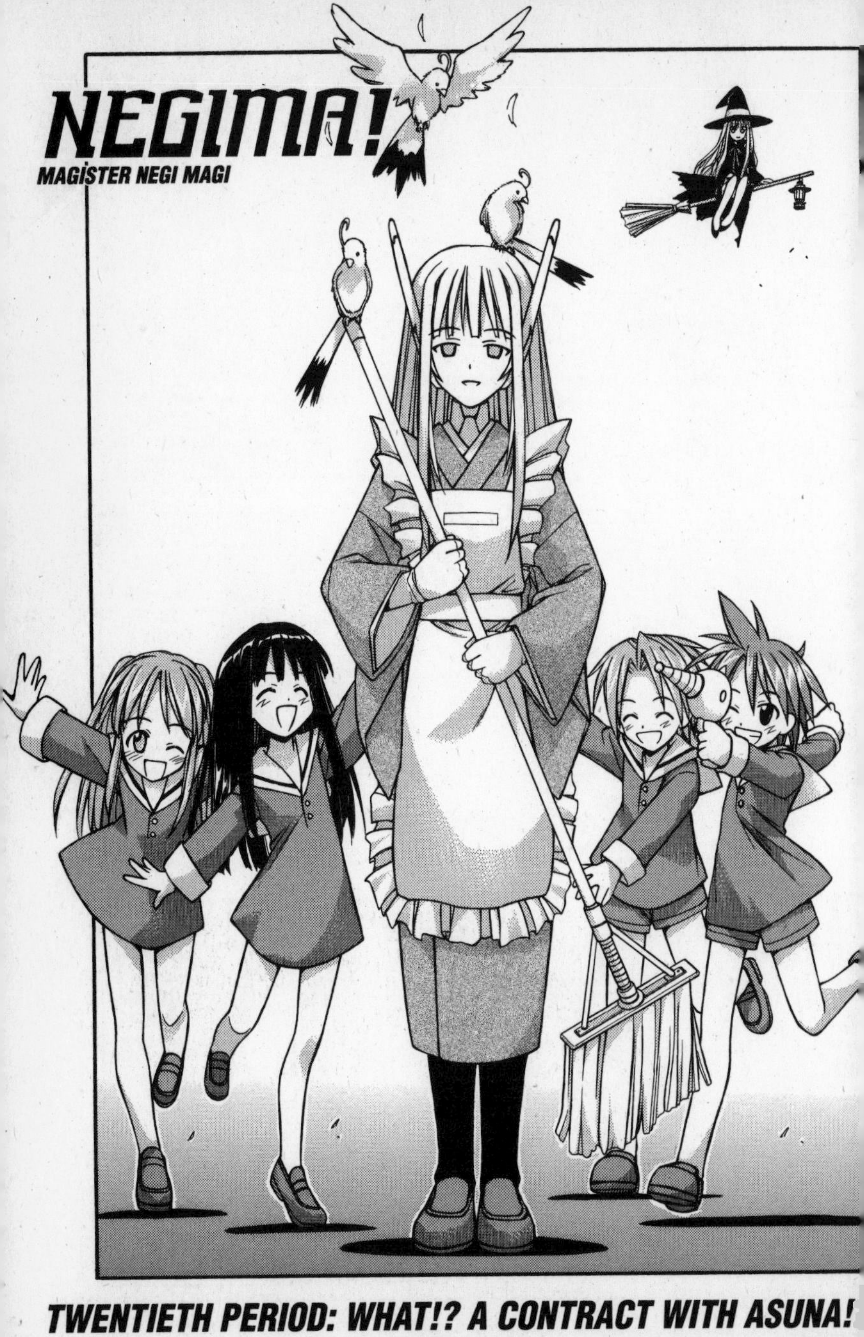
NEGIMA!
MAGISTER NEGI MAGI

TWENTIETH PERIOD: WHAT!? A CONTRACT WITH ASUNA!

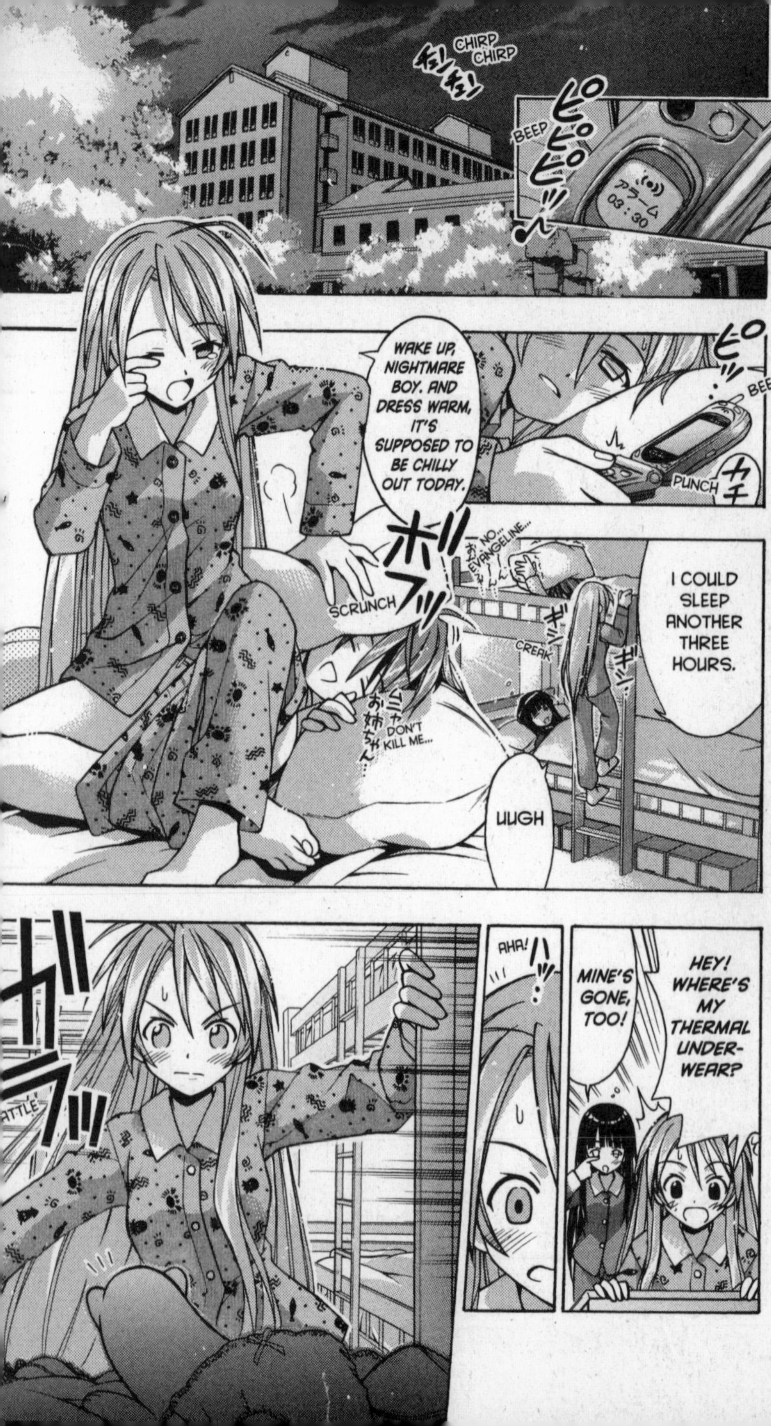
BEEP
アラーム
03 : 30
BEEP
CHIRP CHIRP
BEEP
PUNCH
I COULD SLEEP ANOTHER THREE HOURS.
CREAK
NO... EVANGELINE...
UUGH
WAKE UP, NIGHTMARE BOY. AND DRESS WARM, IT'S SUPPOSED TO BE CHILLY OUT TODAY.
SCRUNCH
DON'T KILL ME...
HEY! WHERE'S MY THERMAL UNDER-WEAR?
MINE'S GONE, TOO!
AHA!

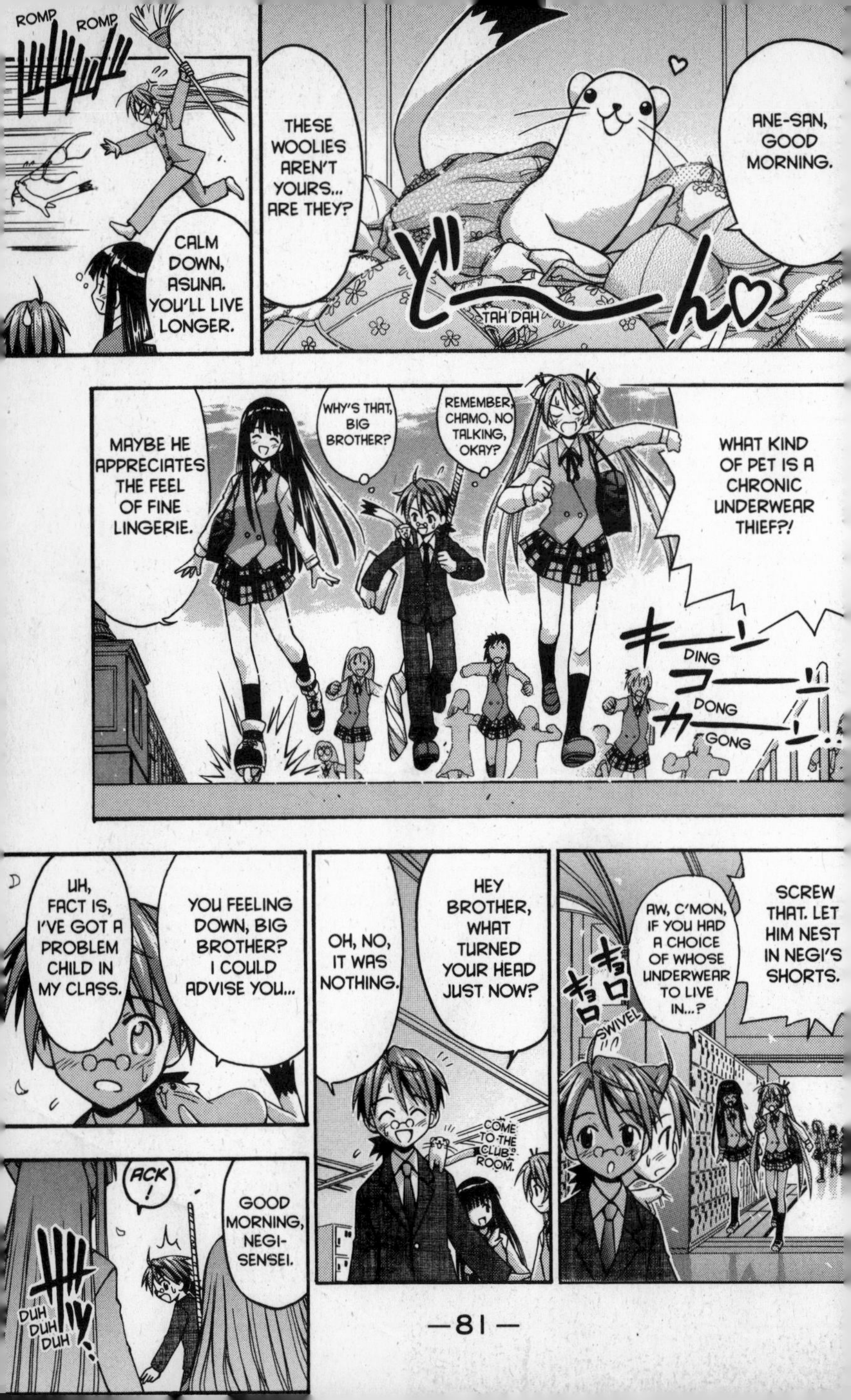

ANE-SAN, GOOD MORNING.
TAH DAH
THESE WOOLIES AREN'T YOURS... ARE THEY?
ROMP ROMP
CALM DOWN, ASUNA. YOU'LL LIVE LONGER.
WHAT KIND OF PET IS A CHRONIC UNDERWEAR THIEF?!
DING
DONG
GONG
REMEMBER, CHAMO, NO TALKING, OKAY?
WHY'S THAT, BIG BROTHER?
MAYBE HE APPRECIATES THE FEEL OF FINE LINGERIE.
SCREW THAT. LET HIM NEST IN NEGI'S SHORTS.
AW, C'MON, IF YOU HAD A CHOICE OF WHOSE UNDERWEAR TO LIVE IN...?
SWIVEL
HEY BROTHER, WHAT TURNED YOUR HEAD JUST NOW?
OH, NO, IT WAS NOTHING.
COME TO THE CLUB ROOM.
YOU FEELING DOWN, BIG BROTHER? I COULD ADVISE YOU...
UH, FACT IS, I'VE GOT A PROBLEM CHILD IN MY CLASS.
GOOD MORNING, NEGI-SENSEI.
ACK!
DUH DUH DUH

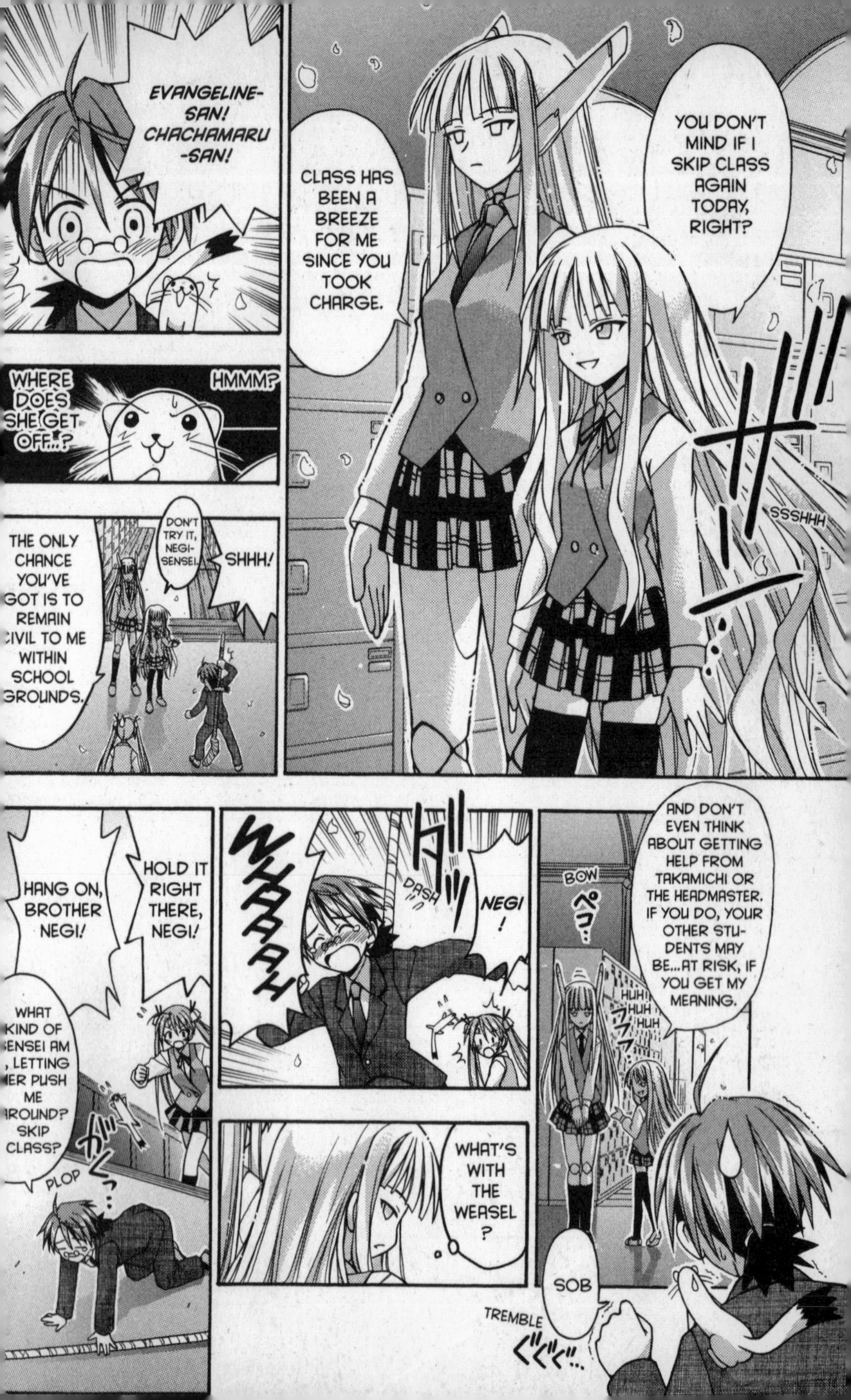
YOU DON'T MIND IF I SKIP CLASS AGAIN TODAY, RIGHT?
CLASS HAS BEEN A BREEZE FOR ME SINCE YOU TOOK CHARGE.
SSSHHH
EVANGELINE-SAN! CHACHAMARU-SAN!
HMMM?
WHERE DOES SHE GET OFF...?
SHHH!
DON'T TRY IT, NEGI-SENSEI.
THE ONLY CHANCE YOU'VE GOT IS TO REMAIN CIVIL TO ME WITHIN SCHOOL GROUNDS.
AND DON'T EVEN THINK ABOUT GETTING HELP FROM TAKAMICHI OR THE HEADMASTER. IF YOU DO, YOUR OTHER STUDENTS MAY BE...AT RISK, IF YOU GET MY MEANING.
BOW
HUH HUH HUH
SOB
TREMBLE
NEGI!
DASH
WHAAAAH
WHAT'S WITH THE WEASEL?
HOLD IT RIGHT THERE, NEGI!
HANG ON, BROTHER NEGI!
WHAT KIND OF SENSEI AM I, LETTING HER PUSH ME AROUND? SKIP CLASS?
PLOP

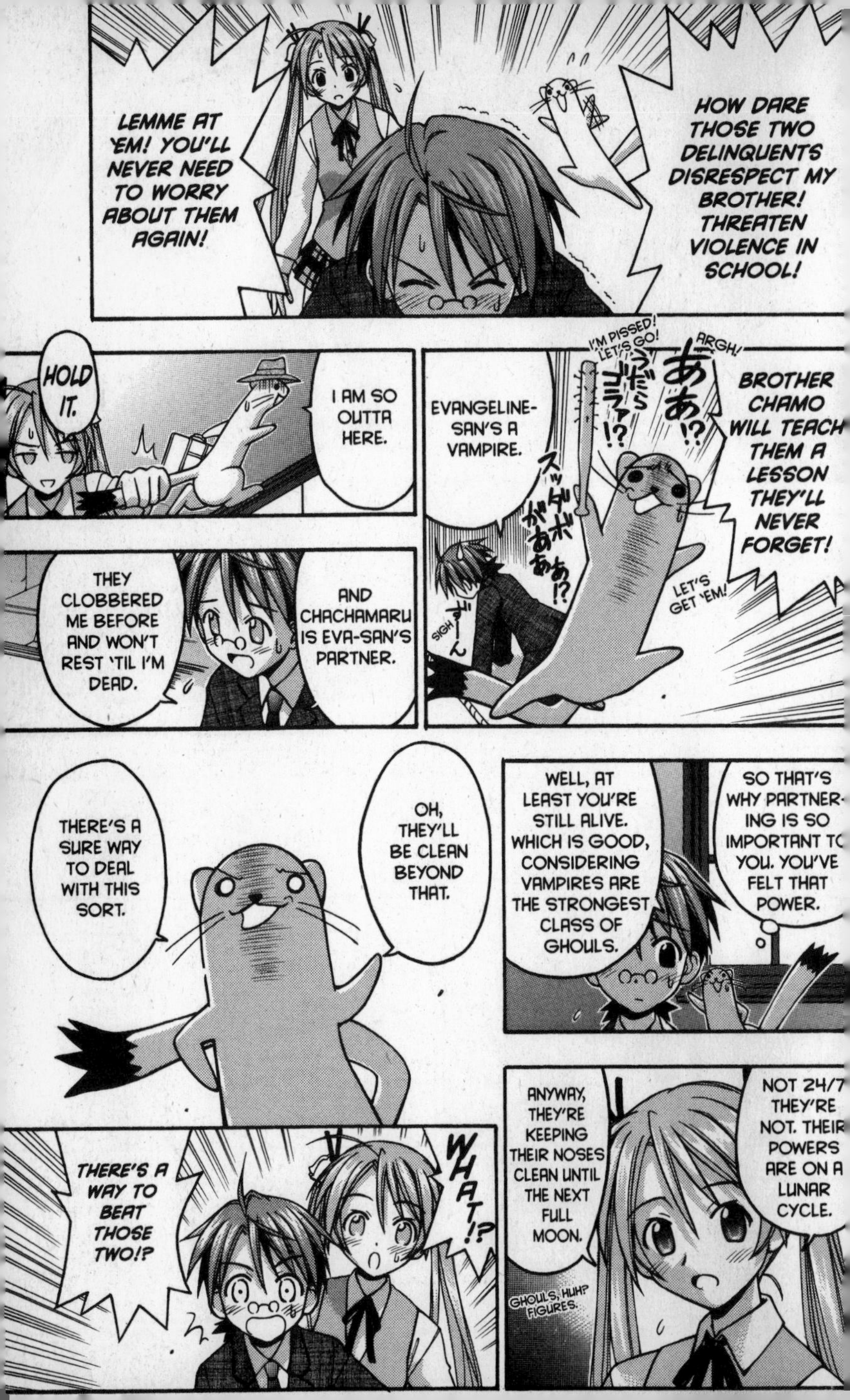
HOW DARE THOSE TWO DELINQUENTS DISRESPECT MY BROTHER! THREATEN VIOLENCE IN SCHOOL!
LEMME AT 'EM! YOU'LL NEVER NEED TO WORRY ABOUT THEM AGAIN!
BROTHER CHAMO WILL TEACH THEM A LESSON THEY'LL NEVER FORGET!
ARGH!
あぁ!?
I'M PISSED! LET'S GO!
うだらゴラァ!?
LET'S GET 'EM!
スッダボがぁぁあ!?
SIGH
ずーん
EVANGELINE-SAN'S A VAMPIRE.
I AM SO OUTTA HERE.
HOLD IT.
AND CHACHAMARU IS EVA-SAN'S PARTNER.
THEY CLOBBERED ME BEFORE AND WON'T REST 'TIL I'M DEAD.
SO THAT'S WHY PARTNERING IS SO IMPORTANT TO YOU. YOU'VE FELT THAT POWER.
WELL, AT LEAST YOU'RE STILL ALIVE. WHICH IS GOOD, CONSIDERING VAMPIRES ARE THE STRONGEST CLASS OF GHOULS.
NOT 24/7 THEY'RE NOT. THEIR POWERS ARE ON A LUNAR CYCLE.
ANYWAY, THEY'RE KEEPING THEIR NOSES CLEAN UNTIL THE NEXT FULL MOON.
GHOULS, HUH? FIGURES.
OH, THEY'LL BE CLEAN BEYOND THAT.
THERE'S A SURE WAY TO DEAL WITH THIS SORT.
WHAT!?
THERE'S A WAY TO BEAT THOSE TWO!?

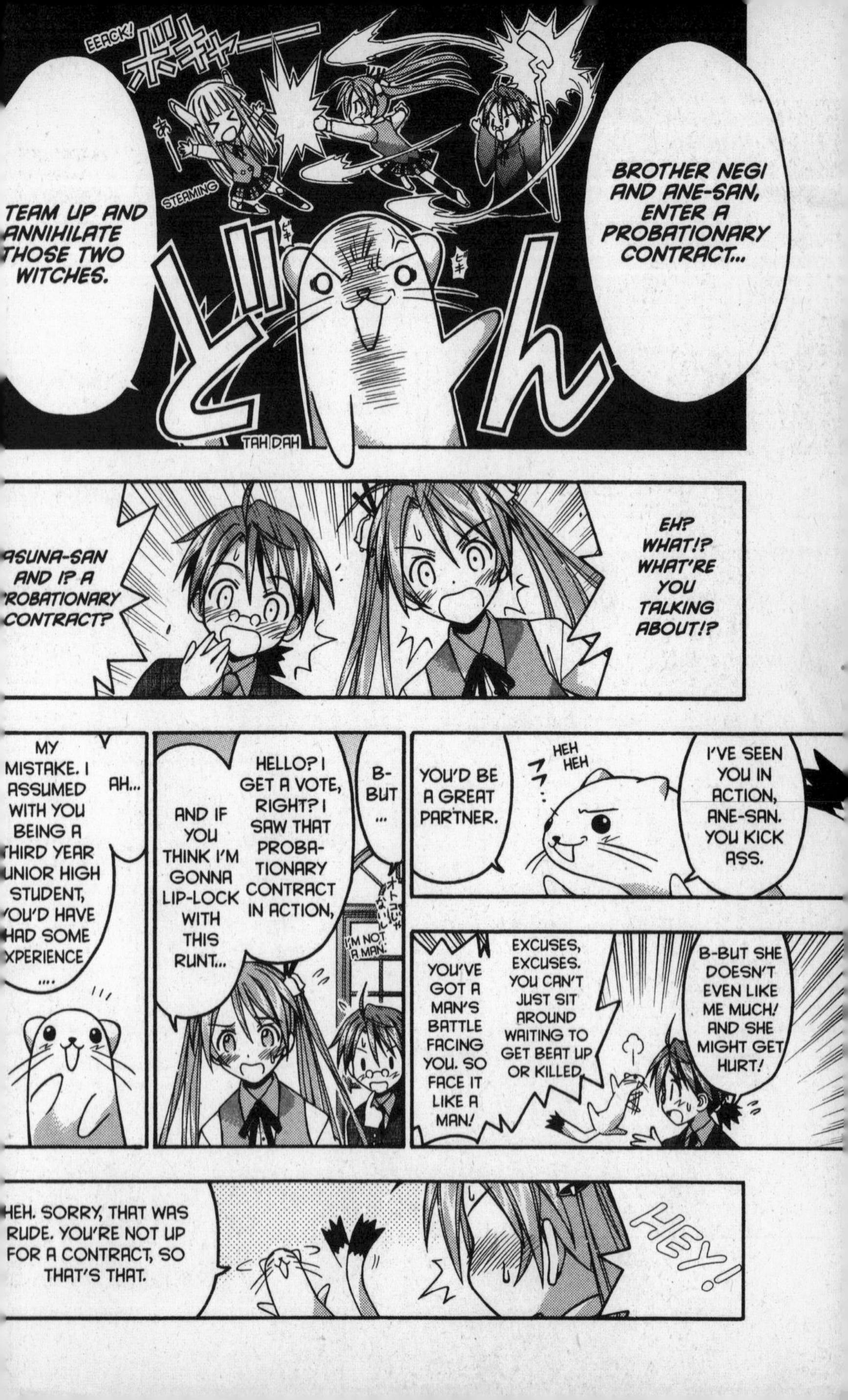
BROTHER NEGI AND ANE-SAN, ENTER A PROBATIONARY CONTRACT...
EEACK!
STEAMING
TEAM UP AND ANNIHILATE THOSE TWO WITCHES.
TAH DAH
EH? WHAT!? WHAT'RE YOU TALKING ABOUT!?
ASUNA-SAN AND I!? A PROBATIONARY CONTRACT?
I'VE SEEN YOU IN ACTION, ANE-SAN. YOU KICK ASS.
HEH HEH
YOU'D BE A GREAT PARTNER.
B-BUT SHE DOESN'T EVEN LIKE ME MUCH! AND SHE MIGHT GET HURT!
EXCUSES, EXCUSES. YOU CAN'T JUST SIT AROUND WAITING TO GET BEAT UP OR KILLED.
YOU'VE GOT A MAN'S BATTLE FACING YOU. SO FACE IT LIKE A MAN!
B-BUT...
HELLO? I GET A VOTE, RIGHT? I SAW THAT PROBATIONARY CONTRACT IN ACTION,
AND IF YOU THINK I'M GONNA LIP-LOCK WITH THIS RUNT...
I'M NOT A MAN.
AH...
MY MISTAKE. I ASSUMED WITH YOU BEING A THIRD YEAR JUNIOR HIGH STUDENT, YOU'D HAVE HAD SOME EXPERIENCE....
HEY!
HEH. SORRY, THAT WAS RUDE. YOU'RE NOT UP FOR A CONTRACT, SO THAT'S THAT.

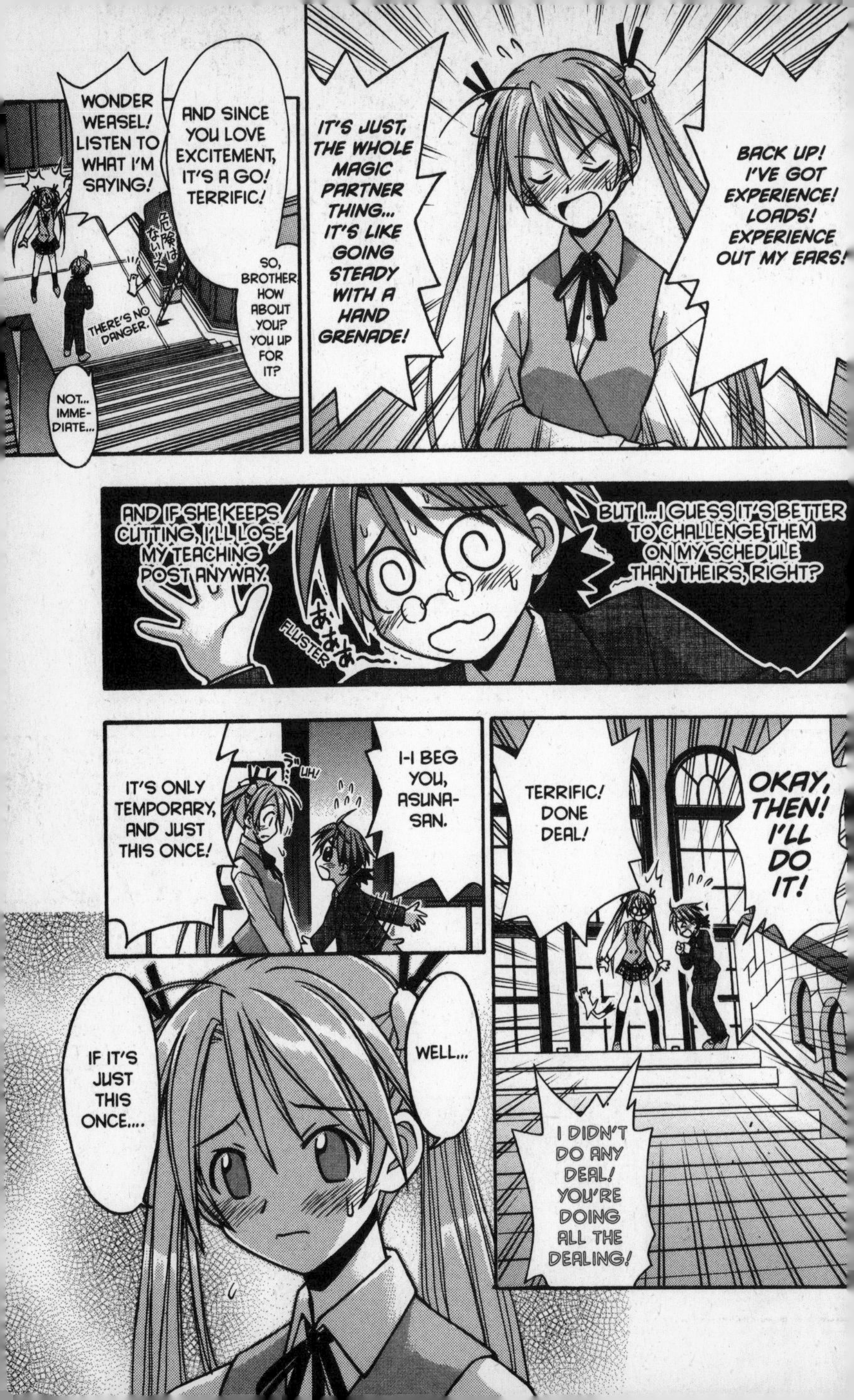
BACK UP! I'VE GOT EXPERIENCE! LOADS! EXPERIENCE OUT MY EARS!
IT'S JUST, THE WHOLE MAGIC PARTNER THING... IT'S LIKE GOING STEADY WITH A HAND GRENADE!
AND SINCE YOU LOVE EXCITEMENT, IT'S A GO! TERRIFIC!
WONDER WEASEL! LISTEN TO WHAT I'M SAYING!
SO, BROTHER HOW ABOUT YOU? YOU UP FOR IT?
危険はないッス
THERE'S NO DANGER.
NOT... IMMEDIATE...
BUT I...I GUESS IT'S BETTER TO CHALLENGE THEM ON MY SCHEDULE THAN THEIRS, RIGHT?
AND IF SHE KEEPS CUTTING, I'LL LOSE MY TEACHING POST ANYWAY.
あああ
FLUSTER
OKAY, THEN! I'LL DO IT!
TERRIFIC! DONE DEAL!
I DIDN'T DO ANY DEAL! YOU'RE DOING ALL THE DEALING!
I-I BEG YOU, ASUNA-SAN.
ウ
UH!
IT'S ONLY TEMPORARY, AND JUST THIS ONCE!
WELL...
IF IT'S JUST THIS ONCE....

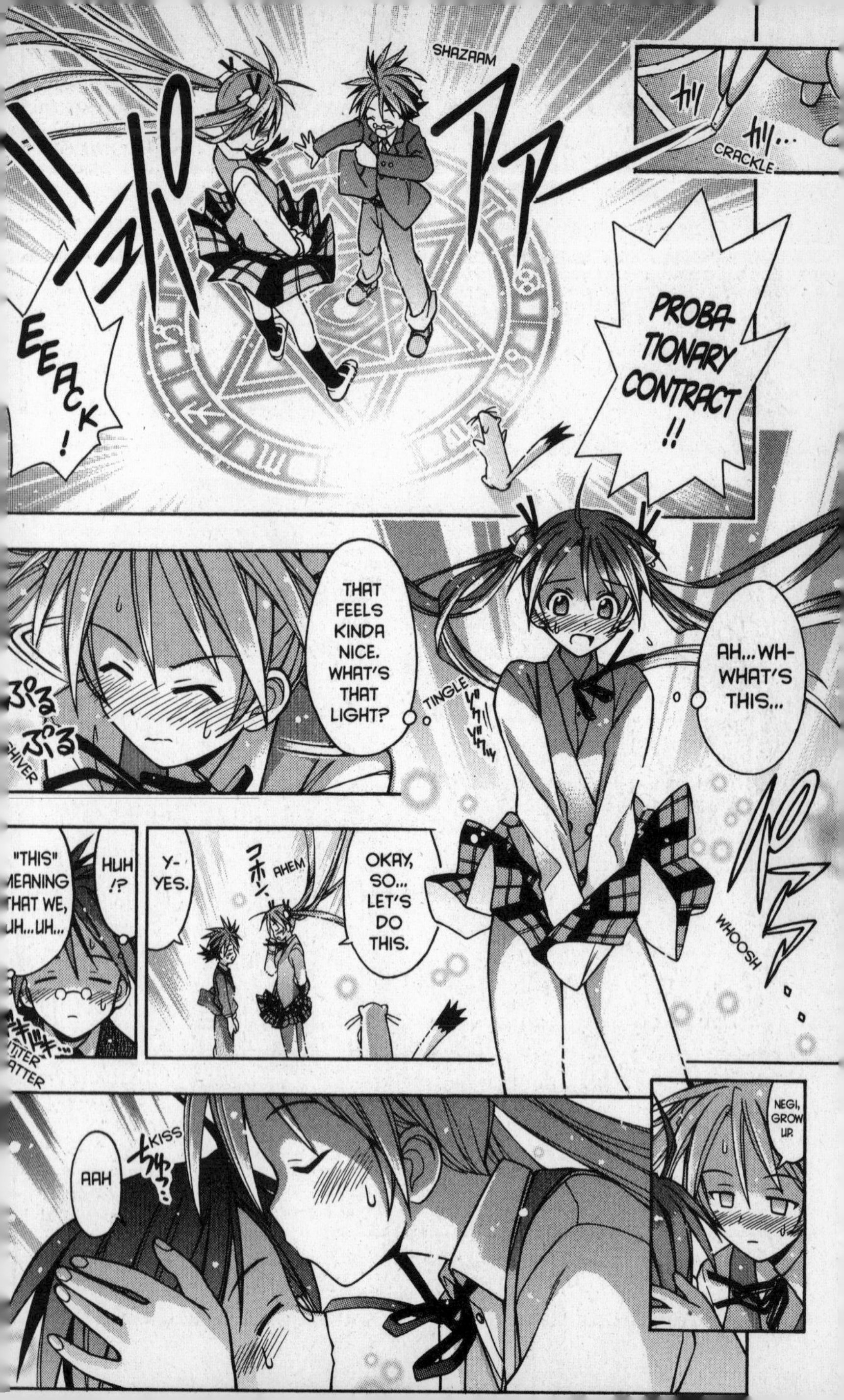
CRACKLE
SHAZAAM
PROBATIONARY CONTRACT!!
EEEACK!
AH...WH-WHAT'S THIS...
WHOOSH
THAT FEELS KINDA NICE. WHAT'S THAT LIGHT?
TINGLE
SHIVER
OKAY, SO... LET'S DO THIS.
AHEM
Y-YES.
HUH!?
"THIS" MEANING THAT WE, UH...UH...
NEGI, GROW UP.
KISS
AAH

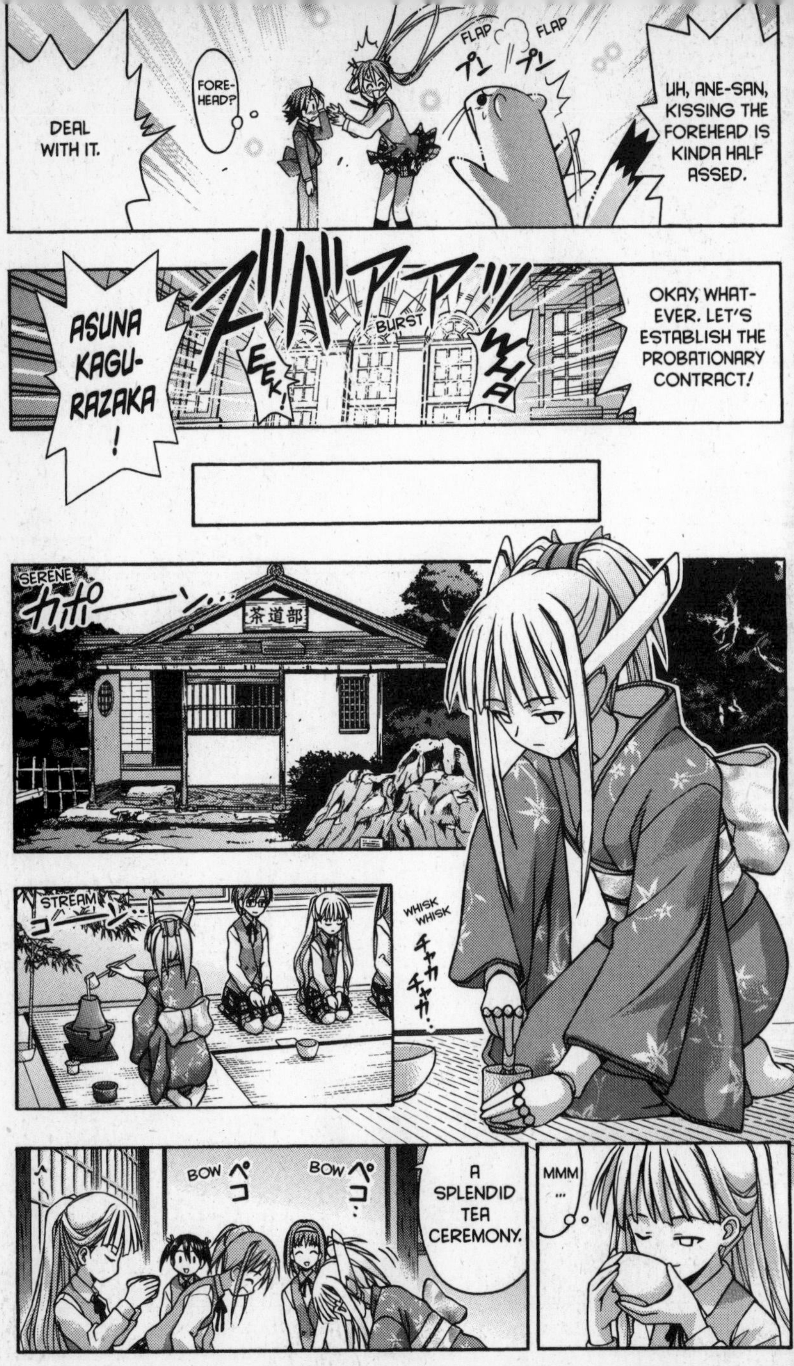
UH, ANE-SAN, KISSING THE FOREHEAD IS KINDA HALF ASSED.
FLAP
FLAP
プン
プン
FORE-HEAD?
DEAL WITH IT.
OKAY, WHAT-EVER. LET'S ESTABLISH THE PROBATIONARY CONTRACT!
WHA
BURST
ズバアアッ
EEK!
ASUNA KAGU-RAZAKA!
WHISK WHISK
チャカチャカ…
SERENE
カポーン…
STREAM
コーン…
MMM…
A SPLENDID TEA CEREMONY.
BOW
ペコ
BOW
ペコ…

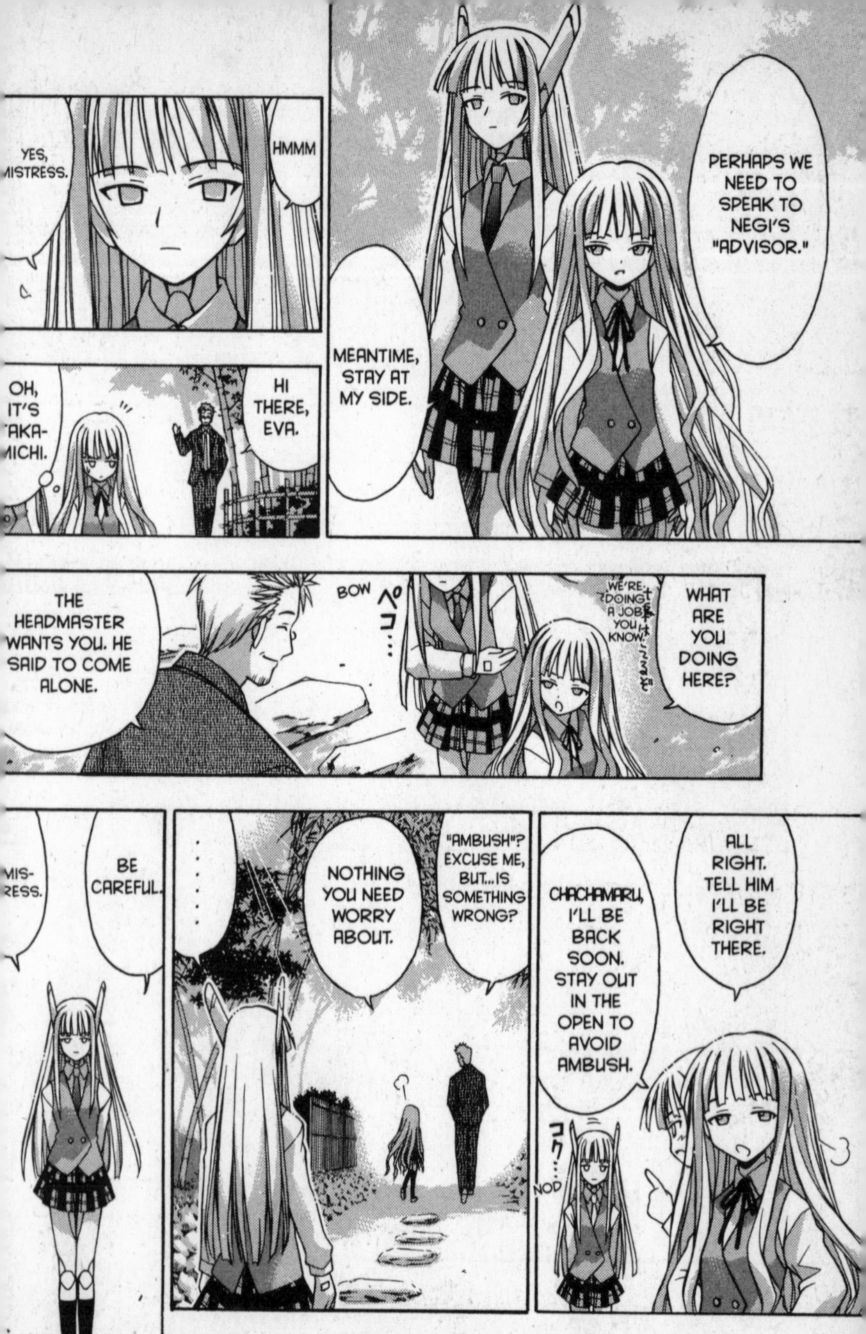
PERHAPS WE NEED TO SPEAK TO NEGI'S "ADVISOR."
MEANTIME, STAY AT MY SIDE.
HMMM
YES, MISTRESS.
HI THERE, EVA.
OH, IT'S AKA-ICHI.
WHAT ARE YOU DOING HERE?
WE'RE DOING A JOB YOU KNOW.
BOW
THE HEADMASTER WANTS YOU. HE SAID TO COME ALONE.
ALL RIGHT. TELL HIM I'LL BE RIGHT THERE.
CHACHAMARU, I'LL BE BACK SOON. STAY OUT IN THE OPEN TO AVOID AMBUSH.
NOD
"AMBUSH"? EXCUSE ME, BUT...IS SOMETHING WRONG?
NOTHING YOU NEED WORRY ABOUT.
......
BE CAREFUL.
MIS-RESS.

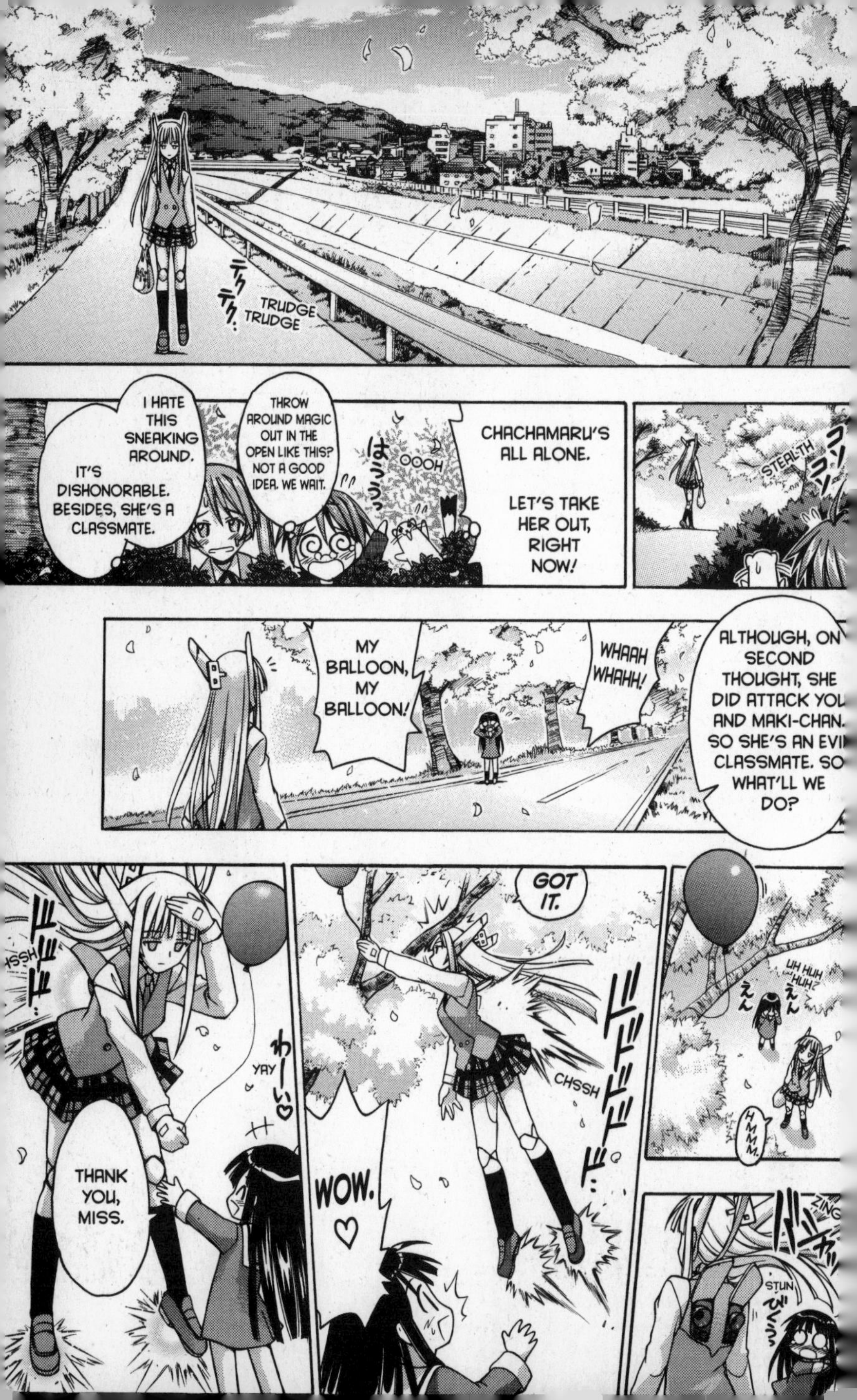
テクテク
TRUDGE TRUDGE
コソコソ
STEALTH
CHACHAMARU'S ALL ALONE.
LET'S TAKE HER OUT, RIGHT NOW!
はううう
OOOH
THROW AROUND MAGIC OUT IN THE OPEN LIKE THIS? NOT A GOOD IDEA. WE WAIT.
I HATE THIS SNEAKING AROUND.
IT'S DISHONORABLE. BESIDES, SHE'S A CLASSMATE.
ALTHOUGH, ON SECOND THOUGHT, SHE DID ATTACK YOU AND MAKI-CHAN. SO SHE'S AN EVIL CLASSMATE. SO WHAT'LL WE DO?
WHAAH WHAHH!
MY BALLOON, MY BALLOON!
UH HUH HUH
えんえん
HMMM.
ZING
STUN
びくっ
GOT IT.
ドドドドド
CHSSH
WOW.
わーい
YAY
THANK YOU, MISS.

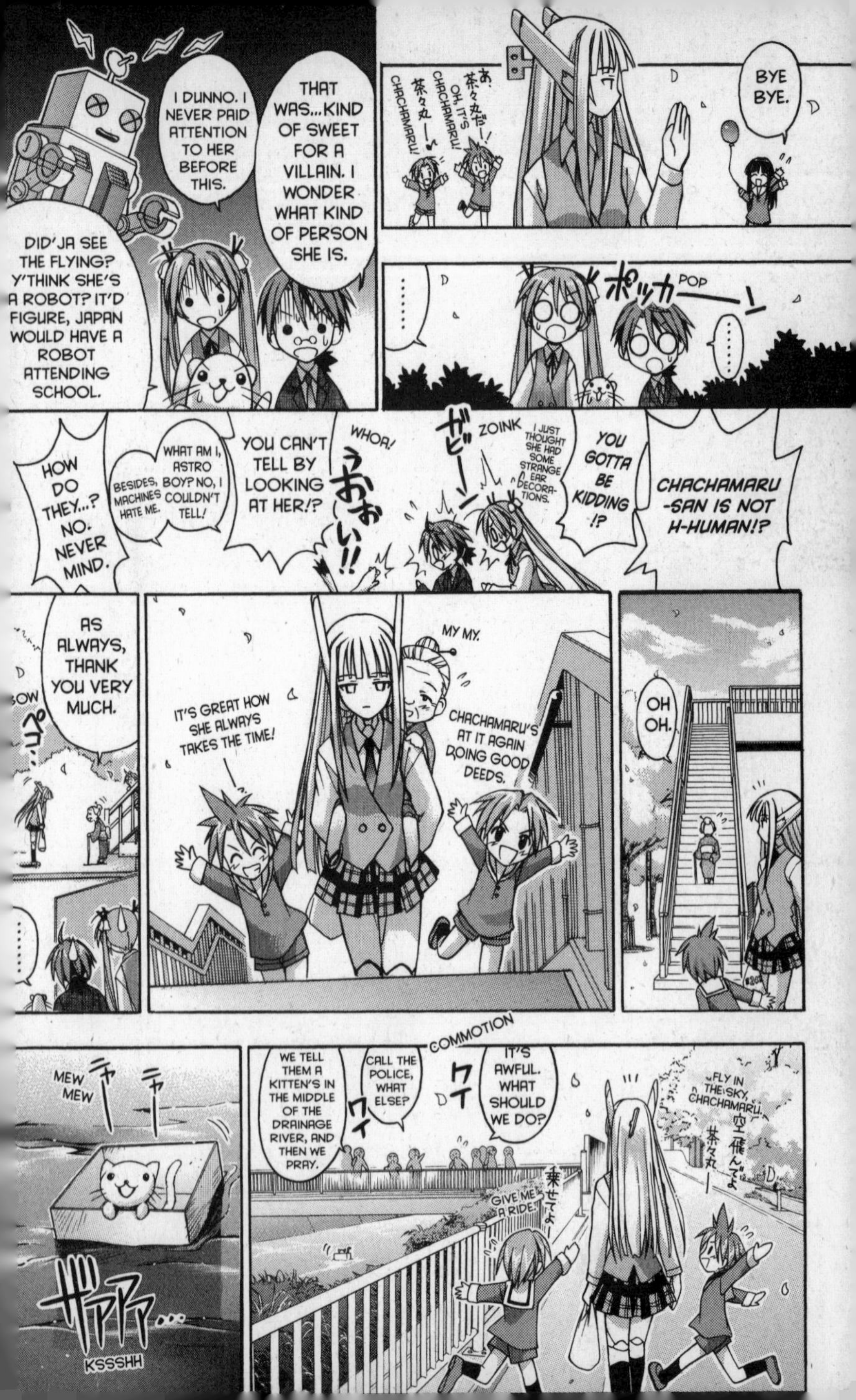
BYE BYE.
あ、茶々丸だー！
OH, IT'S CHACHAMARU!
茶々丸ー♪
CHACHAMARU!
ポッカーン
POP
......
......
THAT WAS...KIND OF SWEET FOR A VILLAIN. I WONDER WHAT KIND OF PERSON SHE IS.
I DUNNO. I NEVER PAID ATTENTION TO HER BEFORE THIS.
DID'JA SEE THE FLYING? Y'THINK SHE'S A ROBOT? IT'D FIGURE, JAPAN WOULD HAVE A ROBOT ATTENDING SCHOOL.
CHACHAMARU-SAN IS NOT H-HUMAN!?
YOU GOTTA BE KIDDING!?
I JUST THOUGHT SHE HAD SOME STRANGE EAR DECORATIONS.
ガビーン
ZOINK
WHOA!
うおおい!!
YOU CAN'T TELL BY LOOKING AT HER!?
WHAT AM I, ASTRO BOY? NO, I COULDN'T TELL!
BESIDES, MACHINES HATE ME.
HOW DO THEY...? NO. NEVER MIND.
OH OH.
MY MY.
CHACHAMARU'S AT IT AGAIN DOING GOOD DEEDS.
IT'S GREAT HOW SHE ALWAYS TAKES THE TIME!
AS ALWAYS, THANK YOU VERY MUCH.
ペコ
BOW
......
FLY IN THE SKY, CHACHAMARU.
空飛んでよ茶々丸ー
乗せてよー
GIVE ME A RIDE.
IT'S AWFUL. WHAT SHOULD WE DO?
ワイワイ
COMMOTION
CALL THE POLICE, WHAT ELSE?
WE TELL THEM A KITTEN'S IN THE MIDDLE OF THE DRAINAGE RIVER, AND THEN WE PRAY.
ニャー ニャー
MEW MEW
ザァァァ
KSSSHH

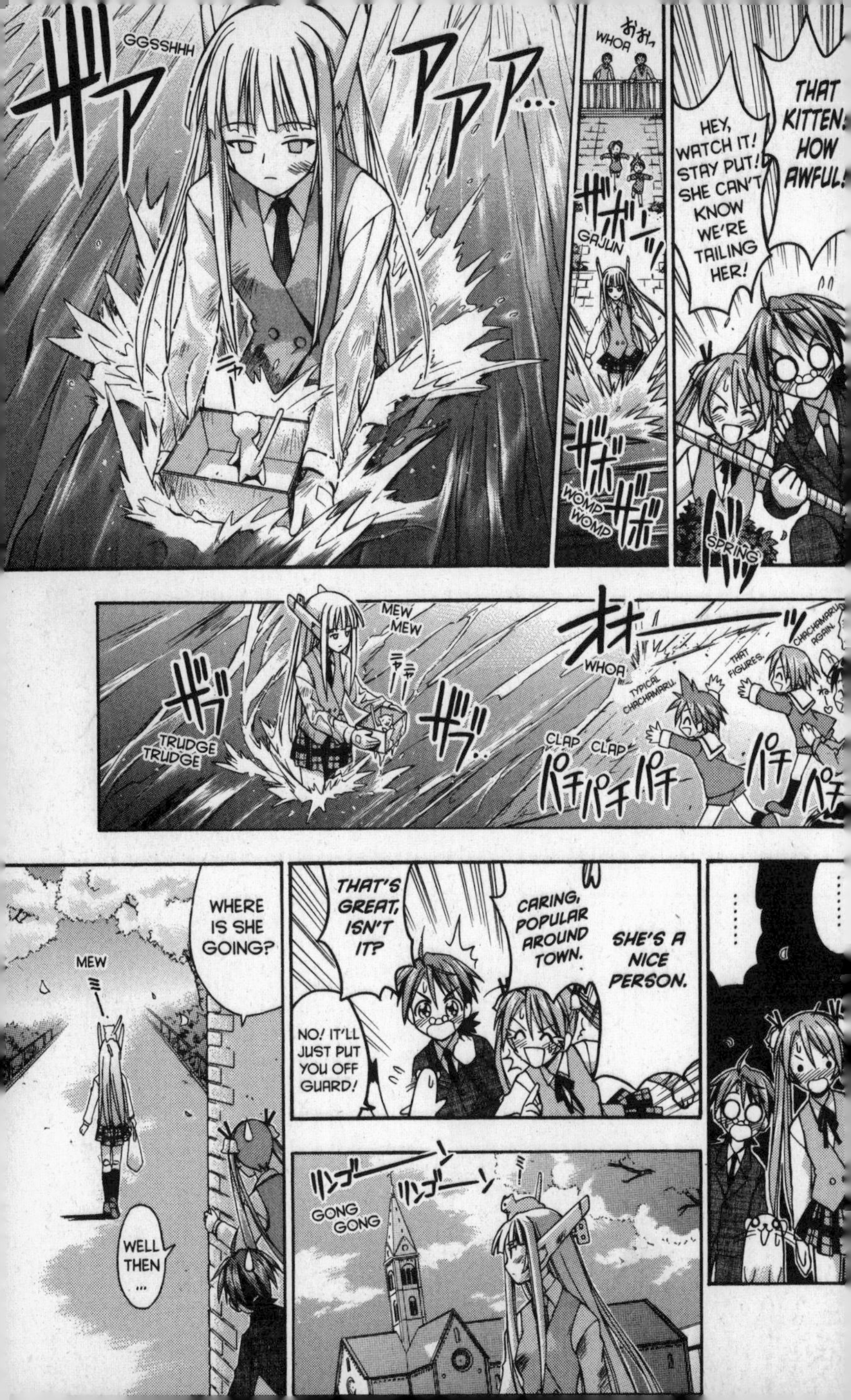
THAT KITTEN. HOW AWFUL!
HEY, WATCH IT! STAY PUT! SHE CAN'T KNOW WE'RE TAILING HER!
SPRING
おお、
WHOA
ザボーンッ
GAJUN
ザボザボ
WOMP WOMP
ザア
GGSSHHH
アアア...
オオーーッ
WHOA
CHACHAMARU AGAIN.
THAT FIGURES.
TYPICAL CHACHAMARU.
パチ
CLAP CLAP
パチパチパチ
MEW MEW
ザブ...
ザブ
TRUDGE TRUDGE
......
SHE'S A NICE PERSON.
CARING, POPULAR AROUND TOWN.
THAT'S GREAT, ISN'T IT?
NO! IT'LL JUST PUT YOU OFF GUARD!
ミー
リンゴーン リンゴーン
GONG GONG
WHERE IS SHE GOING?
MEW
ミー
WELL THEN ...

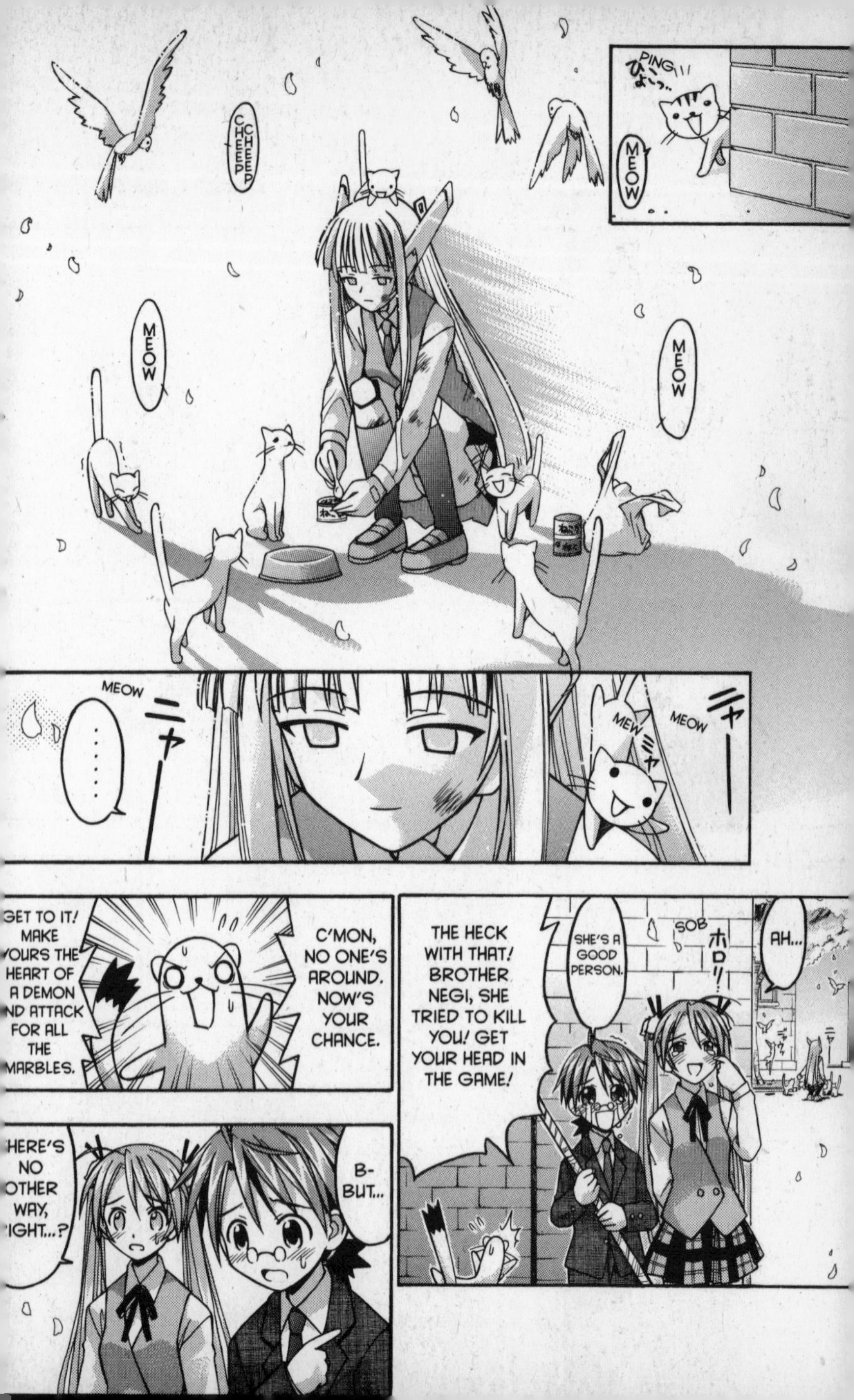

PING ぴょこっ
MEOW
MEOW
CHEEP CHEEP
MEOW
ニャー MEOW
MEW ミャ
ニャ MEOW
......
AH...
SOB ホロリ
SHE'S A GOOD PERSON.
THE HECK WITH THAT! BROTHER NEGI, SHE TRIED TO KILL YOU! GET YOUR HEAD IN THE GAME!
C'MON, NO ONE'S AROUND. NOW'S YOUR CHANCE.
GET TO IT! MAKE YOURS THE HEART OF A DEMON ND ATTACK FOR ALL THE MARBLES.
B-BUT...
HERE'S NO OTHER WAY, IGHT...?

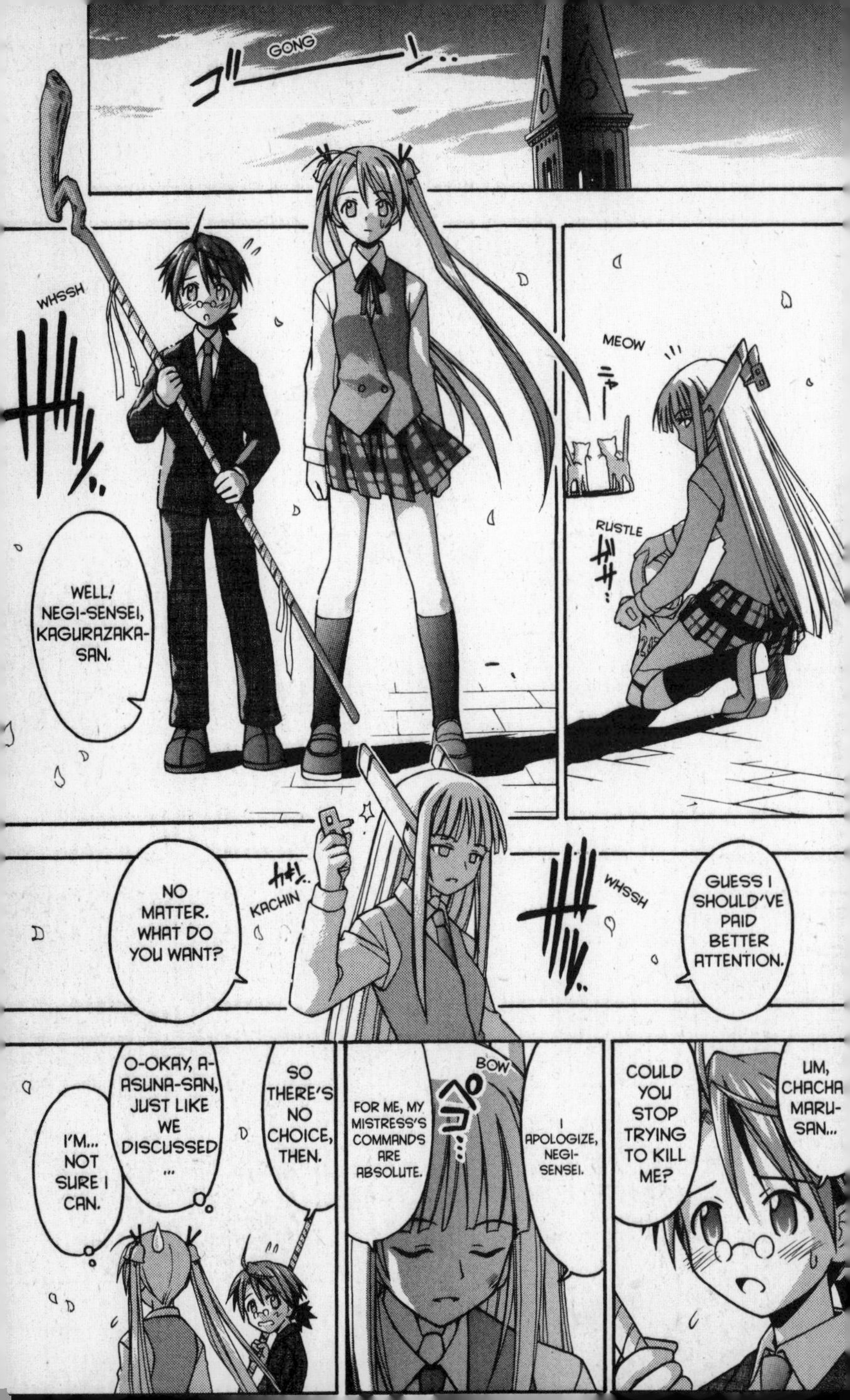
GONG
MEOW
RUSTLE
WHSSH
WELL! NEGI-SENSEI, KAGURAZAKA-SAN.
WHSSH
GUESS I SHOULD'VE PAID BETTER ATTENTION.
KACHIN
NO MATTER. WHAT DO YOU WANT?
UM, CHACHAMARU-SAN...
COULD YOU STOP TRYING TO KILL ME?
I APOLOGIZE, NEGI-SENSEI.
BOW
FOR ME, MY MISTRESS'S COMMANDS ARE ABSOLUTE.
SO THERE'S NO CHOICE, THEN.
O-OKAY, A-ASUNA-SAN, JUST LIKE WE DISCUSSED...
I'M... NOT SURE I CAN.

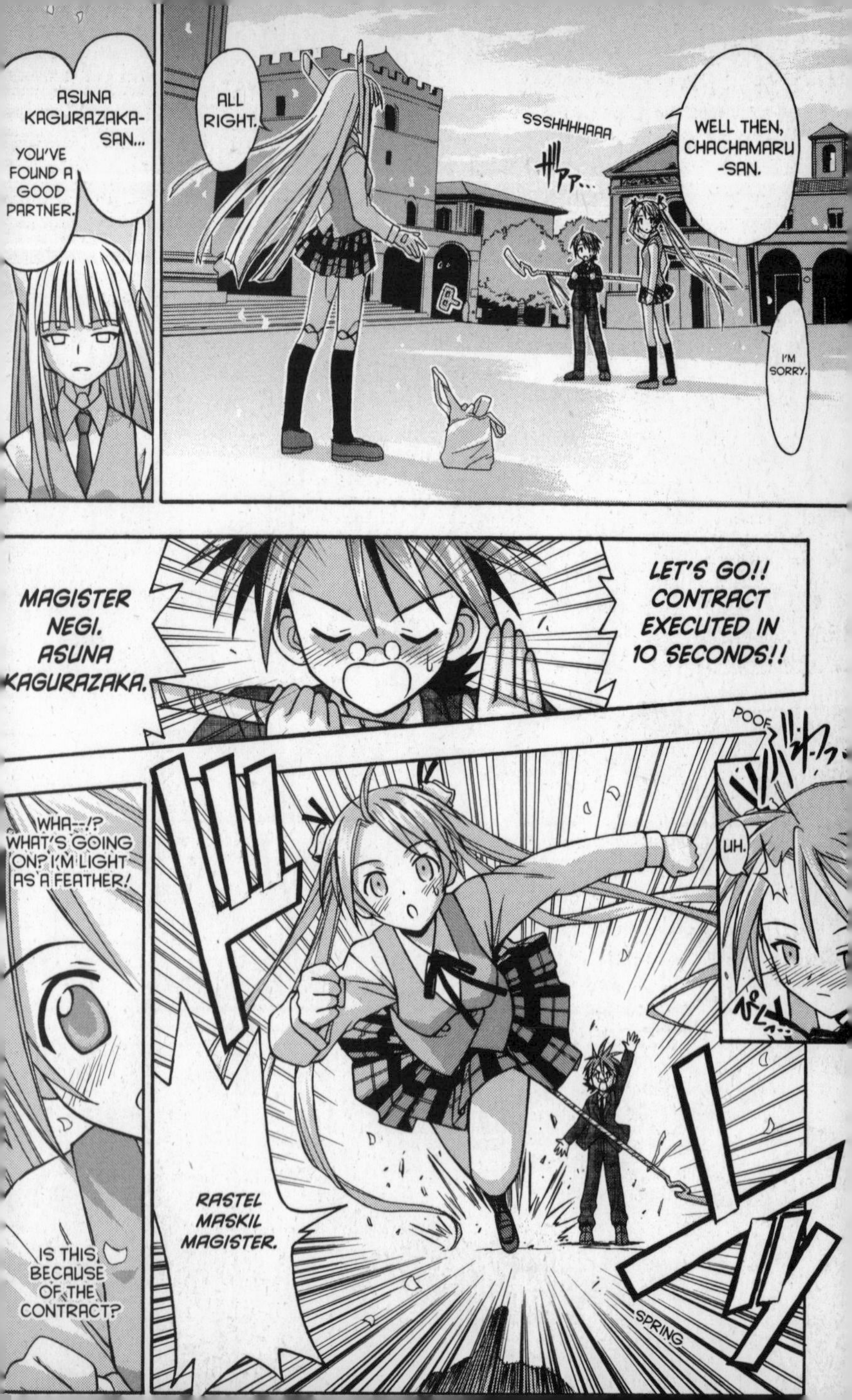
WELL THEN, CHACHAMARU-SAN.
ALL RIGHT.
SSSHHHHAAA
I'M SORRY.
ASUNA KAGURAZAKA-SAN...
YOU'VE FOUND A GOOD PARTNER.
LET'S GO!! CONTRACT EXECUTED IN 10 SECONDS!!
MAGISTER NEGI. ASUNA KAGURAZAKA.
POOF
UH.
RASTEL MASKIL MAGISTER.
SPRING
WHA--!? WHAT'S GOING ON? I'M LIGHT AS A FEATHER!
IS THIS, BECAUSE OF THE CONTRACT?

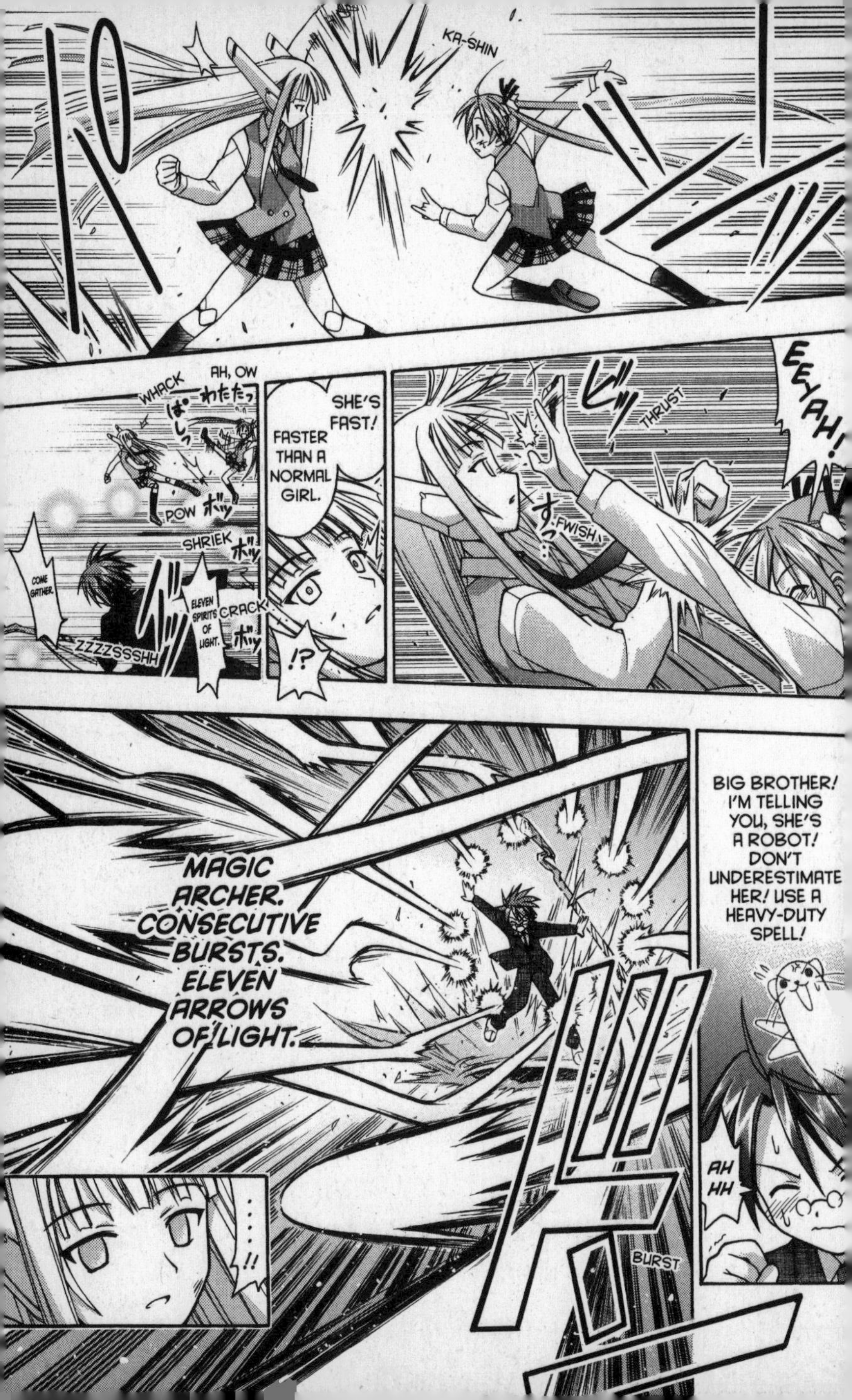
KA-SHIN
EEYAH!
THRUST
FWISH
SHE'S FAST!
FASTER THAN A NORMAL GIRL.
!?
AH, OW わたたっ
WHACK ぱしっ
POW ボッ
SHRIEK ボッ
COME GATHER.
ELEVEN SPIRITS OF LIGHT.
CRACK ボッ
ZZZZSSSHH
BIG BROTHER! I'M TELLING YOU, SHE'S A ROBOT! DON'T UNDERESTIMATE HER! USE A HEAVY-DUTY SPELL!
AH HH
MAGIC ARCHER. CONSECUTIVE BURSTS. ELEVEN ARROWS OF LIGHT.
BURST
...
!!

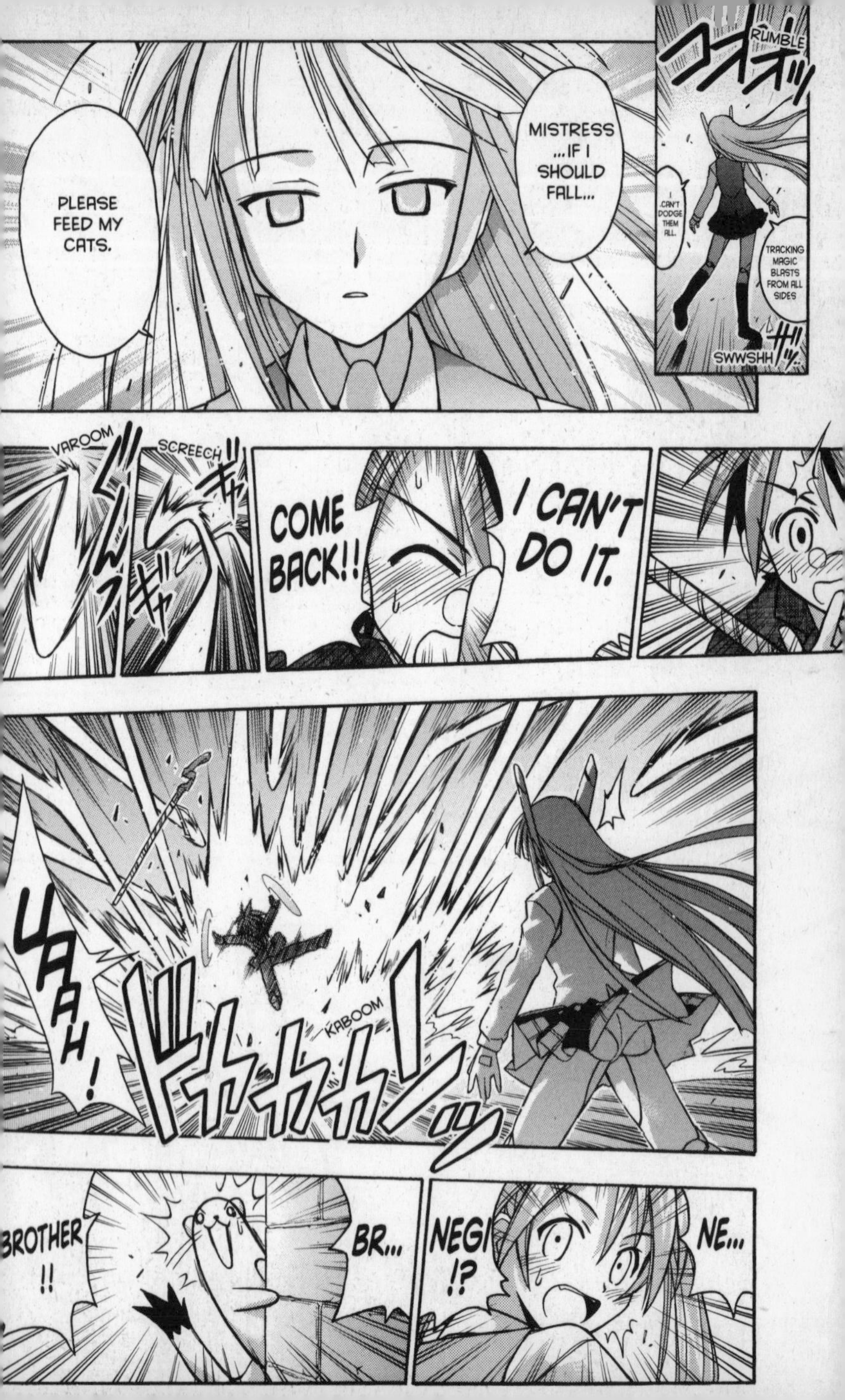
RUMBLE
I CAN'T DODGE THEM ALL.
TRACKING MAGIC BLASTS FROM ALL SIDES
SWWSHH
MISTRESS ...IF I SHOULD FALL...
PLEASE FEED MY CATS.
I CAN'T DO IT.
COME BACK!!
SCREECH
VAROOM
KABOOM
UAAAH!
NE...
NEGI !?
BR...
BROTHER !!

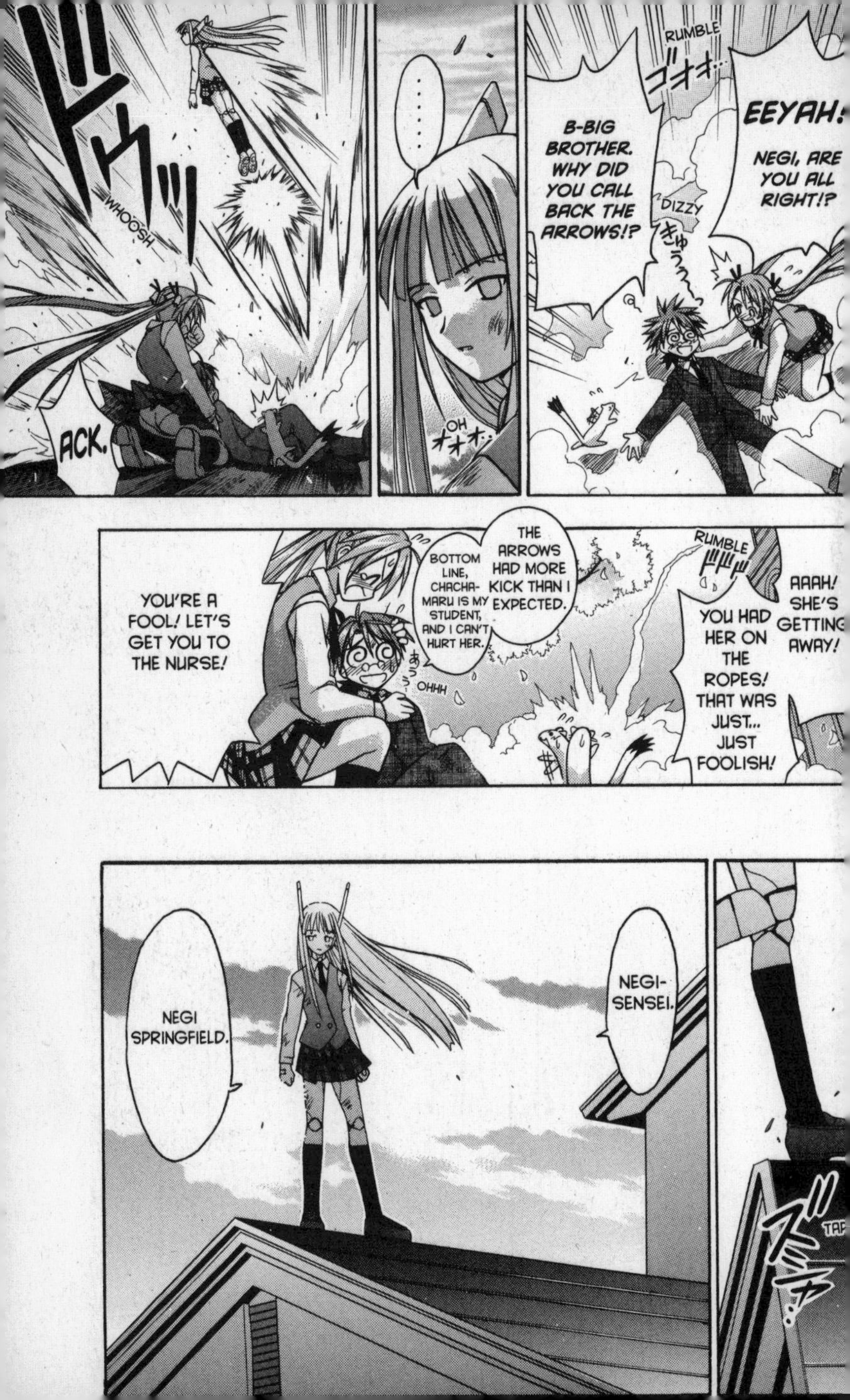
RUMBLE
EEYAH!
NEGI, ARE YOU ALL RIGHT!?
B-BIG BROTHER. WHY DID YOU CALL BACK THE ARROWS!?
DIZZY
…
OH
WHOOSH
ACK.
RUMBLE
AAAH! SHE'S GETTING AWAY!
YOU HAD HER ON THE ROPES! THAT WAS JUST... JUST FOOLISH!
THE ARROWS HAD MORE KICK THAN I EXPECTED.
BOTTOM LINE, CHACHAMARU IS MY STUDENT, AND I CAN'T HURT HER.
OHHH
YOU'RE A FOOL! LET'S GET YOU TO THE NURSE!
NEGI-SENSEI.
NEGI SPRINGFIELD.

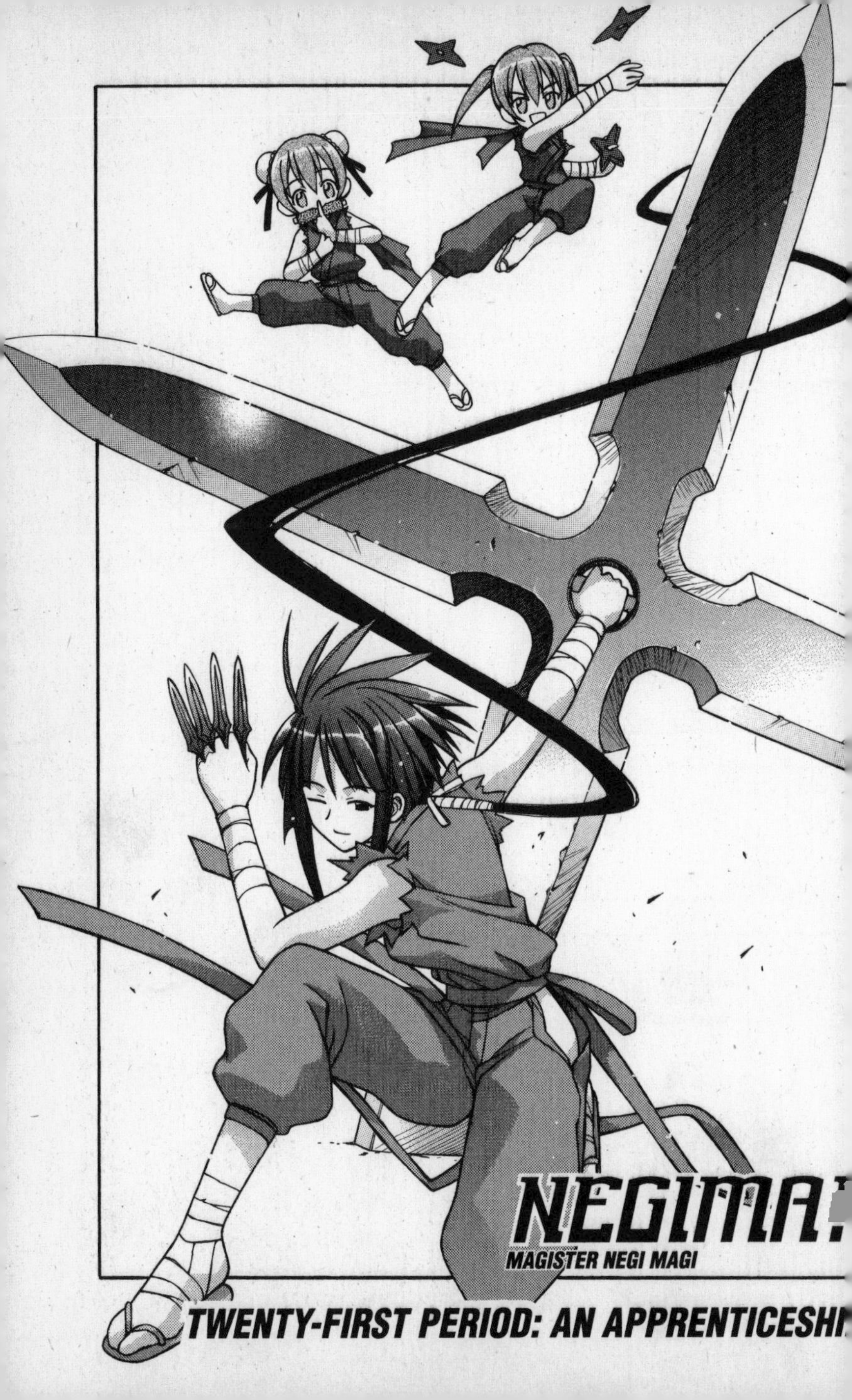
NEGIMA!
MAGISTER NEGI MAGI
TWENTY-FIRST PERIOD: AN APPRENTICESHI

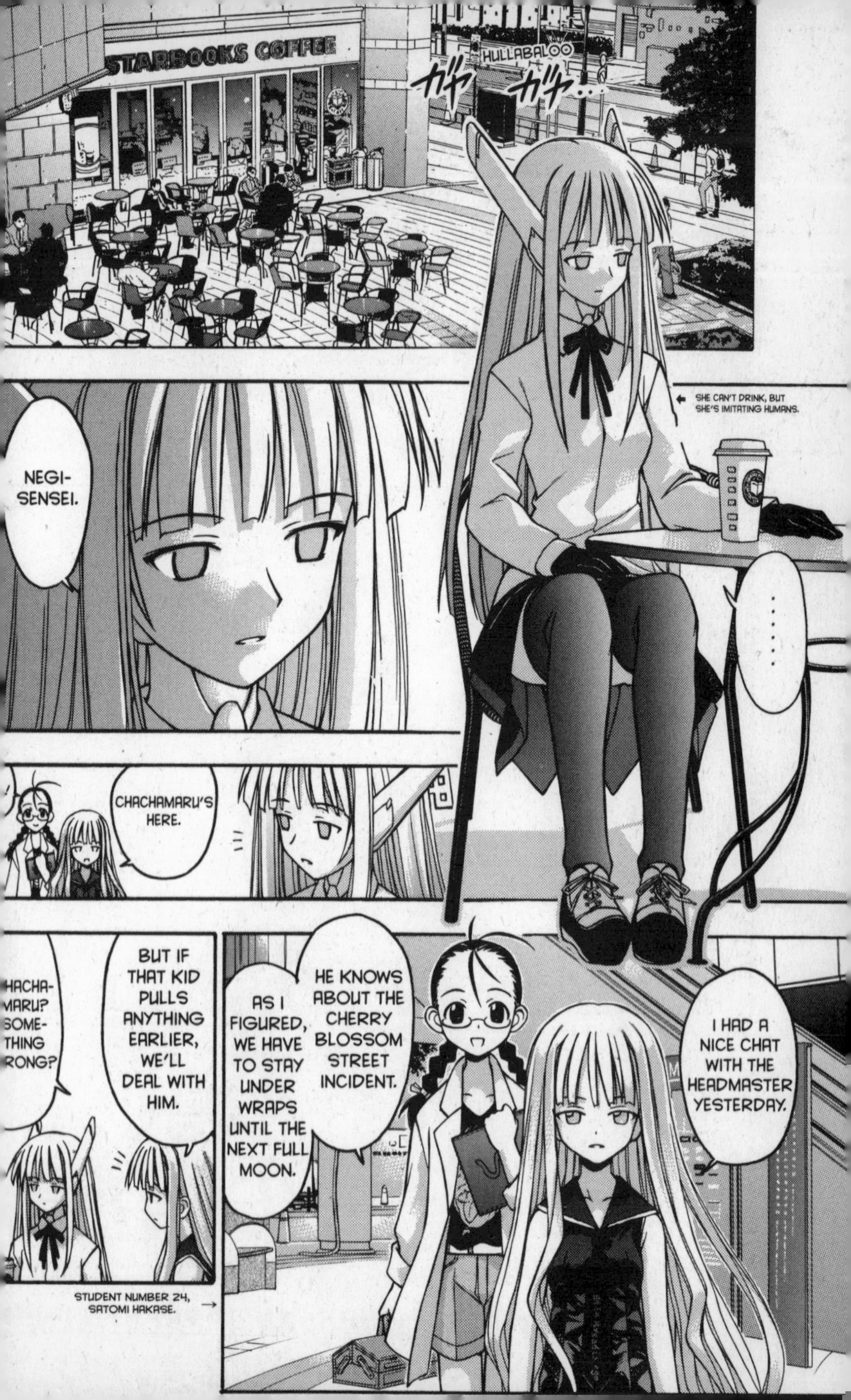
STARBOOKS COFFEE
HULLABALOO
ガヤ ガヤ...
SHE CAN'T DRINK, BUT SHE'S IMITATING HUMANS.
......
NEGI-SENSEI.
CHACHAMARU'S HERE.
I HAD A NICE CHAT WITH THE HEADMASTER YESTERDAY.
HE KNOWS ABOUT THE CHERRY BLOSSOM STREET INCIDENT.
AS I FIGURED, WE HAVE TO STAY UNDER WRAPS UNTIL THE NEXT FULL MOON.
BUT IF THAT KID PULLS ANYTHING EARLIER, WE'LL DEAL WITH HIM.
HACHA-MARU? SOME-THING RONG?
STUDENT NUMBER 24, SATOMI HAKASE.

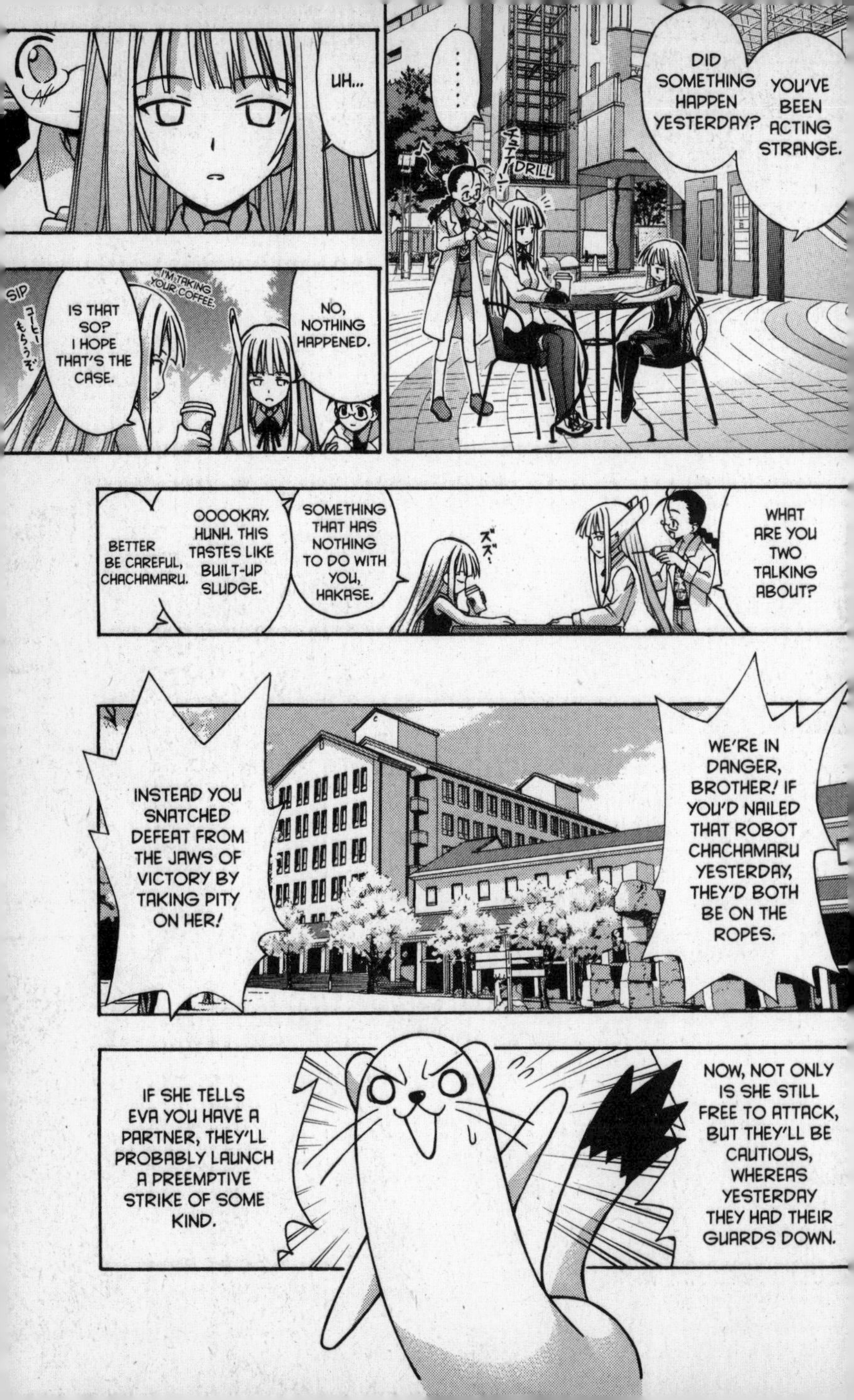
YOU'VE BEEN ACTING STRANGE.
DID SOMETHING HAPPEN YESTERDAY?
......
DRILL
UH...
NO, NOTHING HAPPENED.
I'M TAKING YOUR COFFEE.
IS THAT SO? I HOPE THAT'S THE CASE.
SIP
コーヒーもらうぞ
WHAT ARE YOU TWO TALKING ABOUT?
SOMETHING THAT HAS NOTHING TO DO WITH YOU, HAKASE.
ズズ
OOOOKAY. HUNH. THIS TASTES LIKE BUILT-UP SLUDGE.
BETTER BE CAREFUL, CHACHAMARU.
WE'RE IN DANGER, BROTHER! IF YOU'D NAILED THAT ROBOT CHACHAMARU YESTERDAY, THEY'D BOTH BE ON THE ROPES.
INSTEAD YOU SNATCHED DEFEAT FROM THE JAWS OF VICTORY BY TAKING PITY ON HER!
NOW, NOT ONLY IS SHE STILL FREE TO ATTACK, BUT THEY'LL BE CAUTIOUS, WHEREAS YESTERDAY THEY HAD THEIR GUARDS DOWN.
IF SHE TELLS EVA YOU HAVE A PARTNER, THEY'LL PROBABLY LAUNCH A PREEMPTIVE STRIKE OF SOME KIND.

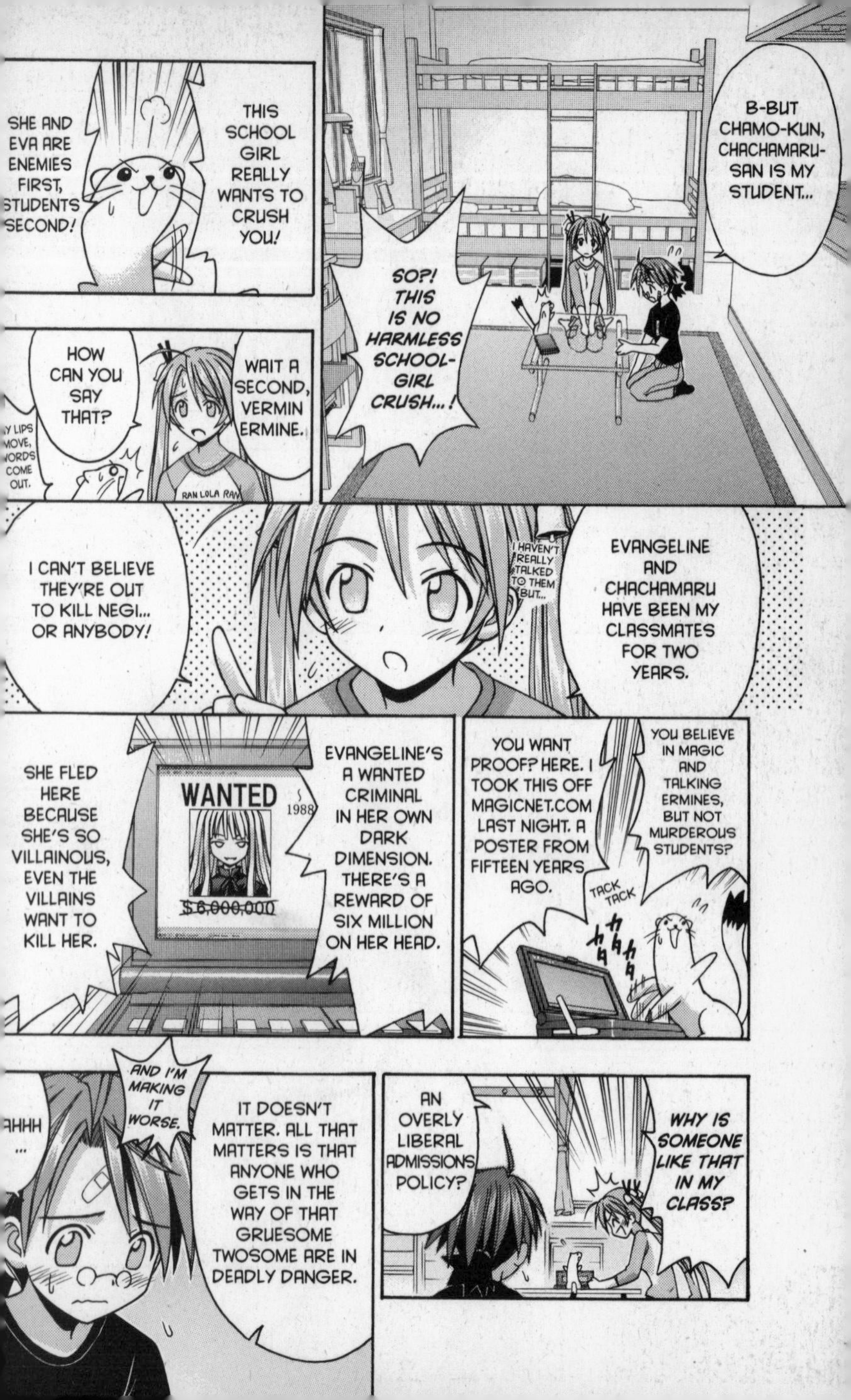
B-BUT CHAMO-KUN, CHACHAMARU-SAN IS MY STUDENT...
SO?! THIS IS NO HARMLESS SCHOOL-GIRL CRUSH...!
THIS SCHOOL GIRL REALLY WANTS TO CRUSH YOU!
SHE AND EVA ARE ENEMIES FIRST, STUDENTS SECOND!
WAIT A SECOND, VERMIN ERMINE.
HOW CAN YOU SAY THAT?
Y LIPS MOVE, WORDS COME OUT.
RAN LOLA RAN
EVANGELINE AND CHACHAMARU HAVE BEEN MY CLASSMATES FOR TWO YEARS.
I HAVEN'T REALLY TALKED TO THEM BUT...
I CAN'T BELIEVE THEY'RE OUT TO KILL NEGI... OR ANYBODY!
YOU BELIEVE IN MAGIC AND TALKING ERMINES, BUT NOT MURDEROUS STUDENTS?
YOU WANT PROOF? HERE. I TOOK THIS OFF MAGICNET.COM LAST NIGHT. A POSTER FROM FIFTEEN YEARS AGO.
TACK TACK
WANTED
1988
$6,000,000
EVANGELINE'S A WANTED CRIMINAL IN HER OWN DARK DIMENSION. THERE'S A REWARD OF SIX MILLION ON HER HEAD.
SHE FLED HERE BECAUSE SHE'S SO VILLAINOUS, EVEN THE VILLAINS WANT TO KILL HER.
WHY IS SOMEONE LIKE THAT IN MY CLASS?
AN OVERLY LIBERAL ADMISSIONS POLICY?
IT DOESN'T MATTER. ALL THAT MATTERS IS THAT ANYONE WHO GETS IN THE WAY OF THAT GRUESOME TWOSOME ARE IN DEADLY DANGER.
AND I'M MAKING IT WORSE.
AHHH ...

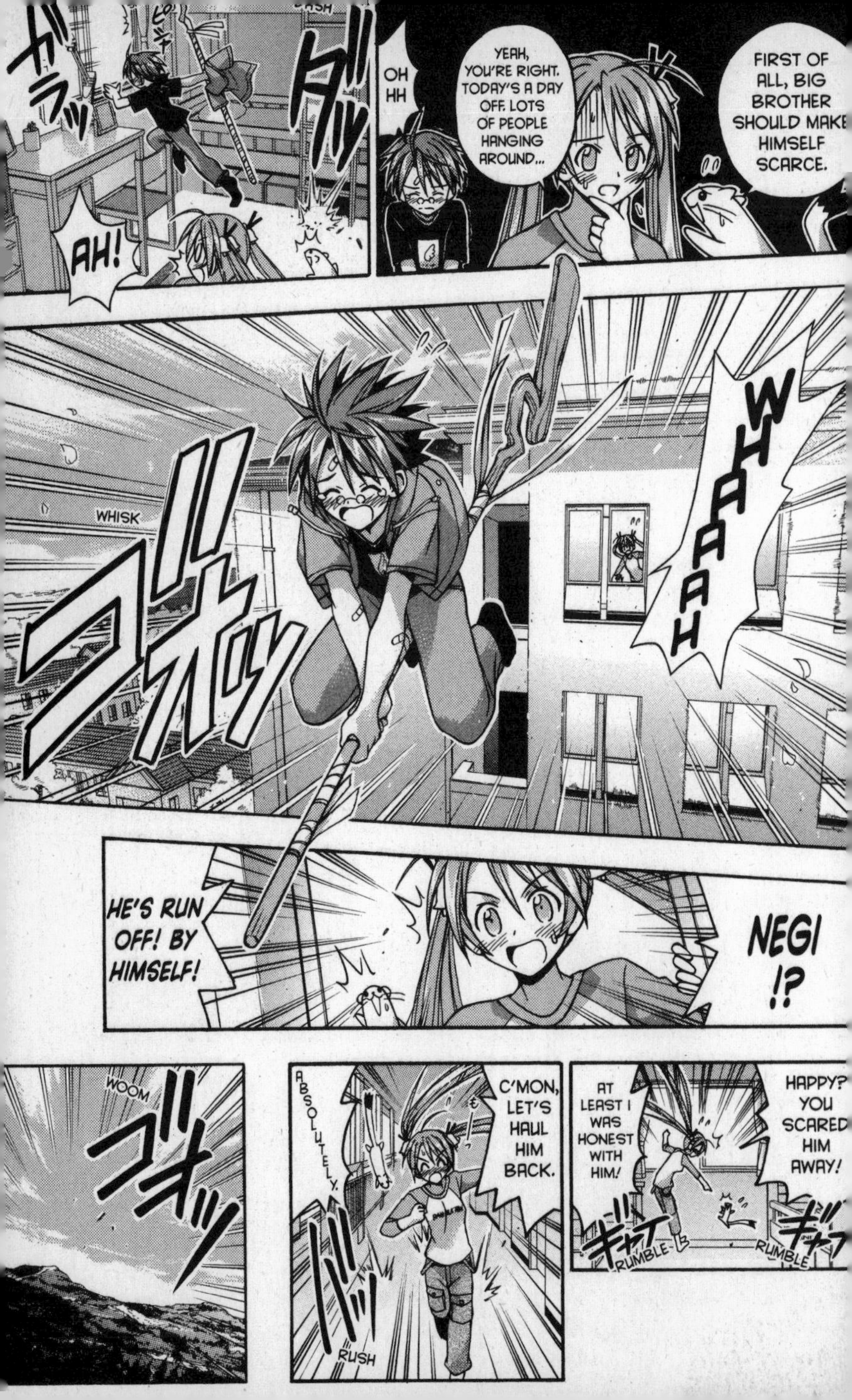
FIRST OF ALL, BIG BROTHER SHOULD MAKE HIMSELF SCARCE.
YEAH, YOU'RE RIGHT. TODAY'S A DAY OFF. LOTS OF PEOPLE HANGING AROUND...
OH HH
AH!
WHAAAAAH
WHISK
NEGI !?
HE'S RUN OFF! BY HIMSELF!
HAPPY? YOU SCARED HIM AWAY!
AT LEAST I WAS HONEST WITH HIM!
RUMBLE
RUMBLE
C'MON, LET'S HAUL HIM BACK.
ABSOLUTELY.
RUSH
WOOM

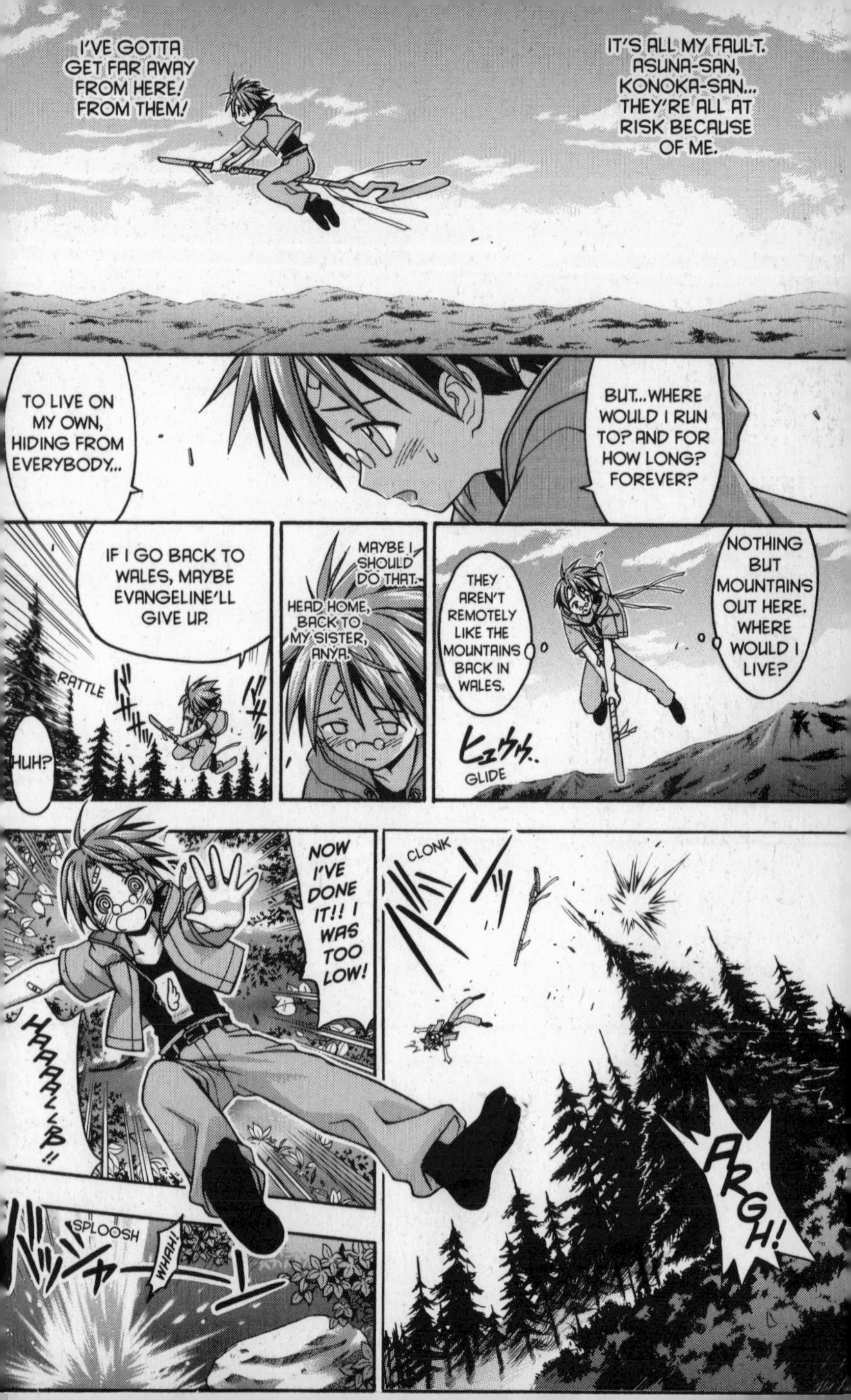
IT'S ALL MY FAULT. ASUNA-SAN, KONOKA-SAN... THEY'RE ALL AT RISK BECAUSE OF ME.
I'VE GOTTA GET FAR AWAY FROM HERE! FROM THEM!
BUT...WHERE WOULD I RUN TO? AND FOR HOW LONG? FOREVER?
TO LIVE ON MY OWN, HIDING FROM EVERYBODY...
NOTHING BUT MOUNTAINS OUT HERE. WHERE WOULD I LIVE?
THEY AREN'T REMOTELY LIKE THE MOUNTAINS BACK IN WALES.
GLIDE
MAYBE I SHOULD DO THAT.
HEAD HOME, BACK TO MY SISTER, ANYA.
IF I GO BACK TO WALES, MAYBE EVANGELINE'LL GIVE UP.
RATTLE
HUH?
CLONK
ARGH!
NOW I'VE DONE IT!! I WAS TOO LOW!
SPLOOSH
WHAH!

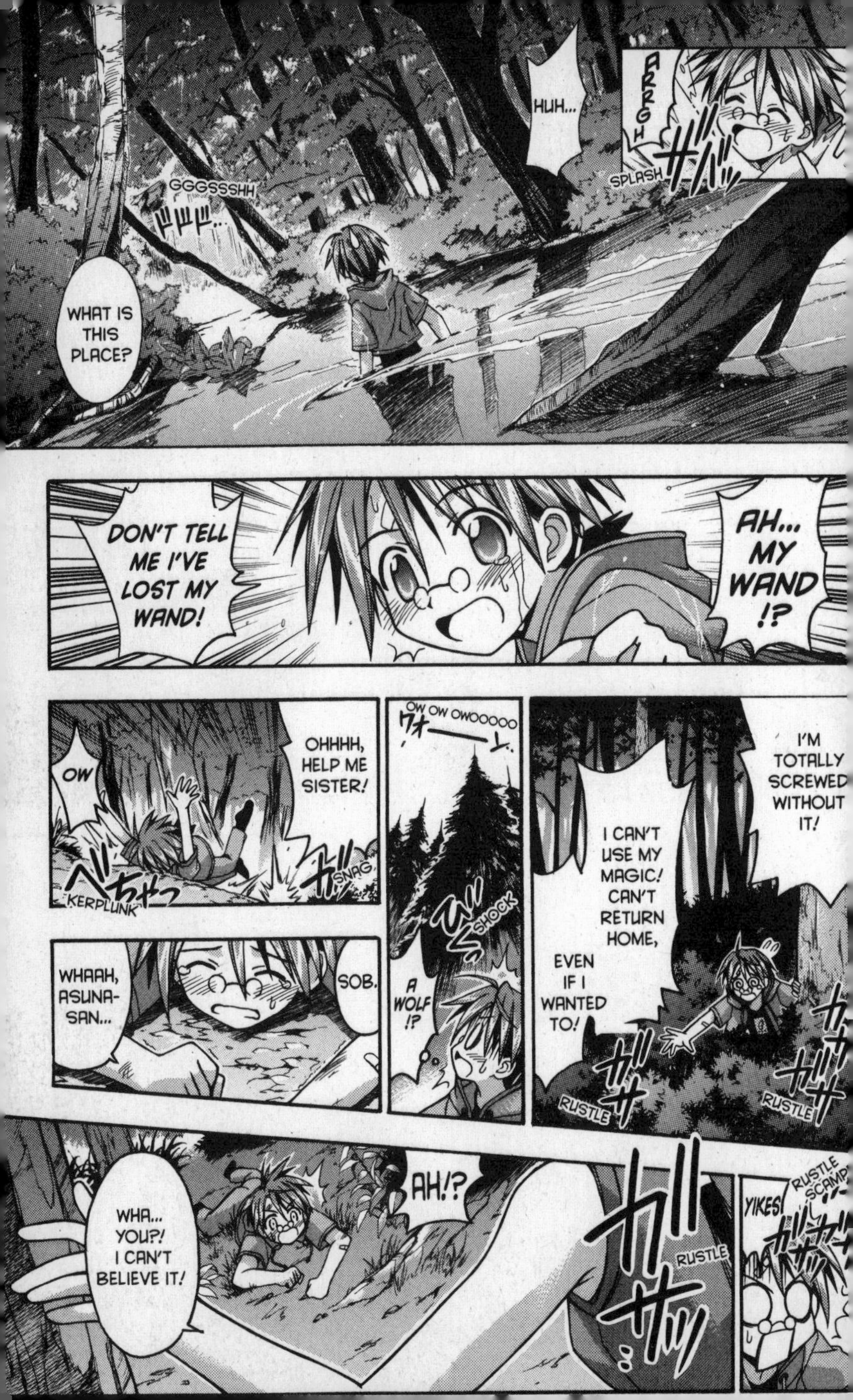

ARRRGH
SPLASH
HUH...
GGGSSSHH
WHAT IS THIS PLACE?
AH... MY WAND!?
DON'T TELL ME I'VE LOST MY WAND!
I'M TOTALLY SCREWED WITHOUT IT!
I CAN'T USE MY MAGIC! CAN'T RETURN HOME,
EVEN IF I WANTED TO!
RUSTLE
RUSTLE
OW OW OWOOOOO
SHOCK
A WOLF!?
OHHHH, HELP ME SISTER!
OW
SNAG
KERPLUNK
SOB.
WHAAH, ASUNA-SAN...
RUSTLE
SCAMP
YIKES!
RUSTLE
AH!?
WHA... YOU?! I CAN'T BELIEVE IT!

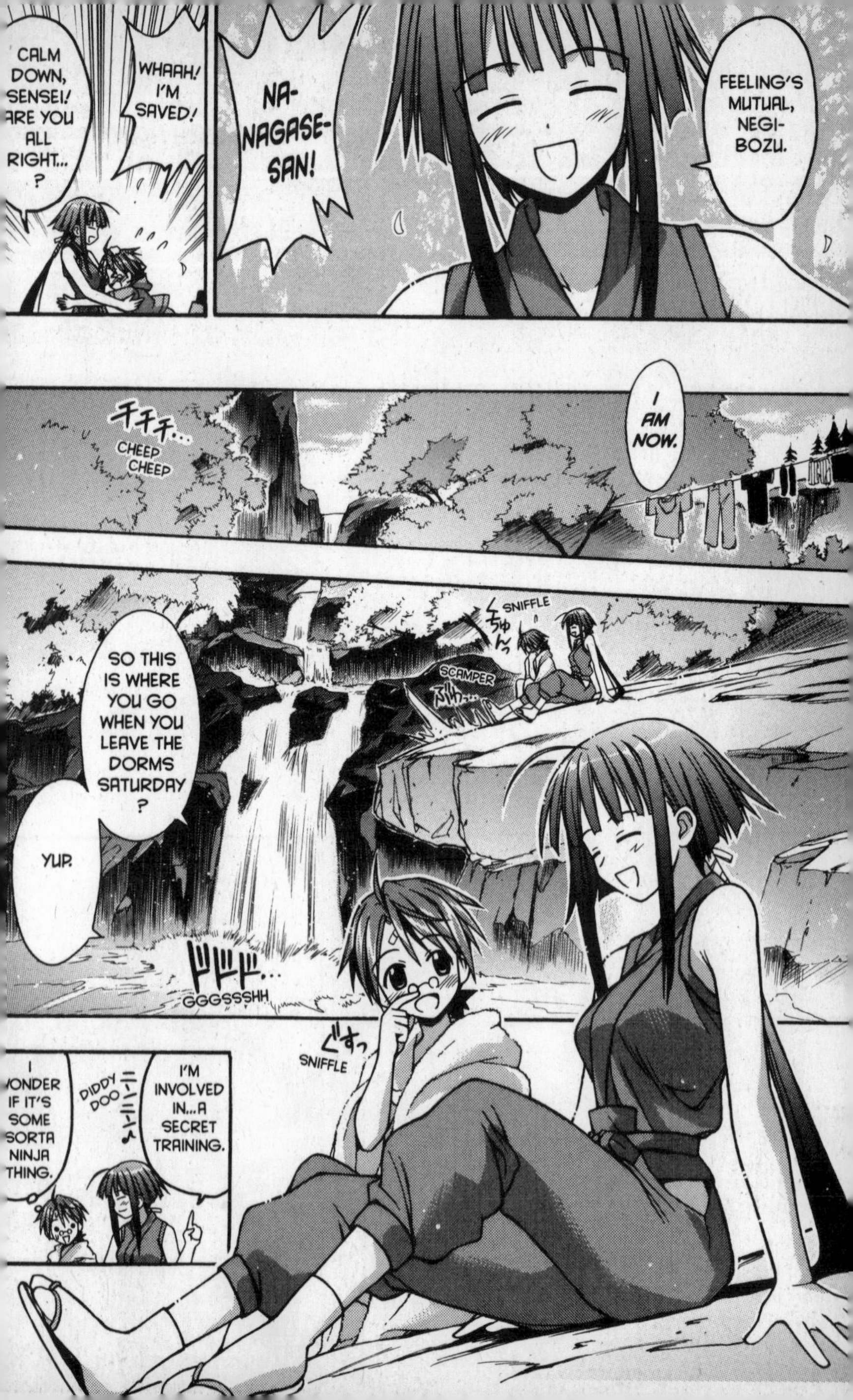

FEELING'S MUTUAL, NEGI-BOZU.
NA-NAGASE-SAN!
WHAAAH! I'M SAVED!
CALM DOWN, SENSEI! ARE YOU ALL RIGHT...?
I AM NOW.
チチチ…
CHEEP CHEEP
SNIFFLE
SCAMPER
SO THIS IS WHERE YOU GO WHEN YOU LEAVE THE DORMS SATURDAY?
YUP.
ドドド…
GGGSSSHH
ぐすっ
SNIFFLE
I'M INVOLVED IN...A SECRET TRAINING.
DIDDY DOO
I WONDER IF IT'S SOME SORTA NINJA THING.

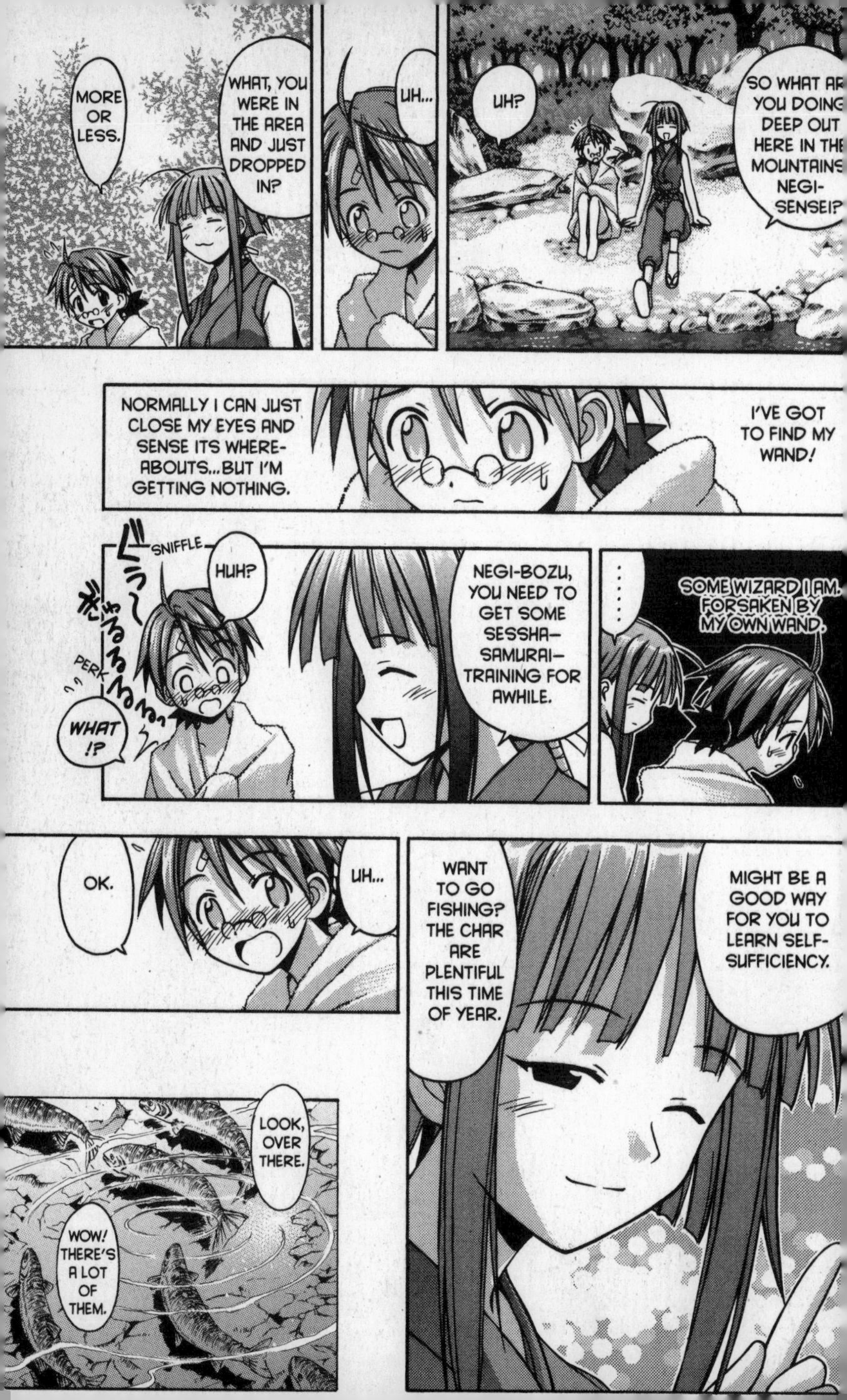
SO WHAT ARE YOU DOING DEEP OUT HERE IN THE MOUNTAINS NEGI-SENSEI?
UH?
UH...
WHAT, YOU WERE IN THE AREA AND JUST DROPPED IN?
MORE OR LESS.
I'VE GOT TO FIND MY WAND!
NORMALLY I CAN JUST CLOSE MY EYES AND SENSE ITS WHEREABOUTS...BUT I'M GETTING NOTHING.
SOME WIZARD I AM. FORSAKEN BY MY OWN WAND.
......
NEGI-BOZU, YOU NEED TO GET SOME SESSHA-SAMURAI-TRAINING FOR AWHILE.
SNIFFLE
HUH?
PERK
WHAT!?
MIGHT BE A GOOD WAY FOR YOU TO LEARN SELF-SUFFICIENCY.
WANT TO GO FISHING? THE CHAR ARE PLENTIFUL THIS TIME OF YEAR.
UH...
OK.
LOOK, OVER THERE.
WOW! THERE'S A LOT OF THEM.

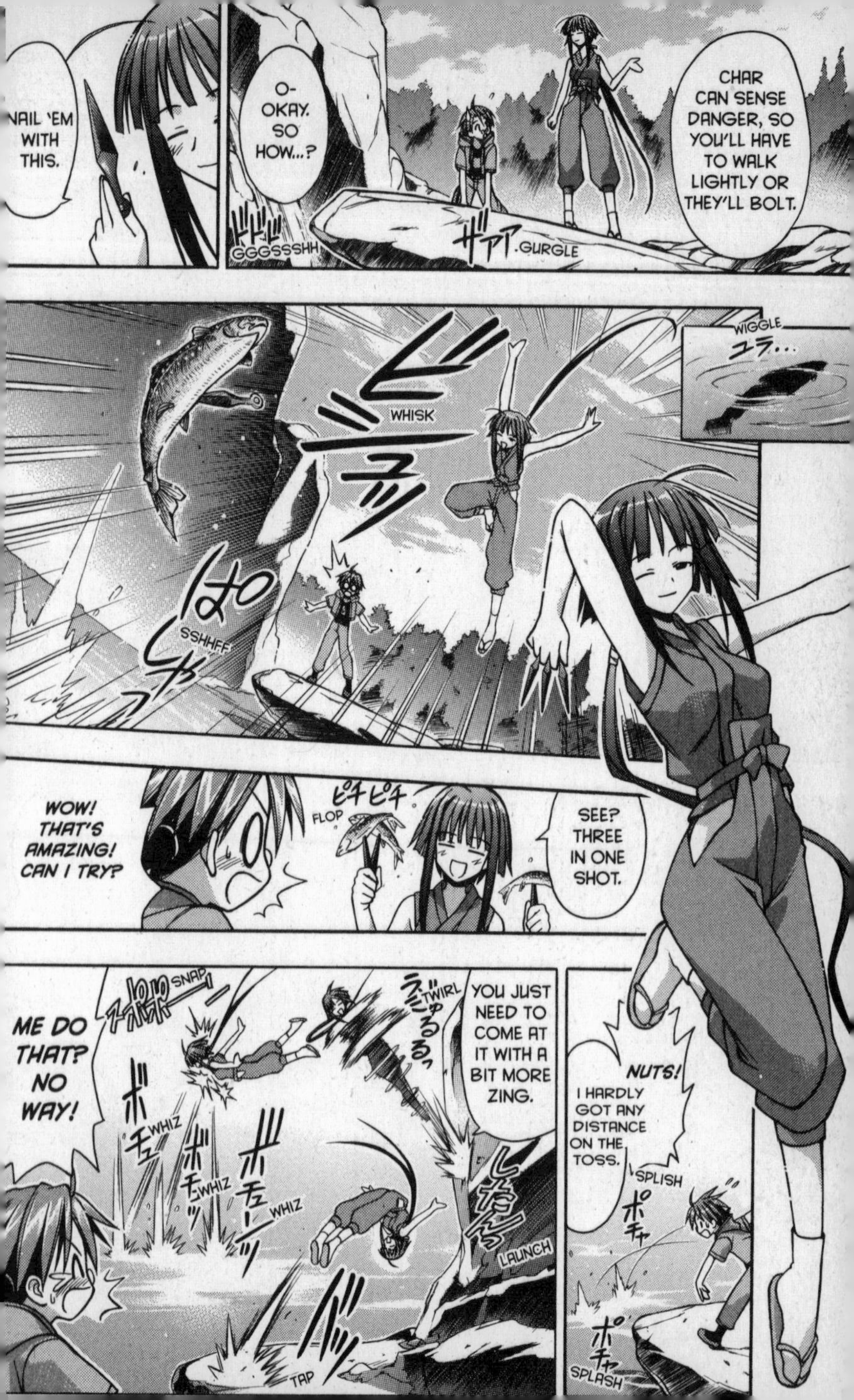
CHAR CAN SENSE DANGER, SO YOU'LL HAVE TO WALK LIGHTLY OR THEY'LL BOLT.
ザァア
GURGLE
O-OKAY. SO HOW...?
ドドド
GGGSSSHH
NAIL 'EM WITH THIS.
ユラ...
WIGGLE
WHISK
SSHHFF
SEE? THREE IN ONE SHOT.
ピチピチ
FLOP
WOW! THAT'S AMAZING! CAN I TRY?
NUTS!
I HARDLY GOT ANY DISTANCE ON THE TOSS.
SPLISH
SPLASH
YOU JUST NEED TO COME AT IT WITH A BIT MORE ZING.
TWIRL
LAUNCH
TAP
SNAP
WHIZ
WHIZ
WHIZ
ME DO THAT? NO WAY!

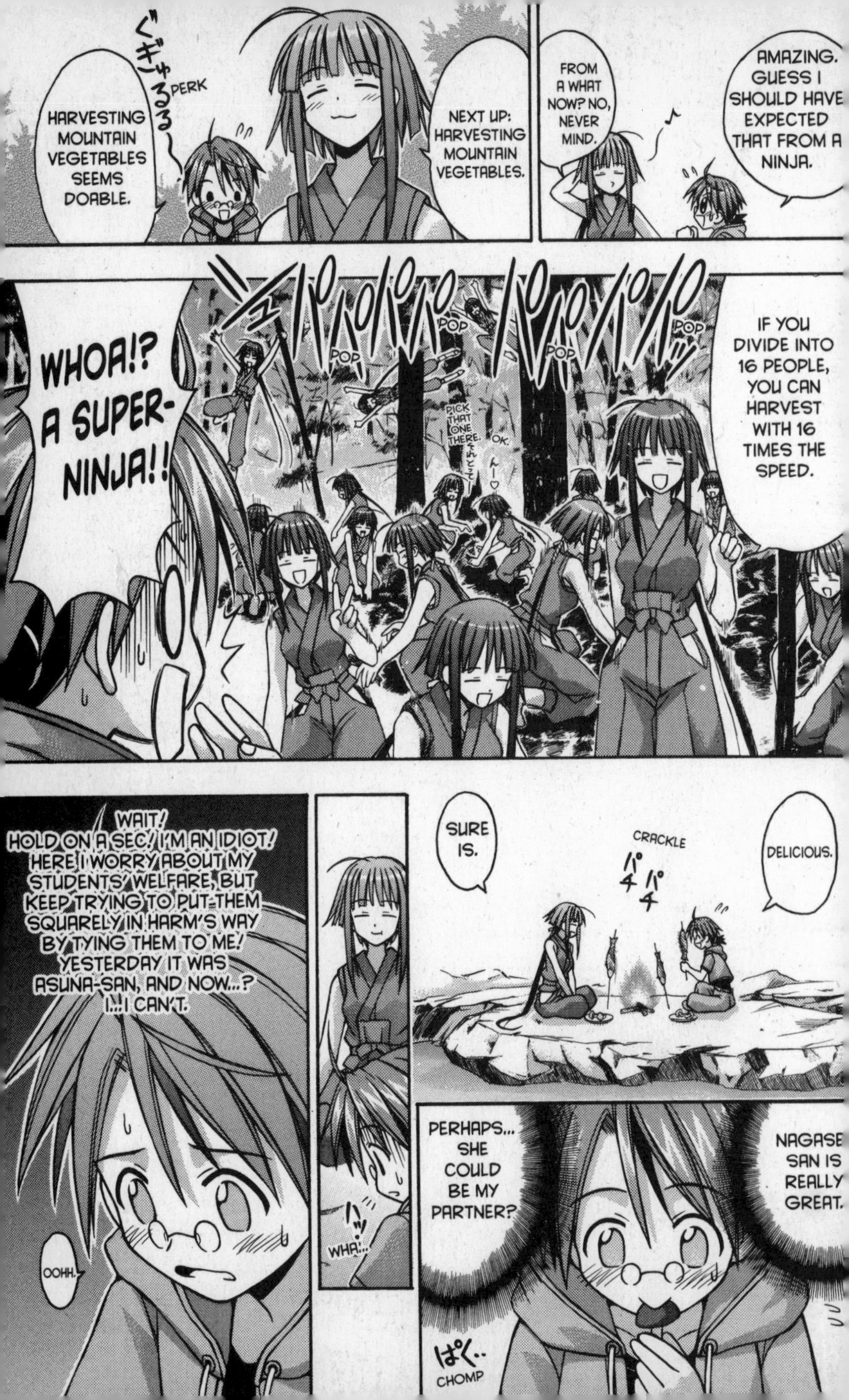
AMAZING. GUESS I SHOULD HAVE EXPECTED THAT FROM A NINJA.
FROM A WHAT NOW? NO, NEVER MIND.
NEXT UP: HARVESTING MOUNTAIN VEGETABLES.
ぐぎゅるる
PERK
HARVESTING MOUNTAIN VEGETABLES SEEMS DOABLE.
IF YOU DIVIDE INTO 16 PEOPLE, YOU CAN HARVEST WITH 16 TIMES THE SPEED.
POP
POP
POP
POP
PICK THAT ONE THERE.
OK.
ん～♡
WHOA!? A SUPER-NINJA!!
DELICIOUS.
CRACKLE
パチパチ
SURE IS.
NAGASE SAN IS REALLY GREAT.
PERHAPS... SHE COULD BE MY PARTNER?
ぱく..
CHOMP
ハッ
WHA!...
WAIT! HOLD ON A SEC! I'M AN IDIOT! HERE I WORRY ABOUT MY STUDENTS' WELFARE, BUT KEEP TRYING TO PUT THEM SQUARELY IN HARM'S WAY BY TYING THEM TO ME! YESTERDAY IT WAS ASUNA-SAN, AND NOW...? I...I CAN'T.
OOHH.

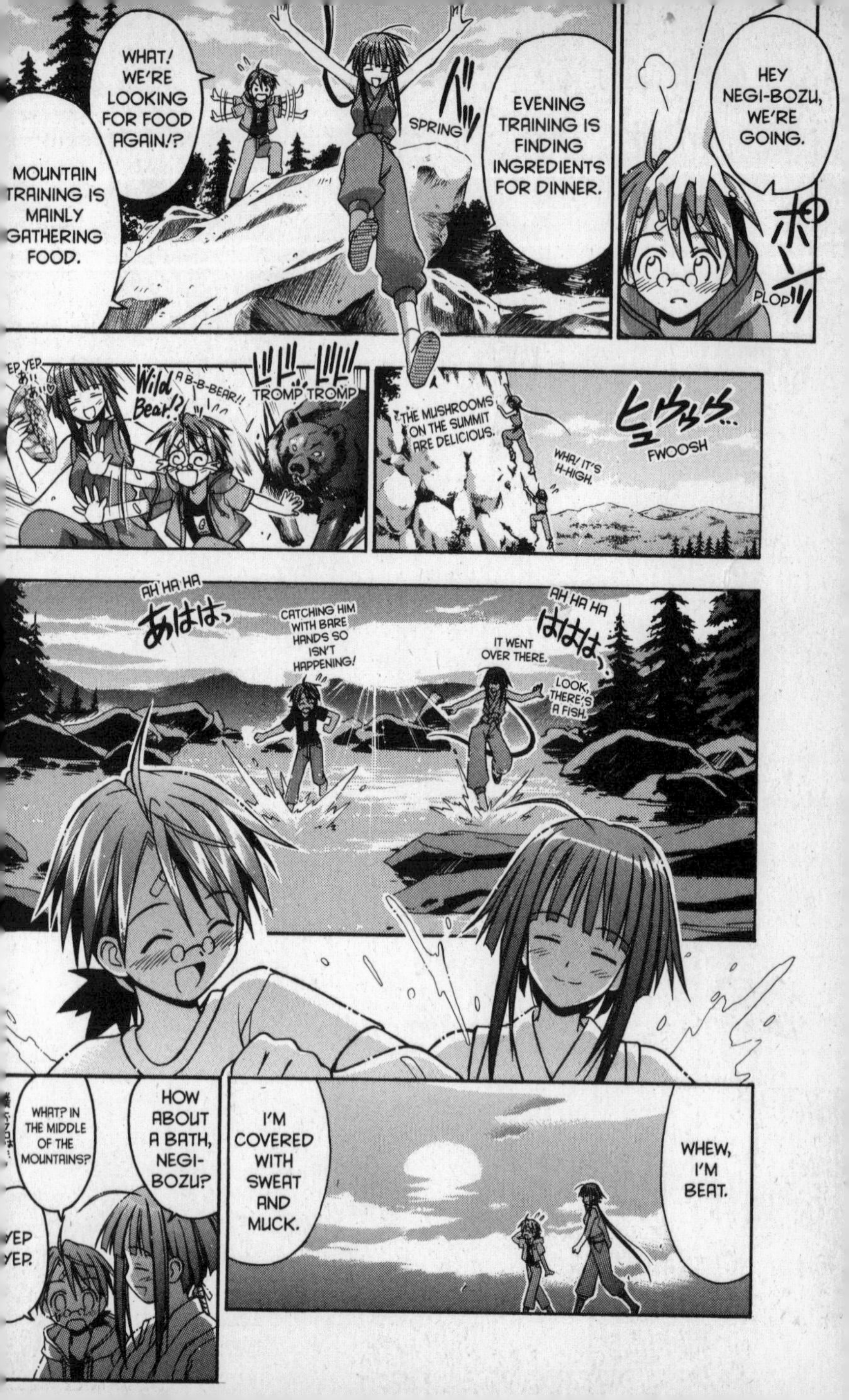
HEY NEGI-BOZU, WE'RE GOING.
PLOP
EVENING TRAINING IS FINDING INGREDIENTS FOR DINNER.
SPRING
WHAT! WE'RE LOOKING FOR FOOD AGAIN!?
MOUNTAIN TRAINING IS MAINLY GATHERING FOOD.
FWOOSH
THE MUSHROOMS ON THE SUMMIT ARE DELICIOUS.
WHA! IT'S H-HIGH.
TROMP TROMP
B-B-BEAR!!
Wild Bear!?
YEP YEP
AH HA HA
ははは
IT WENT OVER THERE.
LOOK, THERE'S A FISH.
CATCHING HIM WITH BARE HANDS SO ISN'T HAPPENING!
AH HA HA
あははっ
WHEW, I'M BEAT.
I'M COVERED WITH SWEAT AND MUCK.
HOW ABOUT A BATH, NEGI-BOZU?
WHAT? IN THE MIDDLE OF THE MOUNTAINS?
YEP YEP.

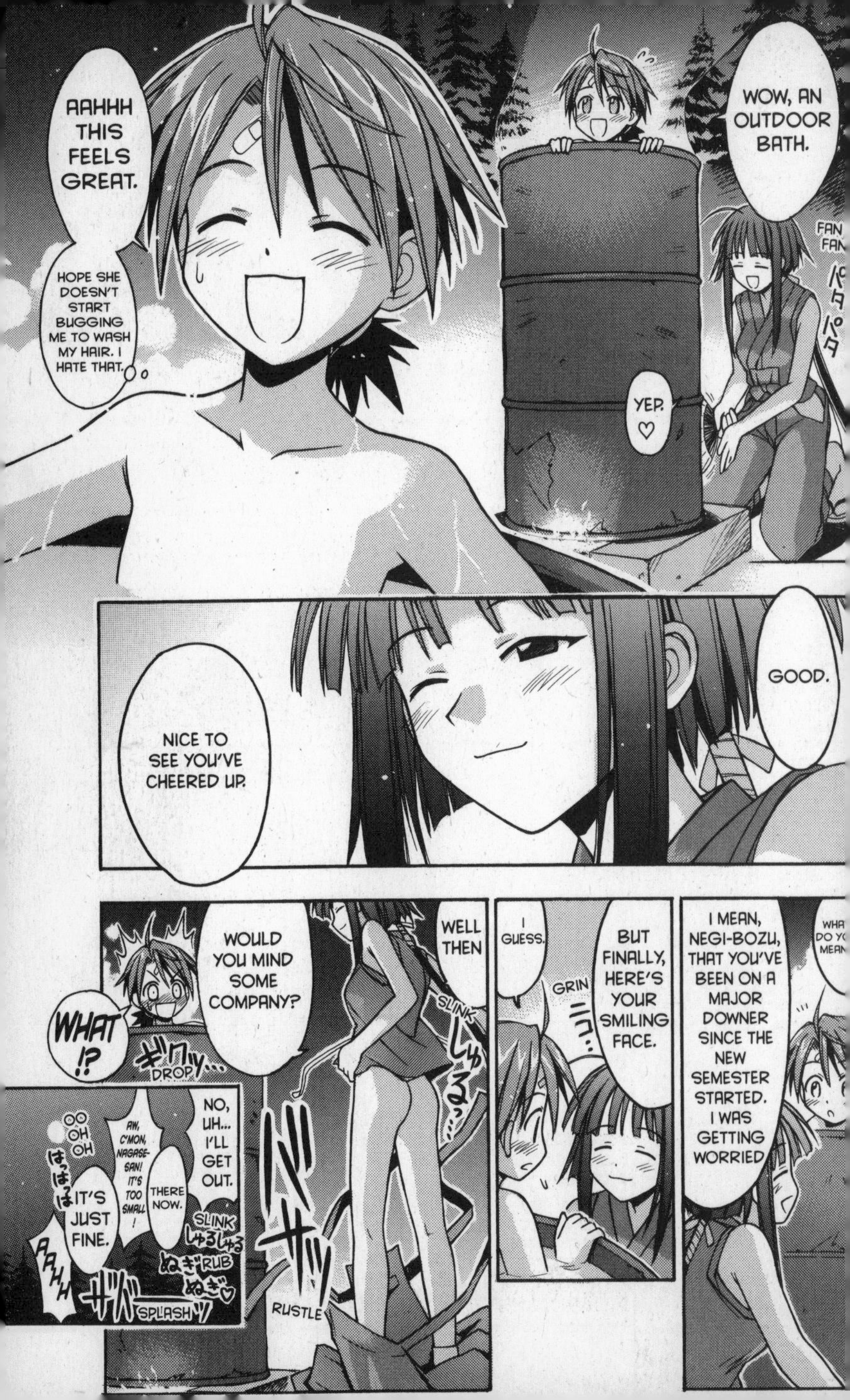
WOW, AN OUTDOOR BATH.
YEP. ♡
FAN FAN
パタ パタ
AAHHH THIS FEELS GREAT.
HOPE SHE DOESN'T START BUGGING ME TO WASH MY HAIR. I HATE THAT.
GOOD.
NICE TO SEE YOU'VE CHEERED UP.
WHA DO YO MEAN
I MEAN, NEGI-BOZU, THAT YOU'VE BEEN ON A MAJOR DOWNER SINCE THE NEW SEMESTER STARTED. I WAS GETTING WORRIED.
I GUESS.
BUT FINALLY, HERE'S YOUR SMILING FACE.
GRIN
ニコ...
WELL THEN
WOULD YOU MIND SOME COMPANY?
SLINK
しゅるっ...
WHAT !?
ギクッ...
DROP
ザッ
RUSTLE
NO, UH... I'LL GET OUT.
AW, C'MON, NAGASE-SAN! IT'S TOO SMALL!
THERE NOW.
OO OH OH
はっはっは
IT'S JUST FINE.
SLINK
しゅるしゅる
ぬぎ RUB
ぬぎ♡
ザバー
SPLASH

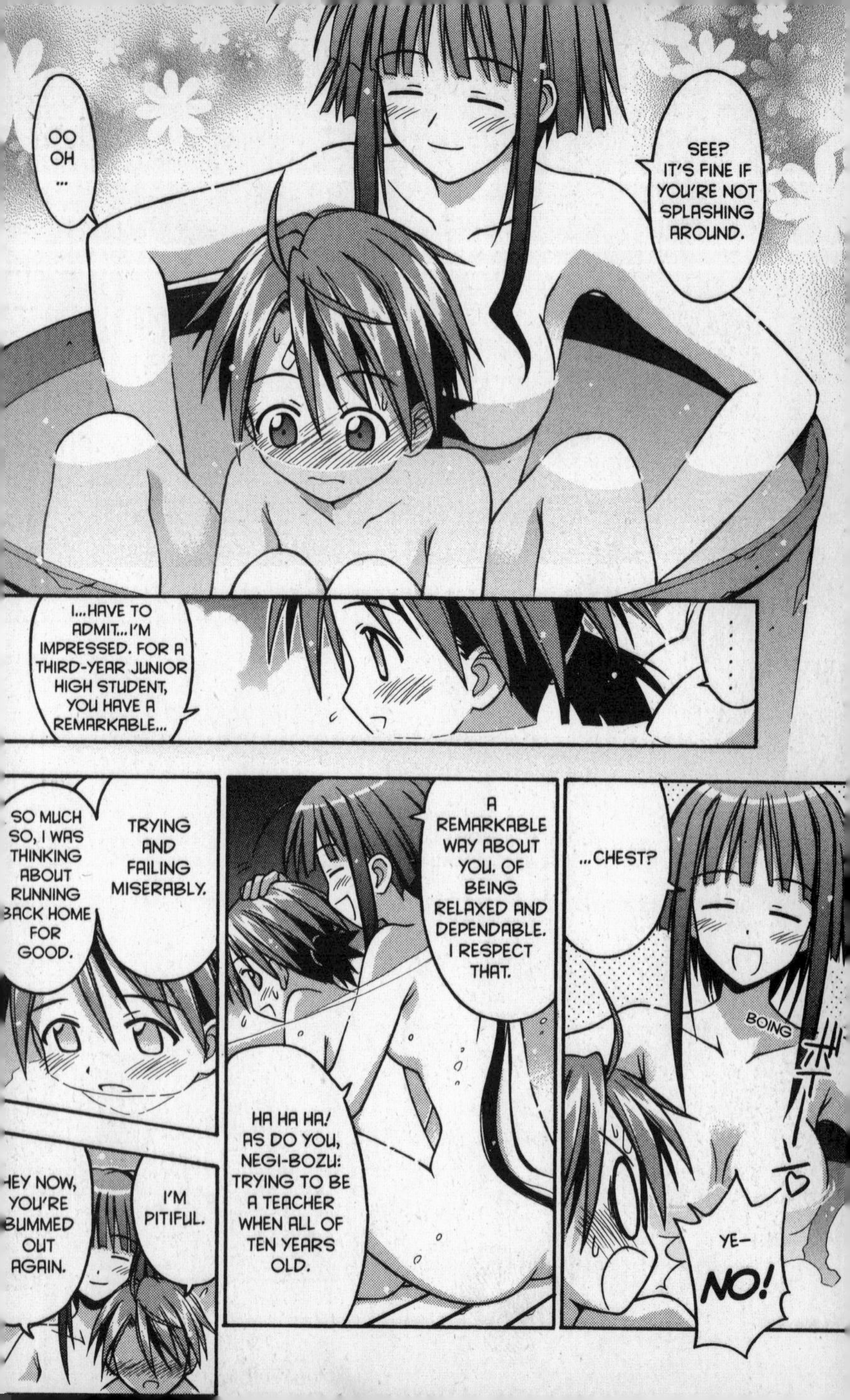
SEE? IT'S FINE IF YOU'RE NOT SPLASHING AROUND.
OO OH ...
......
I...HAVE TO ADMIT...I'M IMPRESSED. FOR A THIRD-YEAR JUNIOR HIGH STUDENT, YOU HAVE A REMARKABLE...
...CHEST?
BOING
YE-
NO!
A REMARKABLE WAY ABOUT YOU. OF BEING RELAXED AND DEPENDABLE. I RESPECT THAT.
HA HA HA! AS DO YOU, NEGI-BOZU: TRYING TO BE A TEACHER WHEN ALL OF TEN YEARS OLD.
TRYING AND FAILING MISERABLY.
SO MUCH SO, I WAS THINKING ABOUT RUNNING BACK HOME FOR GOOD.
I'M PITIFUL.
HEY NOW, YOU'RE BUMMED OUT AGAIN.

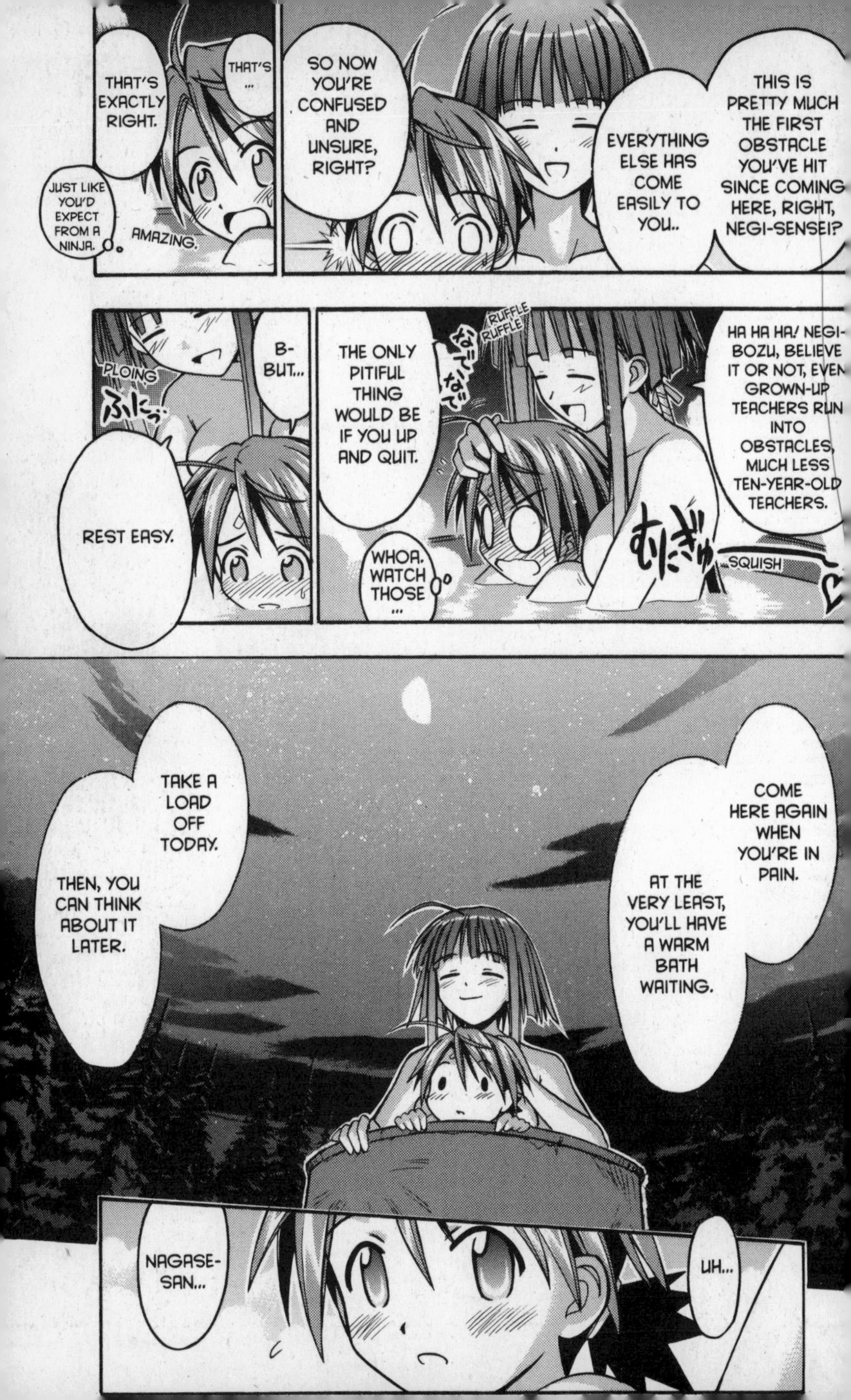
THIS IS PRETTY MUCH THE FIRST OBSTACLE YOU'VE HIT SINCE COMING HERE, RIGHT, NEGI-SENSEI?
EVERYTHING ELSE HAS COME EASILY TO YOU..
SO NOW YOU'RE CONFUSED AND UNSURE, RIGHT?
THAT'S ...
THAT'S EXACTLY RIGHT.
JUST LIKE YOU'D EXPECT FROM A NINJA.
AMAZING.
HA HA HA! NEGI-BOZU, BELIEVE IT OR NOT, EVEN GROWN-UP TEACHERS RUN INTO OBSTACLES, MUCH LESS TEN-YEAR-OLD TEACHERS.
むにぎゅ
SQUISH
RUFFLE RUFFLE
なでなで
THE ONLY PITIFUL THING WOULD BE IF YOU UP AND QUIT.
WHOA. WATCH THOSE ...
B-BUT...
ふにっ
PLOING
REST EASY.
COME HERE AGAIN WHEN YOU'RE IN PAIN.
AT THE VERY LEAST, YOU'LL HAVE A WARM BATH WAITING.
TAKE A LOAD OFF TODAY.
THEN, YOU CAN THINK ABOUT IT LATER.
UH...
NAGASE-SAN...

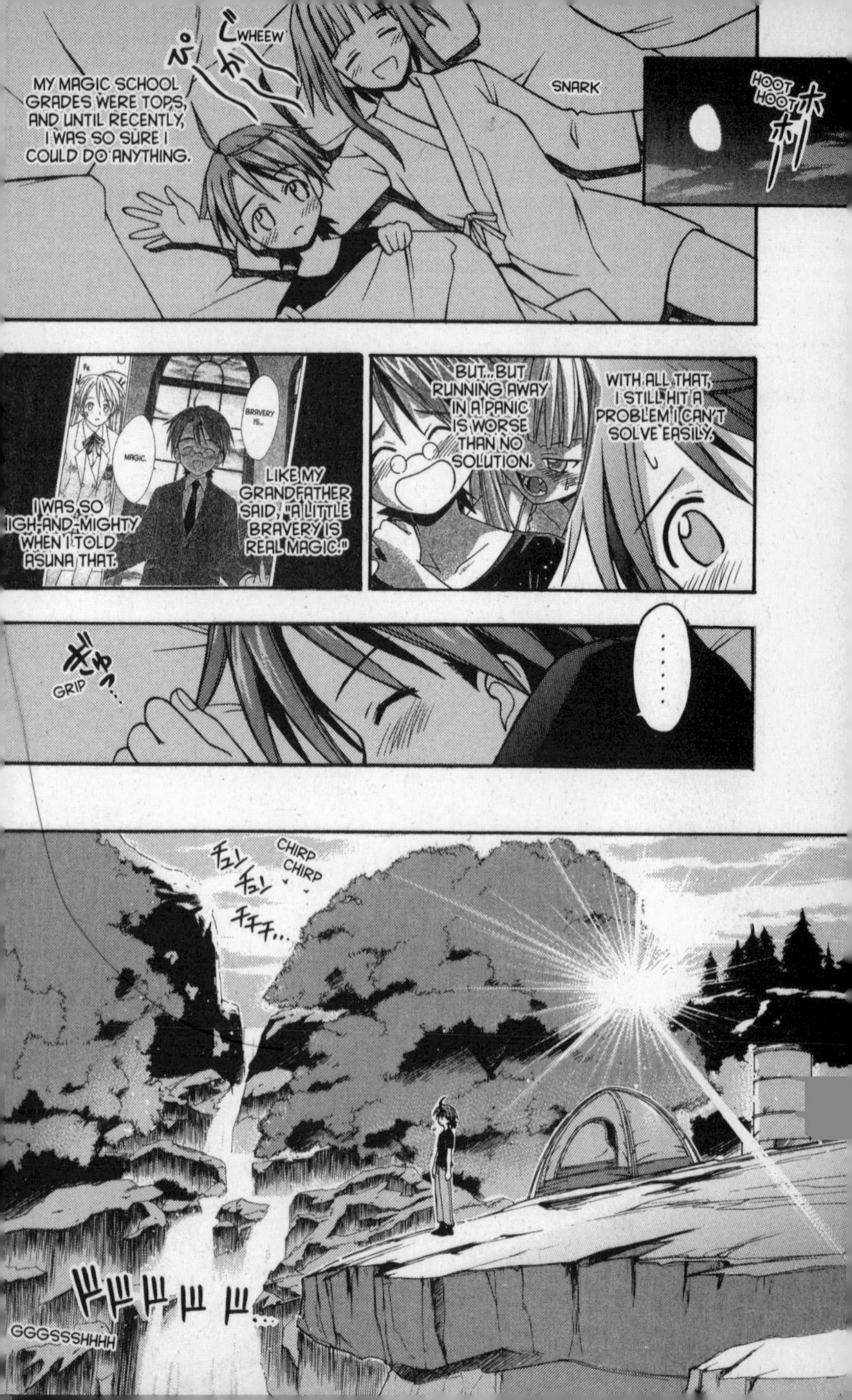

HOOT HOOT
ホーホー
SNARK
WHEEW
MY MAGIC SCHOOL GRADES WERE TOPS, AND UNTIL RECENTLY, I WAS SO SURE I COULD DO ANYTHING.
WITH ALL THAT, I STILL HIT A PROBLEM I CAN'T SOLVE EASILY.
BUT... BUT RUNNING AWAY IN A PANIC IS WORSE THAN NO SOLUTION.
LIKE MY GRANDFATHER SAID, "A LITTLE BRAVERY IS REAL MAGIC."
BRAVERY IS...
MAGIC.
I WAS SO IGH-AND-MIGHTY WHEN I TOLD ASUNA THAT.
......
ぎゅっ...
GRIP
CHIRP CHIRP
チュン チュン チチチ...
ドドドドド...
GGGSSSHHHH

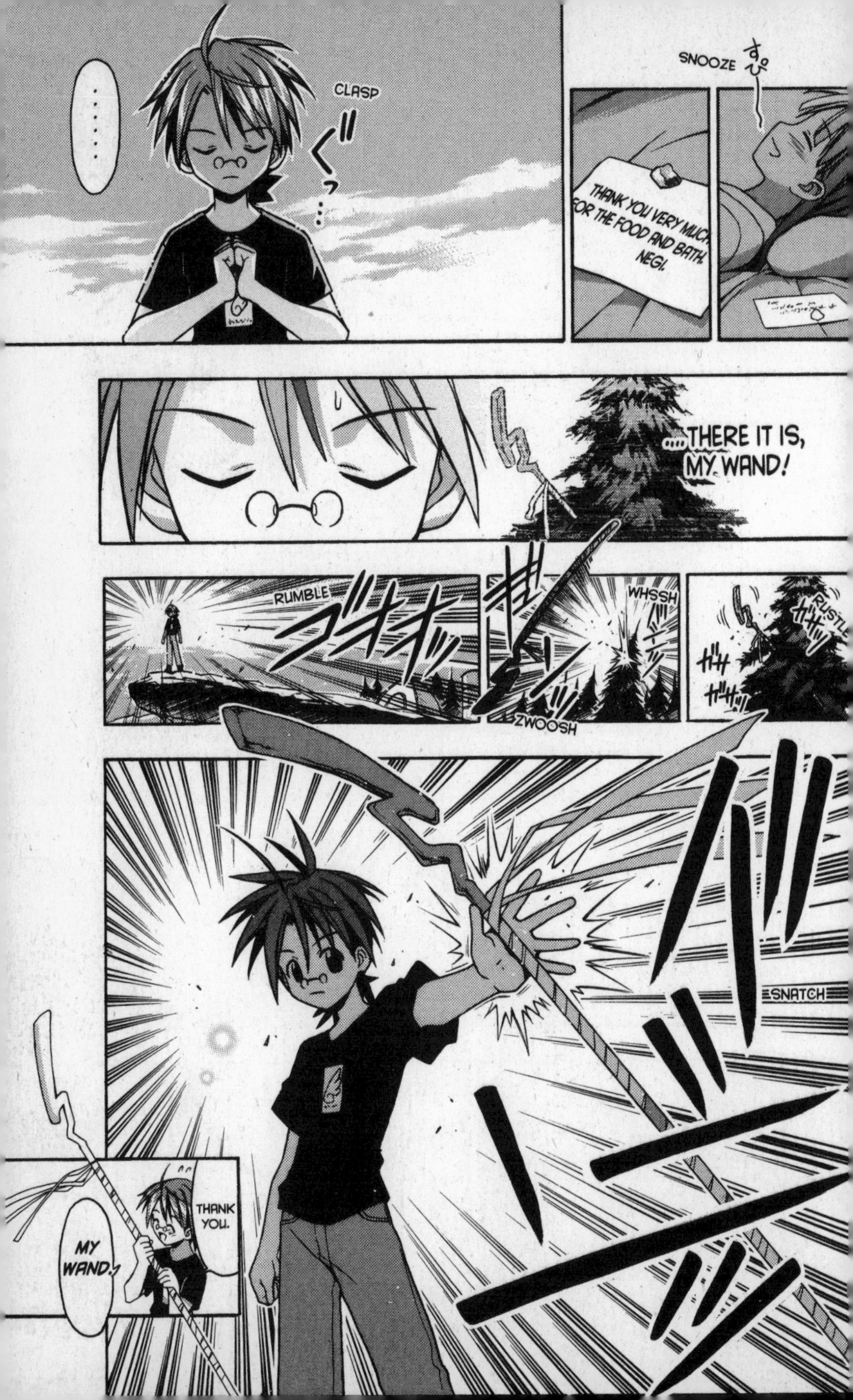

SNOOZE
THANK YOU VERY MUCH FOR THE FOOD AND BATH. NEGI.
CLASP
......
...THERE IT IS, MY WAND!
RUSTLE
WHSSH
ZWOOSH
RUMBLE
SNATCH
THANK YOU.
MY WAND...

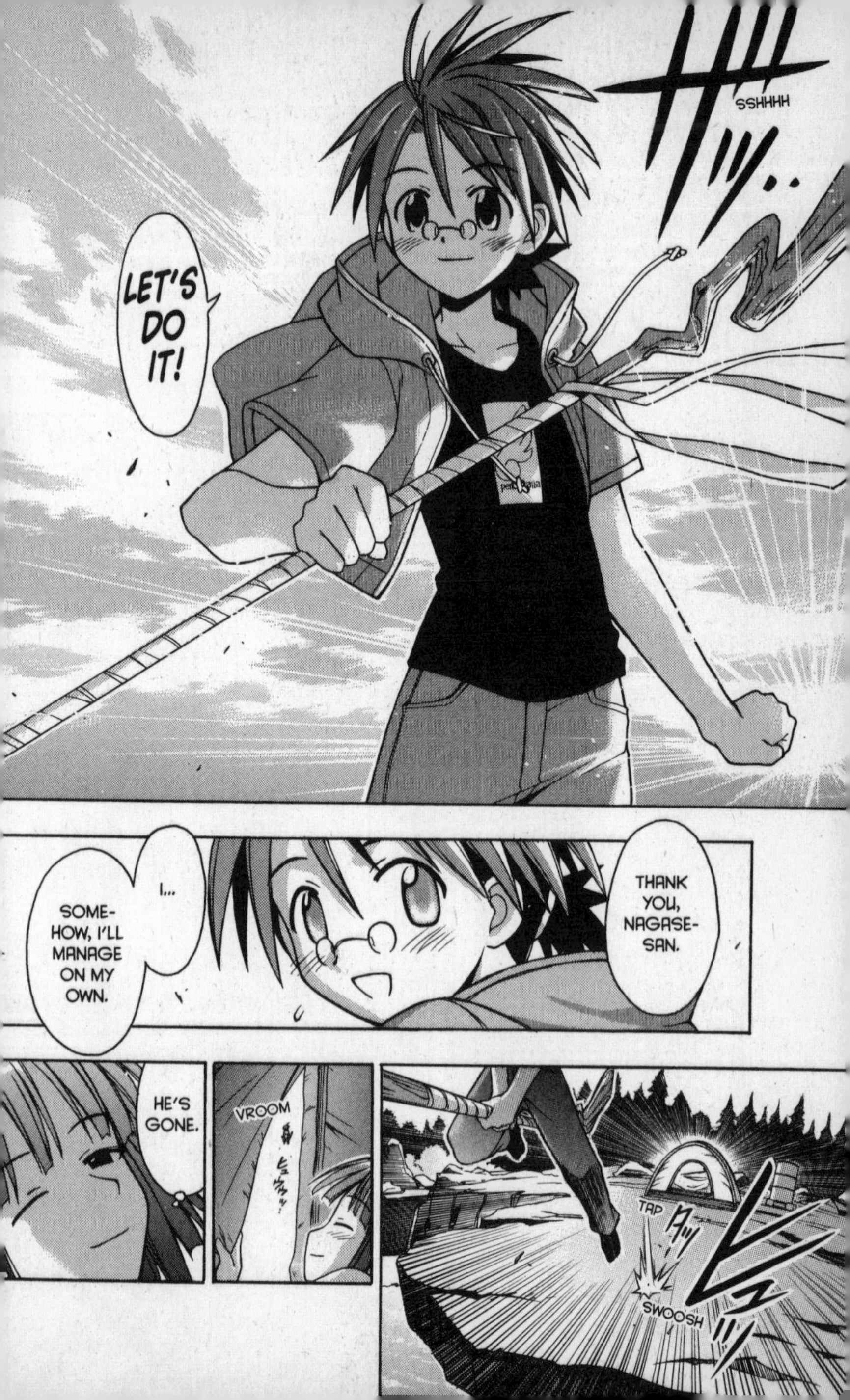
SSHHHH
LET'S DO IT!
THANK YOU, NAGASE-SAN.
I... SOME-HOW, I'LL MANAGE ON MY OWN.
TAP
SWOOSH
VROOM
HE'S GONE.

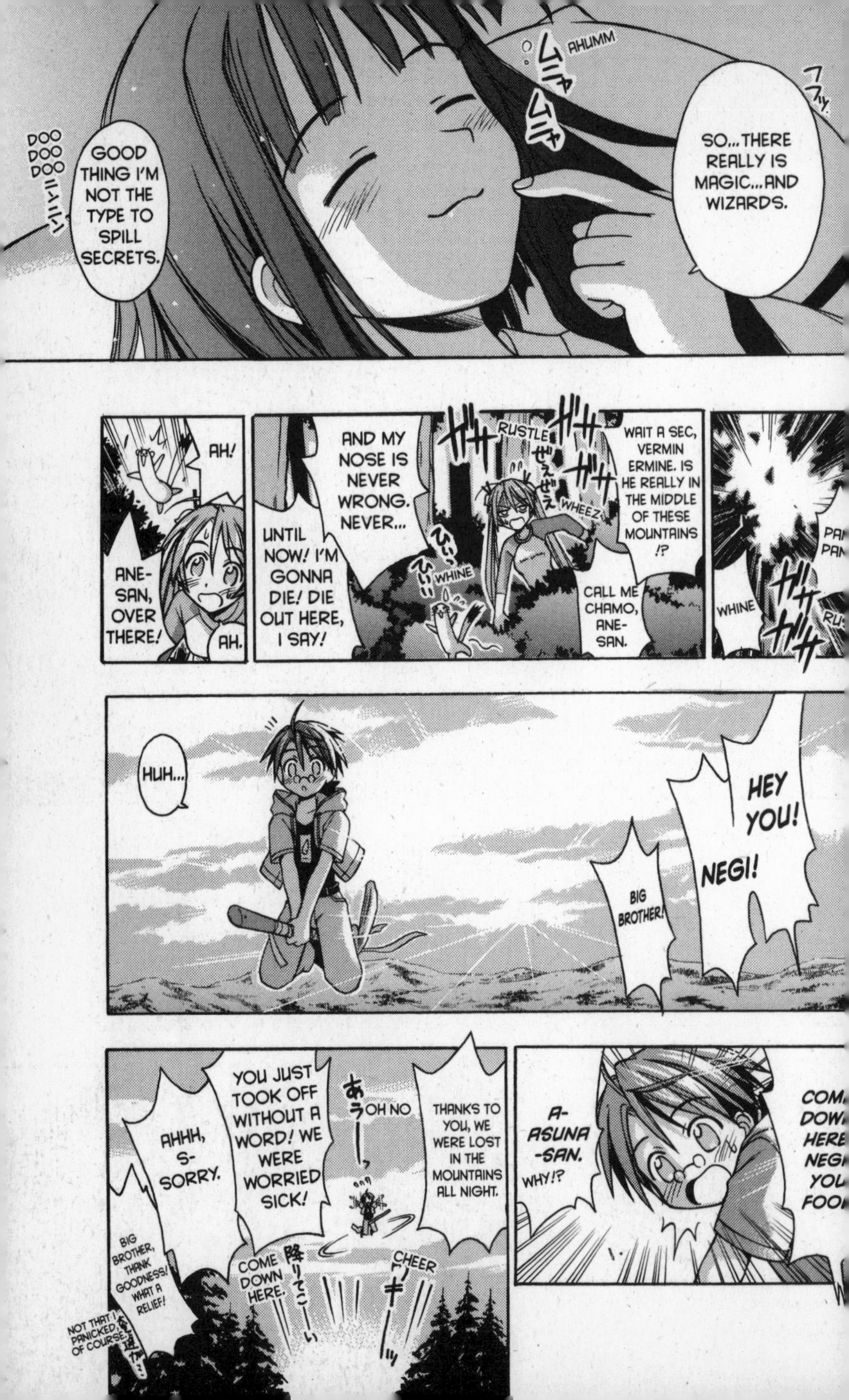

AHUMM
SO...THERE REALLY IS MAGIC...AND WIZARDS.
GOOD THING I'M NOT THE TYPE TO SPILL SECRETS.
DOO DOO DOO
WHINE
WAIT A SEC, VERMIN ERMINE. IS HE REALLY IN THE MIDDLE OF THESE MOUNTAINS!?
RUSTLE
WHEEZ
CALL ME CHAMO, ANE-SAN.
AND MY NOSE IS NEVER WRONG. NEVER...
UNTIL NOW! I'M GONNA DIE! DIE OUT HERE, I SAY!
WHINE
AH!
ANE-SAN, OVER THERE!
AH.
HEY YOU!
NEGI!
BIG BROTHER!
HUH...
A-ASUNA-SAN.
WHY!?
THANKS TO YOU, WE WERE LOST IN THE MOUNTAINS ALL NIGHT.
OH NO
YOU JUST TOOK OFF WITHOUT A WORD! WE WERE WORRIED SICK!
AHHH, S-SORRY.
CHEER
COME DOWN HERE.
BIG BROTHER, THANK GOODNESS! WHAT A RELIEF!
NOT THAT I PANICKED, OF COURSE.

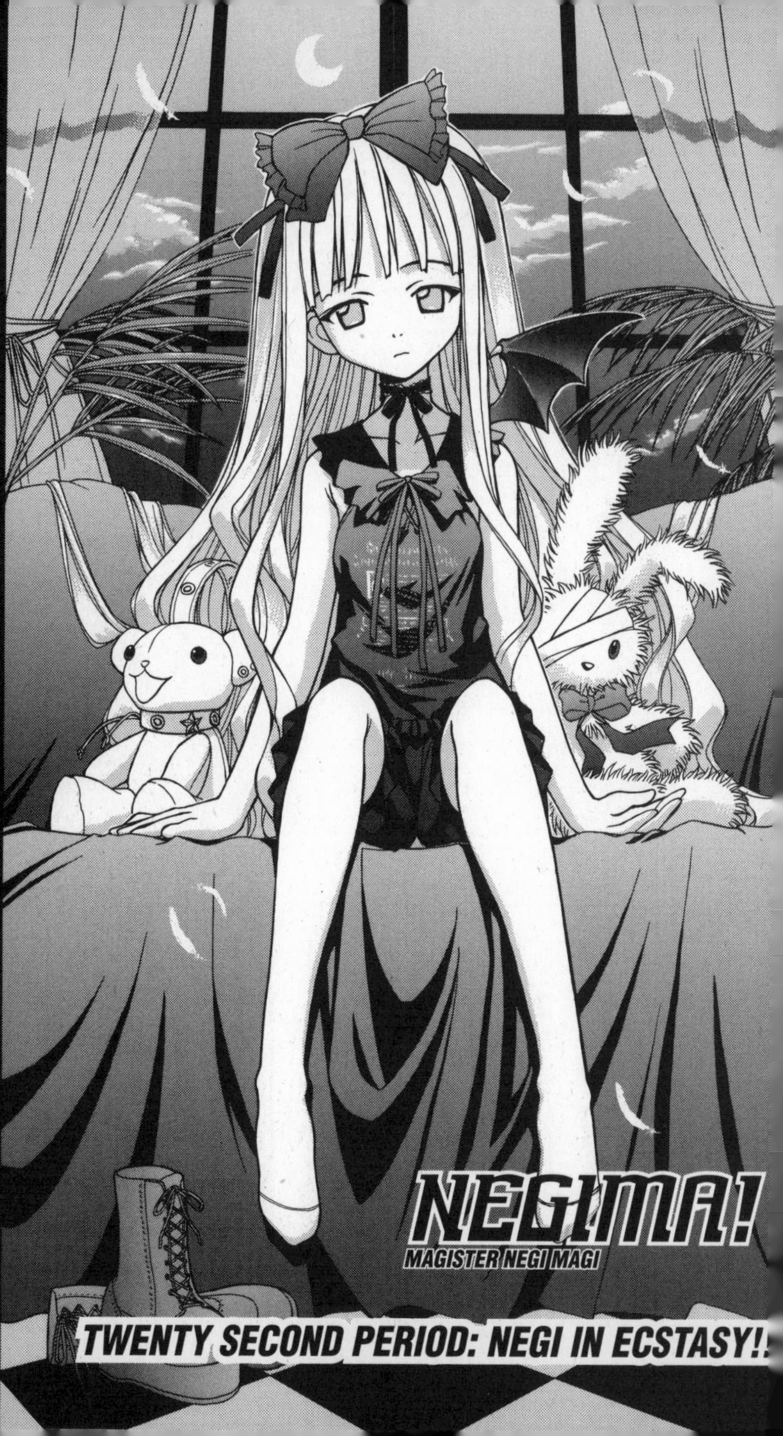
NEGIMA!
MAGISTER NEGI MAGI
TWENTY SECOND PERIOD: NEGI IN ECSTASY!!

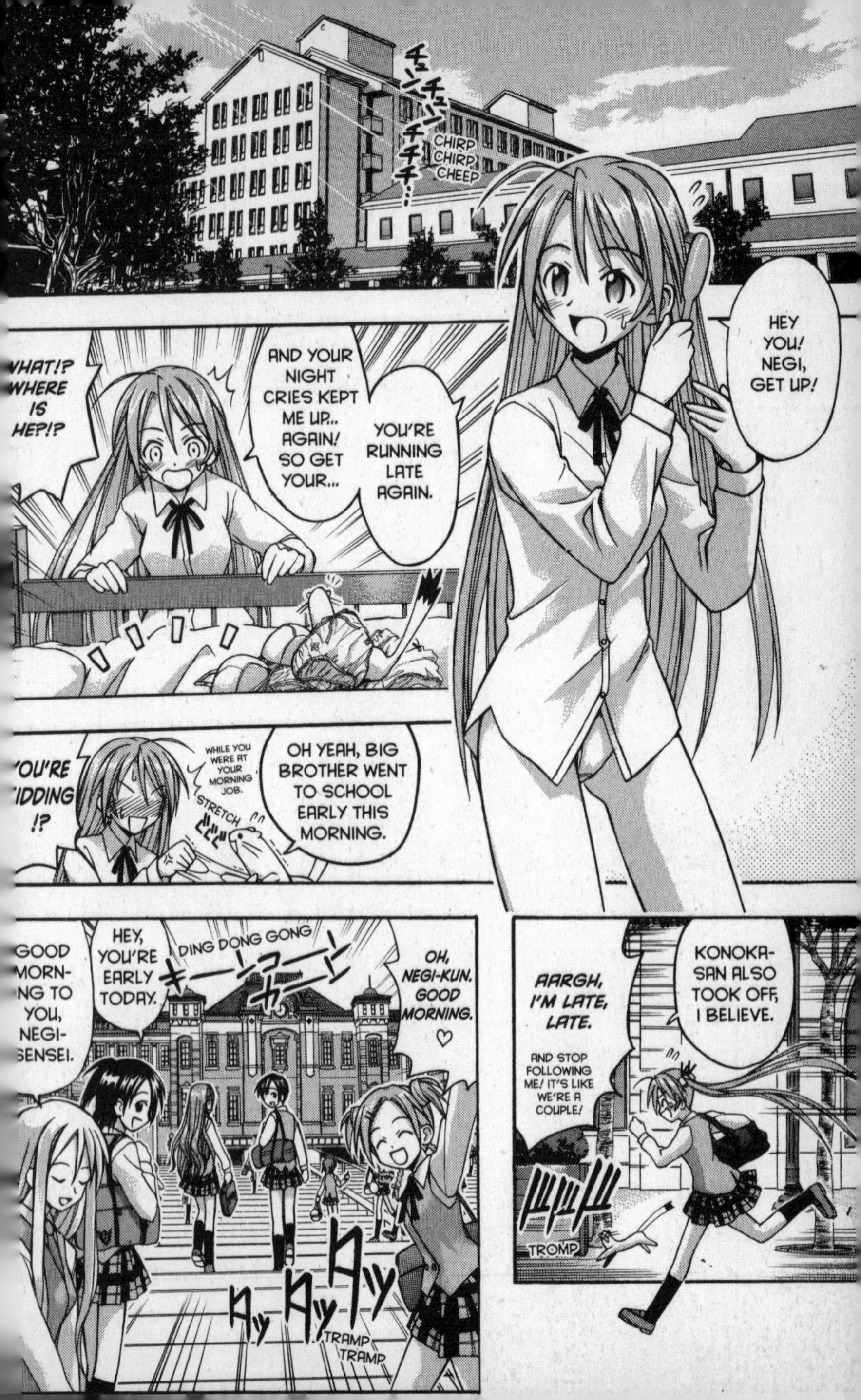

チュンチュン チチチ…
CHIRP CHIRP CHEEP
HEY YOU! NEGI, GET UP!
YOU'RE RUNNING LATE AGAIN.
AND YOUR NIGHT CRIES KEPT ME UP... AGAIN! SO GET YOUR...
WHAT!? WHERE IS HE?!?
OH YEAH, BIG BROTHER WENT TO SCHOOL EARLY THIS MORNING.
WHILE YOU WERE AT YOUR MORNING JOB.
STRETCH
YOU'RE KIDDING !?
KONOKA-SAN ALSO TOOK OFF, I BELIEVE.
AARGH, I'M LATE, LATE.
AND STOP FOLLOWING ME! IT'S LIKE WE'RE A COUPLE!
TROMP
OH, NEGI-KUN. GOOD MORNING.
キーンコーンカーン
DING DONG GONG
HEY, YOU'RE EARLY TODAY.
GOOD MORNING TO YOU, NEGI-SENSEI.
TRAMP TRAMP

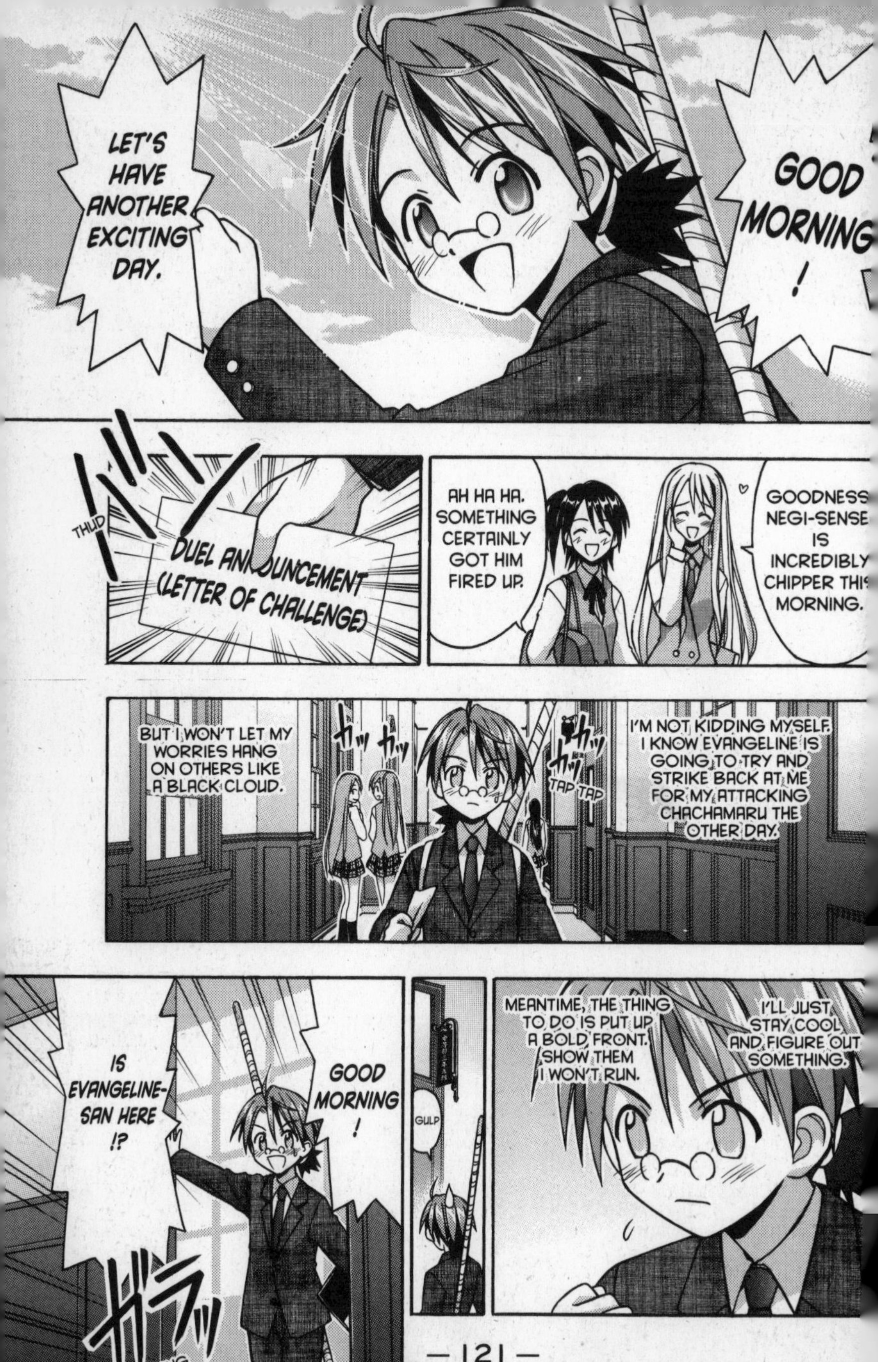
GOOD MORNING!
LET'S HAVE ANOTHER EXCITING DAY.
GOODNESS NEGI-SENSE IS INCREDIBLY CHIPPER THIS MORNING.
AH HA HA. SOMETHING CERTAINLY GOT HIM FIRED UP.
THUD
DUEL ANNOUNCEMENT (LETTER OF CHALLENGE)
I'M NOT KIDDING MYSELF. I KNOW EVANGELINE IS GOING TO TRY AND STRIKE BACK AT ME FOR MY ATTACKING CHACHAMARU THE OTHER DAY.
TAP TAP
BUT I WON'T LET MY WORRIES HANG ON OTHERS LIKE A BLACK CLOUD.
I'LL JUST STAY COOL AND FIGURE OUT SOMETHING.
MEANTIME, THE THING TO DO IS PUT UP A BOLD FRONT. SHOW THEM I WON'T RUN.
GULP
GOOD MORNING!
IS EVANGELINE-SAN HERE!?
BANG

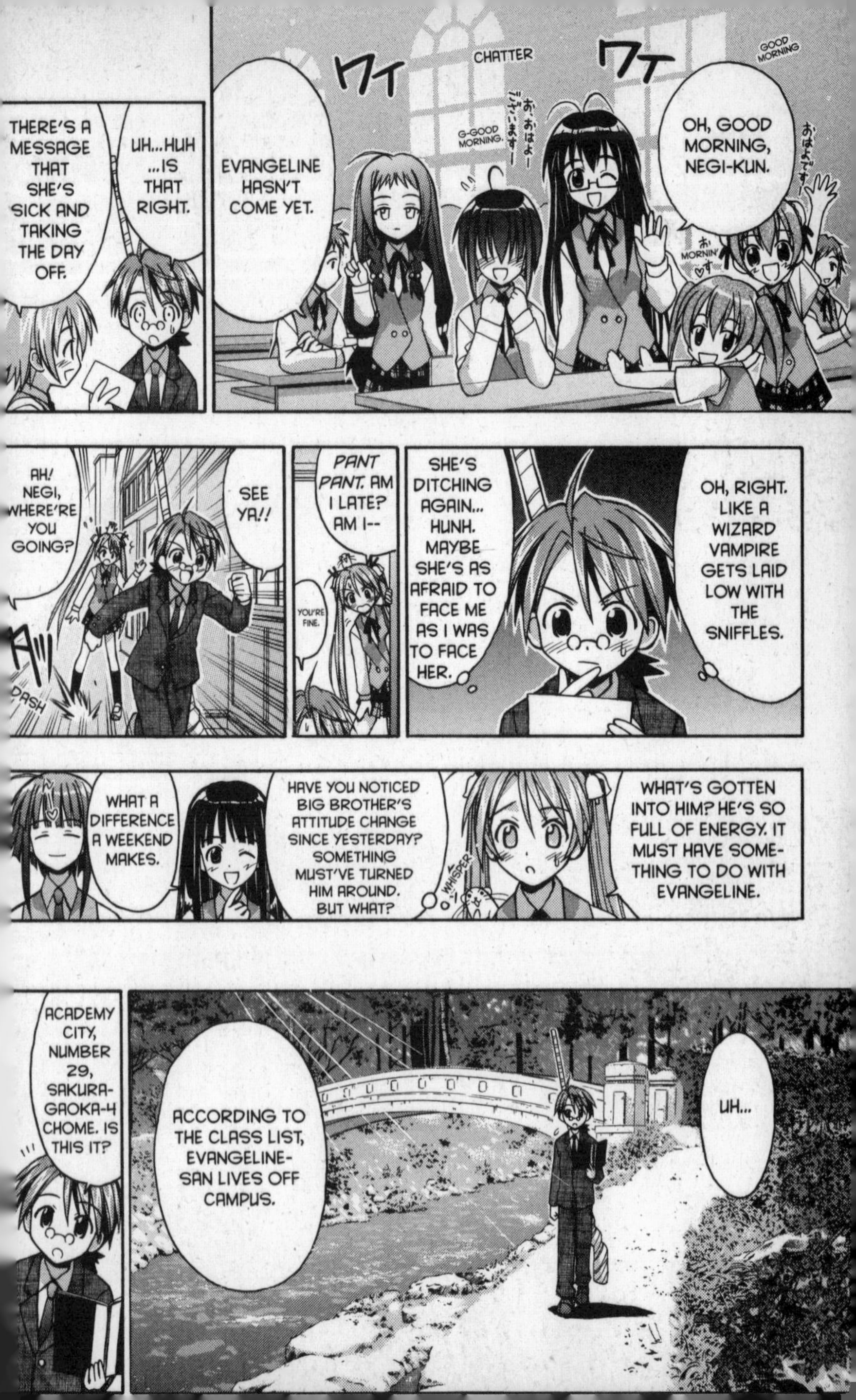
GOOD MORNING
OH, GOOD MORNING, NEGI-KUN.
おはよです
MORNIN'
お♡す
G-GOOD MORNING.
お、おはよーございますー
CHATTER
EVANGELINE HASN'T COME YET.
UH...HUH ...IS THAT RIGHT.
THERE'S A MESSAGE THAT SHE'S SICK AND TAKING THE DAY OFF.
OH, RIGHT. LIKE A WIZARD VAMPIRE GETS LAID LOW WITH THE SNIFFLES.
SHE'S DITCHING AGAIN... HUNH. MAYBE SHE'S AS AFRAID TO FACE ME AS I WAS TO FACE HER.
PANT PANT. AM I LATE? AM I--
YOU'RE FINE.
SEE YA!!
AH! NEGI, WHERE'RE YOU GOING?
DASH
WHAT'S GOTTEN INTO HIM? HE'S SO FULL OF ENERGY. IT MUST HAVE SOMETHING TO DO WITH EVANGELINE.
WHISPER
HAVE YOU NOTICED BIG BROTHER'S ATTITUDE CHANGE SINCE YESTERDAY? SOMETHING MUST'VE TURNED HIM AROUND. BUT WHAT?
WHAT A DIFFERENCE A WEEKEND MAKES.
UH...
ACCORDING TO THE CLASS LIST, EVANGELINE-SAN LIVES OFF CAMPUS.
ACADEMY CITY, NUMBER 29, SAKURA-GAOKA-4 CHOME. IS THIS IT?

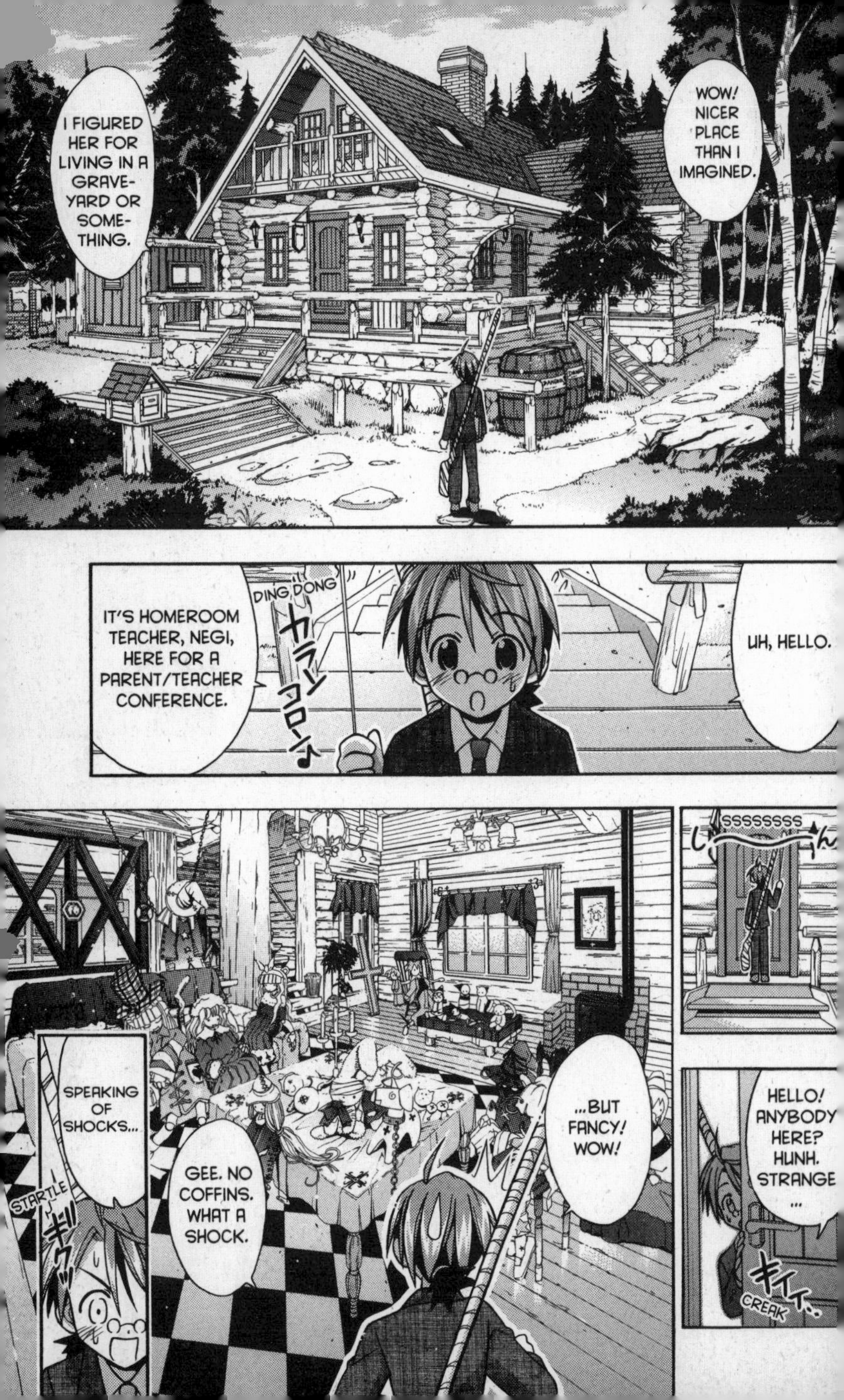
WOW! NICER PLACE THAN I IMAGINED.
I FIGURED HER FOR LIVING IN A GRAVE-YARD OR SOME-THING.
UH, HELLO.
DING DONG
IT'S HOMEROOM TEACHER, NEGI, HERE FOR A PARENT/TEACHER CONFERENCE.
SSSSSSSS
HELLO! ANYBODY HERE? HUNH. STRANGE ...
CREAK
...BUT FANCY! WOW!
GEE. NO COFFINS. WHAT A SHOCK.
SPEAKING OF SHOCKS...
STARTLE

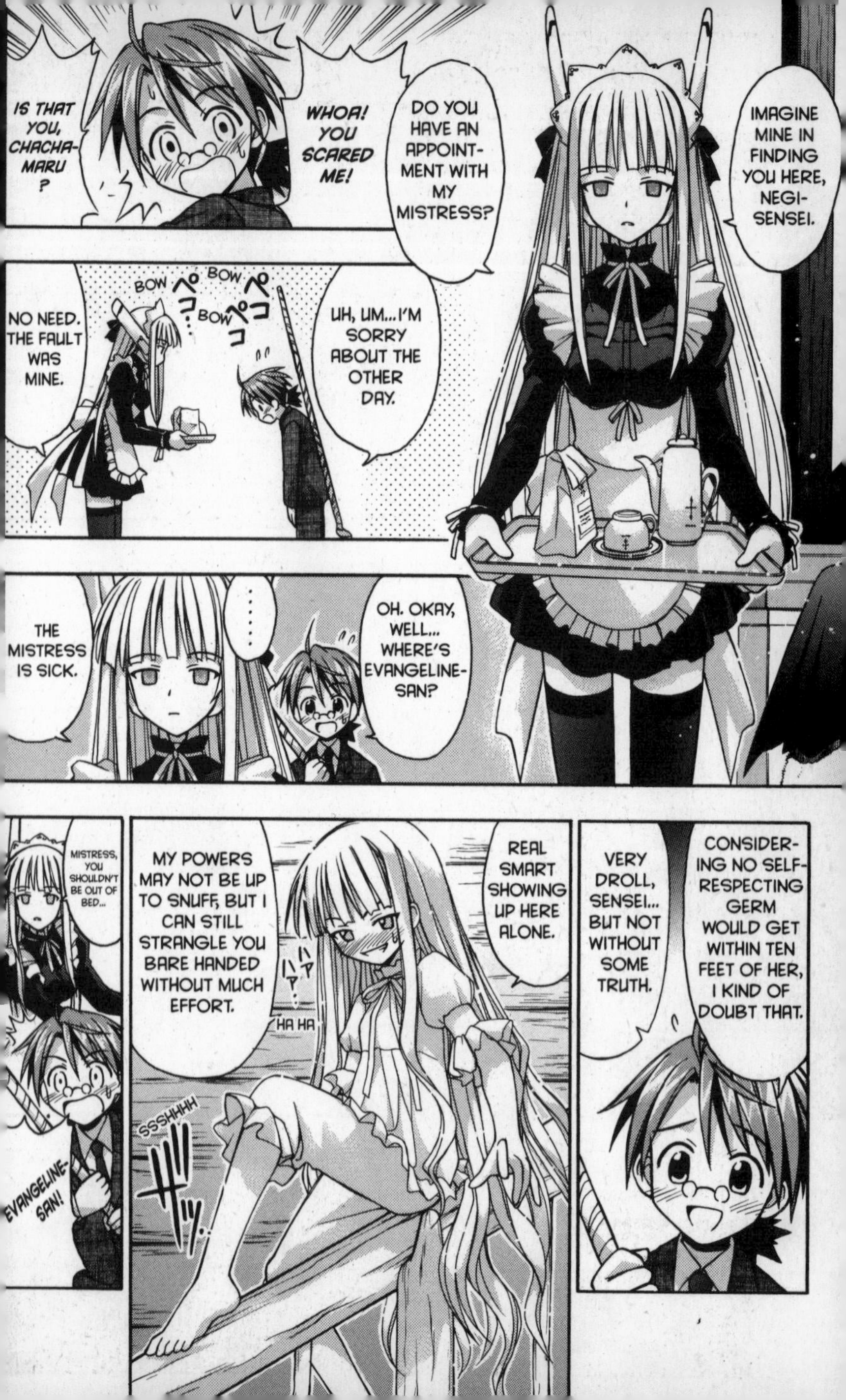
IMAGINE MINE IN FINDING YOU HERE, NEGI-SENSEI.
DO YOU HAVE AN APPOINTMENT WITH MY MISTRESS?
WHOA! YOU SCARED ME!
IS THAT YOU, CHACHAMARU?
UH, UM...I'M SORRY ABOUT THE OTHER DAY.
BOW BOW BOW
NO NEED. THE FAULT WAS MINE.
OH. OKAY, WELL... WHERE'S EVANGELINE-SAN?
......
THE MISTRESS IS SICK.
CONSIDERING NO SELF-RESPECTING GERM WOULD GET WITHIN TEN FEET OF HER, I KIND OF DOUBT THAT.
VERY DROLL, SENSEI... BUT NOT WITHOUT SOME TRUTH.
REAL SMART SHOWING UP HERE ALONE.
MY POWERS MAY NOT BE UP TO SNUFF, BUT I CAN STILL STRANGLE YOU BARE HANDED WITHOUT MUCH EFFORT.
HA HA
SSSHHHH
MISTRESS, YOU SHOULDN'T BE OUT OF BED...
EVANGELINE-SAN!

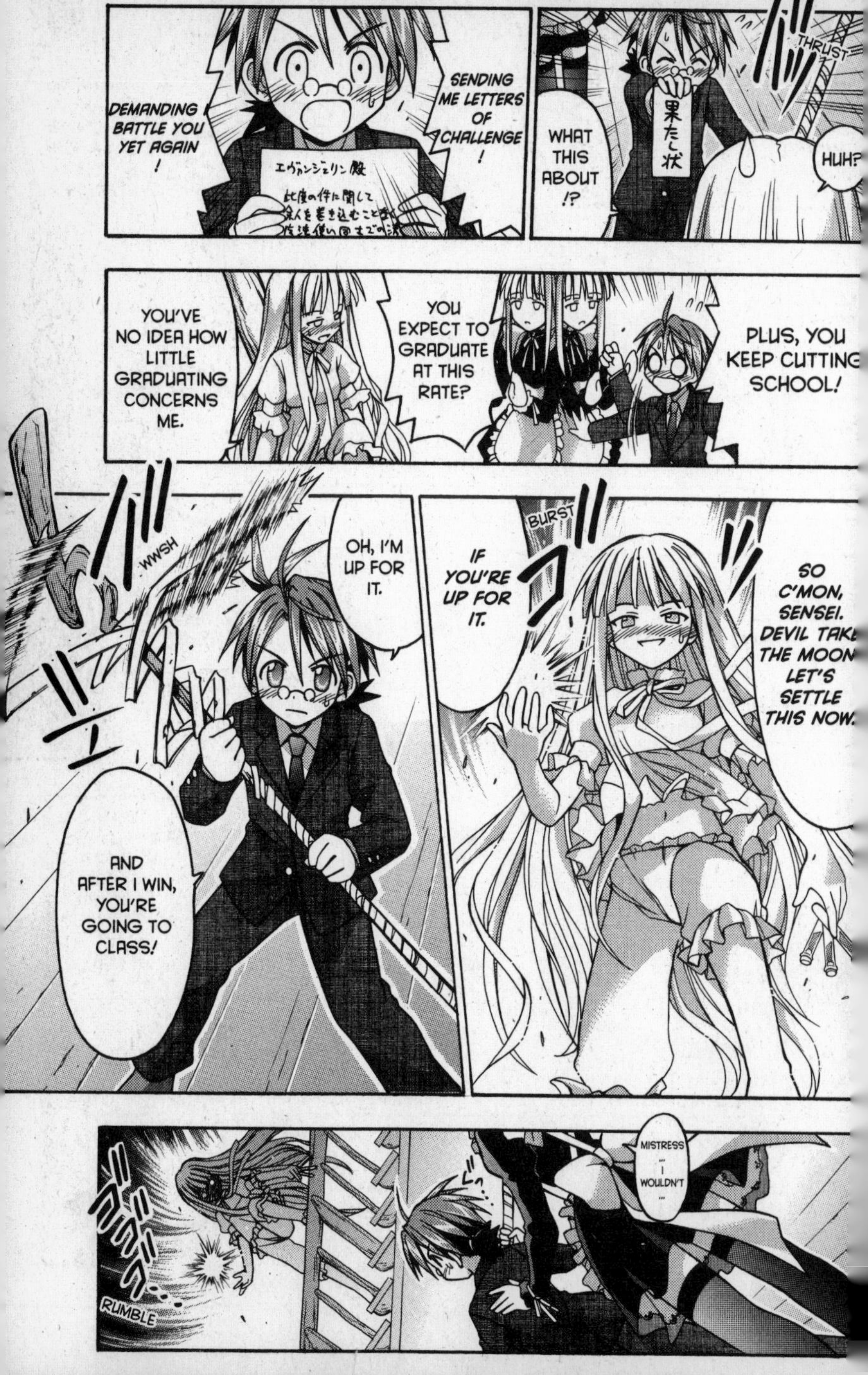
THRUST
果たし状
HUH?
WHAT THIS ABOUT !?
SENDING ME LETTERS OF CHALLENGE !
DEMANDING I BATTLE YOU YET AGAIN !
エヴァンジェリン殿
PLUS, YOU KEEP CUTTING SCHOOL!
YOU EXPECT TO GRADUATE AT THIS RATE?
YOU'VE NO IDEA HOW LITTLE GRADUATING CONCERNS ME.
SO C'MON, SENSEI. DEVIL TAKE THE MOON LET'S SETTLE THIS NOW.
BURST
IF YOU'RE UP FOR IT.
OH, I'M UP FOR IT.
WWSH
AND AFTER I WIN, YOU'RE GOING TO CLASS!
MISTRESS ... I WOULDN'T ...
RUMBLE

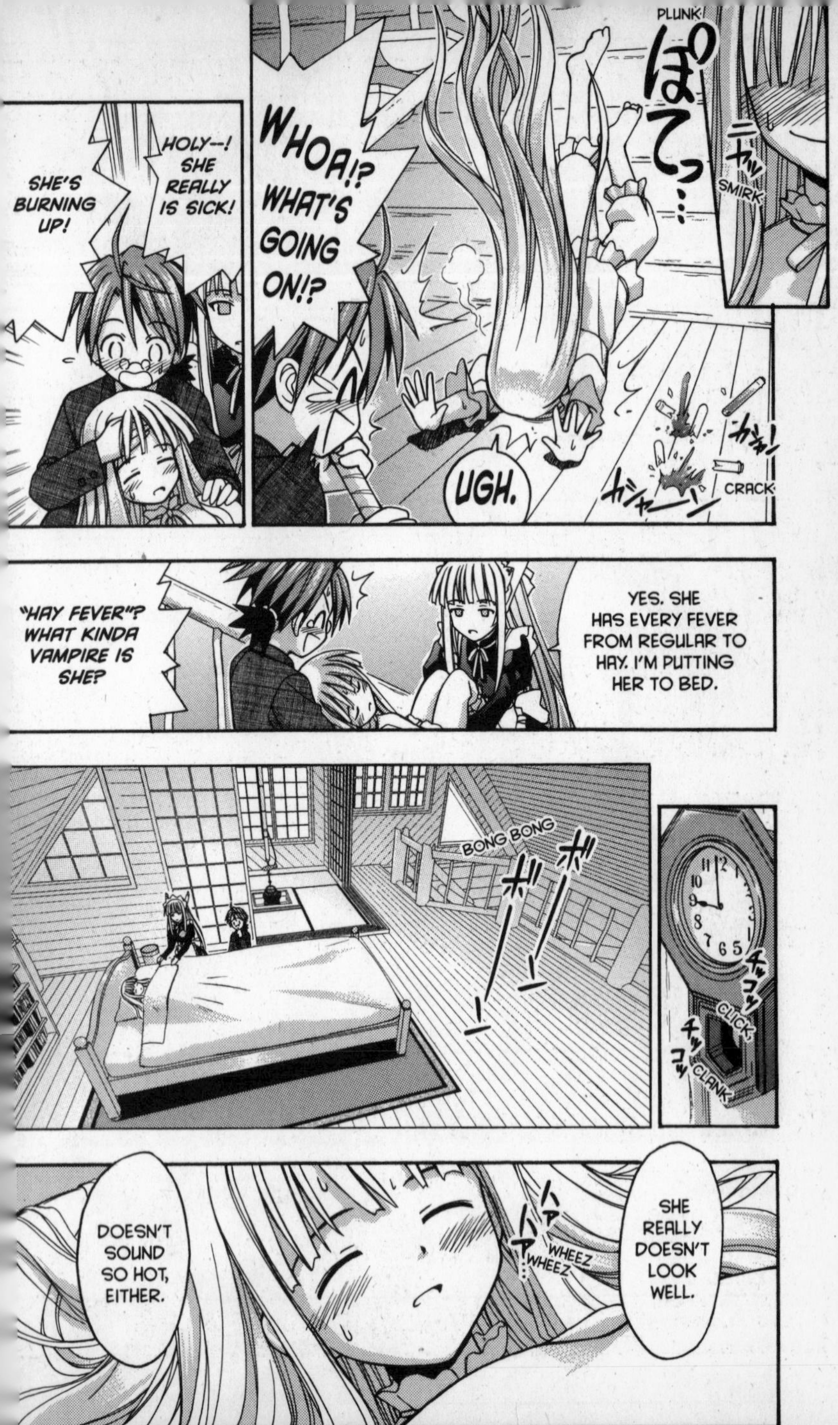
ニヤッ
SMIRK
PLUNK
ぽてっ…
WHOA!? WHAT'S GOING ON!?
UGH.
CRACK
HOLY--! SHE REALLY IS SICK!
SHE'S BURNING UP!
YES. SHE HAS EVERY FEVER FROM REGULAR TO HAY. I'M PUTTING HER TO BED.
"HAY FEVER"? WHAT KINDA VAMPIRE IS SHE?
CLICK
CLANK
BONG BONG
SHE REALLY DOESN'T LOOK WELL.
WHEEZ
WHEEZ
DOESN'T SOUND SO HOT, EITHER.

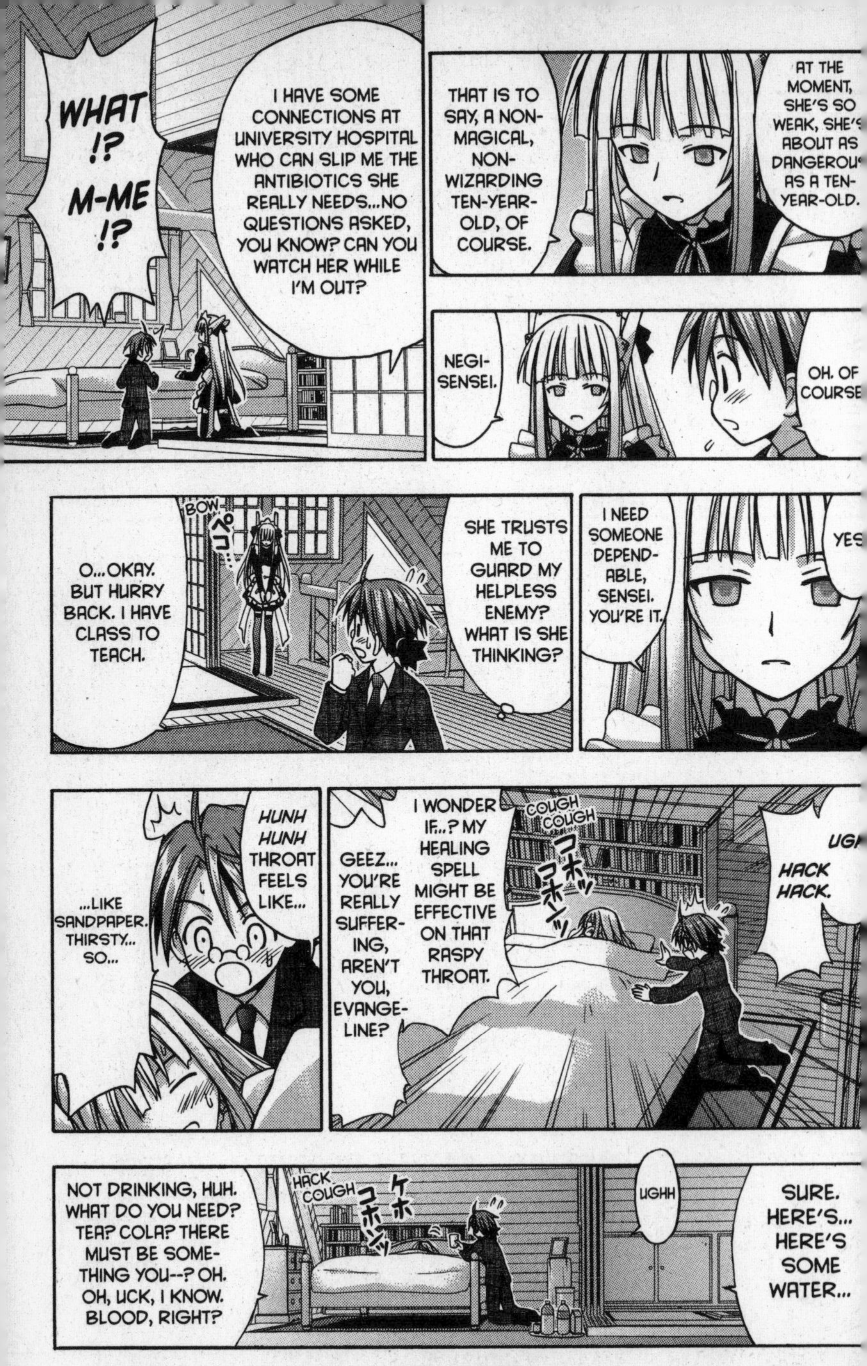

AT THE MOMENT, SHE'S SO WEAK, SHE'S ABOUT AS DANGEROUS AS A TEN-YEAR-OLD.
THAT IS TO SAY, A NON-MAGICAL, NON-WIZARDING TEN-YEAR-OLD, OF COURSE.
OH. OF COURSE
NEGI-SENSEI.
I HAVE SOME CONNECTIONS AT UNIVERSITY HOSPITAL WHO CAN SLIP ME THE ANTIBIOTICS SHE REALLY NEEDS...NO QUESTIONS ASKED, YOU KNOW? CAN YOU WATCH HER WHILE I'M OUT?
WHAT!? M-ME!?
YES
I NEED SOMEONE DEPENDABLE, SENSEI. YOU'RE IT.
SHE TRUSTS ME TO GUARD MY HELPLESS ENEMY? WHAT IS SHE THINKING?
BOW
ペコ
O...OKAY. BUT HURRY BACK. I HAVE CLASS TO TEACH.
HACK HACK.
COUGH COUGH
コホッ コホンッ
I WONDER IF...? MY HEALING SPELL MIGHT BE EFFECTIVE ON THAT RASPY THROAT.
GEEZ... YOU'RE REALLY SUFFERING, AREN'T YOU, EVANGELINE?
HUNH HUNH THROAT FEELS LIKE...
...LIKE SANDPAPER. THIRSTY... SO...
SURE. HERE'S... HERE'S SOME WATER...
UGHH
HACK COUGH
ケホ コホンッ
NOT DRINKING, HUH. WHAT DO YOU NEED? TEA? COLA? THERE MUST BE SOME-THING YOU--? OH. OH, UCK, I KNOW. BLOOD, RIGHT?

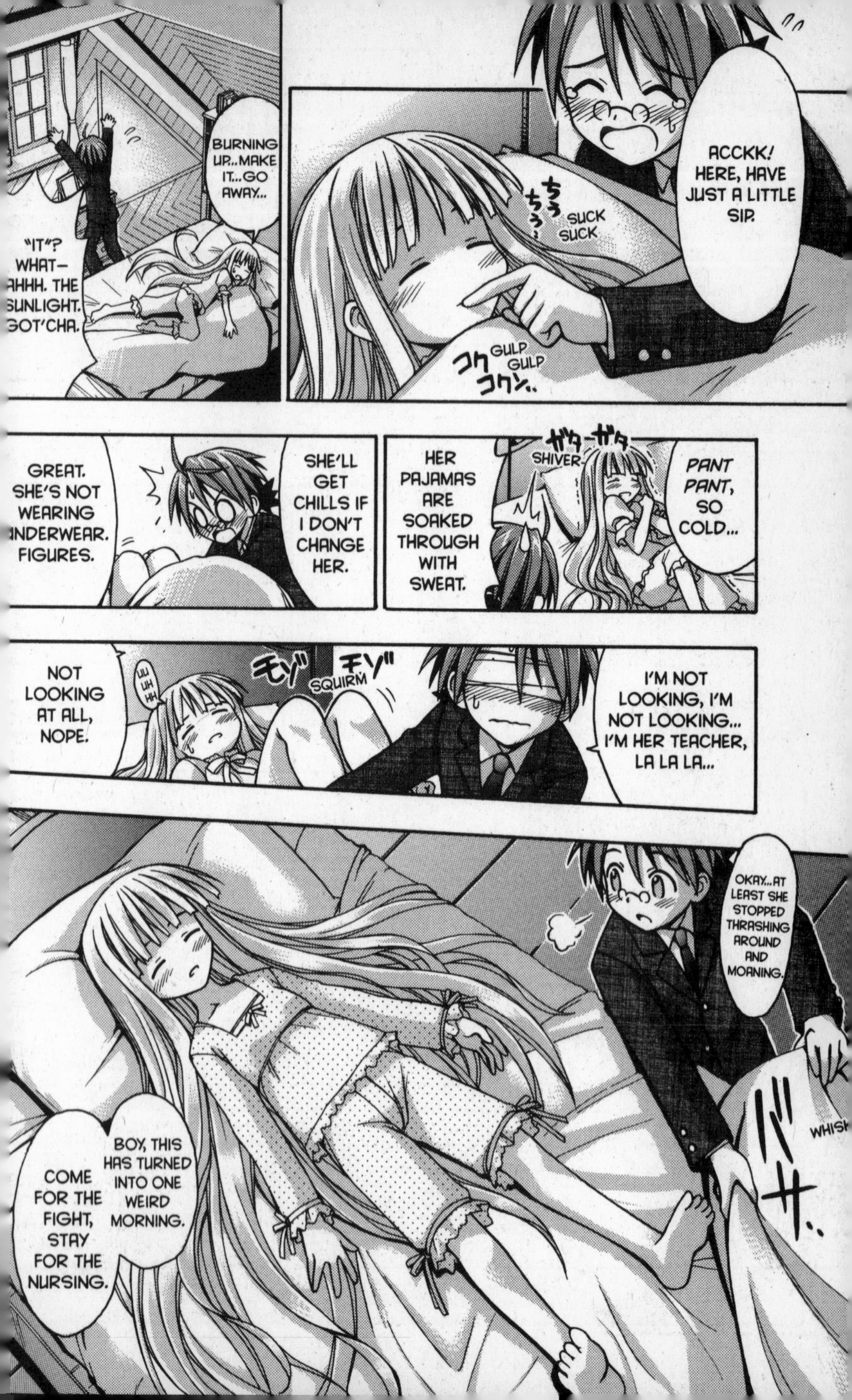
ACCKK! HERE, HAVE JUST A LITTLE SIP.
ちう ちう
SUCK SUCK
コク コクン
GULP GULP
BURNING UP...MAKE IT...GO AWAY...
"IT"? WHAT— AHHH. THE SUNLIGHT. GOT'CHA.
PANT PANT, SO COLD...
ガタガタ
SHIVER
HER PAJAMAS ARE SOAKED THROUGH WITH SWEAT.
SHE'LL GET CHILLS IF I DON'T CHANGE HER.
GREAT. SHE'S NOT WEARING UNDERWEAR. FIGURES.
I'M NOT LOOKING, I'M NOT LOOKING... I'M HER TEACHER, LA LA LA...
モゾ モゾ
SQUIRM
UU UH HH
NOT LOOKING AT ALL, NOPE.
OKAY...AT LEAST SHE STOPPED THRASHING AROUND AND MORNING.
バサ..
WHISH
BOY, THIS HAS TURNED INTO ONE WEIRD MORNING.
COME FOR THE FIGHT, STAY FOR THE NURSING.

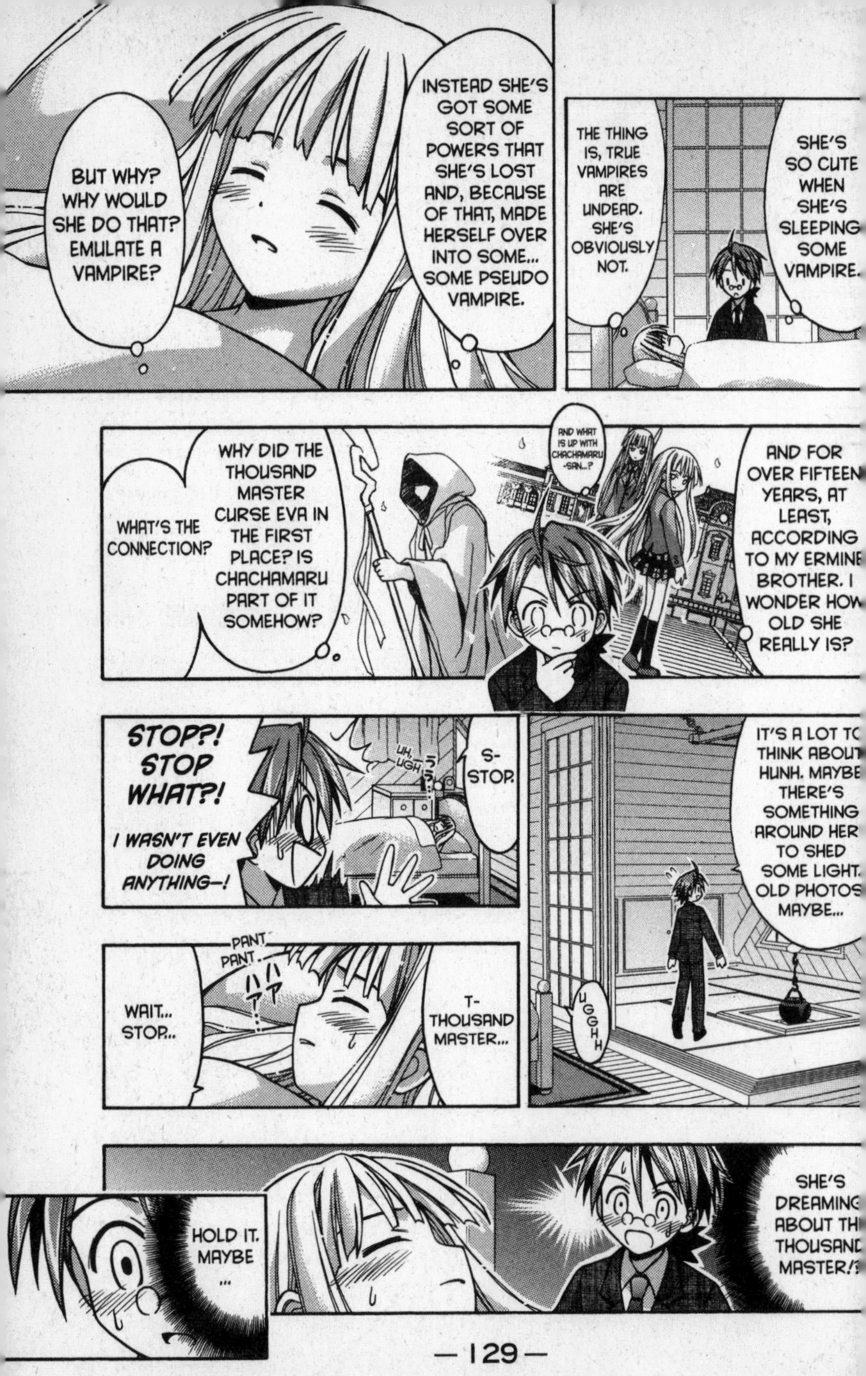
SHE'S SO CUTE WHEN SHE'S SLEEPING SOME VAMPIRE.
THE THING IS, TRUE VAMPIRES ARE UNDEAD. SHE'S OBVIOUSLY NOT.
INSTEAD SHE'S GOT SOME SORT OF POWERS THAT SHE'S LOST AND, BECAUSE OF THAT, MADE HERSELF OVER INTO SOME... SOME PSEUDO VAMPIRE.
BUT WHY? WHY WOULD SHE DO THAT? EMULATE A VAMPIRE?
AND FOR OVER FIFTEEN YEARS, AT LEAST, ACCORDING TO MY ERMINE BROTHER. I WONDER HOW OLD SHE REALLY IS?
AND WHAT IS UP WITH CHACHAMARU-SAN...?
WHY DID THE THOUSAND MASTER CURSE EVA IN THE FIRST PLACE? IS CHACHAMARU PART OF IT SOMEHOW?
WHAT'S THE CONNECTION?
IT'S A LOT TO THINK ABOUT HUNH. MAYBE THERE'S SOMETHING AROUND HER TO SHED SOME LIGHT. OLD PHOTOS MAYBE...
UGGHH
S-STOP.
UH, UGH
STOP?! STOP WHAT?!
I WASN'T EVEN DOING ANYTHING—!
T-THOUSAND MASTER...
PANT PANT
WAIT... STOP...
SHE'S DREAMING ABOUT THE THOUSAND MASTER!?
HOLD IT. MAYBE ...

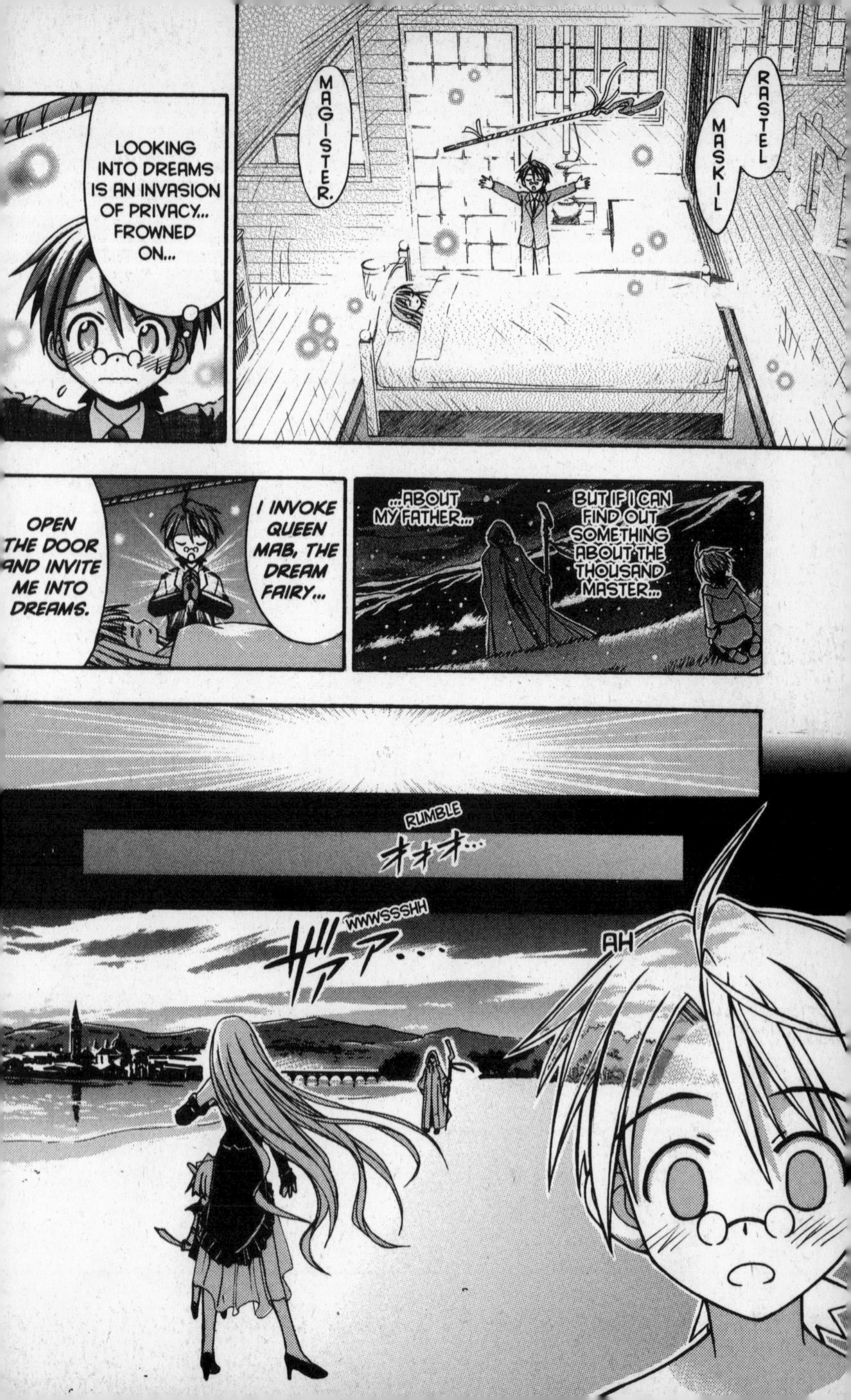
RASTEL MASKIL
MAGISTER.
LOOKING INTO DREAMS IS AN INVASION OF PRIVACY... FROWNED ON...
BUT IF I CAN FIND OUT SOMETHING ABOUT THE THOUSAND MASTER...
...ABOUT MY FATHER...
I INVOKE QUEEN MAB, THE DREAM FAIRY...
OPEN THE DOOR AND INVITE ME INTO DREAMS.
RUMBLE
オオオ...
WWWSSSHH
ザァア...
AH

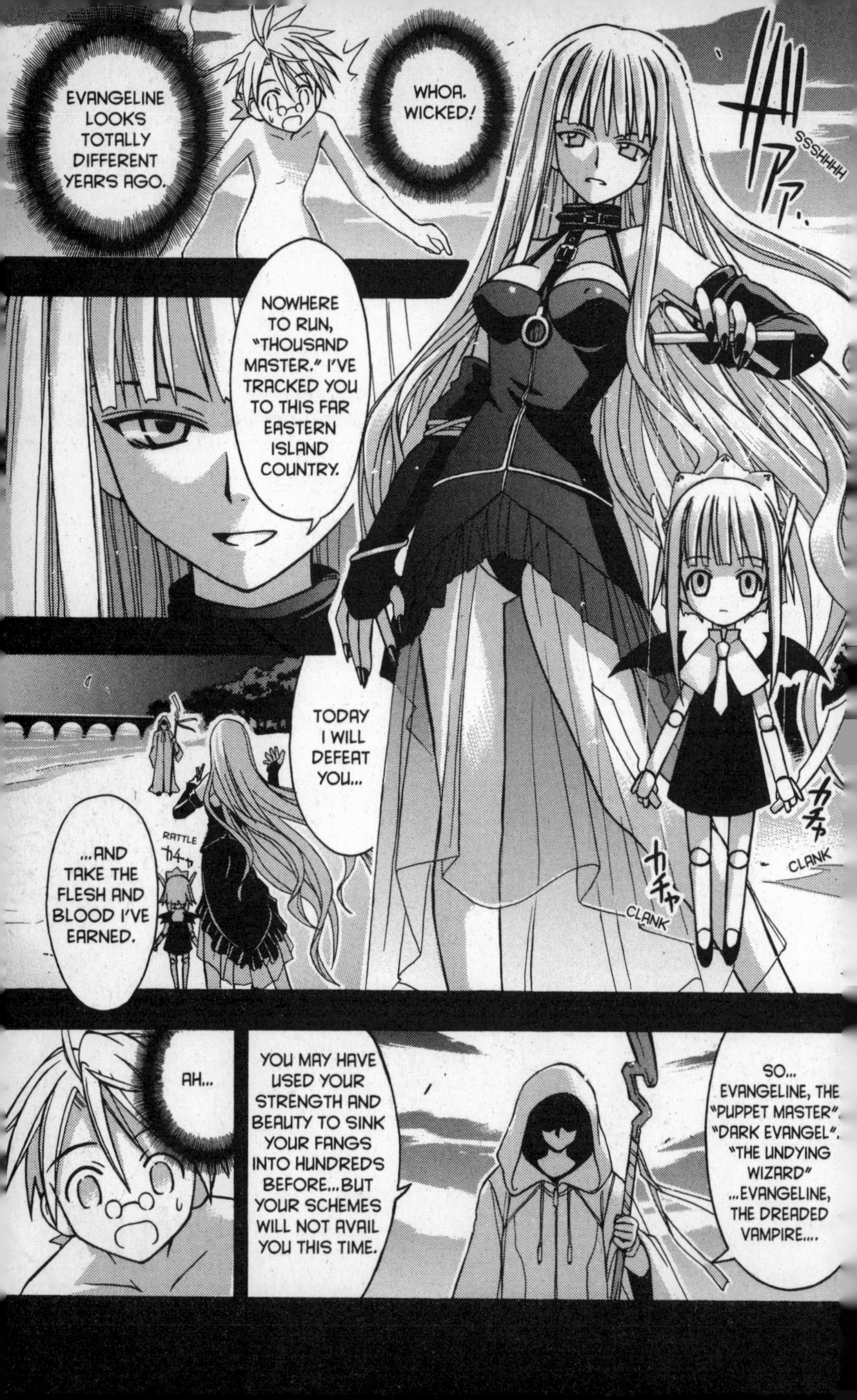
SSSHHHH
WHOA. WICKED!
EVANGELINE LOOKS TOTALLY DIFFERENT YEARS AGO.
NOWHERE TO RUN, "THOUSAND MASTER." I'VE TRACKED YOU TO THIS FAR EASTERN ISLAND COUNTRY.
CLANK
CLANK
TODAY I WILL DEFEAT YOU...
RATTLE
...AND TAKE THE FLESH AND BLOOD I'VE EARNED.
SO... EVANGELINE, THE "PUPPET MASTER", "DARK EVANGEL", "THE UNDYING WIZARD" ...EVANGELINE, THE DREADED VAMPIRE....
YOU MAY HAVE USED YOUR STRENGTH AND BEAUTY TO SINK YOUR FANGS INTO HUNDREDS BEFORE...BUT YOUR SCHEMES WILL NOT AVAIL YOU THIS TIME.
AH...

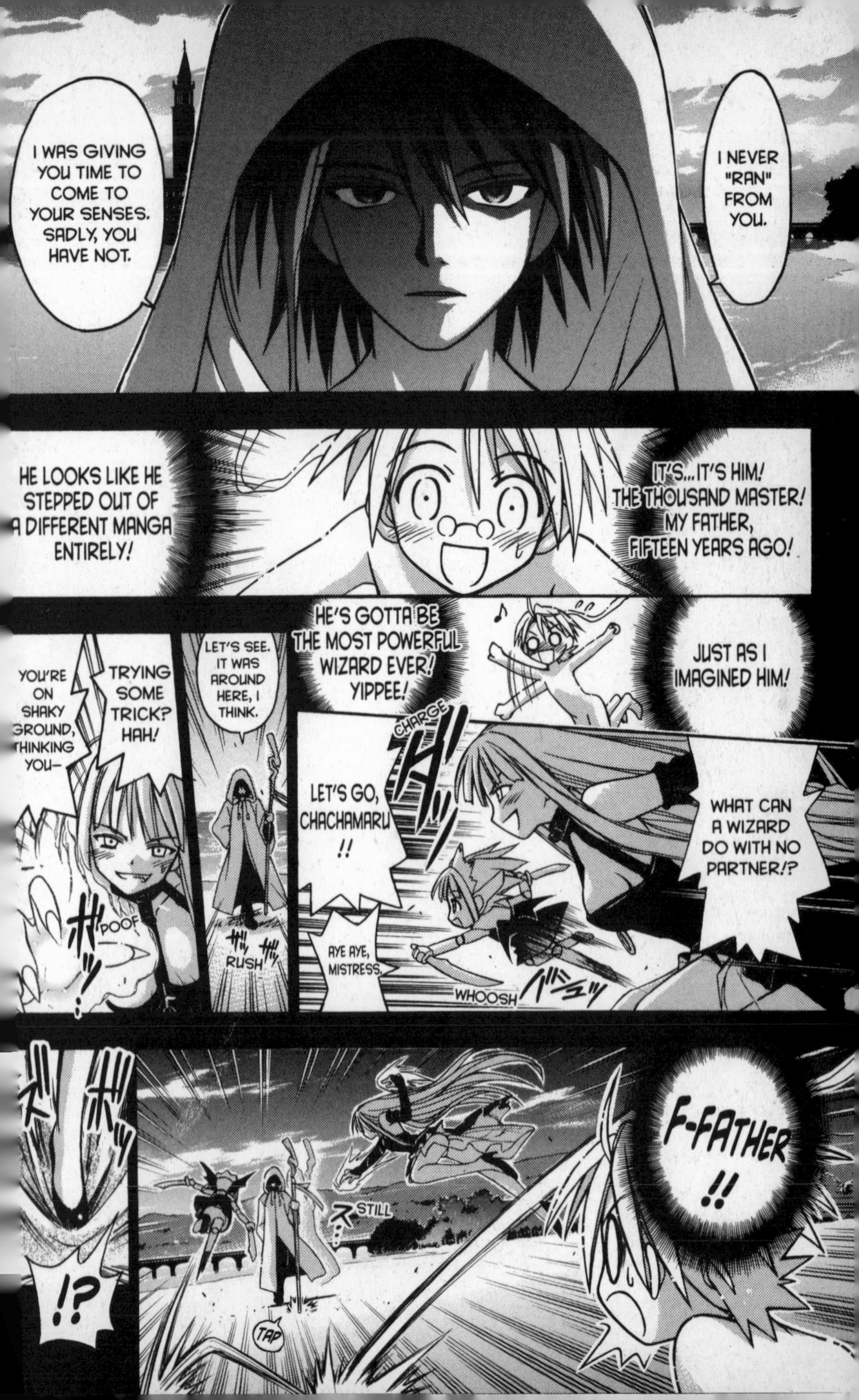
I NEVER "RAN" FROM YOU.
I WAS GIVING YOU TIME TO COME TO YOUR SENSES. SADLY, YOU HAVE NOT.
IT'S...IT'S HIM! THE THOUSAND MASTER! MY FATHER, FIFTEEN YEARS AGO!
HE LOOKS LIKE HE STEPPED OUT OF A DIFFERENT MANGA ENTIRELY!
JUST AS I IMAGINED HIM!
HE'S GOTTA BE THE MOST POWERFUL WIZARD EVER! YIPPEE!
WHAT CAN A WIZARD DO WITH NO PARTNER!?
CHARGE
LET'S GO, CHACHAMARU!!
AYE AYE, MISTRESS.
WHOOSH
LET'S SEE. IT WAS AROUND HERE, I THINK.
RUSH
TRYING SOME TRICK? HAH!
YOU'RE ON SHAKY GROUND, THINKING YOU—
POOF
F-FATHER!!
STILL
TAP
!?

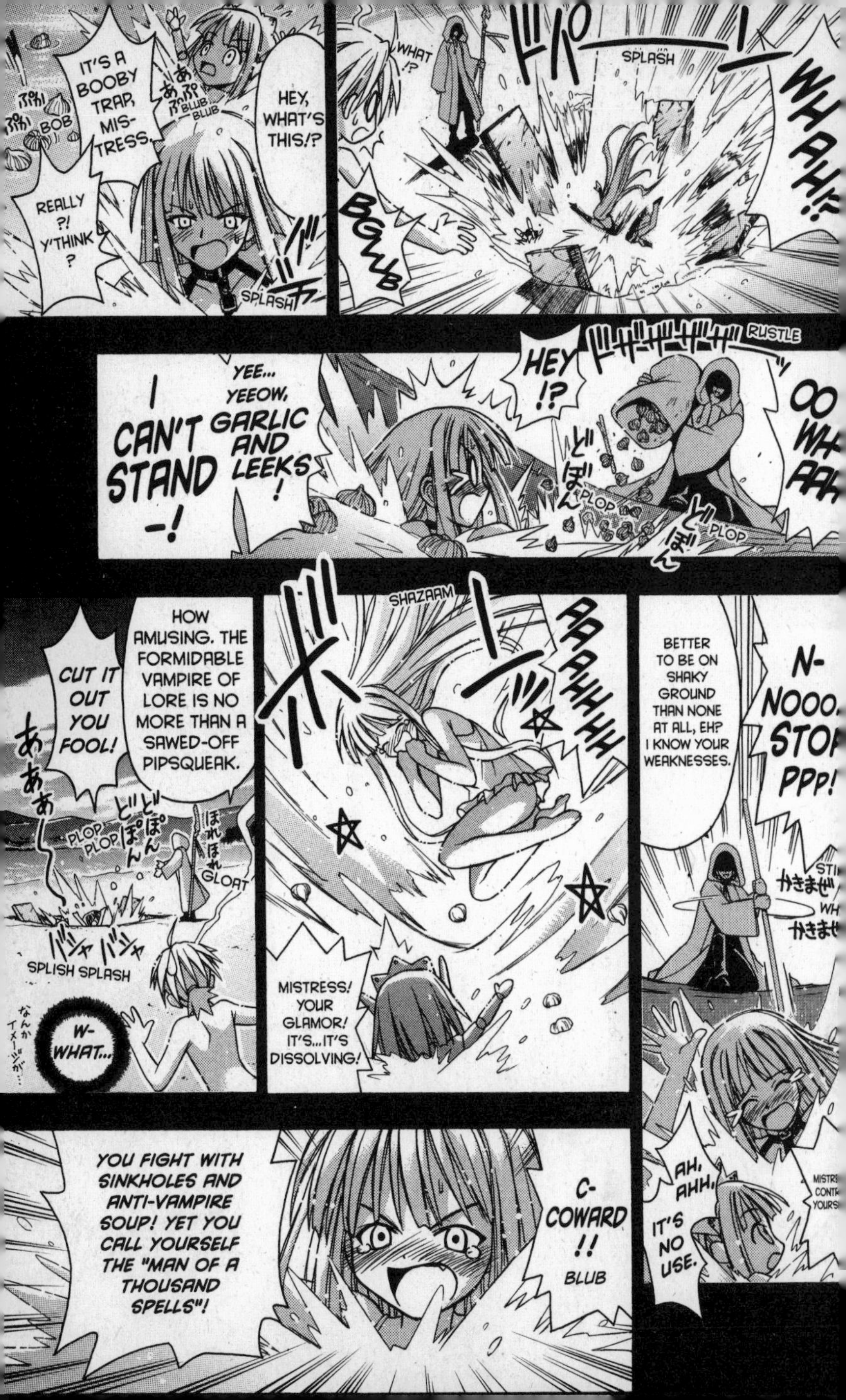

WHAT !?
ドパー
SPLASH
WHAAAH!!?
BGLUB
HEY, WHAT'S THIS!?
あぷあぷ
BLUB BLUB
IT'S A BOOBY TRAP, MISTRESS.
ぷか! ぷか!
BOB
REALLY ?! Y'THINK ?
SPLASH
ドザザーザザー
RUSTLE
OOWHAAAH
HEY !?
どぼん
PLOP
どぼん
PLOP
YEE... YEEOW, GARLIC AND LEEKS!
I CAN'T STAND -!
BETTER TO BE ON SHAKY GROUND THAN NONE AT ALL, EH? I KNOW YOUR WEAKNESSES.
N-NOOO, STOPPPP!
かきまぜ
かきまぜ
SHAZAAM
AAAAHHHH
MISTRESS! YOUR GLAMOR! IT'S...IT'S DISSOLVING!
HOW AMUSING. THE FORMIDABLE VAMPIRE OF LORE IS NO MORE THAN A SAWED-OFF PIPSQUEAK.
CUT IT OUT YOU FOOL!
あああ
どぽん どぽん
PLOP PLOP
ほれほれ
GLOAT
バシャバシャ
SPLISH SPLASH
なんかイメージが…
W-WHAT...
AH, AHH, IT'S NO USE.
C-COWARD !!
BLUB
YOU FIGHT WITH SINKHOLES AND ANTI-VAMPIRE SOUP! YET YOU CALL YOURSELF THE "MAN OF A THOUSAND SPELLS"!

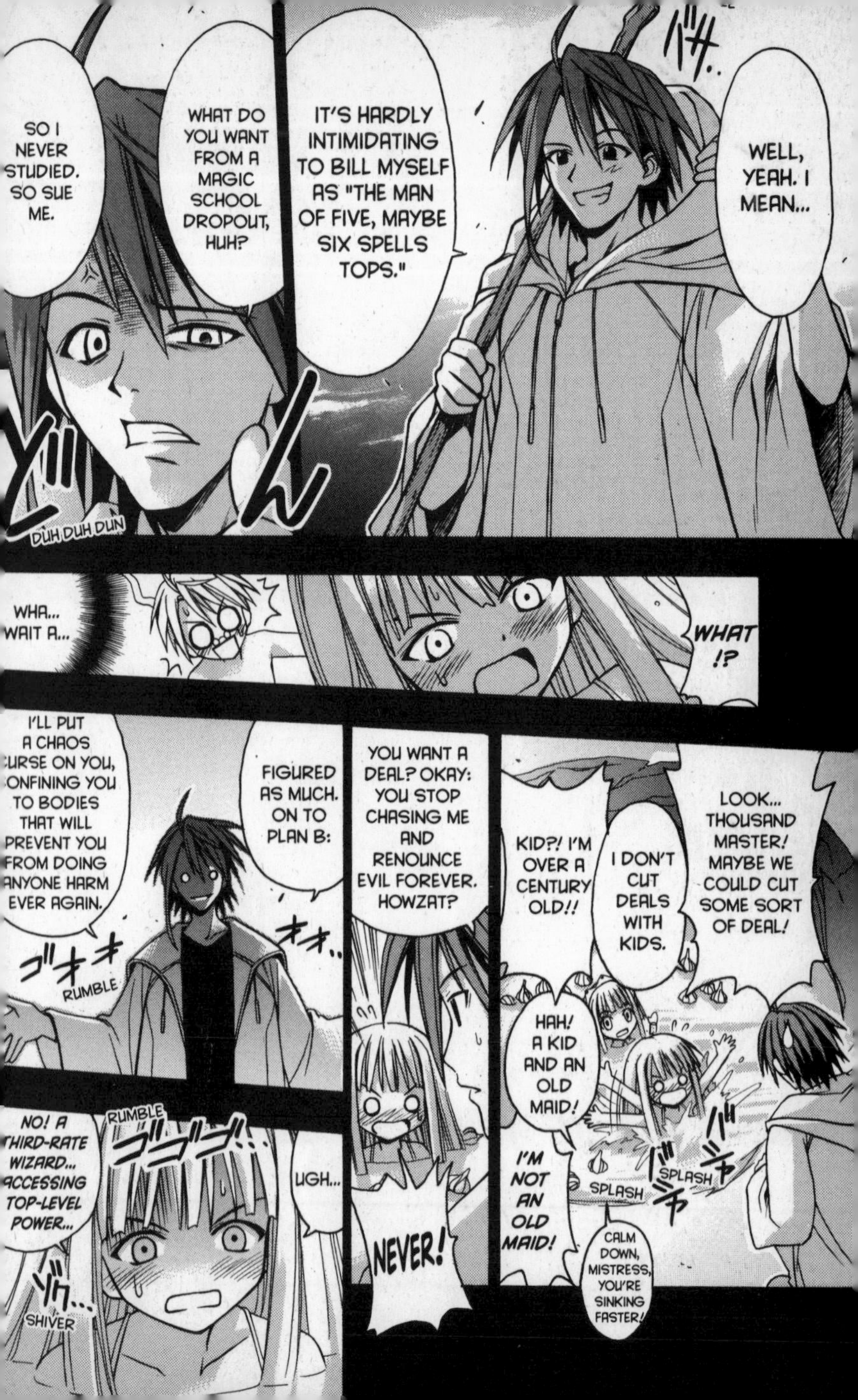
WELL, YEAH. I MEAN...
IT'S HARDLY INTIMIDATING TO BILL MYSELF AS "THE MAN OF FIVE, MAYBE SIX SPELLS TOPS."
WHAT DO YOU WANT FROM A MAGIC SCHOOL DROPOUT, HUH?
SO I NEVER STUDIED. SO SUE ME.
DUH DUH DUN
WHAT!?
WHA... WAIT A...
LOOK... THOUSAND MASTER! MAYBE WE COULD CUT SOME SORT OF DEAL!
I DON'T CUT DEALS WITH KIDS.
KID?! I'M OVER A CENTURY OLD!!
HAH! A KID AND AN OLD MAID!
SPLASH
SPLASH
I'M NOT AN OLD MAID!
CALM DOWN, MISTRESS, YOU'RE SINKING FASTER!
YOU WANT A DEAL? OKAY: YOU STOP CHASING ME AND RENOUNCE EVIL FOREVER. HOWZAT?
NEVER!
FIGURED AS MUCH. ON TO PLAN B:
I'LL PUT A CHAOS URSE ON YOU, ONFINING YOU TO BODIES THAT WILL PREVENT YOU FROM DOING NYONE HARM EVER AGAIN.
RUMBLE
UGH...
RUMBLE
NO! A THIRD-RATE WIZARD... ACCESSING TOP-LEVEL POWER...
SHIVER

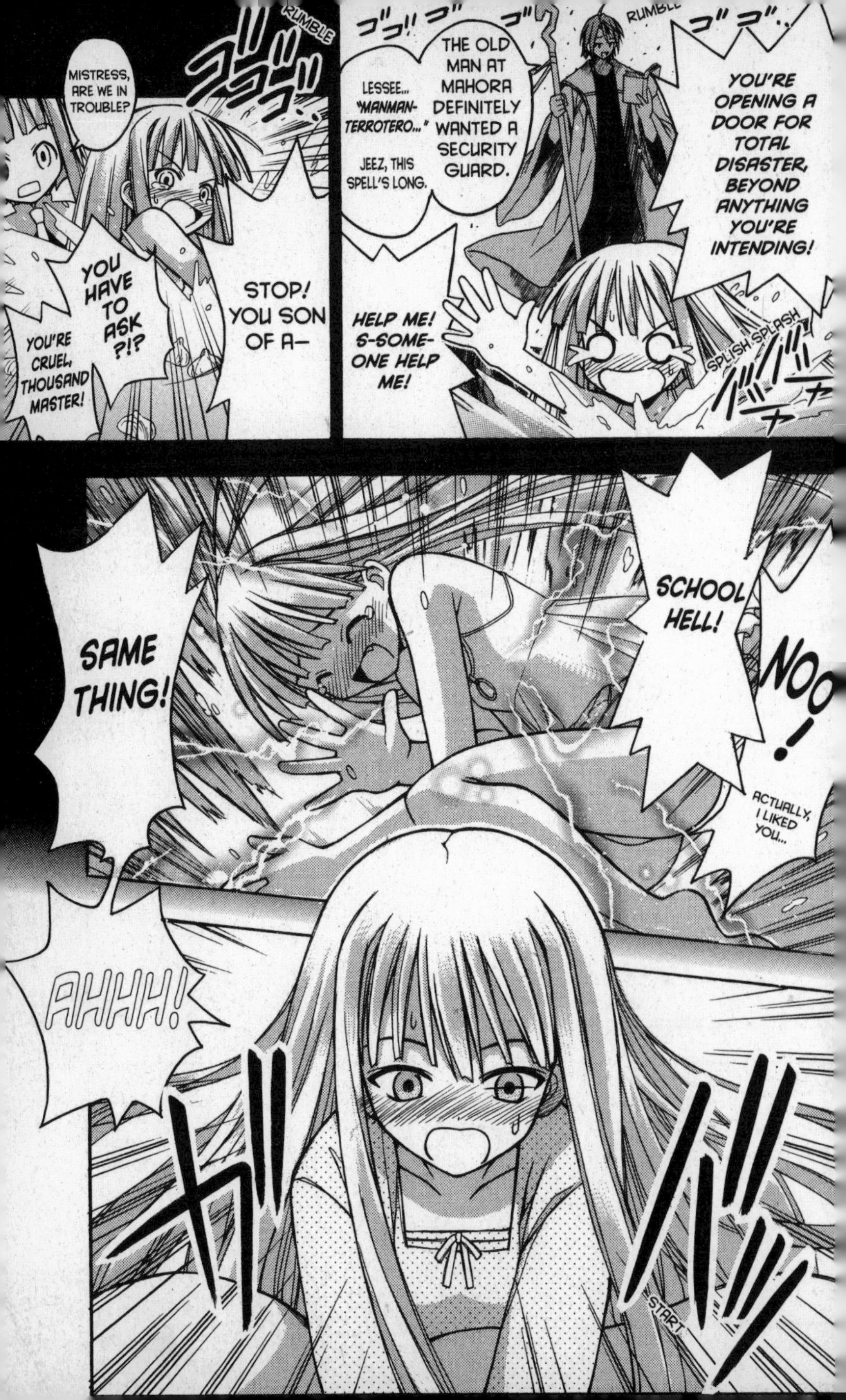
RUMBLE
YOU'RE OPENING A DOOR FOR TOTAL DISASTER, BEYOND ANYTHING YOU'RE INTENDING!
THE OLD MAN AT MAHORA DEFINITELY WANTED A SECURITY GUARD.
LESSEE... "MANMAN-TERROTERO..."
JEEZ, THIS SPELL'S LONG.
HELP ME! S-SOME-ONE HELP ME!
SPLISH SPLASH
RUMBLE
MISTRESS, ARE WE IN TROUBLE?
YOU HAVE TO ASK?!?
STOP! YOU SON OF A—
YOU'RE CRUEL, THOUSAND MASTER!
SCHOOL HELL!
NOO!
ACTUALLY, I LIKED YOU...
SAME THING!
AHHH!
START

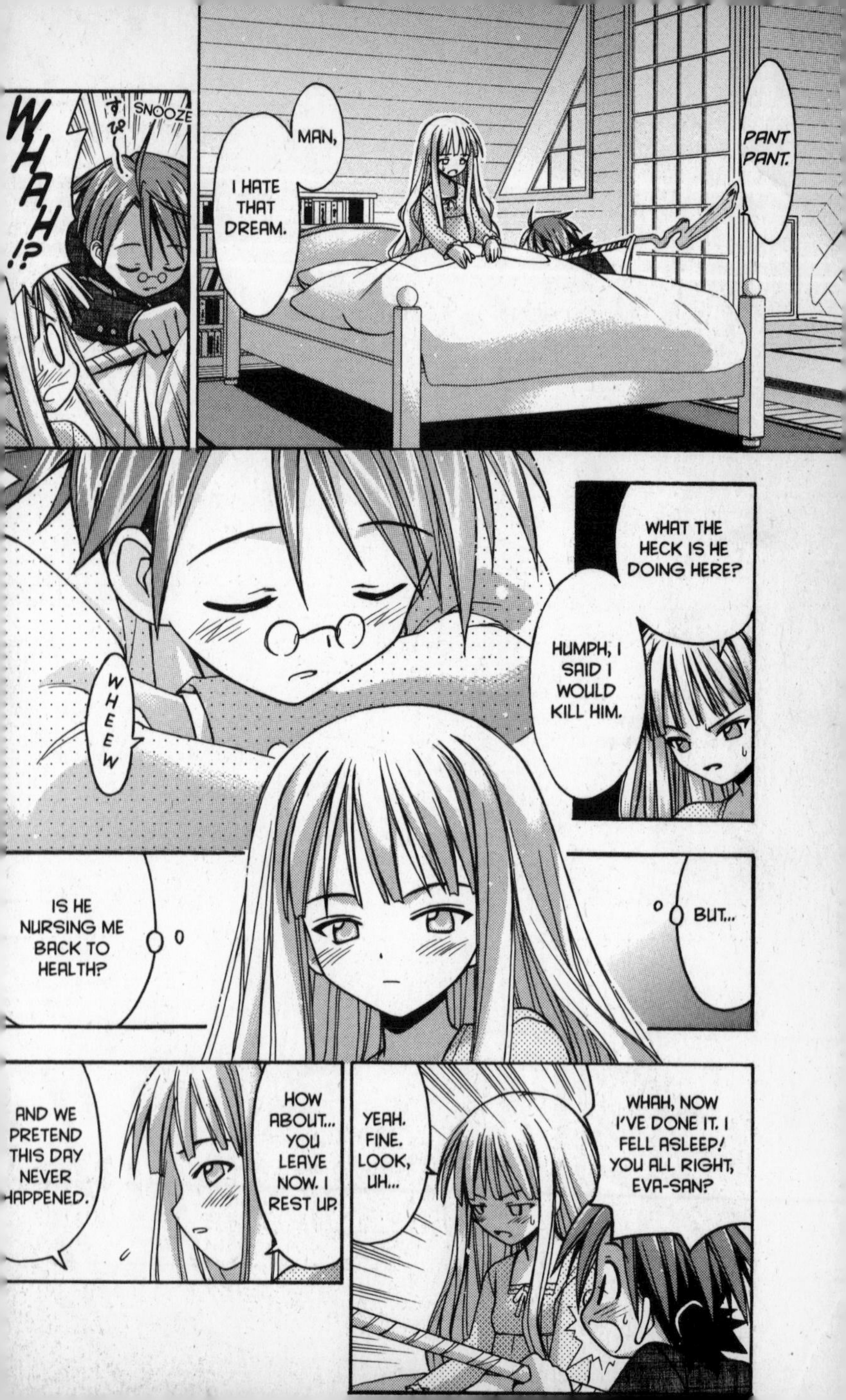
PANT PANT.
MAN,
I HATE THAT DREAM.
すぴ
SNOOZE
WHAH!?
WHAT THE HECK IS HE DOING HERE?
HUMPH, I SAID I WOULD KILL HIM.
WHEEEW
BUT...
IS HE NURSING ME BACK TO HEALTH?
WHAH, NOW I'VE DONE IT. I FELL ASLEEP! YOU ALL RIGHT, EVA-SAN?
YEAH. FINE. LOOK, UH...
HOW ABOUT... YOU LEAVE NOW. I REST UP.
AND WE PRETEND THIS DAY NEVER HAPPENED.

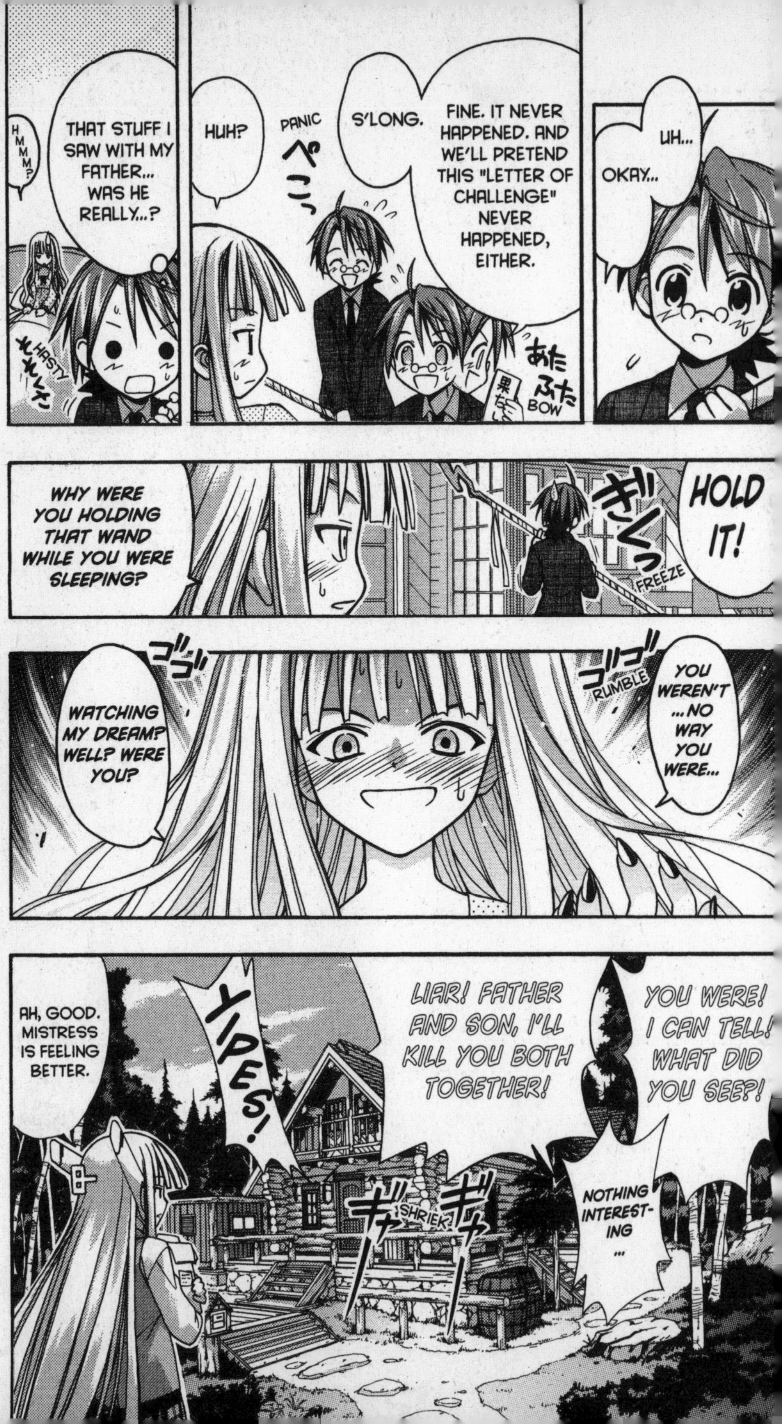
UH... OKAY...
FINE. IT NEVER HAPPENED. AND WE'LL PRETEND THIS "LETTER OF CHALLENGE" NEVER HAPPENED, EITHER.
S'LONG.
PANIC ぺこっ
HUH?
あたふた BOW
果たし
THAT STUFF I SAW WITH MY FATHER... WAS HE REALLY...?
HMMM?
HASTY そそくさ
HOLD IT!
ぎくっ FREEZE
WHY WERE YOU HOLDING THAT WAND WHILE YOU WERE SLEEPING?
YOU WEREN'T ...NO WAY YOU WERE...
ゴゴゴ RUMBLE
ゴゴ
WATCHING MY DREAM? WELL? WERE YOU?
YOU WERE! I CAN TELL! WHAT DID YOU SEE?!
LIAR! FATHER AND SON, I'LL KILL YOU BOTH TOGETHER!
YIPES!
AH, GOOD. MISTRESS IS FEELING BETTER.
NOTHING INTEREST-ING...
ギャー SHRIEK ギャー

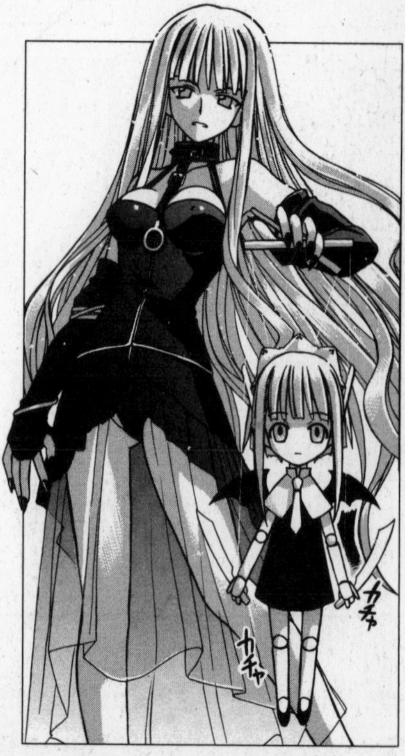
カチャ
カチャ

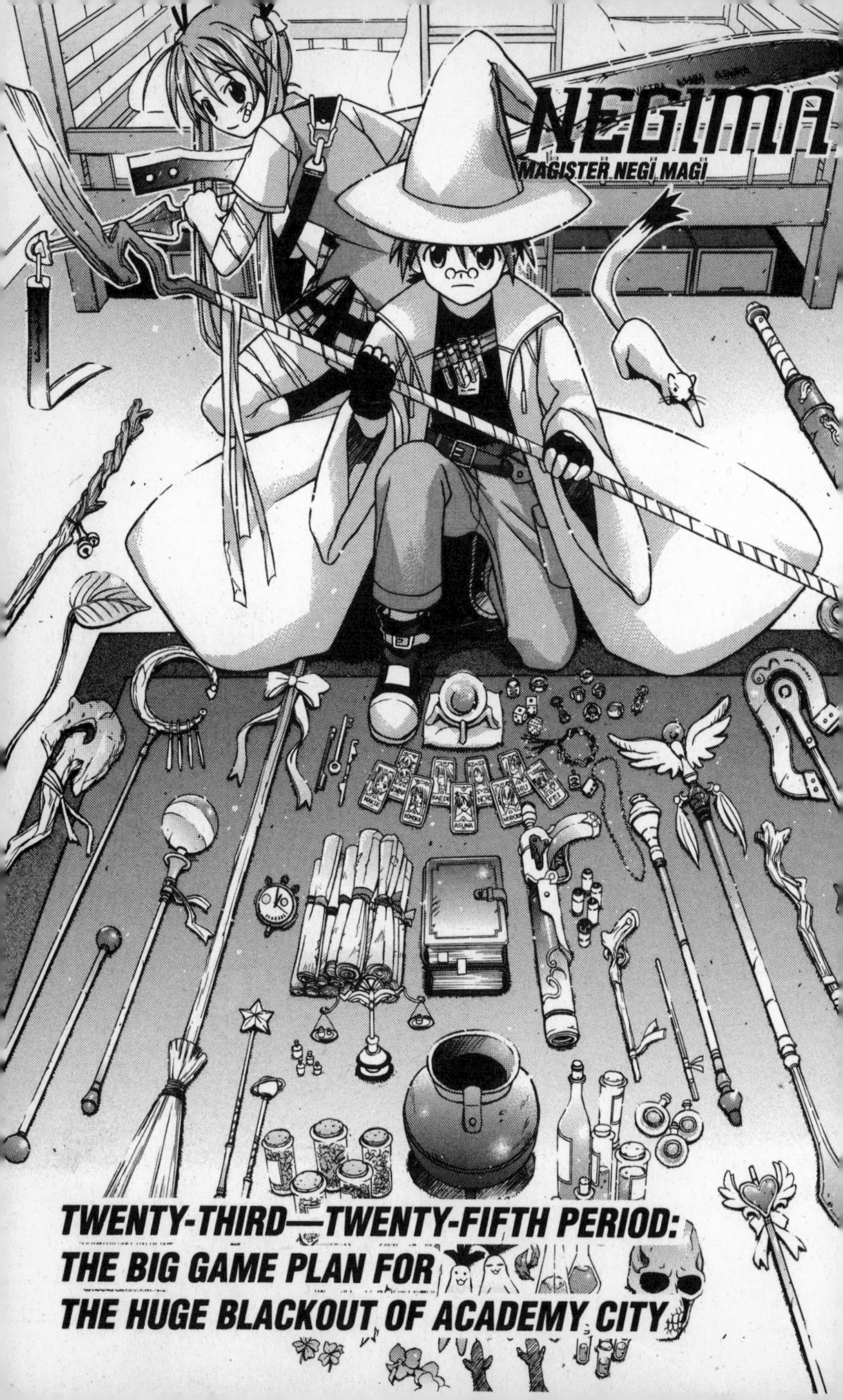
NEGIMA
MAGISTER NEGI MAGI
TWENTY-THIRD—TWENTY-FIFTH PERIOD:
THE BIG GAME PLAN FOR
THE HUGE BLACKOUT OF ACADEMY CITY

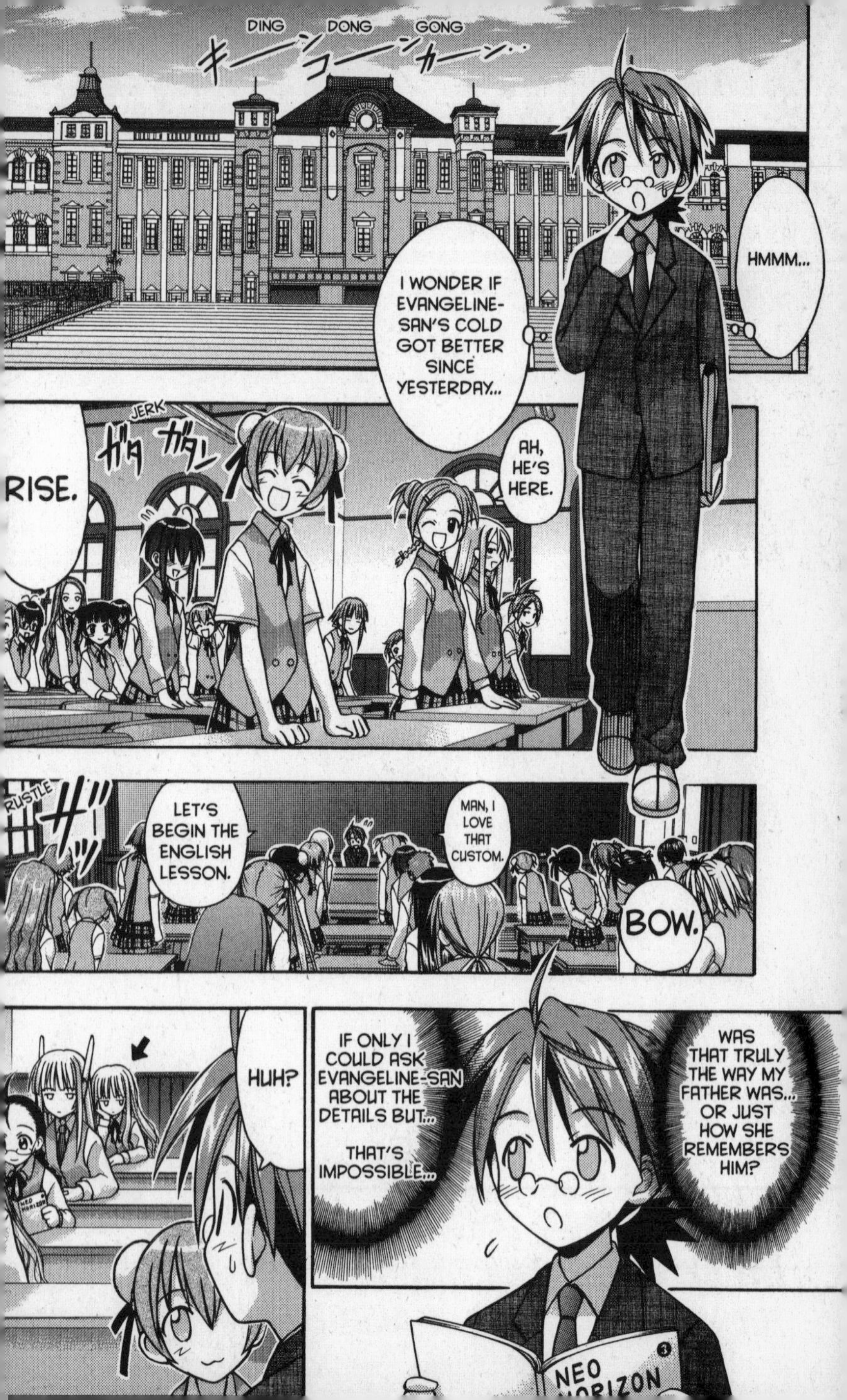

DING DONG GONG
キーンコーンカーン・・
HMMM...
I WONDER IF EVANGELINE-SAN'S COLD GOT BETTER SINCE YESTERDAY...
AH, HE'S HERE.
JERK
ガタ ガタン
RISE.
BOW.
MAN, I LOVE THAT CUSTOM.
LET'S BEGIN THE ENGLISH LESSON.
RUSTLE
WAS THAT TRULY THE WAY MY FATHER WAS... OR JUST HOW SHE REMEMBERS HIM?
IF ONLY I COULD ASK EVANGELINE-SAN ABOUT THE DETAILS BUT...
THAT'S IMPOSSIBLE...
NEO HORIZON
HUH?

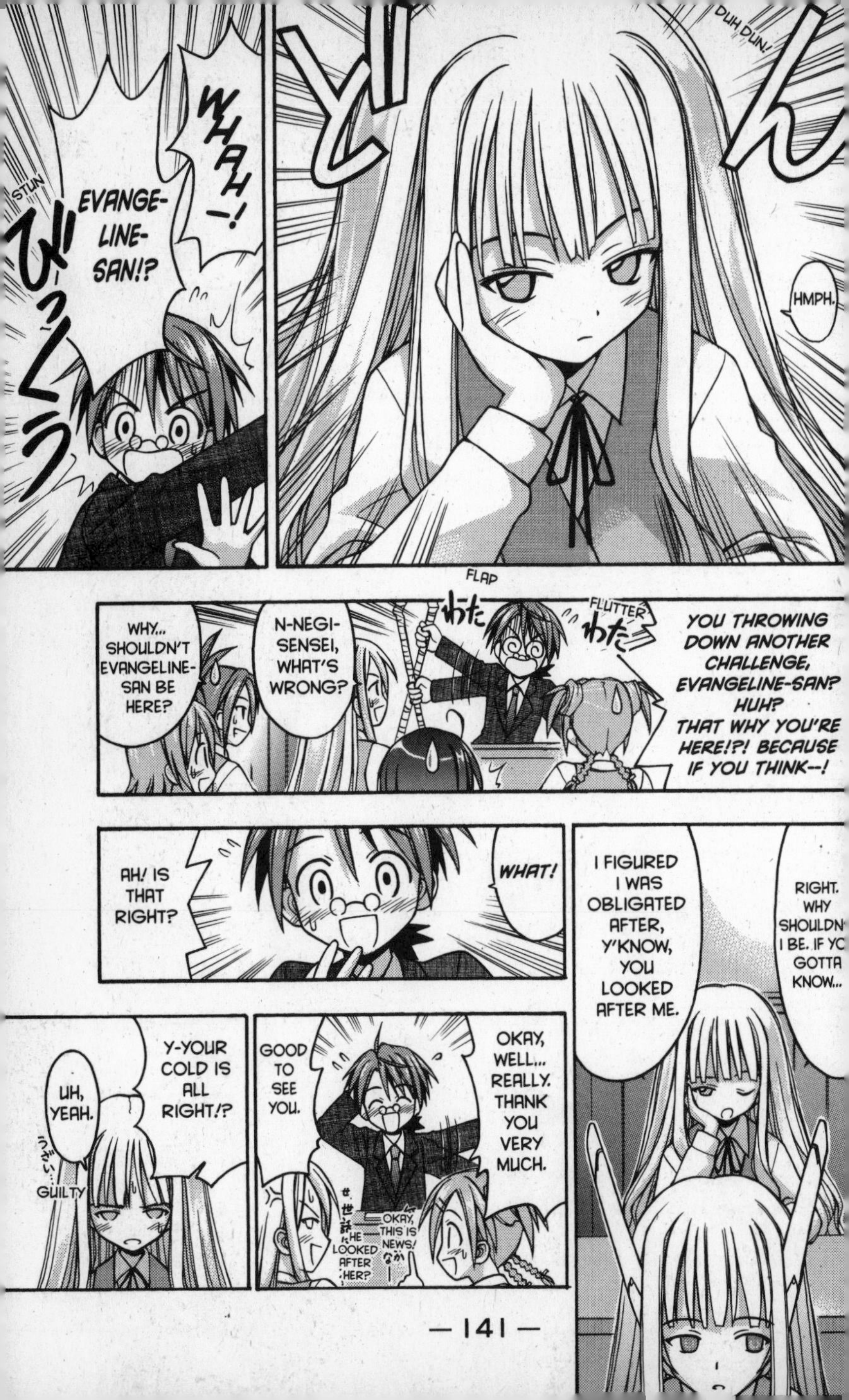
DUH DUN!
HMPH.
WHAAH--!
EVANGE-LINE-SAN!?
STUN
YOU THROWING DOWN ANOTHER CHALLENGE, EVANGELINE-SAN? HUH? THAT WHY YOU'RE HERE!?! BECAUSE IF YOU THINK--!
FLUTTER
FLAP
N-NEGI-SENSEI, WHAT'S WRONG?
WHY... SHOULDN'T EVANGELINE-SAN BE HERE?
RIGHT. WHY SHOULDN I BE. IF YO GOTTA KNOW...
I FIGURED I WAS OBLIGATED AFTER, Y'KNOW, YOU LOOKED AFTER ME.
WHAT!
AH! IS THAT RIGHT?
OKAY, WELL... REALLY. THANK YOU VERY MUCH.
GOOD TO SEE YOU.
OKAY, THIS IS NEWS!
HE LOOKED AFTER HER?
Y-YOUR COLD IS ALL RIGHT!?
UH, YEAH.
GUILTY

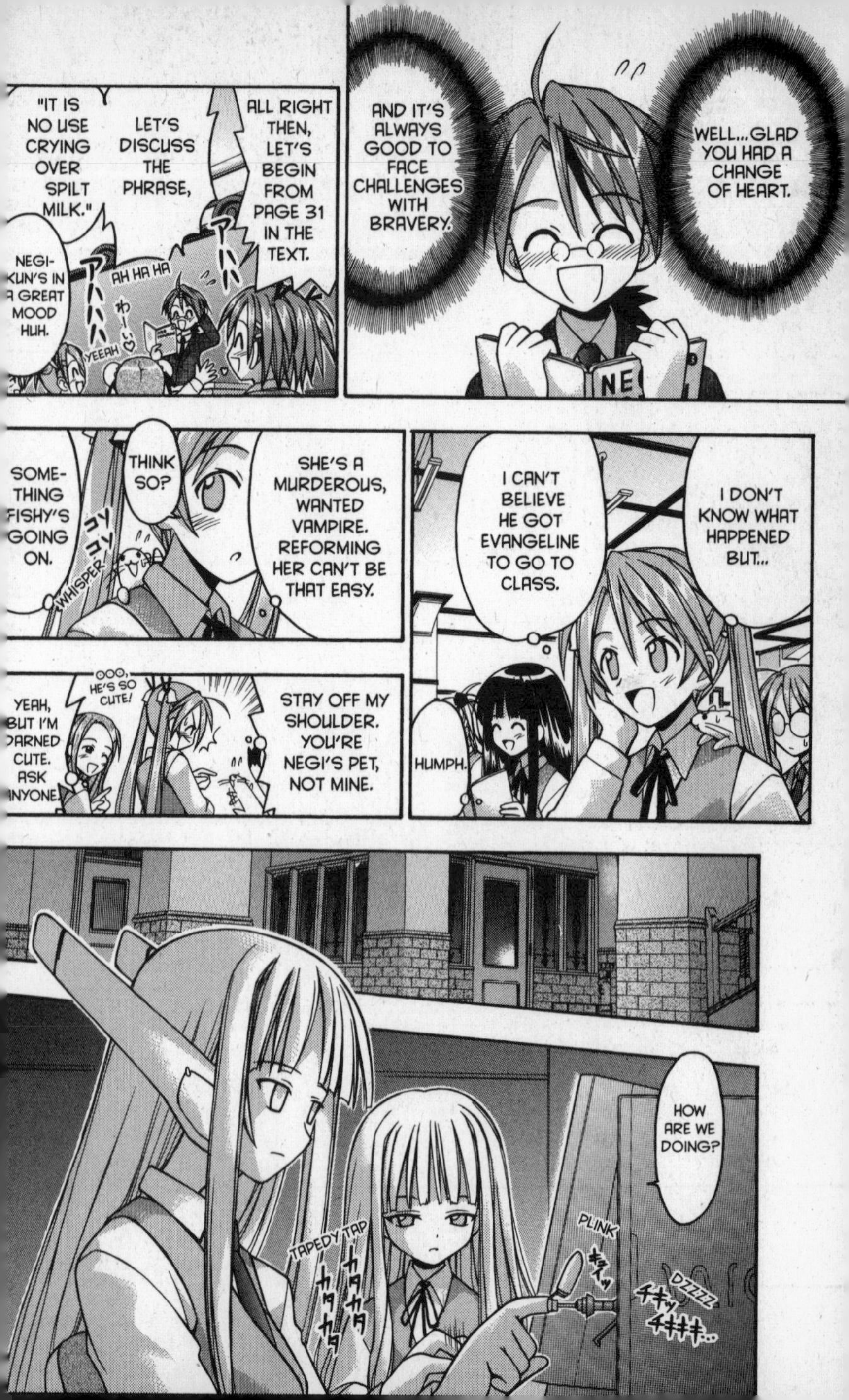
WELL...GLAD YOU HAD A CHANGE OF HEART.
AND IT'S ALWAYS GOOD TO FACE CHALLENGES WITH BRAVERY.
ALL RIGHT THEN, LET'S BEGIN FROM PAGE 31 IN THE TEXT.
LET'S DISCUSS THE PHRASE,
"IT IS NO USE CRYING OVER SPILT MILK."
AH HA HA
NEGI-KUN'S IN A GREAT MOOD HUH.
YEEAH
I DON'T KNOW WHAT HAPPENED BUT...
I CAN'T BELIEVE HE GOT EVANGELINE TO GO TO CLASS.
HUMPH.
SHE'S A MURDEROUS, WANTED VAMPIRE. REFORMING HER CAN'T BE THAT EASY.
THINK SO?
SOMETHING FISHY'S GOING ON.
WHISPER
STAY OFF MY SHOULDER. YOU'RE NEGI'S PET, NOT MINE.
OOO, HE'S SO CUTE!
YEAH, BUT I'M DARNED CUTE. ASK ANYONE.
HOW ARE WE DOING?
PLINK
DZZZZ
TAPEDY TAP

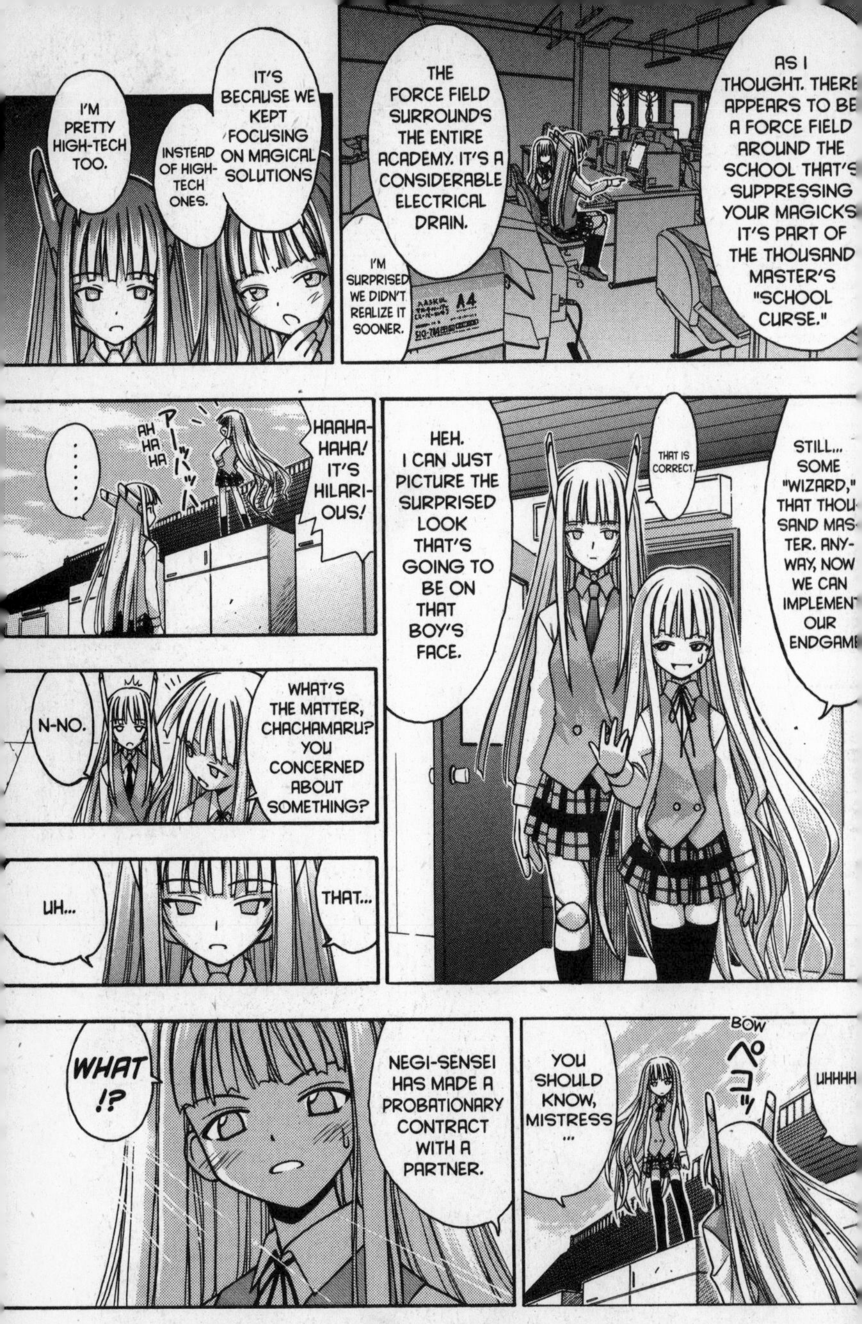
AS I THOUGHT. THERE APPEARS TO BE A FORCE FIELD AROUND THE SCHOOL THAT'S SUPPRESSING YOUR MAGICKS. IT'S PART OF THE THOUSAND MASTER'S "SCHOOL CURSE."
THE FORCE FIELD SURROUNDS THE ENTIRE ACADEMY. IT'S A CONSIDERABLE ELECTRICAL DRAIN.
I'M SURPRISED WE DIDN'T REALIZE IT SOONER.
IT'S BECAUSE WE KEPT FOCUSING ON MAGICAL SOLUTIONS
INSTEAD OF HIGH-TECH ONES.
I'M PRETTY HIGH-TECH TOO.
STILL... SOME "WIZARD," THAT THOUSAND MASTER. ANYWAY, NOW WE CAN IMPLEMENT OUR ENDGAME
THAT IS CORRECT.
HEH. I CAN JUST PICTURE THE SURPRISED LOOK THAT'S GOING TO BE ON THAT BOY'S FACE.
HAAHAHAHA! IT'S HILARIOUS!
AH HA HA
......
WHAT'S THE MATTER, CHACHAMARU? YOU CONCERNED ABOUT SOMETHING?
N-NO.
THAT...
UH...
UHHHH
BOW
YOU SHOULD KNOW, MISTRESS...
NEGI-SENSEI HAS MADE A PROBATIONARY CONTRACT WITH A PARTNER.
WHAT!?

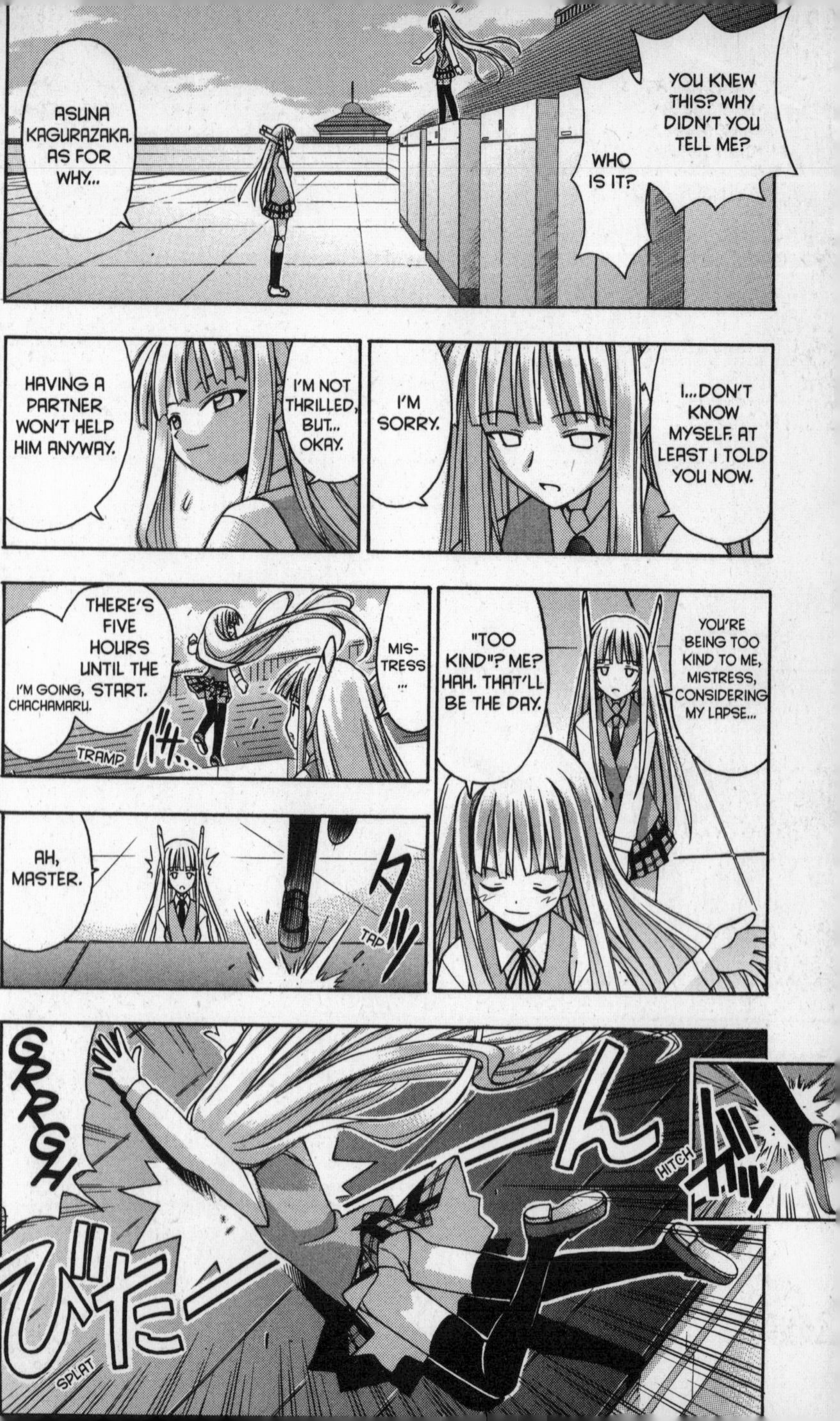
YOU KNEW THIS? WHY DIDN'T YOU TELL ME?
WHO IS IT?
ASUNA KAGURAZAKA. AS FOR WHY...
I...DON'T KNOW MYSELF. AT LEAST I TOLD YOU NOW.
I'M SORRY.
I'M NOT THRILLED, BUT... OKAY.
HAVING A PARTNER WON'T HELP HIM ANYWAY.
YOU'RE BEING TOO KIND TO ME, MISTRESS, CONSIDERING MY LAPSE...
"TOO KIND"? ME? HAH. THAT'LL BE THE DAY.
MISTRESS ...
THERE'S FIVE HOURS UNTIL THE START.
I'M GOING, CHACHAMARU.
バサ...
TRAMP
タッ
TAP
AH, MASTER.
ガッ
HITCH
ーーん
GRRGH
びたーー
SPLAT

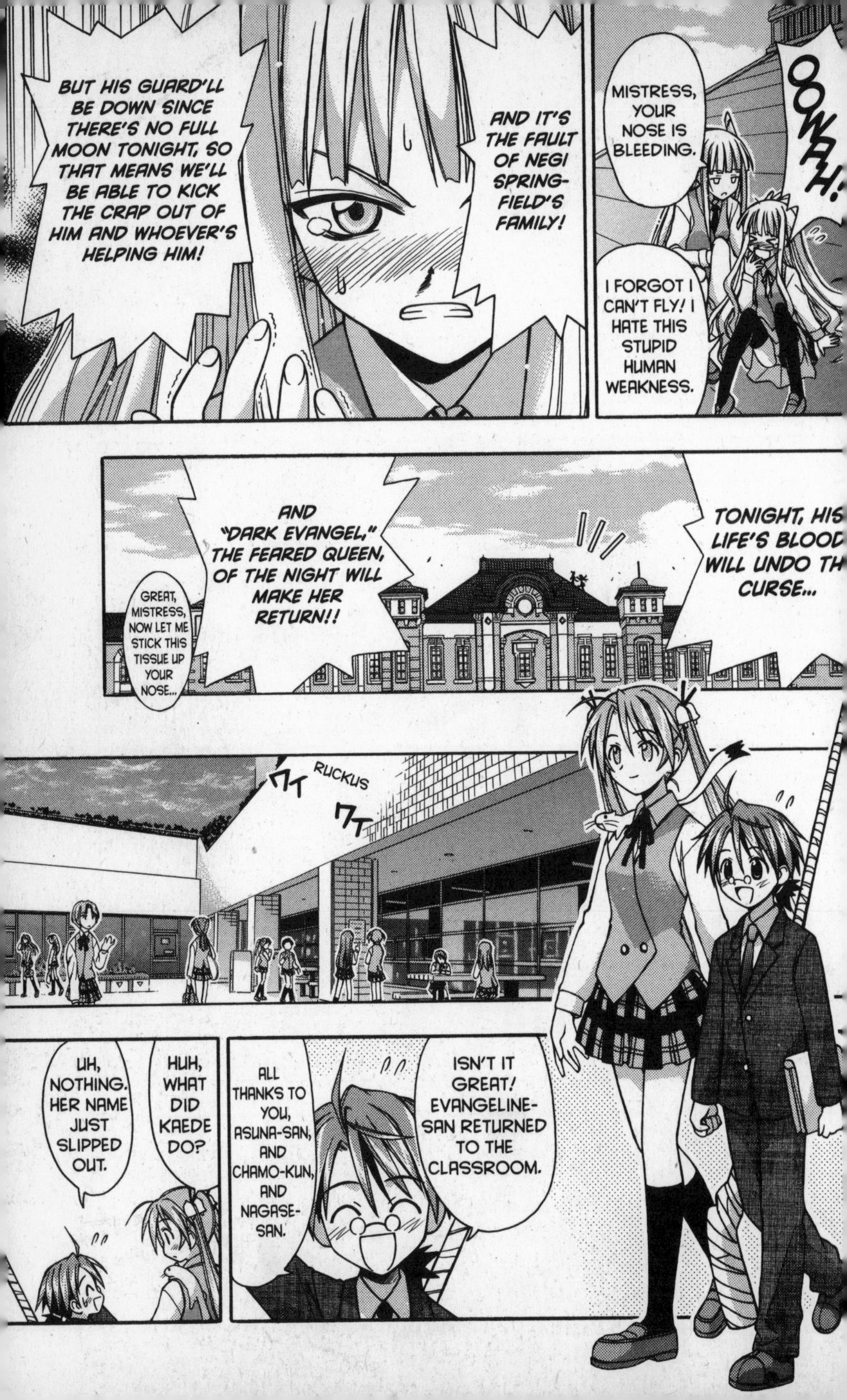
OOWAH!
MISTRESS, YOUR NOSE IS BLEEDING.
I FORGOT I CAN'T FLY! I HATE THIS STUPID HUMAN WEAKNESS.
AND IT'S THE FAULT OF NEGI SPRINGFIELD'S FAMILY!
BUT HIS GUARD'LL BE DOWN SINCE THERE'S NO FULL MOON TONIGHT, SO THAT MEANS WE'LL BE ABLE TO KICK THE CRAP OUT OF HIM AND WHOEVER'S HELPING HIM!
TONIGHT, HIS LIFE'S BLOOD WILL UNDO TH CURSE...
AND "DARK EVANGEL," THE FEARED QUEEN, OF THE NIGHT WILL MAKE HER RETURN!!
GREAT, MISTRESS, NOW LET ME STICK THIS TISSUE UP YOUR NOSE...
ワイ
RUCKUS
ワイ
ISN'T IT GREAT! EVANGELINE-SAN RETURNED TO THE CLASSROOM.
ALL THANKS TO YOU, ASUNA-SAN, AND CHAMO-KUN, AND NAGASE-SAN.
HUH, WHAT DID KAEDE DO?
UH, NOTHING. HER NAME JUST SLIPPED OUT.

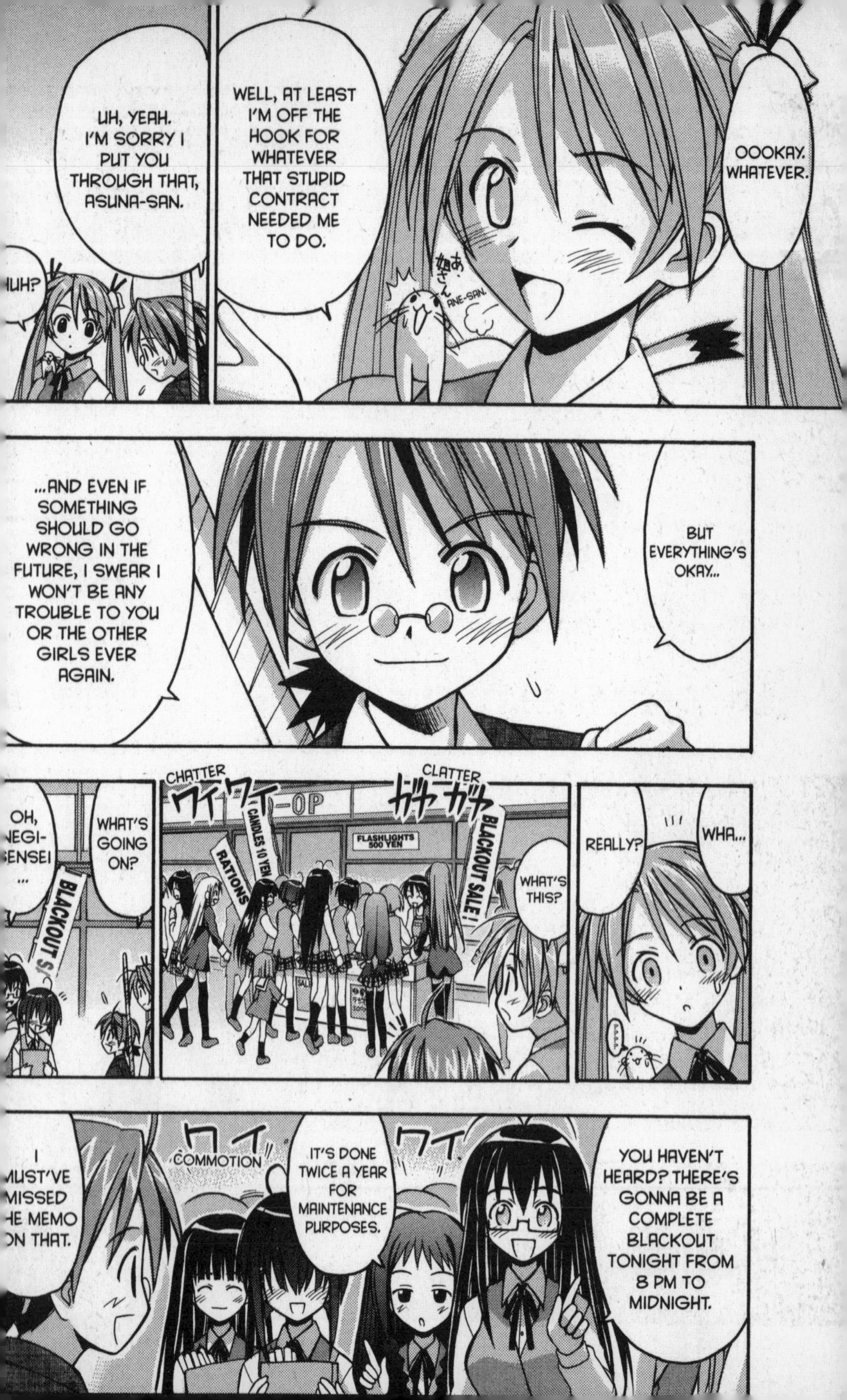
OOOKAY. WHATEVER.
WELL, AT LEAST I'M OFF THE HOOK FOR WHATEVER THAT STUPID CONTRACT NEEDED ME TO DO.
あ…姐さん
ANE-SAN.
UH, YEAH. I'M SORRY I PUT YOU THROUGH THAT, ASUNA-SAN.
HUH?
BUT EVERYTHING'S OKAY...
...AND EVEN IF SOMETHING SHOULD GO WRONG IN THE FUTURE, I SWEAR I WON'T BE ANY TROUBLE TO YOU OR THE OTHER GIRLS EVER AGAIN.
WHA...
REALLY?
WHAT'S THIS?
CLATTER
CHATTER
BLACKOUT SALE!
FLASHLIGHTS 500 YEN
CANDLES 10 YEN
RATIONS
-OP
WHAT'S GOING ON?
OH, NEGI-SENSEI...
BLACKOUT S
YOU HAVEN'T HEARD? THERE'S GONNA BE A COMPLETE BLACKOUT TONIGHT FROM 8 PM TO MIDNIGHT.
IT'S DONE TWICE A YEAR FOR MAINTENANCE PURPOSES.
COMMOTION
I MUST'VE MISSED THE MEMO ON THAT.

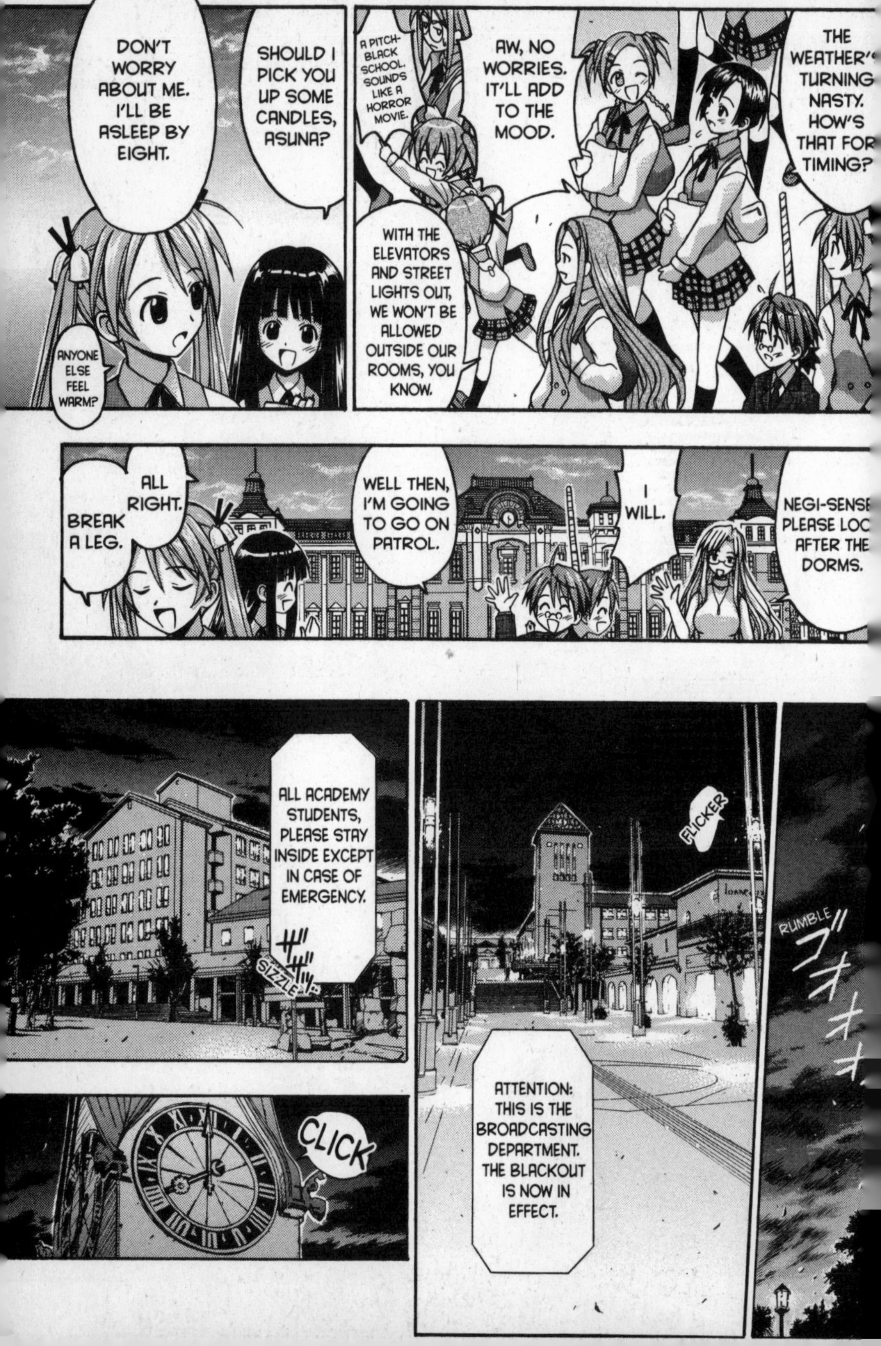
THE WEATHER'S TURNING NASTY. HOW'S THAT FOR TIMING?
AW, NO WORRIES. IT'LL ADD TO THE MOOD.
A PITCH-BLACK SCHOOL. SOUNDS LIKE A HORROR MOVIE.
WITH THE ELEVATORS AND STREET LIGHTS OUT, WE WON'T BE ALLOWED OUTSIDE OUR ROOMS, YOU KNOW.
SHOULD I PICK YOU UP SOME CANDLES, ASUNA?
DON'T WORRY ABOUT ME. I'LL BE ASLEEP BY EIGHT.
ANYONE ELSE FEEL WARM?
NEGI-SENSE PLEASE LOO AFTER THE DORMS.
I WILL.
WELL THEN, I'M GOING TO GO ON PATROL.
ALL RIGHT.
BREAK A LEG.
RUMBLE
FLICKER
ATTENTION: THIS IS THE BROADCASTING DEPARTMENT. THE BLACKOUT IS NOW IN EFFECT.
ALL ACADEMY STUDENTS, PLEASE STAY INSIDE EXCEPT IN CASE OF EMERGENCY.
SIZZLE
CLICK

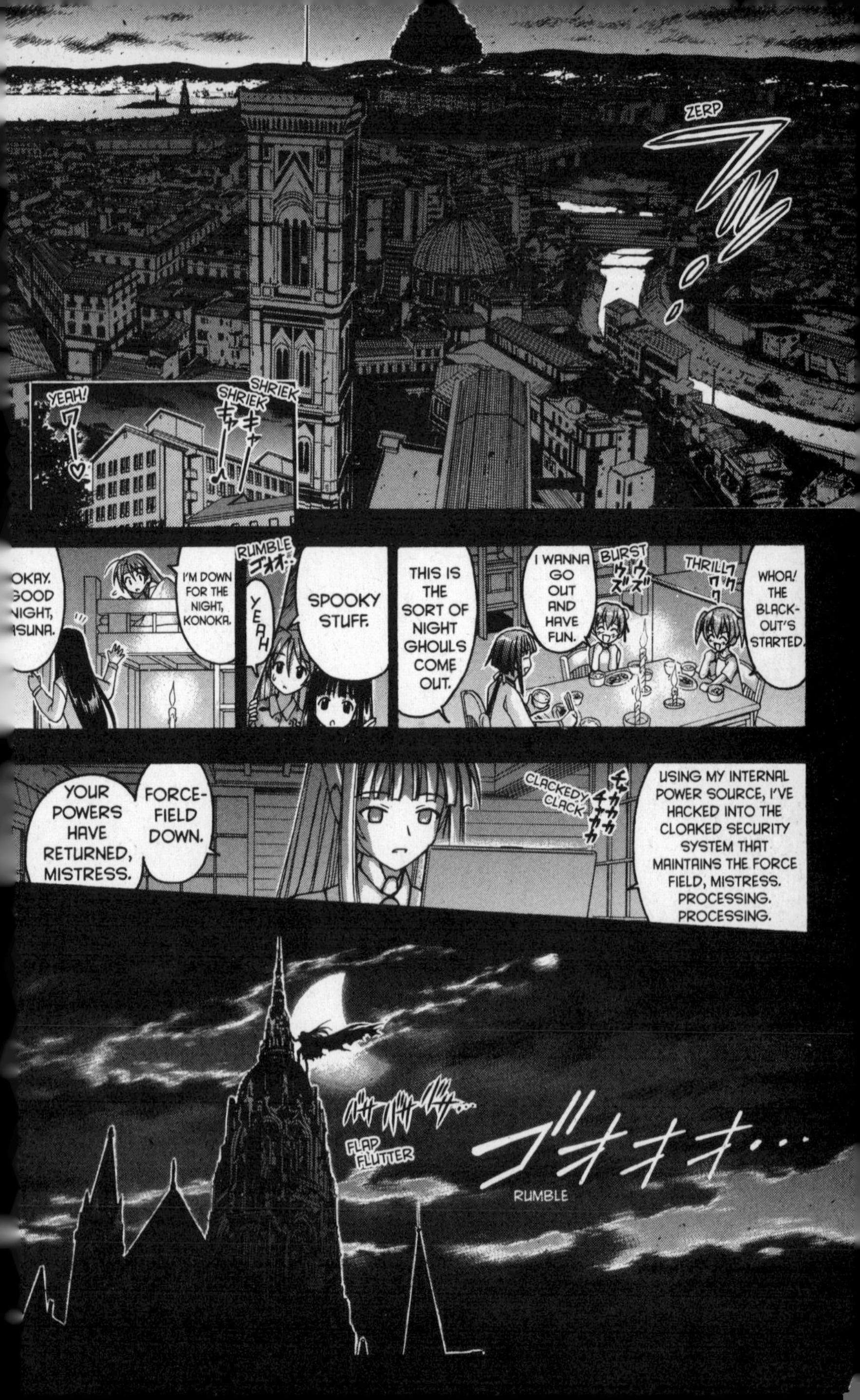
ZERP
SHRIEK SHRIEK
YEAH!
WHOA! THE BLACK-OUT'S STARTED.
THRILL
I WANNA GO OUT AND HAVE FUN.
BURST
THIS IS THE SORT OF NIGHT GHOULS COME OUT.
SPOOKY STUFF.
RUMBLE
YEAH
I'M DOWN FOR THE NIGHT, KONOKA.
OKAY. GOOD NIGHT, ASUNA.
USING MY INTERNAL POWER SOURCE, I'VE HACKED INTO THE CLOAKED SECURITY SYSTEM THAT MAINTAINS THE FORCE FIELD, MISTRESS. PROCESSING. PROCESSING.
CLACKEDY CLACK
FORCE-FIELD DOWN.
YOUR POWERS HAVE RETURNED, MISTRESS.
RUMBLE
FLAP FLUTTER

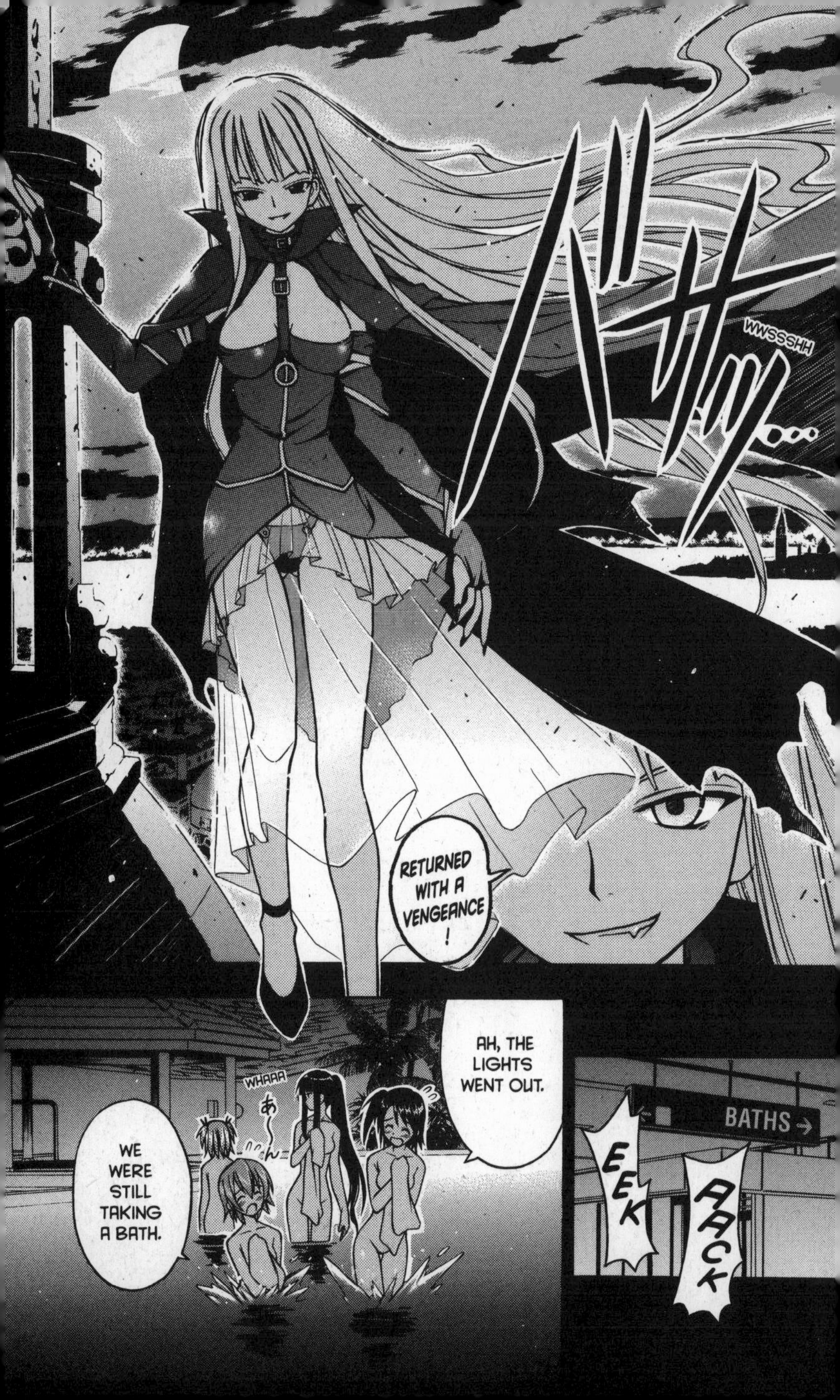
バサッ…
WWSSSHH
RETURNED WITH A VENGEANCE!
BATHS →
EEK
AACK
AH, THE LIGHTS WENT OUT.
WHAAA
あ〜ん
WE WERE STILL TAKING A BATH.

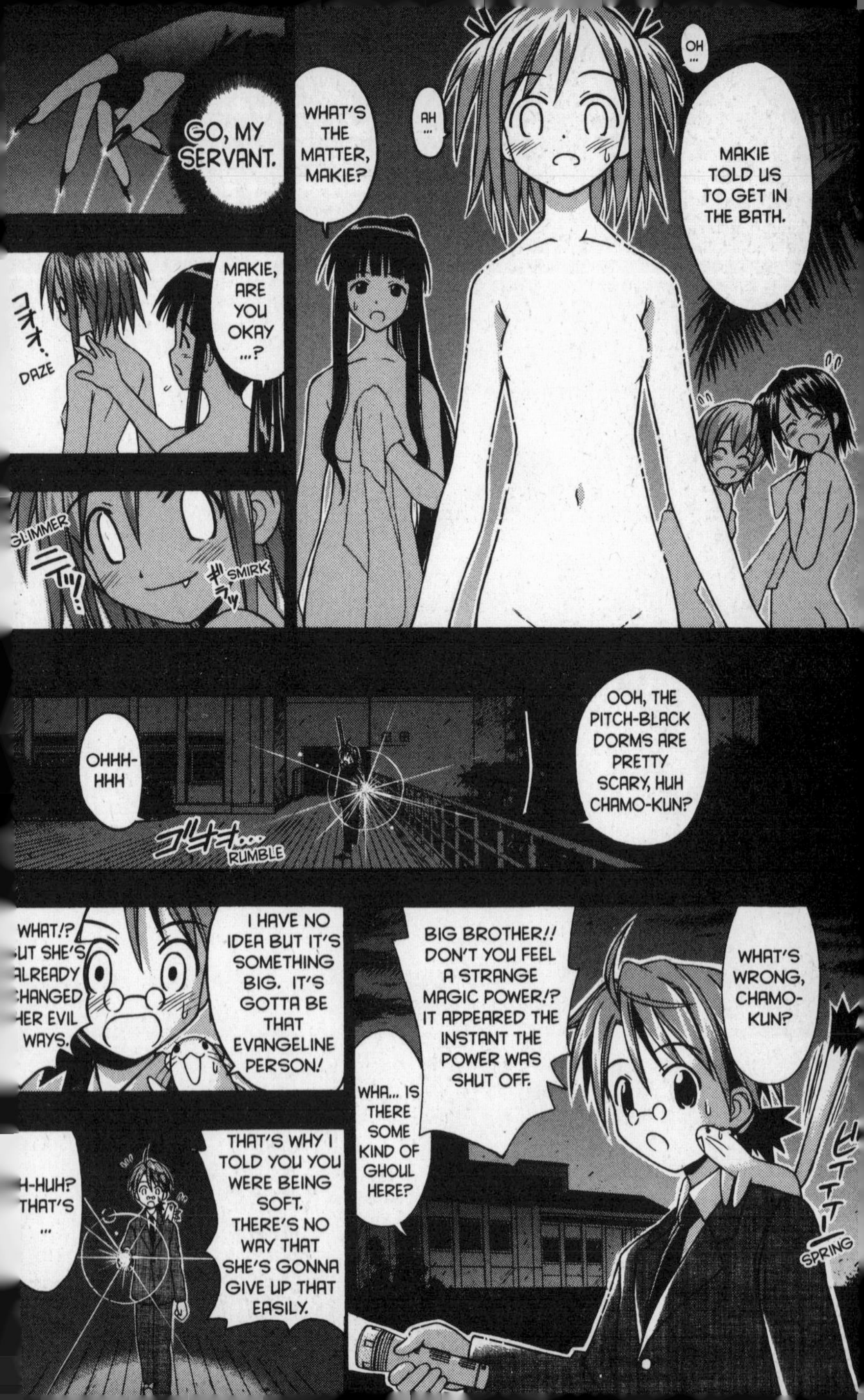
OH ...
MAKIE TOLD US TO GET IN THE BATH.
AH ...
WHAT'S THE MATTER, MAKIE?
GO, MY SERVANT.
MAKIE, ARE YOU OKAY ...?
DAZE
GLIMMER
SMIRK
OOH, THE PITCH-BLACK DORMS ARE PRETTY SCARY, HUH CHAMO-KUN?
OHHH-HHH
RUMBLE
WHAT'S WRONG, CHAMO-KUN?
BIG BROTHER!! DON'T YOU FEEL A STRANGE MAGIC POWER!? IT APPEARED THE INSTANT THE POWER WAS SHUT OFF.
WHA... IS THERE SOME KIND OF GHOUL HERE?
SPRING
I HAVE NO IDEA BUT IT'S SOMETHING BIG. IT'S GOTTA BE THAT EVANGELINE PERSON!
WHAT!? UT SHE'S LREADY HANGED HER EVIL WAYS.
THAT'S WHY I TOLD YOU YOU WERE BEING SOFT. THERE'S NO WAY THAT SHE'S GONNA GIVE UP THAT EASILY.
H-HUH? THAT'S ...

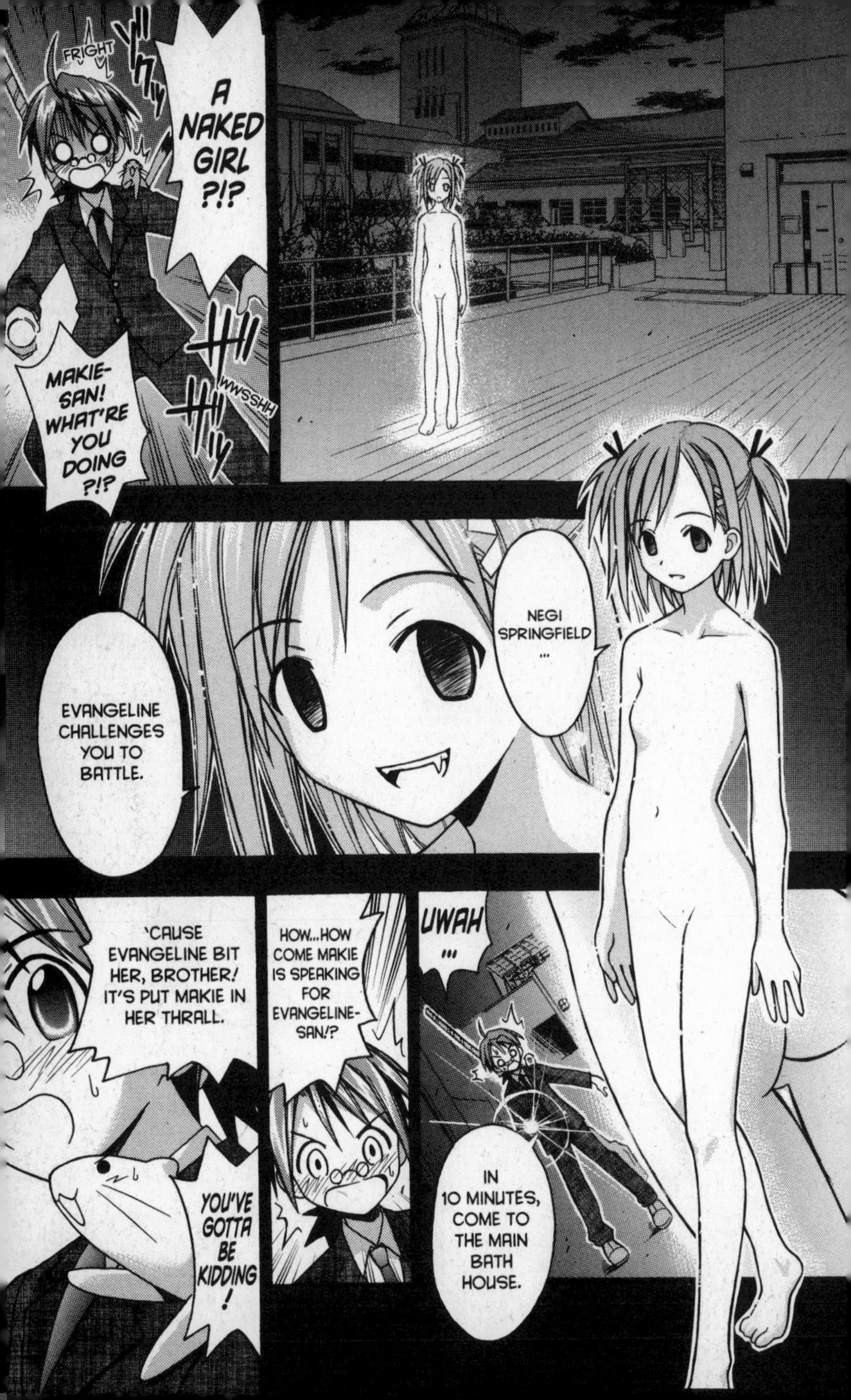
A NAKED GIRL ?!?
FRIGHT
WWSSHH
MAKIE-SAN! WHAT'RE YOU DOING ?!?
NEGI SPRINGFIELD ...
EVANGELINE CHALLENGES YOU TO BATTLE.
UWAH ...
IN 10 MINUTES, COME TO THE MAIN BATH HOUSE.
HOW...HOW COME MAKIE IS SPEAKING FOR EVANGELINE-SAN!?
'CAUSE EVANGELINE BIT HER, BROTHER! IT'S PUT MAKIE IN HER THRALL.
YOU'VE GOTTA BE KIDDING !

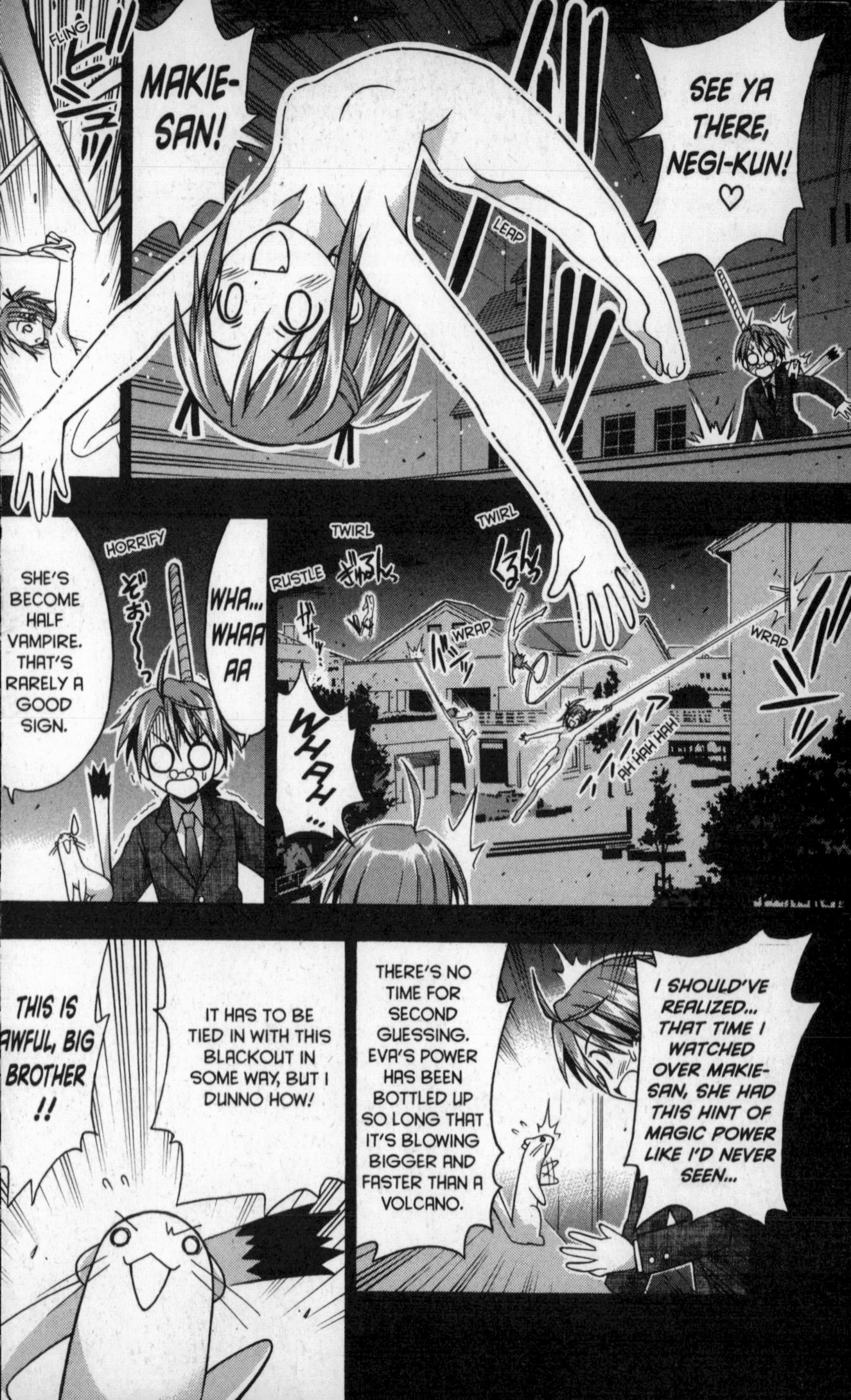
SEE YA THERE, NEGI-KUN! ♡
MAKIE-SAN!
LEAP
FLING
TWIRL
TWIRL
RUSTLE
WRAP
WRAP
AH HAH HAH
WHAH...
WHA... WHAAAA
HORRIFY
SHE'S BECOME HALF VAMPIRE. THAT'S RARELY A GOOD SIGN.
I SHOULD'VE REALIZED... THAT TIME I WATCHED OVER MAKIE-SAN, SHE HAD THIS HINT OF MAGIC POWER LIKE I'D NEVER SEEN...
THERE'S NO TIME FOR SECOND GUESSING. EVA'S POWER HAS BEEN BOTTLED UP SO LONG THAT IT'S BLOWING BIGGER AND FASTER THAN A VOLCANO.
IT HAS TO BE TIED IN WITH THIS BLACKOUT IN SOME WAY, BUT I DUNNO HOW!
THIS IS AWFUL, BIG BROTHER!!

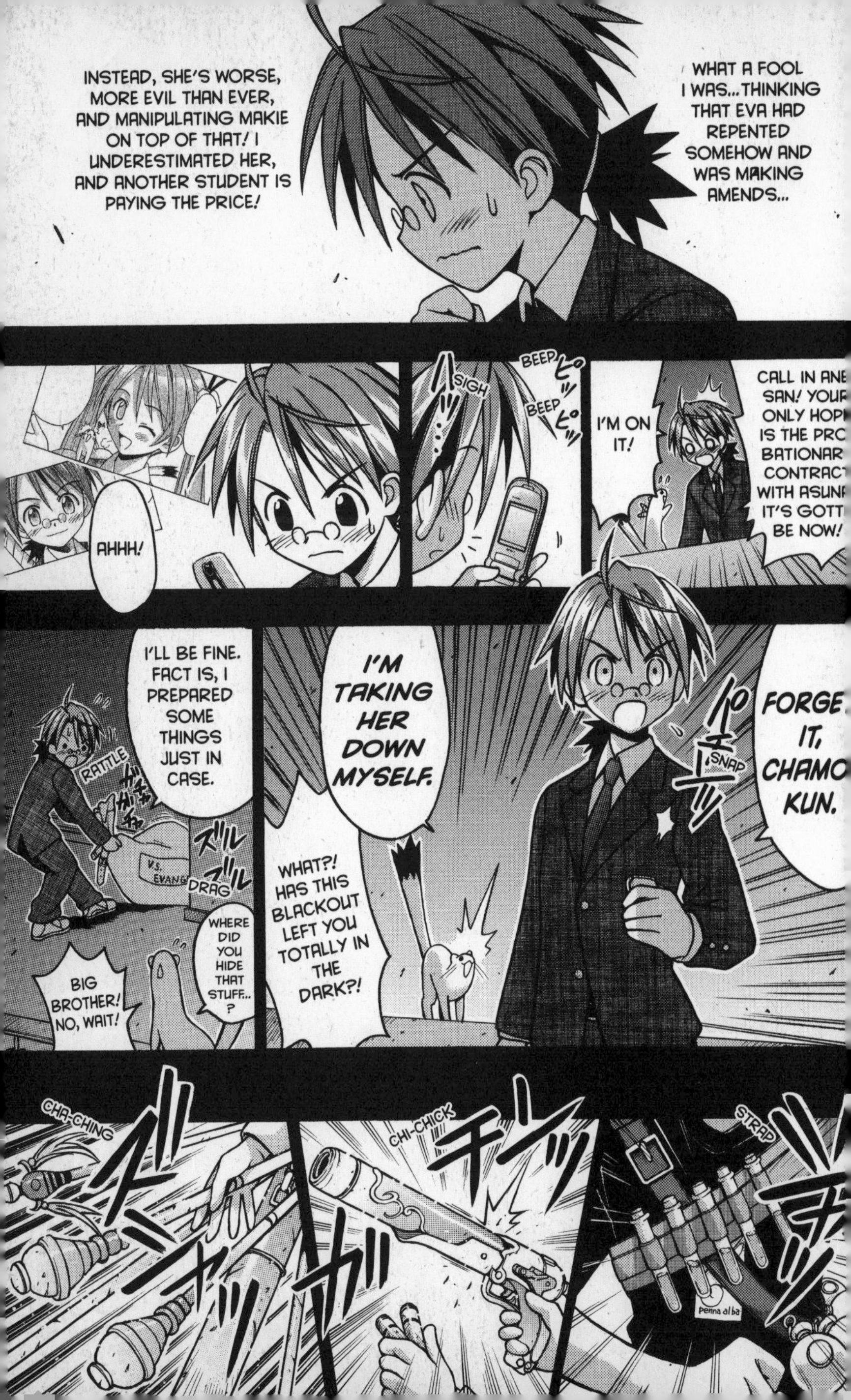
WHAT A FOOL I WAS...THINKING THAT EVA HAD REPENTED SOMEHOW AND WAS MAKING AMENDS...
INSTEAD, SHE'S WORSE, MORE EVIL THAN EVER, AND MANIPULATING MAKIE ON TOP OF THAT! I UNDERESTIMATED HER, AND ANOTHER STUDENT IS PAYING THE PRICE!
CALL IN ANE SAN! YOUR ONLY HOP IS THE PRO BATIONAR CONTRAC WITH ASUN IT'S GOTT BE NOW!
I'M ON IT!
BEEP
BEEP
SIGH
AHHH!
FORGE IT, CHAMO KUN.
SNAP
I'M TAKING HER DOWN MYSELF.
WHAT?! HAS THIS BLACKOUT LEFT YOU TOTALLY IN THE DARK?!
I'LL BE FINE. FACT IS, I PREPARED SOME THINGS JUST IN CASE.
RATTLE
V.S. EVANG
DRAG
WHERE DID YOU HIDE THAT STUFF... ?
BIG BROTHER! NO, WAIT!
STRAP
penna alba
CHI-CHICK
CHA-CHING

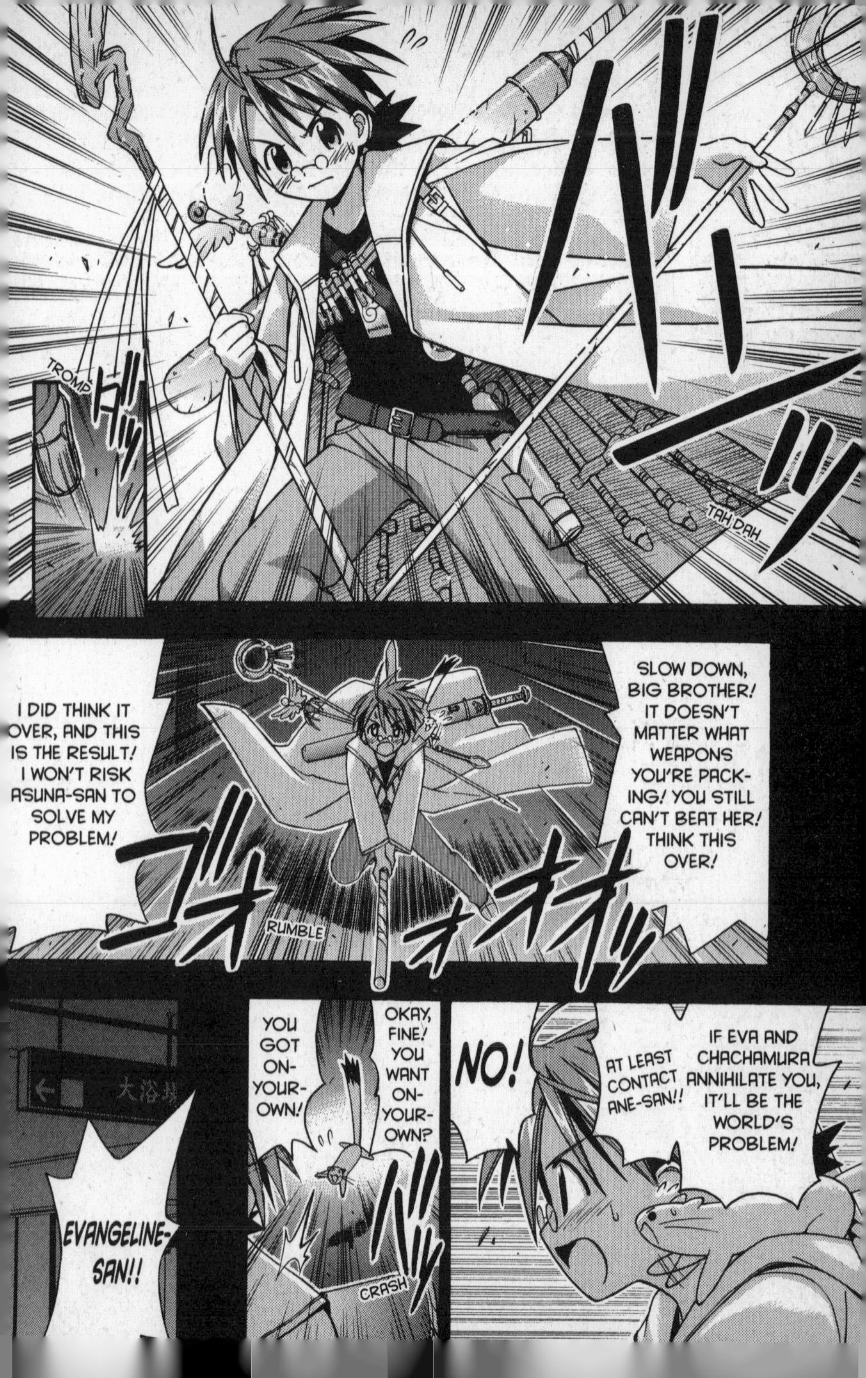

TAH DAH
TROMP
SLOW DOWN, BIG BROTHER! IT DOESN'T MATTER WHAT WEAPONS YOU'RE PACKING! YOU STILL CAN'T BEAT HER! THINK THIS OVER!
I DID THINK IT OVER, AND THIS IS THE RESULT! I WON'T RISK ASUNA-SAN TO SOLVE MY PROBLEM!
RUMBLE
IF EVA AND CHACHAMURA ANNIHILATE YOU, IT'LL BE THE WORLD'S PROBLEM!
AT LEAST CONTACT ANE-SAN!!
NO!
OKAY, FINE! YOU WANT ON-YOUR-OWN?
YOU GOT ON-YOUR-OWN!
CRASH
EVANGELINE-SAN!!

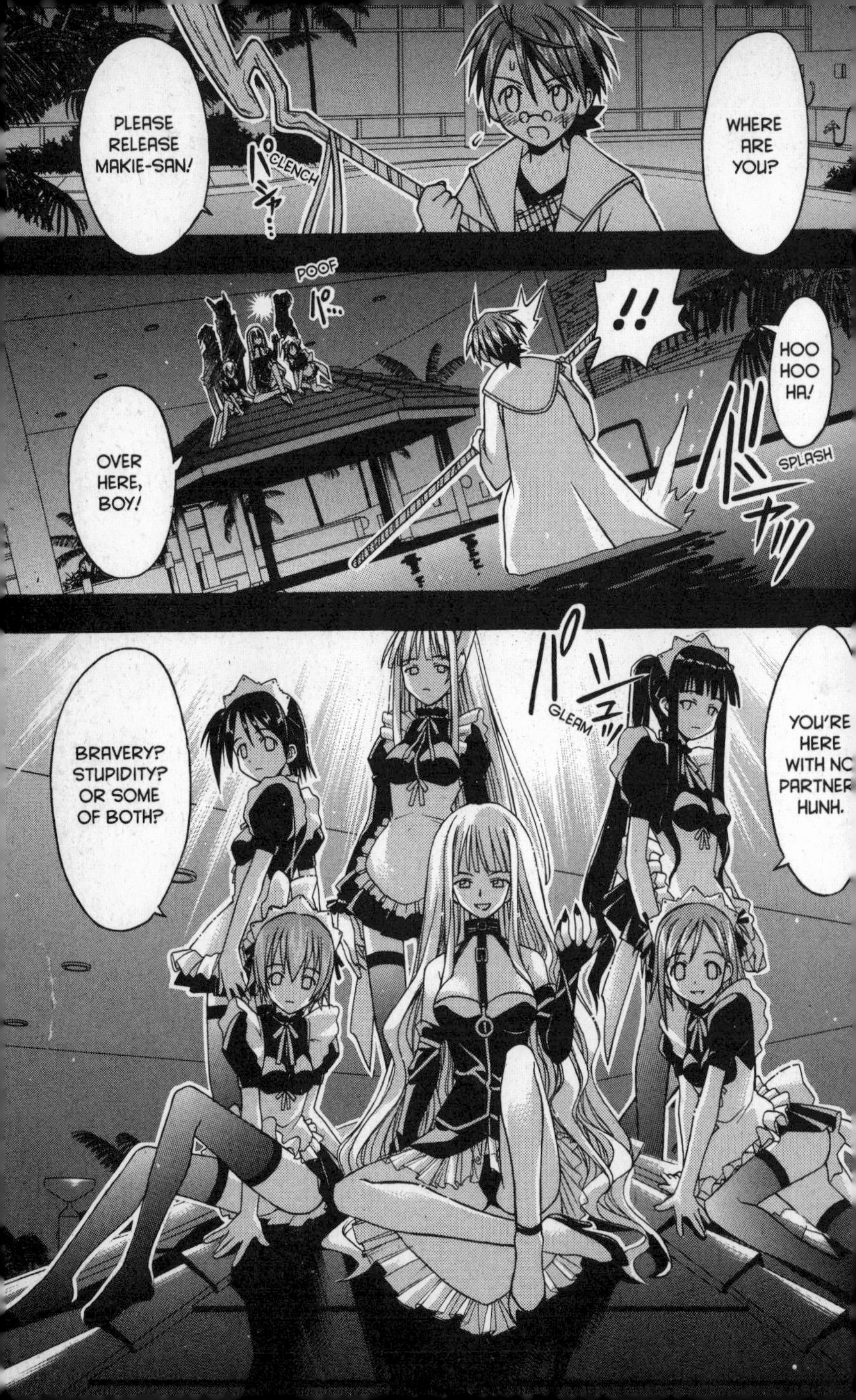
WHERE ARE YOU?
CLENCH
PLEASE RELEASE MAKIE-SAN!
!!
HOO HOO HA!
SPLASH
POOF
OVER HERE, BOY!
YOU'RE HERE WITH NC PARTNER HUNH.
GLEAM
BRAVERY? STUPIDITY? OR SOME OF BOTH?

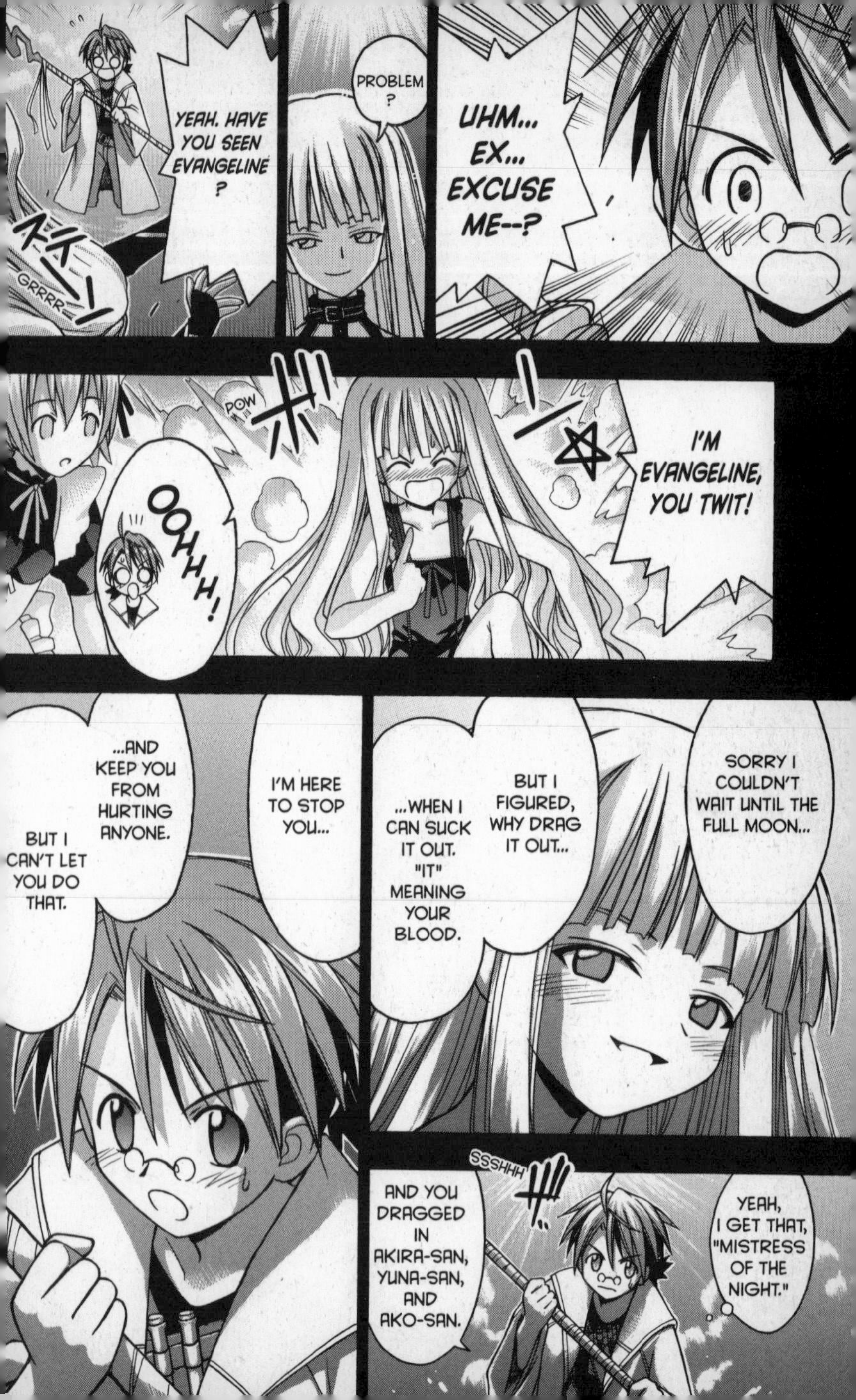

UHM... EX... EXCUSE ME--?
PROBLEM ?
YEAH. HAVE YOU SEEN EVANGELINE ?
GRRRR
I'M EVANGELINE, YOU TWIT!
POW
OOHHHH!
SORRY I COULDN'T WAIT UNTIL THE FULL MOON...
BUT I FIGURED, WHY DRAG IT OUT...
...WHEN I CAN SUCK IT OUT. "IT" MEANING YOUR BLOOD.
YEAH, I GET THAT, "MISTRESS OF THE NIGHT."
SSSHHH
AND YOU DRAGGED IN AKIRA-SAN, YUNA-SAN, AND AKO-SAN.
I'M HERE TO STOP YOU...
...AND KEEP YOU FROM HURTING ANYONE.
BUT I CAN'T LET YOU DO THAT.

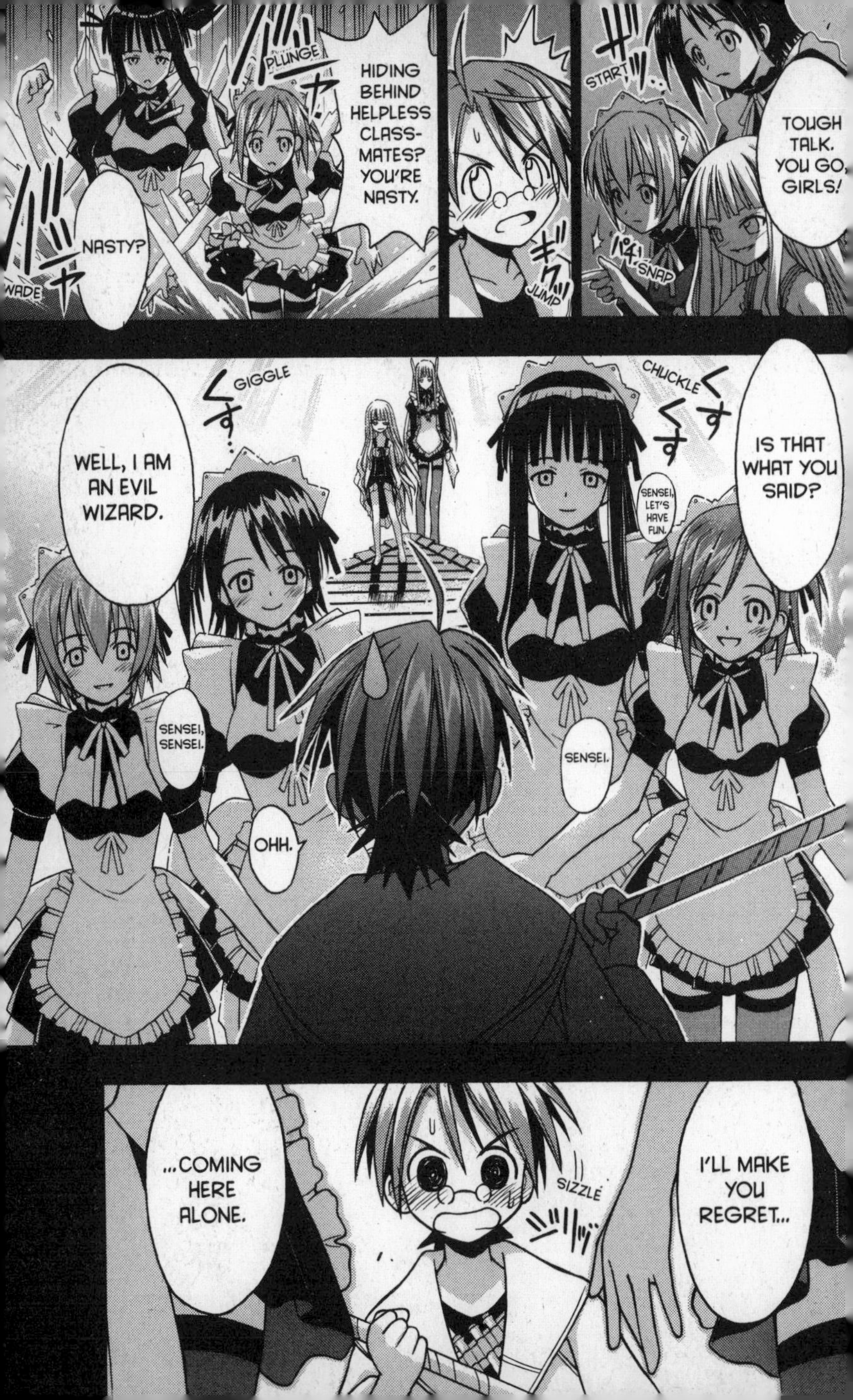
START
TOUGH TALK. YOU GO, GIRLS!
SNAP
JUMP
PLUNGE
HIDING BEHIND HELPLESS CLASSMATES? YOU'RE NASTY.
NASTY?
WADE
CHUCKLE
IS THAT WHAT YOU SAID?
SENSEI, LET'S HAVE FUN.
GIGGLE
WELL, I AM AN EVIL WIZARD.
SENSEI.
SENSEI, SENSEI.
OHH.
I'LL MAKE YOU REGRET...
SIZZLE
...COMING HERE ALONE.

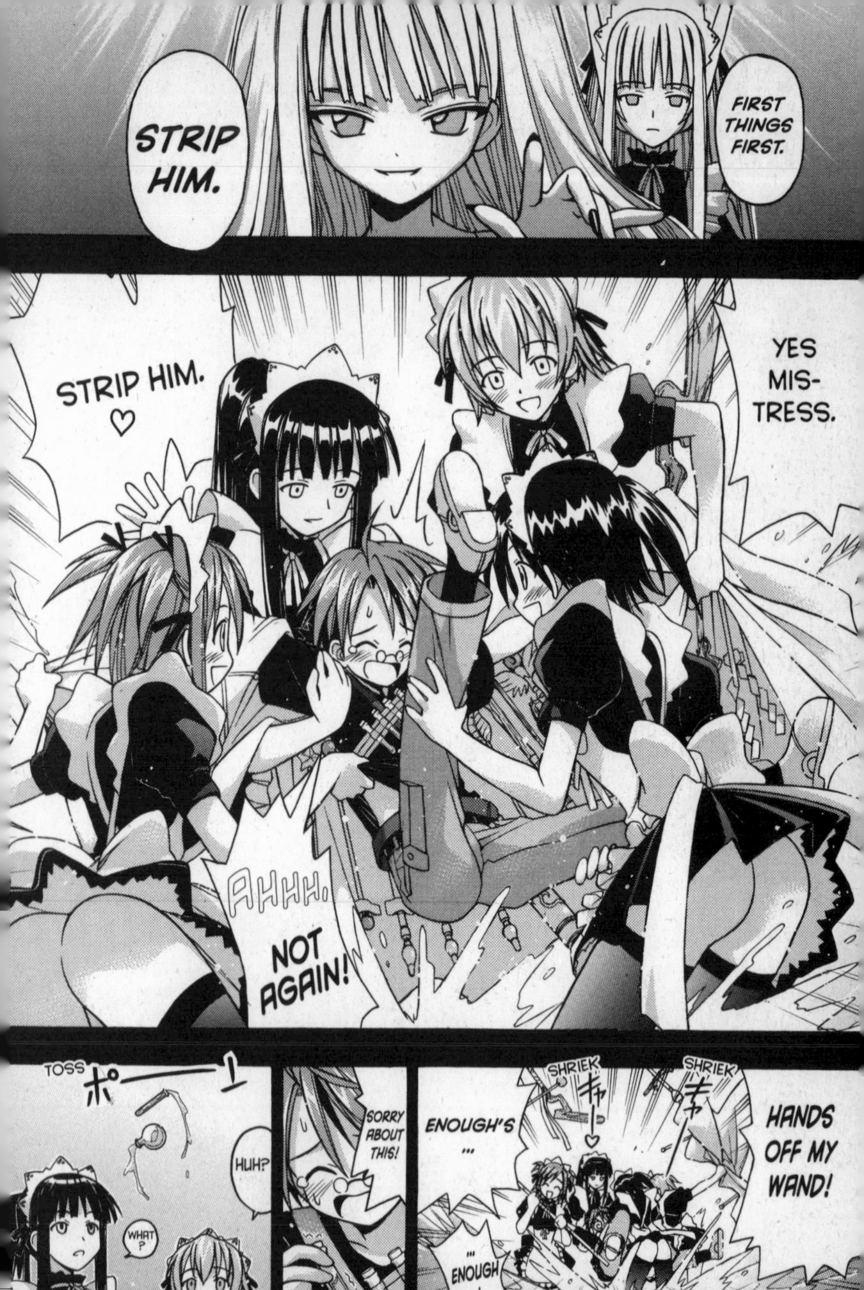
FIRST THINGS FIRST.
STRIP HIM.
YES MIS-TRESS.
STRIP HIM. ♡
AHHH,
NOT AGAIN!
HANDS OFF MY WAND!
SHRIEK
ギャー
SHRIEK
ギャー♡
ENOUGH'S ...
... ENOUGH !
SORRY ABOUT THIS!
HUH?
TOSS
ポーー!
WHAT?

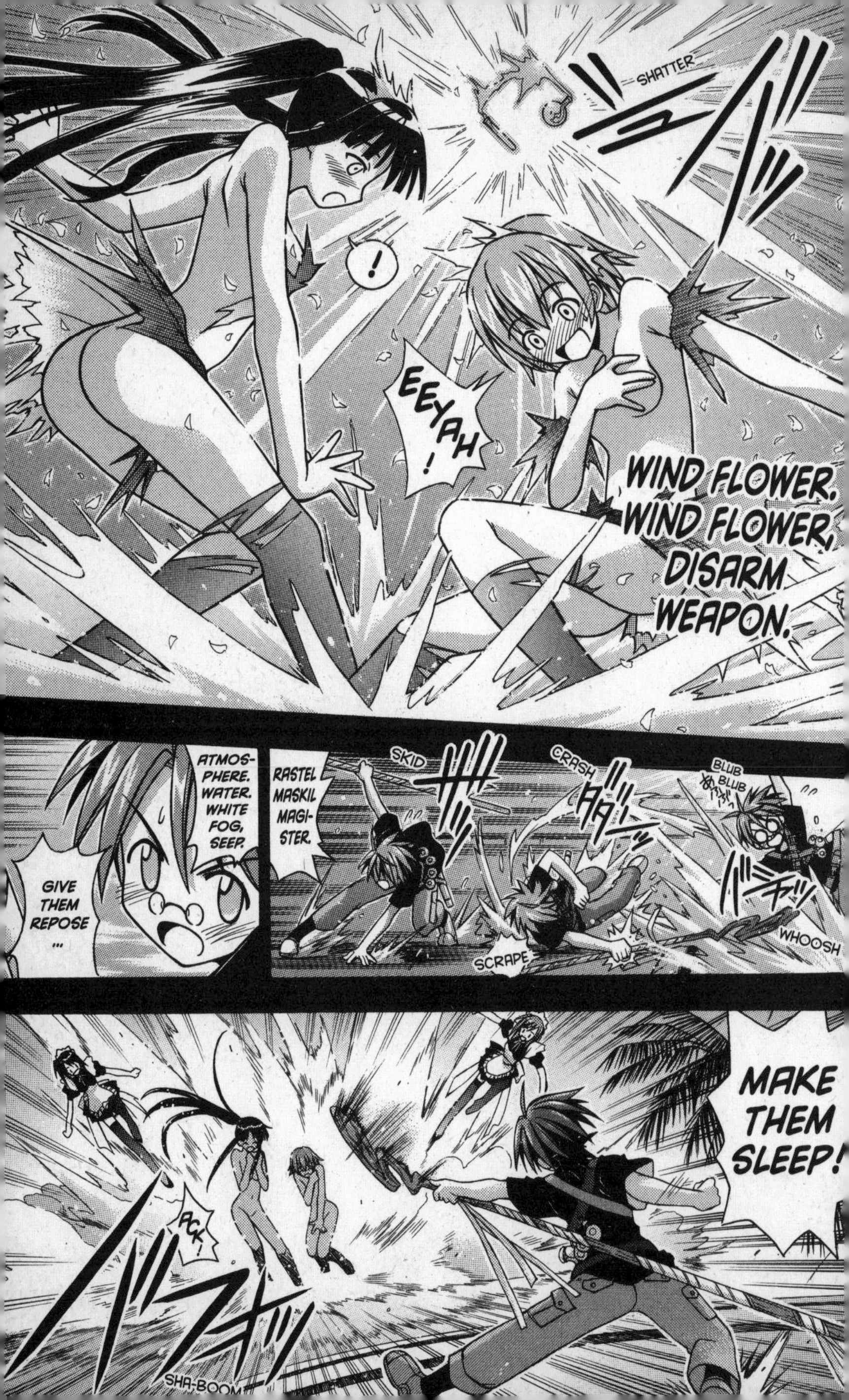
SHATTER
!
EEYAH!
WIND FLOWER. WIND FLOWER. DISARM WEAPON.
BLUB BLUB
CRASH
SKID
RASTEL MASKIL MAGISTER.
WHOOSH
SCRAPE
ATMOSPHERE. WATER. WHITE FOG, SEEP.
GIVE THEM REPOSE ...
MAKE THEM SLEEP!
ACK!
SHA-BOOM

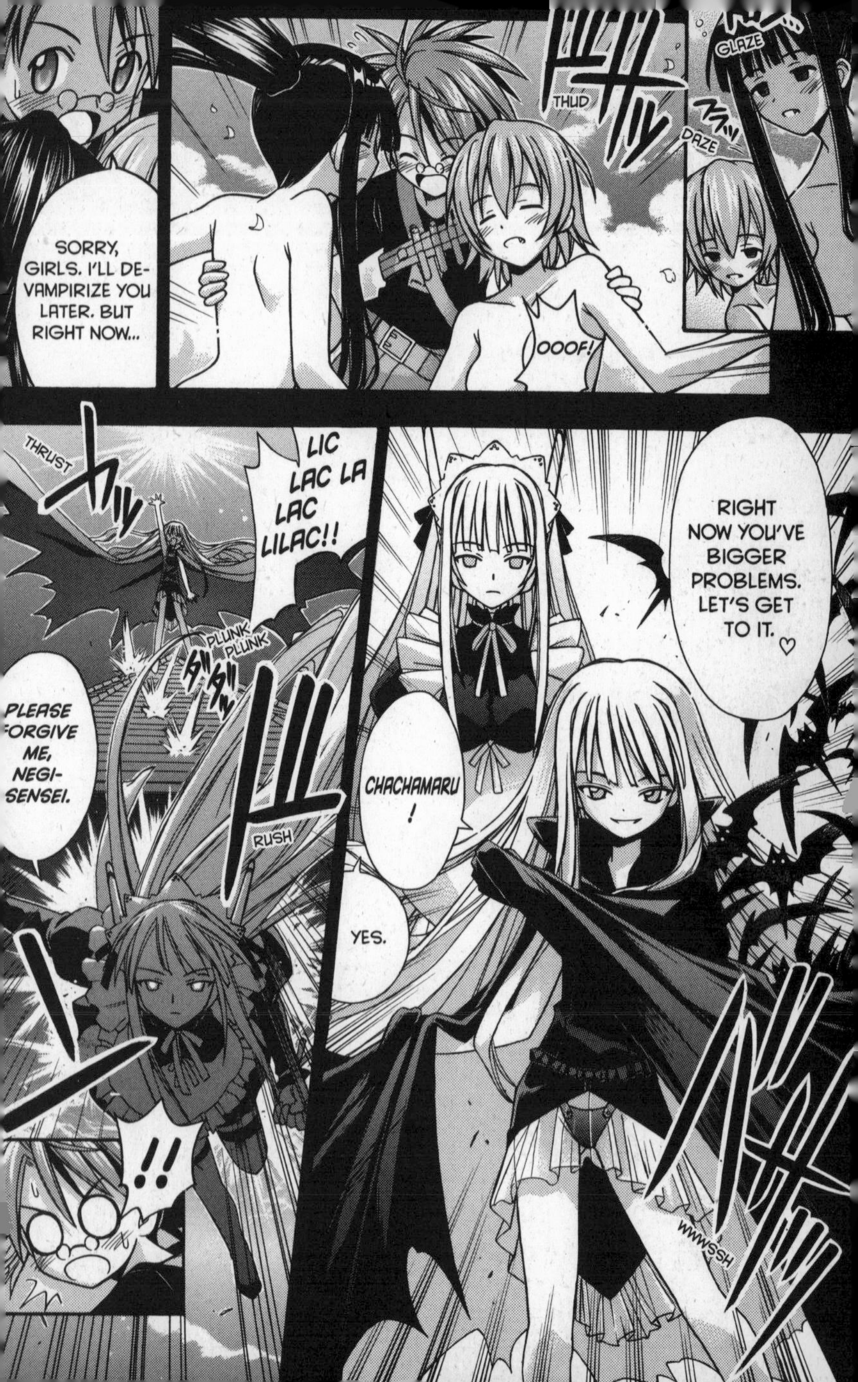
GLAZE
DAZE
THUD
OOOF!
SORRY, GIRLS. I'LL DE-VAMPIRIZE YOU LATER. BUT RIGHT NOW...
RIGHT NOW YOU'VE BIGGER PROBLEMS. LET'S GET TO IT. ♡
CHACHAMARU!
YES.
WWWSSH
THRUST
LIC LAC LA LAC LILAC!!
PLUNK PLUNK
PLEASE FORGIVE ME, NEGI-SENSEI.
RUSH
!!

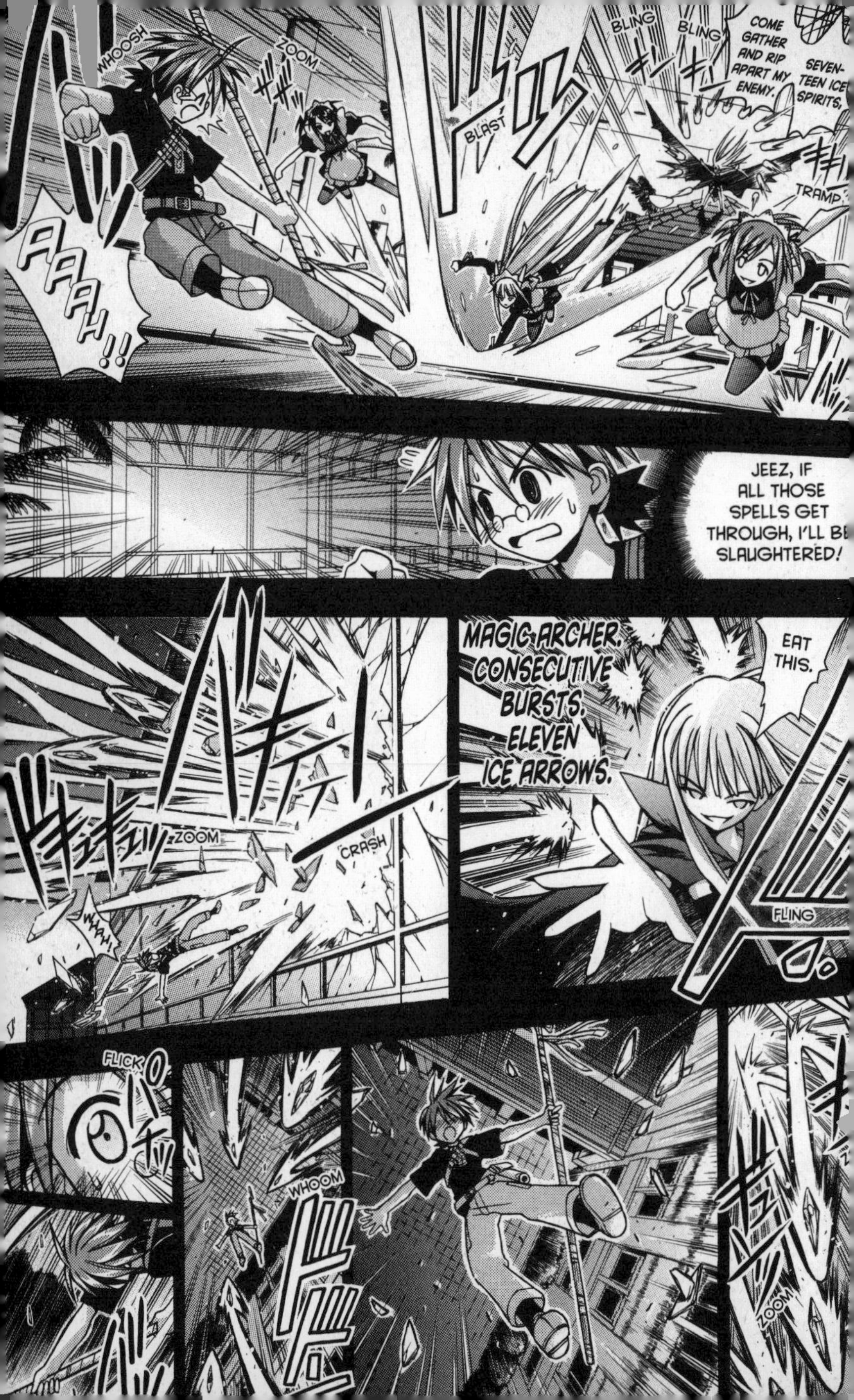
SEVEN-TEEN ICE SPIRITS,
COME GATHER AND RIP APART MY ENEMY.
BLING
BLING
TRAMP
BLAST
ZOOM
WHOOSH
AAAAH!!
JEEZ, IF ALL THOSE SPELLS GET THROUGH, I'LL BE SLAUGHTERED!
EAT THIS.
MAGIC ARCHER. CONSECUTIVE BURSTS. ELEVEN ICE ARROWS.
FLING
CRASH
ZOOM
WHAAH!
ZOOM
WHOOM
FLICK

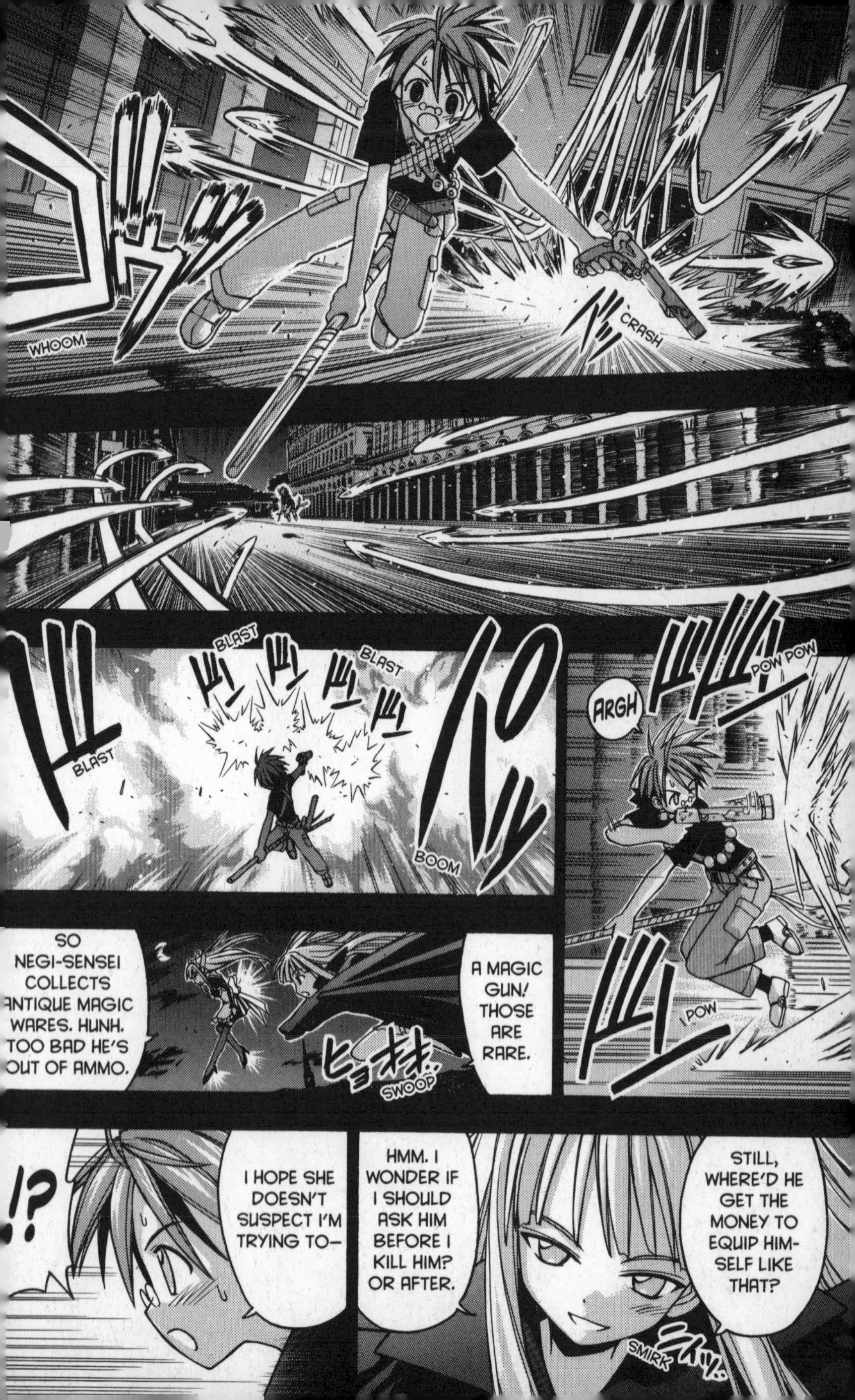
CRASH
WHOOM
POW POW
ARGH
POW
BLAST
BLAST
BOOM
BLAST
A MAGIC GUN! THOSE ARE RARE.
SWOOP
SO NEGI-SENSEI COLLECTS ANTIQUE MAGIC WARES. HUNH. TOO BAD HE'S OUT OF AMMO.
STILL, WHERE'D HE GET THE MONEY TO EQUIP HIMSELF LIKE THAT?
HMM. I WONDER IF I SHOULD ASK HIM BEFORE I KILL HIM? OR AFTER.
SMIRK
I HOPE SHE DOESN'T SUSPECT I'M TRYING TO—
!?

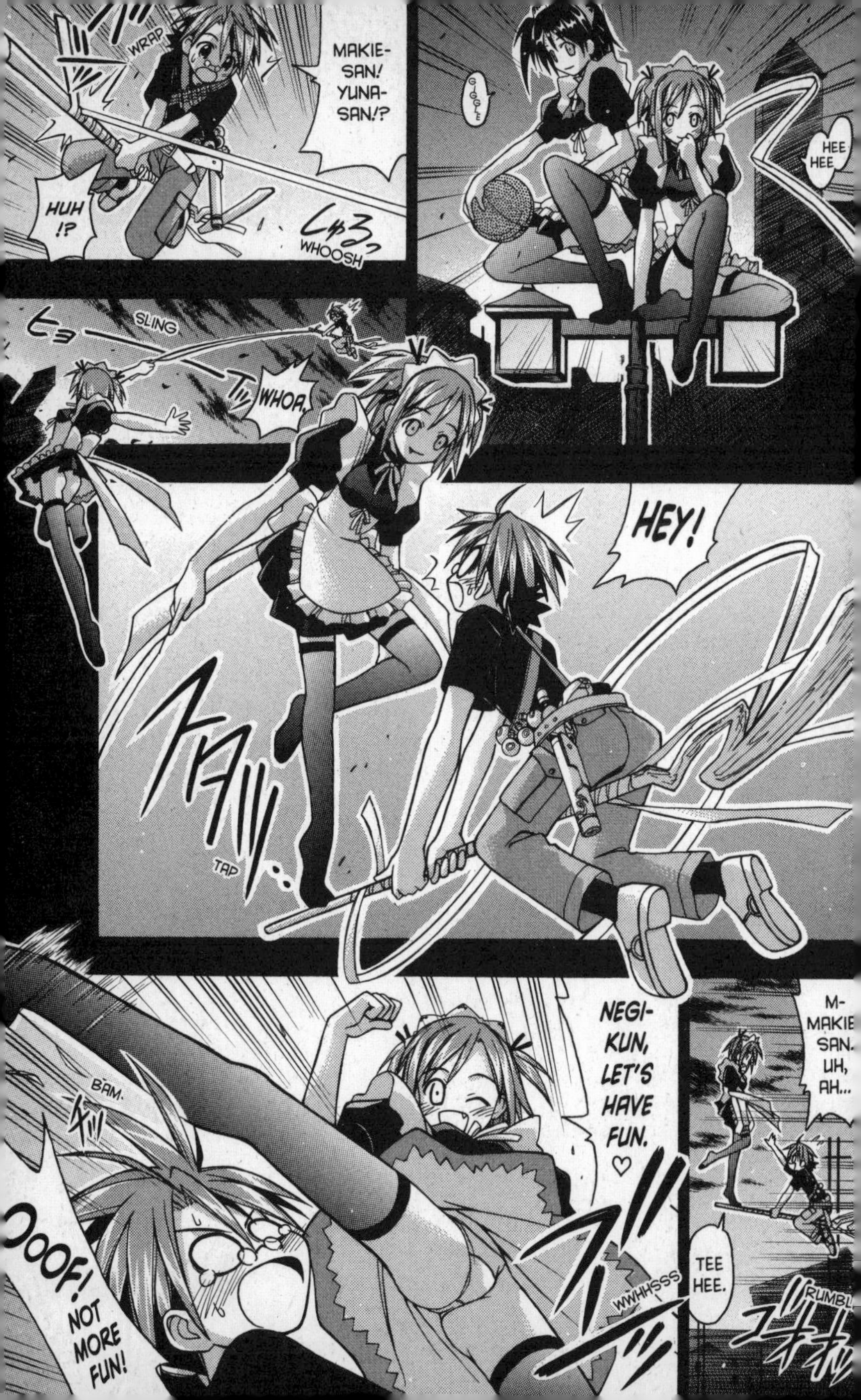

HEE HEE
GIGGLE
MAKIE-SAN! YUNA-SAN!?
WRAP
HUH !?
しゅるっ
WHOOSH
ヒュ
SLING
WHOA
HEY!
TAP
M-MAKIE SAN. UH, AH...
RUMBLE
TEE HEE.
NEGI-KUN, LET'S HAVE FUN. ♡
WWHHSSS
BAM.
OOOF! NOT MORE FUN!

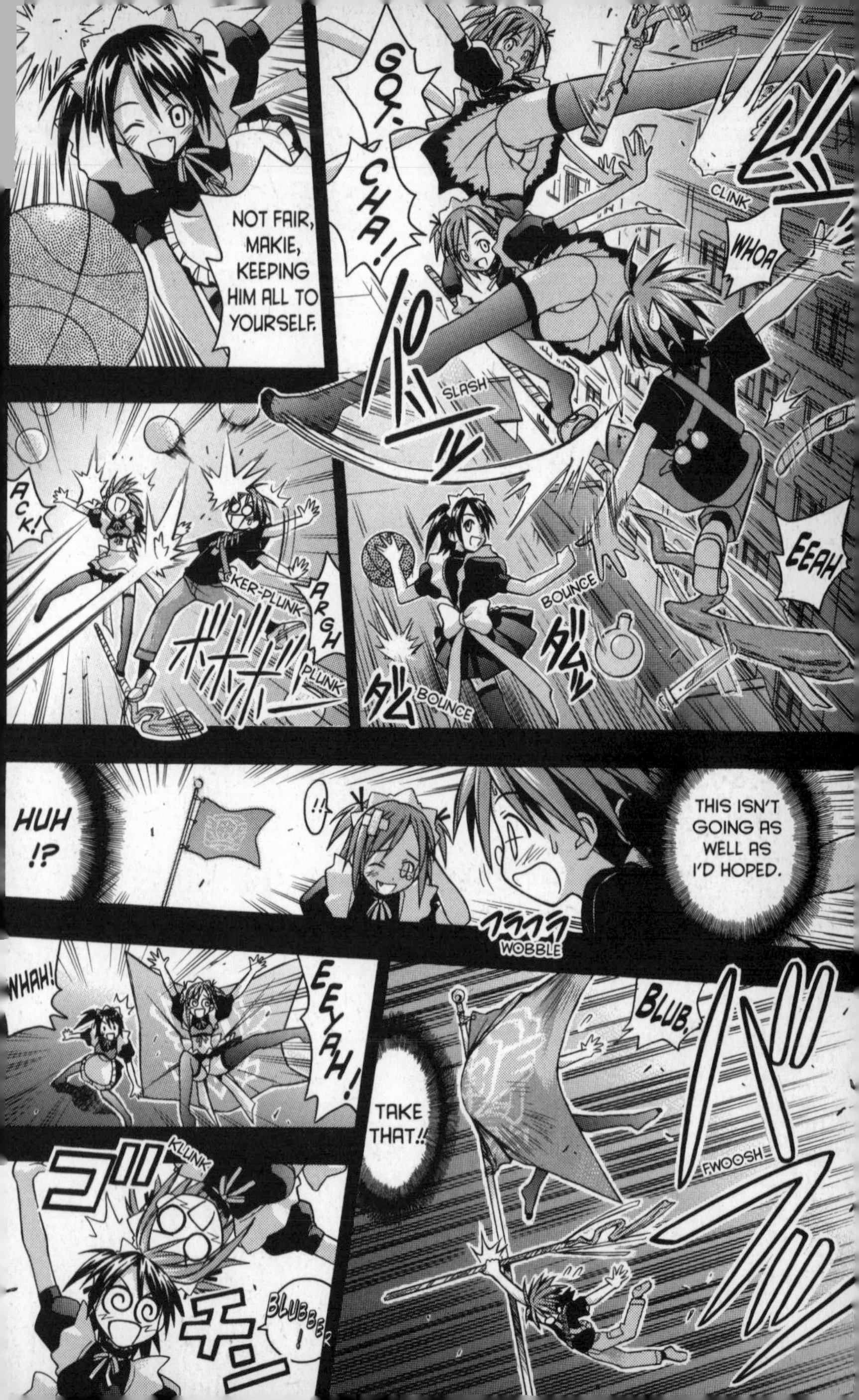
GOT-CHA!
CLINK
WHOA
SLASH
NOT FAIR, MAKIE, KEEPING HIM ALL TO YOURSELF.
EEAH
BOUNCE
BOUNCE
ACK!
KER-PLUNK
ARGH
PLUNK
THIS ISN'T GOING AS WELL AS I'D HOPED.
WOBBLE
!!
HUH !?
BLUB.
FWOOSH
TAKE THAT!!
EEYAH!
WHAH!
KLUNK
BLUBBER!

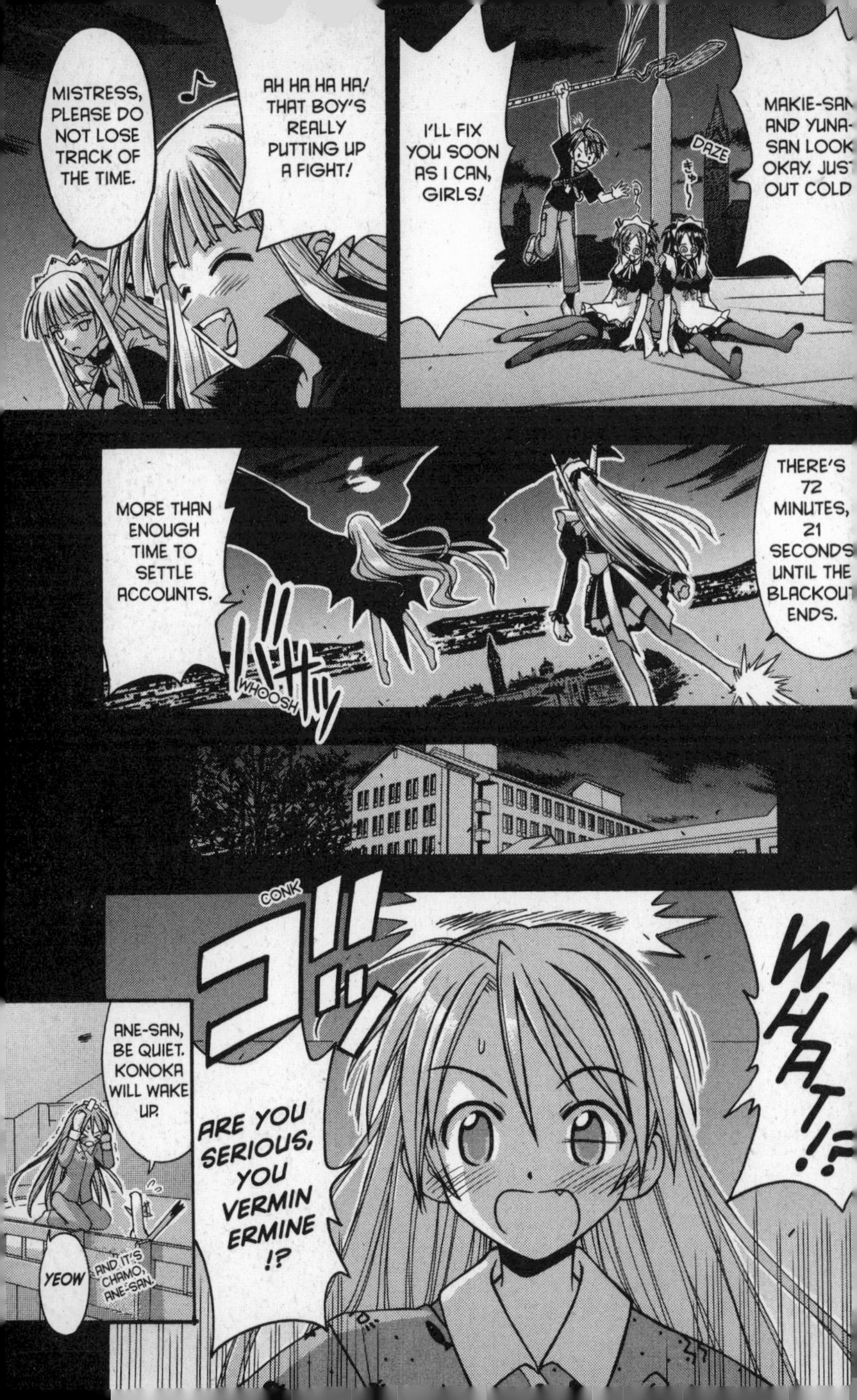
MAKIE-SAN AND YUNA-SAN LOOK OKAY. JUST OUT COLD
DAZE
I'LL FIX YOU SOON AS I CAN, GIRLS!
AH HA HA HA! THAT BOY'S REALLY PUTTING UP A FIGHT!
MISTRESS, PLEASE DO NOT LOSE TRACK OF THE TIME.
THERE'S 72 MINUTES, 21 SECONDS UNTIL THE BLACKOUT ENDS.
MORE THAN ENOUGH TIME TO SETTLE ACCOUNTS.
WHOOSH
CONK
WHAT!!?
ARE YOU SERIOUS, YOU VERMIN ERMINE!?
ANE-SAN, BE QUIET. KONOKA WILL WAKE UP.
AND IT'S CHAMO, ANE-SAN.
YEOW

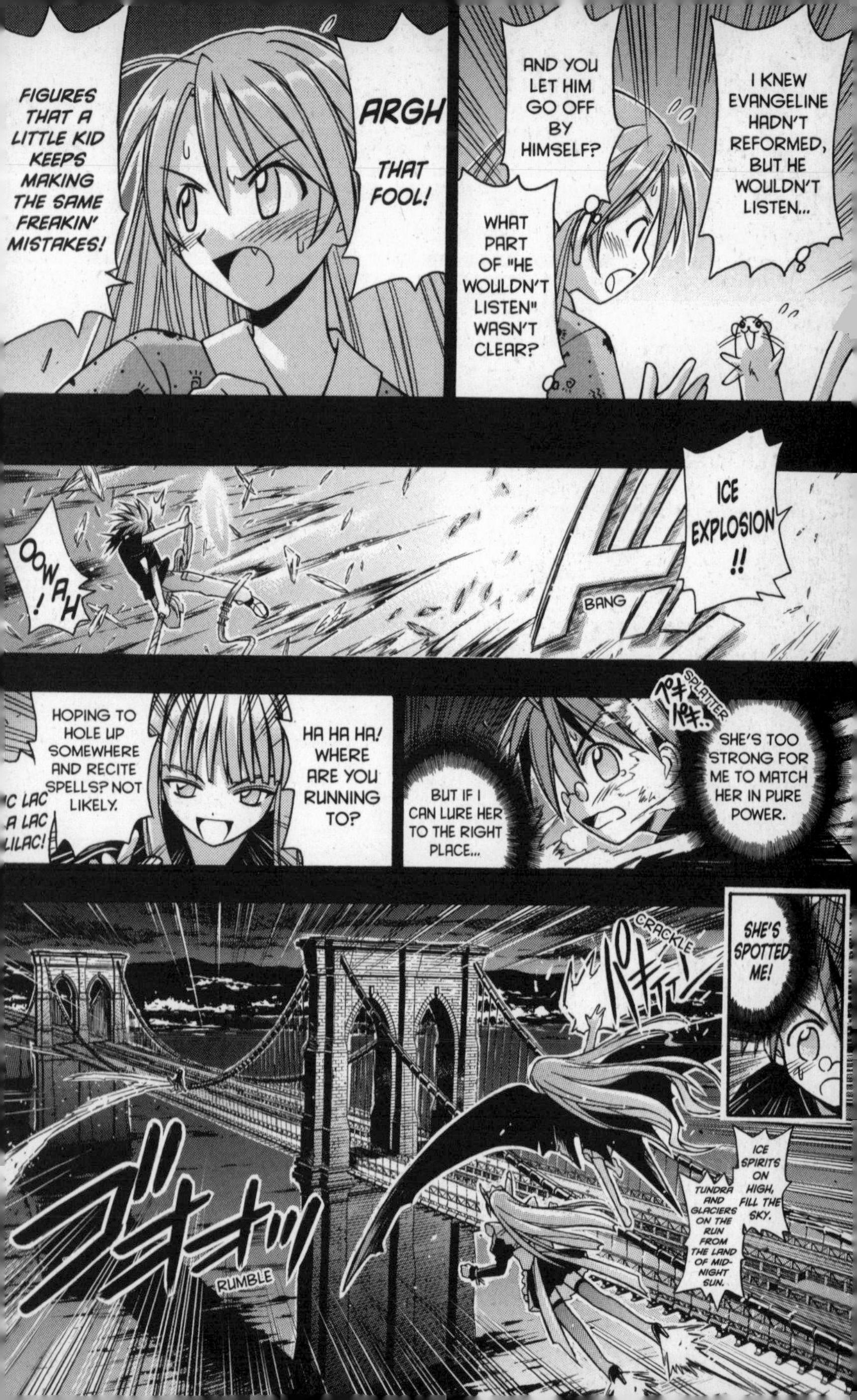
I KNEW EVANGELINE HADN'T REFORMED, BUT HE WOULDN'T LISTEN...
AND YOU LET HIM GO OFF BY HIMSELF?
WHAT PART OF "HE WOULDN'T LISTEN" WASN'T CLEAR?
ARGH
THAT FOOL!
FIGURES THAT A LITTLE KID KEEPS MAKING THE SAME FREAKIN' MISTAKES!
ICE EXPLOSION!!
BANG
OOWAH!
SPLATTER
SHE'S TOO STRONG FOR ME TO MATCH HER IN PURE POWER.
BUT IF I CAN LURE HER TO THE RIGHT PLACE...
HA HA HA! WHERE ARE YOU RUNNING TO?
HOPING TO HOLE UP SOMEWHERE AND RECITE SPELLS? NOT LIKELY.
C LAC A LAC LILAC!
SHE'S SPOTTED ME!
CRACKLE
ICE SPIRITS ON HIGH, FILL THE SKY.
TUNDRA AND GLACIERS ON THE RUN FROM THE LAND OF MID-NIGHT SUN.
RUMBLE

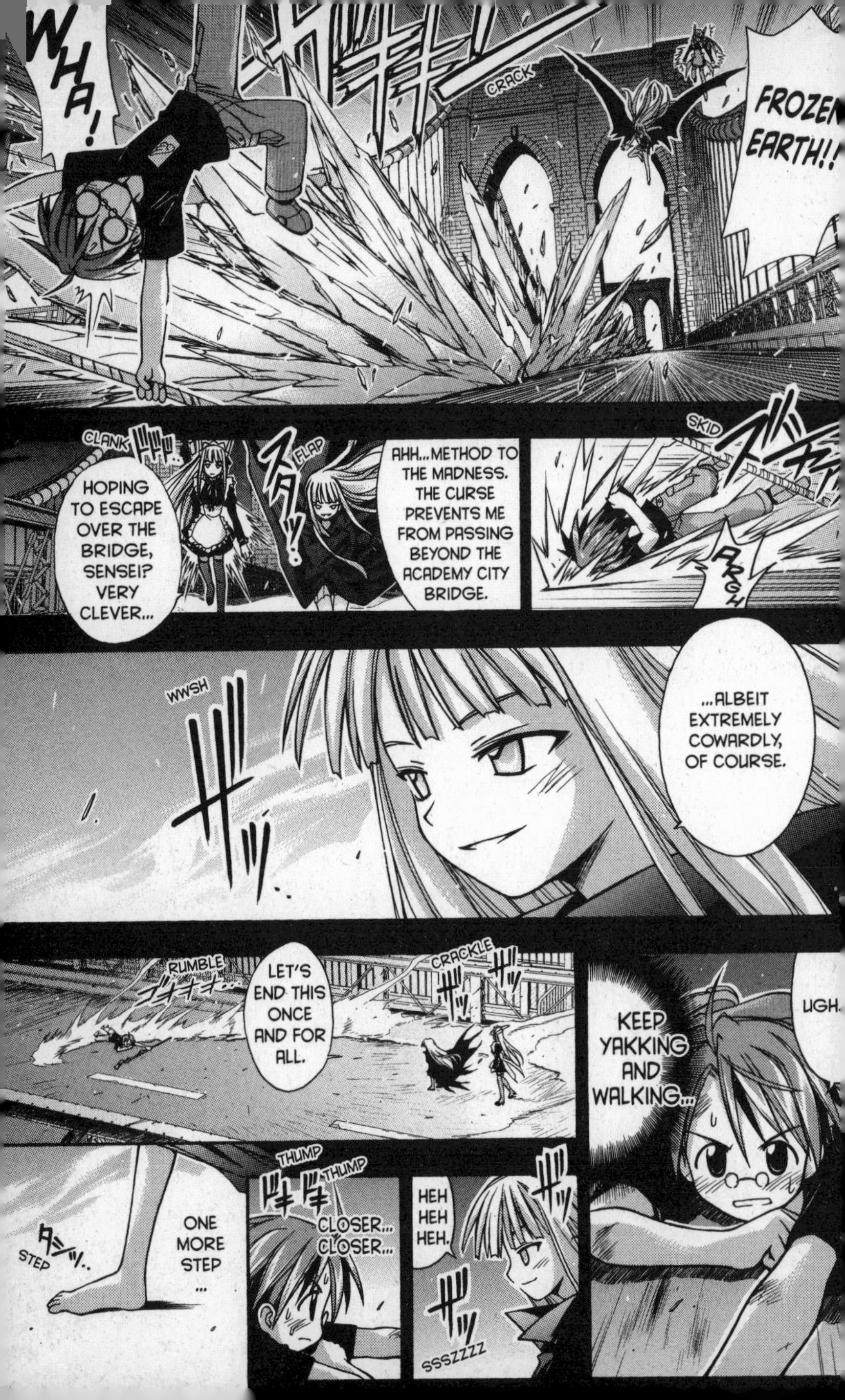

FROZEN EARTH!!
CRACK
WHA!
SKID
ARGH
AHH...METHOD TO THE MADNESS. THE CURSE PREVENTS ME FROM PASSING BEYOND THE ACADEMY CITY BRIDGE.
FLAP
CLANK
HOPING TO ESCAPE OVER THE BRIDGE, SENSEI? VERY CLEVER...
...ALBEIT EXTREMELY COWARDLY, OF COURSE.
WWSH
UGH.
KEEP YAKKING AND WALKING...
CRACKLE
LET'S END THIS ONCE AND FOR ALL.
RUMBLE
HEH HEH HEH.
SSSZZZZ
THUMP
THUMP
CLOSER... CLOSER...
ONE MORE STEP ...
STEP

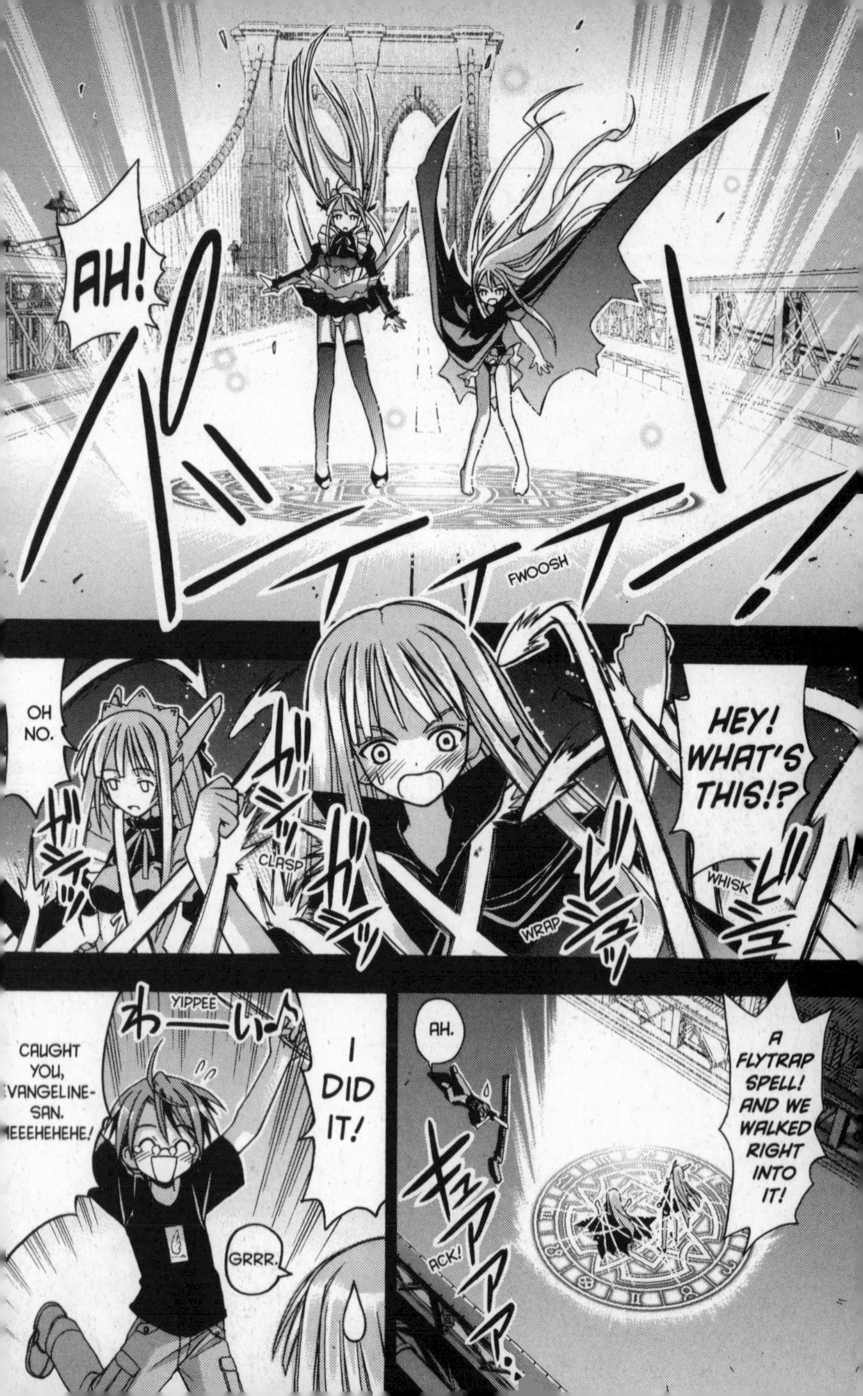
AH!
FWOOSH
HEY! WHAT'S THIS!?
WHISK
WRAP
CLASP
OH NO.
A FLYTRAP SPELL! AND WE WALKED RIGHT INTO IT!
AH.
ACK!
I DID IT!
YIPPEE
CAUGHT YOU, VANGELINE-SAN. EEEEHEHEHE!
GRRR.

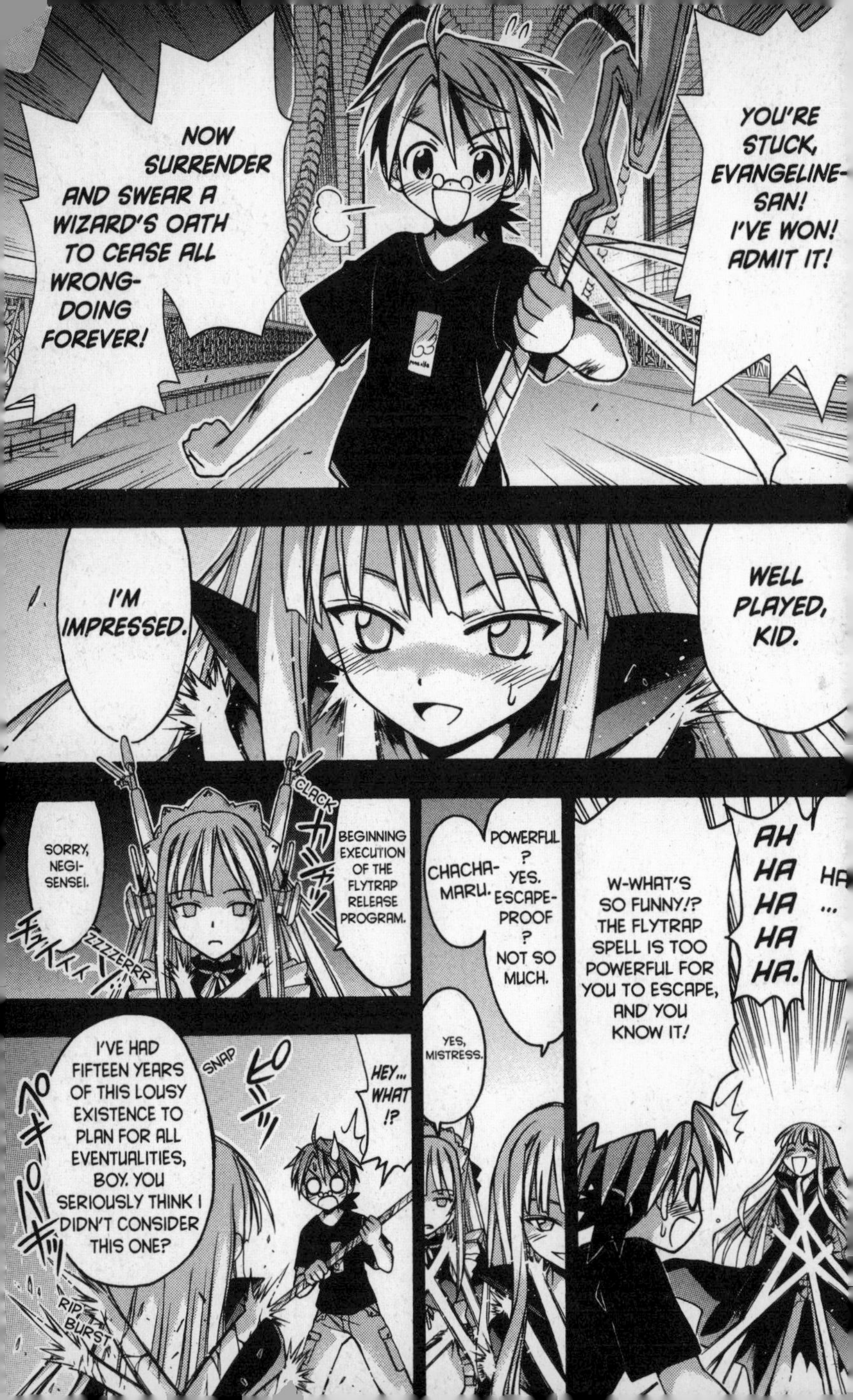
YOU'RE STUCK, EVANGELINE-SAN! I'VE WON! ADMIT IT!
NOW SURRENDER AND SWEAR A WIZARD'S OATH TO CEASE ALL WRONG-DOING FOREVER!
WELL PLAYED, KID.
I'M IMPRESSED.
AH HA HA HA HA.
HA...
W-WHAT'S SO FUNNY!? THE FLYTRAP SPELL IS TOO POWERFUL FOR YOU TO ESCAPE, AND YOU KNOW IT!
POWERFUL? YES. ESCAPE-PROOF? NOT SO MUCH.
CHACHA-MARU.
YES, MISTRESS.
BEGINNING EXECUTION OF THE FLYTRAP RELEASE PROGRAM.
CLACK
SORRY, NEGI-SENSEI.
ZZZZZERRR
HEY... WHAT!?
SNAP
I'VE HAD FIFTEEN YEARS OF THIS LOUSY EXISTENCE TO PLAN FOR ALL EVENTUALITIES, BOY. YOU SERIOUSLY THINK I DIDN'T CONSIDER THIS ONE?
RIP
BURST

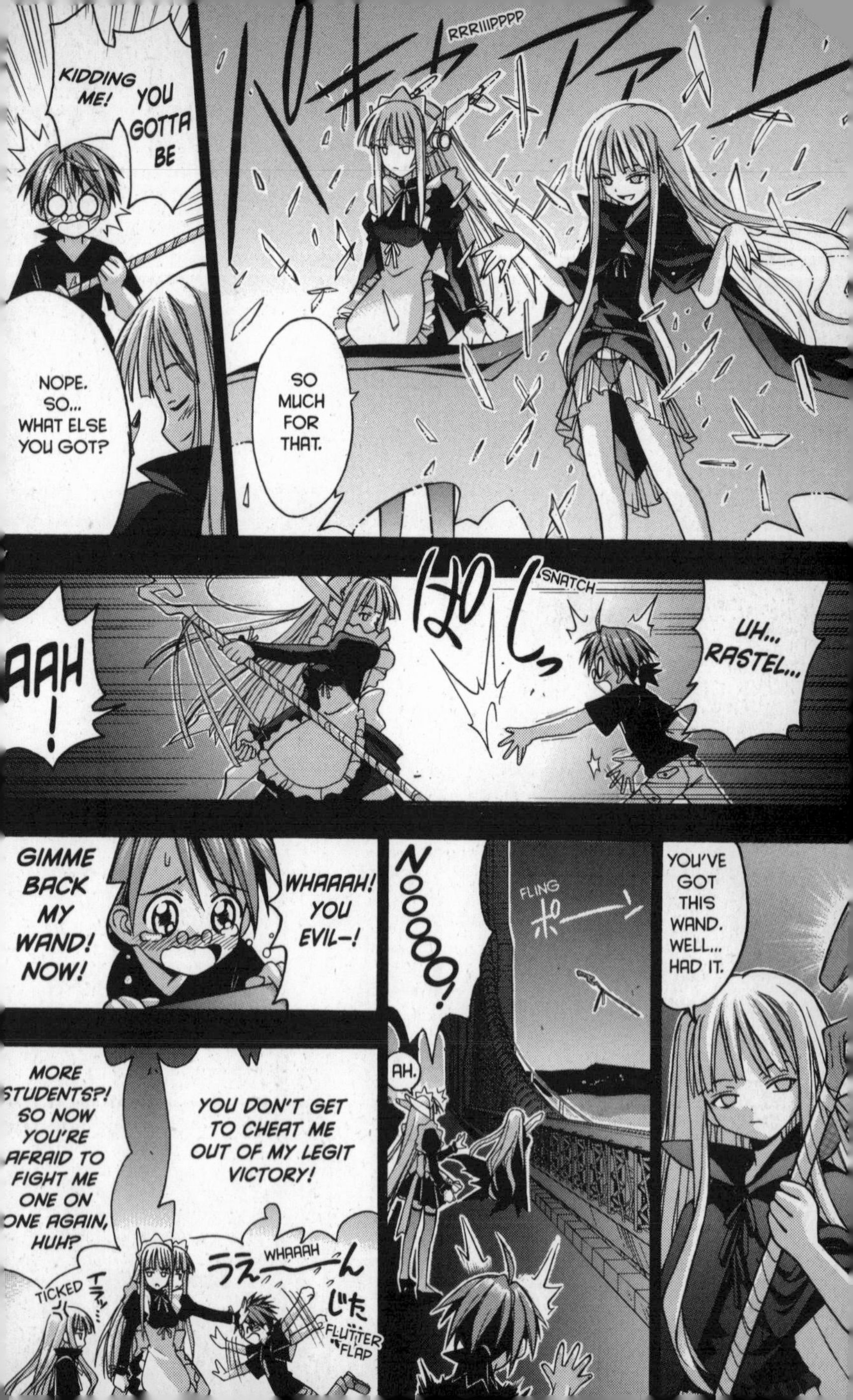
RRRIIIPPPP
SO MUCH FOR THAT.
YOU GOTTA BE KIDDING ME!
NOPE. SO... WHAT ELSE YOU GOT?
UH... RASTEL...
SNATCH
AAH!
YOU'VE GOT THIS WAND. WELL... HAD IT.
FLING
NOOOOO!
AH.
WHAAAH! YOU EVIL-!
GIMME BACK MY WAND! NOW!
YOU DON'T GET TO CHEAT ME OUT OF MY LEGIT VICTORY!
MORE STUDENTS?! SO NOW YOU'RE AFRAID TO FIGHT ME ONE ON ONE AGAIN, HUH?
WHAAAH
FLUTTER FLAP
TICKED

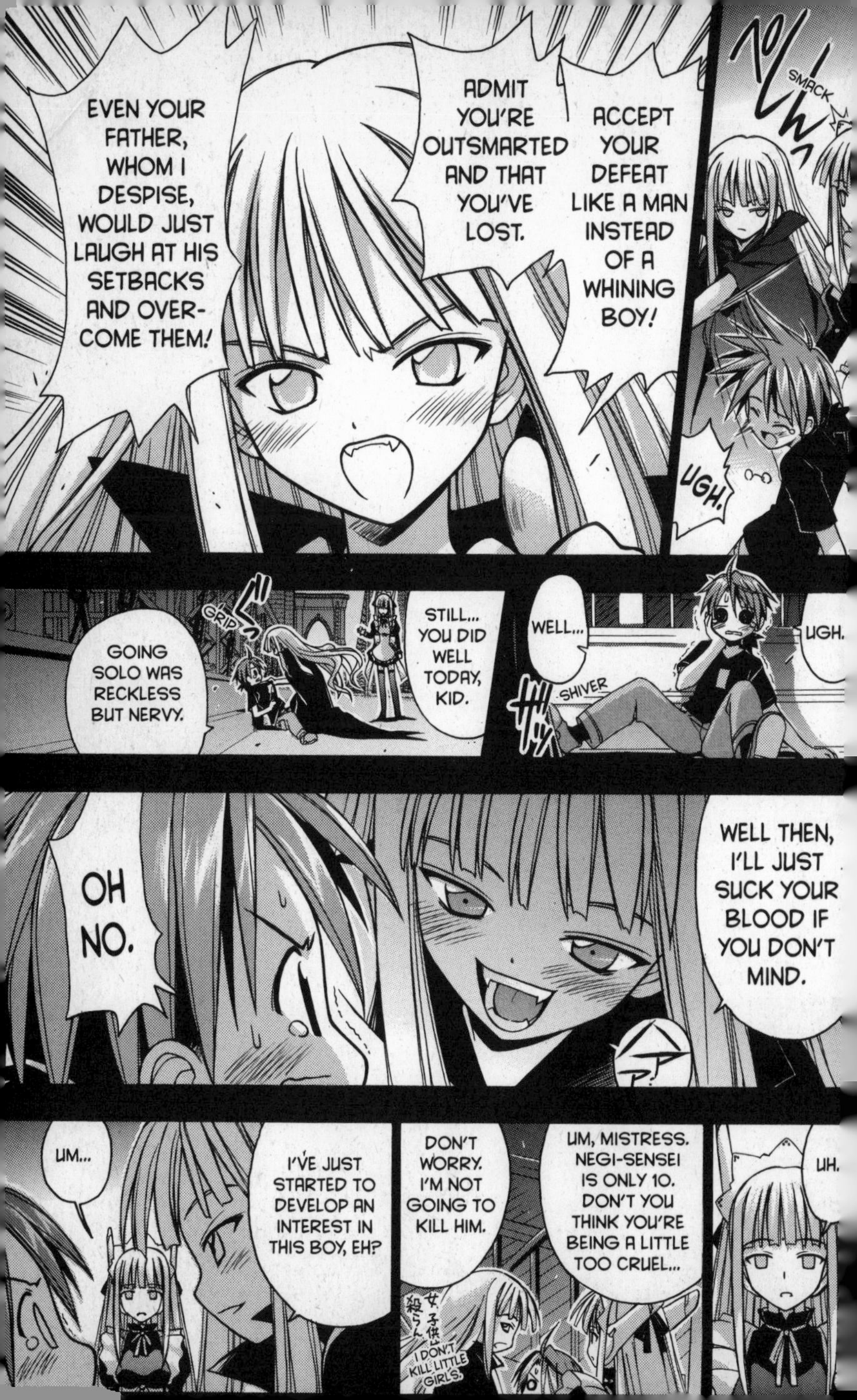
SMACK
UGH.
ACCEPT YOUR DEFEAT LIKE A MAN INSTEAD OF A WHINING BOY!
ADMIT YOU'RE OUTSMARTED AND THAT YOU'VE LOST.
EVEN YOUR FATHER, WHOM I DESPISE, WOULD JUST LAUGH AT HIS SETBACKS AND OVERCOME THEM!
UGH.
WELL...
SHIVER
STILL... YOU DID WELL TODAY, KID.
GRIP
GOING SOLO WAS RECKLESS BUT NERVY.
WELL THEN, I'LL JUST SUCK YOUR BLOOD IF YOU DON'T MIND.
OH NO.
UH.
UM, MISTRESS. NEGI-SENSEI IS ONLY 10. DON'T YOU THINK YOU'RE BEING A LITTLE TOO CRUEL...
DON'T WORRY. I'M NOT GOING TO KILL HIM.
女子供は殺らん
I DON'T KILL LITTLE GIRLS.
I'VE JUST STARTED TO DEVELOP AN INTEREST IN THIS BOY, EH?
UM...

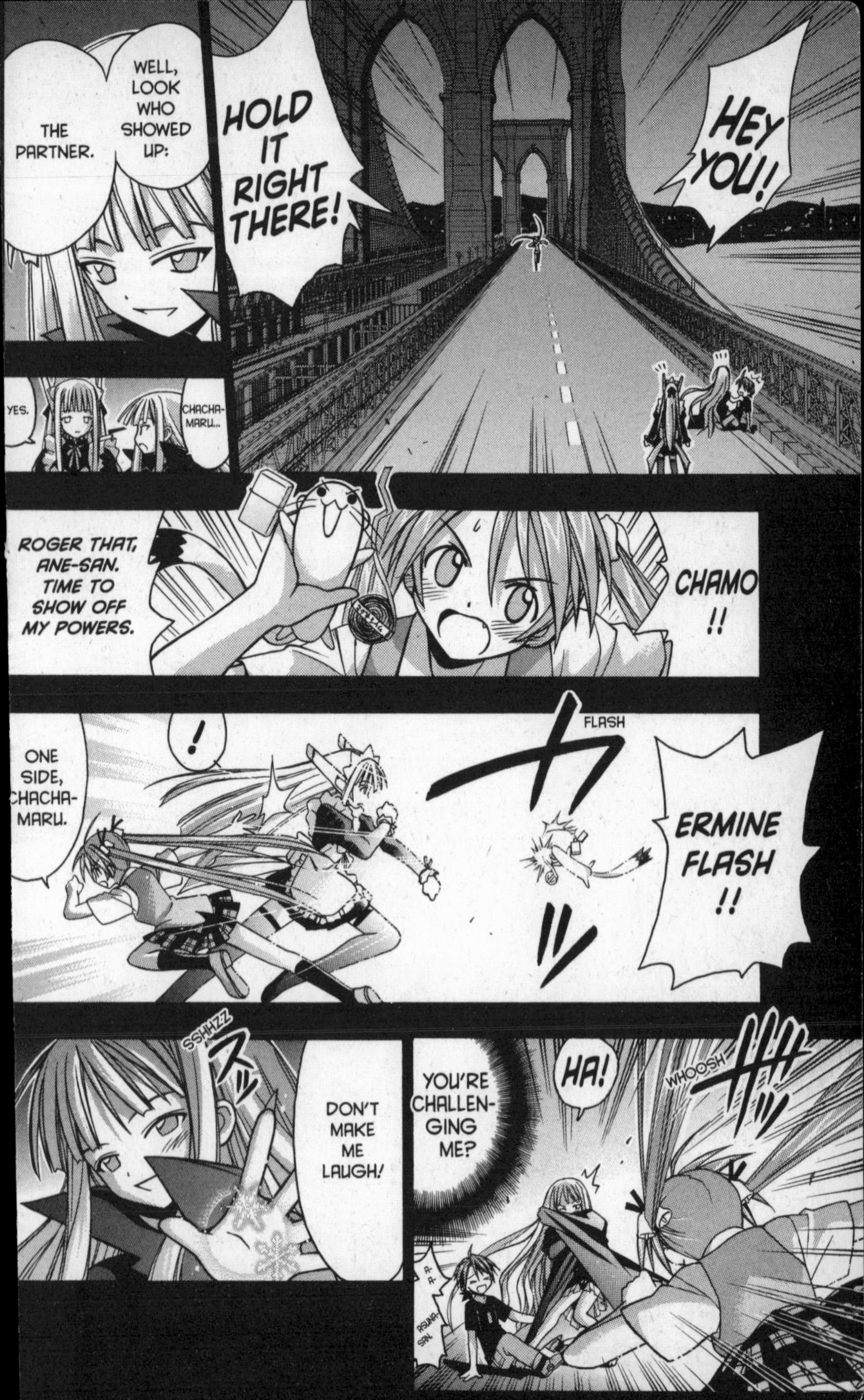
HEY YOU!
HOLD IT RIGHT THERE!
WELL, LOOK WHO SHOWED UP:
THE PARTNER.
CHACHA-MARU...
YES.
CHAMO !!
ROGER THAT, ANE-SAN. TIME TO SHOW OFF MY POWERS.
FLASH
ERMINE FLASH !!
!
ONE SIDE, CHACHA-MARU.
WHOOSH
HA!
YOU'RE CHALLEN-GING ME?
A-A-ASUNA-SAN.
SSHHZZ
DON'T MAKE ME LAUGH!

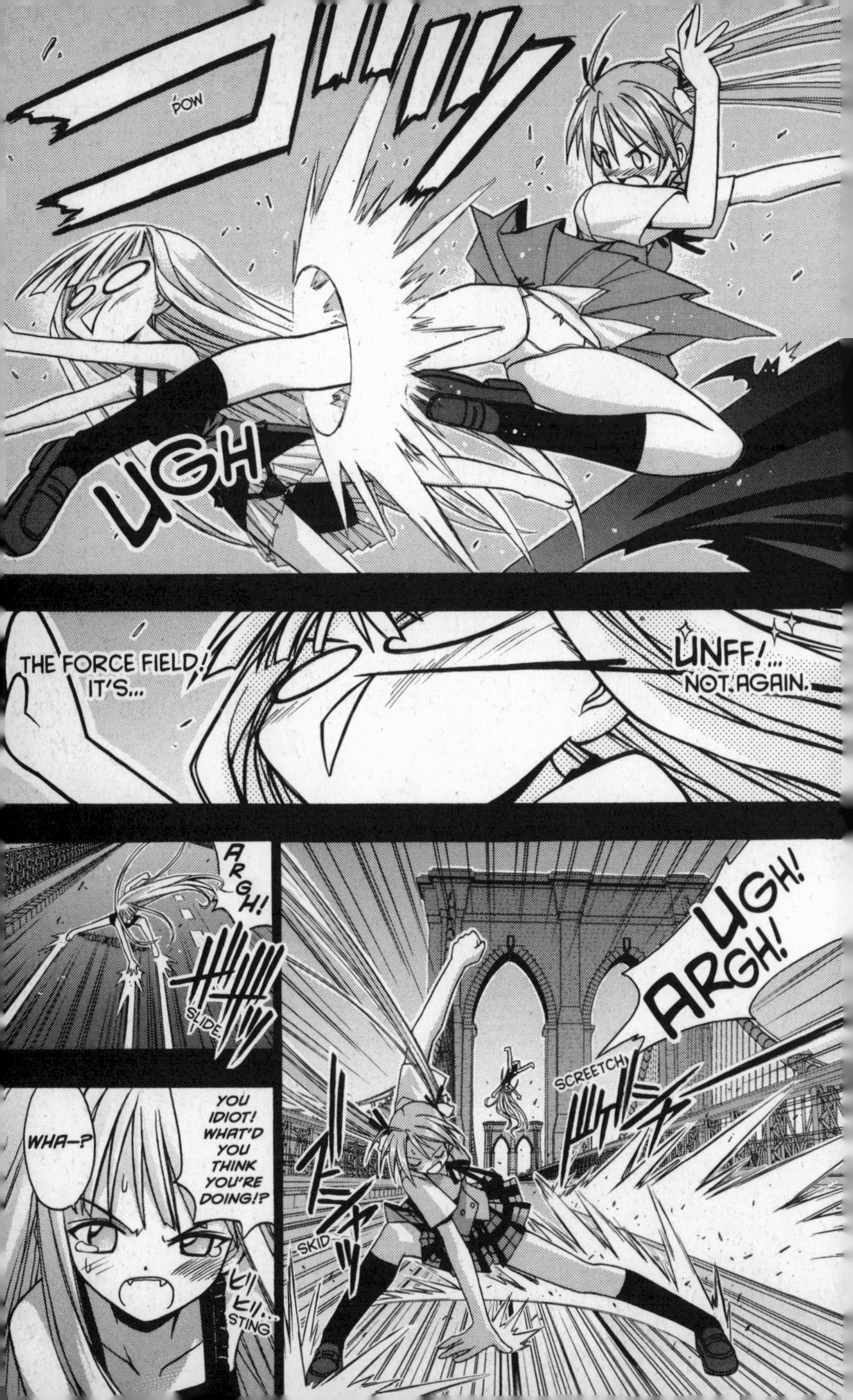
POW
UGH
UNFF!... NOT AGAIN.
THE FORCE FIELD! IT'S...
UGH! ARGH!
SCREETCH
SKID
ARGH!
SLIDE
YOU IDIOT! WHAT'D YOU THINK YOU'RE DOING!?
WHA-?
STING

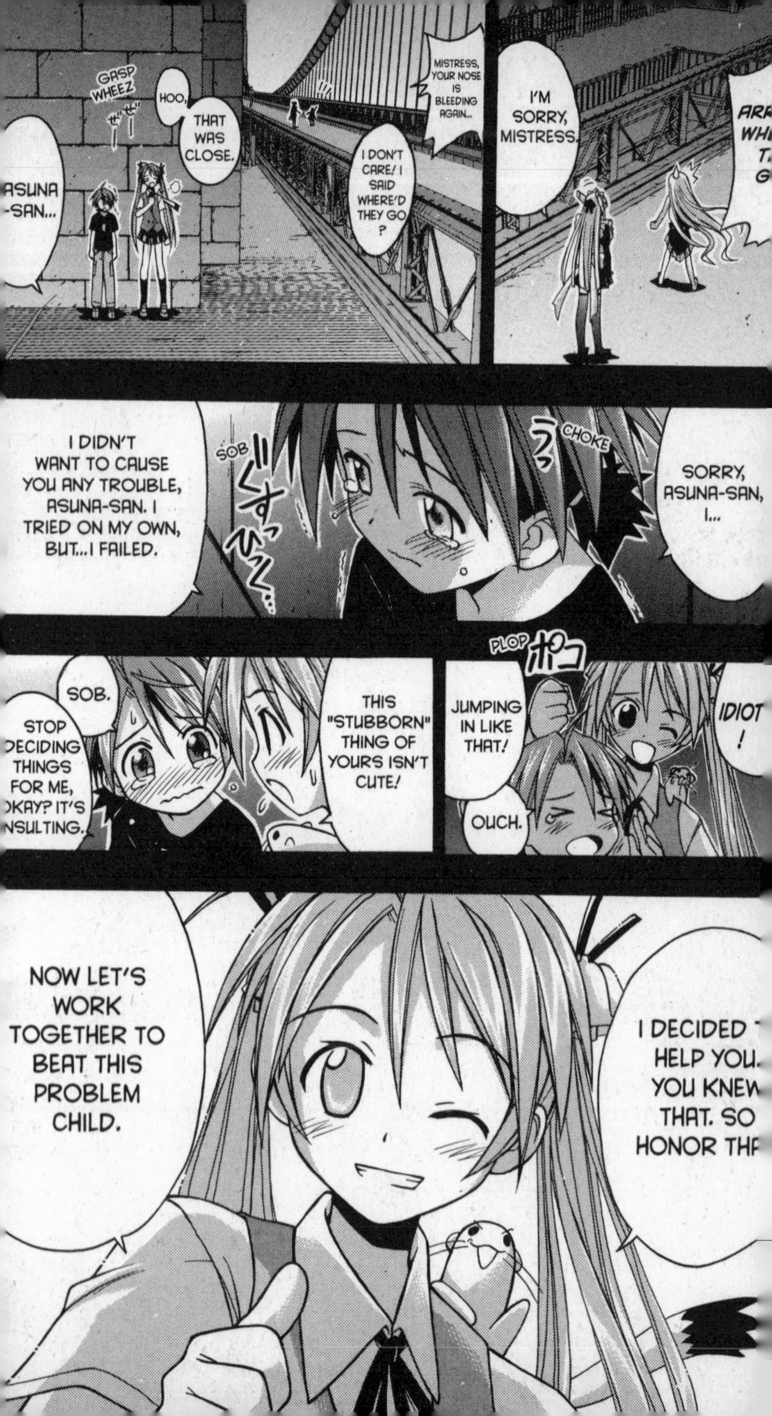
ARR
WH
T
G
I'M SORRY, MISTRESS.
MISTRESS, YOUR NOSE IS BLEEDING AGAIN...
I DON'T CARE! I SAID WHERE'D THEY GO?
HOO, THAT WAS CLOSE.
GASP WHEEZ
ASUNA -SAN...
SORRY, ASUNA-SAN, I...
CHOKE
SOB
I DIDN'T WANT TO CAUSE YOU ANY TROUBLE, ASUNA-SAN. I TRIED ON MY OWN, BUT...I FAILED.
IDIOT!
PLOP
JUMPING IN LIKE THAT!
OUCH.
THIS "STUBBORN" THING OF YOURS ISN'T CUTE!
SOB.
STOP ECIDING THINGS FOR ME, KAY? IT'S NSULTING.
I DECIDED T HELP YOU. YOU KNEW THAT. SO HONOR TH
NOW LET'S WORK TOGETHER TO BEAT THIS PROBLEM CHILD.

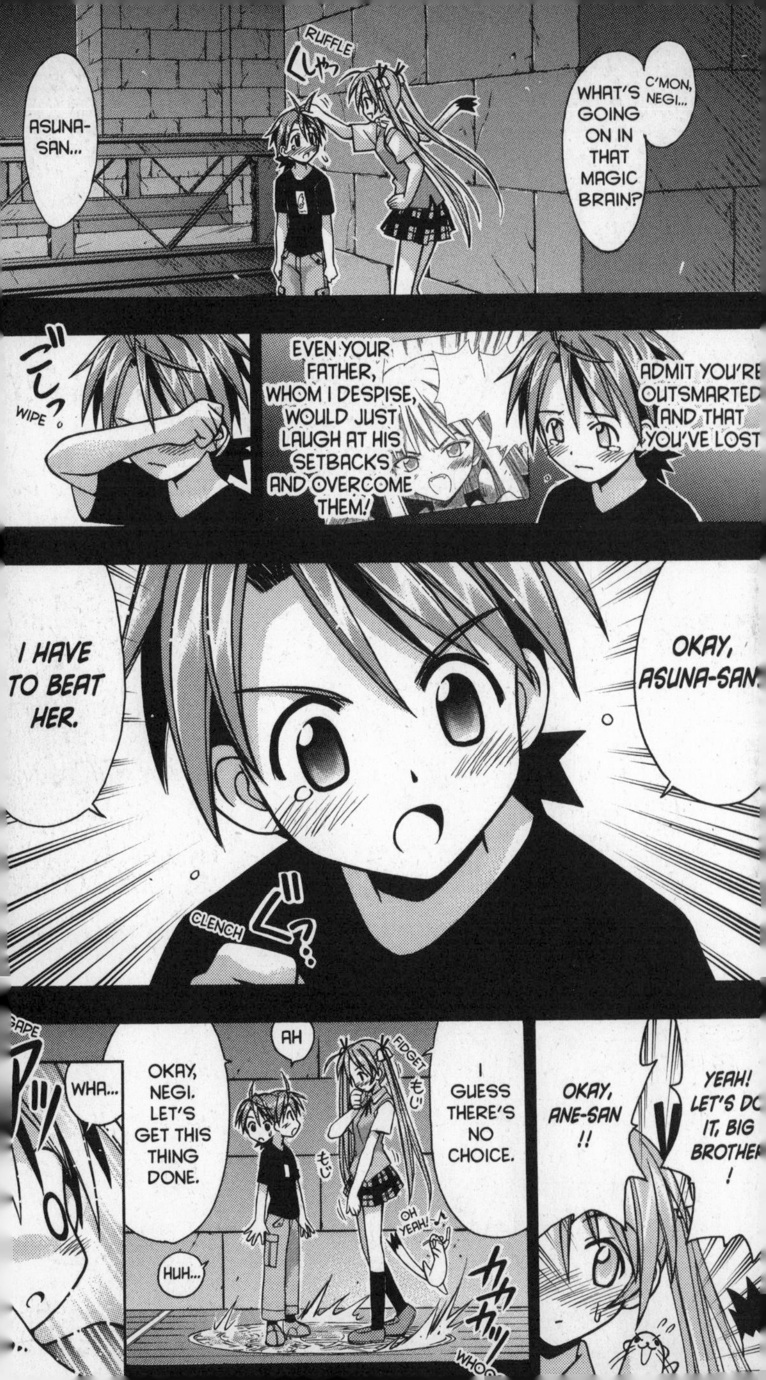
C'MON, NEGI...
WHAT'S GOING ON IN THAT MAGIC BRAIN?
RUFFLE
ASUNA-SAN...
ADMIT YOU'RE OUTSMARTED AND THAT YOU'VE LOST
EVEN YOUR FATHER, WHOM I DESPISE, WOULD JUST LAUGH AT HIS SETBACKS AND OVERCOME THEM!
WIPE
OKAY, ASUNA-SAN.
I HAVE TO BEAT HER.
CLENCH
YEAH! LET'S DO IT, BIG BROTHE !
OKAY, ANE-SAN !!
I GUESS THERE'S NO CHOICE.
FIDGET
AH
OKAY, NEGI. LET'S GET THIS THING DONE.
OH YEAH! ♪
HUH...
WHOO
GAPE
WHA...

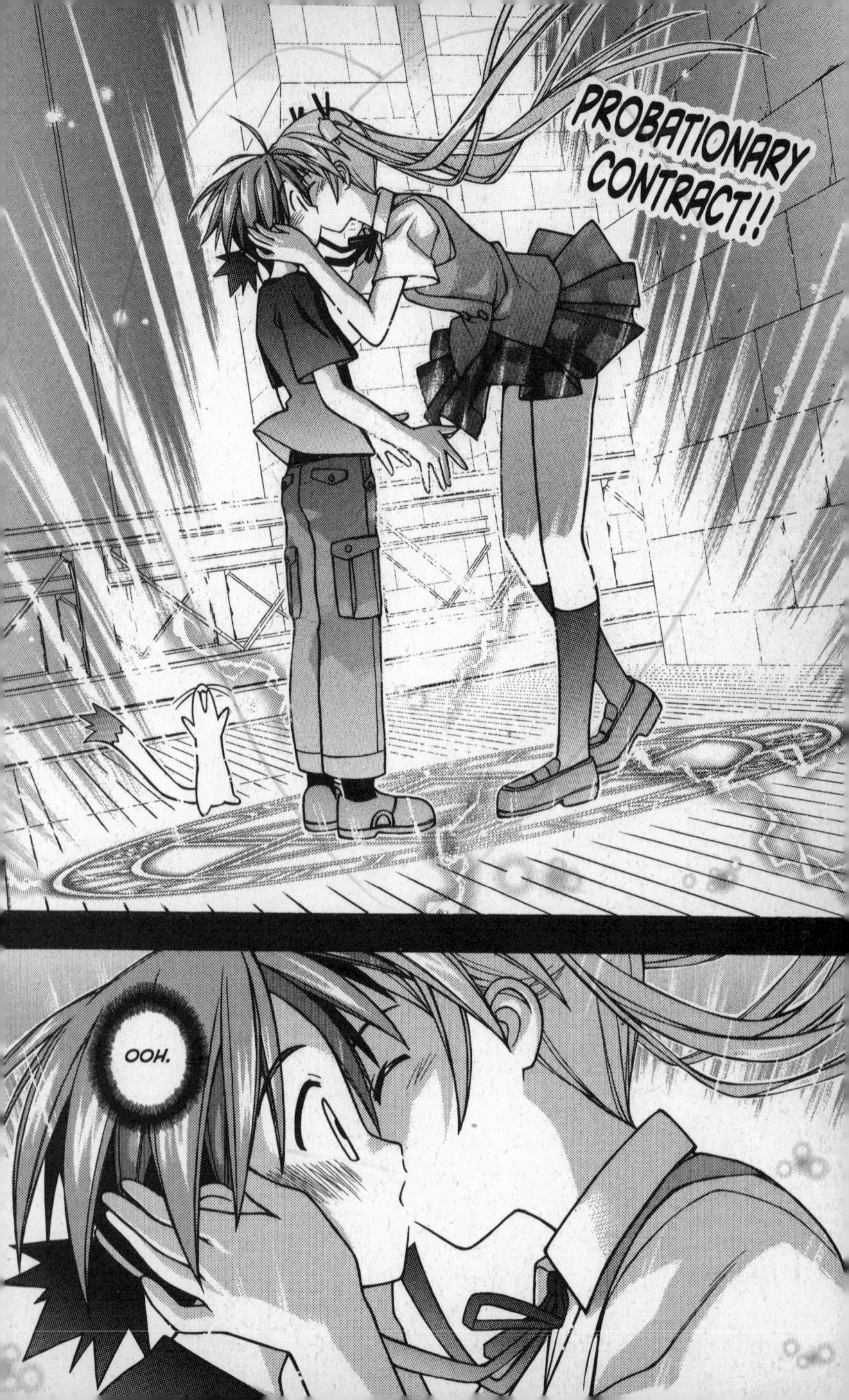
PROBATIONARY CONTRACT!!
OOH.

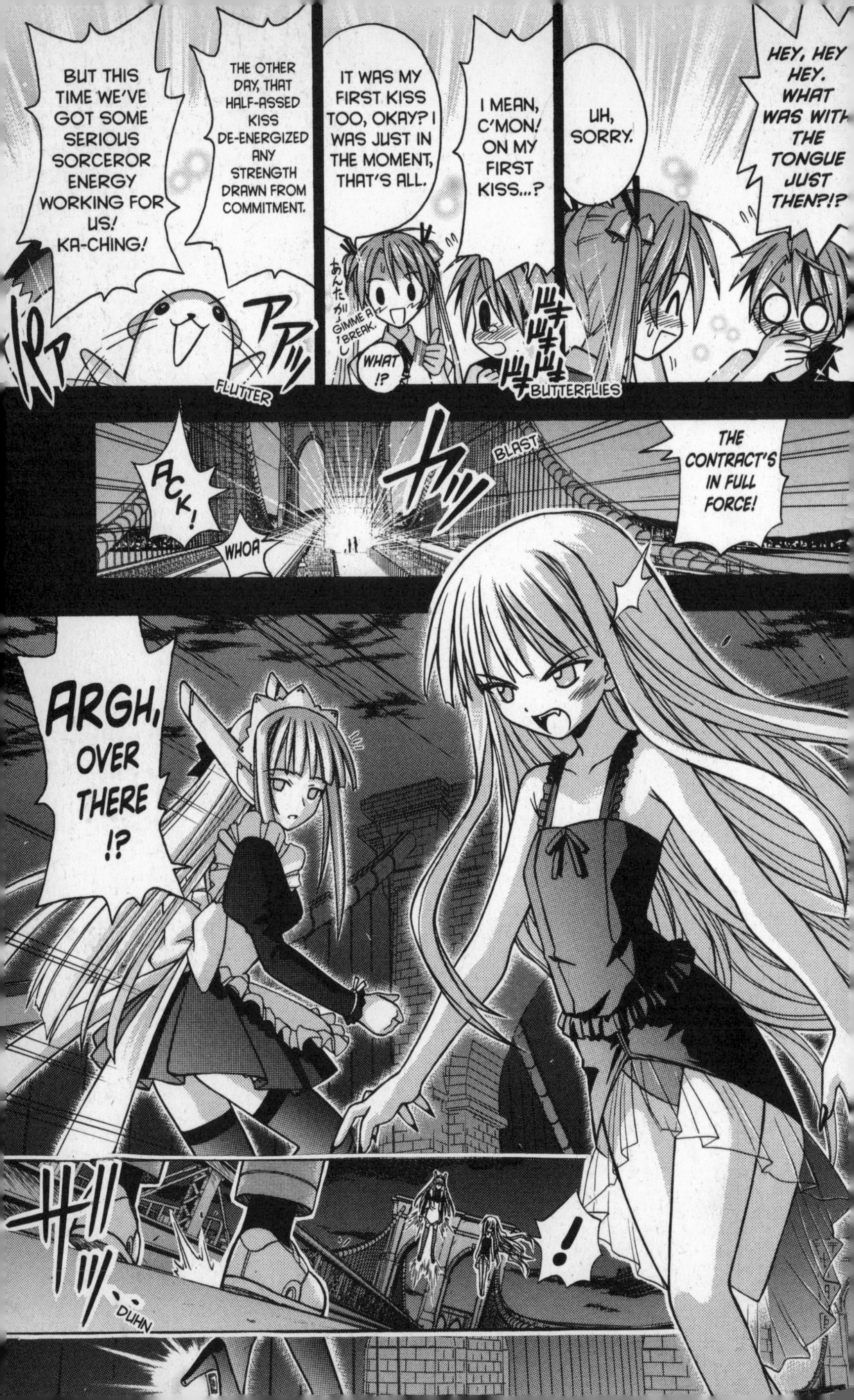
HEY, HEY HEY. WHAT WAS WITH THE TONGUE JUST THEN?!?
UH, SORRY.
I MEAN, C'MON! ON MY FIRST KISS...?
BUTTERFLIES
IT WAS MY FIRST KISS TOO, OKAY? I WAS JUST IN THE MOMENT, THAT'S ALL.
GIMME A BREAK.
WHAT !?
THE OTHER DAY, THAT HALF-ASSED KISS DE-ENERGIZED ANY STRENGTH DRAWN FROM COMMITMENT.
BUT THIS TIME WE'VE GOT SOME SERIOUS SORCEROR ENERGY WORKING FOR US! KA-CHING!
FLUTTER
THE CONTRACT'S IN FULL FORCE!
BLAST
ACK!
WHOA
ARGH, OVER THERE !?
!
DUHN

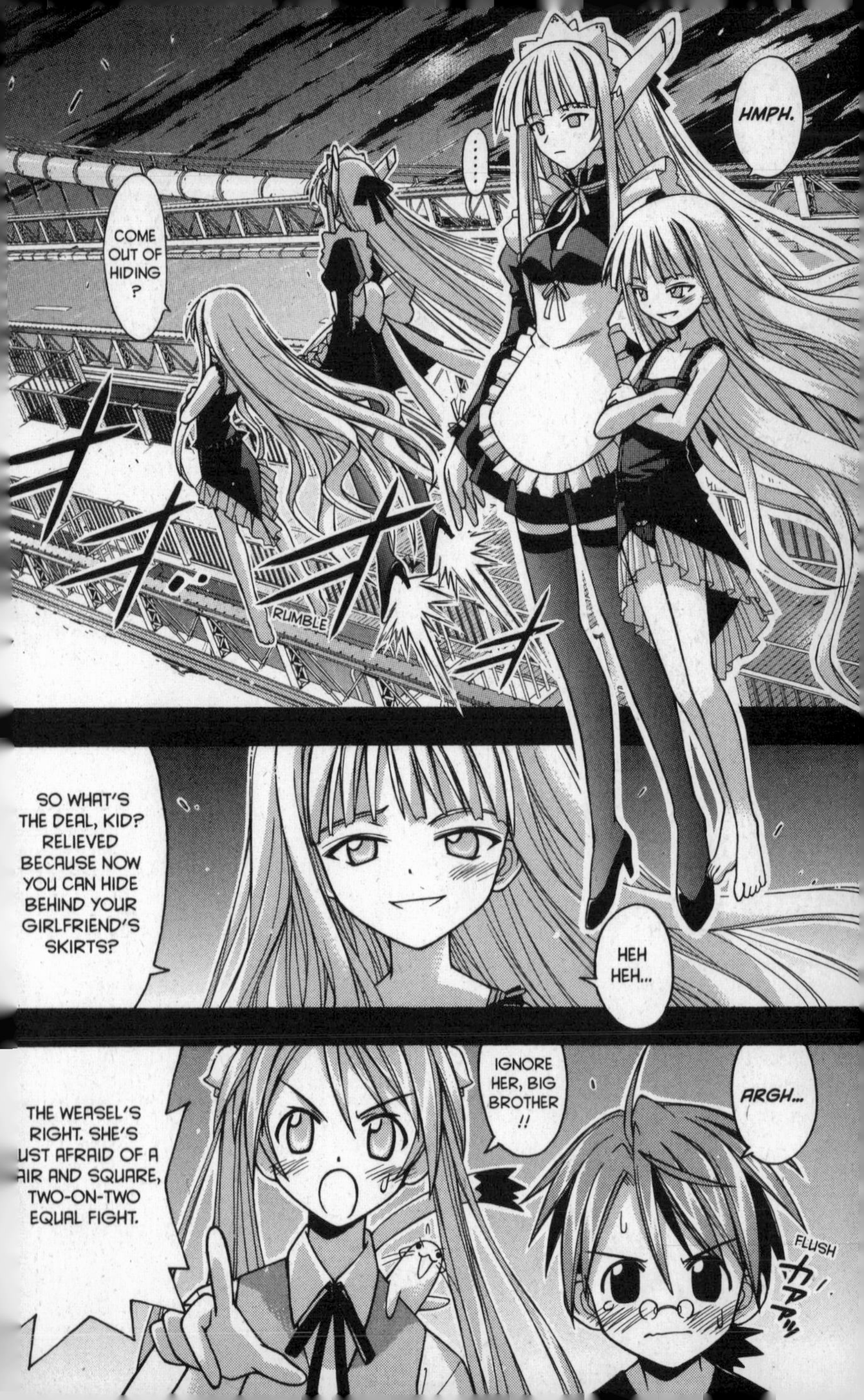
HMPH.
......
COME OUT OF HIDING ?
RUMBLE
HEH HEH...
SO WHAT'S THE DEAL, KID? RELIEVED BECAUSE NOW YOU CAN HIDE BEHIND YOUR GIRLFRIEND'S SKIRTS?
ARGH...
FLUSH
IGNORE HER, BIG BROTHER !!
THE WEASEL'S RIGHT. SHE'S UST AFRAID OF A AIR AND SQUARE, TWO-ON-TWO EQUAL FIGHT.

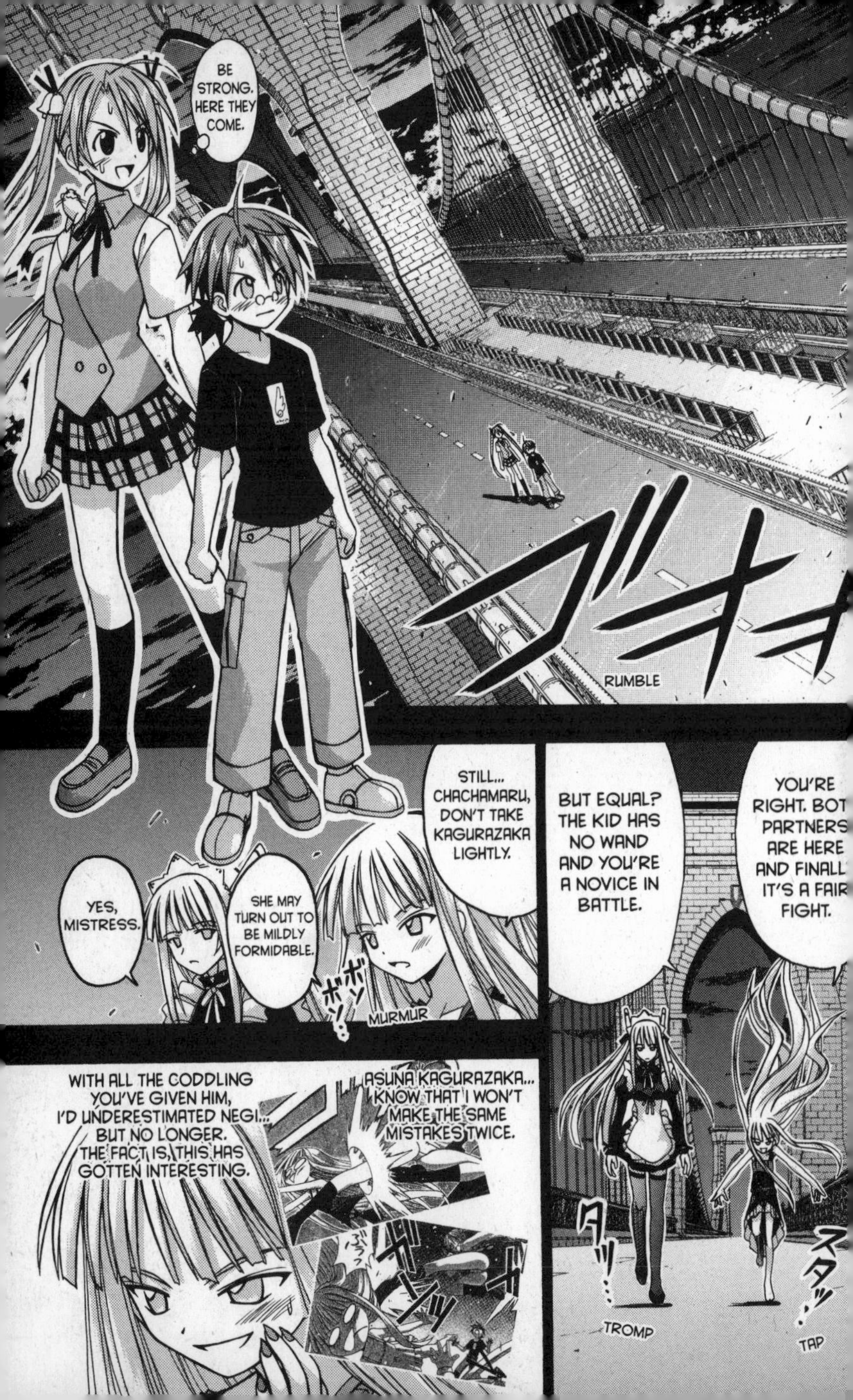
BE STRONG. HERE THEY COME.
RUMBLE
YOU'RE RIGHT. BOT PARTNERS ARE HERE AND FINALL IT'S A FAIR FIGHT.
BUT EQUAL? THE KID HAS NO WAND AND YOU'RE A NOVICE IN BATTLE.
TROMP
TAP
STILL... CHACHAMARU, DON'T TAKE KAGURAZAKA LIGHTLY.
SHE MAY TURN OUT TO BE MILDLY FORMIDABLE.
MURMUR
YES, MISTRESS.
ASUNA KAGURAZAKA... KNOW THAT I WON'T MAKE THE SAME MISTAKES TWICE.
WITH ALL THE CODDLING YOU'VE GIVEN HIM, I'D UNDERESTIMATED NEGI... BUT NO LONGER. THE FACT IS, THIS HAS GOTTEN INTERESTING.

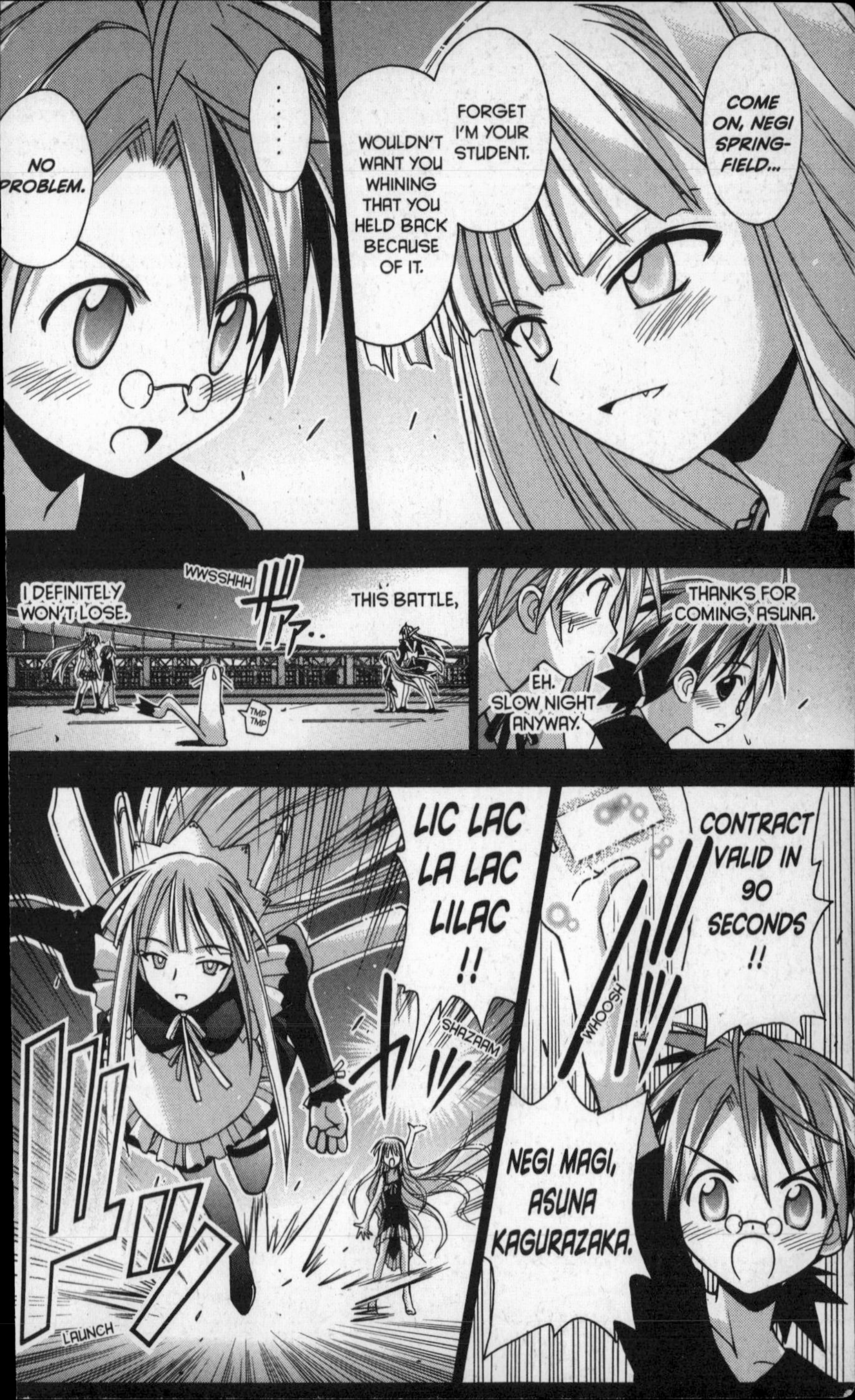
COME ON, NEGI SPRING-FIELD...
FORGET I'M YOUR STUDENT.
WOULDN'T WANT YOU WHINING THAT YOU HELD BACK BECAUSE OF IT.
......
NO PROBLEM.
THANKS FOR COMING, ASUNA.
EH. SLOW NIGHT ANYWAY.
THIS BATTLE,
WWSSHHH
I DEFINITELY WON'T LOSE.
TMP TMP
CONTRACT VALID IN 90 SECONDS !!
WHOOSH
NEGI MAGI, ASUNA KAGURAZAKA.
LIC LAC LA LAC LILAC !!
SHAZAAM
LAUNCH

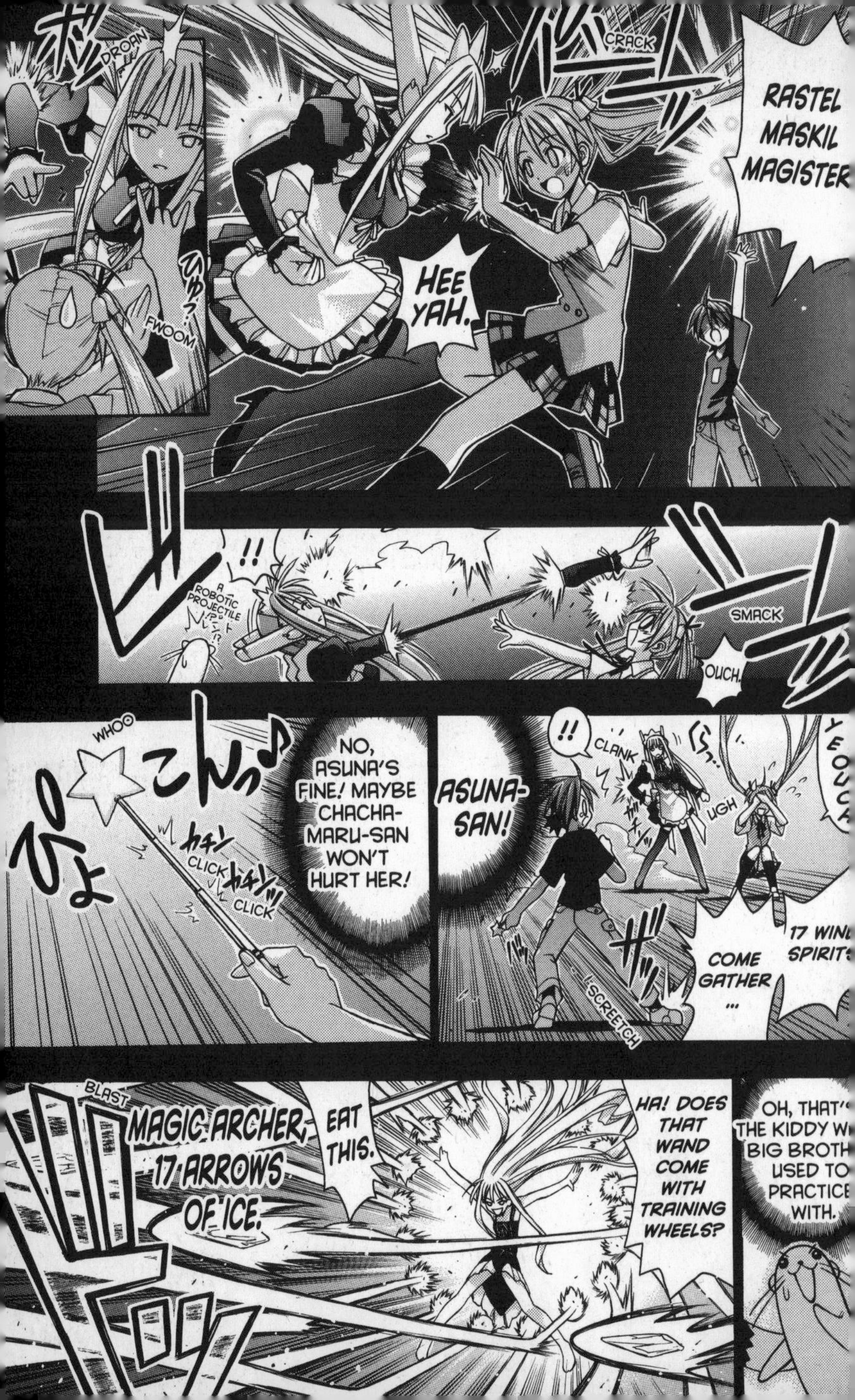
RASTEL MASKIL MAGISTER
CRACK
HEE YAH.
DROAN
FWOOM
SMACK
OUCH.
!!
A ROBOTIC PROJECTILE
YEOUCH
17 WIND SPIRITS
COME GATHER ...
UGH
CLANK
!!
ASUNA-SAN!
SCREECH
NO, ASUNA'S FINE! MAYBE CHACHA-MARU-SAN WON'T HURT HER!
WHOO
CLICK
CLICK
OH, THAT'S THE KIDDY W BIG BROTH USED TO PRACTICE WITH.
HA! DOES THAT WAND COME WITH TRAINING WHEELS?
EAT THIS.
MAGIC ARCHER, 17 ARROWS OF ICE.
BLAST

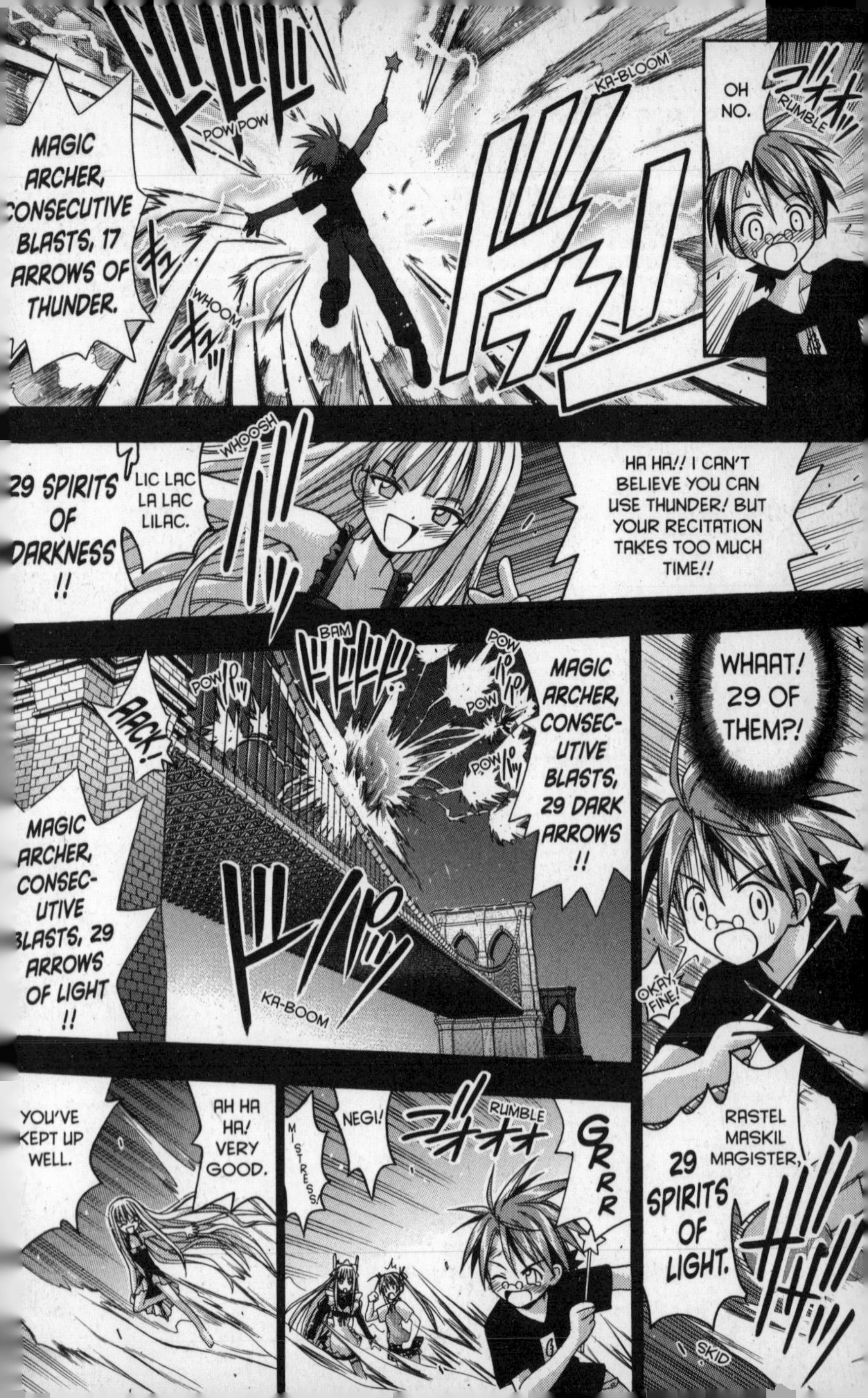
OH NO.
RUMBLE
KA-BLOOM
POW POW
WHOOM
MAGIC ARCHER, CONSECUTIVE BLASTS, 17 ARROWS OF THUNDER.
HA HA!! I CAN'T BELIEVE YOU CAN USE THUNDER! BUT YOUR RECITATION TAKES TOO MUCH TIME!!
WHOOSH
LIC LAC LA LAC LILAC.
29 SPIRITS OF DARKNESS!!
WHAAT! 29 OF THEM?!
OKAY, FINE!
RASTEL MASKIL MAGISTER,
29 SPIRITS OF LIGHT.
SKID
MAGIC ARCHER, CONSECUTIVE BLASTS, 29 DARK ARROWS!!
POW
POW
POW
BAM
POW
AACK!
MAGIC ARCHER, CONSECUTIVE BLASTS, 29 ARROWS OF LIGHT!!
KA-BOOM
RUMBLE
GRRR
NEGI!
MISTRESS!
AH HA HA! VERY GOOD.
YOU'VE KEPT UP WELL.

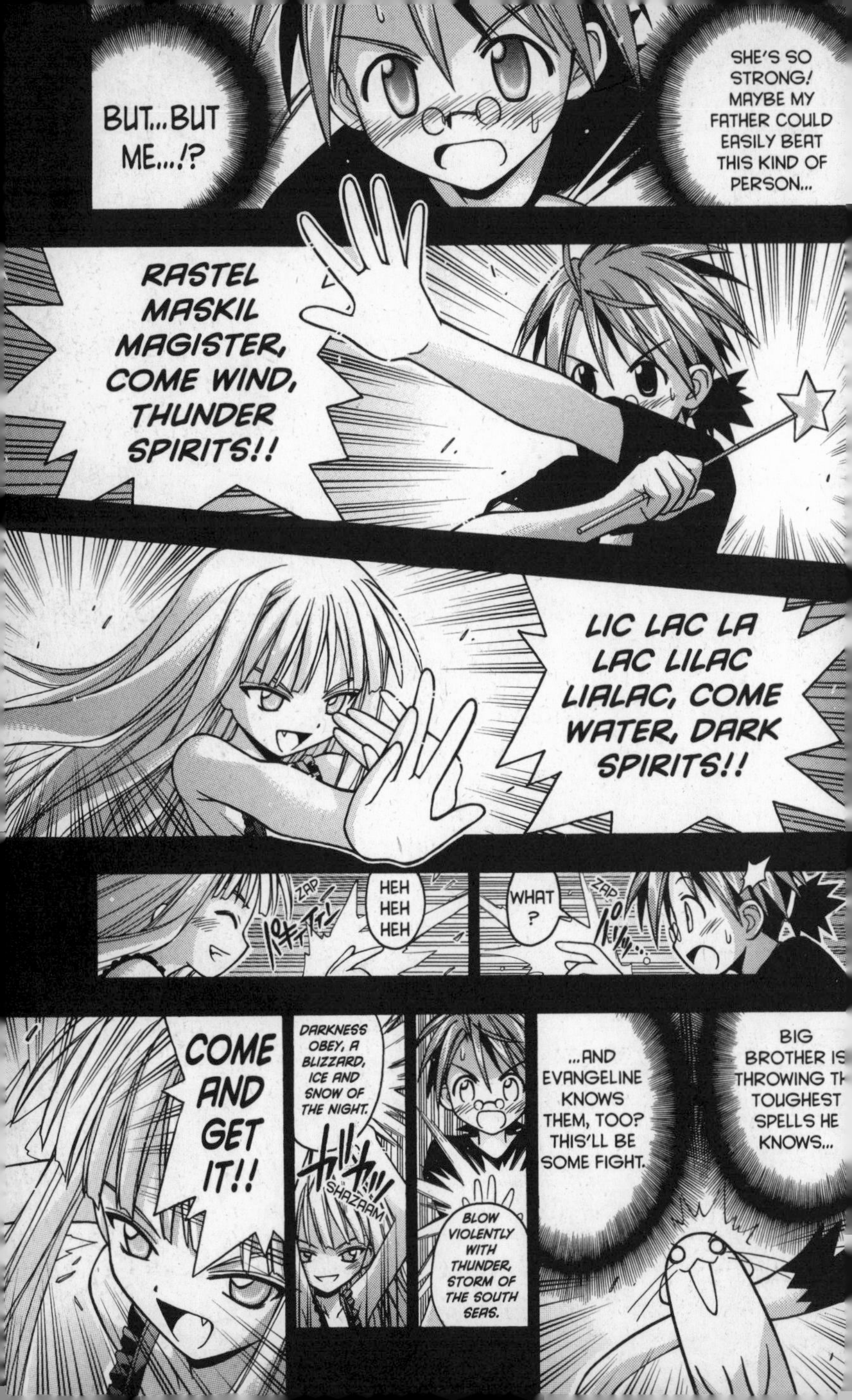
SHE'S SO STRONG! MAYBE MY FATHER COULD EASILY BEAT THIS KIND OF PERSON...
BUT...BUT ME...!?
RASTEL MASKIL MAGISTER, COME WIND, THUNDER SPIRITS!!
LIC LAC LA LAC LILAC LIALAC, COME WATER, DARK SPIRITS!!
WHAT ?
ZAP
HEH HEH HEH
ZAP
BIG BROTHER IS THROWING TH TOUGHEST SPELLS HE KNOWS...
...AND EVANGELINE KNOWS THEM, TOO? THIS'LL BE SOME FIGHT.
BLOW VIOLENTLY WITH THUNDER, STORM OF THE SOUTH SEAS.
DARKNESS OBEY, A BLIZZARD, ICE AND SNOW OF THE NIGHT.
SHAZAAM
COME AND GET IT!!

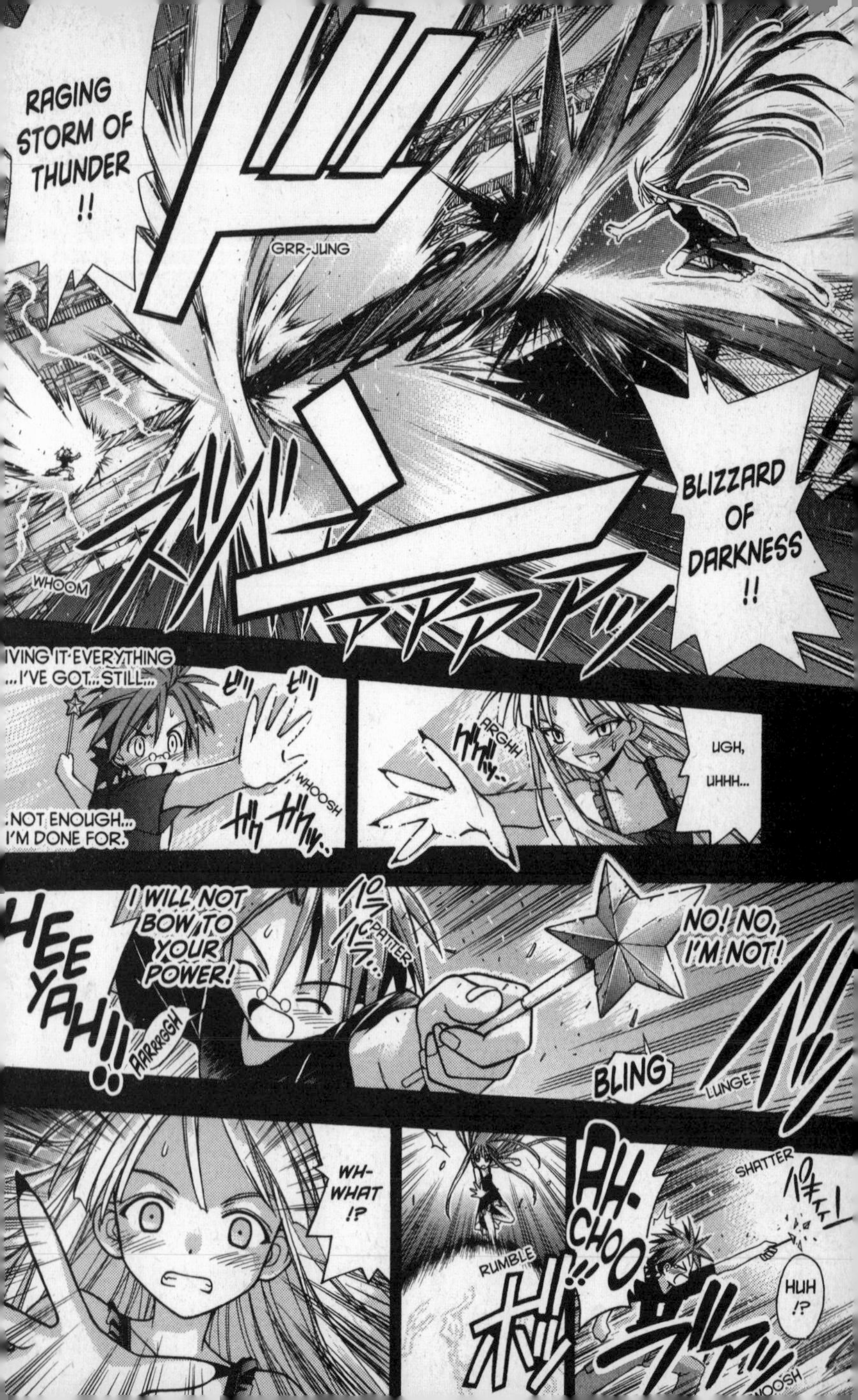
RAGING STORM OF THUNDER !!
GRR-JUNG
BLIZZARD OF DARKNESS !!
WHOOM
ARGHH
UGH, UHHH...
IVING IT EVERYTHING ...I'VE GOT... STILL...
WHOOSH
.NOT ENOUGH... I'M DONE FOR.
NO! NO, I'M NOT!
LUNGE
BLING
CPATTER
I WILL NOT BOW TO YOUR POWER!
AARRRGGH
HEE YAH!!
SHATTER
AH-CHOO!!
HUH !?
RUMBLE
NOOSH
WH-WHAT !?

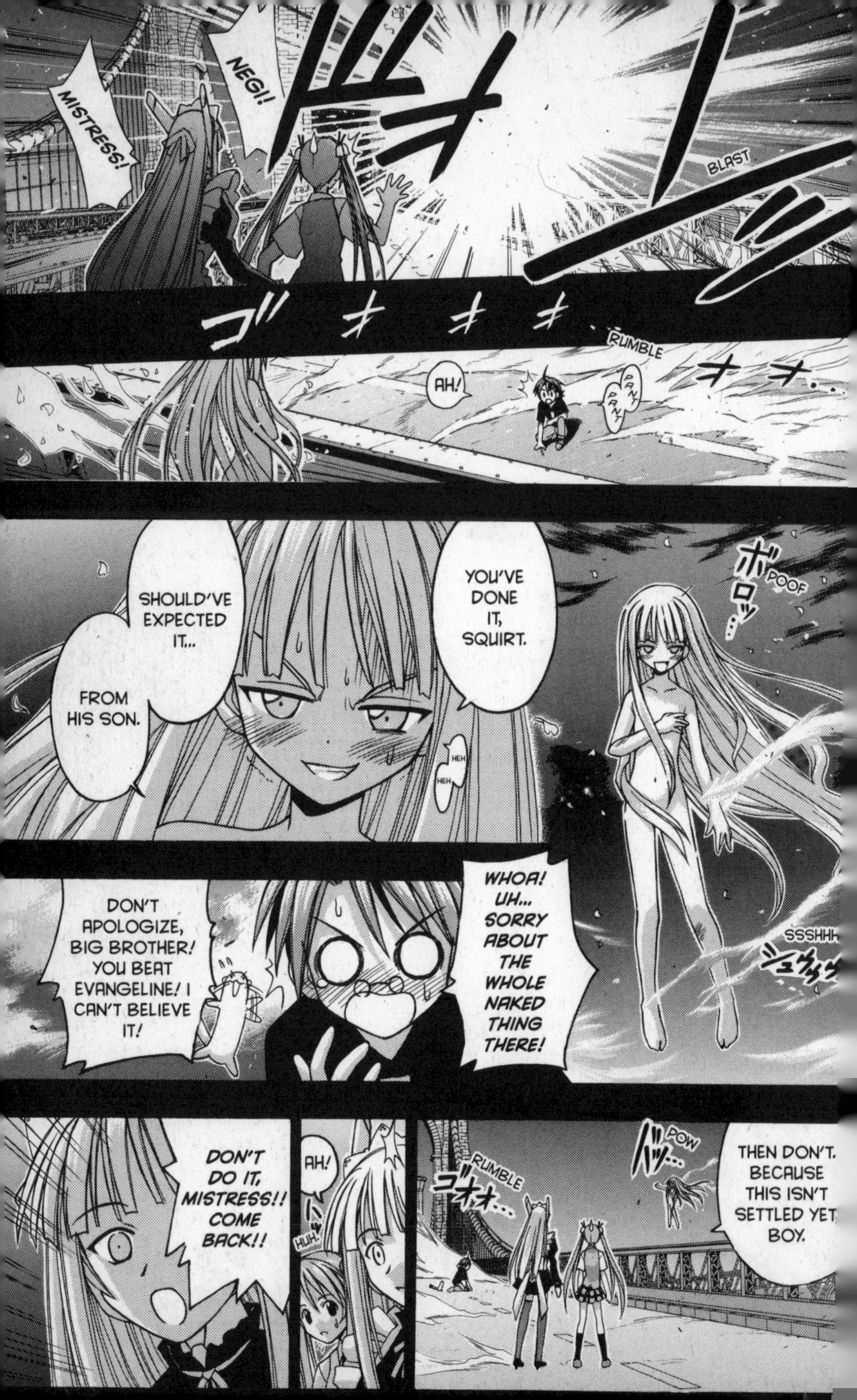
BLAST
NEGI!
MISTRESS!
RUMBLE
PANT PANT
AH!
POOF
YOU'VE DONE IT, SQUIRT.
HEH HEH
SHOULD'VE EXPECTED IT...
FROM HIS SON.
SSSHHH
WHOA! UH... SORRY ABOUT THE WHOLE NAKED THING THERE!
DON'T APOLOGIZE, BIG BROTHER! YOU BEAT EVANGELINE! I CAN'T BELIEVE IT!
THEN DON'T. BECAUSE THIS ISN'T SETTLED YET, BOY.
POW
RUMBLE
AH!
HUH
DON'T DO IT, MISTRESS!! COME BACK!!

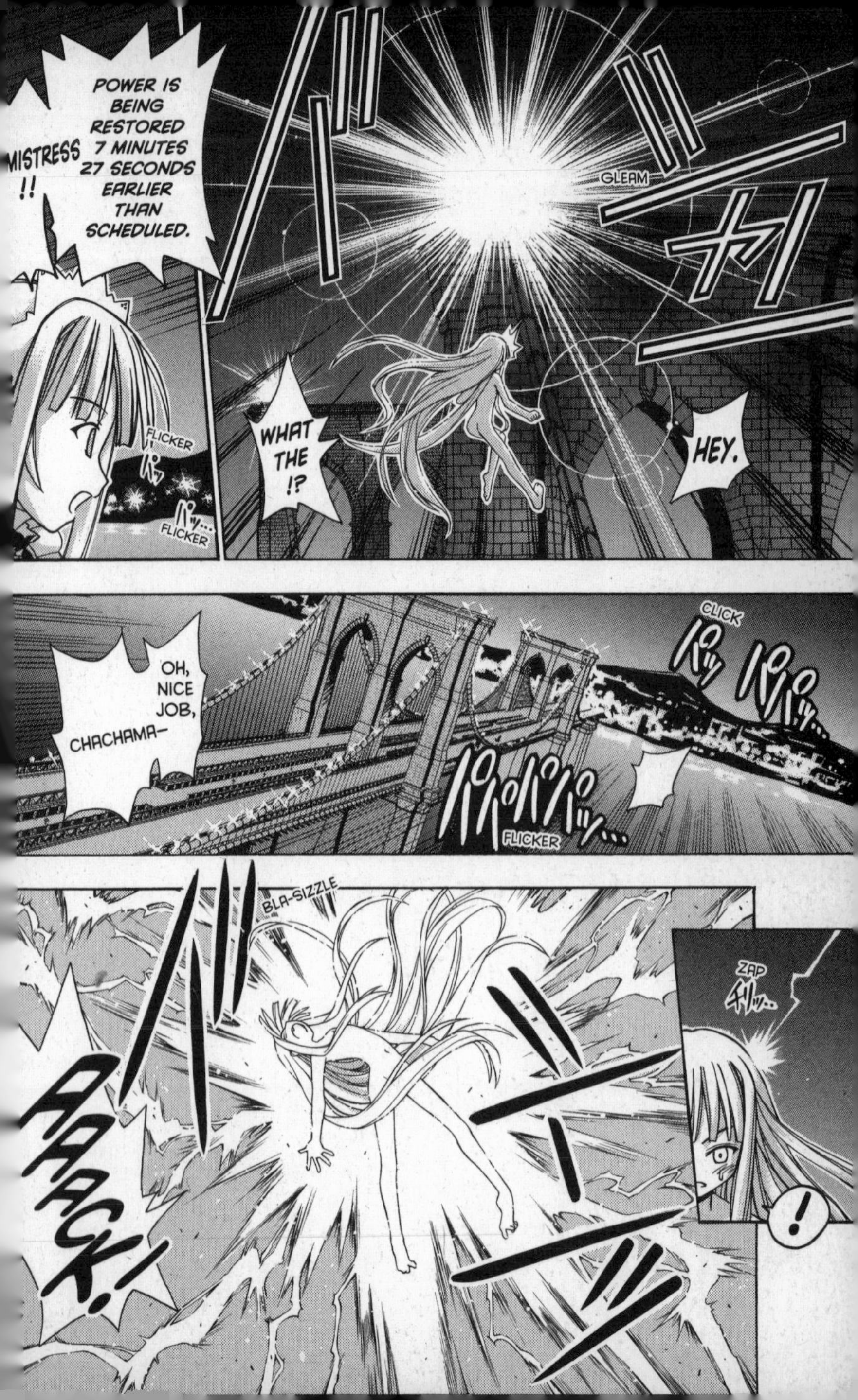
GLEAM
HEY.
WHAT THE !?
POWER IS BEING RESTORED 7 MINUTES 27 SECONDS EARLIER THAN SCHEDULED.
MISTRESS !!
FLICKER
FLICKER
CLICK
OH, NICE JOB, CHACHAMA–
FLICKER
ZAP
!
BLA-SIZZLE
AAACK!

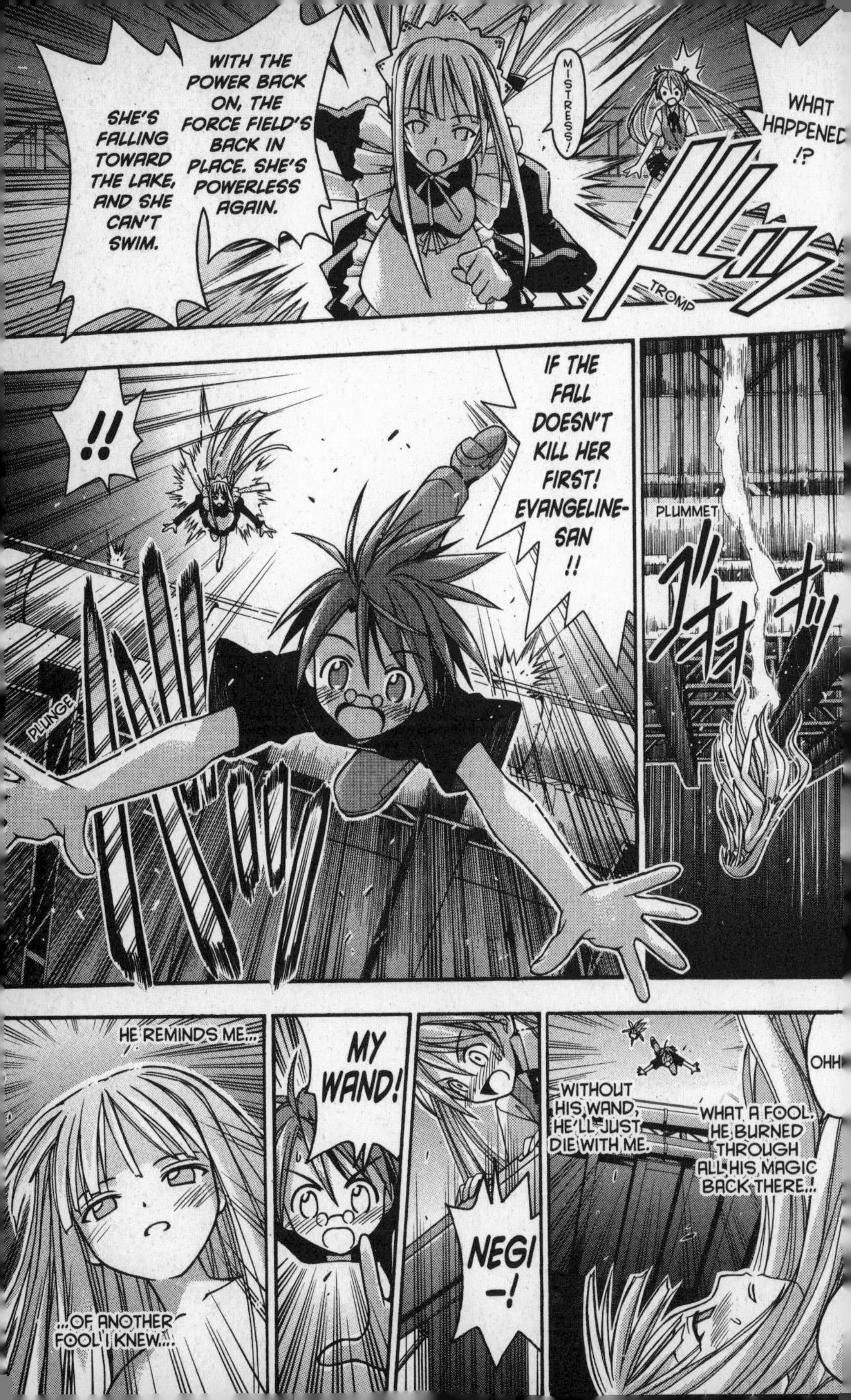
WHAT HAPPENED!?
MISTRESS!
WITH THE POWER BACK ON, THE FORCE FIELD'S BACK IN PLACE. SHE'S POWERLESS AGAIN.
SHE'S FALLING TOWARD THE LAKE, AND SHE CAN'T SWIM.
TROMP
PLUMMET
IF THE FALL DOESN'T KILL HER FIRST! EVANGELINE-SAN!!
!!
PLUNGE
OHH
WHAT A FOOL. HE BURNED THROUGH ALL HIS MAGIC BACK THERE..!
WITHOUT HIS WAND, HE'LL JUST DIE WITH ME.
NEGI-!
MY WAND!
HE REMINDS ME...
...OF ANOTHER FOOL I KNEW...

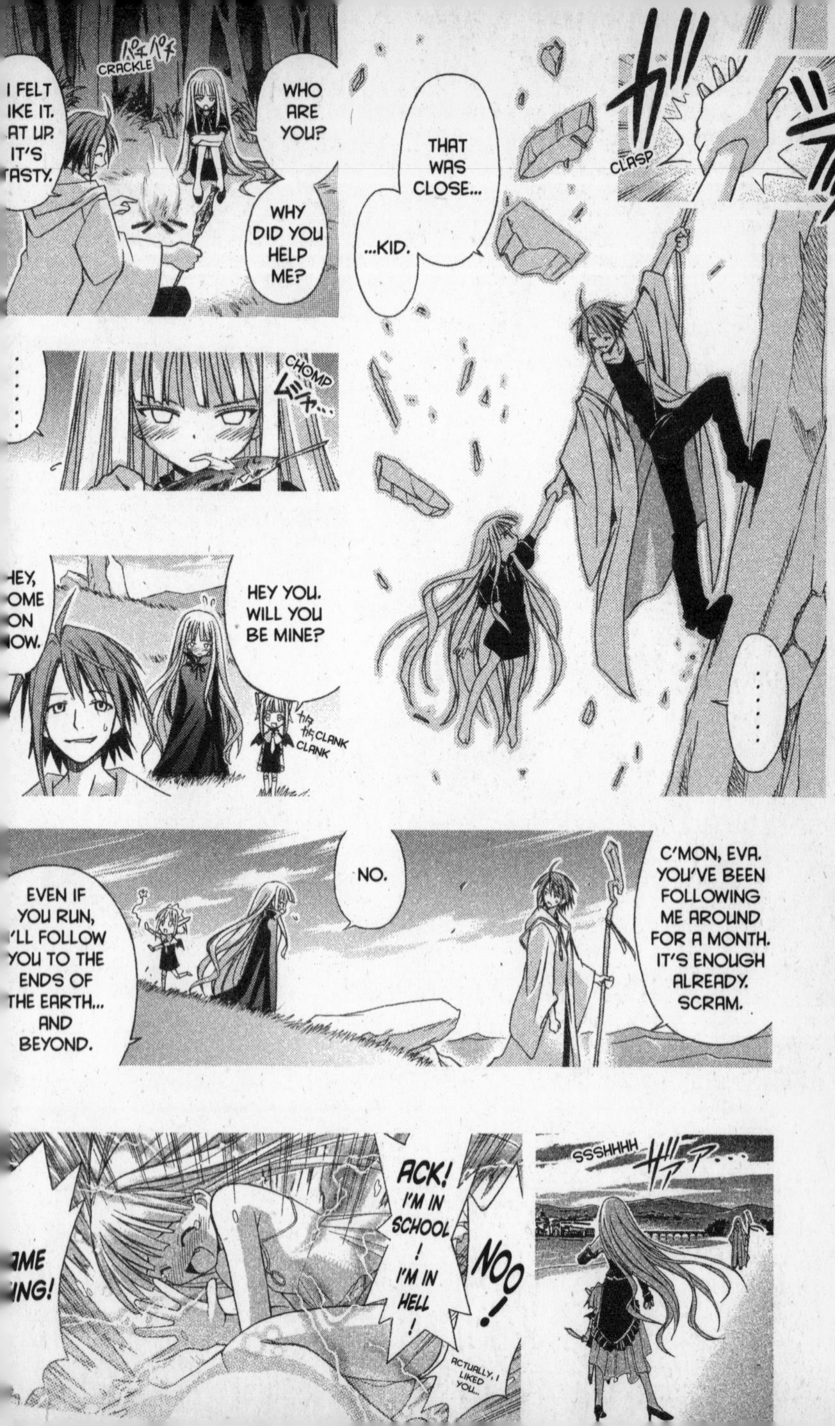
CLASP
THAT WAS CLOSE...
...KID.
......
CRACKLE
WHO ARE YOU?
WHY DID YOU HELP ME?
I FELT IKE IT. AT UP. IT'S TASTY.
CHOMP
......
HEY YOU. WILL YOU BE MINE?
HEY, OME ON OW.
CLANK CLANK
C'MON, EVA. YOU'VE BEEN FOLLOWING ME AROUND FOR A MONTH. IT'S ENOUGH ALREADY. SCRAM.
NO.
EVEN IF YOU RUN, 'LL FOLLOW YOU TO THE ENDS OF THE EARTH... AND BEYOND.
SSSHHHH
ACK! I'M IN SCHOOL! I'M IN HELL!
NOO!
ACTUALLY, I LIKED YOU...
AME ING!

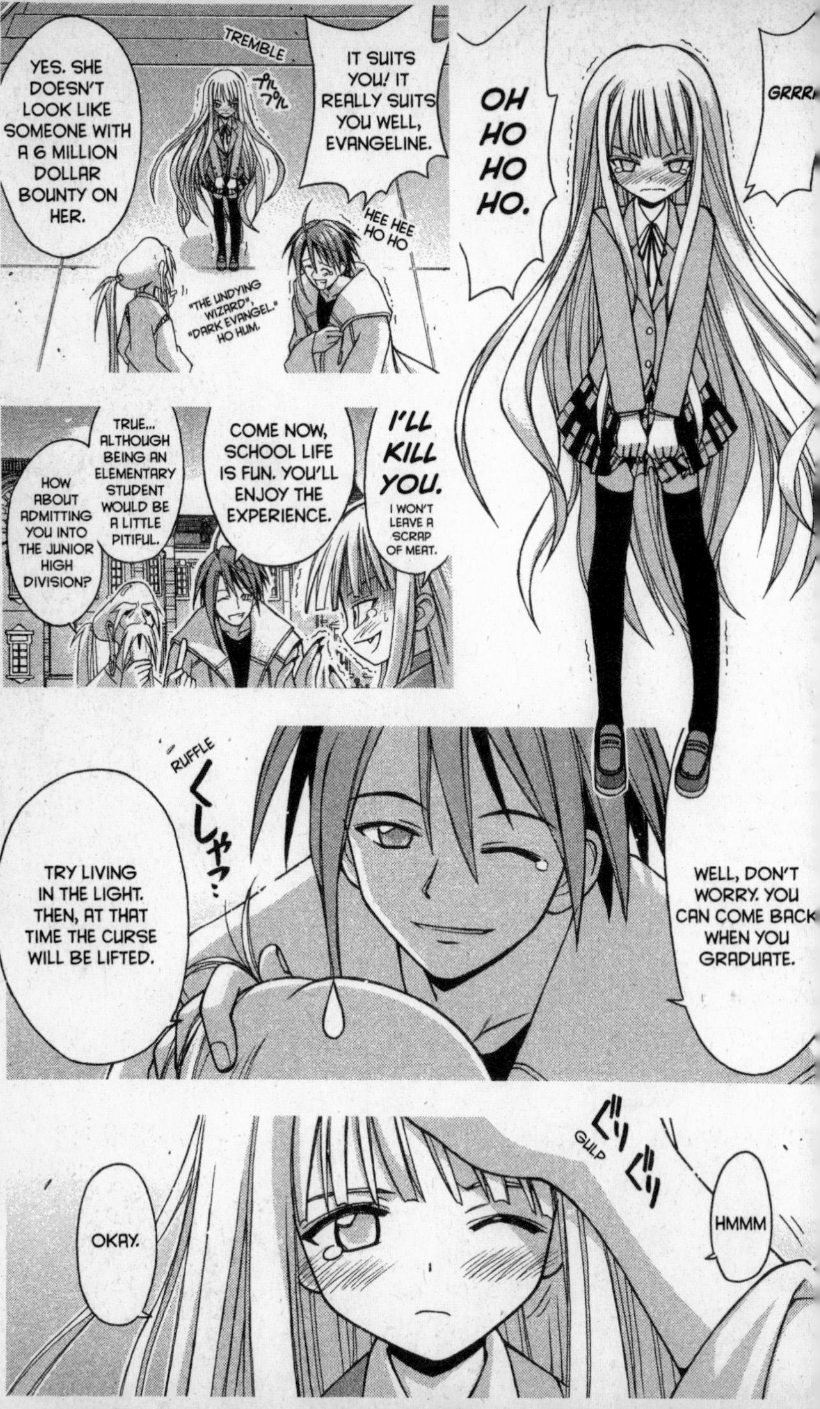
GRRR
OH HO HO HO.
TREMBLE
プルプル
IT SUITS YOU! IT REALLY SUITS YOU WELL, EVANGELINE.
HEE HEE HO HO
YES. SHE DOESN'T LOOK LIKE SOMEONE WITH A 6 MILLION DOLLAR BOUNTY ON HER.
"THE UNDYING WIZARD", "DARK EVANGEL." HO HUM.
I'LL KILL YOU.
I WON'T LEAVE A SCRAP OF MEAT.
COME NOW, SCHOOL LIFE IS FUN. YOU'LL ENJOY THE EXPERIENCE.
TRUE... ALTHOUGH BEING AN ELEMENTARY STUDENT WOULD BE A LITTLE PITIFUL.
HOW ABOUT ADMITTING YOU INTO THE JUNIOR HIGH DIVISION?
WELL, DON'T WORRY. YOU CAN COME BACK WHEN YOU GRADUATE.
RUFFLE
くしゃっ
TRY LIVING IN THE LIGHT. THEN, AT THAT TIME THE CURSE WILL BE LIFTED.
ぐりぐり
GULP
HMMM
OKAY.

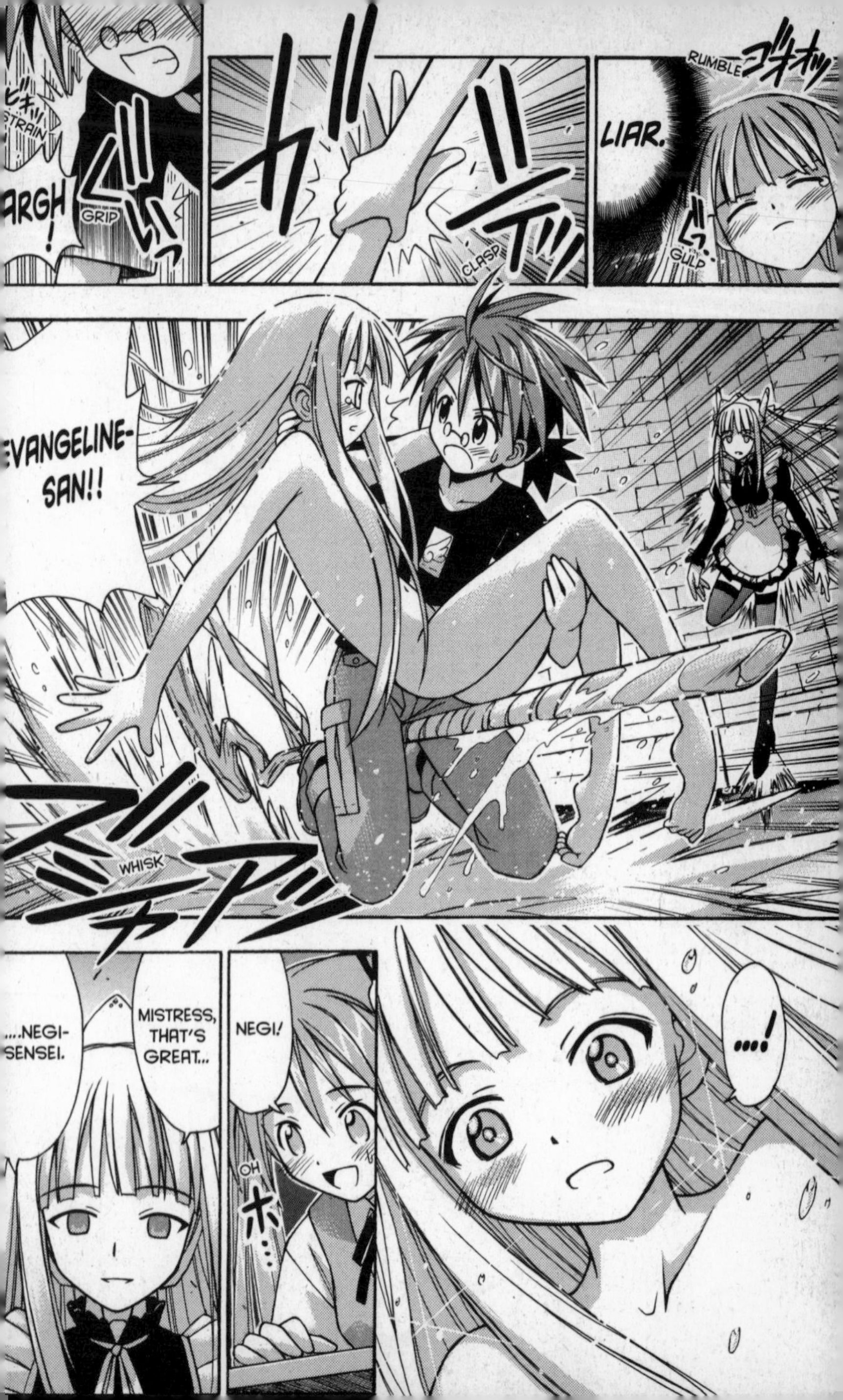
RUMBLE
LIAR.
GULP
CLASP
STRAIN
GRIP
ARGH!
EVANGELINE-SAN!!
WHISK
...!
NEGI!
OH
MISTRESS, THAT'S GREAT...
....NEGI-SENSEI.

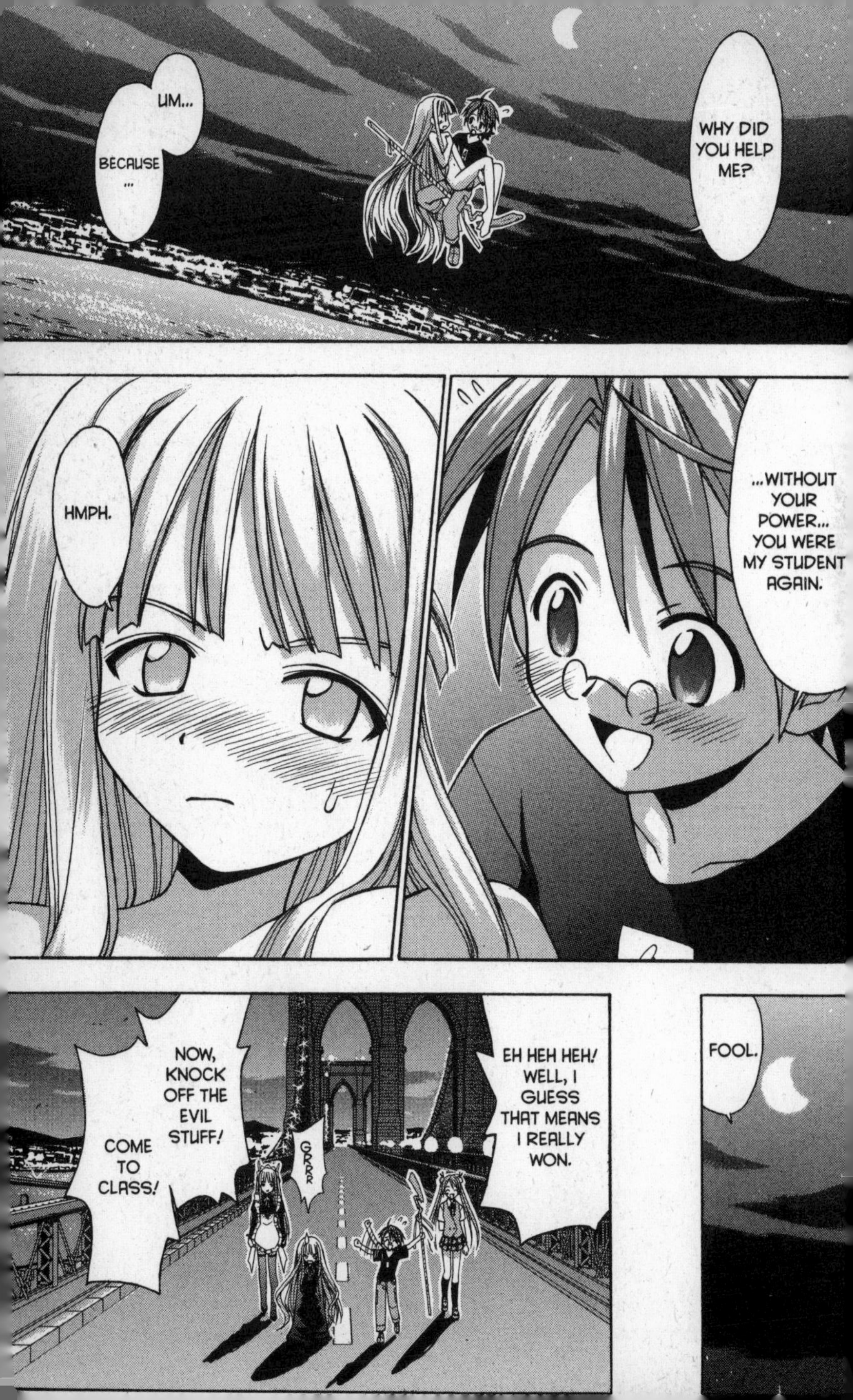
WHY DID YOU HELP ME?
UM... BECAUSE ...
...WITHOUT YOUR POWER... YOU WERE MY STUDENT AGAIN.
HMPH.
FOOL.
EH HEH HEH! WELL, I GUESS THAT MEANS I REALLY WON.
GRRR
NOW, KNOCK OFF THE EVIL STUFF!
COME TO CLASS!

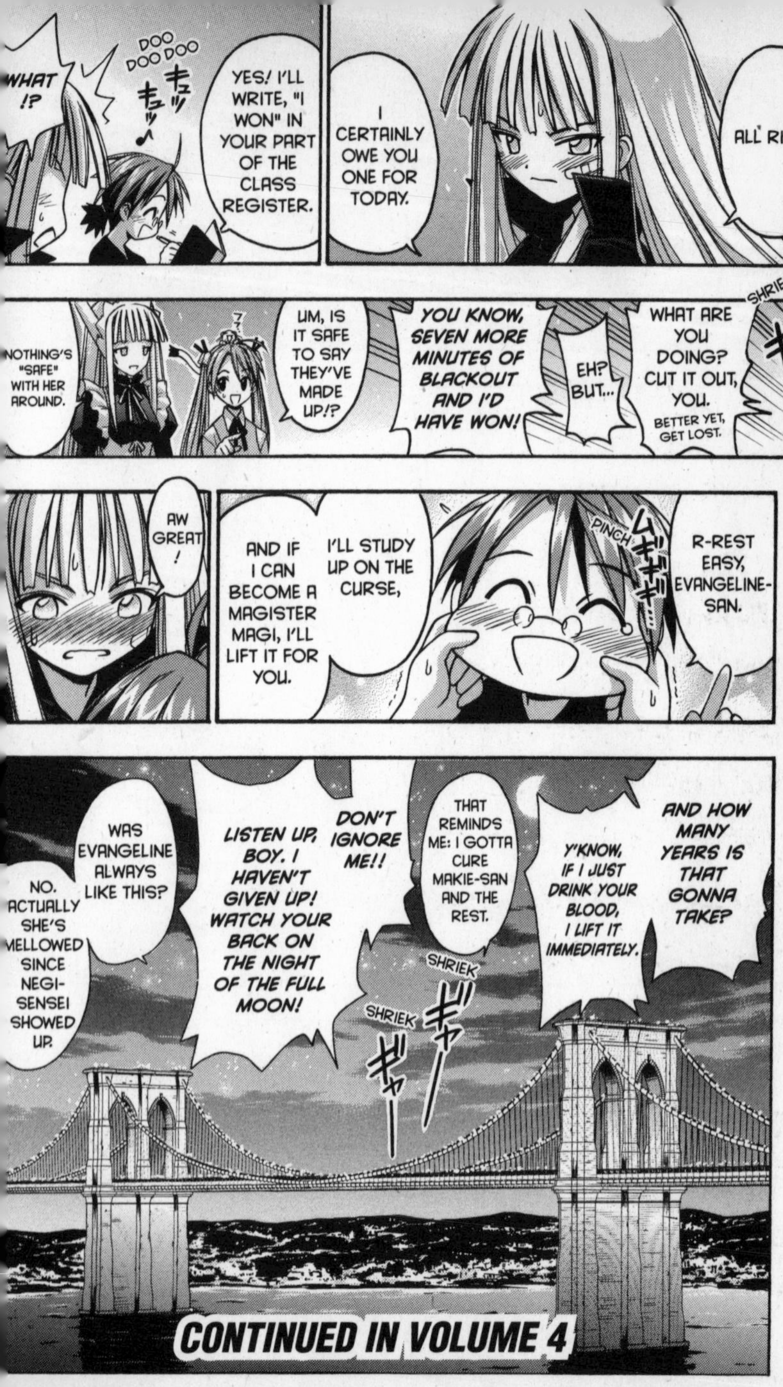
ALL RIGHT.
I CERTAINLY OWE YOU ONE FOR TODAY.
YES! I'LL WRITE, "I WON" IN YOUR PART OF THE CLASS REGISTER.
DOO DOO DOO
キュッキュッ♪
WHAT!?
SHRIEK SHRIEK
ギャーギャー
WHAT ARE YOU DOING? CUT IT OUT, YOU.
BETTER YET, GET LOST.
EH? BUT...
YOU KNOW, SEVEN MORE MINUTES OF BLACKOUT AND I'D HAVE WON!
UM, IS IT SAFE TO SAY THEY'VE MADE UP!?
NOTHING'S "SAFE" WITH HER AROUND.
R-REST EASY, EVANGELINE-SAN.
PINCH
ムギギギ
I'LL STUDY UP ON THE CURSE,
AND IF I CAN BECOME A MAGISTER MAGI, I'LL LIFT IT FOR YOU.
AW GREAT!
AND HOW MANY YEARS IS THAT GONNA TAKE?
Y'KNOW, IF I JUST DRINK YOUR BLOOD, I LIFT IT IMMEDIATELY.
THAT REMINDS ME: I GOTTA CURE MAKIE-SAN AND THE REST.
SHRIEK
ギャー
SHRIEK
ギャー
DON'T IGNORE ME!!
LISTEN UP, BOY. I HAVEN'T GIVEN UP! WATCH YOUR BACK ON THE NIGHT OF THE FULL MOON!
WAS EVANGELINE ALWAYS LIKE THIS?
NO. ACTUALLY SHE'S MELLOWED SINCE NEGI-SENSEI SHOWED UP.
CONTINUED IN VOLUME 4

– STAFF –

Ken Akamatsu
Takashi Takemoto
Kenichi Nakamura
Masaki Ohyama
Keiichi Yamashita
Chigusa Amagasaki
Takaaki Miyahara

Thanks To

Ran Ayanaga
Toshiko Akamatsu

About the Creator

Negima! is only Ken Akamatsu's third manga, although he started working in the field in 1994 with *AI Ga Tomaranai*. Like all of Akamatsu's work to date, it was published in Kodansha's *Shonen Magazine*. *AI Ga Tomaranai* ran for five years before concluding in 1999. In 1998, however, Akamatsu began the work that would make him one of the most popular manga artists in Japan: *Love Hina*. *Love Hina* ran for four years, and before its conclusion in 2002, it would cause Akamatsu to be granted the prestigious Manga of the Year award from Kodansha, as well as going on to become one of the best-selling manga in the United States.

LEXICON NEGIMARIUM DE CANTU
Negima! Glossary Of Spells

Sixteenth Period

Undecim spiritus aerials, vinculum facti iimicum captent. Sagitta magica, aer Capturae. ("11 wind spirits, become a chain that binds and capture my enemy.") Magic that uses the wind to restrain enemies. It is a weak attack and had little effect on the experienced Evangeline.

Reflexio. ("Ice Shield.") A magic shield that is conjured to repel the attacking magic from an enemy. Evangeline is skilled at ice magic so she conjured an "ice shield." *Reflexio* corresponds to the English *reflection.*

Seventeenth Period

Frigerans Exarmatio. ("Release freeze weapon.") Magic that, without causing any frostbite injury to the opponent, freezes the things attached to the body and shatters them, disarming the enemy. Control over complicated magic power is necessary to wield this spell. However, metal and other types of hard materials cannot be shattered, so the most you can do is buy some time against these types of items.

Evocatio valcyriarum, contubernalia gladiaria. ("I summon the wind spirit!! Sword-wielding brothers in arms!!") The word *walkyria* has been Latinized, but corresponds to the old Nordic *valkyrie,* referring here to a "person who chooses immortality." In short, what Negi is summoning is an immortal god. Odin's handmaidens, who appear in Wagner's opera, are popular valkryies, but throughout this work, the term is used as a neuter noun and not a proper entity. "Age capiant" is a form of address that means, "please capture."

Flans exarmatio. ("Wind flower, disarm weapon.") This is, in fact, the magic that appears most frequently in *Negima!* The incantation blows off with a powerful wind items attached to an opponent's body . Clothing and other light things are changed into flower petals. The sole purpose is to disarm an opponent of weapons, so no matter strong the wind is, it will not blow away the opponent herself. When Negi sneezes and blows off the clothes of Asuna and friends, this is the explosion of this magic. Refer to the First, Second, Fifth, Sixth, and Twelfth Periods. (From the Seventeenth Period on.)

Nineteenth Period

Practe bigi nar. This is the "magic release key" and is not a Latin language spell. The formal "release key" is created by each student individually upon graduation from magic school, but *practe bigi nar* is an apprenticeship key given to a schoolchild.

Pactio. ("Probationary Contract.") A spell to enter a probationary contract between a wizard (magus) and a partner (minister) that brings about ecstacy in order to draw out both parties' consciousness from within their egos. A ceremony is necessary for the spell to work. The word *pactio* itself does not indicate that the spell is probationary; this is the same as the proper, permanent contract spell. However, stronger contract magic is used for the so-called real contract. When a wizard enters a probationary contract, certain powers are attained.

Twentieth Period

Sis mea pars per decem secundas. Ministra Negi, Asuna Kagurazaka. ("Contract executed in 10 seconds. Minister Negi, Asuna Kagurazaka.") A spell that sends a wizard's own magic power to the person with whom that wizard has entered a probationary contract; in this case, from Negi to Asuna. *Sis mea pars* means *you are a part of me.* If the contract is incomplete, there are restrictions on the magic powers sent, and it appears that with Negi and friends they were able to use the contract's power only during the first 10 seconds. If the contract is renewed correctly, the magic powers can be used for another 90 seconds (*per nonaginta secundas*).

Undecem spiritus lucis, coeuntes sagitent inimicum. Sagitta magica, series lucis. (11 spirits of light, come gather [shoot the enemy]; Magic Archer, consecutive bursts, 11 arrows of light) A basic battle spell. Light spirit version. *Serius lucis* means "range of light."

Twenty-Second Period

Nympha somni, regina Mab, portam aperiens ad se me alliciat. ("I invoke Queen Mab, the Dream Fairy, open the door and invite me into dreams.") Magic that lets you see into sleeping people's dreams. Mab is the name of a queen who appears in a Celtic myth. She is thought of as a fairy who controls dreams.

Manmanterroterro. The Thousand Master's "release key." A style that's changed considerably.

Infernus scholasticus. (School hell.) A very strange curse. In the past, it was used for making dropouts go to school. This curse has tormented Evangeline for over 15 years.

Twenty-Third—Twenty-Fifth Periods

Aer et aqua, facti nebula illis somnum brevem. Nebula hypnotica. ("Atmosphere. Water. White fog, seep. Give them repose, make them sleep.") Magic that conjures a fog that makes your opponent sleep.

Lic lac la lac lilac. Evangeline's "release key." Lilac thrives where things are difficult to grow, and when a flower is brought inside the house, it brings evil with it. In the language of flowers, the incantation refers to "purity" and "first love."

Septendecim spiritus glaciales, coeuntes inimicum concidant. SAGITTA MAGICA, SERIES GLACIALIS. ("17 Ice Spirits, come gather and rip apart my enemy"; "Magic Archer. Consecutive bursts. Eleven ice arrows.") The ice version of the "Magic Archer." Several sharp ice pillars attack the enemy.

Nivis casus. ("Ice explosion.") Magic that makes large volumes of ice appear in the air and attacks the opponent with both frosty air and a blast of wind. *Nivis casus* means "avalanche".

Veniant spiritus aerials fulgurientes, cum fulgurationi flet tempestas austrina. Jovis tempestas fulguriens. ("Ice spirits on high, fill the sky. Tundra and Glaciers on the run from the land of midnight sun"; "Frozen earth.") Attacks with huge ice pillars that come from the earth in an instant. If not dodged effectively, your feet become frozen to the ground and you aren't able to move. For enemies that can't fly, this magic is very effective to use before an attack.

Septendecim spiritus aerials, coeuntes...Sagitta maigca, wries fulguralis. ("17 Wind Spirits. Come gather..."; "Magic Archer, Consecutive blasts, 17 arrows of thunder.") The lightning version of "Magic Archer." If the user's power becomes too weak it also can be used to stun.

Undetriginta spiritus obscuri...Sagitta magica, series obscuri. ("29 Spirits of Darkness..."; "Magic Archer, consecutive blasts, 29 arrow of darkness.") The dark version of "Magic Archer." It's unknown what kind of power is in the flying dark bullet.

Undetriginata spiritus lucis...Sagitta magica, series lucis. ("29 spirits of light..."; "Magic Archer, consecutive blasts, 29 arrows of light.") Constitutes the opposite of the magic written above. Besides the fact that one is obscuri (dark) and one is lucis (light), they are parallel spells.

Veniant spiritus aerials fulgurientes, cum fulgurationi flet tempestas austrina. Jovis tempestas. ("*Come wind, thunder spirits. Blow violently with thunder, Storm of the South Seas.*") Magic that conjures a strong whirlwind and lightning that attacks the enemy. *Jovis* is another name for the king of Roman gods, Jupiter, who is thought to use lightning as a weapon. In short, *Jovis tempestas* means "Jupiter's storm that unleashes lightning."

Veniant spiritus glaciales obscurants, cum obscurationi flet tempestas nivalis. Nivis tempestas obscurans. ("*Darkness obey, a blizzard, ice and snow of the night.*"; "*Blizzard of darkness.*") Magic that conjures a strong blizzard and darkness that attacks the enemy. As you might have noticed, there are several similar points with the spell above. It seems that Evangeline chose the same type of spells in order to fight Negi. Nivis tempestas obscurans means "snowstorm that brings darkness."

Mea virga. (My wand.) The words used to call the wand that Negi received from the Thousand Master. Mea means "my" and virga means "wand."

NEGI MAGI MAGISTER

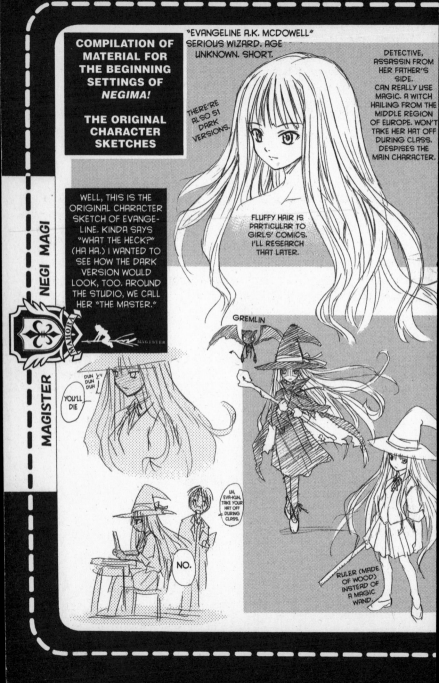

COMPILATION OF MATERIAL FOR THE BEGINNING SETTINGS OF *NEGIMA!*

THE ORIGINAL CHARACTER SKETCHES

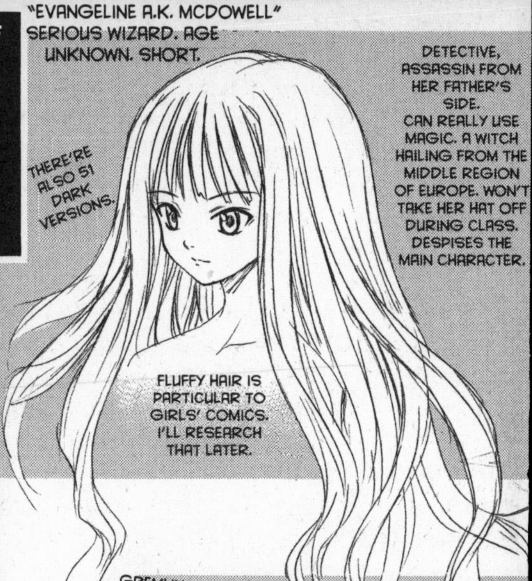

"EVANGELINE A.K. MCDOWELL"
SERIOUS WIZARD. AGE UNKNOWN. SHORT.
DETECTIVE, ASSASSIN FROM HER FATHER'S SIDE.
CAN REALLY USE MAGIC. A WITCH HAILING FROM THE MIDDLE REGION OF EUROPE. WON'T TAKE HER HAT OFF DURING CLASS. DESPISES THE MAIN CHARACTER.
THERE'RE ALSO 51 DARK VERSIONS.
FLUFFY HAIR IS PARTICULAR TO GIRLS' COMICS. I'LL RESEARCH THAT LATER.

WELL, THIS IS THE ORIGINAL CHARACTER SKETCH OF EVANGELINE. KINDA SAYS "WHAT THE HECK?" (HA HA.) I WANTED TO SEE HOW THE DARK VERSION WOULD LOOK, TOO. AROUND THE STUDIO, WE CALL HER "THE MASTER."

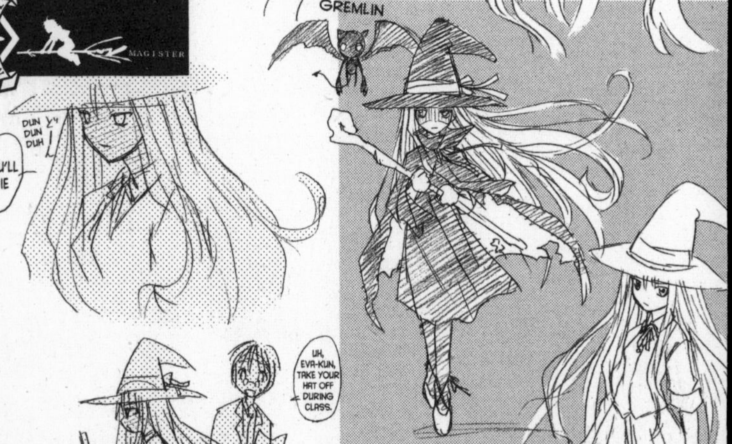

GREMLIN
RULER (MADE OF WOOD) INSTEAD OF A MAGIC WAND.
UH, EVA-KUN, TAKE YOUR HAT OFF DURING CLASS.
NO.
DUN DUN DUH
YOU'LL DIE

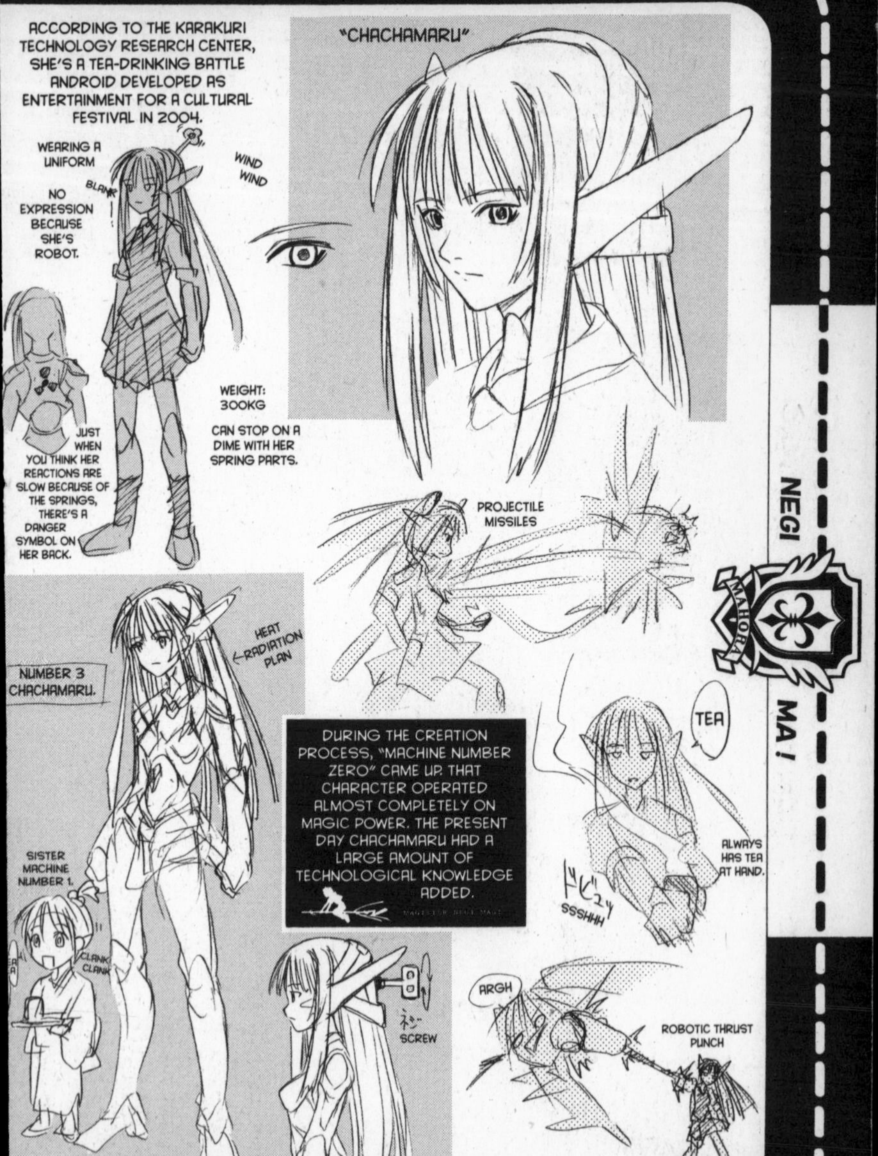
ACCORDING TO THE KARAKURI TECHNOLOGY RESEARCH CENTER, SHE'S A TEA-DRINKING BATTLE ANDROID DEVELOPED AS ENTERTAINMENT FOR A CULTURAL FESTIVAL IN 2004.
"CHACHAMARU"
WEARING A UNIFORM
WIND WIND
BLANK
NO EXPRESSION BECAUSE SHE'S ROBOT.
WEIGHT: 300KG
CAN STOP ON A DIME WITH HER SPRING PARTS.
JUST WHEN YOU THINK HER REACTIONS ARE SLOW BECAUSE OF THE SPRINGS, THERE'S A DANGER SYMBOL ON HER BACK.
PROJECTILE MISSILES
HEAT ←RADIATION PLAN
NUMBER 3 CHACHAMARU.
DURING THE CREATION PROCESS, "MACHINE NUMBER ZERO" CAME UP. THAT CHARACTER OPERATED ALMOST COMPLETELY ON MAGIC POWER. THE PRESENT DAY CHACHAMARU HAD A LARGE AMOUNT OF TECHNOLOGICAL KNOWLEDGE ADDED.
TEA
ALWAYS HAS TEA AT HAND.
SSSHHH
SISTER MACHINE NUMBER 1.
CLANK CLANK
SCREW
ARGH
ROBOTIC THRUST PUNCH
REFER TO DREAM AND M-6
NEGI MA!
MAHORA

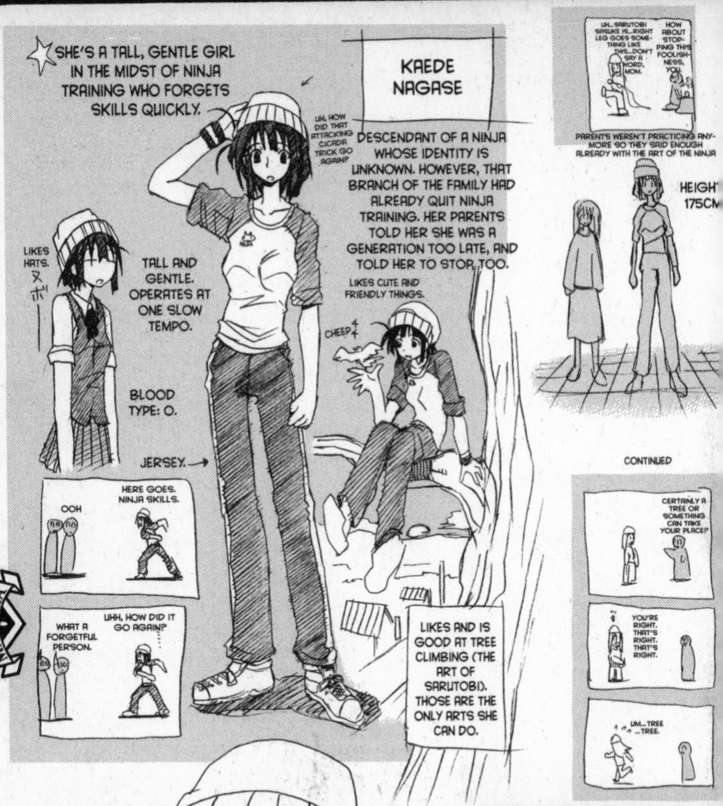
UH...SARUTOBI SASUKE IS...RIGHT LEG GOES SOMETHING LIKE THIS...DON'T SAY A WORD, MOM.
HOW ABOUT STOPPING THIS FOOLISHNESS, YOU.
PARENTS WEREN'T PRACTICING ANYMORE SO THEY SAID ENOUGH ALREADY WITH THE ART OF THE NINJA
HEIGHT 175CM
CONTINUED
CERTAINLY A TREE OR SOMETHING CAN TAKE YOUR PLACE?
YOU'RE RIGHT. THAT'S RIGHT. THAT'S RIGHT.
UM...TREE ...TREE.
KAEDE NAGASE
SHE'S A TALL, GENTLE GIRL IN THE MIDST OF NINJA TRAINING WHO FORGETS SKILLS QUICKLY.
UH, HOW DID THAT ATTACKING CICADA TRICK GO AGAIN?
DESCENDANT OF A NINJA WHOSE IDENTITY IS UNKNOWN. HOWEVER, THAT BRANCH OF THE FAMILY HAD ALREADY QUIT NINJA TRAINING. HER PARENTS TOLD HER SHE WAS A GENERATION TOO LATE, AND TOLD HER TO STOP, TOO.
LIKES CUTE AND FRIENDLY THINGS.
CHEEP
LIKES AND IS GOOD AT TREE CLIMBING (THE ART OF SARUTOBI). THOSE ARE THE ONLY ARTS SHE CAN DO.
TALL AND GENTLE. OPERATES AT ONE SLOW TEMPO.
BLOOD TYPE: O.
JERSEY.
LIKES HATS.
ヌボ
HERE GOES. NINJA SKILLS.
OOH
UHH, HOW DID IT GO AGAIN?
WHAT A FORGETFUL PERSON.

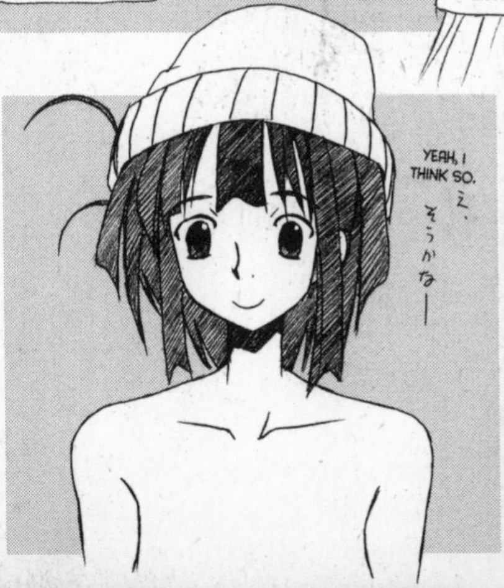
YEAH, I THINK SO.
え.そうかなー

KAEDE HAS CHANGED CONSIDERABLY. THE FIRST VERSION WAS PORTRAYED AS SOMEONE WITH A LOT O ABILITY. IT LOOKS LIKE SHE'LL BE PLAYING A ROLE HENCEFORTH. IN THE NEXT VOLUME 4, THE SCHOOL FIELD TRIP FINALLY STARTS THAT'S EXACTLY THE BEST PART OF NEGIMA! EXPECT QUITE A STORY! --AKAMATS

MAGISTER NEGI MA

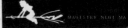

Translation Notes

Japanese is a tricky language for most westerners, and translation is often more art than science. For your edification and reading pleasure, here are notes on some of the places where we could have gone in a different direction in our translation of the work, or where a Japanese cultural reference is used.

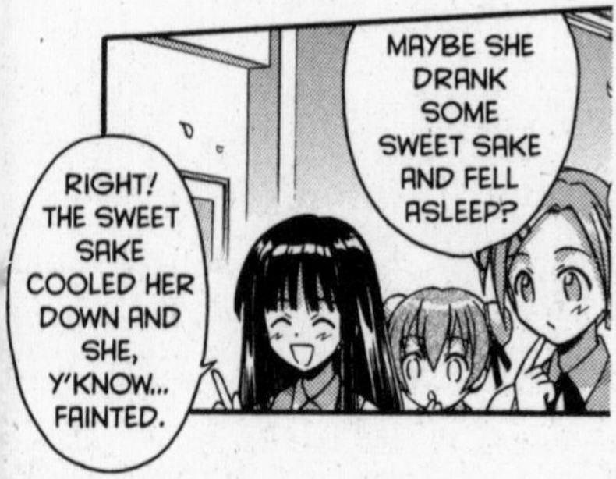

MAYBE SHE DRANK SOME SWEET SAKE AND FELL ASLEEP?
RIGHT! THE SWEET SAKE COOLED HER DOWN AND SHE, Y'KNOW... FAINTED.

Sweet sake, page 15

We've used the phrase *sweet sake* here, instead of the actual Japanese term that appeared in the original, *amazake. Amazake,* which most Japanese are familiar with, is a drink brewed from rice and malt usually drunk in the spring or summer.

Ane-san, page 65

Ane-san is a generic term for a girl, usually older, that means sister. It can be construed as rude or too informal, although it's more likely in this case that Albert Chamomile is just trying to ingratiate himself with Asuna so she won't kick him out.

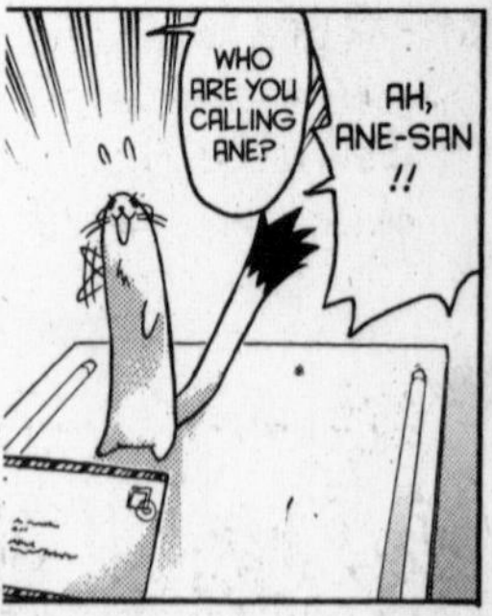

AH, ANE-SAN!!
WHO ARE YOU CALLING ANE?

Garbage, page 66

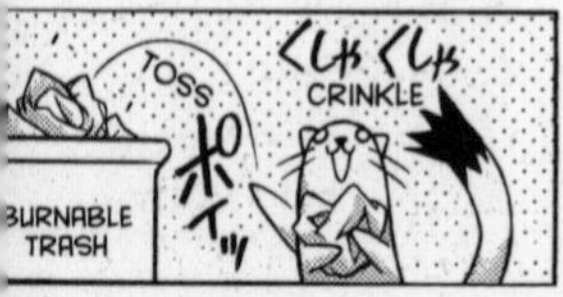

CRINKLE
TOSS
BURNABLE TRASH

Chamo may be destroying the evidence, but at least he's conscientious about it. Dividing garbage in Japan can be a complicated business. Trash is usually divided into burnables, nonburnables, and recyclables.

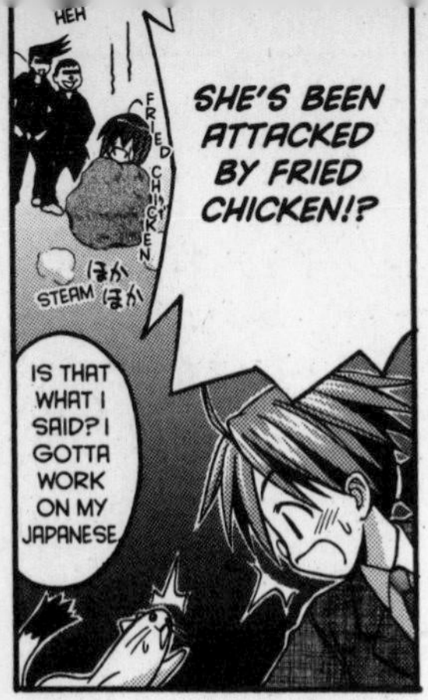
HEH
SHE'S BEEN ATTACKED BY FRIED CHICKEN!?
FRIED CHICKEN
ほか ほか
STEAM
IS THAT WHAT I SAID? I GOTTA WORK ON MY JAPANESE

Karaage, page 67

Chamo rushes in to tell Negi that Nodoka is being attacked by *karaage,* which is Japanese-style fried chicken. Chamo's next comment in the original text is that he's really got to work on his Japanese—remember, he's from Wales, like young Negi. Problem is, the joke doesn't really work in English so we modified it a wee bit.

Tsujigiri, page 89

In the original text, Asuna says that she doesn't like what they're doing because it reminds her too much of *tsujigiri. Tsujigiri* refers to a time when samurais would sharpen their swordsmanship skills on people on the street, a clearly dishonorable act.

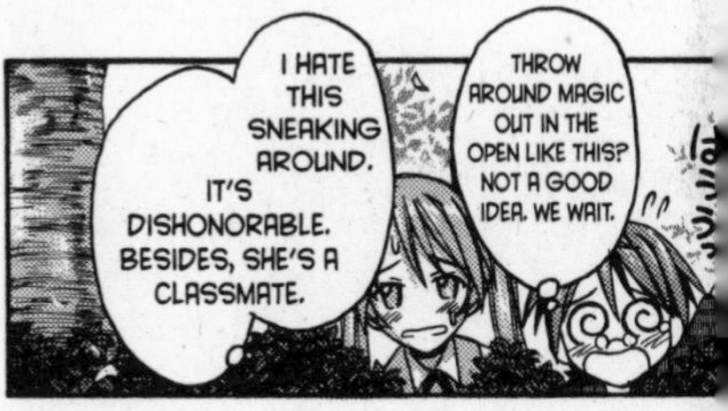
THROW AROUND MAGIC OUT IN THE OPEN LIKE THIS? NOT A GOOD IDEA. WE WAIT.
I HATE THIS SNEAKING AROUND. IT'S DISHONORABLE. BESIDES, SHE'S A CLASSMATE.

Sessha, page 107

Remember this term from volume 2? Just in case you don't: *Sessha* is a condescending word that samurai used to refer to themselves. It also refers to a character from a book written in the seventeenth century who assisted women down on their luck.

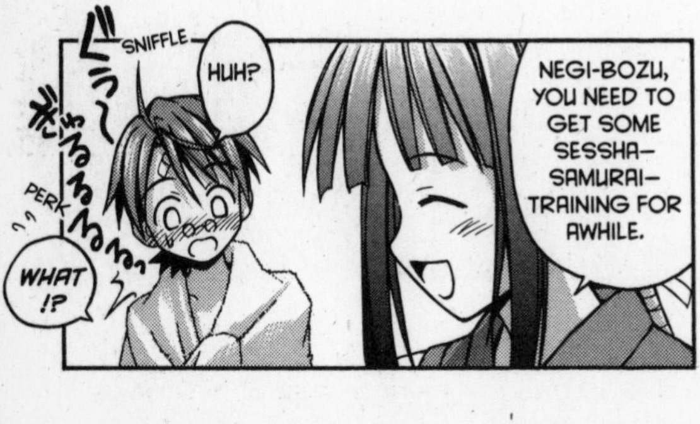
NEGI-BOZU, YOU NEED TO GET SOME SESSHA-SAMURAI-TRAINING FOR AWHILE.
HUH?
SNIFFLE
PERK
WHAT !?

Char, page 107

A char is a fish you might catch in a mountain stream in the summer in Japan or China.

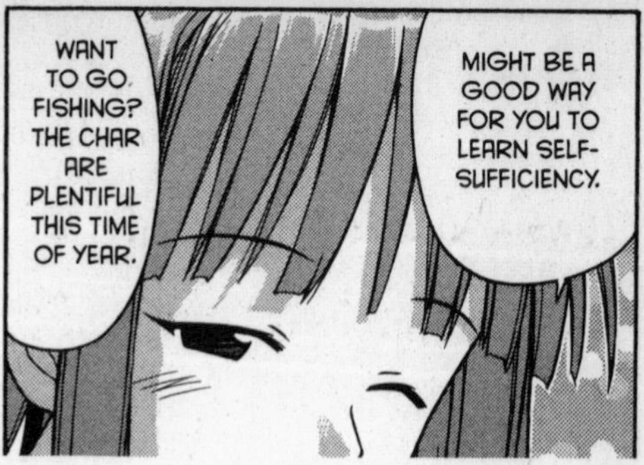
MIGHT BE A GOOD WAY FOR YOU TO LEARN SELF-SUFFICIENCY.
WANT TO GO FISHING? THE CHAR ARE PLENTIFUL THIS TIME OF YEAR.

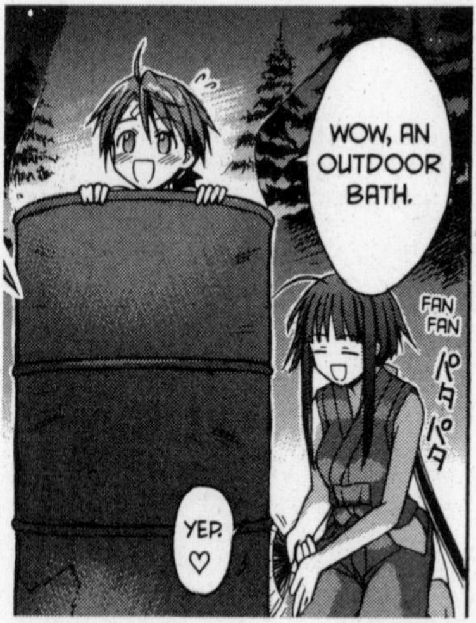
WOW, AN OUTDOOR BATH.
FAN FAN
パタパタ
YEP. ♡

Baths, page 111

As you might know, baths and hot springs are very popular in Japan. Outdoor baths, not necessarily in this style, can be found in the forests and mountains in resorts towns such as Gerou, in Gifu Prefecture.

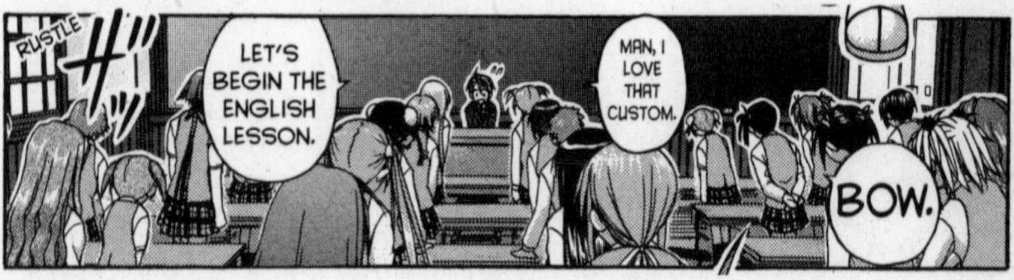
BOW.
MAN, I LOVE THAT CUSTOM.
LET'S BEGIN THE ENGLISH LESSON.
RUSTLE
ザッ

Bowing, page 140

Note that all of the girls are bowing as Negi takes his place at the front of the classroom. This is a daily custom in Japanese primary and secondary schools, and is intended as a sign of respect and gratitude to the teacher.

Preview of Volume 4

Here is an excerpt from Volume 4, on sale in English now.

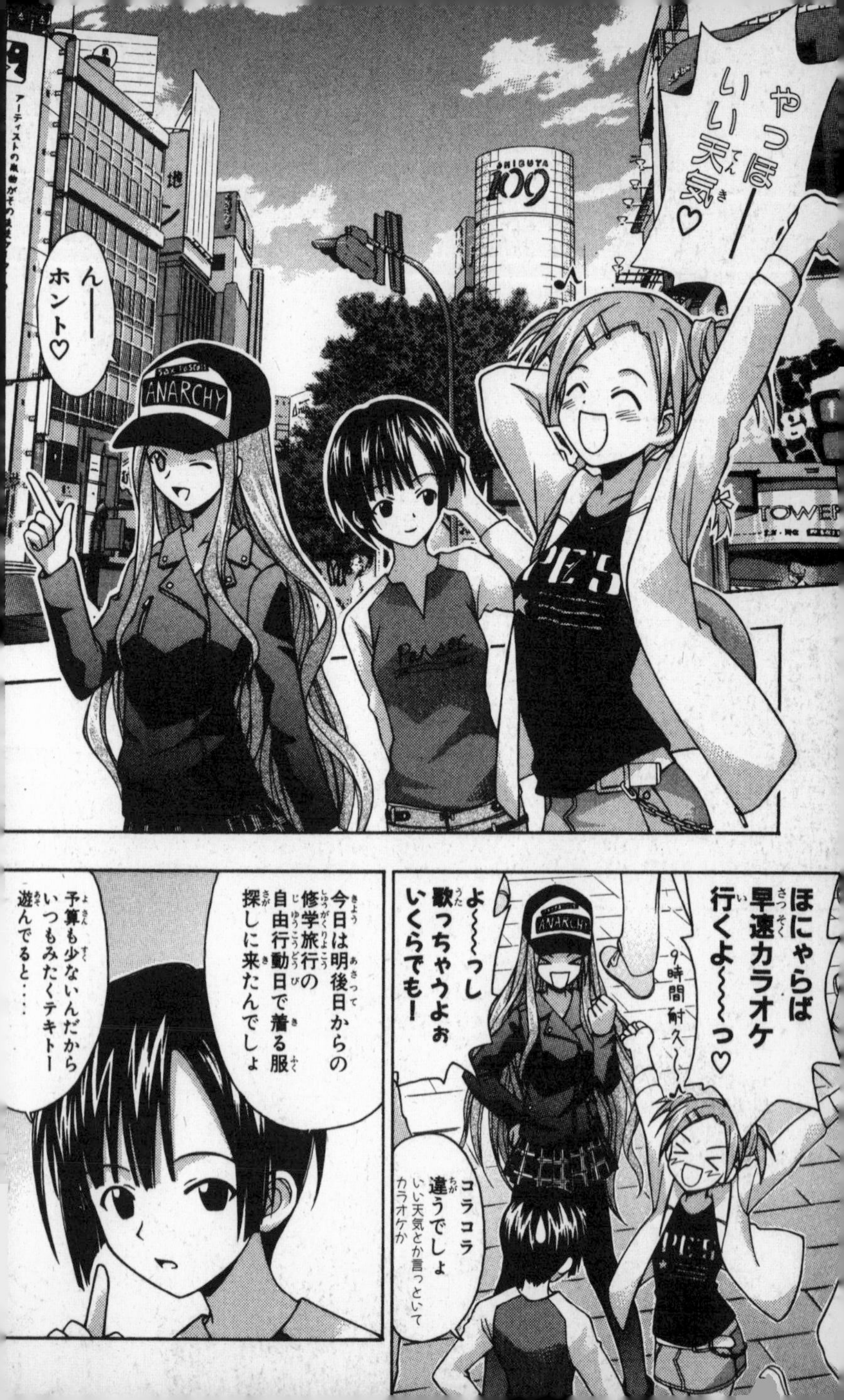
やっほー いい天気♡
SHIBUYA 109
ん―― ホント♡
ANARCHY
TOWER
ほにゃらば 早速カラオケ 行くよ～～っ♡
9時間耐久～
よ～～っし 歌っちゃうよぉ いくらでも！
コラコラ 違うでしょ
いい天気とか言っといて カラオケか
今日は明後日からの 修学旅行の 自由行動日で着る服 探しに来たんでしょ
予算も少ないんだから いつもみたくテキトー 遊んでると‥‥

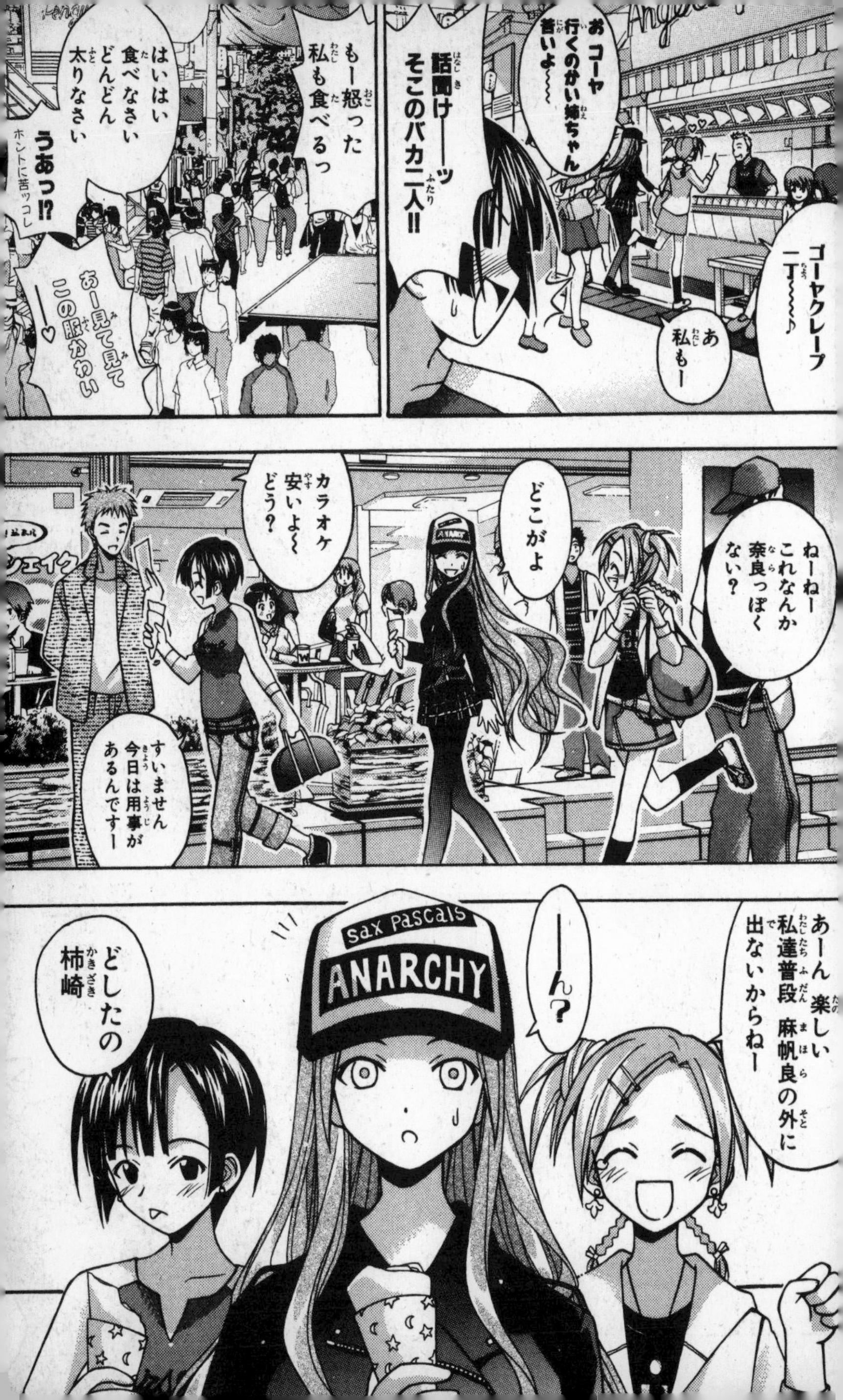
ゴーヤクレープ一丁〜〜〜♪
あ 私もー
おコーヤ行くのかい姉ちゃん 苦いよ〜〜〜
話聞けーーッ そこのバカ二人!!
もー怒った 私も食べるっ
はいはい 食べなさい どんどん太りなさい
うあっ!? ホントに苦ッコレ
あー見て見て この服かわいーー♡
ねーねー これなんか奈良っぽくない？
どこがよ
カラオケ安いよ〜 どう？
すいません 今日は用事があるんですー
あーん 楽しい 私達普段 麻帆良の外に出ないからねー
ーーん？
sax pascals
ANARCHY
どしたの柿崎

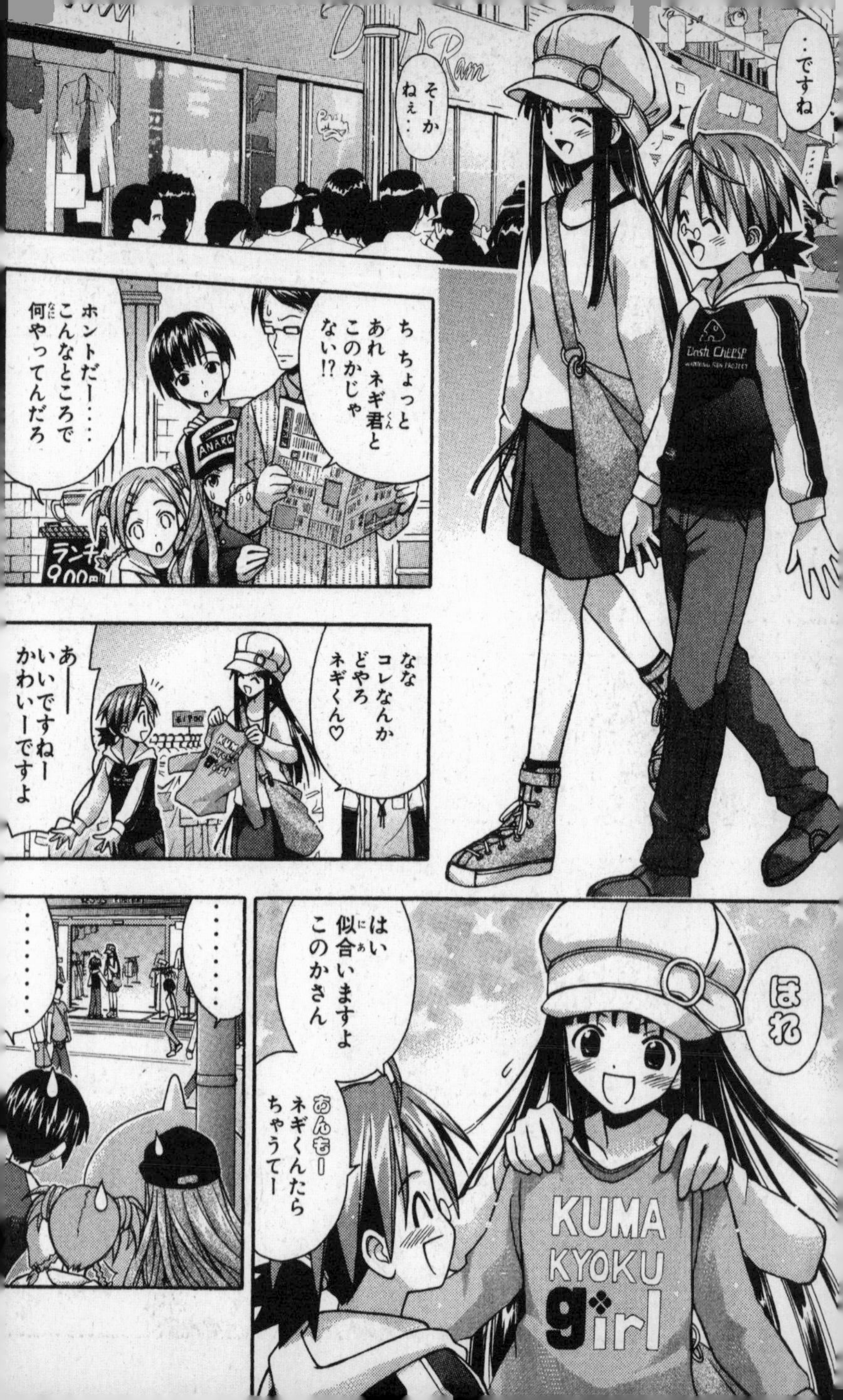
…ですね
そーかねぇ…
ちちょっと あれ ネギ君とこのかじゃない!?
ホントだー…こんなところで何やってんだろ
ランチ 900円
ななコレなんかどやろネギくん♡
あーいいですねーかわいーですよ
ほれ
はい似合いますよこのかさん
おんもーネギくんたらちゃうてー
KUMA KYOKU girl
……
……

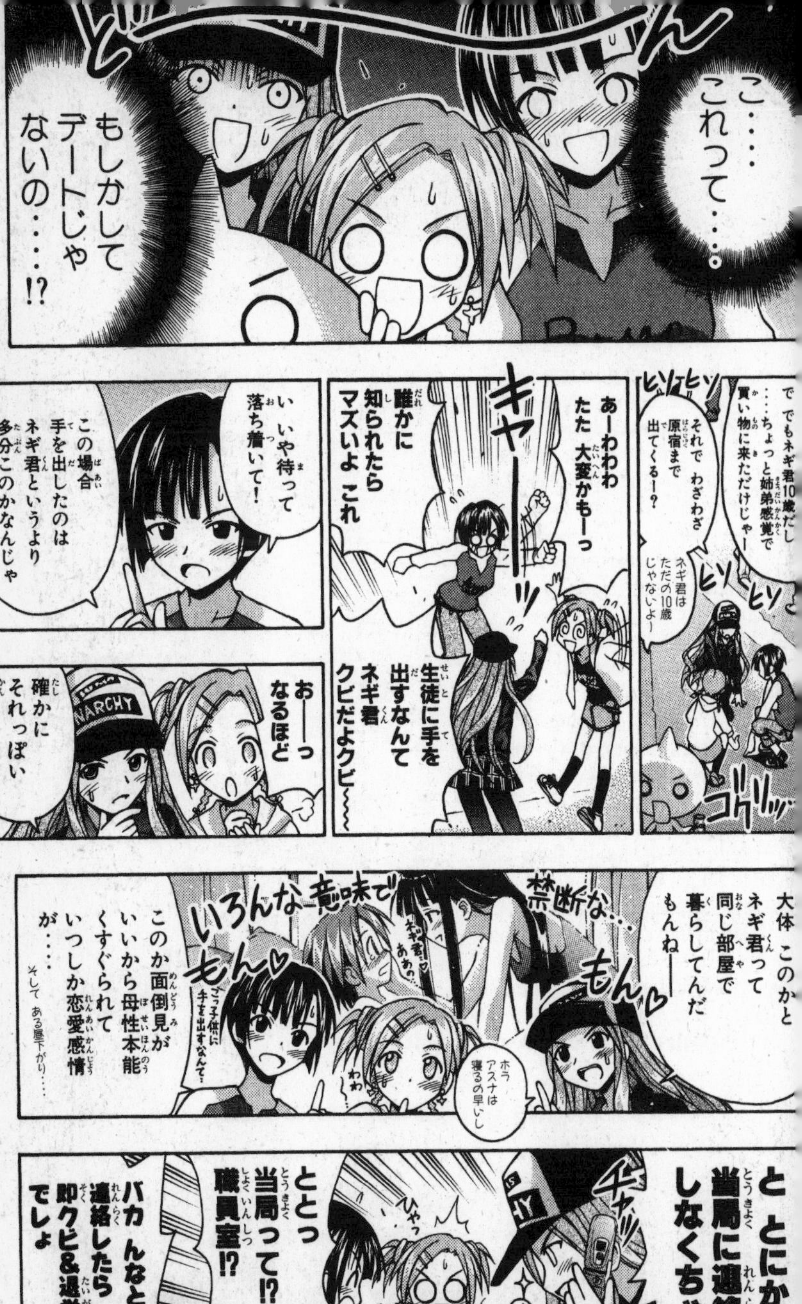
こ……これって……
もしかしてデートじゃないの……!?
で でもネギ君10歳だし……ちょっと姉弟感覚で買い物に来ただけじゃー
それで わざわざ原宿まで出てくるー?
ネギ君はただの10歳じゃないよー
ヒソヒソ
ヒソヒソ
ゴクリッ
あーわわわ たた 大変かもーっ
キャー
誰かに知られたらマズいよ これ
生徒に手を出すなんて ネギ君クビだよクビ~~
いいや待って落ち着いて!
この場合手を出したのはネギ君というより多分このかなんじゃ……?
おーーっ なるほど
確かにそれっぽい感じよね……
大体 このかと ネギ君って同じ部屋で暮らしてんだもんねー
禁断な…もん♥
ホラ アスナは寝るの早いし
わわ~
ネギ君…ああの…
いろんな意味で もん♥
子供に手を出すなんて…
このか面倒見がいいから母性本能くすぐられていつしか恋愛感情が……
そして ある昼下がり……
と とにかく当局に連絡しなくちゃ
トゥルルル トゥルルル
ひゃっ
ととっ当局って!? 職員室!?
バカ んなとこ連絡したら即クビ&退学でしょ

Othello

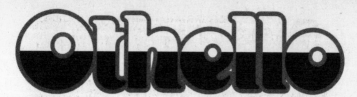

BY SATOMI IKEZAWA

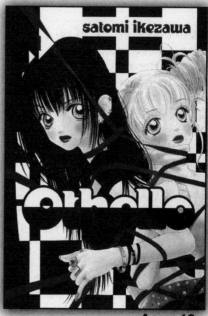

Yaya Higuchi has a rough life. Constantly teased and tormented by her classmates, she takes her solace in dressing up as a member of her favorite rock band, Juliet, on the weekends. Things begin to look up for Yaya when a cute classmate befriends her. Her devotion to Juliet, however, eventually just brings her more of the teasing and harassment she gets at school. Unable to cope, Yaya . . . changes. Suddenly, Yaya is gone—and in the blink of an eye, a new personality emerges. She is now Nana and she is tough, confident, and in charge. Nana can do things that Yaya could never do—like beating up the boys and taking care of all of Yaya's problems. How will Yaya live with this new, super-confident alternate personality? Who will be the dominant one, and who is the REAL Yaya?

satomi ikezawa
Othello

Ages: 16+

Special extras in each volume! Read them all!

DEL REY

VISIT WWW.DELREYMANGA.COM TO:

- View release date calendars for upcoming volumes
- Sign up for Del Rey's free manga e-newsletter
- Find out the latest about new Del Rey Manga series

THE WALLFLOWER

YAMATONADESHIKO SHICHIHENGE

BY TOMOKO HAYAKAWA

It's a beautiful, expansive mansion, and four handsome, fifteen-year-old friends are allowed to live in it for free! But there is one condition—within three years the young men must take the owner's niece and transform her into a proper lady befitting the palace in which they all live! How hard can it be?

Enter Sunako Nakahara, the horror-movie-loving, pock-faced, frizzy-haired, fashion-illiterate hermit who has a tendency to break into explosive nosebleeds whenever she sees anyone attractive. This project is going to take far more than our four heroes ever expected; it needs a miracle!

Ages: 16+

Special extras in each volume! Read them all!

BY CLAMP

Watanuki Kimihiro is haunted by visions. When he finds himself irresistibly drawn into a shop owned by Yûko, a mysterious witch, he is offered the chance to rid himself of the spirits that plague him. He accepts, but soon realizes that he's just been tricked into working for the shop to pay off the cost of Yûko's services! But this isn't any ordinary kind of shop . . . In this shop, Yûko grants wishes to those in need. But they must have the strength of will not only to truly understand their need, but to give up something incredibly precious in return.

Ages: 13+

Special extras in each volume! Read them all!

VISIT WWW.DELREYMANGA.COM TO:
• View release date calendars for upcoming volumes
• Sign up for Del Rey's free manga e-newsletter
• Find out the latest about new Del Rey Manga series

GUNDAM SEED

ART BY MASATSUGU IWASE
ORIGINAL STORY BY HAJIME YATATE
AND YOSHIYUKI TOMINO

In the world of the Cosmic Era, a war is under way between the genetically enhanced humans known as Coordinators and those who remain unmodified, called Naturals. The Natural-dominated Earth Alliance, struggling to catch up with the Coordinators' superior technology, has secretly developed its own Gundam mobile suits at a neutral space colony. But through a twist of fate, a young Coordinator named Kira Yamato becomes the pilot of the Alliance's prototype Strike Gundam, and finds himself forced to fight his own people in order to protect his friends. Featuring all the best elements of the legendary Gundam saga, this thrilling series reimagines the gripping story of men, women, and magnificent fighting machines in epic conflict.

Ages: 13 +

Special extras in each volume! Read them all!

VISIT WWW.DELREYMANGA.COM TO:
- View release date calendars for upcoming volumes
- Sign up for Del Rey's free manga e-newsletter
- Find out the latest about new Del Rey Manga series

TOMARE!

[STOP!]

You're going the wrong way!

Manga is a completely different type of reading experience.

To start at the *beginning*, go to the *end*!

That's right! Authentic manga is read the traditional Japanese way—from right to left. Exactly the *opposite* of how American books are read. It's easy to follow: Just go to the other end of the book, and read each page—and each panel—from right side to left side, starting at the top right. Now you're experiencing manga as it was meant to be.